1

London, March 1940

"Margot, you realize that if a bomb falls on St Margaret's during your wedding, it'll be curtains for the government as well as for your love story. The whole damn Cabinet's on this list!"

Margot Moore, seated at the leather-topped desk in her father's study, paused in her letter writing to turn and make a face at her younger sister.

"You're such a wonderful comfort, Katie. Without you around, I'd be a nervous wreck by now."

The sarcasm was only half intended. Margot adored her eighteen-year-old sister, and she needed her at this time. Not that the prospect of her imminent marriage into English society was unnerving her. On the contrary, the days still left before the wedding seemed to be dragging by much too slowly. Miss Margot Moore of Washington, DC was in a tearing hurry to become Mrs Charles Garland of London. The ceremony at St Margaret's, Westminster would, at a stroke, relieve her of the mundane role of parentally controlled teenager and invest her with the far more interesting, and potentially tragic, role of a woman with a husband at the wars.

"Poor child!" she had overheard Lady Colefax say on the occasion of her January engagement party. "War turns young brides overnight into women far older than their years. It steals part of their wonderful youth from them. It's so unfair!"

Margot had not thought it unfair at all. Whatever part of her youth was about to be stolen from her, it was no part that she was going to miss. She was more than ready to take her place in the adult word. Though six months short of her twentieth birthday, she had for some time been making an effort, usually successful, to have people believe, on first encounter, that she was older. Only last night a British diplomat, albeit slightly in his cups, had sworn that he remembered attending her twenty-first birthday party in Washington on the eve of Roosevelt's re-election in 1936. Margot felt flattered, and quite reluctant to declare a case of mistaken identity. In eighteen months in London as the daughter of a senior American diplomat, and now the daughter-in-law-to-be of a distinguished British politician, Margot had become accustomed to moving amongst the mighty. Ambassadors, Cabinet ministers, captains of industry, knights of the stage and peers of the realm peopled the pages of her assiduously kept diary. She encouraged them to talk, listened to what they said, and recorded the best of what she heard along with her impressions of the characters in question. She felt at ease in their company, sure that her striking good looks and self-confident manner compelled attention. It irked her, therefore, that her doting parents still treated her as a precocious teenager who really shouldn't be marrying quite so young, even while approving her choice.

Katie was delighted that her sister was going to marry such a nice, handsome man, but she nonetheless continued to tease Margot over her addiction to people of importance.

"How come you aren't marrying at least a marquess or a Cabinet minister?" she would ask.

"Because Charlie's just what I want. Besides, no one else whom I *really* like has asked me."

This was not strictly true. Months before discovering Charlie, she had met his rather older first cousin, Jamie, a regular Grenadier officer. Swaying slightly on his feet, he had proposed to her in the floodlit grounds of Blenheim Palace during the Duke and Duchess of Marlborough's spectacular coming-out ball for their daughter. It was only their third meeting.

"You'd make a jolly super mistress of Edmonton Hall,

dear," had been his opening line, adding after a gulp from his champagne glass: "How about it, Yank?"

Margot had smiled sweetly, patted him on the cheek, and told him to go and drink a strong black coffee.

"Margot, save me from the hordes of ghastly horse-faced debs!" he had wailed after her retreating figure. "Do England a good turn!"

The next morning she had received a huge bouquet of flowers accompanied by a note in which her suitor had simply apologized for having made a fool of himself. Margot wondered whether the wealthy young marquess planned to try again after a decent interval. He seemed nice enough when sober, she noted that day in her diary. "Worth getting to know better," she added. She did get to know him better that summer, and grew to like him a lot. But he never proposed to her again, drunk or sober, which mildly irritated her even though she was not in love with him. Or anyone else, for that matter. And by the time Charlie proposed, the war was on and Jamie was in France.

"The list, Katie. Give it back."

She stretched out a hand and beckoned impatiently with a forefinger.

"Wait!"

"No. Now! I need it for this letter."

"What does 'C no R yes' mean against some of the names?"

"Coming to the reception but not to the church. Give it to me."

Katie sighed as she got up from the armchair and brought the list to her sister.

"So Ambassador Kennedy wants to drink, not pray."

"Don't be cheeky."

"I wish it was Joe Junior who was coming."

"Well, he's not," said Margot taking the list from her sister. "And don't you dare embarrass the ambassador at the reception. He doesn't pass messages to his sons from lovesick non-Catholics. Now do leave me alone, for God's sakes, or I'll never get this letter finished. Go play with the soldiers in the park."

"Thank goodness you're getting married! You're no

fun anymore." Katie playfully shook her sister by the shoulders. "Are you writing to the grandparents?"

"I am."

"Can I add a PS?"

"No. Write your own letter. It's Grandpa's seventieth in two weeks, and he'll expect one from you."

"I just wanted to warn them that their first great-grandchild is going to be conceived in an overnight train somewhere between here and Scotland."

"Out, Katie! Out!"

"I'm going. And I'll be out to dinner."

"Lucky me, lucky everyone! Which regiment are you entertaining tonight?"

"Jealous!"

Margot smiled as she heard Katie close the study door behind her. Katie had a passion for men in uniform and confessed that she went weak at the knees every time she passed a handsome young officer on the street. And wartime London's pavements, not to mention its parks, restaurants, theatres and shops, seemed to have been taken over by them. Katie needed watching, Margot had decided. To her family she liked to give the impression that she only had eyes for the ambassador's eldest son, Joe Kennedy Jr, even though she and they knew that the young man was well beyond her reach. But Margot realized that this was something of a smokescreen obscuring her daily quest for the attentions of any Adonis in uniform who might cross her path. Many, Margot suspected, paid her more than passing attention, but Katie covered her tracks well, scrupulously observing the parental two a.m. curfew when not accompanied by her elder sister, and accounting for her daytime forays into the streets of London with a convincing display of knowledge of the storyline of every movie showing in town. She was, she assured her sister, still a virgin. Margot was not so certain of that, but it seemed not to have crossed her parents' mind that Katie could be anything else, so Margot kept her doubts to herself and a watchful eye on her sister.

She scanned the "Cs" among the alphabetically listed acceptances of invitations to her wedding. Good! Duff and Diana Cooper would be there. And the Cranbornes. And Chips Channon. The Vicomte and Vicomtesse de Creçy naturally. She had been accidentally born in their Paris mansion, taking her mother by surprise during a late afternoon social call on the American-born Vicomtesse. Quick-witted Connie de Creçy had looked out on the rain-lashed, traffic-choked avenue Hoche and decided that Elinor and Harland Moore's first child would be better born in a guest bed than a traffic jam. A general practitioner, living across the street, was summoned, and an hour later, apologizing profusely if breathlessly for the inconvenience she was causing her hostess, Elinor was delivered of first a boy and, two minutes later, a girl. Connie finally reached the unsuspecting father at his place of work, the American Embassy, and told him that his twins had gatecrashed her tea party. Henri de Creçy, Margot knew, was now dying of cancer, and she was deeply moved that they had nonetheless written to say that nothing short of a German invasion of France would prevent them from being in London for the wedding.

She looked further down the list. No Noël Coward; he had written from Paris, where he was temporarily a resident. He was a friend of her future in-laws, and had sung and played for her and Charlie at the dinner following their engagement party. If the de Creçy's could make it, why couldn't he? She felt let down. Then she turned the page and read "Winston and Clemmie Churchill." That's more like it! She stuck a pencil between her teeth and gazed out the window at the row of Georgian houses across the street. My God! My Holton Arms classmates will be green with envy when they hear all about this wedding, she mused for the hundredth time. None of them would be there, which was sad; the war in Europe, albeit at a standstill, had seen to that. But she'd promised to send clippings to her closest girlfriends. "So 'Mimi de Paris' has really done it in style!" they'd be saying. "You bet she has! Did you ever doubt it?" Well, they probably never expected me to marry anyone but a Frenchman. But a high society European wedding it was always going to be.

Margot Moore had quickly earned the nickname "Mimi

de Paris" from her schoolmates. As soon as she had been old enough to understand that she had been born in the French capital, where her father had been on his first overseas diplomatic posting, all things French took on a wondrous attraction. She took French at the earliest opportunity in her schooling, and excelled at it. She read French literature and history voraciously, plastered the walls of her bedroom at home with reproductions of France's greatest old masters, especially the Impressionists, and endlessly played French music, both classical and contemporary, on her phonograph. At fifteen, she was praying each night that she would dream of being seduced and deflowered by a handsome Frenchman in some beautiful château. Occasionally her prayers were answered, and she would eventually wake up, shivering and moaning, trying desperately to cling to the fast fading images in her mind.

"Spent the night with Gaston, Mimi?" her school room-mates would enquire laughingly. Gaston had been their invention rather than hers; she thought the name rather common. She was looking for a Thierry, a Pierre-André, an Alexis. For a while she dated the son of a French diplomat, who was a Washington neighbour, but he fell short of what she expected from a Frenchman of noble birth, so she abandoned Jean-Claude and fell briefly in love with a Congressman's son who happily bore the name Louis. Louis knew nothing about France and the French when they started dating, and knew more than he ever wanted to by the time he returned to Des Moines, Iowa, on his father's failure to be re-elected in the Congressional race of 1938. A month later, Margot tearfully kissed twin brother Larry and sister Katie goodbye, and left with her parents for London and the American Embassy there. Katie would join them following graduation from Holton Arms the following summer. Larry was heading for Princeton. Through most of the crossing on the *Athenia*, heavy winter seas kept Margot prostrate with seasickness. She would have suffered this excruciating misery with St Joan-like fortitude if her destination had been Le Havre instead of Liverpool. In her aching head she composed a letter to Louis saying that if

14

she couldn't have Paris she could have done worse than opt for Des Moines and life as the wife of a trainee farm insurance salesman, as he had urged her to consider. But the letter never got written. When the seas calmed on the penultimate day of the voyage, and Margot was able to enjoy her first dinner in the first-class dining room, she fell happily under the spell of a young titled Englishman whom her parents had invited to join them at their table. She danced the night away with him, let him enfold her in a blanket on the chilly deck and kiss her breathlessly in the cloud-filtered moonlight, leaving thoughts of Louis and the cornbelt bobbing into oblivion in the liner's frothing wake.

"I suppose you're still a virgin, being an American," he said, infiltrating a hand into the folds of the blanket and pressing the palm against the two layers of clothing that encased her full young breasts.

"And what's so American about still being a virgin?" she enquired without rancour, letting his hand exert its pleasing pressure

"Basically, you're a race of puritans."

"Is that what they teach you in English schools? How quaint!"

"Prove me wrong then."

"I'm afraid you'll have to take my word for it. Here come my parents looking for me. They worry a helluva lot more about my virginity than I do."

The hand withdrew rapidly from her breast. Margot stayed leaning against the rail, back to the sea, and pulled the blanket closer around her shoulders.

"Yes, I suppose it is a little too chilly now," said the young Englishman, answering an unasked question as he rubbed his hands vigorously together.

"Time to turn in, I think," said Harland Moore.

"Victor thinks we're a race of puritans," said Margot.

"Oh, I'm not – "

"I'm relieved," cut in Elinor Moore, "that you're giving him that impression, Margot."

Margot and her father laughed.

"Typical mother," she said. She shrugged the blanket from her shoulders, dropped it on a stack of folded deck

15

chairs, and stepped forward to take the still blushing Victor by the arm.

"Walk us to our suite," she said.

They dropped back a bit as her parents hurried on.

"I probably won't see you tomorrow in all the rush of packing and disembarking," she told him. "But will we see each other in London?"

"I'm sure we'll run into each other at some stage."

"Well, can't we have a date or something?"

"Well, I suppose – "

Margot stopped and pulled him round to face her.

"I seem to be speaking what should be your lines."

She looked intently at the pink, boyish face, the rather watery blue eyes, the wide, humorous mouth.

"Oh, I see," she said quietly. "Someone waiting for you. Steady girlfriend."

"Wife."

"*Wife?*" Margot laughed. "You naughty boy! You never told us that!"

"I'm sorry." He hung his head.

"Don't be. I think it's fun. I've never been kissed by a married man before."

She glanced down the dimly lit deck and saw that her parents were out of sight.

"Now that I know, I feel like some more."

She put her arms round his neck, pressed the whole length of her body against his, and opened her lips wide as he inclined his face to hers.

"London's going to be fun," she murmured, as their lips met.

And so it proved. But, as it turned out, Victor, fifth Viscount Porterrington, played no part in that. He broke his neck out hunting on New Year's Day 1939, less than a month after his one and only encounter with the tall, honey-blonde diplomat's daughter from Washington, DC. Margot swallowed the pride that had been pricked by Victor's apparent unwillingness to meet her on *terra firma* and slipped into the crowded memorial service held in a fashionable West End church. It was the first time that she had seen London society *en masse*. She was impressed. Even in their evident grief at the untimely departure of one of their number, they seemed to convey a contented self-satisfaction at their collective ability to put on such an effortless show of beauty and elegance. Deeming it appropriate to place herself at the back of the church, she nonetheless secured an end seat on the aisle and was thus treated to a close-up view of the congregation as it good-manneredly left pew by pew, starting from the front, at the close of the service. She found her gaze being returned with interest and realized that London society was getting its first glimpse of her. The exchange of looks between her and the only face she recognized, that of Anthony Eden, sent a shiver of pleasure tinged with fear through her whole body. Her departure from the church was rather more noted than her arrival, and one fur-coated and hatted lady, overcome with curiosity, approached her and enquired:

"Do I know you, my dear?"

"I don't think you do, I'm afraid," said Margot, a little taken aback. "I'm Margot Moore." She held out her hand. "From Washington, DC."

"How very interesting," said the lady. "You must have met Victor out there. He really did treat Daisy quite abominably, but then his father was like that with Maud. Turned her very thirsty. Thank God she was half sober for this little farewell. I mustn't keep you, my dear. That's a pretty hat but much too summery. What did you say your name was?"

"Margot Moore. My father's at the embassy."

"Working for the terrible Mr Kennedy. Oh dear! You know he wore trousers instead of knee breeches when he presented his wife and daughters at Court. Not surprising he was mistaken for a waiter!"

Margot suppressed a giggle.

"I don't know what your Mr Roosevelt thought he was doing sending us an Irish Catholic," the lady continued. "Very poor form! But my son Jamie says everyone likes the Kennedy gel who's running around with Billy Hartington. Of course it won't come to anything. No future Duke of Devonshire can marry a papist, can he? Are you a papist, my dear?"

"Episcopalian. Like your Church of England."

"How very sensible of you. You should talk to Kick Kennedy and tell her to become one too if she wants to be the next Duchess. I must run now. My cook's cat got flattened by a Harrods van this morning and she's bawling the house down. Will you be doing the Season? If so, you'll run into Jamie. He's a Grenadier, but he seems to spend all his time at race meetings and on dance floors. If Herr Hitler has the bad manners to go to war with us during Ascot Week, he'll find every Guards officer *hors de combat* in the Royal Enclosure. It was so nice to meet you, and I'm glad to see you don't chew gum like the Kennedy gel does. The jaw movements do so remind one of the camels at the zoo, don't you think?"

She turned just in time to miss Margot's collapse into helpless giggles, and disappeared back into the slowly dispersing crowd. Recovering, Margot looked about her and saw a well-dressed, middle-aged woman with a notebook and pencil in her hand stepping towards her.

"Forgive me, but I couldn't help overhearing you discussing Kick Kennedy with Lady Edmonton just now. Are you a friend of hers? By the way, I'm Anne Coxwell. I write for the *Tatler*."

"Who did you say I was talking to?"

"The Dowager Marchioness of Edmonton. You don't know her?"

"No. She just came up and started talking to me." Margot held out her hand. "I'm Margot Moore. My father's with the American Embassy."

They shook hands.

"So you must know Kick Kennedy."

"Not yet. I've only been here three weeks, and she's with her mother and brothers and sisters in St Moritz."

"And poor Victor?"

"We met on the *Athenia*."

"I see. Are you going to be presented at Court?"

"I've no idea."

"Since your father's at the embassy, you most likely will be. It's up to the ambassador. May I ask how old you are?"

"Eighteen."

18

"Really? You look a little older." She smiled pleasantly. "That's American sophistication for you! I imagine you'll do the Season then."

"I'm not even sure I know what it is," replied Margot with a laugh. "But I'll do it if it's fun."

"Will your parents give a coming-out party for you?"

"I think they're going to give some sort of party when my sister arrives here in June. That's Katie," she added watching the woman noting something on her pad. "She's a year younger."

"Well, thank you for answering my questions. Just one more: your father's full name and his position."

"Harland A. Moore. A for Austin. He's a political counsellor."

"Thank you. I'm sure we'll be running into each other again. And I'm sure you'll be a very charming and sought-after addition to the Season. Last year, Kick Kennedy; this year, Margot Moore. It seems our American cousins have come to conquer us!"

Margot felt herself blushing, and as the elegant society reporter turned away, she delayed her with a touch on the shoulder.

"Please, I've forgotten her name already; the Marchioness."

"The Marchioness of Edmonton. She's a widow. Her son Jamie is the current marquess. I expect you'll be meeting him."

"I hope so."

They parted, and Margot went in search of a taxi. On the ride home, she congratulated herself on her first ever press interview. The late lamented Victor Porterrington had done her a good turn after all. Kick Kennedy had had the advantage the previous year of all the publicity attendant upon the arrival of a new American ambassador with a wife and nine children. The Moores having arrived unheralded, as indeed the parents both expected and desired, Margot had no alternative but to shift for herself in these early weeks. Maybe when the Kennedys returned home next week from St Moritz, she'd get to meet Kick, and through her some of her society friends. But she wasn't counting on it. Besides, she rather wanted to make it on her own, and she now had the feeling that maybe she was on to a good start. Thanks to poor Victor breaking his neck. You're awful, Margot! she reproached herself with a smile. But the world she had encountered inside that church was a world she was now in a hurry to get to know. So, for the time being, at least, it was goodbye to Thierry, Pierre-André and Alexis.

That evening over dinner, she talked volubly of her afternoon's experience. Her father smiled and said little. Her mother, however, admonished her.

"Don't count on being invited everywhere, dear. You don't enter London society as if you were simply checking into a hotel."

But, as events turned out, it seemed to Margot to be just as simple as that. The ambassador did indeed include Margot and her mother among the chosen few American residents of London to be presented at Court in the second week of May. A dressmaker familiar with the style of dress required by Buckingham Palace made the white tulle gowns with five-foot trains sweeping from the shoulders. On the appointed day, Mrs Kennedy herself came round to the Moores' Hill Street house to ready the presentees and run through the protocol. Satisfied that Elinor and her daughter each had the three regulation Prince of Wales plumes correctly in place on their coiffures and that the tulle veil at the base was of the right length, she asked her charges to rehearse for her the deep curtsy they would execute in unison when they came as a pair before the King and Queen.

"You will do honour to our country," said the ambassador's wife approvingly. "You make a strikingly handsome pair."

Margot thought so too, and she was delighted with the attentions paid to her by the newspaper photographers who surrounded them at the entrance to the Palace. The next day, the *Evening Standard* was among the several papers to publish a photograph of the radiant young American making her formal entry into London society.

"The Kennedy ladies, not to mention our current crop of homegrown beauties, will need to look to their laurels," gushed the accompanying column. "This tall, smiling-eyed honey-blonde from Washington, DC is going to be the catch of the season."

Margot was now well and truly launched. Not that she had been excluded from the London Season prior to her presentation at Court; Kick Kennedy saw to that. The immensely popular second Kennedy daughter was delighted to introduce her to her own wide circle of English friends, as well as to her two brothers, Joe Jr and Jack. Both young men were using London as their base from which to make extensive political study tours of Europe at their father's behest as the threat of war grew daily. Margot saw little of either of them, although Jack twice escorted her to dances. While she found the elder brother somewhat brusque and intimidating, Jack's easy-going style and infectious humour appealed to her. She knew that variety was the spice of the hectic social life he led when in London, and she harboured no ambitions to win his concentrated attention, which she knew would have been a lost cause. Nonetheless she was sorry not to have seen more of him before his return to America at the outbreak of war.

There were, of course, plenty of other young men to distract her. In accordance with the rules of society, it was necessary for her mother to meet the mothers of those debutantes who wished to have Margot at their parties and to acquaint herself with the names and reputations of those young men who might be considered suitable escorts for her daughter. While anxious to respect the conventions and protect her daughter, Elinor Moore found such social protocol time-consuming and not infrequently irritating. And the prospect of having to redouble the duty on the arrival of Katie did little to encourage her. Through May and June she stoically chaperoned Margot to the almost nightly balls, all too rarely accompanied by her husband for whom the press of embassy business grew more burdensome by the week.

"Is all this really necessary?" she asked Margot in a weary voice as a taxi bore them home in the early hours of a late May morning from the third debutante ball that week. "With a war coming it all seems so inappropriate."

"It's because there's a war coming that everyone wants

21

to enjoy the last days of peace. Listen, Mother, I know you hate these long evenings, so why don't you just go home early? I'm perfectly capable of looking after myself. I'm a year older than most of the debs anyway, and when Katie arrives we can chaperon each other."

"I promised your father – "

"I'll talk to him tomorrow," said Margot firmly.

This she did, and in return for a promise that she would not go nightclubbing and would identify to her mother in advance the young man who would escort her home, not later than two o'clock, Elinor would henceforth limit her chaperoning to the first hour or two of the ball.

Margot scrupulously observed the two o'clock curfew, but the ban on nightclubbing she promptly and cheerfully ignored. She recognized the risk of her parents eventually hearing of her midnight visits to the Café de Paris and the Four Hundred, but until they did, she was determined to enjoy her new-found liberty. Her escorts encouraged her by telling her that she looked and was far more sophisticated than the average English debutante, an observation which she welcomed as a high compliment and as a justification for disobeying her parents.

By the time Katie arrived in late June, Margot was a star of the Season. Wherever she went, photographers fell over themselves to take her picture. She had the pick of the young male aristocracy as her escorts, and the rumours, sometimes emerging in print, that the Marquess of This or the Earl of That had set his heart on marrying her amused her enormously. Her weekends were spent at some of the finest country mansions in the land, and speculation as to who would be her escorts to the Derby and Royal Ascot added much grist to the society columnists' mills.

By the time the Season had opened in late April, with the first spring race meeting at Newmarket, she had already devised her strategy. It was based on the possibility, if not probability, that her stay in England would be cut short by a European war. She wanted to make the best of the time available to her, meet as many prominent people as possible, make her mark, and return to the United States, as and when compelled to do so, with a record of social accomplishment enviable enough to secure her instant recognition in New York and Washington society.

Consistent with this strategy, she would seek to avoid any amorous entanglement and would "play the field". Not that she was against having suitors; on the contrary she was sure that she would find it immensely flattering, as indeed she later did. But at the same time she was learning how to keep them at just the distance required to retain their interest in her without raising their hopes unduly. Having gently rebuffed Jamie Edmonton's rather casual proposal, she was delighted that he elected not to take umbrage, but instead to assume the role of brotherly companion as and when she felt the need for such.

But Katie's arrival marked the beginning of a change in her strategy. Her younger sister was, as she herself had been, an instant success, and the last two months of the London Season were to be dominated by The Moore Sisters. Though there was a thirteen-month difference in their ages, they might have passed for near-identical twins. Like her elder sister, Katie had honey-blonde hair falling just short of the shoulders and framing the same high-cheekboned face with pale brown eyes and heart-shaped, full-lipped mouth. Katie conceded an inch in height to Margot, but by any standards they were both tall, long-legged girls. The only striking difference between them was in their voices. While the younger spoke in a lilting soprano, Margot's voice was a richly textured contralto.

In addition to the continuing balls in London and the countryside and the weekend house-parties, there were still important social functions left on the summer calendar. Henley Regatta, Goodwood Race Week, Cowes Yachting Week and the final Garden Party at Buckingham Palace were yet to come, and Margot and Katie had invitations to all of them. Under her elder sister's watchful and delighted eye, Katie flung herself into the revelries with the same infectious enthusiasm that had marked Margot's earlier launching. But now Margot was aware that a change had taken place in her attitude towards the life she was leading. She could accurately pinpoint the

23

origin of the change to a conversation she had had with a
young English diplomat whom she sat next to at a dinner
party just before Katie's arrival. It was a dinner given
by the American-born Member of Parliament, Henry
Channon known to his friends as "Chips", whom she
had met through Kick Kennedy. That evening she was
flattered to find herself the only debutante in a glittering
group, including the Duke and Duchess of Kent. As was
invariably the case these days, the conversation came
round to the dwindling prospects of avoiding war. Could
Hitler really be deterred from invading Poland by the
British guarantee of military support for the beleaguered
country? The consensus was pessimistic.

"Chips is right," said the young diplomat seated at
Margot's right. "We need Churchill at the helm now that
war is inevitable. I suppose you'll be going back to the
States."

"I really don't know. Father's hinted at it often enough,
but he's not said definitely that we will."

He bent his head closer to hers and whispered: "The
middle-aged fellow across the table, and his wife at the
other end, they told me they were leaving for Canada as
soon as war breaks out. He's a wealthy businessman, and
I think it's shocking that he should decide to run from his
own country in its hour of danger."

"Maybe he's Jewish," murmured Margot.

"He's not. On the other hand, one or two of the
Government are, but you won't catch them slinking off
into the night like frightened rats."

He drank from his wine glass, then smiled at her.

"I'm sorry, my dear. I'm being a little emotional. The
point is that when the war comes, you will see Britain and
the British at their very best. Win or lose, it is going to
be one of the most glorious chapters in our history, and
I wouldn't miss being a part of it for anything in the
world!"

Margot stared into the handsome young face and felt
her lips quivering.

"What a wonderful thing to say," she said.

He smiled again, shyly. "I'm joining the Navy early
next month. I want to be in uniform when it starts. I don't

want to be a Johnny-Come-Lately as you Americans say."

"But what if it doesn't come? Can you get back into the Foreign Office?"

"It will come, I promise you."

"It's all so awful!" she said.

"There's no reason for it to be awful for you. You'll be able to go home, and if the isolationists like your Ambassador Kennedy get their way with FDR, you won't have to fight any war."

There was bitterness in his voice, and Margot drew back. "Don't jump to conclusions about us. It's not fair, especially not to people like me who feel very strongly about this country. I don't feel at all like that couple who will be running away to Canada. I could never do that!"

"I'm sorry," he said, gently.

"When I look around at my friends and think about what they may be going through before long I feel awful. I sometimes wish I could share what's coming with them." She broke off. "Let's not carry on this conversation. I don't want to cry and I'm feeling very close to doing so."

Later that night Margot lay awake in bed. In her mind she was beginning to see, if only in hazy outline, a new image of herself. It was definitely a romantic image, but tinged with tragedy: a beautiful American woman, rejecting the security of her home across the oceans to share the dangers and horrors of war with the man to whom she has given her heart, body and soul. She could not get out of her mind the words of the young diplomat. Britain and the British would be at their best when the war came; it was going to be one of the most glorious chapters in their history. She realized now that deep down in her there was a longing to play a part in that splendid drama. The question was: who would be her leading man? She reckoned she could have just about anybody she chose. But she would have to choose fast if she was not to find herself on a boat to New York before the curtain went up, with the prospect of languishing later as a student at Vassar, a mere spectator on the sidelines of history.

2

On 4 July 1939, Harland and Elinor Moore, accompanied by their two daughters, attended the Independence Day Garden Party at the American Ambassador's imposing six-storey residence overlooking Hyde Park. After passing through the receiving line in the formal dining room to be greeted by the ambassador and Mrs Kennedy, the Moores walked through to join the guests mingling in the spacious garden in the rear.

The previous evening, the elder Moores had given a buffet dinner at Hill Street, in honour of their daughters, which most of the young Kennedys, including Joe Jr, Jack and Kick, had attended. It was Katie's first encounter with the eldest Kennedy son, and although he had not stayed long and had paid her only limited if courteous attention, she had announced to her sister after the party that she would never look at another man again. Margot had smiled indulgently and bet her five shillings she'd be looking hard at others by the following weekend. In the crowded embassy garden, Katie put on a brave face as she watched the object of her adoration playing the role of dutiful eldest son, moving from one knot of people to another, hailing visiting Bostonians, decorously greeting distinguished British guests, until eventually his progress through the crowd brought him to where Margot and Katie stood.

"Hi there! That was a great party last night. I wish I could have stayed longer."

"I wish you had too!" said Katie, reluctant to let go of his hand.

"See you all again soon," he said, flashing a wide smile. Then he was gone.

"Might as well go now," said Katie with a pout.

"Don't be silly. Come and talk to Jack over here. He'll cheer you up."

Katie shrugged her shoulders.

The younger brother, handsomely suntanned, and dapper in a dark double-breasted suit with a red carnation in the buttonhole, was engaged in conversation with a distinguished-looking, silver-haired gentleman. Margot thought he looked vaguely familiar.

"May we say hello?" she said, approaching them.

"Hey! The Moore Sisters!" beamed Jack Kennedy. "Recovered from last night?"

He pecked Margot on the cheek and squeezed Katie's hand.

"I want you to meet Sir Walter Garland, a very prominent Member of Parliament. Sir Walter – Margot and Katie Moore. Their father's at the embassy with Dad."

"How do you do, young ladies. How long have you been over here?"

As they chatted, Margot saw a man beckon Jack away. "Please excuse me. Enjoy yourselves," he said cheerfully. Margot blew him a kiss, then turned to answer a question from Sir Walter Garland.

"Yes, I do indeed know Jamie. I'd no idea he was your nephew. Is he here?" She looked around her.

"No, but I brought my son, Charlie, with me. I'd like you to meet him. He's just back from a year in Canada, and he'll be starting a job in the City in a few days."

"Jamie told me about him. We'd love to meet him."

They found Charlie Garland sampling a glass of American wine at the outside bar.

"Almost drinkable, Father," he said with a grin before turning a curious eye on the two pretty girls accompanying him.

"Charlie, these two delightful young ladies are American friends of Jamie's. Margot and – er – Katie isn't it?"

Katie nodded. "Moore," she added.

"Well, I've only been back five days, but I've heard about you already. Jamie filled me in over dinner the other night. I'm jolly glad to meet you."

It was the eyes that immediately drew Margot's attention. They were large brown eyes with almost girlishly long eyelashes. With his free left hand he flicked a forelock of dark brown hair up from his forehead. A tight-lipped grin revealed a deep dimple in the right cheek. He had a suntan to rival Jack Kennedy's, and the cut of his double-breasted grey flannel pin-stripe suit enhanced his tall, thin frame. The black tie with the pale blue stripes announced him, with no surprise to Margot, as an Old Etonian. She thought him very attractive.

"Welcome back," said Margot as they shook hands. "How was Canada?"

He glanced fleetingly at his father.

"Quite a lot of fun, really. But I'm glad to be home."

"My good friend Lord Beaverbrook arranged a job for him at a paper mill," interjected Sir Walter. "Quite an experience, I'd say. Well, I'll leave you young things to get to know each other. I have a few people here to see."

He took his leave.

"Actually, it was monumentally boring," said Charlie as soon as his father was out of earshot. "It was a sort of punishment for refusing to go to Oxford. Father thought I should get myself a degree, but I'd had more than enough of exams by the time I'd left Eton."

"Was he mad at you?" asked Katie, warming to this rebel spirit.

"Absolutely bloody furious!" Charlie laughed with the sisters. " 'Off to the frozen wastes with you!' he bellowed at me. 'No loafing around London!' I'd probably still be indentured labour at the Tallow Creek Paper Mills if I hadn't written to say that I thought I ought to come back and enrol in the reserve list of potential officers, since it looked as though the balloon was going to go up. That rather impressed him, and he sent me the lolly for my passage back by return post."

"But I thought he said you were going to work in the City?" said Margot.

"I am; starting next week. Father has a hare-brained scheme to turn me into a stock-broker. And two evenings a week I report to Wellington Barracks, properly equipped with bowler hat and rolled umbrella and get chased all over the parade ground with a lot of other poor sods by a bellowing Guards drill sergeant. You can come and gawk at us through the railings if you want a good laugh!"

Margot smiled. "I may just do that."

"This Yankee wine is really almost drinkable." He drained his glass. "You should try it."

"It's not Yankee, it's Californian, and it's not *almost* drinkable, it's *very* drinkable. So get me a glass, you dreadful Limey snob!"

For a second Charlie looked taken aback, then he saw the grin spread across Margot's face, and he laughed heartily.

"While you two are trading insults," said Katie, "I'll go and trade endearments with Joe Junior."

"Good luck, little sis!" Margot waved her away. "Poor lovesick child," she added, taking a glass of wine from Charlie.

"Talking of love," he said, "I hear from Jamie and several others that you've been breaking hearts all over London. Having met you, I can see why."

Margot blushed. "Jamie always exaggerates; what else has he said?"

"That we have to make the best of you because you'll be on a boat bound for Yankeeland at the first blast of war."

"Don't count on it."

"Really? That's going to be good news for us reluctant warriors if you actually stay. Will your parents let you?"

"I'm not planning on giving them the choice."

Charlie laughed.

"Plotting a runaway marriage to one of our lot? Not Jamie, I trust. He's too insufferably superior already. None of us will be able to stand him if he pulls off a coup like that."

"I haven't said anything about marrying anyone."

"Thank God for that! You'd provoke a wave of suicides among the losers. Listen, I'm planning a little jollification next Thursday on the eve of my deliverance into the slavering jaws of Mammon. You and your delightful sister must come."

"I'll check. If we're free we'll be there."

"If you're not free, you make yourself free. That's an order!"

"You're not a Guards officer yet, Charlie!"

"And may never make one, old girl. I'll probably fight the whole bloody war polishing Jamie's boots and buttons."

"Come now! Let's see a little ambition, Mr Garland!"

"Absolutely Miss Moore! For a decent whisky and soda, instantly! I thought old man Kennedy had been in the liquor business; he must have some of the proper stuff in the house. Come on, let's go and ingratiate ourselves."

Putting his wine glass down, he took her by the arm and led her across the lawn in the direction of the house. Spotting her parents, Margot pulled Charlie along to introduce him.

"You have a very bewitching daughter, sir," said Charlie, shaking Moore's hand. "The fairest envoy ever sent!"

Moore chuckled. "This one? Don't give her more of a swollen head than she already has after six months here in England. By the time she goes back for college, she'll be impossible."

The two men chatted for a moment while Elinor told her daughter that they would be leaving in fifteen minutes and that she should go and warn Katie.

"What do you think of him, Mother?" Margot whispered into her ear.

"Who, dear?"

"This one; Charlie Garland."

"He looks like all the others to me. Why?"

"Oh really, Mother!"

"I'm sure he's charming, Margot. But all these English boys look so under-nourished. English nannies must starve them from birth."

"Well I think he's very handsome. He's Jamie's first cousin."

"Jamie who, dear?"

Margot heaved a sigh. "Don't you ever remember who any of my dates are any more?"

"Do go and find Katie, dear. There's so much cleaning up after last night still to be done, so I don't want to be late home."

Margot drew Charlie away from her father and they set off in search of Katie and the Scotch and soda.

"So, you're headed for college, Margot."

"That's what they think."

"Come now! A little ambition!"

Margot laughed. *"Touché!"*

"Delighted we have something in common. Down with degrees!" He squeezed her arm. "I like your father."

"I like yours."

"So far, so good, then. I'll ring Jamie tonight and tell him to keep his noble hands off you from now on."

"No need; they're not on me. Jamie's appointed himself honorary elder brother. And don't be so possessive. I've only known you for ten minutes."

"Am I being rather un-British in my haste? It's the Spanish blood coursing through my veins. My maternal great-grandmother was a rather high-class tart from Barcelona. I'm the only one in the family who ever mentions her. There's your sister over there."

She was talking animatedly with a young man in US Navy officer's uniform. Charlie stopped and rested a hand on Margot's shoulder.

"I think I'd better forget the whisky and catch up with Father. He's signalling to leave. Will you dine with me tomorrow? I'd really rather not wait until next Thursday's bash to see you again."

"I'm supposed to be going to an embassy concert. Maybe I can get out of it. Will you call me tomorrow morning after nine?" She gave him the Hill Street number.

"I'll be counting on you," he said, leaning forward to give her a peck on the cheek.

"I'll try to fix it."

She watched him stroll away to rejoin his father at the entrance to the residence. She had a strange feeling that she had known him for some time already. Their conversation had immediately been natural and familiar, and the invitation to dinner and the kiss on the cheek had left

31

her with a warm glow of pleasure but no real feeling of surprise. Of course she would find an excuse not to go to the concert; tomorrow was not a day too soon to find out more about the deliciously attractive Charlie Garland.

She walked over to prise her sister away from her uniformed prey.

That evening, Margot took a telephone call from Jamie Edmonton.

"Well, well, well! So now the Moore magic has cousin Charlie spellbound! He just rang me, gibbering like a demented monkey about you. I told him that in view of what was in store for him next week when he starts work, I'd permit him a little light dalliance with you. The condemned man's hearty breakfast, so to speak."

"Jamie, you're awful!"

She felt a flush of intense pleasure that Charlie had already discussed her with his cousin.

"You'd better get out of that concert tomorrow, old girl, otherwise our desperate Charlie may do himself a mortal injury."

"Don't worry; I'm going to."

And she did. Charlie escorted her to the theatre to see Leslie Banks in *The Man in Half Moon Street*. Over dinner at the Café de Paris he let slip the fact that he'd already seen the play two evenings before.

"I'm afraid I got a bit besotted over Ann Todd, you know, the nurse he falls for. So I immediately got tickets to see her again. Then I met you."

"Killing two birds with one stone, Charlie?"

She laughed loudly to compensate for the slight trace of irritation in her voice.

"No. I just thought you'd like the play."

"Well I did. And I like Ann Todd. So your forty-eight-hour crush on the lady is forgiven. Now how about asking me to dance while we wait for the next course?"

On the dance floor, she beamed happily at the couples around her.

"You're a wonderful dancer, Charlie."

"You think so? I'm glad to hear it. There aren't many things I'm wonderful at."

"I'll probably find out there are a lot."

"I think the City will find out otherwise."

"Why do you always put yourself down?"

"Saves one being disappointed in oneself. Besides, it's better than boasting of qualities one hasn't actually got."

"Well, I want to find out which ones you *have* got, Charlie Garland."

"Then we'd better work fast. In a week or so they'll be trying to find some military qualities in me. And when they inevitably fail to find any at all, Hitler will feel free to start the war."

Margot laughed. "The English taste for self-deprecation! I love it. Underneath all that there's a hero in the making. Right?"

Charlie kissed her on the cheek. "I wouldn't bet on it."

Later, in the taxi on the way to Hill Street, they kissed with a passion that left them both breathless.

"Heavens!" said Charlie quietly. "I didn't know things would happen so quicky."

"Well, you said we had to work fast."

Agreeing eagerly to see each other the next day for lunch at Quaglino's, Margot hurried inside and upstairs to her room. Katie, hearing her return, left her bed and joined her elder sister in her room.

"Well?"

Margot sat at her dresser, staring at herself in the triple mirror.

"I think I've found him, Katie."

"Found who?"

"Someone I'm really going to fall in love with."

"Charlie? Don't tell me it's love at first sight!"

"Not even second. But I really think I'm going to fall in love with him."

"Holy Moses, sis! How in heaven can you tell?"

"It's a feeling. A strong one."

She picked up a tissue and carefully wiped the lipstick from her lips.

"Well, he's a good-looking guy. And nice. But what did he do or say to you tonight to get you into this romantic state? Boy! He must be quite something! Was he all over you in the cab?"

"For God's sakes, Katie, does it always have to be so carnal with you? I just have this feeling about him. It's something which – " She left the sentence unfinished and shrugged her shoulders. "I guess you just wouldn't understand."

"I would if you'd only tell me what it is about him that makes you so sure you're going to fall in love with him."

"Now I wish I hadn't told you. But just wait and see."

"Oh I will!"

"Now go back to bed."

Katie leaned down and kissed her. "Hope your dreams come true, sis. Honestly!"

Margot stroked Katie's hair.

"So do I."

Once in bed she lay awake for a while in the darkness wondering just what dream it was that she wanted to have come true. Just a short time ago she would have settled for nothing less than another Anthony Eden or another Duke of Kent. And since there didn't seem to be many, if any, who combined those exceptional qualifications with availability, she had been resigned to the likelihood that the dream would remain a dream for some, or even all, time. And then there had been born within her this determination to stay in England if, as seemed now inevitable, England went to war. This made a husband a more pressing requirement, and that might entail being a little less exacting in her selection. Then Charlie had appeared. And Charlie, having no power, no position, no title, and seemingly, in his uncertainty of himself, no ambition, could on the face of it meet only the less exacting of her criteria. Yet here she was, imbued with the feeling that she had found the right man. There was something fresh, innocent and unformed about this handsome young man which excited her. He was high quality clay waiting for the creative hands of the sculptor. That was it. She could shape Charlie to her desires. Her lover-husband, the hero returning from the war to climb the ladder of political power. Why not?

The last image in her mind's eye as she fell asleep was of Charlie leaning from the window of a troop train as it pulled out of some London terminus, blowing her a last kiss.

For his part, Charlie had already come to the decision that he could never look at another girl again, now that he had met Margot, and the only thought in his mind now was how to persuade her to become Mrs Charles Garland. Over a lunch of cold salmon and Muscadet at the Guards Club, he consulted his cousin Jamie, the one person in whom he could safely confide and who ought to have some useful insights as an earlier suitor.

"You have everything that is supposed to appeal to an American girl thinking about an English husband, so how in hell did you make a balls of it, Jamie?"

Jamie laughed as he helped himself to more mayonnaise.

"I may have a revered handle to my name, and if you'll pardon the indelicacy, I dare say I wouldn't wholly disappoint the lady between the sheets. But basically she sees me as nothing more than a prettily dressed toy soldier with just enough brain to keep me moving in the right direction at the Changing of the Guard. She wants more than that, old boy."

"In that case, she can scarcely want me," said Charlie gloomily. "What the hell have I got to offer?"

"Not much, Charlie. But women are unpredictable animals. They fall in love with the most unlikely people. Look at Rosie Gledhill! Just when everybody was sure she was about to marry poor old Ferdie and become a Duchess and a millionairess in one fell swoop, she ups and runs off with that impecunious zoologist from Leeds. So don't give up. Anyway, from what you tell me, she's not exactly resisting your charms. And if you're right in thinking that she's looking for a husband as a means of staying over here, she's obviously got you on her list of candidates."

"Along with half the bachelors in Burke's."

"Don't be such a sodding pessimist. You told me she was pressing her knee against yours at lunch at Quaglino's yesterday. That's not exactly an unfriendly act."

"Well, I'm just scared that if I propose to her, she'll run a mile. On the other hand, the longer I wait, the more chance someone else will snap her up."

Jamie poured his cousin another glass of wine.

"Listen, Charlie. It's really dead simple. You must tell her that you're wildly in love with her, but don't breathe a word about marriage yet. Then the ball's in her court. See her as much as possible, and the moment she utters a word about being in love with you, if she's ever going to, pop the question immediately. If she never does, she's the wrong person for you anyway. The point is, don't propose until you know she wants you. That way you won't get hurt."

Charlie silently pondered his cousin's advice as his knife steered a last mouthful of peas onto his fork.

"I'll give it a try," he said finally.

"Good fellow! And you're booking me right now as best man."

At Charlie's "jollification", the cocktail party which Sir Walter and Lady Garland gave for their son the following week, Margot felt in her element. Crowded into the elegant drawing room, dining room and study of the Garlands' Queen Anne house close by Westminster Abbey was an agreeable combination of both Charlie's and his parents' closest friends.

"Just wander round and dazzle them," said Charlie, who had stationed himself at the drawing room dooor to greet the arriving guests. "But come and tell me every now and then how the party's going."

Margot happily did his bidding, moving from room to room, spotting and chatting with friends here and there, and introducing herself boldly to those of Sir Walter's friends whom she recognized as, or who looked as though they might be, people of importance.

"I *adore* Lord Beaverbrook," she reported back to Charlie a little later. "And Randolph Churchill told me a *very* naughty story about Evelyn Waugh!"

She was off again, this time to chat with Kick Kennedy and her beau, Billy Hartington who urged her to join them later for dinner at Ciro's, but she was due to join

Charlie and his parents for dinner at the Savoy, so she declined. A moment later, Jamie Edmonton took her by the arm and led her into a corner of the library.

"How's our favourite Yank doing?" he asked. "You certainly look as though you were the happiest girl in the world. And the most beautiful."

Margot dropped a little curtsey.

"Thank you, kind sir! I'm enjoying myself hugely. Do you like my new dress? It arrived from New York just in time."

Hands on hips, she struck a model's pose, showing off the pale mauve off-the-shoulder dress in shot silk.

"Gorgeous."

"My mother thinks it's too daring. She didn't want me to wear it."

"I'm glad you're a disobedient daughter. What does Charlie think of it?"

"He hasn't said."

Jamie shook his head. "Poor Charlie. He's not really a Philistine; it's just that being head over heels in love has rendered him somewhat inarticulate."

Margot felt herself blushing. What had Charlie been saying to his cousin?

"Who's the lucky girl?"

The words came out almost involuntarily. The wretched cliché had popped out on its own, as if she had been cued in a play by Jamie's line. Embarrassed at the triteness of her question, she sipped at her cocktail and stared at her feet.

"You know all right, sweetie," he laughed. "Your charming blush betrays all!"

"It's news to me."

The false ring to the phrase embarrassed her further, and she looked desperately over Jamie's shoulder for someone to come and change the conversation.

But Jamie was enjoying himself.

"As I said, the dear boy's a little inarticulate at the moment, so don't be surprised if he fumbles his lines. You may have to give him a piece of paper and a pencil to write them down."

"Oh really, Jamie!"

She couldn't think of anything sensible to say, so she turned to stare at the leather-bound volumes in the library shelves behind her.

"Have you read Disraeli's novels?" she asked in an unsteady voice.

"Only a couple. Charlie, on the other hand, has probably read all of them. He's the family know-all when it comes to English literature."

"Perhaps he'd make a good writer himself."

"Who knows? Charlie's one of those people who has to be pushed into doing things. Not enough ambition. His father can't push him because Charlie has an aversion to parental advice."

Margot drained her cocktail glass.

"Don't we all, Jamie. And speaking of which, be an angel and accompany me to get another of these. I need a little Dutch courage for this dinner à quatre with Charlie and his parents. I wish you were coming too."

"Not in Charlie's plans. Besides, I've just asked Katie to join me and some others at the Berkeley. You'll find my uncle and aunt very easy to get on with."

Margot took him by the arm as they left the library and headed for the bar in the drawing room.

"Jamie, if it's true that Charlie's, well, sort of taken to me in rather a big way, do you suppose he's told his parents?"

"Heavens, no! He never tells them anything. Your dinner is his way of letting them find out for themselves that he's mad about you. Typical Charlie tactics."

"You mean he's done this before."

"Before he went to Canada. He got smitten by the daughter of his history tutor at Eton. The day he left Eton, he invited her up to London and took her to lunch with Uncle Walter at the House of Commons. He'd been so busy lusting after her that he'd never bothered to investigate her mind. Over lunch she told Uncle Walter that Oswald Mosley was her political hero, and she was sick in the Central Hall on the way out. Uncle W. was not amused, and Charlie slunk around like a wounded animal for weeks."

Margot laughed. "Maybe I'll be just as big a disappointment!"

"Not you, Yank. You'll bowl them over."

Which she did.

"May I?" asked Sir Walter, and kissed her on the cheek as they parted near midnight in the forecourt of the Savoy. "You must come down to Bowes Court for a weekend soon, my dear."

"I'd love to. And thank you both for such a delightful evening."

Margot turned and embraced Lady Garland.

"Don't keep my son up too late," said Charlie's mother with a smile. "I know he'll want to dance the night away with you." Charlie made a face. "And tell your mother I'm going to ring her and ask her to lunch," added Lady Garland as she stepped into a waiting cab.

Charlie and Margot took a taxi to the Four Hundred. On the way, she told him what lovely people she thought his parents were.

"They were being particularly nice tonight," said Charlie. "They obviously think you're terrific."

"And do you?" She snuggled close to him.

"Stupid question. Of course I do."

She kissed him on the cheek.

"Then don't be a stuffy Englishman and keep it to yourself. I want to hear it!"

At the nightclub they sipped champagne and danced until late. Scarcely moving to the soft, slow music, Margot, her cheek against Charlie's, held his left hand tight against her right breast. Through the mauve silk the pressure of his hand was doing pleasant things to her nipple, and the brushing together of their thighs as they traced almost statically the steps of a slow foxtrot was igniting a fire in her loins. She wanted to tell him that right now, more than anything else in the world, she wished they were in some secret place where he could close the chapter on her virginity. She desperately wanted to surrender to this gentle, appealing young man with the large brown eyes and unruly forelock and the tall, slim frame that she now hugged to her. But realizing how little she still knew him and how unsure she was of his likely reaction, she hesitated. And then she felt against the inside of her thigh the hard evidence of his own arousal.

"I can feel you, Charlie," she whispered in his ear.

He giggled nervously. "I'm afraid you probably can."

He pulled back slightly from her, but she hugged him to her again.

"Don't. It's flattering."

"Well, that's the effect you have on me."

"You're having the same on me. What are we going to do about it, Charlie?" She smothered a laugh on the shoulder of his dinner jacket.

"Nothing we can do, damnit. But it's time to get ourselves home."

"Do you think I'm very forward?" she asked him later as the cab sped down Piccadilly. She was snuggled in his arms, and she had guided one of his hands down the top of her dress and into her bra where he lightly massaged a swollen nipple with his forefinger.

"Yes, thank goodness! And you probably think me very backward."

"You're doing fine, Charlie. Just fine."

They swayed with the cab as it swung into Berkeley Square, and she sought his lips for a kiss that they held until the cab drew up outside 43 Hill Street.

"Hurry home, handsome."

She got quickly out of the cab and disappeared into the house.

The following Monday morning Margot was awakened by a telephone call at nine-thirty from Charlie.

"I thought my first telephone call on my first day at the office should be to you."

"A sweet thought, Charlie. And I'm glad you made it in on time."

There was a pause and she heard Charlie clear his throat.

"Margot, I want to tell you that I've decided that I'm very much in love with you." There was another pause. "Is it awful to say it over the telephone?"

Margot ran her fingers energetically through her unkempt hair.

"No, Charlie, provided you say it to me face to face the moment we next meet."

For a split second she thought of saying that she would tell him then what her own feelings were about him. But she couldn't hold back what she really wanted to tell him right away.

"I think I'm in love with you too, Charlie."

"Think?" said Charlie.

"Yes, 'think'. It's all happening so fast. I need a little more time to be sure. Does that make sense?"

"I suppose so. Yes, of course it does."

Margot turned and saw her mother in the doorway.

"Charlie, I'm standing in my bathrobe in Father's study, and Mother's just come in. Will we see each other today?"

"We'll go together to William Douglas-Home's drinks party. I'll pick you up at six."

"Marvellous! Work hard! And thanks for the call, and everything." She replaced the receiver and turned to her mother. "Charlie. He says he's in love with me."

"Another one. Do you want a boiled egg?"

Margot sighed. "Mother, this is not just 'another one', you know. I didn't tell him I thought I was in love with him too just for kicks."

She strode past her mother onto the landing and turned towards her bedroom.

"Just don't get too deeply involved, darling, that's all. By the look of the news these days, we'll be heading back for Washington quicker than you think."

Margot said nothing. She closed the bedroom door behind her and threw herself back on the bed.

"Head back to Washington?" she said out loud. "Forget it!"

War might break out before I know how much I'm really in love with him, she told herself. But that won't stop me from marrying him. And if he hasn't proposed to me by the time the shooting starts, I'll just have to do the proposing myself.

Pleased with her spirit of defiance, she marched off to the bathroom to start preparing herself for the day.

*

Through the rest of July and all August, as Europe moved nearer to war, Charlie and Margot were inseparable. Their friends, almost without exception, were by now assuming that an engagement was in the offing, indeed that they might already be secretly engaged. Charlie would smile shyly when asked if he had popped the question, and would invariably respond: "What's the hurry?" Margot flatly denied, even to Jamie, that she was about to become engaged. "He hasn't proposed to me. Period." In Katie alone she had confided her true feelings and intentions. She was sure that, come the fall, Charlie would propose marriage, and she would accept. But if war broke out before then and she were threatened with immediate repatriation to the States, she would have to force the issue with Charlie: "We get engaged now, or I go home."

Katie was delighted to be in on her sister's secret plan and swore not to divulge it to anyone. Rumours of an impending engagement nonetheless abounded, and in early August Harland and Elinor Moore decided to have it out with their elder daughter.

"But I keep telling you, he hasn't ever mentioned marriage!" Margot told them with some irritation.

"And if he does? Don't you think your parents have a right to know what your answer is going to be?"

"I don't *know*, Mother, what my answer's going to be," she replied, trying her best to sound convincing. "We're very fond of each other, but marriage is a big step. We both know that, I'm sure."

"You must think carefully," said her father gently, "about what a wartime marriage could mean. He could be away a very long time – "

"Or get killed!" interjected her mother.

Moore glared at his wife.

"I just want you to think carefully, sweetheart," he repeated. "You're very young. You owe it to yourself more than to anyone to be sure in your own mind that you could handle it. And your mother and I want to be sure too."

"Father, if he asks me, I'll think very carefully before giving an answer, I promise. Just don't be surprised if the answer is yes. But it won't be yes unless I'm sure that that's what I really want and that I can handle it."

"How can you possibly know!" snapped her mother. "It would be far better if you went back home now and let time tell how much you really care for this young man."

"For God's sakes, you two! Why are you talking as though Charlie and I were already secretly engaged? Can't I have a good friend without all this talk of war and getting killed and me being sent home!"

"All right, calm down, honey," said her father soothingly. "We don't mean to over-dramatize, and nobody's being sent home, at least not unless things get really bad here in Europe. And we're certainly not discouraging your relationship with Charlie. So let's talk no more of it now."

Elinor sighed, shook her head, and left the room.

"You can't blame your mother for being concerned, Margot," said Harland when she was gone.

"Father, I'm nineteen and I know what I'm doing. That's all I want you to understand. And right now I'm not doing anything that you or Mother could possibly object to. Right?"

Harland nodded.

"OK then, Father. Nobody need get upset."

Margot felt that she had successfully put the lid back on the pot, and for a time there were indeed no further cross-examinations as to her intentions in the matter. Which was just as well, because she was growing daily more determined to become Mrs Charles Garland.

It was Jamie who eventually brought matters to a head – or as Margot later observed, it was really Hitler and Stalin. On 23rd August, to the astonishment of the rest of the world, the two sworn enemies, Germany and the Soviet Union, signed a non-aggression pact. That evening, Jamie was visiting his Uncle Walter and Charlie at the Member of Parliament's Westminster home.

"That's it!" said Sir Walter with an air of finality. "Hitler can now do what he damn well pleases with Danzig and Poland. We'll be at war within a month."

For a while they discussed the dangerous new situation which, as Jamie observed, would almost certainly lead to Charlie's being soon out of the City and into uniform.

"Cynthia tells me that Elinor Moore and the girls will be going home at the declaration of war," said Sir Walter as they helped themselves to a second whisky and soda. "Gloomy as the situation will be, I think we ought to consider giving them a little send-off party, don't you think?"

Jamie looked at Charlie who looked at his feet.

"What do you say, boys?" said Sir Walter.

Charlie was looking stricken.

"Actually, Uncle Walter," said Jamie hesitantly, "I think the best thing would be if Charlie were to waste no time in putting Margot out of her misery and proposed to her. I know that's what she's waiting for."

Charlie opened his mouth to say something, but nothing came out.

"Is that what she wants, Charlie? Is that what *you* want?" Sir Walter's brusque tone discomforted Charlie even more.

"Well, yes, Father. I think it is. Yes, it is." His voice dropped away as though the pain of confessing a mortal sin were overcoming him.

His father's face broke into a wide smile.

"Well, for God's sake, old boy, what on earth are you waiting for, then? Get on with it!"

"I'll drink to that!" said Jamie.

Charlie's brow furrowed, then he matched his father's smile. "You'd approve?"

"I certainly would, Charlie. Nicest and prettiest American girl I've met over here since Thelma Furness, and it's just as well for both of you that this is 1939 and not 1930 or the Prince of Wales would have snapped her up! And don't worry about your mother. I can square her. She'll say you're too young to marry, but these are exceptional times. A word of advice though. You'll be off for full officer training as soon as we're at war. Marry her when you get your commission. Shouldn't take more than a few months."

Charlie got himself invited by the Moore family to dine at their home the following evening. He arrived clutching separate bunches of red and pink roses, a dozen of each.

44

To his relief, he found the womenfolk of the family not yet assembled; Harland Moore greeted him alone, suggested he leave the roses in the hall for the time being, and escorted him into the drawing room for a cocktail.

Charlie wasted no time.

"May I talk to you alone, sir, for a moment?"

"We are alone, Charlie. Go ahead. What can I get you to drink?"

"Gin and tonic, sir. Thank you."

He followed his host to the corner of the room where a drinks wagon stood laden with bottles and glasses.

"Sir, I would like this evening to ask Margot if she would consent to be my wife. Before doing so, I naturally want to ask your permission."

Harland Moore said nothing as he bent over the wagon and poured a gin and tonic. Then he turned and proffered the glass to his guest.

"This comes as no surprise, Charlie, and in normal circumstances I couldn't think of a better match. But are you both sure you love and need each other enough to start a married life as war breaks out? Have you thought of the probability of long separations, lots of anxiety, and all that? Do you think you can both handle it?"

Charlie swallowed hard, then took a first sip at his drink.

"I've thought all about that, sir, and rather imagine that Margot has as well – "

"Thought about what? Isn't someone going to put these lovely roses in water?"

Margot stood in the doorway, cradling the bunches of roses in her arms.

"Well, may I join you?"

"Charlie and I were just having a little private chat," said Harland, pouring himself a bourbon and water. "Why don't you take the roses down to the kitchen and put them in vases."

"The red are for you and the pink for your mother," said Charlie hoarsely.

Margot walked across the room and pecked Charlie on the cheek.

"Very thoughtful of you. Mother will be touched.

Carry on with your 'private chat' about me, but make it brief; I don't want to have to hang around in that hot kitchen for long."

She turned and left the room, and hurried down the back stairs to the kitchen. So Charlie's finally taken the bull by the horns! she told herself excitedly. She was grinning happily when she confronted her mother and Mrs Watts, the cook, across the kitchen table.

"Pink roses for you, Mother, from your future son-in-law. Red roses for his future wife."

"Oh my!" exclaimed Mrs Watts, stopping stirring a sauce.

Elinor Moore, who had just picked up a full water pitcher, put it down again on the table.

"Is that what Charlie's talking to your father about?" Her voice trembled.

"So it seems. I'm expecting a proposal any minute now. So please look happy, Mother! You couldn't possibly ask for a nicer son-in-law."

She came round the table and put an arm around her mother's shoulders.

"You've known him such a short time, and you're so young," said Elinor, tears now welling up in her eyes. "Are you sure you know what you're doing?"

"I certainly do, Mother."

"I'm sure you do," chimed in Mrs Watts. "And they're such a lovely family, the Garlands. Very suitable, my dear."

While she arranged the roses in vases, Margot sought to reassure her mother, talking of the happy tradition of mixing good East Coast American blood with good upper-class English blood. She told her how much she loved Charlie and respected his parents, and vice versa, and how she looked forward to having children and bringing them on visits to the family in America. Throughout the recital of this catalogue of joys, Elinor said nothing, sniffing and dabbing at her eyes as she slowly folded some freshly laundered napkins. There was a look of defeat and resignation on her face as Harland Moore appeared in the kitchen and went straight over to his daughter and hugged and kissed her.

"Go upstairs to Charlie, honey. He has a question to ask you." As Margot hurried away, he turned to his wife. "Come on now, sweetheart. The young man's convinced me," he said with a broad grin of encouragement.

"Nobody's convinced *me*," she retorted with a sniff. "What will she do when the war starts?"

"We'll discuss that with them later. Now go on upstairs and repair the tear damage." He kissed her on the cheek. "And tell that tardy younger daughter of ours to come down and help Mrs Watts."

Margot entered the drawing room carrying the vase of roses.

"Now, where shall we put them?" she asked, trying to sound as casual as possible. Avoiding Charlie's eyes, she looked around the room, selected a pembroke table in the window, and asked Charlie to make space on it by moving aside some trinkets. That done, Charlie took her by the hand and pulled her to him.

"Your father says you can marry me if you want to."

Margot started to giggle. "Well, that's *one* way of proposing, I suppose. Charlie, you are wonderful! May I take it that *you* want to marry me?"

"I didn't put it very well, did I?" he said with a shy smile. "Yes, I very much want to marry you. How about early next year?"

Margot frowned. "Do we have to wait that long?"

"My father feels I ought to get my commission in the Brigade first, and your father seems to agree."

"But do *you* agree?"

"I think it's probably sensible."

"But we can announce the engagement right away, can't we?"

"Of course."

"Sealed with a kiss, then, my darling."

She tipped her head upwards and their lips met.

That night, before going to sleep, an elated Margot wrote in her diary:

This evening C. proposed and I accepted. We'll announce the engagement in the papers on Sept. 1. Marry not later than March. M. put on a brave face this

47

evening, but she's not happy. F. seems delighted. K. too. As for me I'm over the moon. I *do* love him, and I am *thrilled* that my plan has worked out so perfectly. At dinner F. said Amb. Kennedy is still convinced Britain won't go to war. C. says his father expects war any day now. I got C. just in time. We'll buy the engagement ring tomorrow. He's seen a diamond ring at Cartier he'd like me to have. His darling father has given him the money for it. He and Lady G. are delighted, C. says. Happy day! Happy me!

3

The announcement of Margot's and Charlie's engagement appeared in the London papers on the morning that Hitler's divisions swept into Poland. Two days later, Britain was at war. Ten days later, Charlie reported to the Royal Military College at Sandhurst which had been rapidly placed on a wartime footing, converting part-time cadets like Charlie into commissioned officers. He would be there for the next four months.

Assured that her fiancé would be able to get to London to see her at regular intervals, Margot was in good spirits as she waved Charlie goodbye. His officer's training course was all that stood between them and marriage, so the sooner he got on with it the better.

That evening, she attended a farewell party given by Ambassador Kennedy for his children. All but Rosemary would be returning with Mrs Kennedy to the safety of the United States within the next few days. Kick Kennedy confided to Margot her misery at leaving England. The ambassador's repeated predictions that Britain could not possibly win the war made the parting from her English friends, especially Billy Hartington, unbearably painful.

"Don't let them send you home, Margot," she urged. "You have every reason to stay now, and I only wish I was in your position."

"Don't worry; I'm staying all right," she assured her friend. "Whether the Germans come or not!"

The closing months of 1939 were a period of watching and waiting, both in England and on the continent. Jamie, whose Grenadier Guards battalion had gone to

France as part of the British Expeditionary Force, wrote home that sitting on the Belgian frontier waiting for the Germans to come was the most boring thing he'd done since Latin prose at Eton. And back in Britain, the people were beginning to feel the strain of the unnatural inactivity. Sir Walter Garland, like most of his parliamentary colleagues, complained that the Prime Minister's weekly briefing of the House of Commons on the war situation was invariably "as dull as ditchwater". And to add to the general depression, it rained incessantly through the last weeks of the year.

Margot, on the other hand, had never been happier. The declaration of war had come as something of a personal release. Engaged to an Englishman who would soon be a fighting Guards officer, she felt herself to be a part of the British war effort. Her plan had worked. Her mother often referred to some as yet unchosen date in the future when "the girls and I will obviously have to go home", but Margot resisted the temptation to argue any more at this stage. The day, if it came, would be the moment for her to dig her heels into British soil and refuse to go. In the meantime she would keep her counsel and not create domestic friction.

When Charlie was able to get a thirty-six hours leave pass, he would take the train to London, go straight to his parents' house to greet them, and then spend as much as possible of the time at his disposal with Margot. Usually they would lunch together at a favourite restaurant, spend the afternoon holding hands at the movies, meet family or friends for cocktails in the evening, then dine and dance until the early hours when Charlie would take the milk train back to Camberley.

One afternoon, following lunch at Prunier, he hailed a cab and ordered it to Lowndes Square, off Knightsbridge.

"Why are we going to Lowndes Square?" asked Margot.

"A friend at Sandhurst has a small flat there." He smiled and took her hand. "For a modest consideration he has agreed to let me use it whenever I want to, provided he's not using it himself."

"How great! But won't your parents mind you not staying with them when you're up here?"

"If I want to stay overnight at the flat, I just won't tell them that I'm coming to London."

The cab drew up outside a modern apartment block on the west side of the square. Moments later Charlie was turning the key in the door of a third-floor apartment.

"Small but cosy," he announced as he ushered Margot in.

"You've been here before, then."

"Early this morning. On my way to my parents' I cased the joint, as you Americans say."

In the narrow hallway, he took her in his arms and kissed her.

"So my Charlie found us a little hideaway!" said Margot between kisses.

"It's well stocked; he's got a super record collection; and – " he paused, "there are clean sheets on the bed."

"Are there, now?"

"Yes, there are."

She pulled away from him and walked into the living room. Charlie followed, biting his lip.

"There's a fire been made up in the grate," she said, pointing to the fireplace which took up most of one end of the small room. "Can we light it?"

"Why not?"

"Then you get it going while I case the kitchen and see if I can come up with some coffee."

"It's the door on the left off the hall."

Margot found it, put on a kettle, and started opening cupboards in search of coffee and cups. Her thoughts were racing, and she noticed that her hands were shaking badly as she matched two cups with their saucers. So this was to be it. This was the moment. She tried to remember the date which would now be such an important one in her personal history. And how glad she was that it was going to happen at last! She might have waited for marriage if it hadn't been for this ridiculously long engagement. Yes, that was the real justification. She found a bottle of Camp Coffee and poured measures of the dark brown liquid into the cups. She had often wondered whether it was going to hurt, but now she didn't give a damn about that. The thought of Charlie's body finally

51

being revealed to her suddenly made her giggle as there flashed into her mind at the same time a Christmas gift that had stood for days near the decorated Christmas tree many years back. Meticulously packaged in gift wrap, it was nonetheless so easily identifiable by its shape as the beginner's bicycle she had asked for that she had wondered why on earth they had bothered to wrap it. Whenever she could she had sneaked up to it and felt it all over, trying to guess the colour and imagine the brightness of the chrome. Then, when the great moment had arrived on Christmas morning and she had been allowed to tear away the wrappings, she had burst into tears on discovering that it was black, and that instead of gleaming chrome there was only a dull grey metal finish. After all the fantasies she enjoyed about making love with Charlie, would the actual act of love now turn out to be another black bicycle?

The boiling water rattled the lid of the kettle, and she poured it into the cups.

"Oh, bugger!" she heard Charlie exclaim from the next room. "I forgot to open the flue. We're going to be smoked out." Margot hurried to the living room. "Excuse my military language," he said as he searched awkwardly, with a hand thrust up the chimney, for the flue handle.

"For God's sakes don't burn yourself." She winced as she saw the flames beginning to curl up from the ignited paper "Got it!" he shouted as a shower of soot fell, coating the sleeve of his jacket. "Oh, Christ!" He began brushing it off.

"Don't touch anything. Go straight to the bathroom. We'll never be allowed back here if your friend finds black finger marks all over."

"Especially on the sheets!"

Margot smacked him on the bottom as he passed her. "Watch your step, Cadet Garland."

While Charlie cleaned up, she tidied the grate, brought the coffee in, and pulled an armchair nearer the fireplace. She searched through a pile of records by the phonograph, selected a Paderewski recording of Rachmaninov's Second Piano Concerto, wound up the machine and checked the sequence of the three records.

52

Meanwhile she was asking herself what had come over Charlie. He was certainly very confident that she was going to surrender her virginity to him right there and then. She had never known him setting the pace like this; she had always felt that it had been very much up to her to pull him along in such limited sexual intimacies as they had so far enjoyed. Maybe it was pressure from his fellow officer cadets that had induced this new boldness. Whatever the reason his cockiness by no means upset her; it was just unexpected. As was the arrangement he had made about the apartment. If this was the new Charlie, she had no complaints! The army seemed to be having a very desirable effect on him.

They drank their coffee in front of the fire, Charlie sitting in the armchair, Margot crossed-legged on the floor at his feet, resting her back against his knees as she stared into the flames licking the lumps of coal in the hearth. They were silent, listening to the music. When the moment came to turn the records, she rose to her feet. Charlie followed her to the phonograph, watched her put on the second half of the concerto, then took her by the hand and led her wordlessly to the bedroom. A modest-sized double bed took up most of the space in the small room, and at the foot of it they stood for a moment, arms around each other's waist, looking at each other squarely in the eye.

"This is very important to you, Charlie, isn't it?" she said softly. "I mean you really want us to make love before we're married. You're not doing it simply because you think that's what *I* want."

He kissed her lightly on the lips.

"Of course I want it. I can't wait through all that engagement. And you never know," he said, looking towards the window, "things may happen suddenly in this war."

Margot smiled and put a hand up to stroke his cheek.

"Well, this lady here wants it, war or no war, and she wants it badly and now."

She drew back from him and started to undress, un-buckling the belt on her pleated skirt. Charlie sat down on the bed and watched her. In a hesitant voice he asked her whether she had ever undressed in front of a man before.

She laughed. "Only my doctor, darling. Don't worry; I wasn't lying when I told you I was a virgin. You're not about to discover that I'm really a scarlet woman."

She unhooked the single strand of pearls round her neck and laid them on the top of the chest of drawers behind her. After pulling the cashmere sweater over her head she came and sat next to him to detach her stockings from her garter belt. He ran a hand down one firm, warm thigh as she rolled the second stocking off and let it fall to the carpet.

"Unhook my bra for me, sweetheart." She pivoted to turn her back to him. The bra followed the stockings to the floor. "I feel embarrassed being almost naked while you're still fully dressed," she said, standing up. "Off with them, Charlie!" She stood waiting, her thumbs inserted in the waistband of her lace-trimmed silk panties.

Charlie was staring at her breasts, mesmerized by what he had felt but never properly seen. They looked fuller than they had seemed to his earlier touch. He got to his feet and placed his hands over them.

"You're beautiful, Margot," he said in a whisper.

"Hurry up and show me how beautiful you are."

She went and propped the pillows up against the headboard and stretched out against them, watching him.

"Do you realize we've never even seen each other in swimming clothes?" she said. "I had my period and you had a bad cold that one weekend when we could have swum at the Deans."

"Disappointed in what you now see before you?"

"Absolutely not!"

She looked approvingly at the tall, slim young man pulling an undervest over his tousled head.

"You have a wonderful body and I can see that you're in perfect shape. That square-bashing and physical training you complain about seems to be keeping you marvellously trim. You must be feeling terribly well, too."

Charlie stood at the end of the bed, staring at her.

"I'm sorry, Charlie. I think I'm talking too much.

54

Perhaps I am a bit nervous after all. But I know you'll be gentle. And do you have one of those things with you?''

"This?'' said Charlie, opening a clenched fist to reveal a small cardboard container in the palm of his hand.

Margot nodded. "Neither of our families would be wildly happy if I was a pregnant bride.''

As Charlie came round the bed, she reached behind and under her and slid her panties down. Kicking them off her ankles, she pulled the pillows down and lay back. Charlie turned away from her as he dropped his underpants, and for a moment a sudden feeling of shyness overcame her.

There was not much afternoon light filtering through the muslin-draped window, but enough for her to see that her fiancé's penis was impressively stiff, and that the circumcised head appeared to wear a deep blush. She thought of pain and blood, and that made her sit up on her elbows.

"Shouldn't we put a towel on the bed?'' she asked in a hoarse voice.

Charlie nodded, left the room and returned a moment later to spread a bath towel over the pale green sheets. Then, without a word, he left the room again.

"Where are you going?''

There was no answer, but he was quickly back, and Margot saw that he had drawn the filmy sheath over his swollen member. She was disappointed; she had wanted to touch it naked. But she said nothing. She raised her arms to Charlie and drew him down to her.

"I'm ready for you, darling,'' she said softly, as she felt his chest heavy against her breasts. "I know I am.'' She spread her legs wide to let him settle between them, and for a while she felt the tip of his penis brushing gently against her golden-haired mound. Then, guided by his hand, the tip began to exert pressure against her vagina, and she hungrily sought his mouth with her lips, moaning quietly. Suddenly the gentle instrument that had been lightly pressing became a miniature battering-ram. She caught her breath, shuddered, cried out and shook her head violently from side to side. She bit on her lip and then, in a wave of blissful relief from pain, she became aware that the cruel battering-ram had become a silk-smooth piston, gently easing its way forward and backward in a slow, comforting rhythm. A moment later, she felt Charlie's body tauten as he gasped for breath, then shivers convulsed him as his torso lifted then sank back heavily on her. For a while they lay in silence, holding each other tightly, and Margot felt the beads of sweat that moistened Charlie's brow mingling with the tears that now coursed down her own cheeks and trickled coolly into her ears.

It took her a little time to collect her thoughts, and when she did, she told herself that the act of losing her virginity had felt good all right. But not sensational. No exploding fireworks. No shooting stars. Did anyone really feel all that? She kissed the still prone and silent Charlie on the cheek.

"It *was* good, darling," she said as if he might have been reading her thoughts and needed reassurance.

"Didn't hurt?" he mumbled.

"Hardly at all. And I feel wonderful now. Really I do."

Charlie slowly rolled over then raised himself on one elbow.

"But I don't think I gave you much pleasure," he said. "I was too quick, I think." He glanced down to her still spread legs. "Oh God, it must have hurt. You bled quite a lot. I'm so sorry, I – "

She reached and pulled his head down to her, and stopped his words with a long kiss. At the end of it she simply said:

"I love you, Charlie. Please God, don't let the war hurt us."

Then the tears broke again, and he held her tight as she sobbed helplessly in his arms.

The next day, Margot wrote to her twin brother, Larry, just as she had always done when anything particularly wonderful or awful had happened to her. Not that she told him her fiancé had just deflowered her; that would shock him. She merely wanted to reassure him that everything was beautiful between herself and Charlie, and that she was the happiest woman in the world. It pained her somewhat to keep from a brother in whom she normally confided everything the details of her developing intimacy with her husband-to-be. But Larry would not approve. From his early teens he had granted himself the role of diligent overseer of his two sisters' honour, sometimes to their amusement and sometimes to their irritation. In letters written to them from Phillips Academy he would urge them to choose their dates with care, and during vacations he would question them searchingly on the behaviour of their escorts. Margot had found his concern rather endearing, as long as it was confined to advice rather than intervention. Katie was far less tolerant, and would tell her brother to go shut himself up in a monastery where he obviously belonged.

Dear, funny Larry! Margot loved him enough to forgive the streak of hypocrisy which she could not fail to recognize in him. He had once, in a moment of emotional anguish, told her of the strong attraction he felt towards older women, an attraction which tortured him since the objects of his yearning were so obviously untouchable. In particular he had confessed to her his desperate love for the forty-year-old wife of one of his teachers at Andover, and of how for days on end he had hidden his tears of anguish in the john following the announcement of her untimely death from a brain haemorrhage.

Just as she would not share with her twin the facts of her sexual graduation, she would deny that knowledge to her younger sister as well. For the time being. She had no wish, at this stage, to further fan the flames of Katie's desire to lose her virginity as soon as possible.

For the moment, there was little talk of sending the ladies of the Moore family back across the Atlantic. Not a single Nazi bomb had yet fallen on England, and Hitler seemed in no hurry to set his aggressive foot on the soil of the Low Countries or France, let alone on that of the island kingdom across the water. The Soviet invasion of Finland at the end of November provided Europe with the only resounding clash of arms since the subjugation of Poland. As Harland Moore told his family, it seemed quite possible that Hitler was having serious second thoughts about enlarging his field of conquest.

And so life went on at 43 Hill Street much as it had before the outbreak of the war, except that each member of the family now slung a gas mask in a cardboard carrier over one shoulder on leaving the house, and at dusk, whoever was home stepped out into the darkened street no longer lit by street lamps to check that no light filtered through chinks in the blackout curtains that draped every window of the house. The difficulties of moving about London in the blackout in no way discouraged Margot and Katie from pursuing their social life, which showed few signs of slowing down. Charlie had voiced no objection to his fiancée's insistence that their engagement, and his absence, should not be a bar to her continued enjoyment of the company of her wide circle of friends. He would join them whenever he could get away for an evening or a weekend. In the meantime he trusted her without reservation.

Charlie was granted Christmas leave, and Sir Walter and Lady Garland invited the Moores and their two daughters to join them and Charlie for Christmas and New Year at Bowes Court, the family seat in the Hampshire countryside. They were the happiest of days for Margot. Her Charlie was at her side, attentive, loving, funny and so full of life. The war seemed utterly remote, almost unreal. But then, on the morning of New Year's Eve, coming down early before breakfast to retrieve the purse she had left the previous evening in the drawing room, she surprised her hostess arranging flowers, and weeping as she did so.

Lady Garland made no attempt to conceal her tears as Margot stammered an apology for intruding.

"That's all right, dear. Don't rush away. I get like this sometimes these days. The thought that this might be, well, you know –" She sniffed and dabbed at her eyes with the back of her hand. "It could be our last Christmas and New Year together. God knows what 1940 has in store for us. Especially for Charlie."

She choked back more sobs as she inserted chrysanthemums into a tall crystal vase on the grand piano. Margot came to her, wanting but not daring to put an arm around her.

"We mustn't think that way. Maybe there isn't going to be any real war for us. Father's highly doubtful."

"Forgive me for saying so, my dear, but I don't think you Americans really understand what's going on here in Europe. Talk to my husband. He'll tell you there's going to be a real war, and a terrible one. And he knows what he's talking about, I'm afraid."

"But I just know Charlie's going to be all right!" said Margot, trying to sound comforting while she knew how ridiculous a remark it was.

Lady Garland suddenly smiled. "That's what a young woman in love should feel, but you cannot possibly *know*."

"You love him as a mother. So you must feel it too."

"I'm trying, dear. But it isn't easy. Remember, I lost my only two brothers in the last war. The elder, Jamie's father, was killed only five weeks before the Armistice. He was just twenty-three. Eddie was killed the day after his twenty-first birthday."

She seemed to have control of herself now, and she put a hand on Margot's shoulder.

"Go and wake that sister of yours. She's always late for breakfast and it does so upset the routine in the kitchen."

Margot leaned forward and kissed her on her tear-dampened cheek.

"I love you Garlands!" she said.

"Thank you, dear. And we're so happy to have you among us. Now go and give Katie a shove."

Margot left and hurried up the broad, carved-oak staircase and down the long corridor to the guest wing. If what happened to Lady Garland's brothers befell Charlie this time, she thought, she would never break her ties with this lovely family. The elder brother had had time to father Jamie before dying. If the English and the Germans are really going to fight, then Charlie must give her a baby before he goes. She'd bring him up here at Bowes Court. It wasn't the first time she'd had this thought, but somehow it seemed to be impressing itself upon her more strongly than ever after her encounter with the weeping Lady Garland.

She opened the door of Katie's darkened room,

approached the bed and gently shook an exposed shoulder.

"Time to get up if you want breakfast."

Katie rolled over and rubbed her eyes.

"Damn you, sis. Joe Junior and I were just spreading a rug out on the grass, and it wasn't for a picnic!"

"Try again tonight, nympho. Let's hope it starts where it left off."

Charlie was commissioned an ensign in the Grenadier Guards in the second week of February, and immediately joined the training battalion at Windsor. He was informed that his stay would be a short one – only four weeks – after which he would be granted ten days' leave before embarking for France. France! Jamie's battalion! My God I'm going to the front!

He walked hurriedly from the adjutant's office, where this news had been imparted to him, to the Officers' Mess where he poured himself an eleven o'clock cup of tea and sank into a deep leather armchair to collect his thoughts. Margot wasn't going to like this one bit. The odds had been on his joining a battalion remaining in England. Now he would be shipped off to the front immediately after what would obviously have to be a very short honeymoon. The wedding was set for 12th March; he would be leaving for France on the twenty-fourth. Did they have to do this when they knew he was just getting married? The adjutant had expressed his sympathy, but these things happened in wartime, and besides, they thought he'd appreciate joining the battalion in which his cousin was serving. They'd had to pull a string or two to do that.

Charlie decided not to break the news to his fiancée over the telephone. He'd tell her face to face at the weekend. It was only two days away.

Margot took the news calmly. Ever since Charlie's father had convinced her that Hitler intended to fight a full-scale war, she had lived with the knowledge that Charlie would, sooner or later, be sent away to fight. But although Jamie had gone to France within days of the outbreak of war she was, like Charlie, rather taken aback by the haste with which he was now to be dispatched to the front.

"At least you'll be with Jamie, darling. And you mustn't worry about me. I'm going to miss you dreadfully, but I'll manage all right, and I'll be terribly proud of you."

It was only after Charlie returned to Windsor on the Sunday evening, leaving her alone with her thoughts, that she began to appreciate fully what lay in store for her. How was she really going to survive without Charlie after a honeymoon full, she assumed, of frenzied love-making? How could she tell how much she was going to miss him until he was actually gone? It might be far worse than she anticipated. And would they succeed in making her pregnant during their honeymoon? Supposing the fighting started before his first leave – and goodness knows when that might be – and he got killed without having given her a child?

Now she couldn't wait for the wedding. The second half of February seemed to drag by with painful slowness. In the cold, the sleet, and eventually the snow which laid a thin grimy grey mantle on the city, London seemed to be prostrate with both boredom and sloth. Even the growing suspicion that "when the spring comes, so will Hitler" did nothing to jerk people out of their temporary inertia. Margot now normally went out in the evenings only when Charlie was in town, which was rarely more than once a week. To her frustration, the convenient arrangement for the use of the Lowndes Square flat had come to an end. Charlie's fellow cadet, now commissioned in the Coldstream Guards and on guard duty in London, had repossessed their love-nest. They had used it only three times.

She got out of bed late each morning, and spent the remainder of it helping around the house and sometimes assisting Mrs Watts get the lunch which her father and Katie – now working mornings as a volunteer at the embassy library – usually came home for. The afternoons she often spent closeted in her father's study, writing letters to friends and family back home and reading French literature. Although she could think of no logical reason why, Charlie's imminent departure for France had rekindled her fascination with things French, and she had decided to return to her study of the language and her exploration of the classics. She began to envy Charlie going to France even on so potentially perilous a mission, though Jamie had reported in his letters that it was almost like being on holiday there.

This particular afternoon, however, she had been devoting time to checking the wedding invitation replies until she recalled that she owed her grandfather Austin a letter congratulating him on his upcoming seventieth birthday. With Katie now gone, no doubt to a rendezvous with some uniformed admirer, she settled down into an armchair to read through the letter.

43 Hill Street
London W1
2nd March 1940

Dearest Grandpa,

If by some miracle this letter reaches you in time for your birthday, I'll never say another unkind word about the mails again! We are all thinking about you and *wish* that we could be at Adamswood to join in the celebration. I'm sure that if Mr Neville Chamberlain knew you he'd have agreed that greeting you on your seventieth was a high enough priority to let us use the transatlantic line for once. But Father has told us that even Ambassador Kennedy gets only ten minutes every Sunday to call his family, and you know how big *that* is! Incidentally, Katie still dreams about Joe Jr, so she says, but she seems to be doing fine without him when she's awake. No shortage of boyfriends here!

I hope you like the enclosed photo of my Charlie. Doesn't he look just gorgeous in his Guards officer's uniform? I almost cry when I think how long it may be before you get to meet him. You asked in your last letter whether he was taller than me. Yes, thank goodness, and he has a lovely soft baritone voice and isn't a bit pompous like some of his brother officers. I think I told you how fond we are of his parents. Sir Walter's not too popular with the Prime Minister because he was a staunch anti-appeasement ally of Churchill and Eden, so I don't suppose Mr Kennedy has much time for him either. He's pretty gloomy on the subject of the war, and says that it's only a matter of weeks now before the Germans make their next move. Charlie doesn't talk about it much, but I sense that he wants to get to the front before anything blows up even though he keeps saying how much he dreads leaving me. But I don't want him to want to stay behind here just because of me, if you get my meaning. He'll be a brilliant soldier and I'll be so proud of him. All the same, I can't help feeling scared for him. I feel a lot for his sweet mother in all of this. She lost both brothers in the last war.

To happier matters! Father and Mother and Katie and I all went to morning service at St Margaret's, Westminster last Sunday to get a good look at the church in which I'll be married. It's really beautiful; next to Westminster Abbey and across the street from Parliament. The list of guests who will be attending is very impressive. Mr Churchill and Mr Eden are coming, and goodness knows who else of importance. Ambassador Kennedy promises to be at the reception to propose a toast. We are going to close the service with "The Battle Hymn of the Republic" before we go out to the Wedding March. How I'm going to avoid crying I just don't know! The reception is at the Hyde Park Hotel, then Charlie and I leave overnight by train for Scotland. We'll have just eight days in Argyllshire at a lovely castle on Loch Fyne which is owned by friends of the Garlands. They're lending us the "guest tower" and will feed us, lend us a car to explore, and otherwise leave us as much alone as we want. What generous, sweet people! Then my Charlie heads off to join Jamie in saving the world.

Dearest Grandpa, please write and tell me you *don't* think, and Grandma either, that nineteen and a half is too young to marry. Mother said you both had some doubts. I promise you I'm doing the right thing, and I want everybody to be very happy about it. Besides, Englishmen make great husbands, so everyone here tells me!

I miss you both and hope that you will have a

wonderful birthday party. Will Larry get over from Yale
for it? I assume so. Anyway, tell him that his twin sister
hasn't heard from him for over a *month*. That's breaking
our rules. When he last wrote he told me that you were
going to buy him a new hunter from the Cottingham
farm for his twentieth birthday. So you finally gave
in, you weak, generous, lovable grandfather! He
doesn't deserve it, and please make sure he doesn't
break his neck this time. Your wedding present to
us arrived yesterday and I'm going to open it on your
birthday as a sort of double celebration. I *promise* you
we'll all be with you for your seventy-fifth, and with
great-grandchildren for you to spoil rotten.

All the best to Aunt Sarah, the Cootes et al. We shed
many a tear for dear old Nimrod. Will you get another
setter from the Micklems?

A big kiss to you and Grandma. M. and F. and Katie
all send their love. And so does my adored Grenadier
who can't wait to meet the loveliest American grandparents ever!

Your loving
Margot

PS The wedding dress is a dream! And I'll be wearing
Charlie's aunt's tiara. We'll send pictures, of course.

She got up, went to the desk and addressed an airmail
envelope. She sealed the letter in it, stamped it, and put it
on a table by the door. A gilt carriage clock on the mantelpiece showed a quarter to four. The room was cold, but
the house rule was that a coal fire would be lit in only one
room at a time, and not before five o'clock, which would
be early enough to warm the room in which the family
would spend the evening. When there were no guests,
they used the small panelled study on the second floor
in which she now sat. She shivered as she buttoned a
cardigan over her wool blouse. The memory of central
heating back home in Washington only made her feel
colder.

"To hell with house rules!" she suddenly said out loud,
springing from the armchair. Her mother was out, and
Mrs Watts was sure to be taking her afternoon nap. She

picked a box of matches off the mantelpiece, knelt in front of the fireplace and set light to the paper under the kindling wood. As the wood caught, she laid a few lumps of coal on top and with a pair of bellows puffed the small bluish flames into fiery tongues of orange. As she usually did nowadays whenever she lit a fire, she thought of Charlie struggling with the flue in the Lowndes Square flat just before they had made love for the first time.

God, I wish you were here now, lovely Charlie, she thought as she stared into the flames. And if I'm feeling like this now, how in hell am I going to manage when you're gone to fight the war?

4

On the eve of his daughter's wedding, Harland Moore, political counsellor at the United States Embassy in London, was asking himself from whence he would draw the strength to get through the following twenty-four hours. Not that he was not looking forward greatly to the discharge of his duties as father of the bride; nothing short of the invasion of England was going to deprive him of the enjoyment of giving his beloved Margot's hand in marriage to her handsome young Guards officer. He simply wished he was not so tired.

Ambassador Joseph P. Kennedy's customary Christmas and New Year vacation with the family in Palm Beach, Florida, had this year stretched into February, and his staff at the London embassy had begun to wonder whether he would return at all to his post. Then, in mid-February, President Roosevelt had announced that he was sending Under-Secretary of State Sumner Welles, a most polished and skilful diplomat, on a personal mission for him in Europe to assess the chances of halting the war. The Ambassador to the Court of St James, to his intense chagrin, had not been consulted about the Welles mission, and when in the last days of February Kennedy left the Florida sunshine to return to a Europe struggling through its coldest winter in forty-five years, Moore and his colleagues had braced themselves for what they were sure would be a frosting of the atmosphere at the embassy every bit as chilling as the winter weather.

After visits to the German, Italian and French leaders, Under-Secretary Welles had come to London for four days of consultations with Britain's leaders, an exercise of which the ambassador had taken a distinctly jaundiced view. And it was only after Welles' departure that Harland Moore had managed to be free to spend an entire evening with his family. He had every intention of doing so again this evening, come what may. He glanced at the clock set in the wall of his office. In a few minutes he would have to leave for the House of Commons where he was due to lunch with the man who would tomorrow become his daughter's father-in-law.

As he began to tidy the papers on his desk, a clerk came in and handed him a news bulletin. Mussolini would leave that afternoon for the Brenner Pass, it informed him, where, the next day, he would meet with the Führer. Well, thought Moore, as long as the two villains keep each other amused through the next twenty-four hours, the enjoyment of my daughter's wedding is in no jeopardy. He dropped the bulletin into an out-tray and went to collect his coat from the outer office.

"Why don't you just go home this afternoon?" Lois Dell, Moore's secretary, helped him into his overcoat. "I'm sure your family needs you, Mr Moore."

Moore smiled. "No, Lois. I have a feeling that the bride's father is the last person they want around the house right now. But you might call Mrs Moore and find out if there's anything she wants me to pick up on my way home this evening."

"I certainly will." She handed Moore his hat and umbrella. "Now go and have a really swell lunch with that lovely Sir Walter. After Mr Eden, there's no handsomer man in British politics. I get goose pimples every time I see his picture in the papers, so don't be surprised if when I meet him in the flesh tomorrow I faint clean away."

"He'd be deeply impressed, Lois, but we don't want you to miss the fun. I'll be back around three."

Leaving the office he crossed the corridor and set off down the staircase. At the street level he noticed that the waiting room by the main entrance was crowded. The majority of them, Moore knew from experience, would be Americans who had concluded that the so-called "phoney war" could not remain "phoney" much longer and that they had better get back across the Atlantic while the possibility still remained. It would not be easy. They would have to take their turn in securing space on British ships, which was scarce, since American vessels were now barred from entering the combat zones. Each time Moore saw the anxious faces of the would-be voyagers, he thought of his own agonizing over what to do about his own family. Elinor was once again trying to persuade him that, much as she detested the thought of leaving him alone in London, she ought really to take the girls back home as soon as Charlie had gone to France. She saw no point in Margot's waiting around in London for his eventual return. She'd be far better off in Washington, especially if she was pregnant. Harland promised a round-table family conference on the matter after the wedding and before Charlie left. He didn't want Margot upset before the wedding.

It was raining lightly. The tall, lean diplomat paused on the front steps of the five-storey Georgian building on the south-east corner of Grosvenor Square which housed the United States Embassy. He smoothed back the greying hair at his temples before carefully placing a grey homburg at a modestly rakish angle on his head. As he unfurled his umbrella, he glanced across the street into the large garden which now served as the base for the silver anti-aircraft blimp that hovered protectively over the square. That morning it was grounded for maintenance, and he watched for a moment the blue-uniformed Women's Auxiliary Air Force crew that manned it at work on its steel entangling wires.

At the corner he hailed a cab and ordered it to the House of Commons. He smiled at the printed notice pasted on the glass partition in front of him. DID YOU REMEMBER YOUR GAS MASK? Lois, who always carried one, had given up scolding her boss for not following her good example. Few Londoners bothered anymore. The novelty of being at war had long since given way to tedium and aggravation. First the blackout, now food rationing. Why can't we get on with it and over with it? was what the man-in-the-street wanted to know. Moore shared their frustration with the "phoney war", but he was now, if he had not been earlier, wholly convinced that the Nazi offensive against the Low Countries and France, and then Britain, could not now be long in coming. He agreed with Sir Walter: only the icy winter, which must be over soon, was staying the Führer's hand. Speculation that he was wavering between a peace initiative and all-out war was, to Moore's mind, wishful and dangerous thinking. And yet the American ambassador seemed wedded to such speculation.

It had been no secret in Washington, at the time that Moore was preparing for his posting to London, that the ambassador's espousal of the cause of Hitler's appeasers, especially those in Britain, was viewed with considerable distaste by the occupant of the White House. The fateful Munich agreement of 30th September 1938, which met almost all of the Nazi leader's demands while leaving Chamberlain with a worthless pledge of peace, had been hailed by Kennedy in his dispatches to Washington as a triumph of common sense. When Moore had arrived in London some five weeks later, he had found many of the embassy staff mulling gloomily over a dinner speech just delivered by the ambassador in which he had called for an end to emphasizing the differences between the democratic and dictator countries and had urged instead further attempts to re-establish good relations with the Third Reich. It left the anti-appeasers breathless with rage, and it left Moore, like many others, wondering what cogent reasons convinced the President and his Secretary of State, Cordell Hull, that the ambassador should be kept in such a sensitive post at such a portentous moment in history. By the time the inevitable had occurred and Britain had gone to war, Moore knew his ambassador too well to harbour any hopes that he might now express moral support for the British involvement which he had so diligently sought to prevent. From now on, predictions of Britain's early defeat and the vital importance of keeping the United States out of the conflict became the recurring themes of Kennedy's cables to his capital.

But, with the war in its eighth month, Moore could feel reassured by at least one diplomatic development. Churchill, now back in the Government along with Eden, had, to the ambassador's extreme anguish, been invited by Roosevelt to correspond directly and confidentially with him through the embassy pouch. Thus was the President able to balance the reporting of his envoy with the views of the new First Lord of the Admiralty, whom he held to be the most impressive member of the War Cabinet. None welcomed this unique and politically risky arrangement more than Harland Moore.

"Well, my dear Harland, here's to tomorrow's little Anglo-American union!" Sir Walter Garland lifted his glass of claret and grinned affably at his guest.

"Here's to the happy pair, Walter. And may our two countries be as united in purpose as our two offspring are."

"Well said, sir!"

Moore sipped at the claret and smiled back at his host. Having found the Member of Parliament somewhat intimidating at their first meetings, he had since developed an immense affection for him and now felt entirely at ease in his company. He seemed to epitomize that English aristocratic elegance and self-confidence which, in men without a touch of self-deprecating humour, could all too easily invite ridicule. There was nothing ridiculous at all about Sir Walter. He was known as a skilful and experienced politician, yet one with no personal ambition for the high offices of state. He was more than content to be a trusted adviser and confidant to the mighty, and in the very successful pursuit of this calling he had earned the respect and abiding friendship of many powerful men. Always immaculately garbed and never without a dark red carnation in the buttonhole of his formal black jacket, he was a familiar figure in the corridors of power. Furthermore, as Moore had earlier learned before even meeting him, he had an impeccable record as an anti-appeaser, and was close to that influential group of men, both in and out of government, who would surely, and before long, take the reins of power from the ailing and increasingly ineffectual Neville Chamberlain. Moore's friendship with Garland thus not only provided the American with access to the thinking of Chamberlain's probable heirs; it also offered him an effective channel through which to communicate information and ideas that could be usefully weighed against the official pronouncements of his own ambassador.

Today, however, there would not be much talk of politics or the war. After a cursory exchange of views on what Hitler and Mussolini might be up to at the Brenner Pass, the conversation had quickly reverted to the family business at hand.

"How's my lovely daughter-in-law-to-be, Harland?"

"A very, very happy and excited young lady indeed. And a very lucky one. The more I get to know him, the more I see what a fine young man your Charlie is."

"Thank you." Sir Walter bent over a slice of calf's liver and began to dissect it into thin strips. "You know, Cynthia and I really admire the spirit in which you have welcomed our children's decision. It cannot be easy for you and your charming wife to contemplate the day when you will be posted back to Washington and will be leaving Margot behind in a country under a very real threat of occupation. That is, of course – " he paused and raised his eyes from his plate to look directly at Moore – "if Margot intends staying on here when you're gone."

"I'll be frank, Walter. There's been much family discussion on it. We want to stay together as a family as long as we can, but if the war hots up and France falls to a German invasion, I'll want to get Elinor and Katie back to the States as quickly as possible, whatever happens to me, and I don't foresee being recalled to Washington for a year or two unless the whole embassy closes down. As for Margot, she'll make up her own mind and, knowing her, she isn't going to seek refuge in America while a British husband is fighting in Europe, even though her mother is going to do her darndest to persuade her to."

"For Charlie's sake, I'm very touched to hear that, and it only doubles our admiration of the girl. It'll be hard on you and the family, but it'll be the right decision. But of course, having her stay here lays a certain responsibility for her welfare on me which I do not intend to shirk." He replenished Moore's claret glass. "A passable bottle, don't you agree? Lachaise-Laurent. Not one of the really great Médocs, but even they couldn't fail to make a decent wine in '34, what?"

"Very nice indeed," agreed Moore who had had little difficulty in acquiring the British passion for wine, although he sought to limit his intake to the evening meal.

"Now, Harland: that Luftwaffe of which Goering is so boastful wasn't built to take Germans on joy-rides over Warsaw. One day, as you very well know, it's going to come and make life exceedingly uncomfortable for us here. I think you ought to consider, as a matter of urgency, finding somewhere outside London, in the countryside, for the family. Obviously you have to be at your post in London, but there's little point in exposing the women-folk to air-raids. Have you thought about that?"

"Only in a preliminary way."

"Well then, I have a suggestion. I have a spinster cousin living in a rather nice cottage not far from Windsor. She has a married sister in Canada, and she says she's going to go and join her there if things get much worse here. If that happens, I can get you the cottage. Your family should be safe there, and it's close enough to London for you to get down there easily for weekends or even some weekday nights if the trains are running properly. I'd have invited you all to live at my place, Bowes Court – God knows there's room enough – but it would be too far away for you. What do you say?"

"It sounds a splendid idea, and I can't thank you enough. Elinor will be delighted."

"Well then, let's just hope my cousin's nerve gives way in time!" He grinned at Moore. "Coffee?"

"Please."

Sir Walter brushed the tips of his greying moustache with a napkin and sighed. "It'll be distressingly thin and watery, I'm afraid. We elected representatives of the people are not spared the dead hand of rationing even in our place of business, whatever our electors may believe."

He summoned a waitress and ordered coffee for two.

As the two fathers took leave of each other at the House of Commons, Margot, Charlie and Katie finished a merry lunch at the Écu de France and left the table. The bridal couple would next see each other at the altar of St Margaret's at half-past two the following afternoon, and as they kissed goodbye on the rain-washed pavement of Jermyn Street, Katie, hovering discreetly in the restaurant entrance, felt a sudden wrenching sadness. It was a bit stupid and selfish to be sad for herself, she thought, while being happy for Margot, but today was the last day of a part of her life that had been supremely enjoyable. Tomorrow, that toast of the town, that endlessly photographed, written about and gossiped over society phenomenon, "The Moore Girls", would be split asunder, and nothing would ever be the same again for either of them.

"Come on, Katie, you and I are going to walk off this meal or I won't fit into my wedding dress tomorrow." Margot was beckoning Katie as Charlie hailed a cab to return him to his parents' Westminster residence. As he opened the cab door, Margot pulled him round by the arm. "I know it's against your pompous regimental rules to kiss females in public when in uniform, but I need one more."

Charlie removed his black-and-gold trimmed peak cap and bent to plant a chaste kiss on her lips.

"You'll have to do better than that off duty, Ensign Garland!"

"And me?"

Katie stepped forward and received a peck on the cheek from a blushing Charlie.

"Don't get too drunk tonight, sweetheart," admonished Margot as her fiancé got into the cab. He grinned sheepishly as it drew away.

"He'll get roaring drunk," said Katie. "That's what bachelor parties are for."

"Well, I don't want to have to prop him up at the altar. Come on, now; let's move it. I'm late for the final fitting of my gown."

They hurried arm in arm along Jermyn Street and turned up St James's Street to cross Piccadilly. At the corner, an evening newspaper billboard announced ADOLF AND MUSSO SURPRISE.

"Don't tell me," said Katie, "they're coming to the wedding."

"Of course! Everyone who's anyone is coming."

"Scared?"

"Wetting my knickers."

"About the wedding or afterwards?"

"Certainly not afterwards, if by that you mean the so-called wedding night."

"Why on earth did you have to choose a sleeping car compartment for a bridal suite? Neither of you is Houdini. Are you going to give it a try?"

"And risk doing ourselves a permanent injury? Absolutely not."

"One extra night of virginity. How can you stand it?"

Margot thought quickly. If she was going to tell her sister, this was the moment. She'd scarcely believe it, because this was not her image of her elder sister. Margot the cautious; Margot the correct. Well to hell with that image! Women didn't command attention these days by parading their devotion to outmoded mores. An aura of slight naughtiness got you further than a halo of dull respectability. Why should she want anyone, including her sister, to see her as something which she was not?

Katie squeezed her arm. "Don't tell me I touched on a raw nerve!"

"Not at all. It's just that I don't happen to be a virgin any more."

"*What?*" Katie stopped dead in her tracks, causing her sister to stumble. "Margot! You witch! You never told me! When did it happen? My God, are you pregnant?"

"Just calm down, Katie. No, I'm not pregnant. Charlie would probably have impaled himself on his bayonet if I was and his parents found out. We just thought we'd like to find out what it was like together before we got married."

"Well what was it like? Tell! Tell! I can't wait to know!" squealed Katie as they resumed walking.

"It was great, of course. Charlie's a wonderful lover."

"But where did you do it? At some seedy hotel?"

"Of course not! Charlie had the key to a friend's flat. We went there three times."

"And did it each time? God, how fantastic! I honestly didn't think you'd do something like that."

"Well then, you don't know me as well as I know you."

Katie squeezed her sister's arm again. "I want more details. About the first time. Who's idea was it? Did he make the first move?"

"Well, you don't go to the trouble of getting a key to someone else's place just to talk or play cards. Once we were there it just happened sort of naturally."

They turned off Piccadilly by the Berkeley Hotel and headed down toward Berkeley Square.

"We were lunching here before he took me off to the flat," said Margot, pointing to the restaurant entrance. "He never said a word about it until he got me into the cab."

"Love in the afternoon! I can't stand it! Why doesn't that happen to me? All they do is take me to the movies and fumble around there and in taxis."

"You're younger. Wait your turn. Besides, I was already engaged."

"Well, I'm certainly not waiting until I'm engaged before doing it."

"That's what I'm afraid of."

"Tell me, honestly, was it as good as you expected?"

"Better," lied Margot. "And it didn't hurt, which I assume is your next question."

"And you both came?"

Margot sighed. "Maybe we should have had Metro-Goldwyn-Mayer there to film it for you! Yes, is the answer."

"But he wore one of those things."

"Of course."

They turned into Berkeley Square.

"I'm told it rather spoils it, though."

"I wouldn't know; I've never had it without."

"And was it the first time for Charlie?"

"I'm beginning to wish I'd never told you about this."

"Well, was it? I'm curious."

"So I noticed. It might have been; he didn't say, but my guess is it wasn't. Why should I care? I'm just glad he seemed to know what to do."

"Oh God, you are so lucky, sis," sighed Katie as they turned into Hill Street. "If this doesn't happen to me soon, I'll go crazy. You know I honestly never thought you'd beat me to it."

Margot smiled. "Are you honestly telling me that I have?"

"I'm afraid so. I guess the guys think I'm just too young. It's ridiculous; I'm only thirteen months younger than you."

"Why don't you wait until you meet a handsome, nice, kind fellow, someone you're really attracted to and like a lot, and tell him that you've decided that you want him to be the man to give you your first experience? How could he refuse such a request?"

"And where do I find this paragon?"

"Oh, they're around. You just have to start focusing a bit on what men have to offer above the belt. You'll be surprised what you find sometimes."

"Don't be so mean!" Katie giggled and jostled her sister.

They were laughing happily when they reached the front door on Hill Street.

The first order of business for them was to calm down their mother whose patience had been sorely tried by the dressmaker's threats to abandon the final fitting if the bride did not instantly materialize. That done, and the dressmaker pacified, calm reigned for a while until Margot realized she'd left at the restaurant the white satin shoes she had collected that morning from Harrods. A complaining Katie was dispatched to retrieve them, and when Harland eventually arrived home, he immediately sensed panic among the womenfolk and took refuge in his study, emerging just before dinner to open a bottle of champagne. The four of them dined happily *en famille*, and talked excitedly about the morrow. Then, after Margot and her mother had taken a final look at the gown and accessories and checked the clothes laid out for the Scottish honeymoon, Margot said goodnight to her family and closed her bedroom door. Before falling into a deep, untroubled sleep, she prayed rapidly for fine weather, for steady nerves, and for no no-shows among the more famous people who had promised to attend. And she prayed that Charlie wasn't at that moment getting paralytically drunk with the half-dozen brother officers and friends who were wining and dining him at the Embassy Club. Her more spiritual prayers would be reserved for the morning.

One of Margot's prayers was partially anwered. Her wedding day dawned grey and cold, but at least there was no rain. Amid the perpendicular splendours of the great Renaissance parish church of St Margaret's, watched by the cream of society and the political establishment, Margot Whitfield Moore became Mrs Charles Garland. As she had predicted, she felt the tears in her eyes when the choir and congregation burst into the stirring, martial strains of "The Battle Hymn of the Republic", but all in all she was enjoying herself immensely, and her nerves were far steadier than she had dared to hope. On the long walk back down the aisle toward the great West Door, squeezing Charlie's shaking hand, she looked rapidly from side to side, checking out the smiling faces. It seemed that they'd all come: the pink, pudgy face of Winston Churchill was decorated with an impish grin; Anthony Eden looked loftily at her, then winked charmingly; she spotted Lady Astor, Lord Beaverbrook, the actress Anna Neagle, the American Consul-General and his wife, a much bemedalled Admiral she didn't know, poor ailing Henri de Creçy and Connie, over from Paris, Malcolm Sargent, the conductor . . . Oh, heavens, this was all really something to write home about!

They emerged into the cold afternoon under an arch of drawn swords held aloft by a Grenadier guard of honour to face a battery of flashing cameras and a cockney chorus of "Ow, ain't she lovely?" and "Good luck, luv!" from the band of seasoned society wedding watchers at the gate.

"The ultimate accolade, darling," said Charlie as he handed his bride into the waiting Daimler. "You're a real Londoner now!"

Katie leaned into the car to arrange the train at her sister's feet.

"Well done, Mrs Garland. Knickers still dry?"

77

"Oh Katie, really!"

As the car pulled away, she waved regally to the well-wishers and gave them her best smile.

At the reception she blushed delightedly when Anthony Eden kissed her on the cheek and told her she was "lovely beyond words". The Marchioness of Edmonton was her usual forthright self:

"Have a baby quickly, my dear. I'm sure Charlie can manage, if he's anything like his father. Walter was a prodigious trouser-dropper in his day. Until Cynthia cornered him."

Ambassador Kennedy toasted the bride as "one of the fairest flowers of American womanhood" and "America's loveliest gift to Britain since Jennie Jerome married Randolph Churchill".

"I bet you he's praying our Margot doesn't produce another Winston!" whispered Harland Moore into his wife's ear.

As for Margot, she was wondering if Kennedy would have described her thus if he'd known what she'd been doing on her visits to Lowndes Square.

5

"Harland should have done what Joe Kennedy did: sent his wife and children straight back here the moment Britain declared war."

Alice Moore stared across the breakfast table at her husband who remained engrossed in his morning paper.

"And as his father," she continued, "I think you should at least have written him a stern letter telling him to stop putting Elinor's and the girls' lives at risk."

Austin Moore lowered his paper and peered at his wife through the gold-framed pince-nez perched on the bridge of his nose.

"Dearest, I don't disagree that it would have been prudent to send them back, but I cannot and will not dictate to my son how he handles his family. He's a grown man and an experienced diplomat and father. He must make his own judgements. I have no doubt he'll send Elinor and Katie packing if the situation gets any more threatening, but you'd be foolish to count on Margot coming with them. There's nothing in her letter to suggest that she's planning to quit the land of her husband, and she can be as stubborn as a mule that girl. You know that."

Alice Moore sighed and poured more coffee from a silver pot.

"Well, if your first ever great-grandchild ends up being born under Nazi occupation, don't say I didn't warn you. Or if she dies in an air-raid before she even gets pregnant."

"For goodness' sakes, Alice, why take such an apocalyptic view? At the rate that war is going, or rather *not* going, we may yet see Hitler sue for peace on the basis of his conquests so far."

"My dear, you're a distinguished professor of European history, and you know you don't believe that."

Austin Moore picked up his newspaper again.

"Well, anyway Alice, you promised me that today was going to be a day of sunshine and happiness here. We've got the sunshine all right, and if we banish all gloomy thoughts for a while, we'll have the happiness too. Damnit, sweetheart, I want to *enjoy* my seventieth birthday!"

"You shall. Now drink up your coffee. The caterers are due any minute and I want you out of the house and out of their way all morning."

Austin Eliot Moore, distinguished historian and hereditary proprietor of the Adamswood estate on the edge of the town of Millbrook in New York's Dutchess County, was punctilious in his obedience to his wife in any matters pertaining to domestic administration; and so, breakfast completed, he donned his light tweed overcoat, picked a favourite walking stick from a brass stand by the garden doors, and sauntered out into the open air. Selecting the rose garden as his first port of call, he set off up the gravel path which curved round the east wing of the house and, arriving there, settled down on a weather-greyed wooden garden seat.

At the garden's centre, water splashed into a small circular pond from a Florentine sculptured fountain in the form of a leaping dolphin. Paths radiated from the pond, slicing the garden into triangular rose beds, bordered with low-clipped boxwood. With its sweeping view of the Catskills, the Dolphin Garden was one of Moore's most treasured retreats, and he would sit, feasting his eyes on the more than five hundred rose blooms, happily inhaling their fragrance.

Silently but fervently he thanked his Maker for the good health he still enjoyed, a blessing which should, he hoped, allow him a number of years yet in which to pursue his love affair with the great garden of his ancestral home. Often he had told himself that if he were to be allowed to live his life over again, he would find all the happiness he sought in being a simple gardener. He had decided that to aid and abet nature in the creation and husbanding of a beautiful garden was as spiritually satisfying an occupation as he could envision for himself. He reflected approvingly on the words his grandmother had had engraved on the stone base upon which the fountain stood: "I would rather make a garden out of a wilderness for one poor person than build all the great palaces of the mighty."

Ever since completing his life's culminating work, a three-volume history of nineteenth-century European-American relations, Professor Moore had had time on his hands to devote himself to the overseeing and enjoyment of his property. He now wondered how many more generations of Moores would inherit Adamswood. For the moment there was money enough to maintain the place. His family's railroad and real estate interests had survived the horrors of 1929, and both his son, Harland, and his grandson, Larry, were devoted to the place. But the war now unleashed in Europe posed threatening uncertainties for America, and whether or not the old world's democracies survived the assault of the dictator, post-war America would, he was convinced, be a very different place from the America of today. Harland would likely see little of Adamswood before his retirement in another twenty years or so, and despite Roosevelt's protestations to the contrary, the likelihood of the youth of America, Larry among them, being sent to fight in the European war seemed stronger by the day. Alice was smart enough to see through his attempts to calm her down with talk of peace negotiations. There was no end of the war in sight, and probably wouldn't be unless and until America came once more to the rescue. And that could cost Larry his life. Not for the first time, the head of the Moore family pondered sadly on the thought that he might really be the last of the short line of inhabitants of Adamswood, which had started with his grandfather Adam, who had built the place in 1846, to end his days at the place.

But no more gloomy thoughts today, he told himself firmly. He pulled back the cuff of his tweed coat to consult his watch. A minute or two before ten. Larry should arrive at any moment at the end of a sixty-mile cross country drive from New Haven. It'll be good to see the boy! That's what's going to make my day! At least I'll have *one* of my grandchildren here.

Slapping his knees with the pleasure of the prospect, he rose to his feet, retrieved his walking stick, and set off along the path on the north side of the Dolphin Garden which led to The Wilderness, a small wooded area that boasted in season a splendid array of wooded plants and shrubs. Mountain laurel flourished protectively around red trillium, Solomon's Seal, wild azaleas, and a half-dozen species of local fern. Austin's mother had created this wild garden as an eightieth birthday present for his grandmother, Grace, back in 1901, and the Professor had often thought what a nice place it would be in which to be buried instead of in the overcrowded family plot at the parish church. Emerging on the far side of The Wilderness, he strolled across a wide stretch of rough-cut grass, dotted with dogwood, towards the South Drive, an elm-lined road rising gently to the house from the lodge gates on the old Dutchess Turnpike, through which Larry should shortly appear. There was a small bench under one of the elms, and he decided to sit there and await his grandson.

It was of his elder granddaughter, Margot, however, that he thought as he sat there. By heavens! What a time he'd had persuading Alice that her marrying an Englishman wasn't the end of the world. It was partly her southern Irish ancestry stirring, but more strongly it was her intense feeling for family ties and togetherness which caused her to deplore the prospect of a Moore choosing anywhere other than the Eastern United States as a place to live and bring up children. She had never wholly forgiven her son, Harland, for choosing the peripatetic life of a Foreign Service officer, but she had at least expected him to ensure that his offspring were not tempted by their environment to forsake the mother-country. Austin had sought to reason with her by confessing that he too had been less than ecstatic at the news of Margot's choice, and that he had kind of hoped that when the darned war was over the whole family would be back on this side of the Atlantic for keeps. But that, he suggested, was merely the wish of a rather selfish old man. What counted above all was Margot's happiness. This self-critical line of argument gradually had its effect on Alice. Whatever her husband might be prepared to brand himself, she was not going to let him brand her a selfish old woman, indifferent to Margot's happiness. And so, without conceding the point that Margot could and should have found a suitable husband from her own American background, she slowly abandoned her overt opposition to the match.

Austin Moore adored his elder granddaughter, and had recognized in her when still in her mid-teens some sterling qualities of intelligence, self-confidence and courage. He never doubted for a moment that she had arrived at her decision to marry Charlie only after most mature consideration of the need to reconcile the claims of true love with the caution imposed by the explosive events taking place around them. She had known what she was doing all right when she'd walked up that aisle just two days ago. She was that sort of girl, God bless her! And if the war had some terrors and tragedies in store for her, she'd pull through. Provided she lived.

He heard the noise of a car coming up the hill, and in a moment Larry's beige Ford sedan hove into sight on the crest of the incline. Moore got up and strode to the edge of the gravel-surfaced drive, waving his stick. The car pulled up by him, and Larry sprang from it and came round to greet his grandfather.

"Happy birthday, Grandpa!" The young man embraced him warmly. "How does it feel to hit seventy?"

"Fine until you mentioned it." He chuckled as he stepped back to take a look at his grandson. "How are they treating you these days at my *alma mater*?"

"Working me like a cottonpicker."

"Well, by the looks of you, you're thriving on it."

At six-foot one, Larry had his father's athletic build, and, unlike his blonde twin sister, he had his father's light brown hair; but the pale brown eyes, the curving set of the eyebrows, the high cheekbones and the rather full lips were very much his twin's. As a young boy he had suffered the opinion of his peers that he looked effeminate, and this had driven him to seek excellence as an athlete. He had succeeded, becoming the highest scoring running back at Andover in a decade, a first-class cross-country runner, and an accomplished horseman. His grandfather, himself a fine equestrian, had fostered his early love of horses, and during vacations spent at Adamswood, where Austin kept a horse for him, he indulged his growing passion for riding and, in season, hunted regularly with the Millbrook foxhounds.

To the surprise of many, but not of his grandfather, he had decided on arrival at Yale in the fall of 1939 to seek no further honours on the football field, but to concentrate instead on his studies. The outbreak of the war in Europe and the knowledge that his father, mother and two sisters could be swept up in its violence at any moment had deeply affected him. In long conversations with his grandfather, whom he revered and who, in his father's absence, had assumed the role of parent and mentor, he had begun a search for an understanding of why and how Europe had been plunged into war, and what America's proper response should be. The more he talked and listened, the more he felt a kinship with the threatened British, a kinship that had now been much reinforced by Margot's marriage. These feelings he had translated into a ferocious appetite for knowledge of Europe, especially Britain, and its history, an appetite which the history department at Yale and its distinguished former head at Adamswood were well placed to satisfy. Austin, of course was delighted, but Larry began to feel a growing frustration. The democracies faced subjugation by a dictator, while America stood on the sidelines. During Christmas at Adamswood he confided in his grandfather that he was seriously thinking now of abandoning his studies and going to London to offer himself to the British armed forces. Austin had listened sympathetically and had then set about persuading Larry that if the war expanded, as he fully expected it to, America could not stand idly by, however loudly the neutralist lobbies protested, and Larry's turn would come. Reluctantly Larry accepted this counsel of patience and returned to his studies, but not before he had won his grandfather's agreement to give him full backing when he wrote to ask his father if he might start flying lessons during the next vacation. Both he and Austin knew that Harland's approval would not easily be forthcoming. Elinor Moore had, many years earlier, watched her only brother dig a smoking crater for himself and his de Havilland biplane when stunting at a county fair. As she watched them disentangle his remains from the wreckage, she had sworn that no son of hers would ever take up flying. Larry knew that his mother's influence on the decision would be decisive, and he was right. She herself had written by return to say that since he knew her feelings on the subject, his request was somewhat insensitive and was duly denied. But Larry's resolve eventually to join the Army Air Corps was not broken by this. He would simply bide his time.

"Hop in, Grandpa. I'll drive you up to the house."

"Only so that you can greet your grandmother. Then you and I will take a walk. She wants neither hide nor hair of us in the house this morning." Larry opened the passenger door for him. "I'm darned glad they let you off, my boy," said Austin as they pulled away. "Goodness knows what your grandmother and your aunt are up to. I think they're inflicting half of Dutchess County on me tonight. She's even lured that old windbag, Congressman Halder, up here. I've a mind to lock myself up in the stable with a couple of good bottles and to hell with all of them! Want to join me?"

"You're going to love every minute of it, and you know it. The ladies will flirt outrageously with you – "

"God help me! Particularly if the lethal Mrs Burchett gets her claws into me."

"Don't worry; I'll take her off your hands."

They were laughing merrily as the car passed under the great Norway spruce which shaded the semicircular sweep of the driveway up to the portico of the classic white clapboard mansion.

"When you've seen your grandmother, we'll walk over to East Wood. I want you to see what we've done to the Daffodil Walk."

Larry hurried inside with his suitcase, and five minutes later they were striding out towards the woods.

"Grandma says you got a letter from Margot just the day after her wedding."

"We did; I'll give it to you to read when we get back." Austin ran his fingers back and forth through his thick silver-white hair, a sign, as Larry knew, that he was about to broach a sensitive subject. "Apparently you haven't written your parents or sisters in a long while. Knowing your feelings about their situation, I find that surprising. You mustn't neglect them."

Larry kicked a twig in his path. "I know. I'm a lousy letter writer. I promise to write this weekend."

"Good."

"You know, it's funny Grandpa. There are times when I feel that I'm never really out of communication with Margot. It's sort of telepathic. I felt it particularly strongly on her wedding day; a sort of conversation without voices."

"Not unheard of between twins, but still not much of an excuse for not writing your parents."

"I know." Larry hastened to change the subject. "When do you think Hitler's going to make his next move?"

"As soon as that arctic winter they're having over there thaws out, I reckon. He's got little to gain from waiting longer."

"So my new brother-in-law should see some action in the spring. Poor Margot."

"Poor brother-in-law. If the Polish campaign's anything to go by, the Germans are going to be darned hard to push back once they get moving."

"I wish to God I was there, Grandpa."

"One day you will be, although it will be over the dead bodies of Congressman Halder and his ilk. I'd stay off that subject with him tonight, if I were you. For a neutralist he gets mighty belligerent in defence of his cause. I don't want my party turning into a beer-hall brawl!"

"I'll try to remember. Does Margot say anything about Mother and Katie coming home?"

"You're asking me?" He grinned impishly at his grandson. "I thought you talked to her every day."

Larry blushed, and forced a short laugh.

"No, Larry. She mentioned nothing. And *that's* a subject which is absolutely taboo with your grandmother this evening. It sets off a torrent of criticism of your father for not sending them packing, and of me for not telling him to do so. So let's keep well away from that if we want a jolly evening."

The party that evening was, as Larry had predicted, enjoyed by his grandfather as much as anyone. The family and their sixty guests dined by candlelight at elaborately decorated tables set in the pale green panelled dining room. Turtle soup, trout, rack of lamb, and an expertly timed Soufflé Grand Marnier – a favourite of Austin's – were washed down with the pick of the French wines and champagnes from the Adamswood cellars. Music from a five-piece band playing in the great octagonal hall under the domed stairwell wafted in to mingle with the chatter of the diners and the clinking of Adamswood's finest china, silverware and crystal. Toasts were drunk, telegrams read, and, through it all, the elderly gentleman they were honouring sat beaming and wiping an occasional tear from the corners of his eyes. Alice Moore, a regal figure in ruby-red velvet, a small diamond tiara and matching pendant earrings, proudly surveyed the scene through a lorgnette.

Larry had started the evening in a sombre mood. Before showering and changing into formal attire, he had sat in the window-seat of his top-floor room reading Margot's letter. Despite its happy tone, it had left him feeling depressed. She was so obviously in love, and the possibility of her dream world suddenly disappearing in the thunder and lightning of war appalled him. When he had gone downstairs to join the family awaiting the arrival of the guests, his grandmother had commented on the strained look on his face.

"No, there's nothing wrong, Grandma," he had assured her. "I was just wishing we could all be here together tonight."

He had pecked her on the cheek, told her how beautiful she looked, and had slipped off to the champagne bar to do something about his flagging spirits. He had a feeling that he might end up drinking too much that evening, but the feeling did not bother him unduly, and by the time his date had arrived and he had taken her on his arm into dinner, his spirits had risen noticeably. Having no steady girlfriend for the moment, he had left the choice of a date to his grandmother, and had thus found himself paired with the daughter of a local judge. He had met her once before and had found her quite attractive except for her high-pitched, bird-like voice which, on this occasion vying with the animated voices of the other diners, was raised to a pitch which grated irritatingly on his ear.

As the dinner came to an end, Alice Moore moved serenely amongst her guests, accepting graciously their expressions of admiration for the elegance of her cuisine, and inviting them to move to the octagonal hall where, ringed by marble columns topped with flower-filled Chinese vases, they were to dance. In a small portrait-lined corridor linking the hall to Austin's library, Elaine Burchett, displaying as was her habit a great deal more of her voluptuous bosom than any other guest similarly endowed would have dared reveal, was busy adjusting Larry's white bow tie.

"Don't they teach you how to tie a butterfly properly at college?" Her long fingers tipped with scarlet nails completed their business then slipped suggestively down the front of Larry's boiled shirt.

"I never was any good at tying one." Larry looked anxiously at Mrs Burchett's marauding fingers, half afraid that the nail polish would leave scarlet streaks in their path. Her perfume seemed to have been applied with the same disregard for moderation as the mascara that framed her hazel eyes and the lipstick coating her generous lips, the upper of which she was now massaging with the tip of her tongue. She really was very vulgar, he thought, and curiously exciting. He wouldn't really have minded her paying him this close attention in her own house, or in a hotel room, or somewhere in the woods, or anywhere other than in the middle of his grandparents' house in the middle of his grandfather's birthday party.

"Let's get some champagne and have a chat in the library. I don't feel like dancing yet," she said.

Larry collected two glasses from the bar. As they entered the book-lined room, a portly man with a flushed face whom Larry recognized as a regular with the Millbrook hunt, pulled a cigar from his mouth.

"Elaine, I trust you didn't buy that Greenacre mare last week; it's a spavined bag of bones!"

Mrs Burchett continued on towards the fireplace, pretending not to have heard, and sank into a high-backed armchair.

"Nobody around here wants to admit that I'm a good judge of horseflesh," she said, taking a glass from Larry's hand. "They think sizing up men is the limit to my talent."

Larry blushed and looked around for something to sit on. He pulled up a tapestried stool and perched rather awkwardly on it at her feet.

"Who's your charming little date, Larry?"

"Louisa Bayles. Her father's an Albany judge; they just bought a property up at Lithgow. She's not really my type."

"What is your type, then?"

She eyed him with an amused smile and, crossing her legs, tapped his knee with the tip of a satin shoe.

"I'm not sure I know, but I do know what is *not* my type."

Feeling himself safely off the hook, he took a mouthful of champagne.

"I think you're probably finding out that sophisticated women have more to offer. Isn't that it?"

Larry looked up at her and thought again about a hotel room. Or would he have the courage to ask her if she would like to take a stroll down to the pool-house for some fresh air? There could hardly be anyone else down there on a March night. He could not make up his mind whether she was trying to tell him that he was too young or whether she was dropping a hint that while others might think him so, she did not consider him too young for her. His developing fantasy was nipped in the bud.

"Tell me about Margot. I gather from this evening's

speeches that she and her English aristocrat got married this week. I hope she picked one who enjoys sex with women."

"Oh really, Mrs Burchett!"

Larry drowned his embarrassment with more champagne, this time draining the glass. Elaine Burchett laughed.

"I'm sure she picked a winner. By the way, Larry," she said, leaning forward and lowering her voice, "your sugar-plum fairy just looked in here and then hurried away. I'd better not keep you. And I'd better go and find my own boring date."

"Who is he?"

"A veterinarian with far fewer social graces than most of his patients." She rose and, smoothing the chartreuse green satin dress over her hips, pulled her shoulders back as if offering Larry one last privileged view of her impressive cleavage. "I'm giving myself a thirty-fifth birthday party on Ash Wednesday. Would you like to come?"

How odd of her to give her age away like that, thought Larry.

"Well, I'm not sure I can get over. Can I let you know?"

"Of course, my dear." She patted him on the cheek. "Be seeing you."

Larry followed her out of the library, stopping at the champagne bar to refill his glass. It irked him that he could not remember what date Ash Wednesday was and whether he would be on vacation at that time. He drained his glass and as the waiter refilled it, he heard his grandfather's voice behind him.

"Easy, young fellow, easy! We want you still on your feet at the end of the evening."

"Oh, I'm OK, Grandpa. Have you seen Louisa anywhere?"

"Yes. Complaining to the judge that you've been hiding from her since dinner. Shame on you!" He grinned. "Elaine Burchett may be only half my age, but she's nearly twice yours."

He took the full glass from Larry's hand and put it down on the bar.

"Now go dance with your grandmother. You'll be

rescuing her from Congressman Halder's standard lecture on 'America First'."

Larry made his way a little unsteadily towards the octagonal hall and the strains of "I'll Never Smile Again". He did not much relish the prospect of an encounter with the local Congressman. On the few occasions they had met, he had found himself quickly provoked by his ultra-conservatism and unabashed xenophobia. The isolationist view, held in its extreme form by Halder, that no good ever came of America trying to help anyone but Americans, was anathema to him, and he had been bold enough to say so on the occasion of their last encounter, and despite his grandfather's admonition earlier that day, he was all too likely to do so again on this occasion. Scanning the dance floor, he spotted the lanky figure of General Hobart Wooler. Now *there* was a man he'd rather talk to! Holder of a US Pilot Licence numbered in the teens and one of the first Expert Aviator Certificates; flew a Nieuport with the American Air Service's 95th Aero Squadron in combat over France in the summer of 1918. *He'd* tell him how to get into the Air Corps! His train of thought was derailed by the sight of Louisa foxtrotting past, her partner's head cocked at an unnatural and uncomfortable angle, like a hanged man. Poor fellow! He was trying to protect his right eardrum from Louisa's factory-whistle voice.

In a flower-decked alcove halfway round the octagon, Larry found his grandmother seated with the New York Congressman on a sofa. Her immobile face suggested that the legislator's lecture had already achieved its deadening effect.

"Aha! Your ears should be burning, young man!" Congressman Halder grinned affably and kneaded the saliva-soaked end of his cigar between thumb and forefinger.

Larry feigned lack of interest. "Good evening, sir. Would you excuse me if I took my grandmother onto the floor?"

"Of course, of course! But before you deprive me of her charming company, let me just tell you that I think I have set your grandmother's mind at rest."

Halder patted Mrs Moore's velvet-robed knee and puffed out his chest.

"Larry, my boy, you aren't going to go and fight and risk death in any wretched foreign war. We're guarding those Neutrality Acts like they were the Ark of the Covenant! The President is not going to be allowed to sneak round them and drag us into a fight with the German people. If he does, he can kiss goodbye to a third term – and he's had two too many for my liking already – and he'll likely find himself impeached as well."

"And what if a majority of the American people feel that Europe is worth fighting for, sir? Suppose wiser men convince them that the Atlantic isn't wide enough to protect us now?"

Mrs Moore looked alarmed, and a smile spread over the Congressman's face as he turned to her.

"Well now, what do you suppose they're teaching 'em these days?" He turned his attention back to Larry. "Might they be just a little short on red-blooded Americanism up there?"

"I'm as patriotic as you are, Congressman!" Larry felt the first flush of anger warming his cheeks. "I just think isolationists are short-sighted people. The longer we ignore what's going on in Europe, the more of my generation will probably have to die when eventually you have no alternative but to fight, and you'll send us to do so ill-equipped and with the odds running against us."

"Quite the little orator, your grandson, Mrs Moore. When he's older and has something valid to say, he'll be a crowd-puller. Right now I think you should take him on the dance floor and speak to him of the virtues of listening to his elders." He puffed energetically on his cigar. "And, if you permit me, of the virtues of moderation in imbibing, especially at his tender age."

Mrs Moore began to rise to her feet, a pained expression on her face. She motioned Larry wordlessly towards the dance floor.

"One moment, please, Grandma. Congressman, are you by any chance pro-German?"

"Now Larry!" Mrs Moore was visibly angry.

"Just what do you mean by that?" The Congressman spat the words out.

"Well, you have a German-sounding name – Halder –

so maybe for family reasons you have divided loyalties. There must be quite a lot of Americans like that. So maybe you wouldn't mind seeing Hitler master of Europe, particularly of the British whom you probably despise anyway."

"Larry, that's more than enough!" Mrs Moore looked desperately around for her husband. A few couples were now marking time on the dance floor near them, drawn by the raised voices.

"I'll have you know, as everyone else here but you knows, that I'm a full-blooded American, and America's all that matters to me!" Halder stood face to face with Larry, grimacing pugnaciously. "If the Europeans let Hitler or the communists trample all over them, that's their problem, not ours. And where my forefathers came from makes no goddammed difference and is none of your goddammed business!" He turned and switched on a ready smile for Mrs Moore's benefit. "Forgive the slight excess of language, dear Mrs Moore."

"I just thought – " began Larry before the Congressman, returning to the fray, interrupted him loudly.

"You've said enough, young man, to discredit yourself and shame your wonderful family."

"I'll remember that, sir, when I'm called to fight to save your skin!"

Larry bowed mockingly, and taking his now ashen-faced grandmother by the arm, he steered her rapidly past the murmuring semicircle of guests and led her round the hall towards the salon.

Congressman Halder summoned up a grin, finding himself now in the familiar situation of standing before an expectant gathering.

"Not really a bad boy, just high-spirited. A lot too much champagne and a lot too little understanding of the real world. Wouldn't FDR just love him!"

He brushed some cigar ash from his sleeve and plunged in among the dancers who were beginning to pick up the foxtrot beat again. He cut in on a young couple.

"May a battle-weary representative of the people find new strength with one of his prettiest constituents?"

The young man backed reluctantly away, consigning his blonde wife to the arms of a man he'd never voted for anyway.

"I'm really ashamed of you Larry," complained Alice Moore as they entered the salon. "It was highly disrespectful and very upsetting for me personally. You've no right at your age to address people like that, however much you may disagree."

She sank into a chair.

"I'm sorry, Grandma, particularly if I've upset you, but he makes me fighting mad. Why do you invite him? He can't stand Democrats like us."

"He's our Congressman, whatever his party, and you'll apologize to him before he leaves. No guest leaves my house offended by a member of the family. Now please go and fetch me a little champagne. But no more for you."

Larry headed for the bar and ran into his grandfather.

"It seems you overstepped the mark with our Congressman, Larry." He sounded more than a little hurt. "At your age, a little bit more respect and restraint is required. You risked spoiling a lovely evening."

"I'm sorry, Grandpa." Larry was beginning to feel remorse. "I got a bit carried away. I guess I'd better apologize to him."

"You will indeed, and you can do it right now. Here he comes."

Halder was approaching the bar with his blonde dancing partner.

"George, I think my grandson wishes to make an apology."

"Yes," said Larry and held out his hand. "I'm sorry I was so outspoken."

"Well, that's just fine. Just fine." Halder grasped his hand. "If when you grow up you decide to run against me, Larry, just be warned I can be a hell of a lot rougher than that. But if I were you, and had political ambitions, I'd steer clear of someone like me. You'll find me harder to unseat than Lincoln in his Memorial!" He laughed heartily and squeezed the waist of his borrowed blonde so tight that she let out a muffled squeak.

Larry excused himself and went to the bar. He gulped quickly at a glass of champagne before taking another one for his grandmother.

"I hear you had a near knock-down fight with our revered Congressman? I didn't know you were the combative type."

He turned to find Elaine Burchett at his shoulder. "Who won?"

Larry smiled despondently. "Hitler."

He bowed and headed for the salon.

"Don't forget Ash Wednesday!" she called after him.

When the party was finally over, somewhere around two o'clock in the morning, a weary and none too sober Larry, who had already bade goodnight to his grandmother, found his grandfather in the library, labouring to remove the mark of a wet glass that someone had thoughtlessly stood on an antique walnut table.

"Grandfather, I'm really sorry if I messed up your party with that row with the Congressman."

Austin Moore straightened up and squinted at his reparatory handiwork.

"You're forgiven, young man, but just remember that there's a time and a place for that sort of exchange. I dare say it wasn't your fault alone."

"Well, I'm sorry anyway."

The elder Moore grinned. "I'm a bit sorry too. That I missed it. Bart Wooler overheard it, and thought you came out well ahead on points, even if he did think you pretty cheeky. He told me he rather enjoyed it. He's not exactly an admirer of George Halder, you know. He's itching to see the Air Corps readied for war."

"I wish I'd been able to talk to him. I somehow missed him."

"Another time. Now off you go to bed."

"Thanks for everything, Grandpa. Goodnight."

On his way upstairs, Larry thought that Margot would have been proud of him.

6

"The trouble with your being a newly-wed, Charlie, is that it's blocking your urge to do something about that gorgeous piece of local talent sitting over there with the pear-shaped major. She's been eyeing you all through dinner."

Jamie Edmonton lifted a cognac glass to his nostrils and inhaled contentedly. Charlie glanced across the restaurant and was rewarded with a shy smile.

"Don't tempt me, Jamie. As the Bard might have said: boredom doth make rapists of us all."

Jamie sighed. "Awful waste. The pear-shape looks like he'd need a map and compass to find his fly."

"All yours, Jamie. I know the type. She'd get you to take her to Madame Ko-Ko's where she'd dump you immediately for a brigadier. That peasant coyness doesn't fool me one bit."

He looked at his watch; it was nearly ten-thirty. He drained his glass of cognac.

"Don't get nervous, Charlie. Have another. There's no bloody point in being back in the lines before midnight."

"I feel it in my bones that Alex is going to come visiting tomorrow morning, and that the commanding officer's going to lead him straight to my position. I'd rather not have a grandmother of a hangover to add to the misery."

"Come on, now! He can't inspect every platoon of all nine battalions every day, can he? And he's already been to us twice this week." Jamie pulled a leather cigar wallet from the breast pocket of his service-dress jacket and extracted a Corona. "*Garçon!*" he called, waving Charlie's empty cognac glass in the air. *"Un autre pour mon petit cousin!"*

Dinner at "l'Huître", which offered the best *haute cuisine* to be had in 1940 in the northern French city of Lille, had become a twice-weekly ritual for Charlie and his cousin. The chicken stuffed with truffles made a welcome change from the offerings of the Grenadier Officers' Mess, resourceful as the Mess Sergeant was in laying his hands on local produce to supplement the army rations.

On his arrival with the British Expeditionary Force at the end of September, shortly after the outbreak of war, Jamie had set about making life as tolerable for himself as possible. He had bought a battered car from a local garage, daubed khaki paint on it to give it some semblance of camouflage, and had constructed a primitive lean-to shelter for it against a side wall of the cottage which served as sleeping quarters for the junior officers of No 3 Company. As the Company's senior subaltern, he had commandeered the principal bedroom, which conveniently contained a hugh oak chest in which he stored a twelve-bore Purdey shotgun, a number five iron, boxes of golf balls and cartridges, and an elaborate canvas and wood *chaise longue* spirited away from the pool-house at Edmonton Hall. During the mild autumn of 1939, he had found plenty of opportunity to put his creature comforts and sporting equipment to good use, happily ignoring the joshing of his less enterprising brother officers, and hugely enjoying the widespread though false rumour that he had asked his commanding officer if he might invite a girlfriend out to the front for Christmas.

The arrival of Charlie in late March to join the battalion had delighted him. The battalion was part of the First Guards Brigade, itself one of the three infantry brigades forming Major-General Harold Alexander's First Division, which had taken up its position at Cysoign, a few miles south-east of Lille. Nine British divisions were deployed along a forty-five-mile curling stretch of the frontier with neutral Belgium, flanked by one French army on their left manning the frontier stretching north-westwards to the

Channel, and by three French armies on their right, linking up with the massively constructed and heavily defended Maginot Line. For seven undisturbed months, the French and British forces had worked on their defences along the frontier. All through the cold and wet winter, the British divisions, under the watchful eye of their commander-in-chief, General Gort, had dug trenches, erected concrete pillboxes and excavated anti-tank ditches until, as the bitter winter weather gave way to the first hints of warming spring, the "Gort Line" was substantially complete.

"Jolly good of you to join us now that we've done all the hard work, Charlie!" said Jamie, greeting his cousin on his arrival from England.

Given a rifle platoon to command in the same company as Jamie, Charlie had at first had difficulty in believing that he was at last in the "front line". Standing in one of his platoon's trenches and staring across the gently undulating and wooded countryside, he had found it a little ridiculous that all he could see in front of him was an apparently peaceful, neutral country. There was no visible sign that this was even a frontier. And as for the enemy, they were, so he had been told, at least a hundred miles away behind their own borders. His platoon sergeant had immediately been at pains to point out, lest the sporting marquess had given the wrong impression, that there was still plenty of work to do. Each time it rained, the flooded trenches had to be drained and the sagging walls shored up. Each morning the company's fortifications were inspected by the company and battalion commanders, and it was a rare day when the brigadier did not also put in an appearance. The general's visits were only a little less frequent, and his inspection the most searching of all.

"Nobody's idle here, sir!" Sergeant Boakes had barked for the benefit not only of Charlie but also of a group of guardsmen sitting with their backs against a pillbox, enjoying the rare pleasure of sunshine as they cleaned their rifles. The men had sprung to their feet as Sergeant Boakes had thrown out his chest and cleared his throat noisily.

"Mr Garland 'ere is our new Platoon Commander!" he roared huskily.

He seems to want even the Germans to know I've arrived, thought Charlie.

"'E 'asn't come all this way to command a dozey bunch of layabouts! 'E's 'ere to command the best platoon in the battalion, and I'll make life miserable for anyone who disappoints 'im!"

And miserable for me if I disappoint *him*, thought Charlie. But I mustn't be intimidated.

"This isn't just going to be the best in the battalion," said Charlie firmly to his charges who were now staring at him curiously. "It's got to be the best in the brigade!"

"You hear what Mr Garland says!" roared Boakes.

Charlie felt better as he was led to the next section.

That afternoon, over tea, he was put in the "bigger picture" by his company commander. The coldest European winter in decades had obviously discouraged Hitler from launching his offensive, but now, with the weather turning, it could come at any moment. It was more or less accepted by the French High Command and by the British force placed under it that the main thrust of the attack would come across the Flanders plain through Belgium and possibly Holland as well, rather than through the dense and hilly Ardennes Forest to the south-east. The "Gort Line", Charlie was told, was thus of critical importance.

"Utter balls!" exclaimed Jamie confidently, as they sipped Scotch and soda in their billet that evening, when Charlie reported what he had been told.

"If the Germans come with tanks and divebombers as they did in Poland," Jamie continued, "our pathetic little defence line will present as much obstacle as a cobweb. When the offensive starts, we'll either be rushed forward or pulled back. They're not going to let us just sit here and be pushed over like toy soldiers on the nursery floor. Unless, of course, I'm underestimating the stupidity of the frog brass, which wouldn't surprise me one bit!"

Charlie was suitably impressed with his cousin's military analysis and would have been more so if he had known, which neither of them did, that the High Command had in fact reached the same conclusion. In November, the British divisional commanders had been informed that the fortifications on which they were expending so much time and energy would not be defended in the event of the German thrust coming, as confidently expected, through Belgium. Instead, the British Expeditionary Force, together with the two immediately flanking French armies, would instantly swing forward into Belgium. The British would race some sixty-five miles forward, passing Brussels, to take up a new position on the river Dyle astride Louvain and to the rear of the main Belgian forces, who, it was suspected, would soon be thrown back by the German armour onto the same line. Given Belgium's neutrality and thus the impossibility of the Allies' helping to strengthen her internal defences in advance of actual hostilities, Plan D, as it was designated, was the best the High Command could come up with. Nonetheless, the two British corps commanders, Generals Dill and Brooke, continued to point out the dreadful risks inherent in leaving a carefully fortified line for a wholly unprepared position far to their front. The French, however, whose divisions outnumbered the British by ten to one, were in no mood to be dictated to by their junior partners; the plan was firm.

At Charlie's insistence, Jamie reluctantly agreed that they should not prolong their evening on the town and that the uncertain delights of Madame Ko-Ko's nightclub could await their next visit to Lille. Charlie was anxious to finish a half-written letter to Margot in time to catch the battalion's outgoing mail the next morning.

"Bloody shame," complained Jamie as he led the way rather unsteadily across the barely lit street to his bizarrely camouflaged Citroën. "There must be scores of passable women in this God-forsaken town just aching to open their legs to me tonight, and here I am chauffeuring my lovesick little cousin back to an early beddy-bye."

"It's not early; it's almost half-past eleven."

"Hang on a minute, Charlie boy."

Charlie saw his cousin disappear into a dark alley after

which there rapidly followed the unmistakable sound of someone urinating against a wall.

"You should have gone with Ivor to Cairo!" Jamie's voice, raised to a shout and amplified by the confines of the alley, rent the night air. "They go to bed after high tea there, like a bloody nursery!"

"Shut up, Jamie," hissed Charlie. "You'll wake the whole bloody neighbourhood." He knew that Jamie was very fond indeed of his younger brother, Ivor, although he made merciless fun of him. Ivor was the brainy one in the family. After first-class honours at Oxford, he'd come out top of the Foreign Service entrance examinations, and after a brief period in Whitehall had just been posted to Cairo.

Jamie emerged from the alley, struggling with his flies. "You'd think that by the year of our Lord nineteen hundred and bloody forty they'd have invented something more practical than a row of six sodding buttons."

"Give me the car keys, Jamie."

"Something on the principle of a revolving door. Damn useful for fast fornication too."

"The keys! *I'm* driving this mobile biscuit tin, or we'll never get to the war."

Jamie handed over the keys and they got in.

"I'll bet you a bottle of Veuve Clicquot," said Charlie, starting the engine, "that Major-General the Honourable Harold Rupert Leofric George Alexander will be ruining our breakfast tomorrow with a snap inspection of No 3 Company."

"He won't, old boy, and thank you. The bet is on. I find cornflakes desperately dull unless soaked in champers. Now please get me safely to my lonely bed where I have nothing to curl up with but Captain Horatio effing Hornblower. I get seasick just thinking about him."

They fell silent as they headed through the suburbs. After an evening in Lille, the return to the lines and the chill recollection that the fighting could start the next day always had a sobering effect. Reaching the countryside, Charlie saw how clear a night it was. He began thinking again about the single cloudless night during their brief

Scottish honeymoon when Margot had urged him against his protests to walk with her down to the banks of Loch Fyne after dinner. They had wrapped themselves in warm clothes and set off under the full moon and the stars across the sheep meadow that ended in an unfenced ten-foot drop to the rocky water's edge. It was a surprisingly mild March night although a light south-westerly wind was blowing off the loch from the direction of Inveraray. They had sat for a while, cuddling close to one another, on the stump of a felled tree, gazing across the rippling water following the silvery shaft of reflected moonlight to the distant bank and the Argyll hills looming black and deep violet against the clear night sky.

"I want to make love right here," Margot had whispered in his ear.

"So do I, darling, but it's too cold."

"For an Englishman? You're kidding!" She had laughed and pressed a gloved hand into his groin. "Seriously, I want to; then when you are spending nights under the stars in France you'll be better able to imagine yourself making love to me. Come on, my handsome, virile husband. Don't keep your fired-up woman waiting."

After a brief search, they had found a dip in the meadow that would shield them from the wind off the loch. He had laid her down on his stretched-out tweed shooting cape on the soft bed of grass and clover. Quickly she had raised her skirt and eased her knickers down over wool-stockinged legs. Charlie unhooked braces beneath his pullover and stepped out of his corduroy trousers. He shivered.

"Come and lie on me quickly, darling," she said, reaching up to him. "I'll warm you."

He lay down between her legs and immediately she slipped her hand into his groin. Within a minute he was gently entering her.

"Don't rush it," she begged him. "He feels so good in there."

"I won't," said Charlie breathlessly, and took his time.

"Oh Charlie, yes, yes!" She had heard his muffled groan just seconds before he climaxed and then immediately her own body had been convulsed. She had gripped him tightly for a while and then, still panting, had told him: "Don't move, darling. Not yet. Oh God, Charlie, we've never done anything as romantic as this."

They had lain prone for a while, kissing, till Margot, looking over Charlie's shoulder, had started to giggle helplessly.

"What the hell's so funny?" Charlie twisted round and saw in the moonlight two sheep standing motionless not six feet away, staring balefully at the lovers.

"There's a charge for watching!" he shouted, and the two woolly voyeurs had turned and trotted jauntily away.

"This car has gears, Charlie. Would you mind getting your right hand out of your crotch and using them occasionally."

Charlie felt himself blush. Five minutes later, he and Jamie were checking themselves through the first line of sentries in the rear of the brigade area. They reached the battalion sector and once again identified themselves to the guard. The picquet officer appeared out of the shadows and peered in through the car window.

"Don't you two ever spend an evening in the Mess except when you're picquet officer or out of money?"

"Get lost, Blackie, you're spoiling the end of a most agreeable evening." Jamie belched and waved Charlie on. "How did they ever let someone like that into the Brigade, even in wartime? I've even seen him putting the milk first into his teacup."

"You're a bloody snob, Jamie." Charlie brought the car to a halt underneath the canvas shelter.

"Someone's got to be the guardian of standards, old cock." He patted him affectionately on the knee. "Go and have sweet dreams about Margot. I shall be dreaming, with any luck, about what I'm going to do to that nubile piece of French crumpet you so shamefully rejected this evening."

They got out of the car and entered the cottage on tiptoe through the back door.

"Don't forget you'll be owing me champagne for tomorrow's breakfast," Jamie whispered as he started up the creaking staircase.

"Don't be too sure. Maybe the Germans will come instead of Alex and then there won't be any breakfast at all."

Two miles away, in a small moated château, Major-General Harold Alexander slept peacefully on his camp bed. The owners of Château Bersée, still in residence, had warmly welcomed the handsome general when he had arrived to set up his divisional headquarters on their small estate, and had offered him the choicest rooms in the château. But Alexander was a man of modest taste and few demands for creature comforts when he was at war. He had selected a small bedroom in one corner of the château which had a turret room leading off it for his ADC, and he had brought his own bed. This night he had left the usual instruction to be wakened at six, and had now been asleep some five hours. A minute or two after five a.m. the distant but unmistakable sound of falling bombs awoke him. Within minutes, hastily, yet as always immaculately dressed in breeches and boots, he was downstairs conferring with his rapidly assembling head-quarters staff. Shortly after five-thirty, Second Corps headquarters were able to put him in the picture. Arras, where Lord Gort's headquarters was located, was under heavy aerial bombardment. The French High Command had immediately issued the series of alerts that were now bringing the British Expeditionary Force to instant readiness to implement Plan D, the crossing into Belgium and the advance to the Dyle. All that was now needed was confirmation that the Germans had indeed violated Belgium's neutrality. By six-fifteen the order to move had been given.

Jamie clearly wasn't going to get his champagne breakfast, and nobly declared his cousin's wager cancelled.

"Well, Charlie, this is what you came here for, I suppose, so do try to look as though you're thrilled to bits. It does so encourage the men."

The junior officers of the Company were hastily packing their spare uniforms and essential personal kit into canvas hold-alls to be loaded onto the platoon stores trucks. A telephone call had brought the mechanic who had sold Jamie his car up to the company billet. The sporting equipment and *chaise longue* had been carefully stowed on the back seat of the camouflaged Citroën and the mechanic had then signed a receipt prepared by Jamie for the car and its contents "to be recuperated by the Marquess of Edmonton, if still alive, as and when conditions permit."

"You'll never see that lot again," said Charlie. "The way things are going your precious *chaise longue* will end up under the huge arse of some SS general's girlfriend."

"You're all a bunch of defeatists," said Jamie as they set off to join their men.

Amid the feverish activity of the morning that had begun when the battalion got the warning order from brigade at six-thirty, Charlie had no time to find out if the mail would be going out now. He had folded the letter to Margot into the back of his map case with the intention of mailing it as soon as the next collection was organized. She would know well before any letter reached her that his division had gone into action and it worried him that it would be difficult to let her know that he was all right. But then of course, he reminded himself, they would be prompt in telling her if anything had happened to him. She would just have to settle for no news being good news; but it worried him all the same.

The battalion would be crossing the line at fourteen-thirty hours. In the meantime Sergeant Boakes fussed about him, reminding him tactfully of duties and procedures that a novice platoon commander, despite the countless rehearsals, might overlook in the rush and excitement of the real moment.

"When it actually happens, it's never quite the same, sir."

"I suppose not, Sergeant Boakes, but I'm just glad the waiting's over."

"That's the spirit, sir. Now we'd better get that weapons inspection under way. Company wants the platoons up for a hot dinner at twelve hundred sharp."

"I know that, Sergeant." Charlie had no wish to sound irritated, but he felt a need to assert himself somewhat.

Certainly he was grateful to have such an efficient and watchful platoon sergeant under him, and he was conscious of having been in the line a bare two months while Boakes had been there from the beginning, including, under the brigade rotation system, a month of contact with the enemy down on the Maginot Line. But rank was rank, and Charlie was sufficiently confident that his basic leadership qualities would not be found wanting in the fighting ahead. There was therefore no reason to feel that Boakes had to wet-nurse him constantly through his initiation into battle.

"I'll handle the weapons inspection, Sergeant Boakes. I want you to check and see that the W/T equipment we put in for repair last Thursday is all back with us or replaced."

"Sah!" Sergeant Boakes saluted with exaggerated ceremony and marched stiffly away to his assigned duties. Charlie smiled and felt better. He squared his shoulders and set off to carry out the weapons inspection.

From the moment the advance into Belgium began, Charlie had the impression of being swept along in a triumphal procession. Women and children lined the twisting country roads and town and village streets, tossing flowers and cheering the columns of vehicles and marching men as they headed eastward across the Escaut, the Dender and the Zenne rivers towards the plain of Waterloo. The troops were exhilarated by the welcome and were soon taking for granted the fact that the Luftwaffe was virtually nowhere to be seen. As they passed south of Brussels and across the Waterloo plain in the early morning of 11th May the mood began to change along with the terrain. The flat Flanders landscape was giving way to woods and valleys, and the advancing troops, instead of being waved on by an enthusiastic populace, were beginning to encounter an ominously increasing flow of cars, trucks, horse-drawn carts, bicycles, and weary foot-sloggers pushing handcarts, prams and wheelbarrows piled high with whatever load of personal belongings the conveyance would bear. The seemingly endless caravan was headed westward.

"Refugees, sir," announced Sergeant Boakes knowingly as the first group passed by the Grenadiers.

"I can see that, Sergeant Boakes." Charlie and his men were halted along with the rest of the brigade column for a reason not yet revealed to them.

"Good thing to let them get fast to the rear, sir. They only get in the way in the fighting area." The sergeant removed his tin helmet and mopped his brow. "How far would we be from the Dyle now, sir?"

Charlie pored over his map. "A little less than three miles by my reading. That probably accounts for the back-up." He stepped up onto the road and looked along the column for signs of movement ahead.

"Come and look at this, Sergeant Boakes." Boakes doubled up to join him. A ragged formation of soldiers, about company strength, was moving down the road past the column. As they approached, Sergeant Boakes stiffened.

"Belgians on the run, sir. Their front forward of the Dyle must be giving." The vanguard of the group had drawn level with them now, and Charlie noticed that many of them were without weapons and some without boots. Some smiled and waved at the British as they shuffled past. Boakes surveyed them with the irritated and disdainful air of a butler finding a tramp on the front doorstep.

"I can see we're going to have to do their fighting for them, sir. And pretty soon."

Charlie suddenly felt depressed and a little afraid. He leaned against the lowered tailgate of the platoon stores truck and stared with unfocused eyes at his map, thinking of Margot. The nagging feeling that he had not been fair in persuading her to marry him when he was about to go off and quite likely die had returned to him. He kept telling himself that it was ridiculous to have misgivings; they had both pledged their undying love a hundred times since the decision was taken, so why should her earlier hesitancy be troubling him now?

"Mug of tea, sir?"

The cheerful voice of Guardsman Pullen, the stores truck driver, interrupted Charlie's self-examination. Pullen offered him a steaming enamel mug which he accepted gratefully. An officer on a motorcycle stopped his machine by the truck. Charlie recognized him as the Coldstream Guards subaltern from Brigade HQ who'd earlier told him he'd met Katie at a party in London just a month ago.

"You'll be moving in five minutes or so," the subaltern called out. "There's been a bit of a cock-up in the signing of the routes to the battalion areas." He revved his bike and started to slide forward. "By the way, Churchill has just become Prime Minister!" he shouted as he accelerated off down the column.

"So what," muttered Pullen, taking a noisy swig at his tea. But Charlie knew that back in London both his father and his father-in-law would be heaving great sighs of relief.

By midday, the First Guards Brigade was being guided into its allotted sector along the Dyle River, and twenty-four hours later, after the last of the stragglers of the Belgian refugees and troops had crossed back over the river and withdrawn to the rear, the bridges were blown, and within a few hours the forward patrols of the German Sixth Army appeared on the far bank. During the next two days, the British Expeditionary Force sat and watched with grim curiosity as the German divisions edged their way cautiously up to the river and deployed along its eastern banks.

"What the hell are they waiting for?" asked Charlie as he and Jamie crouched in a dugout and peered through binoculars at the enemy.

"An engraved invitation requesting the pleasure of their company on this side of the bloody river. Or maybe my twenty-fifth birthday next Friday. Anyway, if they don't come soon, I swear I'm going over there to fetch them. This is all too boring for words."

"Silly bugger! You really want to give the Krauts the satisfaction of winging a marquess this early in the shoot?"

Jamie grinned. "I'd better get back to my command trench – which, incidentally, is the Ritz compared to your little slum here. Some people just don't know how to fight a war in comfort."

He hauled himself out of the trench. Charlie watched his angular figure loping awkwardly in a semi-crouch back down the line. He couldn't help worrying about him. Somehow, for all his jesting self-confidence, he seemed the more vulnerable, especially now that the start of the fighting must be only hours away.

"Jesus Christ! We've been half-way to bloody Germany and back again for bugger all." Jamie laughed and scowled alternately as he and his fellow platoon officers dispersed from a company briefing. They had just received orders to withdraw again; the fourth withdrawal in a week.

"If you move yourself, you might just make it to Lille in time for a meal at l'Huîtrière and a little hasty fornication before the jerries arrive."

"Shut up, Charlie. I'm too tired to lift a knife and fork, let alone anything else."

Thirty-six hours later, they were on the move, back along the same roads they had covered in the opposite direction, and in lighter mood, just two weeks before. Vehicles and men squeezed their way through and around the endless tangle of refugees, cursing at the time it was taking them to regain the Gort Line, their original starting point. To add to their woes, the Luftwaffe paid them frequent and murderous attention. The whine and drone of approaching aircraft sent troops and civilians scurrying from the roadway into the ditches, hedges and surrounding fields, but the bombs and machine guns took a ghastly toll.

"You don't have to look at it, sir," said Sergeant Boakes sharply. A pair of Stukas had just strafed the crowded road, and Charlie found himself staring mesmerized at a baby lying at his feet in two neat halves, severed at the waist. He started to say something about finding the parents, then turned away and threw up into the hedge. Sergeant Boakes hovered over him until he had recovered himself.

"Best leave them to sort out their own dead. We may have problems of our own."

Charlie straightened up quickly, feeling a twinge of

shame that he had not thought first of his own men. He briskly strode out onto the road amid the defiant refugees gathering themselves up for the onward trek. Blocking his ears to the cries of the wounded and the wailing of the bereaved, he pushed his way to the far side of the road where the platoon was reassembling.

"OK, any casualties?" he asked in a firm voice.

"I think we're in luck again, sir." Lance Corporal Rogers held a grubby handkerchief to his acquiline nose to staunch the bleeding on its bridge.

The platoon sergeant was able to report all present and correct within a couple of minutes, and a runner was sent ahead to the company headquarters vehicle to report that the platoon was ready to move.

The slow progress westward continued until exhausted, hungry and harassed, the First Division reached the French frontier line. The Grenadiers dropped gratefully into the trenches in their allotted sector. For two days, keeping their heads down under an almost constant bombardment from General von Bock's artillery, they sought to rest their weary limbs and sleep between the waves of shelling. Charlie slept fitfully and used his waking hours to crawl from trench to trench and dugout to dugout to talk with his men. He found them in little mood to conceal the frustration he shared with them.

"Jamie, who's the general talking over there on the road with the commander?"

"Ask Blackie; he's the battalion know-all."

"Franklyn. Fifth Division, you military ignoramuses. It's obviously something important."

The battalion was assembling on the edge of a wood to the rear of the line to be served its first substantial hot meal since leaving the Dyle. Charlie, Jamie and a group of junior brother officers were chatting while the men stood in line, waiting patiently for the cooks to receive the order to start dishing out the meal.

"Of course it's something important, Blackie," said Jamie. "The savour of our military *haute cuisine* must have wafted over to his HQ, so he's come trotting over with his mess-tin."

110

They watched the general return briskly to his car, leaving the commanding officer in urgent conversation with the quartermaster and the adjutant. Seconds later, the regimental sergeant-major was getting the battalion fallen in by companies on the road.

"I smell real trouble," said Jamie breathlessly as he and Charlie doubled back to their company. "Anything that could wrest even a half-edible meal from my drooling lips at this moment has to be the worst kind of trouble."

Minutes later their company commander briefed them.

"We're one of three battalions being sent to give a quick hand to the 143rd Brigade which is having a spot of trouble up on the Ypres-Comines Canal. It's a nine-mile march, and we can expect some lively fun when we get there at around twenty-two hundred hours. We'll be going straight into action on arrival. The Black Watch will probably be already hard at it. Sorry about the dinner, gentlemen, but our friends up there would appreciate it if we got a move on."

As they marched off up the road, Charlie looked at his men with pride and admiration. There were no grumbles. Assured that they were at last going to fight, their chins were up and their shoulders squared, even if there was an aching emptiness in their stomachs. Ahead of him in the failing light, he could make out Jamie swinging along with his very un-Grenadier-like gait. Take care of yourself tonight, Jamie, said Charlie to himself, as the column swung off the road and began the long trek across the flat fields towards the rumble and glow of the battle to the north-east.

When they finally reached the battle area, orders were hastily given. The Germans still hung on to a narrow bridgehead over the canal and across the railway line which ran along an embankment parallel to it. The Grenadiers and the other two newly-arrived battalions were to push the Germans back over the railway line and the canal. Within minutes Charlie found himself doubling forward across the flat ground towards the embankment. His platoon, bringing up the rear of the company, was to hold a ridge halfway to the embankment and cover the forward platoons as they rushed the Germans on it. If they were forced back, Charlie's platoon would cover their withdrawal.

His platoon was twenty yards short of the ridge when the German machine guns on the embankment opened up. In the light of the flames leaping from the burning town of Comines, he could see men in his company's forward platoons falling as the bullets cut a swathe through the advancing attackers. He and his men were now giving covering fire from the ridge. A green and white flare, the signal for withdrawal, burst in the sky. Continuing to give covering fire, Charlie and his men watched as the depleted assault group fell rapidly back behind the line of his ridge. When he was sure that they had stopped coming, he turned to give the order to Sergeant Boakes for their own withdrawal. In the excitement and the half-light he had not noticed that the man who had dropped down into cover next to him when they reached the ridge was not Boakes but Lance-Sergeant Timmins.

"Where's Sar'nt Boakes?"

"Caught it on the way in, sir. He's back there. Nothing we can do for him, sir."

"Right, get the sections moving back to the start-line and down into the ditch."

Numb with fury, Charlie sprinted back across the open ground with his men. Back in the dubious safety of the ditch, Timmins started the roll-call. The tally jolted Charlie. Four wounded safely back; eight missing, probably dead, out front.

"Bit of a mauling, I'm afraid," agreed the company commander as he reached Charlie's position half an hour later. "Get well dug in; we can expect plenty of unwelcome visits tomorrow."

"Any news of Jamie?" asked Charlie, his voice too weary to betray his anxiety.

"Jamie? He got into a little hand-to-hand brawl and came out on top."

The major grinned and moved away.

"Good for you, Jamie," whispered Charlie.

At six o'clock the next morning the mortar bombardment started. Charlie peered over the top of the ditch and saw, as he had feared, several platoons of grey-uniformed infantry moving towards the Grenadiers' line. He knew the drill. All along the line the bren-gunners would wait until the enemy was no more than fifty yards away, and then the massacre would begin. No sooner had those Germans left standing begun to fall back than the mortars would open up again.

The process repeated itself three times over the next eight hours, and each time the Germans were driven back. By mid-afternoon, however, the battalion's ammunition was all but exhausted. Charlie crept along his platoon position to pass the word that the position was to be held until twenty-two hundred hours that night, and that every round would have to be made to count if they were going to hang on that long.

"If the worst comes to the worst, sir," said Timmins with a toothy grin, "we'll get Trotter here to sing. That'll keep 'em off!"

The men within earshot joined in the laughter.

The mortar bomb exploded some twenty yards to the rear, and Charlie, who was half out of the dugout, felt as though someone had kicked him hard in the thigh. Timmins stared at him blankly for a moment and then said hoarsely:

"Your leg's bleeding a lot, sir."

Charlie looked down and saw the blood well up through a hole in his battledress trousers. Suddenly the searing pain caught up with him and he sucked in his breath and winced. He reached for the field-dressing in the pocket of his other leg, and Timmins helped him apply it.

"This won't do much good, sir. You've got metal in there. I'll send Trotter to company headquarters to see if that carrier's around to run you down to the RAP."

Ten minutes later, Charlie was crouching painfully and awkwardly in the carrier as it lumbered on its screeching tracks down a twisting path towards a farmhouse where the aid post was located. The mortar bombardment was still in progress, and the driver cursed impressively as he urged the bouncing and slewing vehicle towards the farm.

The mortar bomb missed the carrier by a good ten yards, but it blew the driver's head clean off his shoulders. Charlie was pitched half out of the carrier and slid stunned to the ground. After a while he raised himself painfully into a sitting position and noticed that his leg was bleeding badly again. He somehow had the feeling that he should not be there, and he hauled himself with difficulty to his feet. There was an open gate in the hedge, and he decided to go through it. He hobbled into the field, and although the grass looked soft and inviting, he felt he should not stop now and sit down. He was late for something. He stumbled determinedly on, dragging his left leg with difficulty. Damnit! Jamie should be somewhere around! They were going to drive into London to see a doctor to do something about his leg, and then Margot and Katie were going to join them for a celebration dinner.

The bomb crater received him none too gently and knocked the consciousness out of him.

It was first light the next morning when a Feldwebel of the 176th Regiment of Infantry, advancing with his platoon to the rear of the positions that the Tommies had abandoned the previous night, spotted the Tommy officer in the crater and checked to see whether he was alive. He was, just, so he ordered up a stretcher bearer and carefully lifted him out. A half-track coming up the hedgerow was stopped, and the stretcher placed under the canvas. Charlie was not quite conscious the moment he became a prisoner of war.

7

"Well, Mrs Garland, your pregnancy is one thing that can be said to be going according to plan."

Dr Worsley allowed himself a hint of a smile to complement the slightly grim jest. He was not much given to jesting, but since he had earlier enquired after his patient's husband's welfare and had elicited the information that there was as yet no information on the return of the Third Grenadiers from the beaches of Dunkirk, he felt that a mildly humorous allusion to the differing fortunes of wife and husband would not be wholly out of place.

"Well, that's a relief," said Margot from behind the changing screen as she slipped a cotton print dress over her head. "I certainly *feel* that it's all going well."

With shoes back on and hair tidied, she emerged and took a seat in front of the physician's desk.

"Permit me to tender some advice as to general comportment at this time, Mrs Garland." He brought his long-fingered hands together in front of his face as if in prayer. "The safe return of your husband will, of course, be an emotional occasion and one with cause for celebration. At six weeks we must continue to treat our pregnancy with the utmost respect and gentleness. Things being how they are these days, the emotions cannot but be much exercised, and we should guard against any concomitant over-indulgence. May we therefore exercise reasonable restraint, Mrs Garland?"

Margot suppressed a smile. "It certainly will be a celebration; I don't think Charlie even knows we're having a baby. I can't imagine that my letter reached him. But I promise I'll go easy on myself."

"Good. Then we will see you again in a fortnight. I wish you good luck and good news."

Out in the street, Margot bought an *Evening Standard* and then took a cab home. During the ride she scanned the numerous reports of the miraculous evacuation of the British Expeditionary Force and many French troops as well from the Dunkirk beaches by the astonishing armada of navy vessels, channel ferries, trawlers, motor yachts and tiny pleasure craft, all carrying out their rescue mission under the most murderous conditions.

Come on, Charlie, you've *got* to be on one of those boats! she said to herself. And then her heart leaped as her eye caught a brief paragraph in a dispatch from the channel port of Dover.

> Elements of the First Guards Brigade were among weary but happy troops to reach this port at first light this morning, bringing their wounded with them. Other elements may well be at Folkestone or Margate or on their way there.

There you are; you were right, Father! she thought happily as she re-read the report.

"Of course he'll make it," Harland had assured her the previous evening. "They won't leave a crack brigade like that hanging around, exposed, on those beaches for a moment longer than necessary."

Harland had not been at all sure that such an observation was justified, but he had had to counteract the effect of a call to his daughter earlier in the evening from Sir Walter who, while expressing optimism about Charlie's return, nevertheless told her that there were reports of heavy casualties on the beaches. Her father's words had done much to reassure her, and she had slept well that night.

At the front door of 43 Hill Street she fumbled excitedly with her keys, dropped both them and her gas mask, and rang the bell impatiently. Her mother opened the door.

"Look, Mother!" She thrust the paper at her. "It says the Guards are back. Has Charlie called?"

She stepped inside as her mother took the paper and laid it on the hall table without glancing at it.

116

Margot hung her gas mask in the hall closet.

"Is Katie back? Did she get the job with the Red Cross?"

"Calm down, dearest. You're not meant to get so excited in your condition."

Margot busied herself in front of the hall mirror. Then, reflected in the mirror, she saw her mother properly for the first time since entering the house, and she swung round, frowning.

"Mother! You've been crying! What's happened?"

Her father and Katie now materialized in the living room doorway.

"Margot," her father said softly. "Come in and sit down."

She looked from her mother to her father, her frown translated into a look of terror.

"It's bad news, isn't it?" she said softly. She clasped her hands together and looked beseechingly at her father. "Don't tell me Charlie's dead. Don't!"

Elinor took her by the arm and led her into the living room and sat down with her on the sofa. Her father hovered over them.

"No, darling," he said. "We've heard nothing of that sort. Simply that he's believed to have been wounded and most likely captured."

"Oh my *God*!" She buried her head in her mother's shoulder and started to weep softly.

"It was Jamie who gave us news of him."

Margot looked up. "In other words, no one knows where the hell he is or what's happened to him!" she said angrily.

"Let Father explain, sis," said Katie, mopping away a tear of her own.

"I'm listening."

Harland sat himself in a chair opposite and leaned forward, speaking softly but firmly.

"Jamie called Walter and myself this morning as soon as he could get to a telephone at Dover. He told us that Charlie had been slightly wounded in the leg three days ago. Not on the beach; in some action in the interior. He was last seen going off in a carrier to get his wound seen

117

to. They found the carrier shot up, but no sign of Charlie. He obviously got away and was most likely picked up by the Germans because he didn't return to the Grenadier lines. He might have been concussed when the carrier was hit."

"Or he may be lying dead in a ditch," snapped Margot.

"They looked for that, in what time they had before withdrawing, so Jamie assured us. But they didn't find him, so the chances are very good indeed that he was taken a prisoner and is now having his wounds attended to."

"Or maybe he got past the Germans and is making his way to Dunkirk," volunteered Katie.

"It's a possibility, but I don't think we should lay too much store by it," said her father. "No, Walter's and my guess is that he'll shortly be listed as 'missing in action' and that we shall eventually hear through the International Red Cross that he's in some prisoner-of-war-camp." He rose from his chair and squatted down in front of Margot. "The waiting is going to be awfully tough, sweetheart, I know. But the odds favour his being alive, and that means that as a prisoner he's now out of danger, and he'll be coming back to you when this ghastly war's over."

Margot nodded, rose and quickly left the room. Her mother started to follow her.

"No, Elinor," said Harland. "Leave her be for a moment. She'll want to be alone." He crossed the room and opened a cocktail cabinet. "We must do all we can to cheer her up. Anyone else want a stiff one?"

"She's got the baby to look forward to. That will distract her," said Katie.

"Just pray nothing happens to it now," said Elinor and, feeling the tears coming on again, she hurriedly left the room.

Harland Moore sighed. It wasn't going to be easy.

Margot closed the door of her bedroom, kicked off her shoes and sank face up onto the bed. She bit into her quivering lips as the warm tears coursed down her cheeks. Staring at the ceiling and pressing the palm of one hand against her belly, the words formed silently in her mind: I promise you that your father is alive. Then suddenly the realization returned to her that Charlie might be in great pain.

"My darling, I can't help you!" she shouted out, and began to beat the bedclothes with clenched fists, jerking her head from side to side as if his pain had entered her own body. The spasm lasted a few seconds and then stopped as, in her mind's eye, she now saw him lying peacefully in a hospital bed. They're taking good care of him, she assured herself. There's no way they could let someone as beautiful as him die.

She turned now to look at his photograph on her bed-side table. It was a three-quarter length portrait of him in uniform. The photographer had tried to make him look solemn and arrogant, but Charlie's humour and vulnera-bility had cheated the lens. She lay on her side, staring at it and sobbing quietly, and then she started to pray: a jumble of familiar litany mingled with hurriedly formu-lated entreaties to match the tragedy of the moment. In a while she fell asleep, and slept on when her mother stole in to see if she was all right. At seven o'clock her sister woke her to announce dinner in half an hour.

"Or would you rather we brought you up something here, sis?"

"No, no. I'm coming down. I feel better, and I also feel very hungry, and thirsty. Be an angel and fix me a very dry martini, and to hell with Dr Worsley!"

She yawned as she swung her legs off the bed and stretched.

"That's my girl!" said Katie, bending to plant a kiss on her sister's cheek. She then ran downstairs to report that Margot was back on her feet in more senses than one.

After a long and sombre lunch with Sir Walter and Lady Garland, Jamie walked wearily across St James's Park towards Mayfair. He really felt too tired to walk, but the craving for fresh air was too strong. For days he had breathed nothing but the acrid air of war: burning buildings, burning vehicles, petrol, the stench of rot-ting horse cadavers, the sticky odours of perspiring,

119

unwashed, frightened men, and, in the end, the suffocating, oil-reeking hell below decks on a heaving, overcrowded frigate. The only scene he wanted never to have blotted from the memory of that nightmare was the sight of the remnants of his battalion stepping smartly, heads erect, backs straight, up the gangplank and onto the ship, a painfully-managed show of discipline and defiance as the enemy's artillery and bombers sought to the end to snatch them from the threshold of survival.

Jamie had planned his day carefully. His mother would be coming up from the country to dine with him that evening. The next morning he would have to take the early train to rejoin the battalion for the re-forming and re-equipping of its depleted ranks, after which a proper leave could be taken. Right now, the most difficult part of his day was upon him. He had seen Margot only once since the week that she and Charlie had become engaged. The delicacy of his task was preying on his already tattered nerves, and, to add to his discomfort, the civilian clothes he was wearing, borrowed from his solicitous uncle, were noticeably a size too small, elegant though they were in cloth and cut. Jamie had always aspired to sartorial excellence and to fall so far short of it, even in these extenuating circumstances, made him feel uncomfortable. As he approached Hill Street, he prayed that Margot would be in control of herself. He wasn't much good at coping with weeping, hysterical women, especially when he had little, if anything, of comfort to impart.

As he quickly discovered, he needn't have been so apprehensive.

"Don't you dare blame yourself for not bringing him back, Jamie. He looked up to you and you took care of him, as he told me in his letters. But I can quite understand that when the shooting started, you each had your own men to worry about. So *don't* apologize!"

Jamie was sitting on the sofa in the living room, puffing nervously at a cigarette. Margot was on her knees in front of him. She pressed her hands against his pale cheeks and looked into his tired, sad eyes.

"Come on! This is not the boisterous, laughing Jamie I have always known."

He stubbed out the cigarette in an ashtray on his lap. "You make me feel very ashamed of myself, Margot. Here I am meant to be comforting the wife of someone who's just been taken a prisoner of war, and been wounded into the bargain, and here you are, being a pillar of strength and telling me to cheer up."

What he actually thought was more than he dared say. Christ! For all I know, she may already be a war widow, and she must know that, although she's just said that she's certain he's being taken care of in his captivity. What a woman! If Charlie *is* alive, he must surely be bent on an early attempt at escape to get back to someone like this.

"Well, we all have to cheer up. Things could be a lot worse," she said. "For one thing, I'm carrying his child, even if he doesn't know it yet, so a part of him is with me all the time. And now, I suggest we have a drink."

She rose to her feet, crossed to a cupboard by the door, and bent to extract from it a box marked ASPREY.

"Anthony Eden's wedding gift," she said, opening it and unwrapping from tissue paper a silver cocktail shaker. "I was planning to baptize it on Charlie's return, but since he's going to be a little late – " she grinned at him " – I'm sure he wouldn't mind if we used it to celebrate *your* safe return."

Jamie smiled too. "He's not going to have to. I'll stand for no cheek from a junior subaltern. His lady's wish is my command!"

He rose from the sofa, executed a sweeping bow, and walked over to Margot to hug her. For the first time, he saw tears welling up in her eyes.

"He'll come back, won't he? I mean, that can happen, can't it? He could escape and come back a hero. I mean it's not beyond our Charlie, surely."

"Absolutely not, old girl. And yes, I'd love a good strong martini, particularly one made by the fair hand of a genuine Yank."

"Coming right up. And while I'm making it, tell me what happens to you now. Where will the First Guards Brigade be? Close to London, I hope, so that we can see lots of you."

They chatted on until Jamie looked at his watch and drained his second martini.

"I must be off. I have a couple of errands to run before meeting Mama at Brown's. She's not the sort of person to take the fall of France as an excuse for being late."

"But you must stay to see Katie and my parents; they'll all be here within the hour."

"I'd really love to, but after all I've been through, to risk being maimed by my own mother in a London hotel just isn't on!"

Margot sighed. "You English! You're all in thrall to your mothers."

The expectation Margot still had that Charlie might be among the last of the troops brought away from Dunkirk was extinguished two days later, on 4th June, when the town and port were finally reported to be in enemy hands. Four days later, Margot was officially notified that her husband was listed as "missing in action".

That same afternoon, as news came through to the United States Embassy in London that the Germans were within forty miles of Paris and that the French Government was preparing to flee the capital, Harland Moore had an urgent telephone conversation with his wife. Ambassador Kennedy, he had learned, was planning, the moment France fell – which could now be only a matter of days if not hours away – to tell all four thousand Americans remaining in London who were not on absolutely essential government business to return home as quickly as possible. Moore told his wife that, in his view, which for once coincided with that of his ambassador, prudence required that she and their two daughters pack up and go back to America rather than risk being interned in a Nazi-occupied Britain.

"Of course you're right, dearest, although I do hate the thought of us splitting up and leaving you here alone. We're going to have goodness knows what trouble when we have to persuade Margot to leave. You know her views on the matter. Come what may, including Hitler, she intends to stay. But I can't leave a pregnant daughter here alone with you. You'll have more than enough on your plate. I'm sure Charlie and his parents would see the good sense in her coming home with Katie and me."

They broke the news over dinner at the Dorchester, and Margot left them in no doubt about what she thought of it.

"I absolutely refuse to go," she said as she stabbed angrily at a piece of chicken breast on her plate. "For heaven's sakes, have you forgotten already that I'm a British army officer's wife, carrying his child, and that he happens to be a prisoner of war? How on earth do you think I would feel sitting comfortably in Washington or New York while other wives of prisoners were waiting patiently here where the war is? I'm not sure I'd go if they told me he was dead. This is his country and his child is going to be born right here!"

"But wouldn't Charlie rather you were in a safe place?" argued her father.

"Quite possibly, but he'd respect my wishes. He'd never force me to leave against my will."

"If you stay, I stay," said Katie flatly.

"Out of the question!" snapped her mother. "You, of all of us, have no good reason to stay."

"Yes I have. The American Red Cross Office needs me. It may be a small operation now, but it's going to get very big. So I'm here to stay."

"You'll do as we say, Katie," admonished her father.

Margot came to her sister's defence.

"She's eighteen, Father. She has the right to be foolish enough to risk her own neck, whatever Kennedy says. Anyway, I'll keep an eye on her."

"And vice versa," added Katie.

"I suggest," said Moore calmly, "that we finish our dinner peacefully and discuss this again when we get home."

Later, as they picked their way through the blackout back to Hill Street, Elinor, on her husband's arm a few paces ahead of the girls, tried a little gentle mediation.

"Maybe we're rushing this decision after all. We've got a bit of time left. Margot has a strong claim to stay, you've got to admit. And as you know, I'm reluctant to leave myself, however little sense it may make."

123

She squeezed her husband's arm tightly as they crossed South Audley Street, and Harland began to think that the likelihood of his emerging the victor in this family contest of wills was diminishing rapidly. Despite his efforts at firmness and decisiveness, his heart was not really in it. Even if the French were about to be forced into total submission by the invader, he was a good deal less sure than was his ambassador that the same fate awaited the British.

The family discussion was resumed back at the house, and after it was over Margot sat up late writing a letter to her brother at Yale. She wrote first of the sad news about Charlie, but she avoided any self-pitying and stressed her optimism that he was now being properly cared for as a prisoner of war. Then she wrote:

We had a vigorous (to say the least!) discussion this evening about whether or not all or any of us (excluding Father of course) should follow Kennedy's advice and go home as soon as France falls, the assumption being that England will be next. I have refused to go, for obvious reasons, and Katie, who's now working for the American Red Cross Representative here, was equally adamant. Mother doesn't really want to go either, although she tried to make us believe that we all had to do what Father said, and Father was saying that we had to go. Anyway the argument went on until after midnight (just a few minutes ago) and guess who won? Father was very graceful in defeat, and I'd bet my last dollar that he's happy he lost. We're going to take a cottage in the country to retreat to if the bombing gets going, so you really don't have to worry. If the Nazis come, that's a different story, but as neutrals (except for me, I suppose) the worst that can happen is that Katie and the parents get interned or, as diplomats, get sent packing.

I'm falling asleep, so I'll stop now. Love to you and the grandparents. Write soon!

                                                        Margot

8

"It's the government's duty to remain on the soil of France. We have been defeated in battle, and it is now up to the government to guide us through the misery that lies ahead with dignity and wisdom."

Georges Lemonnier, former member of France's Chamber of Deputies and former mayor of Bordeaux, felt that the occasion called for a little rhetoric. The fact that he had an audience of one and that the two of them were standing in the middle of a Médoc vineyard did not in his view render such solemn rhetoric in any way incongruous. It was, after all, a solemn hour in France's history and he was far from sure that his solider son saw correctly by which path France's ultimate salvation would be reached. He motioned to the young man that they resume their progress down the line of vines.

"My dear Edmond," he continued, "to you Marshal Pétain may seem nothing but a senile octogenarian out of France's more glorious past, but to me he is still the hero of Verdun, a man with a sure sense of history, and at this unhappy hour the only person of great stature capable of looking beyond our moment of humiliation to the perpetuation of eternal France."

"And that, Father, is why you feel we should support his urging of an immediate armistice."

"Precisely."

"Well, I wish I could see it your way, but I cannot. We should be fighting to defend the soil of France to the last hectare, but instead we are talking of laying down our arms. It is not only humiliating, it is downright dishonourable! And if the government will not stand and fight

125

here, it should at least withdraw to some convenient part of our empire and wage war from there."

The elder Lemonnier placed a hand on his son's shoulder.

"My son, you are young and you are courageous, and looking at you walking beside me here in your cavalry officer's uniform, I feel a great surge of pride at the thought of you riding your tank into battle against Hitler's panzers. But that would now be a pointless gesture; France has bled enough these past weeks. For the time being we must accept the inevitable so that we may preserve ourselves for the future."

Edmond Lemonnier stared deep into his father's eyes. He saw an elderly, tired but very determined man, and he knew it was useless to argue with him. He loved him dearly and had no wish to spend these few hours with him locked in futile debate. He would eventually do what he had to do and he suspected that his father knew that, and it made Edmond love him all the more. His father's avowal of pride in him, however, left him feeling uncomfortable. So far, in the battle of France, Edmond had seen not a single shot fired in anger, and for the last three months he had not even climbed aboard a tank. In mid-February he had been transferred from his tank battalion with the First Armoured Division at Châlons to a staff post at the Bordeaux headquarters of the Eighteenth Military Region. The transfer had annoyed him even though it had meant an earlier than expected promotion to captain, and he harboured a lingering suspicion that, despite his father's firm denials, there had been some family string-pulling to bring him close to home. What made him feel all the more uncomfortable was the knowledge that his battalion had, just a month ago, been decimated by Rommel's panzers in the fall of Belgium.

Today, 14th June 1940, Captain Lemonnier had reported to his headquarters in the rue Vital-Carles at seven a.m. Two hours later, he and a group of fellow staff officers had stood grimly around a radio set listening to the broken voice of a radio announcer describing the columns of German troops streaming into Paris. Edmond had

126

been due to begin twenty-four-hours leave at midday and now assumed that it would be cancelled. Instead, his superior told him he was free until seven a.m. the following morning, and he had thereupon hitched a ride out into the Médoc vineyard country to visit his parents.

Château Lachaise-Laurent, the Lemonnier family's country home and vineyard, lay in the heart of the Médoc, some fifty kilometres north-west of the great port city of Bordeaux. Edmond's grandfather, Théophile, had purchased the vineyard with its eighteenth-century turreted château in 1899. The ninety-acre property, ten kilometres from the village of St Julien, lay just inside the western boundary of the commune of that name which boasted, in addition, such famous vineyards as Beychevelle, Gruaud-Larose, Talbot and the Léovilles. Théophile had known a good claret when he drank one – which he did with loyal frequency – but he knew less than he ever cared to admit about making one. During the first quarter of the century he had allowed the quality of his wine to deteriorate sadly and it was left to his son and heir, Georges, to restore to Château Lachaise-Laurent the high reputation of a wine officially classified as a "great growth" among the Médocs. By 1930 he was producing a dark, full-bodied wine bearing all the best features of a fine St Julien. The proprietors of the great neighbouring châteaux, though traditionally modest in their praise of each other, congratulated Georges warmly on restoring the good name of Lachaise-Laurent.

He took his son by the arm.

"Come on, Edmond, let's go and see how the '38 and '39 are coming along. At the last tasting I was none too impressed, but you know how difficult I am to please." He bent to check a section of wire on which the vines were supported. As he straightened up, he sighed. "That's something we're going to be short of; it's all gone for barbed wire."

They set off along the track – just wide enough to accommodate the harvest carts – that cut through that part of the vineyard and up to the château.

"When you've said goodbye to your mother, I'll drive you into Bordeaux. Then would you do your old father the honour of dining with him? I plan to stay the night at the apartment because I have business early tomorrow with our lawyers."

Edmond readily agreed. He himself had moved into the family's spacious town apartment on the Cours Pasteur, just behind the Cathedral of Saint-André, on being posted to Bordeaux. His father usually slept there twice a week when business or the urge to spend an evening at his lady-friend's residence compelled him to stay overnight in the city. Edmond knew about his father's liaison with the handsome widow of a wealthy banker, and his father knew that he knew, but no word about her ever passed between them.

"If what you told me this morning is correct, my boy, the government should be assembling in Bordeaux right now. Who would have thought that Bordeaux would become the centre of what is left of free France?"

He shook his head in disbelief.

"The likely consequence of that dubious honour, Father, will be a hail of Luftwaffe bombs."

They continued in silence up the track towards the château and a few minutes later, in the cool of the white-washed interior of the long, low building which housed the new wines in serried ranks of barrels, they sampled the two latest vintages of Château Lachaise-Laurent, accompanied by Aristide Grenier, the *maître de chai*, who drew the wine into glasses from the barrels for their tasting.

"Thin, little tannin; it'll be a small wine," was Georges Lemonnier's crisp verdict on the '39. Edmond and the *maître de chai* concurred. They passed through a door into an adjoining cellar which housed the barrels of '38.

"I still doubt it will be more than an average one," declared the elder Lemonnier after they had tasted the vintage. "But no one else's I've seen promises any better. They're just all rather dull. We'll do well to drink 'em young."

"If the Boche let us!" Grenier hammered the peg back into the barrel with a whack that would have fractured the skull of any invader imprudently caught helping himself to his precious wine.

128

The Lemonniers smiled.

"*Courage*, Grenier," said the elder. "If they raid this place, you can lead them to the '39. But I warn you here and now that I expect you to die defending our splendid '37!"

They laughed and went out blinking into the still strong sunlight.

Edmond left his father and Grenier to continue their rounds and went in search of his mother in the château. Propped against his khaki kepi on a table in the stone-flagged entrance hall was a note from her. She was resting upstairs and he should come up to see her before leaving.

Giselle Lemonnier was the hapless victim of a severe migraine condition and was forced to spend long hours nursing her discomfort in darkened rooms. Yet she remained courageously good-natured, to the admiration of her family and friends. A handsome woman in her early fifties, she was utterly devoted to her husband of thirty-one years, and lavished equal affection on her son, Edmond, and on her married daughter, Solange, the wife of an eye surgeon in Nice. The surgeon had recently become the source of supply of a Swiss drug that more effectively eased her pain but which left her exhausted. This late afternoon, Edmond found her in just such a condition, her head propped against the pillows of her ornate Empire bed, the heavy grey damask drapes drawn three-quarters across the tall windows. He sat on a chair at her bedside and took her hand in his.

"Edmond, I cannot believe our good fortune that in all this disaster you are still with us."

"It may not be for much longer, Mother."

"But if there's an armistice, you can leave the army, no?"

"Either we'll be demobilized or more likely simply disarmed and assigned to some sort of administration duties – the regular officers, that is."

"Well that sounds all right; at least you won't be fighting."

"No mother, it's a dreadful prospect. For a professional

129

soldier, a graduate of St Cyr, to lay down his arms at the feet of an enemy occupier is the ultimate humiliation."

"But you have no choice."

Edmond saw the look of fear in her eyes.

"Edmond!" She clutched his hand tightly. "For God's sake don't do anything rash. Surely there's no dishonour in accepting what you cannot control."

He rose to his feet and kissed his mother gently on the forehead.

"Father's waiting to drive me into Bordeaux; I must leave now."

"Then at least listen to his advice, *chéri*, and try to do him the honour of following it. He's a wise man."

"I'll listen, Mother, I promise. Now rest; I will call you tomorrow."

He closed the door behind him and went down the stairs to the front hall. He picked up his kepi and briefcase and walked out onto the gravel forecourt. His father was inspecting the polish on the grille of his gleaming maroon Renault Nerva Grand Sport, an eight-cylinder convertible of impressive dimensions that was his pride and joy.

"Father, you really will have to lock her away if the Germans get here. They'll never be able to resist her."

"I've already thought of that," said Georges as he climbed in behind the wheel. "Goutard up at the garage in Pauillac tells me he can dismantle her in twenty-four hours and hide the parts. I believe him, but can he put her together again?" They laughed. "I paid forty thousand francs for her three years ago and have no intention of handing such a beautiful investment over to some bullet-headed German general."

He slipped the car into gear and they headed along the driveway across the flat northern area of the vineyard and out onto the narrow road leading towards the village of St Julien-Beychevelle.

"How did you find your mother?"

"Tired, and she worries too much about me. I'm twenty-four, an army captain, and can take care of myself."

"To her, you're still a boy. Don't deprive her of the privilege of treating you as such from time to time when

130

it does no real harm. Listen to her, and to me, and try to bear in mind what we have to say when you come to make your own decisions."

"I've never been a bad listener, Father."

"No, but you're as stubborn as a mule. Not altogether a bad trait, mind you; but in certain circumstances, like those we find ourselves in now, an ability to compromise can be handy."

"You're asking me to bow to what you believe is inevitable."

"I'm asking you, Edmond, not to beat your head needlessly against Hitler's brick wall, don't make unnecessary heroic gestures that could cost you your freedom or your life. As I keep telling you, this situation won't last for ever."

Edmond fell silent. Once again he found himself wanting to avoid a confrontation with his father. Georges Lemonnier slowed the big convertible as they approached the cluster of buildings marking the centre of the commune of St Julien and then turned right into the village of Beychevelle. They were now on the main road leading south-east through the Haut-Médoc to Bordeaux. As they sped throughout the communes of Margaux and Macau, the conversation turned, to Edmond's relief, to vintages and gossip about the owners of the noted châteaux that flashed past them. But as they approached the northwestern outskirts of the great port city, their carefree conversation came to a halt. The traffic had begun to build up and it soon became clear that the city was being subjected to a massive influx of refugees from the *départements* to the north as the Germans pressed their sweep southwards.

"It's got a lot worse than this morning," said Edmond.

"Another good reason for an early armistice," replied his father. "When the shooting stops, so will the refugees."

They were now moving at a crawl through the traffic-clogged inner suburbs. The pavements were crowded with refugees bearing suitcases, bundles, babies and other portable belongings. At the entrances to hotels, restaurants and bars, groups of weary travellers bid

131

loudly for the last bed or seat at a table while harassed proprietors sought to stem the flood by hanging "Closed" or "Full" signs on their doors and windows.

It took the Lemonniers a further twenty minutes to reach the city centre where an equal if not greater chaos reigned. To Georges' mounting distress, the swirling throng of motorists, cart-pushers, pedestrians, bicyclists, and the occasional unruly beast of burden was taking its toll on the immaculate coachwork of his beloved Nerva Grand Sport. They skirted the Cathedral of St André, turned right onto the Cours Pasteur, and nosed their way slowly between the double-parked rows of cars, in some of which whole families appeared to be preparing to pass an uncomfortable night.

"Incredible!" muttered the elder Lemonnier, and then sighed with relief at finding the entrance to the inner courtyard of his apartment building mercifully unobstructed. They parked, mounted stone steps to a brass-fitted oak door, and enclosed themselves in the ill-lit, fading elegance of the entrance hall. At the foot of the staircase they encountered an elderly couple assembling baggage for a journey.

"Good evening, Monsieur Weissberg; you really have decided to leave?" Georges Lemonnier and his son stepped forward to shake hands. "And madame." The neighbours exchanged solemn greetings.

"We have been lucky, Monsieur Lemonnier; my wife and I have passage and visas to England and then to America. We leave tonight."

André Weissberg, one of Bordeaux's most respected and successful antiquarian booksellers, sounded less than elated at his good fortune. His tall, handsome wife stared almost defiantly at the Lemonniers.

"We are not unpatriotic, my husband and I. But, from everything we have heard and read, it seems clear the Nazis will not treat Jews as real French citizens. We will be an embarrassment to everybody and a danger to ourselves, so it is better we go." Simone Weissberg patted her carefully coiffed grey hair and bent to lift a suitcase.

"Please allow me to help." Edmond sprang forward,

and the four of them began to load the Weissberg's car in the courtyard. Georges Lemonnier assured the couple that they had chosen a wise if heart-rendering course, and as they made their rather uncomfortable farewells, Weissberg explained that his younger brother, Bernard, a shipper, had decided to stay and would be moving into the apartment upstairs. At that moment he was awaiting them at the docks.

"He found us the passage," added Madame Wiessberg, "but he refuses to leave France himself. We do not know whether to celebrate his courage or curse his stubbornness."

Her husband frowned as he settled into the driver's seat, then looked up at Georges.

"If it would really be no embarrassment to you, Monsieur Lemonnier, and of course no danger, I'd be so very grateful if you could check on my brother's well-being from time to time."

As if afraid to hear the answer, he rapidly engaged the gears and steered for the low archway opening onto the street.

"Of course," replied Lemonnier but the Weissbergs could no longer hear him. Edmond saluted. André Weissberg caught the salute in his rear-view mirror and smiled sadly.

As Georges and Edmond Lemonnier were bidding farewell to the emigrant Weissbergs, members of the crumbling government of France's Third Republic were assembling in the city. The mayor of Bordeaux busied himself finding lodgings for his distinguished visitors, an operation which he conducted with a keen political sense. Those members of the government known to favour an immediate armistice were found quarters in the best hotels or in the private homes of like-minded civic leaders. Those disposed to fight on were directed to quarters near the railway station and the docks, likely targets should the Luftwaffe turn its attention to the city.

"I have some business to attend to for about an hour," said the elder Lemonnier. "I suggest we meet in the restaurant at the Hôtel Splendide at eight." He set off on foot without further word, leaving Edmond marvelling at his constancy. As the world fell apart around him, Georges Lemonnier would not fail to keep his bi-weekly tryst with the widow Fauvelle.

Edmond went back in to the building and up to the Lemonniers' second-floor apartment. He put through a call to his headquarters at rue Vital-Carles and learned from a fellow staff officer that the Premier, Paul Reynaud, had just arrived there and was to be lodged in the adjoining residence of the commanding general of the region. The Army High Command was also setting up its temporary headquarters there, and the Under-Secretary of National Defence, General de Gaulle, had already called on the commanding general and was now in private consultation with the Premier. Edmond further learned, not wholly to his pleasure, that his name had appeared on a list earlier in the afternoon designating him one of the region's administrative liaison officers with the Army High Command. Having established that his presence at headquarters was not essential that evening, he thanked the staff officer for the briefing and confirmed that he would be back on duty at seven the next morning.

He now had just over an hour to fill before the rendezvous with his father. He selected a half-bottle of white Graves from the wine cooler and pulled André Malraux's *L'Espoir* from a bookshelf. He had a strong feeling that he was about to arrive at a major crossroad in his life within the next twenty-four hours, and he intended to reach it in as calm a state of mind as possible. For the next forty-five minutes he sipped his wine, explored the mind of Malraux, and felt very much at peace with himself.

Edmond met his father promptly at the Hôtel Splendide, where the scene in the lobby was as chaotic as that on the street outside. Guests and would-be guests stumbled over piles of baggage and vied noisily for the attention of the despairing staff. A venerable senator, hot and irritable after the long trek from Paris, was berating an under-manager for failing to find him a room. Another senator, picking his way unnoticed through the crowd, disappeared into the elevator. Pierre Laval was returning from a meeting with a group of colleagues who shared his view that Premier Reynaud's solemn undertaking given to Prime Minister Churchill that France would not make a separate peace with Germany was an act of folly. The conspiring senator had no worries about accommodation; his admirer, the mayor, had engineered the eviction of the former Queen of Portugal from her suite in the hotel, and there he now hurried to mull over his plans to abet the early eviction of Paul Reynaud from the premiership of France.

The Lemonniers made their way to the comparative peace and quiet of the dining room where the *maître d'hôtel* greeted them extravagantly, happy to see two of his regular clients among the sea of strangers. He hurried them to a reserved table and, with a discreet nod of the head, drew their attention to the presence of an elderly gentleman dining nearby.

"The Marshal himself," whispered Georges Lemonnier to his son. Edmond stared curiously at Pétain. So here was the man who would deliver France into the hands of Adolf Hitler. Surely he was too senile to grasp the full measure of the tragedy he was about to inflict on his country? Dishonourable men wanted him in power so that they could work their evil designs through him. It sickened Edmond, and it sickened him still more to think that his own beloved father could accept – even welcome – such a prospect.

"I met my old Assembly colleague, Lorillard, on my way over here," said the elder Lemonnier. "He says that the number of ministers and Assembly deputies eager to call for an armistice is growing hourly, but that Reynaud remains as stubbornly opposed as ever."

"Good for him!"

Lemonnier let his son's challenge pass.

"General de Gaulle is pushing him to take the government and the navy to Algeria to continue the fight from there. It's crazy!"

"No, Father. With respect, it's the only course. Do you want our navy handed on a plate to the Nazis? And why shouldn't we carry on the war from our African possessions? I'm one hundred per cent with the general."

135

"I'm hungry, my son, so let us agree to disagree and feed ourselves."

Edmond smiled and picked up a menu. As father and son bowed their heads towards the familiar list of dishes, they became aware of a tall, uniformed figure manoeuvring awkwardly through the narrow gap between their table and that of their neighbours. They looked up in time to see General de Gaulle approaching the Marshal's table. Silently, his face devoid of expression, the young general held out his hand to the old marshal. Pétain rose to his feet and shook it. No word passed beteen them. De Gaulle turned about and walked stiffly to a distant table where an aide stood waiting.

For Edmond the moment was electrifying. He drew in a deep breath and looked at his father.

"By all accounts, Edmond, he's a fanatic, and I don't care for fanatics in uniform, especially at a time like the present."

Georges Lemonnier unfolded his napkin and tucked one corner behind the knot of his tie, a sure sign that he intended to start the meal with his favourite onion soup, no matter how warm a June evening it was.

"Shall we dispel the gloom with a bottle of the '29 Haut Brion?" he added, placing a hand over his son's.

For the third time that day, Edmond resisted the temptation to get into an argument with his father.

9

It took no more than three further days for the enemies of Paul Reynaud to work their will. The newspapers of the morning of 17th June carried the official announcement that, following the Premier's resignation, President Lebrun had called on Marshal Pétain to form a new government.

Arriving at his desk at the rue Vital-Carles, promptly at seven a.m., Edmond sat for a while with his head in his hands, thinking doom-laden thoughts. He spoke briefly over the telephone with his father who enquired what the military would now have in store for him, but as yet he knew nothing. The conversation was somewhat strained, but at least, thought Edmond, his father had refrained from gloating over Pétain's victory. He turned his attention, without enthusiasm, to his new liaison duties with the numerous recently arrived staff officers attached to the headquarters of the commander-in-chief, General Weygand. What in heaven's name were so many officers doing so far from the fighting? What, for that matter, was *he*, a trained tank commander, doing booking hotel rooms and requisitioning transport for them?

He rose and walked to the window which looked onto the forecourt below. An English-made car with diplomatic insignia drew up at the main entrance, and Edmond was just able to catch a glimpse of the lofty figure of General de Gaulle uncoiling itself from the passenger seat and hurrying into the building. Suitcases protruded from the overladen trunk of the car. Was the general embarking on a journey? Edmond was still speculating on this when the telephone jangled on his desk.

"Yes, *mon Colonel*. Right away!"

Edmond raced down the corridor to an office in which a staff colonel sat behind a desk looking dazed and far from good-humoured.

"General de Gaulle wants appointments made here this afternoon with the people on this list," he said, thrusting a piece of paper at Edmond. "He is no longer Under-Secretary of Defence, but he is still a general entitled to give us orders." The colonel sounded as though he did not at all approve of this state of affairs. "You will handle this, Captain, and keep me informed of your progress in the scheduling. That is all."

He waved Edmond away.

Edmond glanced rapidly down the list as he hurried back to his office where, without delay, he set about organizing the general's appointments. On an impulse, he rose from his desk after a few moments and glanced out of the window. The English diplomatic car was gone.

By midday, Edmond was able to report to the colonel that all the appointments were set. Back in his office his thoughts turned to the deeply depressing prospect of being a disarmed soldier in a dishonoured army. Surely some who felt as he did would flee to Algeria to continue the fight from there! But how could he arrange to join them? His thoughts were interrupted by a knock on the door and the grinning face of a fellow staff officer peering round it.

"Pétain has just made a broadcast. He said it was necessary to stop the fighting. He's not even waiting for the armistice talks to begin."

Edmond rose and collected his kepi.

"Nothing surprises me any more," he said as he pushed his way past the still grinning officer, "I'm going to lunch."

By the time he got back from lunch, the Eighteenth Military District had already received its orders. All troops were to be disarmed immediately and all officers and men confined to quarters. A court martial awaited any officer failing to execute these orders.

So it's come to this, thought Edmond bitterly. But right now, he had a more urgent problem on his hands: there was no sign of General de Gaulle. One by one, the officals on his carefully prepared list of appointments were calling him to ask, in tones of high exasperation, why the general was standing them up. Edmond apologetically explained that he was unable to enlighten them, but, in his own mind, he was beginning to put two and two together. A telephone call in mid-afternoon confirmed what he had already excitedly come to suspect. It was from an aide to one of the senior War Ministry officials who had been waiting in vain for the general, and the voice was far from friendly,

"The minister's just received a cable from de Gaulle saying he's in London, so what the devil have you been doing wasting our time with these appointments?"

"Why have *I* been wasting everyone's time? How was I supposed to know he's gone there?"

He slammed the receiver down and hurried off to find out what the colonel, who had landed him in this hornet's nest, had to say about it. He found him bawling into his telephone.

"Why didn't he have the common courtesy to tell us he was going?"

A stupid question, thought Edmond as he stood to attention before the colonel's desk. The colonel flung the receiver back on its rest.

"Everybody's going mad!" He ripped open a pack of Gauloises. "The sooner we get this armistice, the better." He turned his head and spat some tobacco strands from the tip of his tongue. "Do you approve, Captain?"

"No, *mon colonel.*"

The colonel eyed him curiously. "Nor does de Gaulle; that's why he fled to the British. Pétain will have his head for that, so people like you should be careful."

Coughing raucously on his cigarette, he dismissed the captain from his office.

It was nearly nine in the evening when Edmond set out on foot for his apartment. As he reached the west end of the cathedral, he noticed that even at this late hour there were people passing in and out through the great west door. He paused and then, on an impulse, went inside.

Banks of flickering candles lit by the late-night worshippers illuminated the west end of the cathedral with a pale golden light. The broad twelfth-century nave, in contrast, lay almost in darkness, a grey-black vastness dotted with shadowy kneeling figures, heads bowed in prayer or erectly gazing through the gloom towards the soaring gothic choir and the richly lit, flower-decked altar at the east end. Edmond took a seat in the darkened nave. He felt the heady combination of the wine from dinner and the spiritual intensity of the moment beginning to loosen his tightly controlled emotions. He mumbled a Pater Noster and then began to pray for strength, courage and, above all, an opportunity to fight for France. He suddenly felt angry at the realization that many, if not most, of the other people also on their knees at that moment were most likely praying fervently for an immediate cease-fire. So much for the French people, one under God. He reached for his kepi and rose. In the centre aisle he genuflected towards the distant high altar; it seemed to him to symbolize a liberating light at the end of a long tunnel of darkness. He turned and marched briskly back to the west door, pausing to cross himself with holy water before stepping outside into the night air. As he headed for the Cours Pasteur, he realized that there were now no doubts left lingering in his mind. He must leave Bordeaux and join General de Gaulle in London. And quickly.

At six o'clock the following evening, after another frustrating day at headquarters, Edmond slipped away. The inflow of refugees had swollen alarmingly over the past twenty-four hours and the streets were even more crowded than before. Although French troops were laying down their arms all over the country, the German offensive continued with undiminished determination. If France's fighting men had mistaken Pétain's expressed desire that the carnage cease as an immediate order to stop fighting, the Wehrmacht and the Luftwaffe, for their part, had received no such order from the Führer.

As Edmond entered the apartment, Annette, the housekeeper, came from the kitchen to meet him.

"That General de Gaulle has just started speaking on the wireless from London, Monsieur Edmond."

He followed her through to the kitchen. The airwaves crackled and the volume surged and retreated like a tide, but the voice was firm, authoritative and unhesitating.

". . . France does not stand alone. She is not isolated. Behind her is a vast Empire, and she can make common cause with the British Empire, which commands the seas and is continuing the struggle."

"What's he trying to do, Monsieur Edmond? I thought we didn't have to fight any more."

Edmond put a finger to his lips. Annette clucked disapprovingly and busied herself at the stove.

The pitch of the voice now rose.

"I, General de Gaulle, now in London, call on all French officers and men who are at present on British soil, or may be in the future, with or without their arms; I call on all engineers and skilled workers from the armaments factories who are at present on British soil, or may be in the future, to make contact with me. Whatever happens, the flames of French resistance must not, and shall not, die!"

The broadcast was over.

"There, Annette, is a man who is, at least, trying to save the honour of France."

"Sounds like he's trying to get us all killed, if you ask me. I think it's cheeky going off to London and telling us all from there what to do. Who does he think he is?"

"He's a fine soldier and patriot, and I hope he had a good audience. France needed to hear that."

Edmond returned to the salon and poured himself a glass of sherry. He then called the Weissberg's apartment on the floor above. Bernard Weissberg, the shipper, came on the line and Edmond invited him to share his dinner.

Over the meal Edmond explained his problem, and Bernard Weissberg promised to arrange his clandestine departure for England as soon as possible. It would, he had assured Edmond, be an honour to assist such a gallant officer, such a dedicated fighter against Nazism. What he had done for his brother and sister-in-law would be done with equal enthusiasm and dispatch for the captain.

141

To lessen the chances of his arrest as a deserter, it was decided that Edmond should remain at his post at rue Vital-Carles until the day of his sailing. Weissberg was confident that he could secure him passage with a friendly ship's master within the next three days. He would aim to give Edmond some twelve hours' notice, and on receipt of the coded notice, he should pack a suitcase, change into civilian clothes, and proceed to a small hotel near the railway station where he should take a room and await the arrival of Weissberg who would brief him on the manner and timing of his departure for England.

After saying goodnight to Weissberg and thanking him profusely, Edmond sat down at his father's writing table to compose a letter to his parents. It hurt that he felt compelled to leave without telling them face to face, but he was concerned lest either of them, in their distress at his action, might do or say something which, albeit unwittingly, might set the military authorities on his track. He wrote briefly of his conviction that France must somehow fight on, and that he saw it as a duty, not disloyalty, to join the leader who had called on all French officers and men who could do so to rally to him. He begged their forgiveness for the manner of his leaving and pledged them his undying love and respect. He would pray daily for their safety and well-being, and looked forward to embracing them again on French soil when he, and those choosing a similar course of action, would return to liberate their country. The letter finished, he went to the windows overlooking the street and poked his head through the thick curtains to inhale some night air. Suddenly the gentle murmur of the great port city settling down to an uneasy sleep was obliterated by the soaring wail of sirens, one joining in after another in a canon of screaming voices. So much for Pétain's request for an armistice, he thought. The bombers were coming to the very city where Pétain slept.

Hurrying to rue Vital-Carles the next morning, Edmond noted with relief that the cathedral appeared to be untouched. He passed just one badly damaged building and concluded that the bombers must have been aiming principally at the dock and railroad areas. If that were indeed the case, Weissberg's search for a ship for him could have been badly hampered. He found a number of windows blown out at the military headquarters, but his own office was unscathed. His first action was to call his parents out at the château to let them know that the apartment had suffered no damage and that he would call them again the following day. No sooner had he put down the receiver than the telephone rang, and he heard Weissberg's voice.

"Good morning, Captain. I have some welcome news for you. The spare parts for your car have arrived. You can pick them up at five p.m."

The message caught Edmond off guard. It seemed incredible that Weissberg could have already located a passage for him, yet the spare parts message was the agreed coded signal that he had, and the rendezvous at the hotel was set for five o'clock that same afternoon.

"That was very quick indeed," said Edmond. "I'm extremely grateful to you, and I shall definitely pick them up at five o'clock today."

He took his kepi from the peg on the door and left the office. As he closed the door, he heard his telephone ring. He thought about it for a moment, cursed, and went back in to answer it. It was the colonel.

"Lemonnier, Weygand's people are howling for new glass in their windows. Get hold of some."

"It won't be too easy, Colonel. Our regular supplier was bombed," he lied. "I'll try to find out where else we can get some."

"And quickly. Go yourself and hunt it down."

"Certainly, Colonel. I'm on my way now."

Edmond grinned as he replaced the receiver, and then proceeded purposefully out of the building. When he arrived on foot at the apartment, he was relieved to find Annette was not there, which saved him having to send her out on some contrived errand. He went straight to his father's dressing room and pulled a strong-box from a closet. His father had given him a key in case of emergencies. This he deemed an emergency. He extracted

143

a hundred and fifty thousand francs from a brown envelope, scribbled a receipt, and locked the box again. He then hurried to his bedroom, changed into a civilian suit, packed his uniform, kepi, service revolver, spare clothes and essentials into a large suitcase, and checked to see that the letter he had written the night before to his parents was in his briefcase. It was not quite ten o'clock when he closed and locked the front door of the apartment, and descended to the street to find a cab. He was anxious not to be caught by Annette returning from whatever errand she had been on, so he crossed the street and took a short cut through an alley to a parallel street. There he found a cab and directed it to the Hôtel des Fleurs, close by the railway station.

The thought belatedly struck him that the night's bombing might have destroyed the hotel, and he therefore heaved a sigh of relief when he saw the sign over the entrance to an inconspicuous, seedy-looking, but still standing establishment. A hundred-franc note slipped across the reception desk helped the clerk locate an unexpectedly vacated room for which Edmond registered under a false name. He went straight up to his room, took his André Malraux volume from his briefcase, stretched out on the bed and began to read. He had six hours to kill before his rendezvous there with Weissberg, and the more he stayed out of sight the better.

An hour later, he began to feel hungry and decided that the chance of being recognized by anyone in the little café attached to the hotel was sufficiently remote to permit him to take the risk. After lunching simply but well, he took a brisk three-minute walk around the block before returning to the shelter of his room. Mounting the narrow staircase, he stepped aside to let an attractive young woman pass on her way down. She wore rather too much make-up and a blood-red carnation in her jet black hair. Stopping on the step above him, she rearranged the top of her blouse to afford him a generous view of her sun-tanned bosom, and asked him if he would like a little company. Edmond hesitated for a moment, feeling a stirring in his groin, and then thanked her and declined.

144

Bernard Weissberg walked into the already crowded and noisy bar punctually at five o'clock and found Edmond waiting for him in a corner booth at the back. After ordering beer, they bent their heads together, and Weissberg came straight to the point.

"I struck lucky on my first try. You leave tomorrow morning at nine. It's a small French cargo boat, the *Fonçillon*, carrying what may well be the last cargo of timber from here to Plymouth. I know Pornichet, the master, well enough. He lost a son, a naval rating, at Dunkirk, and he hates Pétain for giving in. He'll probably hand his ship over to the British when he gets there."

"And he's agreed to take me?"

"He's delighted to help, but you must be on board and hidden by six o'clock tomorrow morning. The boat's below Pont de Pierre at the moment, but will be up at the Quai des Chartrons alongside the Bordat warehouse at first light. You'll recognize her by her pale green superstructure and orange smokestack. He'll be at the foot of the gangway at ten-to-six sharp. Don't arrive early and hang around; you might run into people you don't want to meet. And don't be late either. You should be in Plymouth early Friday morning, unless you get jumped by the Germans. She nearly got hit last night, so just pray her luck holds."

"What do I pay him?"

"You don't; I've paid him well."

"Then how much do I owe you?"

"Nothing, my dear friend. Don't deprive me of the good feeling I have in helping send a brave man off to fight the Nazis. I wish I could do the same, but I'm too old. I have to find a way of doing my bit here in Bordeaux. Helping you is a good start."

Edmond watched the tears welling up in Weissberg's eyes. They drank a silent toast to each other, then the shipper rose.

"You'll forgive me if I'm not on the dock to see you off; the fewer people there, the better."

Edmond accompanied him through the bar's direct exit onto the street. On the sidewalk they embraced briefly.

"Bernard, I will not forget you, and I will not forget to

pray for you. When you next see my father, tell him you helped me. I didn't have the chance."

Weissberg smiled. "He'll probably have me arrested."

"No. He'll understand, and he'll be indebted to you."

"If you say so, my friend. And now, good luck."

As Weissberg hurried off down the street, Edmond crossed it to drop the letter to his parents into a mail box opposite the hotel. If all went according to plan, he would be at sea when it reached Lachaise-Laurent. Seven hours had passed since he walked out of the regional military headquarters, and even if no full-scale search for him had yet been ordered, he could not afford to run into any military personnel in the city centre who might be from rue Vital-Carles, so he reluctantly returned to the solitude of his dingy room.

Lying on the bed, he reflected on the absurdity of his situation. He was setting out on the most noble mission of his life, to help save France, and yet he was being forced to steal silently away from mother country and family, wanted as a deserter and a traitor by the army he had served so loyally. And the only person who had been there to say goodbye and wish him God-speed was a Jewish benefactor whom he hardly knew and whom he would most likely never see again. For him there could be no sumptuous farewell dinner with one of his several lady friends, no last act of love, no tear-stained cheeks to mark the parting. Just a simple dinner alone in a run-down back-street hotel, a fitful sleep for a few short hours, and a fugitive's escape at first light.

He read and dozed for a while, and then, at eight o'clock, went down to the café and ordered a steak with *pommes frites*, a salad and cheese, and a carafe of red *vin ordinaire*. He lingered long over the meal, being in no hurry to return to the gloomy little room upstairs. Over coffee and a cognac, he wondered if the Luftwaffe would return that night, and he uttered a silent prayer that if they did, they would leave the *Fonçillon* unscathed. After a second cognac and more coffee, he began to feel a little emotional, and he resisted with difficulty an urge to call his parents to say goodbye.

At ten o'clock he ordered himself to his feet. The café

and bar were nearly empty; the previous night's air-raid had obviously deterred all but a few of the quarter's inhabitants from spending the evening out. He walked through the back of the café and into the lobby of the hotel, and as he did so, his heart sank. There at the reception desk, talking rapidly with the night-clerk, was the girl with the carnation in her hair, and leaning heavily on her arm was someone all too familiar to him: a staff sergeant from rue Vital-Carles.

There was no retreat; he would have to pass the desk to get to the staircase, and the night-clerk was bound to ask him to identify himself with a room key. At that moment the sergeant spied him.

"*Et alors!*" he roared, swaying off balance and all but falling. "My friend, the captain! He'll lend me a few sous so that I can fuck this girl!"

"Shut up and leave me alone," said the girl angrily as she sought to unhook his arm from hers.

Edmond felt mightily relieved that the sergeant was obviously royally drunk. The man detached himself from the girl and lurched towards him.

"You're my friend, Captain. Just a few francs for a room."

"Get him out of here, Janine," hissed the night-clerk.

"If monsieur here will help me." She pointed to Edmond.

Having no wish to leave the sergeant with any further opportunity to reveal his identity, Edmond seized him by the arm.

"Out of here, Sergeant, and that's an order!" He started to steer him towards the door. "Another time, when you've got money in your pockets, I'm sure she'll be happy to entertain you."

To Edmond's relief, the sergeant allowed himself to be led to the door.

"That's not very friendly, Captain," he whined.

Edmond pulled the glass door open.

"And it's not very wise of you to be out when all troops are confined to quarters."

"And what about you, Captain?"

Edmond pushed him through the door and quickly

147

pulled it closed. The sergeant gave him a puzzled look, staggered, and then turned away. In a moment he was gone. Edmond heaved a sigh of relief and turned back to the reception desk.

"*Merci*, monsieur!" chimed the girl and the clerk in chorus.

"You are his captain?" enquired the girl.

Edmond smiled. "No. I'm not even in the army. I suppose I must look something like him. He'd had a skinful."

He showed the clerk his key.

"I'll be leaving early. The room is already paid."

"Then goodnight, monsieur. If there is a raid, you may come down to the cellar."

"Thanks."

He looked at the girl. "Goodnight, mademoiselle."

"But you retire so early?" She was straining to see the number on his key.

"I'm afraid so." He turned and headed for the stairs.

He had been in his room no more than a couple of minutes when, not much to his surprise, he heard a tapping on the door. He went to open it.

"You needn't have been so shy and correct in front of Michel," she said. "He is my brother and he could see that you are a gentleman. May I come in?"

Edmond stood aside. When he had closed the door behind her, she put her arms around his neck and kissed him gently on the lips.

"You give me a little present, and I give you a lot of love. All right, *chéri*?"

Edmond fished in his billfold and handed her a couple of notes.

"For that we play some very nice games," she said, unbuckling the belt around her waist. "You like me to keep anything on?" She snapped a suspender on her garter belt.

Later on, when the siren sounded, Edmond at first heard nothing, his ears being blocked between her thighs.

"Are you afraid, *chéri*? You want to go down to the cellar?"

"No. We stay here."

"Very good, my courageous captain!"

Edmond frowned, and the girl nodded to his suitcase, the lid of which was unlatched and open just enough to leave visible his uniform inside.

He laughed.

"You're running away because you don't want to fight?"

"No, Janine. I'm running away because I *want* to fight!"

There was a crashing explosion which shook the building, and a light shower of plaster floated down. The girl slid down over his perspiration-flecked body, and quickly impaled herself on him.

"*Oh là là!*" she giggled excitedly. "Someone down here seems to thrive on danger!"

At a quarter to six Edmond stepped onto the quay in front of the Bordat warehouse and surveyed the looming hull of the SS *Fonçillon*. He was five minutes early, and Pornichet was not yet to be seen. Suitcase and briefcase in hand, he took cover between two stacks of crates, from which vantage point he could watch the ship's gangplank. Promptly at ten minutes to six, a paunchy figure in a rumpled merchant marine master's uniform and squashed cap made its way down the gangplank. Edmond emerged from his refuge and strode across the quay toward him. Silently the master beckoned to him to follow. Once aboard, they crossed to the starboard side of the ship and down two flights of a companionway into a dimly lit passage. Pornichet unlocked a door and ushered Edmond into a cramped little cabin with a bunk, a squeaking fan and no porthole.

"No luxury stateroom, I'm afraid, Captain." They were Pornichet's first words to him. "But welcome aboard anyway." He held out his hand and Edmond shook it.

"I'm very grateful to you."

"Don't mention it. I'm afraid we'll have to keep you hidden here until we're clear of Pointe de Grave in the early afternoon; too many ships being searched in the Gironde. But don't worry; we won't forget you if the ship goes down!" The master laughed heartily and pointed to

149

a metal container on the floor. "Bread, cheese, wine and a thermos of hot coffee to see you through your incarceration. Good luck. See you at sea."

He closed the door on Edmond and a key turned in the lock. Pornichet spoke through the door.

"Just in case any of my crew who have no business yet knowing you're on board should stumble in on you. The key's safe with me."

Edmond wondered why he could not be trusted to keep the door locked from the inside, and then he noticed that there was no keyhole. He was in the ship's lock-up. He flung himself exhausted on the hard bunk. He had finally thrown the insatiable Janine out of his hotel room at a quarter to four, and he now craved sleep. It came to him just as a church clock, somewhere beyond the warehouses, began to strike six.

"It's very simple," said Pornichet. "I shall cable the ship's owner and tell him that the British have impounded her for the duration of the war. Any of my crew who don't like it can take the next boat home."

It was early on Sunday morning, and Edmond, dressed once again in his uniform, had joined the master on the bridge as the ship slipped past Rame Head into the grey-green waters of Plymouth Sound at the end of their forty-two-hour voyage. It had been a calm and uneventful journey, and when the *Fonçillon* finally docked, Edmond was profuse in his thanks as he took leave of Pornichet.

"Don't mention it," said the master gripping Edmond's hand. "You do your bit for France and I do mine, and may we both have better luck than my poor boy." His face clouded over suddenly at the mention of his slain son, and then, just as quickly, the broad smile returned. "And now get the hell off my boat; I've got treasonous work to do!"

At the foot of the gangplank, a Royal Navy petty officer saluted Edmond smartly.

"Captain Lemonnier?"

"Yes," said Edmond with a surprised look. He wasn't expecting a welcoming party.

"You speak English, sir?"

"Yes, I do."

"Then could you come with me? There are certain formalities to be gone through."

"Formalities? I just need a train to London."

"I'm sure they'll arrange that, sir. But first there are the formalities."

Edmond shrugged his shoulders and set off with the petty officer, feeling somewhat uneasy.

"You must stay as long as you like, my boy, and don't apologize for the short notice. War is full of surprises and few are as agreeable as this one."

Gerald Anstey, a portly, grey-whiskered wine merchant, and his petite, bird-like wife, Nora, had responded instantly to Edmond's telephone call when he had finally been released from interrogation by British military and civilian intelligence officials. The Anstey and Lemonnier families had known each other through the wine trade for nearly thirty years, and Edmond had learned his English on exchange summer visits with his Anstey contemporary, his hosts' only son.

"Sorry you had to go through all that nonsense at Plymouth and again here in London. They're eager beavers our intelligence chaps, and they have to be careful. The country's crawling with refugees from the continent, and who knows how many are really Nazi agents preparing for the invasion?" Anstey refilled his guest's wine glass. "Nothing personal, you see."

"No, but they certainly gave the impression they were more scared of de Gaulle's supporters than they were of Hitler's! They did everything to try to stop me joining him, and when they told me I should probably be sent with the other French troops in the country to the French armies in North Africa, I told them very firmly that I hadn't deserted my post in Bordeaux and escaped to England just to be put at the mercy of Pétainist generals in North Africa."

"Good for you. I'm afraid that's our bloody British island character for you. We hate the Germans, but we distrust the French." Anstey guffawed merrily.

151

"You shouldn't laugh, dear, at our prejudices," said Nora reprovingly. Her husband ignored her.

"How are you going to tackle this chap de Gaulle?"

"Find out where he is and offer him my services, I suppose."

"I may be able to help you there. Ran into a French naval officer yesterday. Came over from Dunkirk with our fellows. He's just been to see the man, so he'll know the form. His father owns a few hectares in Beaujolais. We'll call him tomorrow. Now," said Anstey, "let's drink to your parents. I'm sure they'll be more than a match for the Boche invader, what?"

"We will surely be in the same predicament ourselves very soon," said Mrs Anstey, eyes cast sadly down, dabbing genteelly at the corners of her thin mouth with a napkin.

"Quite likely, so drink up!" Anstey raised his brimming glass. "I'm damned if I'll leave a single decent bottle around for that hippo Goering to flush his insides with."

Nora Anstey winced, and rose to leave the gentlemen to their drinking.

10

"Jamie, my mother's going to crucify me for staying out so late in my condition."

Margot pulled a tortoise-shell powder compact from her purse, flipped open the lid, and studied her face in the little round mirror.

"Don't worry, old girl; they can't possibly object to your doing a little celebrating tonight." Jamie patted her hand soothingly. "I'll square her tomorrow with a heart-stopping bunch of roses."

Margot dabbed a little powder on her nose and chin.

"It seems a bit odd, really, to be celebrating hearing that your husband's a prisoner of war," she said in a matter-of-fact tone. "Until you remember that they might have been telling you that he was dead."

Jamie exchanged fleeting glances with the other two people at the table, then turned to Margot again.

"What about one last shuffle around the floor?"

"Absolutely the last." Margot pressed her hand to her belly. "Both I and my little lodger in here have danced more than enough for one night." She leaned across the table towards the other uniformed Grenadier officer. "Giles, come and rescue me if I'm not off the dance floor in five minutes."

"Will do." Lieutenant Giles Leeds turned to the pale, dark-haired girl seated next to him. "Come on, Kay. On your feet! We need to keep a close eye on his lustful lordship."

The four of them made their way to the dance floor where a half-dozen couples swayed on barely moving feet to the muted music of a small ensemble. Margot offered no protest when, as they began to dance, Jamie's cheek brushed against hers and then gently came to rest there. She was happy to be with the three people whom she especially cherished as friends these days: dear, funny, protective Jamie; Giles Leeds, the gentle six-foot-five-inch giant and fellow Dunkirk survivor; and pretty Kay Lawton, talented young portrait artist, half English, half American, whom she had met only three weeks before and with whom she had struck up an immediate and easy friendship. Tonight, at the Four Hundred, in the company of these three friends, she felt relaxed and content. She liked the womb-like atmosphere of the club with its wine-red, cloth-draped walls, and the little table-lamps illuminating pale, well-bred faces in a theatrical pink and golden glow. She felt secure and at home in the place.

Jamie steered her towards the band and asked her what she would like for her last dance of the evening.

" 'Falling In Love With Love', please."

The pianist smiled and nodded his head. A few moments later, Jamie felt a tear trickle from Margot's cheek onto his own.

"Tears of relief, old girl?"

"I guess so."

She smiled nervously. She *was* relieved that the weeks of waiting for news were over, and the tears were certainly tears of happiness. But there was no denying to herself that it was happiness at her own circumstances as much as at Charlie's. That very moment, dancing cheek-to-cheek with Jamie, to her favourite tune, in her favourite nightclub, with her favourite friends, was a moment of exquisite pleasure. Well, why not? she asked herself. A wife, even a pregnant one, with a husband incarcerated in a prison camp in a distant land didn't have to stay home, isolated and pining. Friends supported one; life went on. All she had to do was wait for her husband's return. And she saw no point in waiting in sorrowful seclusion.

The letter from the War Office had arrived that morning. It was short and to the point. Ensign Charles Garland of the Third Grenadiers was, according to the International Red Cross, a prisoner of war of the Germans.

After two weeks in a French hospital in the occupied zone for treatment of a wound, he was now listed as held in Oflag XIV C near Munich. There followed instructions on addressing a letter or parcel to him, and that was all.

Elinor Moore had tearfully hugged her daughter to her, told her that their prayers had been answered, and had hurried to telephone the good news to her husband at the embassy. Margot had sat alone for a while at the breakfast table, dry-eyed, telling herself that she was not after all a war widow. She was mightily relieved that the time which she had spent in an emotional limbo, half wife, half widow, was finally over. She now knew where she stood. Charlie was alive, and the future now offered two possibilities: he might escape and return a hero, which would be wonderful. Or he might sit out the war as a prisoner, in which case her ambitions for Charlie to *be* somebody would just have to be put on ice until the war was over, whenever that would be. Of the two possibilities, Charlie the heroic escapee obviously had the greater appeal, but was he up to it? She prayed that he was, and would just have to wait and see.

"Well, darling, your father's thrilled and sends you his and Lois's congratulations. He's also left word to have the ambassador informed."

Elinor had returned to the dining room and had started clearing dishes. Margot poured herself another cup of coffee and lit the first of her one-after-meals-only cigarettes of the day.

"I'll write to him today," she said. "The news of the baby will cheer him up. Don't take the sugar away."

Elinor paused in her clearing and studied her daughter as she put the sugar bowl back on the table.

"I don't know about you, Margot," she said, shaking her head. "Inside you must be feeling all this a great deal, but ever since we heard that he was missing you've shown no real emotion over it at all. Where do you get all this self-control from? Certainly not from me!"

Margot smiled. She knew that her self-control over the past three weeks had come close to irritating her more emotional family.

"I'm feeling it all right, Mother," she said.

"I mean, after all, you should be dancing for joy that Charlie's alive and that your baby will now grow up knowing a father, and will, God willing, have brothers and sisters."

It was Margot's turn to feel irritated.

"Do you really think I *don't* feel all that just because I don't show it as much as all of you do? For God's sakes!"

She got up from the table, tightened the bow around the waist of her bathrobe, and hurried from the dining room to seek the solitude of her bedroom. For a while she lay on the bed staring at Charlie's photograph on the dresser.

"I really do love you, Charlie," she whispered. "And, God, how I miss you! There's no one to make love to me. You're no damn use to me, yourself, or the war effort where you are now, so you've got to get back here. And quickly!"

The aggravation of sexual frustration occupied her thoughts for the next few minutes, and she wondered whether she would end up having an affair with someone. The prospect of an entanglement didn't much appeal to her. Men were so lucky; they could go out and buy relief on the street as easily as buying aspirin.

She got up and dressed, then went down to her father's study to make some telephone calls. First she called her new friend, Kay, who immediately suggested that they celebrate the good news that evening with dinner and a visit to a nightclub. Margot happily fell in with the plan and called to leave a message for Jamie whom she knew would be in town that day and lunching at the Guards Club.

"In your condition, you ought to be taking it easy," remonstrated her mother. "Whooping it up on the town until all hours won't do you or the baby any good at all. And it's not fair on Charlie to put your pregnancy at risk like that."

"You fuss too much, Mother," was Margot's only response.

The manager of The Four Hundred beamed at her as he

opened the door onto the street. "I'm so glad to hear that your husband is alive and well, Mrs Garland."

"It's good news, isn't it? Thanks for a lovely evening."

"Margot and her three companions stepped out into the near-darkness of Leicester Square.

"Let's walk for a while," she said. "It's such a nice moonlit night."

"Only until you feel you have had enough," insisted Jamie, linking his arm through hers. They set off around the square heading for Piccadilly and Mayfair. As they walked briskly westwards down Piccadilly, Kay started singing.

> Jeepers! Creepers!
> Where'd you get those peepers?

"Come on everyone, let's hear it!"

They sang merrily as they marched in step along the broad pavement towards Bond Street. They were within twenty yards of it and in full voice when the sirens began to wail.

"Well, for God's sake," said Jamie. "I thought they were never coming." They all stopped and stared up into the almost perfectly clear night sky.

"What do we do?" asked Margot.

"We ignore it, dear heart, that's what," said Jamie firmly. "We've nearly got you home, and if the monsters are really bent on blasting Mayfair, we'll all take refuge in your father's basement. So step lively!"

They quickened their pace as they turned northwards up Bond Street. The streets, which had been nearly deserted before the air-raid warning sounded, were now beginning to show signs of life. Shadowy figures, hastily garbed against the cool night air, were appearing in un-lighted doorways, and there was a patter of feet down basement steps. As Margot and her friends reached the foot of Hay Hill and turned into Berkeley Square, a tin-hatted ARP warden loomed out of the darkness in front of them and blocked their passage. A firm but friendly voice halted them.

"Everybody down into the public shelter, please. Just thirty yards up on your right."

"We've only got to get as far as Hill Street," protested Jamie. "Just another five minutes' walk at most."

"Sorry, sir. No exceptions. You have to take shelter when the alarm sounds; it's for your own safety."

"Come on, Jamie." Giles Leeds nudged him gently forward. "No point arguing. It won't be for long, anyway."

They could see an orderly line of people descending the narrow concrete steps cut into the edge of the grass-covered, fenced-in square.

"I bet it's a false alarm," said Kay as they arrived to take their places in the line.

"False or not, I think it's rather exciting," said Margot as she peered at the ground, anxious not to miss the first step down. A commotion broke out behind them as a woman's voice pierced the air with loud obscenities.

"Drunks; that's all we need," moaned Jamie. Suddenly he felt himself propelled forward, and he just managed to recover his balance on the second step by slapping his left hand against the concrete wall of the shelter entrance. He saw a large woman in a voluminous overcoat, her face panic-stricken, arms flailing, pitching forward down the steep steps.

"For Christ's sake let me in!" she shrieked as she lost the last vestige of her balance and slammed into Margot's half-turned back. There was another shriek, this time Margot's, and Jamie watched helplessly as the two women, in a tangle of limbs and flapping clothes, plunged down into the dark well of the staircase.

"Oh my God!" shouted Jamie, and raced down the remaining steps to the shelter floor, with Giles Leeds and Kay on his heels. Earlier arrivals in the shelter appeared, drawn by the shouting. One of them shone a torch unsteadily on the two prone figures. The fat woman's face was blood-smeared and she was whimpering. Margot lay still, silent, white as a sheet. She was out cold. Jamie and Giles bent over her, and Kay pushed in between them.

"Don't move her; she may have broken something." Jamie's voice had regained it's calm. He began to unbutton his khaki service-dress tunic to lay over her as a cover. "Giles, old fellow, you'd better get back up onto the street and ask that ARP warden how we can get an ambulance here immediately. There should be one not far away now the air-raid's on."

Leeds pushed his way back up the steps and disappeared.

Kay was shaking badly.

"It's all right," said Jamie, "she's breathing; she's just out for the count. At least I hope that's all that's wrong."

Kay looked back over her shoulder at the fat woman who was now sitting propped against the wall, dabbing at the cuts on her face with the sleeve of her coat and muttering imprecations under her port-laden breath.

"Stupid bloody bitch!" said Kay loudly. The woman took no notice.

"She should be arrested," said an onlooker. "I saw what happened."

Margot's eyelids were beginning to quiver as, five minutes later, the clatter of feet on the concrete entrance steps heralded the arrival of a St John Ambulance team with a stretcher.

"Good work, Giles," said Jamie approvingly as the tall figure appeared at the foot of the steps. Brief explanations were given, and Margot was gently lifted onto the stretcher. A policeman waving a torch flattened himself against the wall of the staircase as the stretcher party climbed up to the street.

"One of you only can go with her," he said firmly. "The raid has only just started. Who's the husband?"

"Neither of them," volunteered Kay. "I'm going with her." Without more ado she raced up the steps.

"Which hospital?" shouted Jamie after her. A moment later they heard her voice at the top of the steps.

"St George's, Hyde Park Corner. Come as soon as you can."

During the next three hours Jamie and Giles made several fruitless attempts to persuade the stubborn ARP warden to let them leave the shelter. No one had heard a single bomb fall, but neither had they heard yet the comforting sound of the All Clear, and until that happened there was no getting past the stern and sturdy warden.

"Damnit, we should have insisted on going with her too," said Jamie angrily.

"Shall we try the warden once more?"

The words were hardly off Giles' lips when the unmistakable whine of the All Clear filled the air. Jamie and his friend dashed up the steps and quickly found a taxi. They were not surprised to find Harland and Elinor Moore already there in the emergency wing waiting room. Jamie began to apologize for not taking proper care of Margot, but Harland Moore cut him off.

"It wasn't your fault, Jamie. Don't blame yourself."

Elinor Moore stayed silent, staring grimly at the stained carpet at her feet.

"Just pray that she *and* the child are all right," said Kay. "We should be hearing any moment now from the doctor."

Jamie buried his face in his hands.

"I'm so sorry, Charlie," he half whispered to himself.

"Pain gone?"

Margot nodded.

"You're a strong, healthy young lady, Mrs Garland. You can bear any number of children, so you mustn't think for a moment that the ending of this particular pregnancy is the end of the world."

Margot stared through a film of tears at the benign, owl-like visage of the doctor at her bedside.

"I understand," he went on, "that your husband's a prisoner of war. Well, when he returns to you, which I'm sure will be in the not too distant future, you'll be in perfect shape to start again." He smiled and patted her hand. "Dr Worsley and I will be in to see you tomorrow morning. The soreness will be easing rapidly and I don't think those bruises are going to be discomforting you for much longer, so we should very likely be able to send you home at the weekend."

He saw the unrelieved grief in her face, and tried again to find some words of comfort.

"I know that this is a very sad moment for you, Mrs Garland, but believe you me, we have some things to be thankful for. Now get some rest, my dear."

When he closed the door behind him, Margot turned over and stared through her tears at the row of filled flower vases on the window shelf. One thought alone now filled her agonized mind. She had been carrying a part of Charlie in her. Now she had nothing of him – nothing! First the war had taken him from her, then it had taken what he had left her. Why didn't it just take her as well? And to think that the air-raid warning had been a false alarm, so Jamie had told her! What sort of a goddamned cruel trick was that?

She heard the door open gently behind her and she rolled over.

"Oh Father. You must please let Larry know what's happened."

"Of course, sweetheart. Just take it easy."

She started to sob again as her father picked up her hand from the coverlet and squeezed it.

"Father, tell me this is all a nightmare and that I'm going to wake up."

Harland Moore looked sadly at his daughter and asked himself reproachfully: why, oh why didn't I send you all home?

Margot was duly declared fit to leave hospital at the weekend, and on the Saturday morning her mother fetched her in a taxi. Reluctantly she allowed herself to be persuaded to spend the weekend propped up in her own bed, and she gazed fretfully through the window at the perfect June day outside, wishing that she could take a stroll through Hyde Park and maybe sit by the calm waters of the Serpentine for a while. But she had to admit that one leg was still aching from the fall, and she had been warned that too much walking at this stage would aggravate the slowly fading soreness occasioned by the curettage. She was grateful for the distraction of visitors: Kay Lawton came in the afternoon, and the Garlands in the evening. Katie amused her with accounts of her work with the American Red Cross, and she and her parents kept her company through the evening until she fell asleep.

The next morning, she decided that she must do something about the letter to Charlie which she had completed on the day of the accident. She had been rehearsing in her mind how she might tell him of the misfortune that had befallen her and their baby. Try as she might, she could do no other than assign the ultimate blame to herself. If she had not been out nightclubbing it wouldn't ever have happened. She should have been more careful with herself and her unborn infant. On the other hand, a self-pitying, self-reproaching, maudlin letter would only depress Charlie further. Somehow she had to soften the blow.

"Help me, Katie," she appealed to her sister that Sunday morning. "How should I tell him?"

"Very simple, sis. You send him the letter as it is, and then you add a PS saying that since you wrote it you'd had a little accident which resulted in the ending of the pregnancy, but that you're perfectly all right and the two of you can start again as soon as he's home."

"But that sounds so cold-blooded."

"Not really. It'll convince him that you're not in a suicidal mood at all. You've accepted it and are quite calm about it. The object is that he shouldn't drive himself into a frenzy worrying about you."

"I'll buy that, Katie. You're not so dumb after all."

But as the days passed, the calm acceptance and self-control began to give way to a deepening depression which she could not hide from her family and friends. Hoping that a change of scenery might help, Charlie's parents persuaded her to come and stay a few days at Bowes Court. The weather was perfect, and she spent most of each day stretched out on a *chaise longue* in the garden, pampered by a solicitous Cynthia and waited on hand and foot by her domestic staff. But the depression remained unrelieved, and at the end of five days she thanked her hosts profusely, pretended that she was feeling much better, and asked to be put on a train back to London. The bouts of weeping had become less frequent now, but even Katie's ebullience couldn't lift the pall of gloom from her. She saw her friends sparingly, convinced that her misery would only bore them. Jamie alone seemed capable of raising her morale, but he was now posted as a staff officer at Southern Command near Salisbury, and rarely managed to come to London.

To distract herself, she began paying regular visits to the movies. One afternoon in mid-July, leaving a cinema in Leicester Square after watching a rerun of Leslie Howard in *Pygmalion*, she was caught up in the street by a young RAF officer whom she had noticed sitting alone at the end of her row in the theatre. He wore pilot's wings and a decoration on his chest, and his voice was soft and pleasant when he asked her very politely whether she would give him the great pleasure of letting him buy her a cup of tea at a teashop in the Haymarket. Why the hell not? she thought. Another half-hour or so of distraction before taking the bus back to gloomy Hill Street would suit her fine, and anyway he looked and sounded charming. His name, he said, was Luke McGill.

Walking to the teashop, they talked about the film, avoiding asking each other personal questions. It was only when they sat down and ordered a pot of tea that she told him, responding to his query, that she was the American wife of an English army officer, taken prisoner just before the Dunkirk evacuation. He then told her that he was with a fighter group in Kent, and had flown against the Luftwaffe over the Dunkirk beaches.

"Is that where you won that decoration?" she asked, pointing to the mauve and white ribbon on his chest.

He smiled shyly. "The King pinned the medal on me just yesterday," he said, blushing now. "My sister came to the Palace with me for the investiture. My parents are in Rio de Janeiro; my father's a diplomat."

"Mine too," said Margot after a moment's hesitation. They chatted on.

"Will you have dinner with me tonight, Margot?" he asked eventually.

"No, I'm afraid I can't."

"You don't want to?"

"My father-in-law's coming to dinner at home. I must be there."

That was true, and she was regretting it. She would rather like to have dinner, somewhere discreet where

163

her friends wouldn't see her, with this attractive young fighter pilot

"I see. What a pity. I have to go back early tomorrow."

"Yes, it is a pity," she said, staring at the tea leaves in the bottom of her cup.

"I have a small flat just across St James's Park. If we walked there, we'd feel ready for a drink by the time we got there. Will you come?"

"Let me think about it while you order me another cup of tea."

The full import of what she was doing was just now beginning to sink in. For the first time in her life she'd allowed herself to be picked up on a street by a perfect stranger, and she had needed no cajoling. He must think her an easy lay, and undoubtedly that was what he had been looking for. He must be as pleased as hell to think that he had struck lucky so easily. Yet somehow he didn't look to her to be the type. Did he think that *she* looked the type to do what she'd just done? Two diplomats' offspring playing a game alien to their upbringing. It was ridiculous! But, God, he was so attractive! The blue eyes, the wavy corn-coloured hair. If she hadn't still been quite sore from the curettage, she might have decided that this could be an excusable venture into infidelity. Maybe it was for the better that she was still hurting. But what a pity they couldn't just have dinner together. Just that. But the invitation to the flat made his intentions quite obvious. No. She'd have to say no. She must be sensible.

He watched her intently as the waitress brought them both another cup of tea.

"I think I'd better not come to your flat," she said when the waitress had gone. She dropped two lumps of sugar into the tea and began to stir it with exaggerated vigour. "The truth is, I – well, I've just recently, very recently had a miscarriage, and for the moment I can't – you know."

She felt her cheeks burning with embarrassment. Why was she saying all this? She hadn't intended to. For heaven's sakes, there was no need to! Now she couldn't summon up the courage to look him in the face.

"No, please, you misunderstood," he said agitatedly. "I just wanted you to come back and meet my sister. I'm awfully sorry if I gave some other impression. I just thought we'd all have a drink together. She's staying with me. She works in Oxford."

The anger welled up in her.

"Then what in hell were you doing picking me up?" she hissed between clenched teeth. "Don't tell me you go around picking up women you think might like to meet your sister!"

His look was one of utter mortification.

"Please believe me. I felt lonely and just wanted some company, and I plucked up my courage to ask you because you didn't look at all like the sort of girl whose business it is to be picked up."

"I should damn well think not!"

Her fury at his leading her into making such a fool of herself demanded retribution. She gulped at her tea, burned the inside of her mouth, and slammed the teacup down on the saucer.

"Please don't be angry," he pleaded.

She got to her feet.

"If I were you, Luke whatever-your-name-is, I wouldn't go round picking up women and then putting on the sweet innocent act like that." She leaned down to him as she lowered her voice. "You could get yourself hurt where it really hurts!"

She turned and walked rapidly out into the steet. After a few seconds she glanced over her shoulder, and saw to her relief that he wasn't following. By the time she reached Pall Mall her anger was fast changing to amusement, and by the time she had hailed a cab, she was giggling. So much for her first brush with infidelity. What a glorious fiasco! He was so attractive – but now she'd enjoyed paying him back for making her look such an idiot!

The next morning her depression was gone. And she went to Bond Street and bought an expensive new hat.

11

"So it was a false alarm," said Edmond, scanning a paper.

"What did I tell you?" boomed Gerald Anstey. "They couldn't even find their way up the bloody Thames to the City!"

He transferred a halo of egg yolk from the circumference of his mouth to a gleaming white napkin.

"Dropped their bombs somewhere in Kent, so the radio said. Pathetic! You won't get me out of bed again for a night in the basement until those Luftwaffe loonies learn how to read a map. With any luck they never will."

Edmond sipped his breakfast coffee and smiled at his host.

"They may have just been testing your air defences."

"Rubbish, young man. There aren't any to speak of, and if they didn't know that, they don't know anything."

Anstey manoeuvred a triangle of buttered toast into position under a spoon piled high with Cooper's Oxford Marmalade and tipped the load squarely onto its target.

"If they do ever find their way to London in any numbers, they'll turn a thousand years of English history into a smoking ash heap. We've got virtually nothing to stop them with: a few useless barrage balloons, anti-aircraft units that probably couldn't hit a zeppelin at fifty feet, and night-fighters held together with fish-glue."

"I'm sure you're in better shape than that."

"Not much, old boy. It'll improve, of course; Winston will see to that. But he'd better get a bloody move on. Sure you won't finish the kippers? My brother sends 'em down from Scotland in exchange for an occasional case of

166

rather inferior Burgundy. His wife drinks it; no taste-buds so she doesn't know the difference, poor dear. Archie's drunk nothing but Scotch since his last year at Eton."

Anstey pulled a gold watch from his waistcoat pocket, consulted it, and, turning towards the open dining room door, bellowed for his wife.

"Nora, what have you done with my white handker-chiefs?" He turned to Edmond and winked. "She's prob-ably stitching them together into parachutes, or maybe making a damn great white flag. Women always panic in war."

He guffawed merrily and rose to his feet.

Edmond also rose. "I'll be calling your French naval friend shortly. Thanks again for the very useful lead."

"Delighted, dear fellow. I hope you get your general. In the meantime, if you're at a loose end, pop in on us. We're still in Bury Street, and there's always a decent glass of sherry any time after twelve."

Anstey wandered off into the nether regions of the flat in search of his wife and his white handkerchiefs.

By noon, Edmond had the information he needed from the French naval officer. General de Gaulle and his small staff, he learned, were installed in a two-room office overlooking the Thames in St Stephen's House, across the street from the House of Commons. Edmond called the office and spoke with the General's aide-de-camp. De Gaulle, he was told, would certainly wish to meet the captain. If he cared to come by that afternoon, the aide would be delighted to receive him, hear what he had to say, and brief him on the procedures for joining the Free French before seeing the General.

At half-past two that afternoon, Edmond walked into St Stephen's House and was taken up in a rickety elevator to the third floor. A tall, fair-haired young cavalry officer greeted him.

"Please come in, Captain Lemonnier. You must excuse our primitive furnishings; our good friend General Spears has been kind enough to get us these two rooms and a few pieces of furniture as a start. Now it's up to us."

He led Edmond to a cluttered trestle table and they sat facing each other across it.

"First of all," said the aide, "I must congratulate you on your arrival here."

"I think it's rather for me to be thanking the General for providing the rallying point."

The aide nodded towards a door behind him.

"You'll have your chance to do so personally in a little while. Perhaps you could tell me some more about yourself and how you came to London."

Edmond briefly recounted his background, military career, the circumstances under which he came to take his decision to join de Gaulle, and the manner of his escape from Bordeaux. The aide made some notes on a pad then pushed his chair back and stretched out his long legs.

"We've just set up a Free French Recruiting Centre at the Olympia Stadium in west London," he began. "It's imperative we mount a really effective campaign to pull in as many as possible of the several thousand of our forces now here, most of them from Dunkirk, and some from the Norwegian campaign. The General has Churchill's permission to address a large number of these units at the weekend and he'll try to persuade them to stay on here rather than go to North Africa. We also have a lot of wounded in hospitals. The embassy is offering them repatriation, so we have to make sure they know there's an alternative: signing up with us. In other words, we've got a hell of a lot of work on our hands."

"I'll be happy to help, then"

"You'll be more than welcome. What we need is another good 'fisher of men'. That's what the General will want you to do. But for a start, you should go down to Olympia and sign on officially with the Free French. I suggest that you go immediately after seeing him. If you'll wait here a moment, I'll just have a word with him."

He disappeared into the adjoining office, closing the door behind him. Edmond wondered what his father would be thinking if he knew that his son was about to have a private audience with the man he so distrusted.

"The General will see you now."

The aide smiled encouragingly as he held the door open for him. Edmond entered and briskly crossed the room. De Gaulle rose from behind a large desk and held out his hand. Edmond saluted, shook the proffered hand, and fixed his look on the expressionless face of his new leader. It seemed to Edmond to have been assembled from a remnant stock of unmatching parts. The small forehead contrasted strangely with the prominent nose and the outsize ears which in turn accentuated the inadequacy of the chin and the narrow setting of the hooded eyes. The arc of slicked-down dark hair that framed this unusual face helped to convey to him the inappropriately comic impression of a pompous head waiter.

The General resumed his seat, waving Edmond to a chair opposite him.

"When did you leave Bordeaux, monsieur?" De Gaulle spoke slowly and precisely.

"Four days ago, *mon Général*."

"You were a tank officer?"

"With the First Armoured Division, but I was transferred to staff duties with the Eighteenth District before the Division went into action."

"Waste of a tank commander," said the General sharply. "I need help with the recruiting to our fighting forces here. I want you to make propaganda among the officers and men who seem to have difficulty seeing that the only course of action is to rally to General de Gaulle. I did not come over here to preside over their repatriation to occupied France or their delivery into the ranks of forces loyal to a defeatist government."

"It would be an honour, *mon Général*. I can start immediately."

"My ADC tells me you are proficient in English. That being so, there may be other assignments for you connected with the development of more beneficial relations with the British military." De Gaulle rose and lit a cigarette before offering his hand once more to Edmond. "I am gratified that you answered our appeal so promptly." The General stared straight past Edmond as he spoke, and there was no warmth in his voice.

"Thank you, *mon Général*. It was a privilege to do so."

He saluted smartly and left the room. In the outer office the aide completed writing and signing a note.

"Take this with you to Olympia. Once they've inducted you, they'll give you a thorough briefing on the recruiting effort to date. Tomorrow you can come back here and we'll discuss how you're going to operate. We hope to have some sort of a military bureau set up here within a week, and you'll be fitted into that. Now, what about accommodation?"

"I'm staying with friends of the family for the moment, but I obviously have to find a place of my own soon."

The aide wrote another rapid note. "There's a room with bath and small kitchen available in Bolton Place in Kensington. The landlady's a retired teacher of French who'd like to have a Free French officer there. Three pounds a week, breakfast included, if you can afford it; two pounds without the breakfast. I'm afraid we can't pay you for the moment. You're a volunteer in the truest sense of the word."

"I can manage. I'll go round there right away and take it."

And so, a few minutes later, Edmond left St Stephen's House and set off to secure his lodgings, to sign up with the Free French, and to launch himself as a recruiter of his compatriots to the banner of Charles de Gaulle.

12

Charlie Garland sat down at the long wooden table which took up most of the space between the facing rows of bunk beds, two-tiered, seven on either side, in Room 14 of Oflag XIV C. He massaged his aching thigh slowly, in circular movements and with minimum pressure of the palm of his right hand, as the nurse in the hospital in Lille had told him. He stared at the grubby sheet of paper on the table in front of him on which, since arriving at the prisoner-of-war camp, he had been recording the passage of the days. A large printed calendar hung on the high, white-washed wall at the end of the room, but Charlie preferred to maintain his own personal score.

Today was 12th August, exactly two months to the day since, escorted by Wehrmacht guards, he had hauled himself painfully into the back of a truck outside the Lille hospital and had been driven, along with six other recuperating British officers, to the train that would take them to their confinement in Germany. Deposited fourteen hours later in the inner courtyard of a pictur-esque little Bavarian castle hastily converted into a camp for British officer prisoners, Charlie had experienced a brief sensation of relief, even contentment, at finding himself at this particular journey's end. But within a few hours, despite the friendly reception of those already incarcerated there, he had sunk into a deep depression, a depression in whose grip he was to remain for the next two weeks. And then, during the third week, he had begun to cheer up. His mind, which had been filled with disturb-ing images of all that he had so recently lost had now begun to concentrate on what was immediately to hand.

His fellow prisoners, who had sympathetically accepted his urge to remain withdrawn and largely uncommunicative, had suddenly become the object of his intense interest. The daily routine of camp life, which he had so far followed with cold indifference, had now become an exercise rich in opportunities for self-expression and boredom-breaking exploitation. To his own surprise, he had become alive again, and although life seemed only tolerably worth living, at least it no longer seemed to be utterly devoid of purpose.

Charlie folded his primitive calendar and slid it back into the hip pocket of his battledress trousers. He looked across the room at the figure lying face downwards on one of the lower level bunks.

"Mickey, how the hell are we going to escape from this God-forsaken hole?"

The figure rolled over slowly onto its back and groaned.

"Why did you have to wake me, you sod? I was just about to dip my wick into a gorgeous girl on a beach somewhere. Not Dunkirk, I hasten to add."

"You'd have woken up before you put it in. One always does."

Lieutenant Mickey Weatherall of the Sixtieth Rifles raised himself on his elbows and blinked.

"You know as well as I do, Charlie, that if you aren't a member of Alec Ritchie's little club, you haven't a hope of escaping."

"Then I think it's high time we applied for membership."

"You don't apply; you get invited. And that's not likely to happen to us. Ritchie's under the mistaken impression that Grenadiers and Green Jackets are too effete a breed to do anything so dashing as popping over walls or burrowing through tunnels."

"OK. We'll just have to start our own little club. Fuck Ritchie. Fuck Auntie Jean."

"Now, now, Charles. You know the goons don't like bad language, particularly bad King's English."

Charlie returned to his bunk and sat with his head in his hands. Somehow they had to get round the two leaders of the Escape Committee. Major Alec Ritchie of the Black Watch had been appointed chairman by the senior officer among the prisoners, Colonel Anthony Jeans. The colonel had made it known that while he recognized that it was the duty of all officers to try to escape, individual attempts made outside the auspices of the committee would be much frowned on. If any officer thought up an ingenious scheme for getting out, it was his duty to present it to the Escape Committee for vetting. If approved, the author or authors could prepare the scheme under the overall supervision of the committee. If disapproved, the attempt would under no circumstances be made.

"There must be a hundred ways of getting out, Mickey."

"If there are, you can bet Ritchie and his eager beavers are already working on them, and the goons probably know they are and are just waiting for the right moment to catch the maximum number of them at it."

"Christ, you're such a bloody defeatist!"

Weatherall swung his long legs off the bunk.

"I think a little stroll around this charming property before lunch would be good for the constitution, don't you think?"

"It's standing-room only in the courtyard at this hour."

"No worse than a good day in the Royal Enclosure at Ascot. Besides, we don't want to get a reputation for being unsociable, do we? The Jerries are hell bent on our enjoying our stay."

Rumours were rife in the camp that afternoon and evening that the first batch of mail since the camp had opened had arrived the day before, and it was an expectant crowd of prisoners who hurried down to the courtyard the next morning when the eight-thirty bell rang for the "Appell". Colonel Jeans made a brisk inspection of his men, formed up in contingents by dormitories, then took his place out in front to await the arrival of the German commandant or whomever the commandant had designated to take the parade that morning.

"If Winterfeldt doesn't show up," whispered Mickey, "no mail. He'd certainly not miss the opportunity to make an ingratiating little announcement on so important an occasion."

"We're in luck; he's here," said Charlie as the silver-haired commandant with the pronounced limp emerged from a doorway at the north end of the yard, accompanied by his senior staff, and marched stiffly towards the waiting British colonel. Salutes were exchanged, and junior Wehrmacht officers began to check the count of the numbers on parade. Two hundred and thirty-one prisoners were reported present on parade, the absent fourteen being accounted for in the camp hospital. The camp adjutant, whose absurdly high-pitched voice was a source of endless hilarity for the prisoners, reported angrily on the theft of two pairs of coveralls from a party of plumbers working on the castle's ancient water supply system. The removal of certain privileges would be announced if they were not handed over before midday.

"Two more items for Ritchie's midnight tailors," observed Mickey. "They won't be recognizable by now."

The camp commandant stepped forward. Colonel Baron von Winterfeldt was every inch the aristocrat. Badly wounded in the closing days of the First World War, his role in the Second was confined to that of guarding prisoners. To him it was an utterly distasteful and degrading role, but having never questioned an order in his military career he had accepted it stoically and now sought to make the best of it. He was a man of few words, and they were firmly but never offensively delivered. His message today was typically brief and to the point, and was imparted in near-faultless English as befitted the brother-in-law of an English baronet.

"I regret that because of the aforementioned theft, it was necessary for me to delay by one day the distribution of the mail. It will be distributed immediately following this parade. That is all."

The two colonels exchanged stiff salutes, and the parade was dismissed amid boisterous roars of approval, as much at the announcement of the theft as at the arrival of the mail.

Within ten minutes, Charlie was racing up the stone staircase to his dormitory, clutching letters from both

Margot and his parents. He sat down at the table in the middle of the room. The letters had already been unsealed by the German censors. He pulled Margot's letter first from its envelope, and his eyes immediately fell on a postscript on the back fold of the outer sheet of paper.

My darling – you have just read the letter I wrote you as soon as we got news of you. I saw no point in starting over after what happened later that same day because the letter still expressed all I wanted to say to you about how much I love and miss you. I had a stupid accident, which honestly wasn't my fault. I got knocked down the steps of an air-raid shelter during a false alarm – for London at least. My friend Kay got me to hospital, quite badly bruised and concussed, but no bones broken. I am afraid, however, my darling, that I lost our baby as a result of the wretched fall. I know how dreadfully miserable this will make you on top of everything you have had to go through. But *please* remember that we *can* have other children when you get back; no permanent damage was done to me. I'm so sorry, darling, but we will start over. I love you. I love you. M.

Charlie sank his head in his hands, and Mickey, entering the room, saw his young Grenadier friend's shoulders heaving. He walked over to the table and patted him gently on the back.

"Anything you want to tell me about?"

Charlie looked up, the tears streaming down his face. "Mickey, I have *got* to get out of here. I just must get home. I must!"

He banged his fist down hard on the table before reaching into his pocket for a handkerchief.

"Bad news from home?"

Charlie gulped and then gritted his teeth in an effort to stop his sobbing.

"Margot had an accident. We lost a baby I didn't even know was on the way."

"Oh Christ! Is she all right?"

"She sounds fine, but she must be absolutely bloody

miserable." He stood up and blew his nose. "I'll be all right, Mickey."

"Well, it's a nasty shock, but at least she *says* she's OK."

"She'll get over it. All the same, Mickey, you've got to put on your bloody thinking cap and help me work out how we're going to say an early goodbye to this wretched place."

13

It was a Saturday morning, and Margot got up late. The day was cold and overcast, and she shivered as she pulled the latticed windows closed in the small bedroom. Even though the room was over the kitchen where the coke-fired cooker burned round the clock, she still felt the cold and dreaded surfacing from beneath the thick blankets and puffy eiderdown. It was nearly ten o'clock, and she could hear her parents' and Katie's voices in the kitchen below. Out of bed, she stretched energetically, her finger tips tapping an oak beam on the low ceiling, and then surveyed herself in a full-length mirror as she pulled a blue wool robe around her. She had lost a lot of weight after the accident, but in recent months had regained all of it and more. Despite long country walks and a lot of bicycling, she was losing the struggle to stay as slim as she had been when living in London, and she was now more or less decided that that wartime staple, the potato, would simply have to be banished from her already rather dull diet.

As she brushed her hair, she recalled the difficult conversation that she and her sister had conducted with their parents over dinner the evening before. Well, why shouldn't they go and spend a night in London? It would be Katie's last chance before what she called her "forced repatriation" and there hadn't been an air-raid for weeks. She hoped she would hear no more parental complaints over breakfast.

Throughout the autumn and early winter of 1940, London had been subjected to a horrifying reign of aerial terror. From 7th September to 17th November, Londoners had known only two nights when the bombers were not over the city, and the weary, frightened survivors wondered each morning how long they and the shattered city could take it. And then, quite suddenly in mid-November, the Luftwaffe had switched targets. For the next ten weeks, it was the unhappy turn of the provincial cities, beginning with Coventry, to suffer the nightmare and the anguish through which the capital had barely lived. During those weeks, London was raided only eight times, and from 19th January onwards, only a single raid had forced Londoners into their underground shelters.

In the early days of the blitz, Harland Moore had taken up Sir Walter Garland's suggestion that they rent his cousin's now vacant cottage which stood on the edge of Windsor's Great Park. Elinor and Margot installed themselves in Verbena Cottage on a full-time basis, while Katie and her father braved four nights of their working week at Hill Street, arriving at the cottage on Friday nights. The arrangement, however, did little to dispel Moore's growing doubts over the wisdom of keeping his family together in England. Each time that he and Katie were forced to repair to camp beds in the basement at Hill Street, he steeled himself to announce the very next day that his mind was irrevocably made up that Elinor and his younger daughter must leave for home, and each morning, when he telephoned the cottage to report their survival of yet another night, his resolve had weakened. Then, on one of the few nights in early January when the bombers came, two young secretaries at the embassy, sharing a flat in Chelsea, had died in a direct hit, and that decided the matter for him. Elinor, who had long sensed her husband's silent approach to this decision, accepted it stoically. She could have argued that they were perfectly safe in their country retreat, but she knew that he was also still thinking about the invasion threat, a threat that remained very real. Katie, on the other hand, exploded in anger, threatening to marry the first Englishman to propose to her that week, or bullying one into doing so. She badgered the American Red Cross Representative to call her father to tell him that she was indispensable, but all her stratagems were to no avail. Moore refused any appeal of his decision, and berths were finally secured for

178

her and her mother on the Pan American Clipper flight departing on 10th March.

Margot, while dreading their departure, comforted herself with the knowledge that taking care of her father would be a welcome distraction. If the lull in the bombing continued she could spend more time with him in London, and if the raids resumed she would at least be able to ensure him rest and comfort at the weekends at the cottage. For Harland, the splitting of the family was no less of a wrench, but there was one aspect of his life in London which had much brightened, as if in timely compensation for the domestic upheaval. Joseph Kennedy was gone for good. When he had left just before the November presidential election on a visit to the United States, his embassy staff had assumed a last-ditch attempt on his part to head off a third term for the incumbent. Instead he astonished them with a ringing eleventh-hour endorsement of Roosevelt, which the President rewarded with a fulsome public welcome for his ambassador. Moore reckoned that his twenty-dollar wager that Kennedy would not be returning to the Court of St James was as good as lost. But then, shortly after the returns were in re-electing the President, Kennedy's resignation was announced. Unknown to his London staff, he had handed in his letter of resignation at the White House a week before the election, with every intention that it be accepted. He had had enough. And Roosevelt had had enough of the ambassador.

In the first, cold, days of February, the new ambassador, John G. Winant, had arrived in England to be personally welcomed by the King at an overnight stay at Windsor Castle, and by Churchill over a dinner for two a few days later. The message was unmistakable and, for Moore and his colleagues, full of comfort and cheer. A new era in British-American diplomacy had opened. None had been more relieved for her father than Margot, as indeed she had been relieved for herself. If for the foreseeable future she was to share her wartime life in England with him alone, the state of his morale as a senior embassy staffer was a factor of some importance to her own peace of mind.

She hurried down to the kitchen to join the family at a late breakfast, and found her parents in a sombre mood. Her mother looked as though she had recently been crying, and her father was nervously drumming his fingers on the kitchen table at which he sat drinking tea. Katie had her face buried in a newspaper.

"Something's bothering you," she said. "Out with it!"

Moore pointed to an airmail letter lying beside his wife's plate. Margot immediately recognized her brother's handwriting.

"So Larry finally wrote! Miracle of miracles! May I read it?"

"Help yourself," said Elinor, pushing it across the table. "Now you'll find out what else there is for me to worry myself sick about besides leaving you and your father here in England."

"Well, what's happened to him?" Margot looked anxiously from her mother to her father. It was Katie who responded from behind her paper.

"He's enrolled in Army Flying School."

"Well good for him. He's always wanted to fly."

"Put another way," said Elinor, her voice trembling, "he's dropped out of Yale to go and get himself killed."

"Now, now, Elinor dear," said Moore. "That's no way to look at it. I'm as disappointed as you are that he decided to drop out of college, but if we do end up in this war, he'll have a head start on other kids, and he won't risk being drafted into the infantry. You should look on that side of it."

"For heaven's sakes, Mother, you mustn't allow what happened to Uncle Jack to destroy your faith in your own son."

"You didn't have to bring up Uncle Jack, Margot," she said. "You'll never understand my feelings, any of you!"

Starting to weep, she hurried from the kitchen. Moore rose to his feet and followed her. The two sisters could hear her choking words out in the hallway.

"None of you seem to care that this war could take you, Margot and Larry from me for ever, leaving me with only Katie!"

Katie got up and closed the kitchen door before

resuming her perusal of the paper. Margot began to read Larry's brief letter. They were interrupted a moment later by their father's return.

"Listen, girls, do you really have to go to London tonight? Your mother's upset, and this being our last weekend together as a family, I really think you should stay here."

"It's too late to change now, Father, honestly," said Katie. "And besides, you did promise that we could have one last night on the town before I'm exiled."

Moore sighed. "Is this Frenchman Lemourier – "

"Lemonnier, Father."

"Lemonnier; is he so important to you?"

"I've already told you, Father; it's his twenty-fifth birthday. He's a lonely man in a strange country who happens to be extremely nice and speaks impeccable English. I promised him we'd get together tonight, and I don't intend to let him down."

He appealed to Margot. "Well, maybe *you* could stay?"

"No!" Katie intervened. "She's got to come too. Edmond's bringing a brother officer. I thought you'd be pleased that I'm being chaperoned."

"How well do you know this fellow?"

"We met at the Nicolsons'; he's dated me twice, and you met him once when he came to take me out. And what difference does that make, anyway? Heavens, Father, we went through all this last night!"

Margot decided to stay out of it and let her younger sister carry the ball. She herself had met the Frenchman fleetingly on the Hill Street doorstep and she could understand Katie's enthusiasm for a last night out with him. There was no doubt that he was very attractive. Her only fear for the evening was that her blind date, the brother officer, might turn out to be anything but attractive. But she was ready to risk the sacrifice to give Katie a good send-off.

Katie resumed her speech for the defence.

"Father, I promise you that we'll be on the early train back to Windsor tomorrow morning and we'll have all Sunday together." She rose and kissed him on the cheek.

Harland Moore shrugged his shoulders and smiled wanly.

"All right, you win. But God help you if you're not both back early Sunday."

When the two sisters arrived at Hill Street that evening, Margot felt a pang of disappointment at not finding a letter from Charlie on the door-mat. Not that she had held out much hope of there being one; the last had arrived only two weeks ago. In it he had apologized rather pathetically for having nothing new or interesting to say. Prisoner-of-war life went on according to its depressingly unvarying routine, and all he could really do was comment on what she had told him in her own letters and tell her how much he loved and missed her. At times she had pondered on the possibility of him escaping, and, while the thought of any early reunion thrilled her, she could not conquer the accompanying fear of the mortal risks he would be taking in attempting it. On balance, her mind was more easily at rest when she thought of him stoically bearing the frustrations of prison life than when she pictured him risking death in a bid for liberty, however great would be her joy if he succeeded.

There was, however, a letter from Jamie, informing her that his younger brother, Ivor, would shortly be arriving on leave from Cairo, and suggesting a welcoming party for him.

"Ivor's a bore," said Katie. "He's so serious; you can't really let your hair down with him."

"In your case, your panties. It just happens that he has a remarkable brain, and that end of the human anatomy sadly means nothing to you."

Katie stuck her tongue out at her sister and went upstairs to change. Margot poured herself a drink in the living room and sat for a while thinking frustrating thoughts about Charlie's anatomy until the clock on the mantelpiece struck seven and she hurried upstairs. She found Katie luxuriating in the bathtub, up to her neck in dark green water, the heavy aroma of pine essence wafting with the steam through the open bathroom door.

"There's a war on, Katie, in case you forgot. You're

only meant to fill the tub one third of the way. What's good enough for the Royal Family obviously isn't good enough for you."

"The Royal Family isn't about to spend the evening with the most wickedly handsome Frenchman in the world."

"Mine or yours, as if I can't guess?"

"Mine, I'm afraid. Will you be a nice sister and keep your mouth shut if I go the whole way with him tonight?"

"For God's sakes, Katie! You really want to end up pregnant? What will you tell them back in Washington?"

"I won't be. The French practically invented contraception."

"So what!"

"If he wants me, he can have me. And at his place. I'll join you here for breakfast." She sat up in the tub and began massaging her breasts with a large sponge.

"Katie, you're an incorrigible little whore! Four months ago you boasted of losing your virginity to the Royal Navy. Last month you told me you'd been having it off with a Life Guards officer. Now it's the Free French. How in hell do you think the Allies are going to win this war if half the officer corps is sprawled between your hot little legs?"

"Jealous!" Katie aimed the water-filled sponge at her sister and giggled merrily as it missed her and sploshed against the bathroom door.

Margot retreated to her room. She wasn't jealous, she told herself. She wasn't looking for lovers. But there was no denying to herself that she was finding life without physical love harder to bear than she had anticipated. Seeking relief by re-enacting in her mind her love-making with Charlie was by now affording her only marginal pleasure. Replaying those few love scenes was more and more like going to the same few movies over and over. Other men, faceless and nameless were beginning to people new fantasies, and she knew she would have to exercise careful control over herself if she was going to avoid sliding into adultery. And Katie, damn her, was no help!

183

She opened the hanging closet and unhesitatingly chose a long black satin Molyneux dress, split to the knee and lined with primrose crêpe. It was Charlie's last gift to her, and she had rarely worn it. She laid it carefully on the bed and went to the door to call out to Katie.

"I assume you're wearing long?"

"Right; with nothing underneath."

"Oh for God's sakes, Katie!" Margot slammed her door shut and began preparing for the evening.

Fifty minutes later the front door bell rang. Margot descended the stairs to the front hall. Before opening the door, she paused before a gilt-framed mirror to look herself over once more. Running low on hard-to-get make-up, she had decided to try *Vogue*'s recommended alternative, a non-greasy, all-purpose cream dusted with powder. From duchesses downwards they were trying it, the magazine had assured its readers. Margot was happy with the results; on impeccable skin like hers, it was hard to tell the difference. She pushed her long blonde hair back over her shoulders and checked the grips of her pearl earrings. Then, smoothing the black satin down over her hips she rendered her verdict: stunning! She turned to open the door.

"*Bonsoir*, Madame Garland." Edmond Lemonnier saluted and stepped forward to take and kiss her hand. "Please permit me to present Lieutenant Yves Fossé."

A lanky young man, staring myopically through thick metal-framed spectacles, stepped forward and saluted.

"I am enchanted to meet you, madame," he said in a pleasant if heavily accented voice as he bent towards Margot's proffered hand. She smiled sweetly and invited them into the living room.

She looked at Lemonnier. Lucky Katie, she thought.

"Happy birthday, Captain!"

"Thank you."

"You must forgive me for a moment," she said. "I have to tell my sister to hurry. Please help yourselves to drinks, if you wish."

"You permit me to smoke, madame?" asked Fossé.

"Of course," said Margot, studying the Lieutenant's close-cropped, bullet-shaped head with curiosity. She hurried upstairs to Katie's room and found her sister zipping herself into a long white crêpe sheath skirt.

"Katie, you've got to be kidding! Are you expecting me to carouse around London with someone looking like Himmler's younger brother?"

"I'm told he has a great sense of humour," said Katie, slipping her arms into a white bolero top.

"He'd damn well better. And where on earth did you get *that* outfit?" The bolero top left a good four inches of bare midriff, and the scooped-out neckline compounded the audacity. "You look like a cheap blonde imitation of Dorothy Lamour. Where's the turban?"

"Don't be rude; Himmler's brother would approve of a blonde Lamour. Anyway, this is a very expensive new model. Why don't you go down and amuse the troops for a couple more minutes?"

Fifteen minutes later, Katie made her grand entrance downstairs, by which time Margot had made up her mind that she was going to dislike the whole evening intensely. The fact that, at Edmond's suggestion, it was going to be spent, or rather wasted, dining at the Café de Paris, one of her very favourite restaurants, added to her misery.

As they stepped from the taxi in Coventry Street, they heard, for the first time in six weeks, the wailing of the sirens.

"Hitler must have known it was your birthday, Edmond," said Katie gaily.

"I guessed he'd come looking for me; that's why I chose the safest restaurant in London."

The Café de Paris was underground, beneath a cinema, and during the worst of the blitz it had become a haunt of the less daunted elements of London's café society. Once ensconced in its plush bowels, diners were happily oblivious to the thunder and crash of war up above. The two sisters and their escorts now hurried down the long flight of stairs to the foyer. From the balcony overlooking the dance floor and dining tables, Margot surveyed the animated crowd below. Almost all the men seemed to be in officers' uniforms, and almost all the women were attractive and elegantly dressed.

185

"I have never been here before," said Lieutenant Fossé softly at her shoulder. "It is very impressive."

"You might be interested to know," said Margot coolly, "that it is modelled on the first-class dining room of the *Titanic*."

The Frenchman laughed nervously. "It doesn't seem to worry anyone much."

The four of them descended the curved stairway to the restaurant floor where Charles beamed at the sight of two of his most favoured ladies.

"Why have my two beautiful Americans been neglecting me these past weeks? You only come here when there is an air-raid now?" He led them to one of the best-placed banquette tables, and bowed low before plunging back into the throng of diners and dancers.

As she had already determined, Margot did not enjoy her dinner. Not that the food was bad; it was amongst the best to be had in wartime London. Her problem was Yves Fossé who had set out with evangelistic zeal to teach her far more about General de Gaulle and the Free French than she could ever conceive of wanting to know. She listened with strained politeness, managing somehow to conceal her impatience, and seizing those precious moments when the human Larousse at her side had a mouthful to escape briefly into Katie's and Edmond's world. But Katie was being of little help, concentrating with starry-eyed steadfastness on her handsome captain. Finally Margot suggested that they all dance. Edmond looked across the table at her.

"Since I have most rudely neglected you so far, may I have the honour of the first dance?"

"Delighted," said Margot, rising immediately to forestall any objections from Katie.

"Your sister is very charming," said Edmond as they reached the dance floor and slipped easily into a slow foxtrot.

"I'm glad you think so."

"No moment with her is dull."

"I won't argue with that." Margot looked around the floor at the other dancers. If he's going to talk about her all night, she thought, the sooner we change partners the

186

better. She'd rather settle for that well of unwanted information. She looked across towards the bandstand and caught the eye of Ken "Snakehips" Johnson, the leader. Recognizing her, he winked, and seeing the good-looking young man in the French officer's uniform, gave her a "not bad" nod of the head.

For a while now, she and Edmond danced in silence. Eventually he broke it.

"If you were both single, it would be very difficult indeed to choose between you."

On an impulse, Margot freed a hand and lightly stroked his cheek.

"How sweet of you to say so, Edmond." It was the first time she had addressed him by his given name, or by any name. "But luckily you don't have to make the choice."

She now watched with some amusement her sister, a few feet away, coping as best she could with Lieutenant Fossé whose stilted movements resembled those of a poorly handled marionette.

The melody ended, and Margot immediately detached herself from Edmond.

"That was very nice, thank you. Maybe now you should dance with my sister."

"But first some more champagne." He began to lead her back to the table. The music had started again, and Margot glanced over her shoulder at the dancers. Katie, now laughing merrily, was once more in the uncertain grip of her bespectacled marionette. At the table, Edmond motioned to Margot to sit beside him, and as she sank onto the banquette, she suddenly felt her head being violently pressed down onto her chest. An eerie blue light filled the room for a brief second, and turned red as the table was sucked away from in front of her. As she fell forward, she felt the top half of her dress disengage itself effortlessly from her body, and she sank in blackness to the floor.

It was the screaming that awoke her, and she started to cough as she inhaled the dust and the acrid smell swirling around her. She looked up in the faint light and saw what she thought at first was a face in clown's make-up leaning over her. Then she recognized it as Edmond's face, plastered with white dust and streaked with what must be blood.

"Are you all right?" he asked calmly.

Margot nodded and began to raise herself to a sitting position. One leg was immobile.

"I think you're sitting on my leg."

"No."

Margot looked at her trapped leg and recognized the form of the waiter who had been pulling back the table for them when they resumed their seats. With her free foot, she pushed hard against the inert body and it rolled over onto its back. A small wedge of glass, shaped like a child's paper dart, was buried in the man's face just above the bridge of the nose. She eased herself up onto the banquette and winced as the screaming assailed her ears. She then started to brush the dust from herself and looked down in curiosity as her hands immediately came into contact with her naked breasts.

Edmond had found a napkin and was mopping blood from his face. A nearly full bottle of champagne stood bizarrely upright on the floor at his feet. He bent down, picked it up, drank a mouthful from the neck of the bottle and handed it to Margot. She let it slip through her fingers and it exploded on the floor.

Voices were calling out names. Upright figures began to move unsteadily about. Margot's eyes were slowly becoming adjusted to the poor light cast by a single lamp burning somewhere up in the balcony. An elderly man in a dinner jacket materialized and handed her what appeared to be a piece of tablecloth.

"Here you are, my dear; you can cover yourself with this." He passed on into the gloom. Margot draped it around her neck and let the ends hang down over her chest.

"Stay there, Margot. I have to look for the others." Edmond stepped over the dead waiter and made his way precariously into the dreadful devastation.

"Oh my God!" Margot's befuddled mind suddenly recalled the fact that Katie had been with her. She leapt to her feet and fell immediately back again, head spinning, nausea overwhelming her. She retched violently and threw up over the daintily-crossed feet of the outstretched waiter. She pressed one end of the piece of tablecloth to her mouth and sank back again on the banquette.

"Just stay still, my dear. Help will be coming. You're alive, so all is well." Margot looked up into an extraordinarily lovely middle-aged woman's face. She seemed completely unscathed, immaculately beautiful in white satin and diamonds. Not a hair out of place.

"My sister," whispered Margot. "My sister. We have to find her."

Edmond worked his way towards the dance floor. His legs were shaking as he stopped by a table near the floor to steady himself. A couple were seated at it, their heads thrown back as though enjoying a hearty laugh. The blast must have killed them instantly. He heard someone with a French accent asking people to collect up napkins and bring them to him. The voice was authoritative and he guessed it must be a doctor. Another light came on now, illuminating the scene on the dance floor.

"It fell straight through the fucking cinema!" said a high-pitched male voice.

A young couple, covered in white dust, were picking their way gingerly among the tangle of bodies on the floor, looking for signs of life. Edmond glanced towards the bandstand between the two curved stairways; it seemed he had last seen Katie and Fossé in that general area. A musician with a trumpet in his hand was carefully brushing dust from his jacket. Another, sobbing loudly, was standing staring at the twisted, bloodied remnants of his leader sprawled on the floor below

Edmond reached the centre of the dance floor and immediately spotted his brother officer. He was half buried under a naked female who was not Katie. There was just enough of a French officer's tunic left on the torso to make it identifiable. The shattered remains of a pair of metal-framed glasses hung casually from the mouth of the scarcely recognizable face. Edmond started to call out for Katie. The dust in his throat brought on coughing, and then, a moment later, he found himself staring down incredulously at her. Her face appeared miraculously untouched save for a scratch across the width of her forehead. Her eyes were open and her expression untroubled. The white bolero top hung loosely around her neck like a scarf. From the rib cage downward, there remained little that could be easily identified as the lower half of a human body. Edmond felt the wave of nausea hit him, and he turned quickly and started lurching back across the floor, retracing as best he could his path back through the carnage to where he had left Margot.

"They're dead," he said firmly, well before he was within Margot's earshot. "They're dead!" he repeated again and again until Margot heard him. Then he fainted.

They buried Katie four days later in a small green churchyard not two hundred yards from the back gate of Verbena Cottage. Edmond Lemonnier, his head still bandaged where they had removed the slivers of glass, made the journey to Windsor to see her laid to rest. He stood discreetly at the back of the little fourteenth-century church, eyes cast down. As she followed the coffin out for the burial, Margot, on the steadying arm of Jamie, paused for a fleeting moment by his pew. Edmond looked into her eyes and saw behind the film of tears and tiredness an unquenchable strength.

"Thank you for coming," she said simply, and passed on behind her parents through the arched doorway out into the light drizzle now falling on the churchyard.

14

According to Charlie's calculation, this should be the day his solitary confinement ended. He had scrupulously kept the score, and today was the thirtieth day that he had spent in the small cell in the punishment wing of the camp. The wing was, in fact, a converted stables at the northern extremity of the castle compound. Loose-boxes for some twenty horses had been converted by army bricklayers into twenty closed-in cells with reinforced doors. The narrow windows, high in the outer walls, had newly fixed bars and were without panes. When the wind blew from the north, the temperature in the cells dropped to a bone-chilling level, and when it snowed or rained, the occupants soon found out in which corner of the cell to huddle or to push the rickety cot in order to avoid a soaking or a blanket of snow.

"I am fully aware that you believe it your duty to try to escape," Colonel Baron von Winterfeldt had said to Charlie on the fateful day just a month ago. "It is, however, my duty to prevent you from doing so, and to punish you for any attempt. You will have time during your solitary confinement to ponder on how lucky you are that you were not shot by the guards. That may convince you not to try anything so foolish again."

Charlie had said nothing. He was still seething with anger – not at the courtly Winterfeldt, but at himself. It had been an unplanned, spur-of-the-moment, desperately foolhardy try. He had been to the camp hospital to have his thigh wound examined. For two days he had been feeling considerable pain, and he wanted to know why. The doctor had told him that it was probably the

191

bitterly cold weather, and had given him some ointment and a length of lint and cotton to wrap around it to keep the heat in.

As he had left the doctor's dispensary and stepped out into the alley which ran down between the curtain wall at the east end of the castle and the camp administration block towards the heavily guarded east gate, a military ambulance had drawn up. Charlie had paused to watch. Leaning casually against the curtain wall, fiddling with his roll of dressing, he had watched the driver get out and come round to open the rear doors of the vehicle. With the aid of a second orderly inside, an English officer whom Charlie had never seen before was helped out of the ambulance. He was emaciated, and the yellow pallor of his taut skin suggested severe jaundice. Slowly the three had made their way across the cobble-stoned alley to the back entrance of the hospital wing from which Charlie had just emerged.

Poor bugger! thought Charlie as he set off back to the main courtyard and his dormitory. Then, as he passed the ambulance, it suddenly hit him: the driver and the orderly had left it unattended. His first thought was simply to drive it away, but a few seconds of reflection convinced him it was absurd to think he could bluff his was past the guards on the gate. Through the rear doors, he could see a fixed stretcher, more like a bunk, with a large blanket draped over it.

It's now or never, Charlie; get cracking, she's waiting for you! The words sang in his head as he cast a quick glance at the hospital entrance before darting to the ambulance. Springing inside he rapidly adjusted the blanket so that it reached to the floor around the stretcher, then he rolled himself under it. Thank God! He had judged right: there was just enough clearance and just enough length. For once in his military life he was thankful to be one of the less lofty of the Grenadier Guards officers.

Barely a minute later, he heard boots on the cobblestones and the rear doors of the ambulance were slammed shut. Once more, he had guessed right; the orderly, with no prisoner-patient to watch over, was going to ride up front with the driver. A moment later they were moving. A sudden pattering on the roof told him that heavy rain was falling. The vehicle jerked to a halt; they must have reached the east gate. The guards would probably open the rear doors. Charlie held his breath. There was a crack of thunder, and the pattering on the roof now sounded like machine-gun fire. No one opened the door. Lazy sods, thought Charlie happily; they don't want to get wet by coming out of the guard post. The ambulance moved on and accelerated. He now turned his mind quickly to the daunting question of when and how he was to extricate himself from the vehicle and make good his escape from his unwitting accomplices. The odds seemed stacked impressively against him. He was in an ambulance driven by two armed medical orderlies; he had no idea where he was going except that it was, at least for the moment, away from the camp; he had no maps, no money, and worst of all he was clothed in an instantly recognizable British officer's battledress uniform. He tried to think calmly, but the only thought in his head was that he had just embarked on a costly round trip ending up in a punishment cell.

Which is precisely what it turned out to be. He had been frantically seeking to choose between jumping from the ambulance when it next slowed down - perhaps in full view of a battalion of SS - or of waiting until it reached its destination, whatever that might be, and then hoping to remain undetected until his two hosts were clear of the vehicle. But he never did arrive at a final decision. The ambulance had suddenly stopped, the rear doors had opened, and the blanket had been yanked from the stretcher. His desperate attempt to win freedom had been foiled by a medical orderly whose feet were getting cold.

"I hope any other escape attempts are as stupid as yours, although I doubt that any could be," Captain Zenker, the camp adjutant had sneered loftily as he escorted Charlie to his cell following the commandant's swift pronouncement of sentence. Tired and dispirited as he was, Charlie had managed to summon up a passably insulting imitation of Zenker's high-pitched voice as the cell door clanked shut on him. Flinging himself down on the cot, he had pondered unhappily on the fact that the adjutant's doubt was almost certain to be proven well-founded.

Today, he was sure, was to be his last day in the dank and drafty cell. The punishment diet had taken a toll on his physical strength, but his morale was high. There would certainly be a letter from Margot awaiting him, and maybe the books he had asked her for. He would have a good laugh with Mickey, and doubtless his kinder colleagues would have set aside some goodies for him from the Red Cross food parcels that would have arrived during his forced absence. There was only one cloud, or rather two, on the immediate horizon: Major Ritchie and Auntie Jean. What they would have to say to him about his madcap escapade, he shuddered to think. Without doubt, he was in for a royal roasting, and the prospect, though not unduly alarming on the wartime scale of things, was nonetheless discomforting.

Charlie's solitary confinement was terminated in time for the eight o'clock "Appell" on the morning of 11th March, one whole annoying day later than he had calculated. There was no letter from Margot awaiting him, nor any books. Mickey Weatherall was in hospital with an ear infection, and the pickings from the Red Cross parcels were scant and unappetizing.

"I might just as well have stayed where I bloody well was!" lamented Charlie as his room-mates welcomed him back.

The roasting at the hands of the two senior British officers was, as he had feared, nothing less than memorable.

15

For the next several weeks, Margot scarcely stirred from Verbena Cottage. Prostrate with grief, she simply wanted the hours of each ugly day to pass while she hoped against hope that her desperately wounded spirit would somehow heal. In the past, she had sometimes wondered what it would be like if either Katie or Larry were suddenly to die, and the grief had appeared so unimaginable that there had been no point in speculating on it. Now she knew, and on mornings following nights haunted by images of the carnage in which Katie had died, she despaired of ever recovering. Her condition was not helped by the sufferings of her mother who had collapsed emotionally and physically within hours of watching her younger daughter's remains lowered into the grave. Harland had his wife hospitalized while he made plans for her return to the United States where she would be properly cared for in her mother's comfortable, well-staffed Manhattan apartment. Ambassador Winant helped secure passage for her on the flying boat service, and by the end of March she was gone.

With her mother's departure, and despite her father's misgivings about leaving her so much alone, Margot's spirits began to revive. She worked to restore the neglected garden, once the spring thaw set in; she read voraciously from the well-stocked bookshelves in the little living room; and she wrote frequently to her mother and brother. She felt a particular concern for Larry. The ghastly news of Katie's death had reached him only two days after the local Cadet Examining Board had accepted him as an aviation cadet and two weeks before he had

entered military flying school. He spoke bravely in his
letters of burying his grief in the excitement of his new
physically and mentally taxing activities, but she could
sense that his emotions were still in turmoil, and she
resented her mother's reported attempts, vigorous and
repeated, to have him pull out of flying lest she lose two
children in rapid succession. Margot urged her to desist
from undermining Larry in the one activity that could
quickly restore his spirits.

Each Friday evening her father joined her for the
weekend. There was now no let up in the bombing and
Margot waited anxiously each morning for his call reporting that he had survived the night. Kay Lawton came
frequently to see her, bolstering her morale with her
gaiety and humour, and made her sit for a series of
charcoal portrait sketches.

"You know, Margot, you'd make a marvellous fashion
model," said Kay one morning as she sat sketching
her friend. "You have the figure and the features,
and you wear clothes like a dream. Ever thought
about it?"

"No, I don't think I have; anyway, I've been putting on
too much weight."

"Not that it shows. You only feel it because you've been
largely inactive of late. We're going to have to get some
action back in to your life."

"I'm not sure I'm ready for it yet. When I am, and if it's
safe to go back to London, I think I'd like to work for the
Red Cross like Katie did."

"That's not entirely what I was talking about," said
Kay with a restrained smile, "but let it pass."

Margot looked puzzled, and said nothing.

One morning a letter from Charlie arrived which threw
her into a panic. In it he confessed that he had been "a
naughty boy" and had incurred the grave displeasure of
his hosts, who had rewarded him with "a room of my
own in which to contemplate my waywardness, and a
rather longer occupancy than I would have volunteered
for."

"Poor fellow," said Harland. "He has obviously been
in solitary confinement."

"Then he must have tried to escape!" she cried excitedly. "Oh, Charlie, you wonderful brave man! You *must* try again." She kissed the letter.

"He could get killed doing that, honey," said Harland quietly.

"Officers are supposed to try to escape."

That evening she called Jamie to tell him the news. He was delighted.

"Good for Charlie! Knew he had it in him. I bet he got the goons properly rattled. He's obviously in one hell of a hurry to get back to you, old girl."

"Just as well, Jamie. The celibate life is killing me."

Towards the end of April, Margot had a surprise visit. It was a sunny morning and she had been tending to her flourishing victory vegetable garden when the telephone rang.

"Edmond, what a lovely surprise! Where are you?"

"I'm in Windsor on official business."

"Would you be through in time to take the bus out here for some lunch?"

"I'm finished now. I would like to see you and to put some flowers on Katie's grave."

"Then take the bus to Clewer and call me from the post office. I'll ride over with a bicycle for you; I've got rather good at riding two at once."

The crisply uniformed cavalry captain, his briefcase balanced on the handlebars, pedalled a trifle self-consciously alongside Margot as they covered the mile from the village bus stop to Verbena Cottage. He found her a very bewitching sight, her blonde hair streaming out in the wind, the full skirt of her blue and white cotton dress billowing out around her long slim legs. This was his first real sight of her relaxed and smiling. She had worn a bored pout most of that fateful evening, and he'd not seen her since the funeral. Now, as they rode, she chided him gently.

"Not a word from you for more than a month; you should keep in touch. Mother's gone back home. Charlie's been in solitary confinement, probably for trying to escape – the censors won't let him tell us. Such a lot's happened."

Edmond looked surprised; it was as though she was scolding a truant member of her own family. He felt flattered.

At the cottage, they took glasses of ale into the garden and settled into deck chairs in the sun. They chatted easily for a while, catching up on each other's news, until Margot excused herself to finish preparing the lunch. Over a simple meal of ham, potato salad and apple pie, she let Edmond do most of the talking. She had decided that she wanted to know more about him, his family, what he was doing, what he thought of the war. He spoke eloquently and animatedly in his admirable English, and she revelled in his soft French accent. It was only when he spoke of his family in Bordeaux that his face clouded over and he looked sad. Getting news of them was difficult, and he worried about them a lot. She then asked him if he had left a steady girlfriend behind. He hesitated for a moment and then smiled wistfully. No, he had had no one he could describe as a steady girlfriend in Bordeaux. Between leaving his armoured regiment and escaping to England, he hadn't been long enough in the city to develop such a relationship.

"And what about in London?"

Margot immediately regretted the question. It was tactless. He had obviously been fond of Katie, and she of him. His genuine grief of her horrible death could scarcely be healed enough for him to be lavishing affection on anyone else yet.

"There's no one," said Edmond simply. He had no difficulty in saying that in good conscience. The plump little secretary at his headquarters was not a girlfriend. He had never even taken her out for a meal. She liked to be visited, preferably with a bottle of champagne, in the late evening in her basement bed-sitter. It was not a bad place to be during an air-raid, and love-making helped them both take their minds off the death and destruction being meted out above.

After coffee, they walked out through the back gate in the garden and crossed the grassy common to the church-yard. Margot carried a water-filled vase and Edmond a large bunch of daffodils. They arranged the flowers against the recently erected headstone and then stood silently for a moment staring down at the grave. A light breeze blew Margot's hair across her face, and as she pushed it aside she swept a few warm tears from her cheeks. Edmond turned and took her hand.

"*Elle va bien ici.*"

They walked silently, still holding hands, back to the cottage. A little while later, as she waited with him at the bus-stop, Margot made him promise to come and see her again.

"Maybe you will come to London," he said. "We can also meet there, maybe for a meal."

"Why not?"

Back at the cottage, she stood in front of a mirror in the little living room.

"Charlie, Charlie," she sighed, "why can't you be here to protect me and keep me on the straight and narrow?"

She went to the telephone and called Kay Lawton.

"Enjoy yourself, Margot," Kay told her. "You're old enough and wise enough to keep control of the situation."

Margot laughed. "I wish I had your confidence in me, Kay! It's not that I really see myself leaping into bed with someone, although who knows how long one can keep up this nun-like life? My problem is that when I see a man as gorgeous and seductive as Edmond, my nerves go completely to pieces. I get hot flushes and start dropping plates and tripping over rugs. I was never like this before. My *sang froid* seems to have deserted me, and I suppose it's something to do with this enforced abstinence. Edmond behaved like a perfect gentleman through it all, which unnerved me even more."

"Beware a Frenchman behaving like a perfect gentleman. If he wasn't interested in getting somewhere with you, he'd flirt with you right away, and outrageously, because he'd have nothing to lose. Did he ask to see you again?"

"He said that when I decided I could face London again, I should let him know and we'd have lunch together. Not exactly the pitch of a man lusting desperately after me."

"Gallic cunning. You've read your French literature, so you told me. So you should know all about it. Anyway, give me a call if you need help."

"Dear Kay. Your brand of help is guaranteed to land me in trouble before I know what's hit me."

"Always happy to oblige."

Repairing to the kitchen to wash the dishes, Margot began to ponder the revisions she might decide to make in her attitude toward Edmond. Following Katie's death, she had looked upon him as someone who, through his sharing of the horror of that night, had gained a special entrée into the Moore family circle, as if he had been a long-standing friend of all of them. But Kay was right; she had to look at him differently now.

On the night of 10th May, Edmond thought the world was coming to an end. So did Denise, his little Bretonne, snuggling her warm, plump body closer against the lean, taut frame of her naughty captain. The champagne, sipped between each change of position – *mon Dieu!* How many different positions did the captain know? – had at first made her drowsy, but now the banging, crashing, shaking and thundering of the raid was keeping her on edge, and the fingers of one small hand tugged at the sparse hair on the captain's chest at each new explosion. When the ceiling shook, the patter of plaster falling onto the linoleum floor of her Bayswater basement apartment elicited a throaty *merde!* from her as she pulled the covers higher around her head.

Edmond lay silently, thinking of Margot. He was relieved that, this being a weekend, she would certainly be down at the cottage with her father, away from this deadly bombardment. To his knowledge, she had anyway been only once to London since his visit to her. They had met for a drink at the Ritz, and the conversation had been stilted. She had talked mainly about Charlie and had seemed nervous. All in all it had been an unsatisfactory encounter, and she had left him puzzled and disappointed. Maybe he was wasting his time. On the other hand he was finding it more and more difficult to free his mind of her, and by now he was simply not trying to do so. Clearly for better or for worse, he was going to persevere.

"You'll have to stay till morning, won't you?" said Denise in her croaking voice, the product of a recent childhood spent shrieking at and with eight younger brothers and sisters and her short-tempered parents, compounded by the inhalation of two packets of Gitanes a day since the age of sixteen.

Edmond glanced at his watch; it was nearly three and the raid was showing no signs of slackening. How many had they sent over tonight, for goodness sake?

"I'm not moving," he said in a tired voice.

She giggled. "Well, a part of you is."

She was gently forcing a hand between their locked thighs. Edmond felt no obligation whatsoever to let her be the beneficiary of his thoughts about Margot, but the matter was now literally in Denise's grasping hands, and by the time it was in her small, eager mouth, he saw no further point in being selfish, especially to an exiled compatriot.

Shortly after dawn, the raid stopped, and a little before eight o'clock Edmond abandoned a protesting Denise and climbed up the outside steps onto Inverness Terrace. It was a sunny day, but a thick black pall of smoke hanging over the city was blocking out most of the sun's rays. The grimly familiar smell of burning buildings filled the air, and ragged petals of ash floated in zigzag patterns to the ground. He found a cab and directed it to his Bolton Place address. As they circled round the inner perimeter of Hyde Park, the cabbie recited the details of the night's devastation. Almost the whole of the City of London and the docks to the east had been – and over a great area still were – ablaze. Westminster Abbey, St Paul's, the House of Commons and Scotland Yard had all been hit. The ever-suffering working-class inhabitants of crowded East and West Ham and Silvertown had taken another terrible beating. All the Thames bridges and eight of the nine main railway stations were out of action, and the main telephone exchange had been destroyed. Edmond felt dizzy listening to the appalling litany.

"We can't take this much longer, guv," said the cabbie

with conviction. "If I didn't hate the bleedin' Germans so much, I'd say let 'em occupy us. At least they wouldn't be shittin' on their bleedin' selves every night, now would they?"

"Personally, I don't recommend the Germans as occupiers," said Edmond as he paid the fare. "Anything is better than that."

The cabbie shrugged his shoulders and drove off.

None of the survivors of that murderous raid in which, as it turned out, more than fourteen hundred Londoners died, could have known at the time that that was to be the last major bombing of any English city. It would have made all the more poignant the memorial service which a saddened Edmond attended for the jovial and fearless Gerald Anstey and his twittering Nora who had been blown to bits in a taxi returning from a dinner party in Greenwich. Some six weeks were to pass before it became clear to the battered and dispirited public just why the raids had stopped.

When Margot came down to the kitchen of Verbena Cottage on the morning of Sunday, 23rd June to fix a leisurely breakfast for her father, she found him dressed in a grey business suit, sipping a cup of coffee.

"Hitler's invaded Russia," he said quietly. "It was on the seven o'clock news. I'm wanted back at the embassy."

"*Russia*? What sort of a maniac is he?"

"That at least accounts for the end of the blitz. He must have switched the whole of the Luftwaffe to the east."

"Poor Father! The weather's so great and you do badly need a rest. Hitler's timing is just lousy."

"Let's indeed hope so, sweetheart. If the Red Army can hold him off until winter, he may learn the same awful lesson that Napoleon learned."

"Will this bring us into the war?"

"No chance. There are enough people back home in Congress, like our Representative Halder, who'd get one helluva kick out of seeing the Reds take a whipping from Hitler." Moore drained his coffee cup and rose. "I'm sorry to have to ask you to use precious gas for a ride to the station when there's no shopping to be done. I'm getting the ten o'clock. Can we make it?"

"Of course. Relax. I'll be ready in fifteen minutes."

After a hurried breakfast, Margot dressed, and as she did so she took the decision to spend a couple of days of the following week in London. For one thing she wanted to go to her hairdresser. For another, Mrs Watts would be going on holiday and she wanted to make sure that her father would be properly supplied with food, fresh clothes and linen. And then, of course, there was Edmond. Since their meeting at the Ritz, which she knew she had handled badly, she had spoken to him only twice, briefly, on the telephone, on both occasions excusing herself from making a trip to London to see him. She had spent a day with Kay and had again told her that the mental promise she had made to Charlie not to seek out temptation was becoming harder and harder to keep, but she was still persevering. That was loyal of her, Kay said, but scarcely realistic, and certainly not very healthy. Then, in the ensuing days, Margot began to reassess the situation, not least because Edmond had not called her in nearly two weeks, and that was beginning to irritate her.

She unhooked a beige cotton frock from a hanger and began to rummage in a drawer for suitable underwear. Just as well she didn't have a lover for the moment, she thought; her underwear looked too worn and boring for words. She found nothing appealing in the London shops; the war had seen to that. And she couldn't very well write to her mother asking her to send sexy bras, garter belts and panties. She'd want to know why. She threw some underwear onto the bed, slipped out of her bathrobe and nightgown and stood in front of the long mirror. She struck a three-quarter profile pose, left hand on hip, right hand sweeping her hair up over her right temple, left foot on the toes with knee bent: the classic pin-up pose.

"Not bad, Margot. In fact, damned good," she said out loud.

She noted with approval how nicely flat her stomach remained, and how slim her thighs. The work in the garden, her daily bicycling, and the diet of her own garden produce was keeping her in excellent shape. She cupped a hand under her left breast, weighing its firm fullness, and sighed.

What a waste! What a waste of a *great* body! Damn you, Charlie, for going and getting yourself caught. How long is this body expected to go unappreciated and untouched?

She spread her legs apart and putting a hand down between them started a gentle massage. Why should I deny this to Edmond if he asks for it, she thought as the massaging grew more urgent and her forefinger pushed deeper. I was probably going to do it with Luke, the pilot, until he ruined everything. Why don't you just ask for it, Edmond? Ask for it, damn you! It's wartime; everything's allowed in wartime! Breathless, and gritting her teeth, her thighs quivering, she felt the orgasm swell and explode in her. Then she sank down onto the bed, panting.

Moments later, she heard her father's footsteps crunching on the gravel driveway in front of the garage. She called out that she would be down immediately and rapidly started to dress.

"I'll be coming up to London for two or maybe three days next week," she told him as she settled behind the wheel of the car.

"Well, I'm delighted. It'll do you good. I have an invitation to dine with the Garlands on Wednesday. I know they'll be thrilled to have you along if you care to accompany your old father."

"Of course. Maybe I can find some work to do in London if the bombing is really over. I know someone at the British Red Cross."

"Sure, why not?" He patted her on the knee. "I'm truly proud of you, honey. You've come through this nightmare just wonderfully."

"So have you, Father."

"Charlie's a damn lucky man to have a girl like you to come home to when all this is over."

Margot ground the gears noisily as she turned onto the main road to Windsor. The grating matched the jarring of her thoughts as images of Charlie and Edmond collided in her mind. Why in hell couldn't she make up her mind what to do? Just a few minutes ago she was committing the most exquisite mental adultery with Edmond, and now her father's mention of Charlie had triggered off new pangs of conscience.

After delivering her father to Windsor railway station, she tried to set her confused thoughts in order and draw up a plan of action for dealing with Edmond. Gradually she reached the conclusion that she would do best to leave the ball in Edmond's court. She'd make herself available, as a friend. She'd tell him that she liked him but didn't want any emotional involvement. He ought to be able to understand that that excluded love – her heart was with Charlie – but not necessarily sex. She couldn't spell that out; he'd have to work it out for himself. And she might refuse him. By maintaining her options, she could keep her conscience quiet. For the time being, at least.

She called Edmond as soon as she reached the cottage.

"I've decided I need to come and spend some time in London. Well, I'll be there on Wednesday and Thursday . . . No, I'm dining with my father and my in-laws Wednesday; how about lunch? . . . That would be nice. I'll be there at one. *Au revoir.*"

"I'm sorry, Edmond, I've been talking too much and you've been too polite to stop me." Margot looked guiltily at her barely-touched food. He had been so solicitous in ordering the dish just as she liked it, and now she had let it get cold.

Edmond gestured dismissal of her apology.

"No, it's true," she went on. "I've been babbling on, and it's all trivial and I'm probably boring you stiff." She took a sip of white wine. "It's a sort of defence because although I need to have a serious conversation with you about us, I keep wanting to postpone it. I'm sorry; maybe that was an odd thing to say. I'm not expressing myself very well, I'm afraid."

She blushed at her own words, and then, flashing him a quick, nervous smile, she began to delve in her purse for cigarettes.

"Please, Margot, you must not for one moment think that I am trying to put you in an awkward position."

"Dear Edmond, you're so kind and understanding, and so wickedly handsome in that uniform. Who could resist you without the will-power of a saint?" She leaned forward to let him light her cigarette. "The truth is that you're putting me in an awkward position without probably being conscious of it. I came here today to tell you that I want your friendship and companionship and will give the same in return, but that I don't want an emotional entanglement with you or with anyone else. Does that make sense?"

"Yes, it does."

"The trouble is, Edmond, I just don't know whether you're the sort of person who can stand that type of limited relationship."

Edmond thought for a moment and decided that exemplary caution wrapped in a little humour was what his longer term interests now called for. He gave her a broad smile.

"You just have to think of me as the typical American's idea of a typical Frenchman: an incurable chaser after beautiful women, with a heart big enough to accommodate whatever number of conquests he thinks he has made."

Margot laughed.

"No, seriously," he continued. "I find you a most enchanting woman and I love your company. Who would not? But at the same time, I respect the fact you are married, and I sincerely hope that your Charlie comes back safely to you. If in the meantime I appear to behave a little bit too much like the proverbial French lover, you must slap me down like you would a naughty dog!"

"Worse; I'll lock you in a kennel and throw away the key."

He smiled. "Yes, I was always told American women were very tough."

"But they have a soft side to them, too. You just have to appeal to it. For example, you could order me a sumptuous dessert."

Edmond hailed a waiter. He was beginning to feel that victory might not be so far away as he had imagined. He wished he could order some champagne, but unhappily he was short of funds for the moment. He really must stop buying champagne for Denise, he admonished himself. She certainly wasn't worth it.

Half an hour later, he saw Margot off in a cab. They embraced briefly on parting and promised to keep in touch. Edmond now set off on foot for Carlton Gardens, the new Headquarters of the Free French, a ten-minute walk away. As he strode down St James's Street, he congratulated himself on his handling of Margot. The more she protested that she did not want an affair with him, the more certain he became that that was exactly what she did want, and that his gentlemanly responses were heightening her frustration to the point where she would soon be ready to capitulate to a proposal that they become lovers. All in all, the situation was full of promise.

As he passed through the heavily sandbagged entrance to the headquarters in Carlton Gardens and acknowledged the salute of the Free French sentry, he turned his mind reluctantly to military matters. Delicate negotiations in which he was engaged with the British to secure a new supply of arms were on the verge of collapse. All had been going well at the start. Then British fury over what was seen as particularly high-handed behaviour on the part of General de Gaulle in Syria had burst over Carlton Gardens, affecting almost every aspect of Free French-British cooperation. There were indeed times when Edmond wished his hero had a rather lighter touch with the British, and this was one of them. He reached his office fifteen minutes ahead of the hour scheduled for an emergency meeting to coordinate the Free French effort to save the arms talks. He found, however, a different type of emergency waiting for him.

"Passy wants to see you the moment you come in," said the clerk in the adjoining office. "He's already called twice."

Why on earth would the head of Free French Intelligence want him in such a hurry? Edmond retraced his steps to the main staircase. For reasons that he could not fathom, he had a slightly uneasy feeling.

André Derwavrin, *nom de guerre* "Colonel Passy", a twenty-nine-year-old engineer officer now head of the Bureau de Contre-Espionnage, Renseignements et d'Action (BCRA), rose and shook Edmond's hand. Fairhaired, with a high forehead and intently focused eyes, Dewavrin was known as a tough, resourceful, hard-driving operator who happened also to be a highly articulate intellectual. Edmond had dealt with him on a number of occasions and had quickly gained a healthy respect for him. He hoped that he was not now about to find himself on the wrong side of the man.

"Let me come straight to the point, Lemonnier, as we are both particularly busy today. I have asked that you be released from your present duties for transfer to the BCRA. It would be effective as soon as your arms talks have been concluded. Would you have any objection?"

"None whatever, *mon Commandant*. I would be honoured to join you."

"In a couple of days I will have time to discuss your precise duties with you. In the meantime I merely wanted your transfer settled. My selection of you was, of course, very carefully made, and I look forward to your loyal assistance."

"Thank you, sir."

Edmond returned to his office in a state of elation. Working for Passy! Only those whose utter devotion to de Gaulle had been fully recognized were ever recruited to his intelligence service. These were the elite, who could be trusted to do anything they were ordered to in furthering de Gaulle's cause. *This* was the type of war Edmond wanted to fight!

He gathered up his files on the arms negotiations and hurried down to the basement meeting room. Through an open door he spotted Denise at work at her typewriter, the inevitable cigarette drooping from one corner of her sensuous little mouth, her full breasts encased in a canary-yellow blouse vibrating absurdly as she pounded the keys. There'll be less time for you from now on, *ma petite*, thought Edmond. What with Margot and the BCRA, his hands were going to be more than full.

*

That evening, Margot accompanied her father to dinner with the Garlands at their Westminster home. They were delighted to find her looking so well but chided her gently for not coming to see them more often.

"Come to Bowes Court any weekend you want to," said Sir Walter. "We manage to keep it pretty comfortable still, and the country air is good. Bring your father with you." Margot promised she would. "Ah, here's the Lord Chancellor arriving," he said, taking her by the arm. "Come and meet him. I see your father's already latched onto his compatriot, Mr Murrow, the radio correspondent. You know him already, I'm sure."

Margot was dazzled by the company that evening, and it seemed that she dazzled them in return. The chain-smoking Mr Murrow seemed particularly taken by her and asked her probing questions about what it was like to be the American wife of a British prisoner of war. She suddenly found herself feeling uncomfortable, even a little ashamed, at the recollection of her conversation with Edmond at lunch that day. What was she expected to say to Murrow? "I distract myself by discussing over lunch with a handsome Free French officer whether or not I should have an affair with him. . . ."

This was the world in which she fitted best, she told herself as she looked around the candle-lit table. Here were persons of political power and social eminence who found her attractive and interesting. Here she was, not yet twenty-one years old, being accepted into the circles of the mighty. The Lord Chancellor had told her how impressed he was by her views on countering neutralism back in the States (how many times had she listened to her father on that issue!), and a lady Member of Parliament had asked her to come and talk to the wives in her constituency who had husbands overseas. But she was there not because she was the pretty daughter of an American diplomat, but because she was the daughter-in-law of a prominent English politician. She owed it all to Charlie, so how could she let herself get so pre-occupied with what might or might not be her relationship with a Free French captain about whom she knew so little? He had no place in all of this.

"You looked radiant and you were obviously enjoying yourself," said Harland delightedly as he escorted his daughter home in a cab at the end of the evening.

"It was very good fun, Father. I was a bit scared to start with, but everyone was so nice. I really will get that job at the Red Cross, not just because it will be nice doing something useful, but because it will give me more opportunities, I hope, to spend evenings like this one."

"I'm sure the Garlands will appreciate that. They're proud of you and very fond of you, and you'd do well to spend a little more time with them."

"I will, Father."

But that night, as she lay in bed trying to get to sleep, her thoughts kept coming back to Edmond, and when she awoke in the morning, she realized, with a mixture of pleasure and concern, that she had just been dreaming erotically of him.

16

Margot had thought of going to work as a volunteer, probably part-time, almost immediately, but an agitated letter from her mother imploring her to wait until it was certain that the blitz was truly over caused her to delay. Her decision was taken reluctantly: she was getting bored at Verbena Cottage, but she needed an excuse to move back to London now that Mrs Watts had returned to Hill Street to look after her employer. Margot could not claim to be indispensable to her father's domestic well-being anymore, and so, for the rest of the summer she divided her days between the cottage at Clewer and the Hill Street house, and thus managed to see Edmond from time to time.

Although he never said as much to her, she had the growing impression that he was in love with her. It suited her well that he never declared his true feelings because she simply did not want to confront the situation openly if it were indeed the case. She surmised that he was holding back from telling her that he was in love for fear of losing her, as well he might. She prayed, therefore, that his restraint might be maintained, so that they could continue to behave towards each other as very good friends who rejoiced in each other's company.

Harland Moore remained happily unaware of the potentially dangerous undercurrents in what he considered to be an unexceptional friendship between his daughter and the young Frenchman, and as he hurried to keep a lunch engagement on a bright September day, he was thinking how well Margot was handling this lengthy and unnatural separation from her husband.

Moore's host that day was a British Foreign Office official, Maurice Drake by name, whom he had known some fifteen years ago *en poste* in Paris. Their paths had not crossed again until the summer of 1939 when they had met at a cocktail party in London. Although they had no official relationship, they had since made it their practice to lunch together every so often to exchange views on the war and on Anglo-American relations. Moore found the stocky, sandy-haired Scotsman well-informed and forthcoming, and he hoped that Drake found him as stimulating in return. Their lunches alternated between the Connaught and the Travellers' Club, and today it was at the latter. In the morning room he found his host bent over a table by the tall windows, turning the pages of *Country Life*.

"Maurice, I'm sorry to have kept you waiting."

"You're not late, old boy," said Drake, slipping off a pair of gold-rimmed spectacles and dropping them down behind a voluminous cream silk handkerchief in his breast pocket.

"You'll take a Scotch and soda, won't you?" He pressed a bell in the wall and led Moore to a pair of leather armchairs in a deserted corner of the room. An elderly member, shuffling towards the same corner, bowed to their superior speed with a glare.

"How fares the Republic?" asked Drake as they settled down to await their drinks. They chatted for a while and then, drinks consumed, climbed the broad staircase to the elegantly chandeliered dining room overlooking Pall Mall. As they ate they talked animatedly of developments on the Russian and North African fronts and of war-related activities in their two countries' respective legislatures. They were discussing the increasing threat to American shipping in the Atlantic posed by the ever-expanding fleet of U-Boats, when the head waiter discreetly intervened to recommend some fine Cheddar on which the club had been most fortunate to lay its hands.

"Bring it here!" said Drake, and turned to his guest. "How about bending your rules and joining me in a glass of decent port? Good cheese without port is a little sad, I always think."

212

"Why not? My work schedule this afternoon isn't going to result in any diplomatic history being made."

"The Taylor '18, Mr Drake?"

"The Taylor '18."

The head waiter hurried off.

"The last bottle of Taylor '18 I drank was under rather sad circumstances," said Drake. "My wine merchant, Gerald Anstey of Burgess and Blunt in Bury Street – maybe you knew him – got himself and his wife killed in a raid back in May; that very big one that rang down the curtain. In his will he said that he wanted a group of his closest friends to give a dinner party at his club after the funeral and enjoy some of the best wines from his private cellar. Every bottle, right through to the Taylor '18, was a gem. A pity the wartime food was so unworthy of them."

Drake paused while the cheese and port were served, then he went on.

"I met a young Frenchman there: one of de Gaulle's boys, called Lemonnier. He told me his is the Lemonnier family that owns that quite respectable St Julien vineyard, Lachaise-Laurent. I believe he knows your daughter."

Moore swallowed a mouthful of cheese and looked curiously at his host.

"Did he tell you that?"

"No, but I remember reading that he had been with your two daughters at the Café de Paris that night."

"Yes, he was. I've met him myself only a couple of times, I think. He seemed a nice enough fellow."

"I understand he's quite close to de Gaulle's inner circle. He was one of the early ones to join him."

"Yes, so Margot has told me."

"Does she know him well?"

Moore paused. He thought he recognized a trend in the conversation.

"Forgive me for asking, Maurice, but are you probing?"

Drake began assembling flakes of Cheddar on a biscuit, and took his time answering.

"I think you ought to know," he said eventually, looking Moore straight in the eye, "that we are rather

213

interested in the young captain. Our information is that he is working for the intelligence service."

"So what has that to do with me?" asked Moore as affably as possible.

"Let me put it this way, Harland. You know as well as I do that no Allied leader, if that's what we should call him, irritates either your President or my Prime Minister more than our friend de Gaulle. In fact, as we earlier agreed, over Syria he's been nothing less than a bloody menace." Moore nodded assent, and Drake continued. "Our problem is that we never know what he's going to do next."

"I would have said the exact opposite," interrupted Moore. "His arrogant behaviour in Damascus was wholly in keeping with his character."

"He's not always that predictable. Look at his handling of the Muselier affair. Besides, he seems to welcome well-publicized altercations with Churchill; that way he believes he's demonstrating to the world that he's nobody's puppet. That's what makes him dangerous, and that's why we want to know more about his thinking and his plans. At the moment we're particularly interested in his efforts to build up his own resistance forces in occupied France which would owe total allegiance to him and to no one else."

"And so?" Moore had a nasty suspicion of what was to come next.

"It brings me back to your daughter, Margot. If she knows Lemonnier well enough, she might possibly pick up a few pointers that could be useful not just to our people but to yours as well."

Moore put down his port glass.

"I wish you hadn't brought this up, Maurice."

"I wish I hadn't had to."

"You know I wouldn't involve Margot in something like that. Besides, you seem to forget that she's a very happily married young lady, albeit forcibly separated for the time being. You're just reading far too much into the extent of their acquaintanceship."

"I thought they knew each other quite well," said Drake nonchalantly. "But anyway, let's not let this excellent port go to waste." He held the decanter out to Moore, who declined.

Over the next few minutes they managed to talk of other matters in a rather awkward way, and Moore was relieved when Drake looked at his watch and mentioned an engagement at the Foreign Office twenty minutes hence. Downstairs in the club's front hall, after retrieving their hats, Drake paused before the double doors leading to the steps down to Pall Mall.

"Harland, I do hope you were not unduly offended by my line of questioning." He stared intently into the interior of his bowler hat as if half expecting something to emerge from it.

"No offence taken, Maurice. I'm sure you were duty-bound to ask. But I think I ought to let you know that I am very protective of my remaining daughter and don't want her involved in anything like that."

Drake was still standing watch over the brilliantine-stained inside of his hat. He spoke hesitantly.

"If, by any chance, Harland, you should just happen to hear from her anything, you know, without soliciting it, of course, that could be of interest . . ." He left the sentence unfinished.

"Maurice, I enjoyed the lunch enormously, as always. We'll stay in touch."

Harland pressed his grey homburg onto his head and pushed on the glass door. Drake followed him out onto the steps where they shook hands and smiled a little stiffly before going their separate ways.

That afternoon, Moore did some discreet checking at the embassy. Yes, he was told, there were excellent ground for believing that Mr Drake was a senior intelligence officer. Moore felt no particular relief that his suspicions had been confirmed. He kept recalling now one particular remark of Drake's which, at the time, he had barely digested! "I thought they knew each other quite well." Lemonnier had never mentioned Margot to Drake when they met at the wine merchant's wake, so on what did he base his belief that they knew each other quite well? Moore came to an unhappy and provocative conclusion. The British were watching Lemonnier, and in

215

doing so were seeing Margot with him. Obviously rather frequently, as well. There was now no alternative; he would have to discuss it with her.

While Moore was agonizing in his office, Margot was returning in high spirits to Hill Street. She and Edmond had been to a midday concert at the National Gallery, followed by a pub lunch, and over sandwiches and beer Edmond had told her how wonderful it would be if they could go away for a weekend together somewhere in the country.

So Edmond was at last making his move! Margot bit into her sandwich to give herself time to think. Her skin was tingling at the thought of what must be going on in his mind. He was drawing her to the Rubicon, and inviting her to cross. She had been waiting for this moment, and she knew now that she was going to cross. But she didn't want to say that to him in so many words right now. She wondered if he already had some discreet country hotel in mind. His next remark surprised her.

"We could stay with friends, so that we'd be chaperoned, and you'd have nothing to worry about."

"My friends are all Charlie's friends too. They'd scarcely approve of my arriving for a weekend with a handsome Frenchman in tow."

"But your friend, Kay, whom you talk about so much. She doesn't know Charlie. And she has a place in the country, doesn't she?"

She smiled. Edmond had it all worked out, and he wasn't about to let her off the hook.

"Yes, she has a country house. I'll have to think about it carefully, Edmond. In my position I have to."

As soon as she'd finished speaking she knew that she'd given the game away. And so did he.

"You want us to be together then, but you're just afraid of what people might say. Isn't that it?"

"You're jumping to conclusions."

"The right ones," he said, smiling.

She smiled back. "I'll let you know. I can't answer you right now."

*

That evening, before her father's return, she called Kay Lawton.

"What would you say if I brought Edmond for a weekend?"

"I'd say 'Hallelujah!' It's about time."

"Look, don't read too much into this."

Kay laughed. "Have it your own way, my pet, if you can. I just want you to know that I'm the soul of discretion as a weekend hostess, and the double bed in the guest room is a dream."

"You're sinful, Kay, but I love you. Just don't count on me to live up to your prurient expectations. I may lose my nerve at the last minute, and you may have a furious and frustrated Frenchman rampaging around your house."

"I'll cope. My family's motto is *Nil Nisi Audax*, meaning 'Nothing If Not Bold'. I'll lend it to you for the weekend."

17

The social life of wartime London held no attractions whatsoever for Charles de Gaulle, but the fostering of good relations with those in positions of influence and authority who might be useful to him required that on occasion he entertain. This he preferred to do at the Connaught Hotel, where he often stayed in mid-week, and where the food was as good as anywhere in the capital. From time to time, Edmond Lemonnier found himself summoned to lunch, usually for no more flattering reason than that his impeccable English could be put to use in seeking support for the General from some influential British politician. On such occasions de Gaulle scarcely acknowledged his presence at the table, as if to remind the young Free French officer that he was there to perform a humble duty for his country rather than to enjoy a good meal in stimulating company. His meal-ticket today turned out to be a jovial and portly Conservative Member of Parliament, Mr Reggie Kempton, who was known to have the ear, whenever he wished, of Mr Eden, the Foreign Secretary. He was also, he told Edmond, a connoisseur of fine claret, and the two were soon exchanging expert views on the most recent pre-war vintages while, across the table, the General was busy giving a lecture in the rudiments of modern tank warfare to a member of the Polish Government in Exile.

Engrossed in congenial discussion, Edmond almost missed Margot's entrance on the arm of her father. As they passed behind de Gaulle's chair, she acknowledged Edmond's rather startled recognition of her with a broad grin. Harland Moore looked fleetingly straight through him. Edmond's line of vision to the table at which Margot and her father were now being seated was largely obstructed by the imposing frame of the General seated diagonally across from him. He waited until his leader was once again engrossed in dissecting his grilled trout, the knife and fork in his strangely feminine hands darting agitatedly about the carcass. He then craned his neck as far as he felt good manners allowed to get a better view of Margot over the General's shoulder.

He noted with a tingle of satisfaction that her honey-blonde hair was swept back over one ear and held in place with a tortoise-shell comb. He had suggested a little hesitantly that she try this style just a few days ago when they had lunched together at the pub near Trafalgar Square, but she had seemed doubtful. Now he also remembered telling her then that he was likely to be lunching with the General at the Connaught today, so she must have persuaded her father to bring her here. It was, after all, the nearest good restaurant to the American Embassy. Margot looked up and, seeing Edmond's face peering awkwardly over de Gaulle's shoulder, began to giggle and took refuge behind her menu.

Reggie Kempton followed Edmond's gaze.

"Moore from the American Embassy, isn't it? Who's he with? Do you know her? Stunning girl."

"Yes, I know her. It's his daughter, sir. I met her through her sister. In fact I was with them both that night at the Café de Paris. You probably remember that her sister was among the killed."

"Ghastly affair. Glad you survived at any rate. And your friend as well." He nodded in the direction of Margot before impaling a brussel sprout on his fork. "My wife lost a godson there, day before he was to join his regiment. Took them some time to find an arm that had been blown off him. Had a valuable family signet ring on the hand, you see. But someone had spotted it first and pulled it off. Incredible."

Edmond winced and looked anxiously across the table at the General. The remnants of the trout still held his undivided attention.

"It's almost unbelievable how anyone can be so

dazzling and vivacious after what she has been through in the last year." Edmond spoke in a half whisper and seemingly to himself. "Husband a prisoner of war; baby lost in a miscarriage; sister dead in the blitz. How much can she take?"

"Obviously a great deal." The Englishman raised his glass in Margot's direction as if in a toast. "If their men are anything like as tough as that, the sooner they get into this war, the better off we shall all be. Not so, General?"

De Gaulle's hooded eyes bore down coldly on the Member of Parliament. "We shall see, monsieur." They then reverted to the skeletal remains on his plate.

"Please don't be upset." Margot looked imploringly at her father. "I know he sometimes lunches here with the General, and we happen to have hit a day when he is doing just that. But they're out of earshot, so you can easily say to me what it is that you want to say about him."

Moore drummed nervously on the tablecloth with a fork as he studied the menu.

"I'm not upset. It's just that this fellow seems to be everywhere in our lives, and I'm not at all sure that it's a good thing."

"Oh, come on, Father, you're exaggerating a bit, aren't you? He's a friend who's shared in the most horrible tragedy to hit our family within living memory. He's also a young man exiled from his own country who needs and appreciates some warm human relationships." She found herself enjoying the task of pulling the wool over her father's eyes. You bet he'll appreciate *one* warm human relationship! "So why shouldn't he be our good friend?"

"It just isn't as simple as all that, Margot. His boss over there is the subject of continuous and growing controversy and unease in US and British official circles. He's a courageous and patriotic man, we all agree. But he's also one hell of a troublemaker, and that suggests to me – "

"Just a minute, just a minute!" Margot felt her anger rising as she interrupted her father. "What exactly has that got to do with my being nice to one of the hundreds of Frenchmen working for him here, who happens to have been the boyfriend of my slaughtered sister!''

Moore placed a hand over Margot's clenched fist which was grinding some imaginary object of her wrath into the table-top. ''Take it easy, honey,'' he said softly. ''There's something you don't know which I had not wanted to bother you with, but I think maybe that it's best you *do* know so that you can better judge for yourself how to handle your young friend over there.''

''I'm all ears, Father. He's a Nazi spy? He's a killer rapist? Maybe only a blackmailer?''

Moore sighed. ''Will you do your father the small favour of hearing him out calmly? Please, Margot.''

''So tell me!'' She crushed a cracker between her fingers and the palm of her hand and let the bits fall back onto the plate.

''British Intelligence are very interested to know much more about what's going on in de Gaulle's camp. That's understandable; we'd like to know a lot more ourselves. They know that Lemonnier is close to the centre of de Gaulle's operations even if he isn't one of the real decision-makers. But at least he's an observer of what is happening. They also know that he is friendly with us, as a family, that is. And particularly with you. Believe it or not, they actually asked me if you would be willing to pass on any information you might gather about de Gaulle's activities through your contacts with Edmond. Of course I told them that it was out of the question. They said that as the wife of a British army officer, you might consider it something in the nature of a patriotic duty to help them in this way. But I wasn't buying that!''

Margot was stunned. The British wanted her, an American, to spy on the Free French . . . The grieving grass widow becomes a key player in an international intrigue. Wouldn't *that* be something to write home about! . . . But those were thoughts to keep to herself. In front of her father, righteous indignation was called for.

''How utterly contemptible!'' She put as much venom into her voice as she could muster. ''Not only contemptible; comical as well. They're asking the daughter of a diplomat from a neutral country to spy for her husband's far-from-neutral government on its closest comrade in arms. Worthy of the Marx Brothers, Father!"

A hovering waiter interrupted their exchange, and they ordered quickly. Then Harland took a deep breath and looked his daughter squarely in the eye.

"Margot, I have to tell you that the British are having Edmond followed, and that means that they know when you two are meeting."

"But, for God's sakes, Father – "

"I know, I know. You meet only rarely, and when you do, it's openly, as good friends, and nothing more. But I think that in view of their rather special interest, you ought to stop seeing him."

"Father, maybe to you I'm only your little blonde daughter, but I'm telling you that this is absolutely not the right way to handle this situation. You should go straight to Winant, and he should go straight to Eden, and Eden should tell whoever's responsible to get those idiot intelligence people off my back!" Her voice had risen, and Moore looked anxiously around to see if they were attracting undue attention. It appeared that they were not. He shrugged his shoulders.

"I'm only trying to help and protect you, honey. But you're a grown girl now, a married woman. I have to let you make your own decisions, and I believe that you have the sound judgement not to make wrong ones in this case." He forced a not very convincing smile.

"Then," said Margot, "I suggest we enjoy our lunch and agree that I will handle this matter in my own way."

"Just remember that you've got an experienced diplomat for a father and he hopes that you will not only respect his wishes to get in his two cents' worth of advice, but that you will also turn to him when you feel you need help."

Margot clutched her father's forearm and squeezed it. "Don't fret so much, you old worrier. I'm not going to embarrass you by calling the Prime Minister. Just tell your cloak-and-dagger friends that they're wasting their time. If they want to spy on de Gaulle, they should get themselves invited to his lunches here at the Connaught."

Moore laughed and lifted his knife and fork.

"Why is it, General," Reggie Kempton was asking, "that the Americans are refusing diplomatic recognition of your National Committee?"

The General lit a cigarette and left it hanging precariously from the corner of his mouth as he spoke.

"Because they are listening to the wrong people. The representation of Free France is not yet strong in the United States, while the emissaries of Vichy there never cease to denounce de Gaulle. But America will wake up to an understanding of who represents the real France and who does not, and you must help her wake up soon."

Edmond was relieved at the mildness of the General's reply. At the last lunch to which he had been bidden, he had witnessed his leader deliver himself of such a scathing attack on the United States that a noted British diplomat, whose wife happened to be a Bostonian, pleaded heartburn and left the lunch table, never to return. Kempton now asked de Gaulle what chance he saw of America eventually extending Lend Lease to Free France, but at that moment a waiter began serving apple pie, which prompted the General to extol the superiority of Normandy apples over all others, leaving Kempton's question unanswered.

"What do you think then, young man?" The Englishman turned expectantly to Edmond. Edmond waited until the General was once more in conversation with his Polish neighbour before speaking in a low voice.

"We hear that the State Department may receive our Finance Commissioner, Pleven, any day now. It is at least a step in the right direction."

"That is pure speculation!" de Gaulle barked the words out in French, startling the Pole who was in mid-sentence and causing Edmond to put down his wine glass rather unsteadily under the General's piercing stare. He struggled to find his voice, which had taken refuge somewhere in the pit of his stomach.

223

"Of course, *mon Général*," he finally managed, but the General had already turned back to the Pole and was waiting impatiently for him to remember what it was he had been saying before the interruption. The General's ADC grinned encouragingly at Edmond and offered him a cigarette.

"Sorry if I raised a prickly question there," said Kempton, and changed the subject to the worsening news from the Russian front.

Through the remainder of the meal, Edmond's mind was far from the imperilled cities of Leningrad and Moscow. He was wondering if he might find time that afternoon to see Margot alone for a little while, but he had a problem. The National Committee would be holding its weekly meeting the following morning at Carlton Gardens, and that meant that this afternoon there would, as usual, be a meeting at BCRA headquarters in Duke Street, chaired by Colonel Passy, to finalize the weekly intelligence briefing paper to be set before the Committee. As a major contributor to that paper, Edmond could not afford not to be there. The meeting would most likely be over soon after five, but Margot, he recalled, was going to a special viewing for American diplomats of a new movie, *Citizen Kane*, scheduled for six o'clock at the embassy. There just wasn't going to be time, and the following morning she would be returning early to Windsor for the weekend. Once again he leaned back in his chair and craned sideways to get a glimpse of her. He saw that she was engaged in animated conversation with her father. He maintained his unnatural posture for as long as he felt he could without drawing the General's attention to himself, but Margot did not look his way. He slumped back, disappointed, and turned his attention once more to the conversation at hand.

"I regret you are in error, monsieur." It was the ADC talking. "It was not Napoleon's troops who set fire to Moscow; it was the carelessness of the inhabitants that started a blaze in the bazaar."

The General nodded approvingly, a motion which detached an inch of ash from the tip of the cigarette drooping from his mouth and deposited it on the sleeve of his khaki uniform. He brushed it off, stubbed out the cigarette and rose to his feet.

"Gentlemen, I thank you for coming," he said, and started to shake hands with his guests. A moment later, followed by his ADC, he strode from the dining room, bestowing a glance of barely perceptible recognition on the *maître d'hôtel* as he passed. Margot was now beckoning to Edmond, but Kempton took him aside.

"General de Gaulle obviously *wants* Lend Lease, doesn't he?"

"He's desperate for it, sir," replied Edmond as he signalled to Margot that he would join her and her father in a moment.

"Well, is there anything I can do to help?" continued the Member of Parliament.

"We know that the Foreign Secretary is in favour of it, but we suspect at the same time that the Prime Minister is reluctant to push President Roosevelt too hard on it; we all know what he thinks of the General."

"I'll talk to Anthony about it; that's the least I can do. And maybe stir up some back-bench support."

"That would be very helpful, sir." Edmond held out his hand to the Englishman.

"Going to join your friend?" Kempton grinned and nodded in Margot's direction. "Lucky devil! But I promise not to tell Walter when I see him in the House that you've been making eyes at his daughter-in-law all the way through lunch." He gave a fruity laugh, gripped Edmond's hand briefly, then set off rather unsteadily between the tables to the door. The Pole had already gone, and Edmond went straight over to the table where Moore and his daughter were finishing their meal. He shook hands formally with both of them.

"Sit down, Lemonnier," said Moore affably, "and tell us what's on the great leader's mind today."

"Thank you, sir, but I have to hurry back to a meeting."

"Your man, Pleven, is going to Washington again, isn't he? Maybe this time he'll succeed in charming Sumner Welles."

"I certainly hope so." Edmond looked desperately at Margot.

"I'm going to be home at Hill Street all afternoon, Edmond. Can you call me? I need some names of well-to-do French exiles to help me with a hospital charity."

What an elegant little fabrication, thought Edmond. Her resourcefulness delighted him, and he caught the fleeting conspiratorial smile. Damn the intelligence briefing! He found himself staring at the middle button of her off-white silk blouse: it had come unbuttoned. The jacket of her navy blue two-piece suit was slung casually around her shoulders, and the fall of blonde hair almost obscured a diamond brooch, set in the form of a Grenadier Guards badge, on the lapel.

"Well, we won't detain you, then. It was good to see you." Moore proffered his hand.

"I'll certainly telephone you," said Edmond, looking at Margot as he shook Moore's hand. She had an amused smile on her face as he turned and left.

Colonel Passy was irritable that afternoon, and Edmond's written contribution to the intelligence briefing paper had certainly contributed to the irritation. It noted the brief visit to London from France's unoccupied zone of two middle-rank resistance leaders who had reported directly to the head of Britain's Special Operations Executive, the service obtaining intelligence from France. Such a procedure was to be expected in the case of British-controlled resistance fighters, but these two had been recruited by the Free French and assigned to a group in Normandy controlled wholly by Passy. Worse still, the British had spirited them back to France before the BCRA could find out from the men why the SOE now controlled them. As the bearer of the bad tidings, Edmond feared that Passy's wrath would descend on him, a scapegoat at hand being worth two in France. But he was spared, and after imprecations had been poured down on the two resistance men, their entire group in Normandy, and their British seducers in London, the meeting closed and Edmond was glad to get back to the comparative peace and safety of his own office. Those bastards at SOE! he thought as he stood staring out of the window. Who the hell did they think they were, stealing from our network? And as for the two wretches who'd let themselves be seduced by them, it didn't say much for the BCRA that it had been incapable of kidnapping them and bringing them to account. BCRA should play tougher in such situations. There was too much at stake.

Turning from the window, he noticed a sealed white envelope on his desk. He turned it over and at once recognized the cramped handwriting of Denise. The intent of the circuitously phrased message inside was also easily recognizable. The writer was disappointed that the captain had not taken up her most recent invitation to let her cook him supper at either his place or hers. She would forgive him for making her wait ten days for his reply if he would accept right away and fix the date for not later than tomorrow night.

Poor little Denise! Not getting enough sex, it seemed. He stuffed the message in the breast pocket of his tunic, picked his kepi off the top of the filing cabinet, and left the office, locking the door behind him. He took the back stairs in order to improve his chances of not running into the forlorn and deprived little Bretonne and emerged through a side entrance of the building. He hurried to a call-box and dialled Margot's number. It was already five-thirty and he cursed the possibility of having missed her. But he was in luck.

"Edmond, you just caught me on my way out. Listen, if you'd like to you can come with me to Kay's place next weekend. She has her own boyfriend coming."

Her voice was very matter-of-fact.

"I am thrilled, Margot. Of course I will come."

"Good, I'll call you next week and tell you how we get there. Now I've got to run. I don't want to be late for the movie." She rang off.

Edmond stood in the call-box for a moment, marvelling at Margot's coolness. How could she announce what must be one of the biggest decisions in her life with no more passion than if she were telling what she had decided to eat for dinner? These Americans! They really were very like the English.

Margot, meanwhile, set off on foot to cover the short distance from Hill Street to the embassy. She was in high spirits. The final decision to cross the Rubicon had turned out to be not at all difficult to take. Lunch with her father had seen to that. If one was going into the risky business of taking a lover, one might as well take one who was of more than passing interest as well as being devastatingly attractive. And Edmond was getting more interesting by the minute.

18

Margot spent the next seven days quietly at Verbena
Cottage. She started a new flower bed in the garden,
wrote letters to her mother, Larry and her grandparents
at Adamswood, read a Nancy Mitford novel, and worked
at her French vocabulary. She put off writing her next
letter to Charlie until the following week. For reasons
which she could not fathom, not that she tried very hard,
she had a strong feeling that it would be easier to write
guilelessly to him after what was going to happen at
the weekend had happened rather than when it was still
on the horizon. She was most of the time quite relaxed at
the prospect of the coming weekend, but because she
didn't want it to preoccupy her, she made no attempt
to get in touch with Edmond until near the end of the
week when she called him to fix the Friday afternoon
rendezvous.

She had already decided that, at an appropriate moment
during the weekend, she would tell Edmond what her
father had told her about British Intelligence's interest
in him and in his relationship with herself. If they were
going to be seeing each other on a more regular basis after
becoming lovers, they were going to have to be doubly
discreet in their arrangements, and she didn't want him
to think that it was solely her desire to avoid being seen
by friends in his company that necessitated this extra
caution. Moreover, by sharing her father's confidences
with Edmond, she stood to learn more from him about
himself.

On Friday, she took the train to London and went by
taxi to Hill Street. As she turned the key in the front door,

she had a premonition of what was awaiting her: a letter from Charlie lying on the hall table. I might have known it! she said to herself as she carried it and her suitcase up to her room. She was not to be allowed to go through with the weekend without first being confronted with a tangible and very discomforting reminder of her status as Charlie's wife. She sat on the bed and stared morosely at the envelope. It seemed to be an immutable law of life, of hers in particular, that every indulgence, every transgression, carried a price tag, and payment was on the nail; in this case in the hard currency of a poor conscience.

For a moment she thought of leaving the letter unopened until she returned; its arrival was a sufficient jolt already, so why compound the discomfort by seeing his protestations of love in black and white? But that was unnecessarily mean-spirited and cowardly, she decided, so she tore open the envelope. It was brief. He had been delighted with her last letter and with the Conan Doyle volumes which had arrived safely a few days later. The weather had been marvellous, and with the arrival of cricket equipment through the Red Cross they were able to play a game almost every day in a small field recently incorporated into the camp perimeter. Food parcels were coming in more regularly now, and he had regained all the weight lost during his month in solitary. He loved her very much and prayed for her safety. And that was it. She went to her father's study and left the letter on his desk for him to read, and then returned to her room to pack what she needed for the weekend.

She was back at the station promptly for her five forty-five rendezvous with Edmond. At the entrance to the platform she found him leaning against a baggage trolley, engrossed in a copy of the Free French journal, *La France Libre*. She was used to seeing him in uniform, and in the grey double-breasted suit he was now wearing, he looked, she thought, even slimmer and younger than usual. She approached him silently and peeked over the top of his newspaper.

"Captain Lemonnier, I presume."

Edmond quickly folded the paper and kissed her lightly on both cheeks.

"Exactly on time. Don't American women ever keep their men waiting? How disciplined you are!"

"You sound disapproving. Maybe you prefer your women unpredictable and a touch irresponsible."

He smiled. "I don't prefer, but I understand and forgive."

"Guard the suitcases for a moment; I want to get an evening paper."

She walked across to a nearby news-stand and, as she returned, a man browsing casually through a magazine put it back on the counter, and turned slowly to look over his shoulder at the retreating figure. Each time he saw this girl, he recalled Mr Drake's words: "You can't miss her. She's got Hollywood star quality. You know Veronica Lake? Something like that but with her hair not covering half her face." She certainly was a beautiful young woman, and they made a handsome couple, he thought as he watched them pass through the gate onto the platform. He lingered in front of the news-stand until he saw the train move out, then he replaced the magazine on the counter and hurried off to a call-box.

Kay Lawton met her guests at Sunningdale Station in a pony cart. She was accompanied by her latest romantic interest, a young film director making propaganda films about the RAF. His name was Derry Fleming.

"The pony's a bit temperamental and he farts a lot," said Kay as they climbed aboard the cart, "but he's solved my transportation problem. His name's Tommy."

Margot beamed delightedly as they clattered out of the station yard and headed through the town towards the countryside. The light was beginning to fade and Kay slapped at Tommy's broad hindquarters with the reins.

"I haven't yet masked the lamps to meet blackout regulations. A job for you, Derry darling. But don't worry; we'll be home well before dark."

Twenty minutes later they bounced into the small stable yard behind Kay's converted farmhouse. The cart was put away and the sweating pony rubbed down, fed

231

and turned loose in a stubbly paddock behind the stable. As they walked to the front door of the house, Kay pulled Margot aside.

"I'll offer Edmond the single room. I just hope he doesn't actually sleep there."

Margot blushed. "He can if he wants to. I just don't know how it's going to turn out."

"Oh, I do!" said Kay merrily. "That's what this whole weekend is for."

"Don't ask Derry where he got it all from; he might incriminate himself. Just enjoy it." Kay laid the fruits of her lover's foraging on the candle-lit table: gull's eggs, fresh liver paté, river trout, and a Stilton cheese to follow.

"I could get six months for that lot," said Fleming, grinning mischieviously, "not to mention the ham and eggs you'll be getting for breakfast if you choose to get out of bed tomorrow."

"And here's to Edmond," said Margot. "Thanks to him we'll be washing it down with a couple of fine bottles unwittingly donated by Carlton Gardens; so we must toast the General as well."

"And pray he doesn't find out how generous he's been," added Edmond. "I'm too young to die."

In a jovial mood, they sat down to dine. Margot had not felt so happy and relaxed in a long while, and as she looked across the table at pretty, elfin Kay, all giggles and sparkling dark eyes, she silently blessed her for bringing this moment to pass. Beside her, Edmond, animated, bubbling over with anecdotes of life with the Free French that kept them laughing, seemed to her to be more seductive than she had even known him. Derry Fleming caught her eye, cocked his head towards Edmond and nodded approvingly. Margot smiled appreciatively and sipped at her wine. This evening could have only one ending, and her calm contemplation of it was rapidly turning to burning impatience.

By ten o'clock, the table had been cleared and pushed back, and they were dancing to the restful, romantic strains of Ambrose and his orchestra on the phonograph. Margot and Edmond danced on when Kay and Derry eventually sank into a sofa, nestling close in each other's arms. In a moment the music stopped.

"Turn the records over and help yourselves to drinks," said Kay. "I think I'm taking my man upstairs before he gets too sozzled to give satisfaction."

"Speak for yourself, little nymph," said Fleming, draining his Scotch and water. "Or, rather, nympho."

Kay smacked him playfully on the cheek, rose, and pulled him to his feet. "Just turn the lights out when you come up, darlings."

She and her lover disappeared upstairs.

Margot picked up their empty glasses and started towards the kitchen. As she reached the door, she felt Edmond's hands on her shoulder, and she turned to face him. There was an almost childlike look on his face, at once shy and softly appealing. Yet the hand on her shoulder was strong, so that she read the message through his touch rather than his look. She put the two glasses down and immediately his arms enfolded her.

"You were in really sparkling form tonight, Edmond. May I assume that *mon capitaine* is enjoying himself?"

"I certainly am. And you?"

"Doesn't it show?"

He kissed her lightly on the lips.

"On your face, yes. But I never know what's going on in that pretty head of yours."

"Really? Am I such a mystery woman to you?"

"Sometimes I can read your mind."

"Can your read it now?" She stared intently into his deep brown eyes.

"I think so. You are trying to make up your mind whether to say 'yes' or 'no' if I ask you to sleep with me tonight. Correct?"

Margot shook her head and smiled. "Incorrect, Edmond. It's gallant of you to put it that way, but I've already made up my mind. Some time ago." She patted him on the cheek. "As if you didn't know, my Gallic rascal!"

He bent his head, and their lips met for a long, searching kiss.

"Mmm. I like!" she said, pressing her cheek against his

233

and running her fingers through his thick black hair. "Help me turn out the lights, *chéri*, then let's continue this upstairs."

Upstairs in the gaily chintz-decorated guest room, he gently undressed her, running his long fingers over each successively uncovered part of her body. Naked, she lay back on the bed, pushed the blankets to its foot and covered herself with the pale pink sheet. She watched him remove his clothes and was quite shocked to see that his slimness bordered on emaciation. Not a word had passed between them from the moment they had climbed the stairs, and now, as Edmond slipped under the sheet and locked her tenderly in his embrace, she kissed him hungrily on the mouth before pressing her lips to his ear.

"Make love to me beautifully, Edmond," she whispered.

She submitted joyfully to his feverish exploration of her body, and when his tongue flitted urgently, like the wings of a trapped butterfly, between the lips of her vagina, she reached her first climax. Locking Edmond's tousled head between her knees, she moaned as the explosion in her loins coursed like lightning through her body. As the shivering subsided, she grasped him by the arms and pulled him up on her, impatiently seeking his mouth and the savour of her own sexuality. In a moment he raised himself on his arms and looked down at her. She could feel now his rigidly extending penis pressing hard against the base of her abdomen.

"I have a contraceptive," he said breathlessly.

She cupped his face in her hands.

"I want to feel you inside me, but not like that. Just don't . . ." Her voice trailed off as she felt him enter her. She started to squeeze her full breasts together, and then, pulling her knees up she pressed her calves against his thrusting hips. Droplets of perspiration fell from his brow onto her breasts and face as she rocked from side to side in a fever of ecstasy. She knew that she would very soon reach her second orgasm, and as the flood-tide swirled up on her, Edmond's thrusting rose to a frenzied pitch and he suddenly jerked back from her. She felt the warm juices spattering her stomach and thighs as he

234

fell forward on her, burying his face in her shoulder. She ran her fingers through his damp hair and smiled contentedly.

"Don't move, darling. Please, don't move."

It was nearly nine o'clock the next morning when Margot was awoken by sunlight filtering through the pink and white chintz curtains, shedding a rosy glow on the bedroom. Edmond slept peacefully, curled up in foetal position, his slim buttocks tucked against her right thigh. There was no sound from the rest of the house, and she lay there watching the flickering shadows on the ceiling and thinking about where she was and what had happened to her. She felt a wonderful contentment, and such earlier qualms as she had had about living with the fact that she had taken a lover seemed comfortably remote.

Edmond stirred beside her and rolled over onto his back. His long, dark eyelashes quivered as the sun penetrated his eyelids, and he awoke. Margot propped herself on one elbow, bent over and kissed him lightly on the lips.

"Good morning, my handsome lover. Do you know where you are and whom you are with?"

"I think I am dead and have undeservedly gone to heaven."

"Undeservedly in heaven, yes; dead, no. Not by a long shot!" She had slipped a hand under the covers and now felt his penis beginning to stiffen and grow. She pushed back the covers and eased herself down the bed.

"Do I have *mon capitaine*'s permission?" she asked coquettishly as she lifted his swelling member and reached for the head with her tongue.

By the time they ate breakfast, the weather had changed and it was raining. But the sun came out again in the afternoon, and Margot and Edmond spent an hour strolling around the perimeter of the golf course, hand in hand, chatting happily, stopping every now and then to kiss, and planning their future rendezvous.

"You know that we have to be extra careful now about being seen together in public," she said.

"We always have been; what has changed to make you say that? Has your father, or maybe the Garlands, said something?"

"It's not the family I'm worried about. It's the British."

Edmond halted and swung her round to face him.

"What do you mean, 'the British'?"

"This may sound as crazy to you as it does to me, but my father says he thinks we're being watched and followed by British Intelligence. Ridiculous isn't it? I mean, what could they possibly want to do that for?"

Edmond smiled and kissed her lightly on the forehead.

"Very simple, *ma chérie*. They want you to sell your ravishing body to me in exchange for highly secret information about General de Gaulle's plans to rule the world after we have disposed of the Nazis."

"No, be serious, Edmond. I don't like being followed."

Edmond laughed. "I do love the British; they are such gentlemen. They even ask your father's permission before having you followed!"

"Well, a Foreign Office friend of my father said that he had met you and that he knew you knew me, and he asked a few questions. Father, being the suspicious type, put two and two together."

"And made five?"

"No. The man from the Foreign Office told father that I might be of some use to them. Just like that!"

"And what did your father say?"

"He told him to go to hell, of course."

"Good for him. Let's walk on; it's getting a little chilly."

"You don't seem at all concerned."

"I'm not." He grinned. "Unless of course you *are* planning to spy on us. Mata Hari Margot!"

"Oh, for heavens sakes, Edmond!"

"I think you'd be rather good at it."

"That I don't doubt." Her tone suddenly lightened. "I think I'd be pretty good at getting information out of people." She laughed. "Maybe you'd better watch out after all, Edmond."

"I'll be on my guard."

"But seriously, what are we going to do? It isn't going to make life very easy for us if we are being followed. I know it's your movements they're interested in rather than mine, but if they're going to keep this up, every meeting we have is going to be noted, and before long it'll get back to Father through his nasty little friend."

"We'll just have to think of ways of giving them the slip. Unless, of course, you think your father's right and that we should just not see each other any more."

"No. That's not the answer."

"I'm glad."

He halted her in her tracks and kissed her, then they walked on. For a while neither spoke. They left the golf course through a wicket gate and crossed a tract of bracken and brush separating the course from Kay's paddock where Tommy grazed contentedly.

"Father says that de Gaulle is a thorn in the side of Roosevelt and Churchill; a real troublemaker. What grounds have they got for that?"

Margot smiled in anticipation of some crack about Mata Hari Margot.

"None whatsoever!" he snapped. "Those fools stop at nothing to undermine him."

"Hey, you're talking about my President!"

He ignored her protest. "They hate him because he won't play their game. He's damned if he'll let them decide where France's best interests lie and how they should be secured. That's our business. Don't ever forget that, Margot."

"All right, all right! Calm down. I'm sure I'd feel the same way if I were in your position. It's natural."

"But the British and the Americans ought to feel the same way even though they're not in our position. That's the point. We Free French here, and millions of my countrymen in France, acknowledge de Gaulle as the real leader of the true France. Only he can decide where and when the French will fight for France. And only he can rule the French once we have recovered our territory. That's what you Americans and British have got to understand."

They had halted in the knee-high bracken while

Edmond was stating his case. Margot now put her arms around his neck.

"You're shaking, *chéri*. You really feel all this with a passion, don't you."

Edmond nodded his head.

"Well, I admire you," she went on. "And I think *I* understand. But you must teach me more. Will you?"

"Of course."

"Good. Now let's hurry back. If Kay and Derry are still out, we've got time for a little visit to our guest room before the ghastly ritual of afternoon tea. All right?"

He smiled and kissed her.

Edmond returned to London on Sunday afternoon, leaving Margot to spend one more night with Kay. As the train rattled through the dormitory suburbs toward the capital, he savoured the exquisite delight of his conquest. He felt he had played his cards with consummate skill. After his initial suggestion that they go away for a weekend, he had allowed her to make all the moves leading up to their first passionate love-making. And she had not put a foot wrong. There was something else, too. He had hitherto had only vague thoughts about the possibility of Margot being politically useful to him; he had been more concerned with simply becoming her lover. But her reaction to his outburst the day before on the heath, when he had spoken up for his master, had set him thinking again. Margot moved in important political and social circles. Properly coached by himself, she could be a most effective aid to the Free French in their struggle to secure the full support of Britain's political establishment. A delicate operation, and one which, wrongly handled, could back-fire. But handled with skill, the payoff could be considerable.

At a suburban stop, his compartment door opened and a pretty young woman in the blue uniform of an officer in the Women's Royal Auxiliary Air Force came in and sat in a vacant seat facing him. He nodded acknowledgement of her presence to which she responded with the faintest of smiles, and he suddenly wished he'd been wearing his uniform instead of the now rather crumpled grey cotton suit. She took off her peaked cap, pulled a book from her shoulder bag, and settled down to read. Edmond studied her elegantly crossed legs. They were long, slim, and with beautiful ankles. They were very like Margot's. He thought again of their love-making. How expert she had been! Had there been others besides himself and Charlie? So what!

His thoughts returned to the vexing question of British Intelligence's unwelcome interest in his relationship with an American diplomat's daughter. He had deliberately kept from her that he was now working for the BCRA, recruiting agents to send to France under Free French control. At an appropriate moment he might tell her, but at present he would risk nothing that might conceivably alarm her further. British Intelligence knew, of course; Passy's operation and the French section of MI6 had been working together from the day the former had been charged by de Gaulle with Free France's intelligence functions. They had needed each other in those early days. The young Frenchman had started with no money and no agents; MI6 had money, experience and equipment, but few people knew the territory of occupied France well enough to operate there. So Churchill and de Gaulle had signed an agreement whereby the British financed and equipped an operation under Passy's direction in return for a regular flow of military intelligence gathered in France by agents recruited by him. It was not long, however, before the Free French came to resent risking their people's lives simply to satisfy British intelligence needs, and soon Passy's expanded networks in France were working primarily for de Gaulle, who was out to gain control of the entire resistance effort. Edmond knew perfectly well why: the General was forging a political base in France for future exploitation, and Edmond thoroughly approved. The British did not. For them, the purpose of the resistance was to make life untenable for the German occupiers and to help prepare the way for the eventual liberation of the country; it was not meant to be diverted into the furthering of the General's personal and seemingly boundless political ambitions. The marriage of intelligence convenience was over. No wonder, then, that the British were anxious to know what was going on inside the BCRA, and if the wife of a British officer, albeit an American by birth, was presumed to be having an affair with a Free French officer from the heart of the BCRA's operations, they would be foolish not to try to solicit her cooperation with appeals to her loyalty to her husband's country.

As soon as Margot had told him what her father had revealed to her, Edmond considered whether he should inform Passy. Duty clearly indicated that he should; the risk of being told not to see his American lady friend again persuaded him firmly not to. For the present he would take no action on the matter beyond seeking to obtain from Margot the name of the British official who was friendly with her father and so anxious to recruit her. He was confident that Margot was being honest with him in her protestations of anger at the British move to gain her cooperation. Nonetheless, he would be on his guard.

Back at Kay Lawton's Sunningdale house, Margot was in effervescent form as she, Kay and Derry Fleming drank cocktails before their Sunday night dinner.

"No really, he's a damn nice chap for a Frog," said Derry assuming a mock-serious look and tone of voice.

"And by the sound of it, one hell of a lover," added Kay. "Doesn't suffer from 'brewer's droop' like some English film producers we know well."

Margot blushed. "By God, if after plucking up all that courage I'd discovered otherwise, I'd have killed him!"

She sank into a sofa, giggling. She knew that the wine and cocktails drunk at lunch and again now had gone to her head, but she was far past caring. Ever since waking that morning she had felt a sense of release. Her inhibitions had floated away like ashes in the wind. She had given herself over to total physical pleasure and had enjoyed it to a degree and in a manner that she had never known before, even in the better moments with Charlie. Edmond had unearthed feelings, revealed vistas, harnessed senses and unravelled mysteries that she had never dreamed of finding in the act of love, even in her wilder moments of fantasizing. Where had he learned to do that to women? Or was it something in her that brought out in him a genius for giving pleasure that even he did know he possessed?

"Just don't fall in love with him," said Kay. "He told me he can't wait to get back to France to have a go at the Germans, and I somehow doubt he has plans to stuff you into his knapsack."

"Don't worry. I probably won't. He's my wartime fling, that's all. I just want to enjoy him before he goes off and gets himself killed."

"Christ, you're talking like a world-weary thirty-five-year-old," said Derry. "Amazing what war does to young innocents."

"War is my alibi," retorted Margot. "I don't think you'd catch me doing this in peacetime."

"Bullshit, sweetie!" Kay took her glass from her. "You obviously need another drink."

Margot travelled to London early the next morning with a splitting headache. At half-past eleven she was scheduled to visit the British Red Cross headquarters to talk about taking a part-time position in their administration. She considered cancelling the meeting, but then, as the train neared London, the aspirin which Kay had given her began to exercise its healing powers, and by lunchtime she was able to call her father and report to him that she would henceforth be working two mornings and one afternoon a week as a volunteer in the central records office. She then called Edmond.

"So now you will have to stay in London most of the week," he said with enthusiasm.

"At least three nights."

"I wish you could spend them with me."

"We both know that's not possible."

"When do I see you again?"

"I don't know. But soon, I hope. I'm relying on you to think up some way in which we can meet without half the government knowing about it."

"There's a back way of getting into my building, through a mews off Wetherby Gardens. They made a hole in the wall when they were building the air-raid shelter. Nobody uses it except the landlady. It's difficult to find, and I'm damned sure whoever's watching me doesn't know about it."

"But will your landlady let us use it?"

"She was a French teacher, remember. And she's a romantic."

"Then shall I come round for a drink this evening?"

"Meet me just inside the entrance to the mews at six-fifteen. I'll lead you in."

"Sounds exciting. I'll be there."

Summer gave way to autumn, and through the remaining months of 1941 Margot led a full, complicated but exhilarating life. With the friendly connivance of Edmond's francophile landlady, she was able to have frequent, undetected meetings with her lover. They limited their visits to restaurants, where they might be seen by anyone following Edmond, to an unremarkable once every two weeks or so, and they always behaved with the utmost decorum, giving no overt indication of the true nature of their relationship. At all other times, they would meet in the privacy of his Bolton Place flat, either for an hour of love-making in the early evening, or, when Margot could plausibly invent, for the benefit of her father, an evening out with friends, they would cook dinner at his place and she would stay with him until past midnight. Edmond nonetheless encouraged her to keep up her regular social life. With gentle persuasion, he had imbued her with an enthusiasm for the Free French cause and its leader, and had encouraged her to share her enthusiasm with her political friends and acquaintances. This she did with some caution, citing as the basis for her interest her longstanding fascination with all things French. Nonetheless, her knowledge of Anglo-Free French relations astonished some, not least the consummate francophile among Conversative Members of Parliament, Harold Nicolson, whom she occasionally met at Lady Colefax's dinners. And Randolph Churchill, on leave from the Middle East, and in one of his more exuberant moods, whispered in her ear that French pillow talk was notoriously unreliable. She laughed nervously but took no offence. Randolph, after all, was Randolph.

She had quickly got used to leading a rigidly compartmentalized life. Edmond was kept largely invisible from her family and friends, so much so that Harland commended his daughter on having seen the wisdom of his advice that she stay away from the young Gaullist. Margot concluded that if British Intelligence was noting their occasional public lunch dates, the news was not being filtered through to her father. Thus no cloud hung over the father-daughter relationship. Her relations with Charlie's parents also remained unaffected. She made a point of seeing them frequently, not only because it seemed the natural thing to do – and in any case she was genuinely fond of them – but also because they remained her most important entrée into the highest political circles.

In short, she was managing her double life with considerable skill. It was only when she received tender letters from Charlie, and sat down to pen her replies, that sadness and feelings of guilt weighed upon her. Poor Charlie! They had met for the first time just thirty months ago, and he had been gone from her these last twenty. What was it about him, she asked herself, that she could still love him while with each passing day she seemed to know him less? And then she would dismiss her guilt feelings with the rationalization that as long as she still loved him, their marriage could be resumed on his return without him knowing of any reason why the resumption should not be joyful.

That's what she told herself. But there were times when she wondered how long she could go on believing herself.

19

Larry Moore looked at his watch and sighed.

"I think we'd better go. It's twenty to four and I haven't packed my bag."

"Your watch is fast; it's not yet three-thirty and the car is ordered for five, so you told me. So relax. We can make it back in ten minutes if we canter all the way."

Elaine Burchett raised herself on one elbow and leaned over to kiss him. He put his arms tightly around her neck and pulled her onto him. Outside the barn, one of the horses whinnied and stamped its hooves on the rock-hard dirt.

"This is crazy!" said Elaine. "We should have gone straight to my house and had a gorgeous afternoon romping in the raw, but young Lochinvar here wanted a romantic ride over the hills and dales."

"Nothing to stop you getting into the raw here," said Larry, inserting a hand inside her tweed riding jacket and squeezing the generously full breast that strained so hard against the dark green wool of her polo-neck jersey that the white of the bra underneath was visible between the threads.

"Straw gives me a rash, darling, unless you were simply planning to bend me over that handcart, in which case you should have said so earlier."

"It never occurred to me. You're the one with the pervert's mind; you should have thought of it."

She slapped his cheek playfully.

"You just wait till I get you to my place on your next leave."

"And you just remember that mutilation is not

considered much of a physical qualification for becoming a bomber pilot.''

She grinned, and patted his riding breeches at his groin. ''You don't need *this* to fly!''

Larry stared up at the lofty wooden vaulting of the old barn, then closed his eyes as Elaine laid her head against his shoulder and continued gently to tap on his breeches with the tips of her fingers. Elaine always made him feel a bit guilty. He was not in love with her; he was simply in thrall to her voluptuous body and her sensuous ways with him. Yet she kept on dropping heavy hints, urging him that age differences were no bar to two people living happily together. But how in hell could he live with someone sixteen years older than himself? The very idea was mad. She was mad. His parents and grandparents would banish him from the family for ever and Margot would probably kill him. Why couldn't Elaine just enjoy their sex together and stop all this talk about permanent attachments? The situation was completely cockeyed; it was supposed to be the infatuated young man who pleaded tearfully for the hand of the older woman who had enthralled him, and she who gently discouraged him from such folly.

He was the first to confess that he was fascinated by older women. His grandfather had sensed it and had assured him that it happened among boys his age, and that he was not to worry; it would pass in due time. Worry! He wasn't worrying about his own feelings; he was worrying about Elaine's. She was the one who wasn't playing by the rules. He sometimes wished she'd married her wretched veterinarian, then he would never have touched her again. He was not against lusting after another man's wife – sometimes one just couldn't help it – but he drew the line firmly at adultery. Not that he'd ever been faced with the dilemma. The late lamented wife of his teacher at Andover had never so much as hinted that she'd noticed his infatuation.

His relationship with Elaine had dated from her thirty-fifth birthday party some twenty months previously. At the small buffet supper she had given, at which they had danced afterwards, she had almost totally ignored him.

As the evening had worn on and the drinks had taken their hold on him, his puzzlement had turned to irritation. He had sought her out in the kitchen, where he found her resisting the veterinarian's advances, and had told her he was going home.

"You're in no condition to drive, pet," she had said. "Go join the others and enjoy yourself, and I'll drive you home when the party's over."

"You don't have to do that," interjected the veterinarian, casting a murderous look at Larry. "Someone else can handle that."

But she did, at three in the morning, but not before she had persuaded him to undress, sober up under a cold shower, and make love to her – or at least attempt to. Larry was a flop. His eyes and hands had feasted on a body that he believed only existed on the easel of a pin-up artist, but his night's imbibing had left him as limp as an overcooked asparagus.

"Better luck next time," she had said with a sigh, and then struck him hard on the backside with the palm of her hand.

The next time had turned out to be the following afternoon, and on this occasion his performance had been highly applauded. It was only as he had risen from the bed that he had noticed a riding crop on the floor beside it.

"I didn't have to use it, did I, pet?" she had said with a sweet smile. Larry had retreated rapidly to the bathroom. He had no wish to compare what he had seen Elaine doing to her mounts in the hunting field with what she might be in a mind to do with her lover in the bedroom.

"Come on, we absolutely have to go," said Larry, picking a piece of straw out of Elaine's dark brown hair.

"If you insist. But don't worry; you're not going to be late. When we get back to Adamswood, I'll rub down Prince Igor for you while you pack. Then I'll ride on home when you've gone."

They got up and brushed themselves and each other off.

"Next time you want to cuddle me in a barn, bring a clothes-brush."

"Next time, Elaine, take your clothes off, then they won't get messed up."

She swung at his rear end with her riding crop, and he dodged it, laughing.

"Come on, woman. To horse!"

They went outside into the cold, bright afternoon, and unhitched their horses from the sturdy wooden fence that encircled the forecourt.

"Someone ought to take this little farm in hand again," said Elaine as she swung into the saddle. "It's a crime to leave it abandoned like this."

"Why don't you buy it then?"

"Come and live with me here, lover?"

She laughed and, digging her heels into her roan mare's flanks, she cantered down the path.

Larry swung his black stallion, Prince Igor, around and took off after her. Riding, flying and fucking! What more could a man ask? he mused as he revelled in the cold air rushing into his face.

Ten minutes later they clattered into the stable-yard at Adamswood.

"A good gallop like that makes me horny," said Elaine breathlessly as she slid her feet out of the stirrups and crossed her right leg over her mount's withers. "Damn your flying training!"

Larry dismounted, pulled the reins forward over Prince Igor's noble head, looped them over his forearm, and led the stallion over to where Elaine still perched in her saddle. He held his arms up and she slid down into them. They kissed for a moment, then she pushed him away, taking Prince Igor's reins as she did so.

"Go and get packed. I'll take care of these two beauties."

As Larry started to walk towards the door in the wall which gave access to the front driveway and the house, his grandfather came through it.

"Hello, you two. Had a good ride?"

"Great, thank you Grandpa."

He was relieved that his grandfather hadn't caught him

kissing Elaine. He knew that Austin Moore didn't object to them indulging together in their shared love of horses from time to time, but he also knew that his grandfather was at last getting impatient to see him around with girls more his own age.

"It was a perfect afternoon," said Elaine with rather more feeling than Larry would have wished under the circumstances.

Austin Moore patted Prince Igor's sweating neck. "Well, I'm sorry then to have to spoil it."

Elaine and Larry frowned.

"What's happened, Grandpa?"

"The Japanese have attacked Hawaii. They've bombed the fleet at Pearl Harbor. We had it on the radio just a little while back."

"Holy Moses!" Larry clamped the palm of his hand to his forehead. "So we finally go to war!"

"Has the President declared war?" asked Elaine.

"That's Congress's prerogative. But they will, of course. Tomorrow I should guess. Larry, you'd better hurry in and talk to your grandmother and then call your mother in New York. They're both in a state about you, so try to calm them down. I don't seem to be able to. I'll help Elaine with the horses."

Larry hurried to the house and found his grandmother arranging flowers in the octagonal hall. She came to him and silently embraced him.

"Go and call your mother, Larry," she said simply. "She needs to talk to you."

Larry walked down to his grandfather's study and called a Manhattan number. The conversation was not easy.

Later, changed into his khaki Air Corps Aviation Cadet's uniform, he returned to the stable-yard and found Elaine seated on a mounting block, holding her mare by the reins.

"Sorry I kept you so long. I had a difficult time on the telephone with Mother."

"I'm not surprised. She must be going out of her mind with worry."

"No, she's all right."

"Does this mean no more leave for you?"

"Oh, there'll be leave. But once I'm commissioned, you may not see me for dust."

"But you promise you'll be up to see me before then."

"Heavens, yes! I won't be going overseas, if ever, for months yet."

Elaine got to her feet, and Larry, after glancing round to see that the stable-yard was empty but for themselves, put his arms around her.

"Take great care of yourself, won't you, pet?" she said. "Don't do anything silly like suddenly getting married just because there's a war. Some people do that."

"On my pay? You've got to be kidding!"

"But if you really must, there's always me."

Larry laughed nervously. "I'm not the marrying type. Not for another decade or so."

"You must think I'm crazy, Larry."

"No, I'm flattered. Really."

"Come on, off you go, and leave this pining cradle-snatcher to ride off into the sunset." She kissed him hard on the lips and then detached herself from his arms and quickly mounted. "Write to me, pet!"

"And you to me!"

She trotted out of the yard, her lips tightly pursed as she tried to hold back a tear.

Larry went into the nearby loose-box to see that Prince Igor was settled. He stroked the horse's glossy black flanks and pressed his face to the white muzzle.

"See you again soon, boy," he said, and left quickly.

The car to take him to the station was already drawn up at the front door. He hurried into the house to say good-bye to his grandparents.

"Did you calm your mother down?"

"I think so, Grandpa. I'll call her again next week. And I don't want you two worrying about me either."

"We will, but that's our privilege," said Austin.

20

On 23rd June, Margot wrote a letter to her brother.

Dear Larry,

Well, you made it! Congratulations, big boy! Second Lieutenant at last! Now I suppose I really will have to look up to my twin. Father is naturally preening himself with paternal pride and delight, so don't write and tell us that Mother is crying her eyes out with fear of what happens to you next. When do you actually get to Gowan Field (if that's not a state secret) and what after that?

My life has been fairly uneventful, which you'll probably think is a good thing. The American Red Cross is now firmly established over here, especially in London, so I switched since they seem in greater need of volunteers than the British RC. I'm helping out at an ARC Club on Curzon Street. Hard work, but fun. Maybe one day they'll actually pay me!

Charlie's letters sound a bit depressed, poor love. Well, it's two years now. Enough to keep anyone down in the dumps. I'll tell him you've got your wings. He'll be thrilled.

Jamie wrote from North Africa. Things are pretty hot over there in both senses of the adjective, but he's in good spirits, it seems. Ivor is just back from Cairo and is now an Assistant Private Secretary to the Foreign Secretary which sounds mighty impressive. It's nice to have him around. You asked about Edmond. He seems terribly busy and we hardly ever see him. But he catches me for lunch once in a while.

Father's just back from a trip to Wales with the Ambassador. Winant and he get on terrifically, and Father's work on Lend Lease has won him many accolades from his boss, but he's much too modest to tell you that.

That's it for the moment. Please call Mother and tell her I'll write her next week. Fly safely, dear one, and God bless.

Your loving Margot.

PS. You write *nothing* about your love life! Anything new? Don't tell me Big Boobs Burchett is still after you!

As Sir Walter Garland emerged from the House of Commons and waited for the traffic signal to yield him passage across the street into the shadow of Westminster Abbey, he concluded that 24th June 1942 had been one of the most depressing days in recent memory.

It had begun with the morning newspapers at breakfast. Rommel's Afrika Corps was in hot pursuit of the allied Eighth Army, fleeing helter-skelter across the Libyan desert back towards the Egyptian frontier. Tobruk, the vital port, was lost, together with 25,000 men and God knows how much equipment. Next it would be Alexandria, then Cairo, and then the Suez Canal. And at this moment of all crisis-laden moments, Churchill was returning from Washington to face a motion of censure on the Government's conduct of the war put down by a member of his own Tory party. It was not the Government as a whole, however, that the dissidents were after; it was the Prime Minister himself, and their intention was to embarrass him into surrendering the Defence portfolio and leave the conduct of the war to the generals. And that, in Garland's view, would be an unmitigated disaster.

If those had been his only causes for unhappiness that day, they would already have been enough. But there were more. That morning he had received a letter from his prisoner-of-war son, an event that was usually a cause for much joy. In this letter, however, Charlie poured out to his father and mother his misery and frustration over the inexplicable behaviour of his wife. She had written only twice to him in the last two months – she used to write once a week – and although the letters were affectionate enough, their infrequency and the fact that she was ignoring his pleas to write more often were causing him to wonder whether all was well with her. Obviously all was not well, concluded Sir Walter, but it would be best not to show the letter to the boy's mother until he had done a little discreet investigating. He had heard that his daughter-in-law had been seen a couple of times in public with the young Frenchman who had been with the two sisters that night at the Café de Paris. Nothing wrong with that, on the face of it; but maybe there was more to it. He prayed not, but felt bound to find out. He hesitated to confront Margot directly: the better first step would be to talk to the girl's father. They would lunch together later in the week.

Burdened with his unhappy thoughts, the Member of Parliament for East Hampshire turned into Great College Street and walked slowly down the row of houses until he reached his elegant little Queen Anne residence. His butler opened the door to him and relieved him of his black homburg and neatly furled umbrella.

"A beautiful summer evening, sir."

Sir Walter nodded. "Bring me a whisky and soda in the study."

He climbed the stairs, entered the book-filled room and sank into his favourite high-backed armchair. On a table at his elbow a signed portrait photograph of Churchill stared pugnaciously at him. He returned the stare and felt more depressed than ever. Surely they couldn't be so stupid as to pinion the wings of the one man capable of leading the country at this critical moment! But Winston could be his own worst enemy, and if he met his critics with a display of petulant arrogance, he might succeed in undoing himself.

The butler entered and placed the drink and an evening newspaper beside his master.

"There was a message from the House shortly before you arrived, sir. The censure motion will be debated on the first of July."

"The first of July? Oh, for heaven's sake!" He slapped his knee in irritation. "That will be all, Locke. Thank you. Just call me a cab at a quarter to eight. I'll be dining at the Carlton Club in case her ladyship should ring from the country."

The first of July was his wife's fiftieth birthday, and he had planned a dinner at the Savoy. A wonderful celebration that would be if Winston lost the censure vote that afternoon!

He took a deep pull at his whisky and soda, unfolded the newspaper, and began to scan the columns. Nothing much new there but at least a Beaverbrook paper could be relied on to give the Prime Minister solid backing. A short item on an inside page contained a name that rang a bell faintly in the nether regions of his memory. Poor, silly girl, he said to himself. Asking for trouble driving without adequate lights after dark. Illegal too. He felt almost sorry for the driver of the three-ton army truck which smashed into the pony cart. Must have been a horrible mess. Kay Lawton. Rang a bell somewhere. He turned to the racing results.

The former Washington Hotel on Curzon Street, in the heart of Mayfair, was about to complete its first week as the American Red Cross Washington Club for US Servicemen. It had been a hive of activity from the day it had opened; almost all the rooms (half a crown or fifty cents for bed and breakfast) were occupied, and the dining room, where dinner could be had for a shilling, had been crowded every night. There had been the expected teething troubles and Margot, who had dealt with a fair share of them as assistant to the public relations officer, was exhausted. It was after six o'clock when she locked the door of her small office, picked up a newspaper at the reception desk, politely rejected a request for a dinner date from a young Army Engineer sergeant from Kansas City, and set off on the short two-block walk to Hill Street and home.

It was while she was waiting to cross Charles Street that she glanced inside the evening paper and found herself staring mesmerized at the words ARTIST DIES IN

PONY-CART CRASH. Feeling suddenly faint, she retreated from the kerb. She just managed to absorb the ten-line report before tears began to blind her and she started to shake uncontrollably. She looked up and saw an empty cab halt at the crossing. Impulsively she rushed forward and asked the driver to take her to 14 Bolton Place. Edmond just had to be there, she told herself, and at this moment, in her panic-stricken state, she had to be there with him. As she huddled in the dark corner of the back seat, she started to sob helplessly. Why, oh why was she being punished like this? Why in God's name was she always being confronted with death? Her unborn baby, her sister, and now her best and dearest friend. Why? She was crying loudly, and the cabbie pulled over to the kerb, got out and opened the passenger door.

"Are you all right, miss?"

"Yes, please go on. I'll be all right. I'm sorry." She got the words out with difficulty, her whole body shaking convulsively. The cabbie studied her for a moment, a look of deep concern on his face, then closed the door and got back into his driver's seat. Margot nestled again into the corner and tried to pull herself together. Transgressing Edmond's rule of arrival and departure, this being an emergency, she told the cab to stop at the front entrance. She hurried up to the third floor and pressed the bell on Edmond's door. She heaved a sigh of relief as she heard footsteps on the other side, and in a moment she was in his arms, struggling through renewed sobs to tell him what had happened and how much she needed to be comforted by him. He led her to the living room and sat with her on the sofa. While she buried her head in his shoulder and wept, Edmond hastily read the news item.

"Oh, darling, why is this such a cruel world?" she stuttered.

"I wish I knew." He took her in his arms and hugged her tight. For the next hour he consoled her, gave her a glass of wine, and laid her down on his bed to let her rest from the sheer fatigue of so much weeping.

"I want to stay here tonight, Edmond," she whispered, clutching his hand.

"You may. I can give you dinner here, if you feel like

254

some. I've got cold chicken and plenty of vegetables. But what about your father?"

"I'll call him in a little while and tell him what's happened, and tell him I'm going to Kay's mother immediately. I'd be going tomorrow in any case. I'd better call her too."

"Well then, you make your telephone calls while I just slip downstairs and borrow some butter from my very accommodating landlady."

He kissed her on the cheek and slipped out of the flat. As Margot reached for the telephone by the bed, it rang. She lifted the receiver and listened. Without introduction, a plaintive female voice came across the wires.

"*Edmond, mon chéri, tu viens ou tu viens pas ce soir? Ta petite Denise veut faire l'amour avec toi. Alors, tu viens?*"

Margot replaced the receiver. Her understanding of French was more than sufficient to absorb the message. She sank back on the pillow and took a deep breath. Then she exploded.

"God *damn* you!" she shouted as she leaped from the bed. She searched frantically for her shoes, cursing and sobbing, and eventually located them by the sofa in the living room. Grabbing her purse, she darted to the door, pausing for a second in front of a mirror in the tiny hall to sweep back her hair and curse the streaks of mascara beneath her puffy, tear-stained eyes. She pulled the door open violently and Edmond stumbled in. She pushed past him and turned in the doorway to face him.

"My God, Margot, what's the matter? Where are you going?"

"I don't wish to intrude on your love life!" She spat the words out. "Your little Denise is waiting for you." She reached for the door handle to pull the door shut behind her, but Edmond lunged forward and seized the inside handle.

"Margot! Stop this nonsense at once; you don't know what you're talking about."

"Oh yes I do! I know exactly what I'm talking about!" She pulled again on the door, but Edmond had a firm grip on it. "Just let me go, and then you can run off and fuck your little French whore to your heart's content!"

She let go of the handle and retreated towards the head of the stairs. Edmond followed her and grabbed her arm.

"If you leave now without letting me explain why you are mistaken about me and Denise," he said very calmly, "it is all over between you and me. I really mean that. So come back in and let's talk. Then, if you want, you can go."

"You're hurting me!"

He let go of her arm and she slumped against the wall, gritting her teeth and trying desperately to hold back another onrush of tears. But it was no good. She slid slowly to the floor, shaking pitifully as the sobbing gripped her. Edmond bent and raised her gently to her feet. With an arm firmly around her heaving shoulders, he led her back into the apartment and into the bedroom. She sank onto the bed and buried her head in the pillow. Edmond sat on the edge of the bed, one hand resting on the small of her back. Silently he cursed Denise. The stupid peasant! That was really the end for her. From now on the bitch could find somebody else's cock to suck!

A few moments later, Margot's crying subsided and she turned over on her back. She rubbed her eyes and sniffed.

"There's a handkerchief in my purse. Can I have it please?"

Edmond picked the bag off the floor by the bed and extracted the handkerchief. Margot blew her nose vigorously and lay back again on the pillow, staring sadly at Edmond's worried face.

"Why, Edmond? Am I really so inadequate? Have you just been playing a game with me all along?"

"Listen, *chérie*; you are all that I could possibly want. It is Denise who has been the plaything, and I have not been firm enough in insisting that it has all been over with her once you and I came together. She is persistent, but as far as I am concerned, it is all over. I promise you."

"It just didn't sound like it when she called."

"She doesn't want it to sound like it. That's the trouble."

"Well if you still want each other, go ahead. But you can't have me as well."

"For God's sake, Margot, you're not listening! What she wants doesn't matter a damn. The point is that I don't want to have anything more to do with her, because I have you."

"Then call her now and tell her, once and for all." Margot reached over and handed him the telephone receiver.

"No. That is not the right way to do it. It would be unnecessarily embarrassing for all of us."

"I'm perfectly ready to be embarrassed if it will put a final stop to her chasing you, and vice versa if that is still the case."

Edmond sighed, took the receiver from her and replaced it.

"I will talk to her tomorrow. You must trust me."

"But she's waiting for you tonight."

"Did you say anything to her?"

"Certainly not."

"Well, she still will have got the message. She's not totally stupid. She won't call again tonight."

Edmond gently gripped a silk-stockinged ankle, and slipped his hand slowly up her calf.

"If you ladder these precious stockings, I'll murder you."

"Will you stay with me tonight?"

"Does she work at Carlton Gardens?"

"I don't wish to discuss her, Margot, and I asked you a question. Will you stay with me?"

Margot looked at him silently and bit on her lip.

"Will you?" he repeated.

"No. I want to sleep at home tonight. I will have to go early to Sunningdale, and I want to see my father."

Edmond looked crestfallen.

"But you can give me dinner here. That's the least you can do to make it up to me." She smiled as she leaned forward to take his hand. "In fact, there's so much that

257

you have to make up for, I think you'd better make love to me right now."

Fresh tears glistened in the corners of her eyes as she pulled him down on her.

When Sir Walter Garland called Harland Moore to invite him to lunch, he learned that his daughter-in-law was mourning the accidental death of her closest friend, Kay Lawton. So that was how he'd heard the name! Poor Margot. Sir Walter was a compassionate man, and he now felt uncomfortable at the prospect of raising with her father the extremely delicate question of her fidelity towards his son. He felt, nonetheless, that he should not shirk his duty towards Charlie; he would simply go about it in the very gentlest of ways.

The conversation at lunch somewhat reassured the parliamentarian. Moore was surprised and upset to hear that his daughter had been writing so seldom to her husband, but suggested that it might have something to do with the fact that she was now working very hard: five, sometimes six, days a week with the American Red Cross. In any case, he would mention the matter to her and encourage her to find the time to write more often. When Garland then asked, in the most apologetic manner, whether Moore might have any reason to believe that Margot was being a little distracted by the young Free French officer, Moore told him that he was aware of the friendship and had raised the matter with his daughter. He had fully accepted her protestations that, in the light of their shared tragic experience, she looked on him as almost a member of the family and somebody, being a foreigner, separated by war from his nearest and dearest, to be treated with kindness and concern. Moore was sure that there was nothing more to it than that, he told Sir Walter. What he did not tell him was that while Maurice Drake had never again mentioned Margot and Edmond's friendship to him, he could not help worrying that his daughter remained vulnerable to the machinations of Britain's intelligence services. In fact, he had never mentioned the Drake matter to Sir Walter at all. It seemed to him that such a move risked the Member of Parliament's intervention, and Moore preferred to let that particular sleeping dog lie.

"I'm awfully glad we've had this very frank chat," said Garland as they walked down the steps of the Carlton Club, "and I never doubted that you would take it in the most sympathetic of spirits." He took the American by the arm as they walked up St James's Street. "My dear wife has agreed that we should celebrate her fiftieth birthday a day late, on 2nd July, as I shall have to be in the House on the first for this wretched censure debate. It may go into a second day, but only briefly. I hope the new date of our dinner at the Savoy is all right with you; we do count on both you and Margot being with us."

"We are greatly looking forward to it, Walter. I hope we can celebrate a Winston victory at the same time."

Indeed they did. The Prime Minister, at his bulldog best, saw off the dissidents snapping at his heels, dared them to dismiss him, and carried the day by 476 votes to 25. No one was happier than Sir Walter Garland, his most loyal supporter, and the postponed birthday dinner for Lady Cynthia was a particularly joyous occasion, rendered solemn only at that point at which Sir Walter rose wet-eyed to toast his absent son and to pour blessings on his beautiful daughter-in-law. Margot, in attendance over Edmond's protests, smiled graciously while her father squeezed her hand in case she cried. She almost did. But not quite.

21

Through the summer and autumn of 1942, Margot immersed herself in her work at the Washington Club. Since the beginning of the year, more than a hundred and thirty thousand American troops had arrived in the British Isles as the build-up in the US Army's European Theatre of Operations proceeded apace. London was suddenly full of them. The rapidly expanding Theatre headquarters in Grosvenor Square accounted for many, but even more numerous were the officers and men pouring in from the provinces to take a look at Britain's capital city. Catering to their needs and wishes had become a monumental task for the American Red Cross, and Margot had never worked so hard in her life.

Not surprisingly, finding time to be with Edmond was becoming more and more of a problem for her. Getting to Bolton Place in the blackout at the end of a long day's work at the club was often an exhausting operation, and barely worth the struggle if she was due at a dinner party later. On the infrequent occasions when her father went out of town with the ambassador for a day or two, she would stay over. But Kay's death had deprived them of a venue for weekend trysts and, apart from a couple of weekends spent nervously incognito in a run-down country inn near Canterbury, Margot loyally devoted her Saturdays and Sundays to her father at Verbena Cottage.

The shock of discovering Edmond's liaison with the typist at Carlton Gardens had quickly subsided. Margot had accepted Edmond's solemn pledge that he would never touch the little Bretonne again. If he wished to remain her lover, he must promise total fidelity to her, and this he had readily done. She then felt that she had the relationship very much under control. She was flattered by Edmond's declarations of love, and although she still stopped short of making any such declaration to him, his ardour convinced her that he would rather suffer this frustration than abandon her. But, as the year neared its end, Margot began to realize that her physical dependency on him was now coupled with a deepening affection in which, as the days passed, she sensed the flowering of love. She could now no longer close her mind, as she had so far done, to the consequences of the return into her life of her lawful husband. Hitherto, Edmond had been a comfort and a joy to a lonely and deprived woman whose need for him would last as long as the loneliness and the deprivation threatened. But his role now risked changing from lover to loved one, and writing him out of the script if and when Charlie came home might prove traumatic – if even possible at all. In confronting the dilemma, she admitted to herself that the social standing and political entrée that she had acquired in London, and which she had no inclination to lose, weighed heavily in Charlie's favour. On the other hand, how could she be sure that her feelings for Edmond at the moment when the choice had to be made might not be such as to lead her to abandon all for him? The message now seemed alarmingly clear: Charlie had better come back very soon or risk losing her.

She felt a desperate need to talk to someone about her problem, and now more than ever she missed Kay. Even though her advice would surely have been biased in Edmond's favour, she would at least have afforded her the opportunity to talk it out. She considered writing to Larry, knowing full well that he would come down firmly, even angrily, on Charlie's side, and would lecture her on the unacceptability of adultery. Twice she sat down to write to him, but on both occasions she tore up the sheet of writing paper before she had even broached the subject. Larry should not be troubled with this, she told herself in justification. He was having a bad enough time as it was, according to his letters, training in worn-out B-17 bombers over the desolate, wind-swept salt flats of Utah. Why off-load her troubles on her tired, frozen and no doubt frightened brother? Censorship prevented Larry from telling his sister if and when his bomber group would be sent to join the United States Eighth Air Force in Britain, but their father was sure he would be coming. Maybe when he did arrive, she thought, it would be time enough to tell him all and seek his advice. Unless, of course, by then Charlie had come home. In the meantime she kept her counsel, immersed herself in her work, made love passionately with Edmond, and waited to see what the fates would decree.

One Sunday in early November, as Margot and her father ate a leisurely breakfast in the kitchen at Verbena Cottage, they heard over the radio that American forces, supported by the British, had invaded Vichy-controlled Morocco and Algeria.

"Excellent!" said Harland. "The sooner they mop up there and move east to help poor battle-weary Monty and his Eighth Army, the sooner Rommel will be finished."

"Jamie's mother hasn't heard from him since Alamein. I do hope he's all right."

"Jamie's indestructible."

"It's bad luck to say something like that."

Harland changed the subject. "Your friend Edmond must be pleased about the invasion, not to mention de Gaulle."

"Yes, I suppose so," said Margot in a bored voice and got up to take the dishes to the sink.

"De Gaulle is absolutely furious!" said Edmond as he and Margot sat down to lunch in a crowded little restaurant in Soho the following day. "He knew there was to be an invasion, of course, but you Americans and British refused to bring him in on the planning or even let him know the date."

"There must have been some good reason," said Margot, not looking up from her menu.

"None. And when they woke him at five yesterday morning to tell him it had happened, do you know what he said? He said: 'Well then, I hope the Vichyites hurl them back into the sea.'"

"That angry?" Margot smiled.

"Well, he calmed down later. He went to the BBC and broadcast a call to all Frenchmen in North Africa to help the invaders. After all, we're going to need those North African possessions of ours as a base for launching the liberation of France."

"Yes, I suppose so. Pea soup and the fish cakes for me."

"But that's not all. The General hit the roof again when he heard that Eisenhower had appointed General Giraud commander of the French Army of Africa."

"Why should he object?"

"He's a five-star general, and therefore much senior to de Gaulle. He's also a bit of a hero because he recently escaped from a fortress POW prison in Germany. And now he has an army ten times bigger than ours over here. It's obvious: you're trying to get him accepted as an alternative leader of the French. That's totally unacceptable to us!"

"Edmond, dearest, I do wish you wouldn't equate little me with the British and American governments. I may dine with ambassadors and carouse with Cabinet ministers, but I'm not directing this war any more than your man seems to be. Now, please do order. I'm starving."

"I sometimes think you don't appreciate what de Gaulle's destiny is, Margot," he said, scanning the meagre menu with a jaundiced look.

"Come off it, lover! You'll spoil my lunch, such as it is, if you lecture me all the time. You should be lunching with Maurice Drake; he'd hang on every word, and give you a better lunch into the bargain."

Edmond laughed. "One just can't be serious with you some days. How would you like to come and hear him address a rally at the Albert Hall tomorrow?"

"All right. But don't blame me if we get spotted by Drake. He's bound to weasel his way in. And positively *no* photographs!"

"Your enthusiasm overwhelms me, Margot. I'm beginning to wonder whether you really give a damn for what we stand for and what we're trying to do. I thought you

263

had understood just how vital de Gaulle is to the future of France. He is every bit as important to us now as George Washington was to you in the War of Independence."

"Edmond, don't exhaust yourself converting the converted. I believe in your cause. You've taught me to do so. Maybe I shouldn't; a lot of people, including both my father and father-in-law, two highly intelligent men, believe I shouldn't. But I do, and much of the reason why I do is because I respect and admire you as well as being very fond of you. You took a courageous decision back there in Bordeaux because you believed in a man and a cause, and I find that very moving. I am thrilled by patriotism of that sort; not the flag-waving, national anthem-bawling sort of patriotism. Anyone can indulge in that. But your sort. The sort that carries a price. Exile, being separated from one's family; that sort of thing."

She took a sip of wine.

Edmond stared at her, a look of wonder on his face. He said nothing.

"So don't doubt me, *chéri*," she went on. "And above all, don't doubt my belief in you. I feel it in my bones that you are going to be as great as de Gaulle one day, and I find that very exciting. One day I'll look back and say: I knew Edmond Lemonnier when he was a young officer in London during the war. I watched him start on the ladder to greatness. Maybe I even helped him up it a few rungs. And look where he is today."

Edmond smiled. "The Elysée?"

"Why not? Just survive the war, do your duty supremely well, and the sky should be your limit. I honestly believe you have it in you."

"You do?"

"I do, Edmond. So don't disappoint me."

It seemed to Margot that every French citizen in the United Kingdom was there in the Albert Hall, which was, of course, the General's intention. This was 11th November, the anniversary of the armistice which ended the First World War, and de Gaulle wanted to remind his compatriots and anyone else who would listen that while some armistices were honourable, there were others which were not. But he also had a more immediate message for his listeners. Erect and imposing before a back drop of a huge Cross of Lorraine, he declared the liberation of France to be under the sole, indisputable direction of Fighting France, the name that now replaced the Free French, and Fighting France's unquestioned leader was General Charles de Gaulle.

"So much for Giraud!" exulted Edmond as the General finished.

"Quite a performance, I have to admit," said Margot. "He rather frightens me."

In a lull after the applause, a frail, quavering voice made itself heard in the hall.

"What's he saying, Edmond? Translate for me."

"Senile old fool!" barked Edmond. "He's telling de Gaulle to subordinate himself to Giraud."

Margot looked round and saw an elderly gentleman being hustled roughly from the hall.

"Why do they do that? A little bit of vocal opposition can't harm a strong leader, surely."

"France is a Nazi-occupied country," snapped Edmond, his face red with anger. "We will never tolerate people who hinder our efforts to liberate her!"

"Gracious! Don't get so worked up."

"I'm sorry, *chérie*. It's not you I'm angry with." He rose to his feet. "Come on, it's over."

They made their way with the crowd out into the curving vestibule.

"Can you wait here a moment? I have to have a word with Passy back in the hall."

Margot shrugged her shoulders.

"All right. Just don't lose me. I'll wait in that alcove."

She had been sitting on a bench in the alcove for no more than a minute when a quiet, hesitant, French-accented voice interrupted her thoughts.

"Madame Garland? Forgive me. I believe you are she?"

She looked up into a pair of deep-set dark eyes in a pale, thin face. She frowned in puzzlement.

"Yes, I'm Mrs Garland."

"My name is Pierre Mouret." He held out his hand and she shook it.

"I'm happy to meet you, Mr Mouret. Are you a friend of Edmond? Edmond Lemonnier, that is?"

Mouret left her question unanswered. He glanced rapidly over one and then the other shoulder. Clearly he was not at ease, and neither now was Margot.

"Is there something wrong?" she asked.

"No, no. You must forgive my boldness in approaching you, but it is important that I speak with you."

"I see. What about? And how did you know my name?"

Realizing that the man did not wish to raise his voice much above a whisper, Margot stood up, the better to catch what he was saying.

"I have to tell you about your husband."

"My husband? Edmond's not my husband. He's just a friend."

"I know that, madame. I am referring to Charles Garland."

"To *Charlie!* I don't understand. Do you know him? Have you seen him? He's a prisoner of war, you know."

Margot felt thoroughly confused and a little afraid.

"I cannot talk to you here, madame." He fumbled in the pocket of his jacket and withdrew a slip of paper. "Please call me tomorrow or the next day anytime before midday at that number."

"But what about my husband? You must tell me now! Please, you must!"

Margot shot her hand out to clutch at the man's arm. He gently disengaged himself and turned to leave.

"Please call me," he said, then disappeared rapidly in the flow of people streaming through the foyer to the exits.

Margot decided it was useless to try to follow him. She glanced at the piece of paper. "MOURET WES 9091." She felt a little frightened. The man had known who she was, and whom she was with. He had information about Charlie. But why was he so furtive?

"Sorry to make you wait. Let's go."

Edmond appeared at her side, placed his kepi on his head, and took her arm.

"Edmond, a strange man, a Frenchman, just came up to me, introduced himself as Pierre Mouret, and said he had information about Charlie which he couldn't pass on to me here. He gave me a number to call. Do you know him?"

"I don't know any Mouret. Describe him to me."

Edmond looked agitated.

"Medium height, thin face, dark receding hair, wearing grey flannels and a grey herring-bone tweed jacket under a ratty looking raincoat."

"A very observant witness, I must say!" He smiled nervously and began to steer her towards the exit. "I'll check on him tomorrow. Don't call him until I've found out who he is."

"But how could he know anything about Charlie? And how did he recognize me?"

"That's what I intend to find out."

"By calling him yourself?"

"No. There are other ways. Let me have the note he gave you."

Margot handed him the piece of paper, having rapidly committed the contents to memory.

"Remember we've only got two days; he said so."

"That'll be enough for me. We have to be cautious; it might be some sort of a trap."

"Why on earth?"

"Just trust me and do as I say."

They were now outside on Kensington Gore.

"If we find a taxi, can you drop me on the corner of Hill Street?"

"You don't want to come home?"

"No, chéri, I'm very tired. And Father's not been at all well today. I want to go home and make sure he is all right."

"As you wish," said a disappointed Edmond and started searching for a cab.

Margot spent the greater part of the morning at the Washington Club in a state of considerable frustration. Several times she had nearly called Edmond to find out if he had anything to report, and several times she came close to disobeying his strict instructions not to call the number Mouret had given her. Then, just after midday, Edmond called.

"Nothing on him yet. He's quite likely using an assumed name. So don't make any contact yet."

He rang off hurriedly, and Margot banged her fist down on the desk. She wished she could seek her father's advice, but she did not want him to know the circumstances under which she'd been approached.

"Damnit, I'm going to call Mouret!" she exclaimed, and dialled the number.

The call was answered and she recognized the voice immediately.

"I'm glad you called, Madame. I was just about to leave this address. Would you be able to meet me in the foyer of the Rembrandt Hotel at two o'clock this afternoon?"

"Monsieur Mouret, can't you possibly tell me whatever it is you want to tell me over the phone?"

"No, because there is someone else you have to meet with me who has the information."

"Someone else? Who?"

"Please be there at two o'clock, Madame. Everything will be explained then."

Margot sighed. "All right. I'll be there."

Margot kept the rendezvous punctually. She quickly spotted Mouret in the foyer, and he led her into a nearby sitting room, in the far corner of which sat a stocky red-faced man with sandy hair. He got up as they approached.

"This is Mr Maurice Drake, an English friend of mine," said Mouret.

Taken aback though she was, Margot managed to maintain her composure as they shook hands.

"You're a friend of my father's, aren't you?" she said as amiably as possible.

"I am indeed, Mrs Garland, and I'm delighted to be meeting you at last."

I bet you are! thought Margot. Edmond was right; I've walked into a trap.

"I think it's quiet enough for us to talk here," said

Drake, motioning her to an armchair. He studied her intently for a moment before speaking again.

"I will be brief and to the point, my dear, since I do not wish to waste your time. I am, as your father has doubtless told you, a Foreign Office employee working on certain aspects of our relations with France, amongst other things. I have two matters to discuss with you, and I must ask you to respect strictly the confidentiality of what I and my friend Mouret will be telling you. Understood?"

Margot nodded.

"Good! Then let me tell you first that an organization called MI9, which has been set up to assist and monitor escapes by Allied prisoners of war and evasions by those wandering uncaptured in occupied territories, such as downed air-crews, has made a rare exception to strict procedures and passed on to me information concerning your husband. I can give you no precise details at this stage, and I particularly do not wish to raise your hopes unduly, but it sounds as if he is in the hands of a reliable underground escape line run by some very brave friends of ours on the continent, having managed to get himself out of Oflag XIV C. How, we do not know. If he now manages to make it to Spain, he should be able to get to Gibraltar without too much difficulty, and from there home. I'm sure we all wish him good luck."

Drake sat back and thrust his forefingers into the little pockets of his waistcoat.

"I don't know what to say," said Margot, shaking her head and smiling nervously. "It's wonderful but rather frightening news. He must be in awful danger."

"Possibly, but he's in good hands. If he does exactly what his helpers tell him to, has patience and a decent slice of good luck, he should make it. But don't expect him back tomorrow. These things take time. Maybe several weeks more yet. Possibly months, but I rather doubt that. Let me emphasize," he said leaning forward again, "that we do not normally divulge such information even to next of kin like yourself. For good security reasons. One could betray a whole escape network through unnecessary communication of even the barest facts."

"Then why are you making an exception in Charlie's case?" asked Margot. There had to be a catch in it, and she was beginning to feel scared.

"We are doing you this favour in the hopes that it will encourage you to do us one. And that is why Mouret's here."

I might have known, thought Margot. It's Edmond they're after.

"First of all," said Drake, "I should tell you, also in strictest confidence, that Monsieur Mouret is here on a visit from occupied France – a risky business at the best of times. I need scarcely add that he is a very brave and effective resistance leader with whom we have close connections. He will be returning to France shortly."

Margot looked at Mouret with a mixture of curiosity and admiration. He just didn't look the type. But then, she admitted to herself, she was not at all sure what the type was meant to be. Her examination of Mouret was interrupted with a jolt by what Drake had next to say.

"Mrs Garland, we feel it our duty to warn you of what your friend Captain Lemonnier is up to here in London. He may not have told you that he is working for General de Gaulle's secret intelligence service, the BCRA. That in itself is nothing to be ashamed of. Their service had been very helpful to us in a lot of respects, and we have been very happy to help them in return."

He paused and looked expectantly at Margot.

"No, he had not told me about working for intelligence," she said. "But since it's secret work, why should he?"

"Why indeed, Mrs Garland? And so I am here with my friend Mouret to fill you in. You see, one of Lemonnier's principal responsibilities is to prevent anyone being recruited here in London for the French resistance who does not swear personal allegiance to General de Gaulle. People like Mouret believe that that hampers our resistance war against the Germans, and my people agree with him. But we are up against a tough competitor and a far from scrupulous one. Your friend Lemonnier is, I'm afraid, a master at the art of intimidation, all too often through violence."

"*Edmond?* I don't believe you! He's a gentle being."

"I'm afraid Monsieur Drake is right, Madame," said Mouret softly. "We know the facts. He has done some quite unpleasant things, and we suspect that he is going beyond his orders. His own superiors may well not know what he is up to."

"Mrs Garland, your Edmond is hounding and threatening a number of highly patriotic Frenchmen and Frenchwomen whose only crime is that they do not see why they should be forced to swear allegiance to de Gaulle if they want to join the resistance. De Gaulle has admittedly been remarkably successful in uniting the majority of the different resistance movements under his banner, but there are still significant elements who need to operate independently, particularly in relation to our own well-established networks in France. And such people *must* be protected from the sort of treatment being meted out to them by your friend."

Margot stared at the carpet, confused. "Why are you telling me all this? Do you honestly expect me to stop him? If indeed there is anything that should be stopped."

"No, no, heavens no!" said Drake with a little smile. "We were simply thinking that if in the course of your time spent with Lemonnier you happened to hear him mention any names in an angry sort of way, you know, in a way that might suggest that they were people who were causing him annoyance or trouble in his work, you might care to pass those names along to me."

Margot felt her irritation rising. "Since he hasn't even told me what his job is, it's scarcely likely that he's going to start telling me who his enemies are! Besides, I don't spy on my friends."

"Of course not," said Drake, sounding hurt. "But you should bear in mind that some of the people whom Edmond might not treat too kindly are just the sort of people who have been helping your husband." He brought his hands together as in prayer and tapped his lips with the finger tips as he transfixed Margot with a stare.

"Ah! Now it's all clear to me, Mr Drake," she said, trying to control her quavering voice. "You're calling in your IOUs. In return for getting Charlie home safely, I start spying on my friends for you."

"No, no, madame!" broke in Mouret. "You must not think that! There is no connection between your husband's escape and what Monsieur Drake has been saying about Lemonnier."

"No indeed," said Drake. "And I apologize if I mistakenly conveyed that impression. You are under no obligations whatsoever, Mrs Garland. We are simply sharing some confidential information with you and leaving it entirely to you to see whether or not there is anything you might feel inclined to do about it."

"Well, there isn't, gentlemen, I'm afraid. I'm an American diplomat's daughter, and the wife of a British army officer, and what the French do to each other is simply not my business." She rose, and the two men quickly followed her to their feet. "Did you mention to my father that you were seeing me?"

"No, I did not. This is strictly between us and you."

"One more thing, Mr Drake. Now that you know that I'm not in the spying business, would you do me the great courtesy of not having me spied upon by your own people?"

Drake smiled. "Nobody's spying on *you*, Mrs Garland. But we cannot help it if Captain Lemonnier's admirable taste in ladies leads you into our line of vision from time to time."

"Well, thank you both anyway for the very good news about my husband. I hope he will be back soon."

She shook hands first with Mouret and then with Drake.

"Thank you for agreeing to see us," said Drake.

Margot thought of saying that she had only ever agreed to see Mouret, but thought better of it.

"Good day, gentlemen." She turned and hurried to the hotel exit.

In a taxi bound for the Washington Club, she tried to pull her confused thoughts together. Charlie coming home; Edmond an intelligence agent and alleged political thug; herself in demand as a spy for the British and the French. It was all too much. Back in the privacy of her small office, she put her head in her hands and tried to think what, if anything, she was going to tell Edmond. Then she noticed a slip of paper noting that he had called her. She was to call back urgently. She picked up the receiver, her hand trembling.

"I'm glad you called back promptly, *chérie*. I just wanted to tell you that you must on no account have anything to do with this man Mouret. That's not his real name anyway. He has absolutely nothing to tell you about Charlie; that's just a trick to get you to meet him. He's a very dangerous man and he's probably wanting to find out through our relationship one or two things that he has no business knowing. That's all I can tell you, but you just have to trust me, *chérie*, and above all obey me on this. Don't even call him. All right?"

Margot said nothing for a moment.

"He's really that bad?"

"He's high in the communist hierarchy. I'll tell you that much. But all this is strictly between you and me. Now I have to go. *Au revoir, ma belle.*"

He rang off.

Margot sank her head once more in her hands.

"Oh Jesus! What have I gotten myself into now?"

22

The call Margot received from her father disturbed her. She was to cancel whatever lunch plans she had and come straight home. There was a matter of utmost seriousness to discuss without delay, and he could not elaborate on the telephone. There could be only one reason for it, she concluded with a shudder; somehow he had discovered that she had been lying to him about her whereabouts over the previous weekend. She had told him that she was going to Oxford with a colleague from the Red Cross to help advise in the conversion of a private house into a Servicemen's Club. In fact, she and Edmond had spent the weekend in a small hotel in Abingdon, not far from the university city, which was owned by a retired French cavalry officer and his English wife. No sooner had they returned to London than Margot had begun searching in her mind for a plausible alibi which she could use to cover a return visit. There was no doubt that her father had found her out; the forbidding tenor of his voice over the telephone had convinced her of that. But how? Had the wretched Drake had them followed even to the backwaters of the Berkshire countryside?

As she walked the short distance through Mayfair from the club to Hill Street, she decided she had better make a clean breast of it. She knew she was not very adept at arguing a false case; better that she admit the deception and plead that she had deceived him only because she did not want to hurt him, and that her loneliness and frustration had finally got the better of her. That, after all, was near enough to the truth.

Reaching the house, she turned the key in the lock and entered the hallway.

"Is that you, Margot?"

Her father's voice, calling from the living room, sounded friendlier than it had been on the telephone. Maybe the confrontation was not going to be too traumatic after all.

"Yes, it's me!" she called, shrugging her overcoat from her shoulders and dropping it onto a chair. In front of the mirror she removed her blue felt brimmed hat and primped her hair. Her last thought before going in to face her father was that she had yet to provide him with a plausible reason for being out to dinner later that evening, since she and Edmond had a rendezvous at his flat.

She found her father standing in front of the fireplace, grinning broadly. She frowned, puzzled by the marked change in his mood. Then she felt two hands grip her shoulders from behind. She let out a gasp of fright and swung round to find herself in Charlie's arms.

She felt weak at the knees, and both her breath and her voice deserted her as Charlie crushed her to him, then pushed her gently back to look at her.

"Charlie!" She looked over her shoulder at her father. "What sort of a lousy trick was that?"

Her father laughed. "Charlie's idea, darling."

"Don't I get a homecoming kiss?"

She turned back to Charlie and they kissed. It was brief and chaste, their lips barely parted.

"I can't believe it!" she said, pulling back. "Let me look at you."

Charlie, smartly dressed in service dress uniform, stepped back a pace and stood rigidly at attention in his best parade ground manner.

"How's that?"

"Not bad! Not bad at all! You're not as thin as I expected."

Charlie relaxed his stance. "They fed me up like a goose for the slaughter in San Sebastian and then again in Gibraltar. And you!" He stepped up to her again and took her two hands in his. "You look even more gorgeous than I remember you. Don't tell me grass widowhood has been *that* good for you!"

"I'll leave you two," said Harland, walking to the door. "I've a couple of calls to make, then you're my guests to lunch at the Dorchester. This evening you'll no doubt want to dine out on the town together. We can leave in ten minutes," he called after him as he disappeared upstairs to his study.

"I need a drink," said Margot, sinking onto the sofa. "Can you fix me a strong Scotch and water, Charlie?"

"Right away." He went to the cocktail cabinet.

"You're beasts to have played that trick on me," she said, searching in her purse for her cigarettes. Her hands were now trembling so much that she had difficulty in opening the little silver case, and the flame of her lighter danced maddeningly in front of the tip before she succeeded in bringing the two together.

Charlie brought her her Scotch and sat down beside her. Then suddenly she burst into tears. He took the lit cigarette from her shaking fingers, threw it into the fireplace, and placed her glass on a table. Then he took her in his arms and let her weep uncontrollably on his shoulder while he ran his fingers gently through her hair.

"That's all right, darling. Have a good cry. It's natural and good for you. I feel like a good cry myself, but maybe I'm just too tired at the moment."

After a moment the sobbing ceased and she sat up straight, took the handkerchief offered by Charlie and dabbed at her eyes and blew her nose.

"You didn't throw the cigarette away, did you? That's criminal in wartime!" She laughed and leaned over the grate to see if she could find it on the unlit heap of kindling wood. "Just because you POWs were flush with them." She gave up the search and straightened up again. Charlie lit another one for her, and she inhaled deeply. "I'll have the Scotch too," she said with a shy smile. "I'm sorry; I must look a mess."

"Nonsense, darling."

"Now you'd better tell me how you got here."

"Details of the heroics can wait till lunch," he said with a laugh. "I got into Bristol on a plane this morning from Gibraltar."

"Did you call your parents?"

"From Bristol. They were at Bowes Court. They left immediately for London and are joining us at the Dorchester. They'd like us to go down to the country with them on Saturday morning."

For the first time since entering the room Margot thought of Edmond. She had to call him as soon as possible. She'd do it during lunch, using a trip to the ladies' room as an excuse to leave the table. She just prayed he'd be in his office. Her train of thought led from Edmond to Drake, and she wondered whether she could risk telling Charlie that she had known he was on his way back. She decided against it, at least for the moment. On Drake's instructions, she hadn't even told her father. It would raise too many complicating questions from Charlie if she were to share the secret with him now.

"Penny for your thoughts, darling," said Charlie.

"I'm sorry." As if compensating for the thoughts of Edmond, she put her hand on Charlie's knee. "My head is only just beginning to stop spinning."

She took a full mouthful of Scotch and gulped it down.

"You know Ivor's in London."

"Yes, you told me in your last letter before I got out. And my father told me that Jamie's on Alexander's staff and got a Mention in Dispatches."

"Shall we ask Ivor to join us with a girlfriend this evening? He'll be longing to see you."

Charlie frowned. "No, darling. Cousins can wait. I want you all to myself this first evening. Don't you think that's better?"

"Of course. It was a silly idea." She put down her glass. "Darling, if you'll excuse me a moment; I'll go and repair my face. I should be looking my best for you at our first meal together in two years."

They rose together and Charlie put his arms around her waist.

"It must be a shock for you."

"In a way, Charlie. But a lovely one, of course. You just have to forgive me if I'm not behaving quite in the way you expected me to do, but it's only the effect of the shock." She laughed nervously. "I'll be the old Margot again very quickly." She kissed him on the cheek and gently took his hands from her waist. "Have another drink. I'll be five minutes, then we can leave."

She saw a slight look of sadness in Charlie's face as she turned from him and left the room. As she mounted the stairs to her bedroom she told herself that she had handled the scene pretty badly, and she felt sorry for Charlie, but what could she do? In her room she sat on the edge of the bed and felt herself to be on the edge of a precipice. At least Charlie had thought her performance natural under the circumstances, but then he didn't know that she had been daily expecting his return and that her behaviour was not the result of shock but of the sudden realization that time had finally run out, and that she now faced the crossroads which before had always seemed sufficiently distant to allow her to prepare for a decision.

She got up and walked to her dresser and sat down, gazing forlornly into the mirror. What a mess! She picked up a powder puff and went to work. As she restored her make-up, she recalled with a jolt that she had not even said anything to Charlie to show that she was aware that he must have escaped from his POW camp in order to get home. He must think my behaviour very strange, whatever he may say to the contrary, she told herself. Over lunch with the three parents, she would have to be a great deal more careful.

At the Dorchester, as they ate, Charlie described the manner of his escape from Oflag XIV C. He and his friend, Mickey Weatherall, had taken advantage of the confusion caused when a gasoline wagon blew up as it was entering the prison gates. Being fortuitously in the right place at the right time, they had slipped past the panicking guards and walked briskly up a nearby hill and into some woods, where they hid until next morning. Having observed what appeared to be a whole family taking off from a nearby farmhouse in a car, they visited the farm, found it empty, and helped themselves to clothes and a few Reichmarks. They just managed to outflank a search party on their way back into the hills, where they lay up for the rest of the day, and then, at dusk, set off on a westward course in the general direction of Switzerland.

278

Not being in possession of the forged passes that the camp escape committee was able to provide to participants in "approved" escape plans, there was no possibility for the two of them to use the railroads. It was dangerous enough just walking. Neither of them spoke more than a few words of German, and at one critical juncture they had to pretend they were deaf mutes, conversing in sign language, in order to divest themselves of the attention of a village policeman. For eleven days and nights they continued their dangerous journey, scarcely daring to believe in their good luck as they came closer and closer to the Swiss border.

On the eleventh morning they knew that they had at last reached the frontier when they saw the barriers and the sentries a quarter of a mile up the road on which they were travelling. They took cover on some higher ground and surveyed the border. They picked what looked like a reasonable crossing point about three hundred yards to the left of the road, and hid on the edge of a copse, about a quarter of a mile from it, to await darkness.

"It was freezing cold," continued Charlie, as his audience listened in respectful silence. "We'd had nothing to eat for three days except some rotting turnips we'd found along the way, and we were both weak from exhaustion. Mickey suddenly had second thoughts about the choice of crossing point, and we had a bit of an argument. Just before dark, he got up and went off on his own, over my protests, to see if he couldn't spot a safer crossing point further south. Twenty minutes later I saw him being marched down the road, surrounded by a jubilant group of Hitler Jugend who had presumably been patrolling the frontier area. I just burst into tears when I saw him. All that way just to be captured within sight of freedom by a bunch of boys. Mickey did me one last good turn. He must have convinced his captors that he was a lone escapee, since the Hitler Jugend attempted no further search of the area in which I was still hiding.

"That night I got across without difficulty at our originally chosen spot where the wire fencing was, as we thought we had spotted from a distance, only loosely secured at ground level. I was able to crawl under quite easily. Since the Swiss intern escapees if they catch them, I had to continue the evasion for the two days it took me to reach Bern. We had known back at the camp, from information smuggled in by MI9, that the Military Attaché in Bern could help escapees cross into France where they would be put in touch with a French-run escape line to Spain and Gibraltar. He got me into France within a week and the French took me down to the western Pyrenees and over into Spain. It was a fantastic operation and they were absolutely marvellous people. That, in a nutshell, is how yours truly comes to be having lunch at the Dorchester with his family today."

"A fascinating story, my boy," said Sir Walter, beaming. "We're all proud of you." He raised his glass. "To your courage and determination!"

"And here's to an absent and gallant comrade: Mickey Weatherall!" added Charlie.

As Margot joined in the toasts, she felt a growing sense of desperation grip her. She had been moved and greatly impressed by what she had heard. How had the shy, boyish young officer who had gone off to war just two years ago been transformed into a man of such courage and strength, a storybook hero? His escape, she had to admit, made Edmond's flight from France seem like a Cook's Tour in comparison. As he had been recounting his adventure, she had been studying his face. It was thinner now, and the eyes seemed to be deeper set. The almost girl-like creamy smoothness of the skin, as she had known it previously, had given way to a coarser, grained complexion. As they had walked to the Dorchester from Hill Street, she had detected just a hint of a limp, and she had asked about the wound suffered just before his capture. It was causing him no trouble, he had assured her. The damp, cold nights on the run had brought on a painful ache, and he had worried that the leg might let him down when it came to the wearying climb over the Pyrenees, but in fact he had managed without difficulty, and it was now in excellent shape again.

Yes, she thought; Charlie had grown up into a real man. For two years she had lived with the image in her mind of Charlie as he had left her. Now, suddenly, she was face to face with a very different Charlie. Was he now the sort of man who could wean her, albeit unaware of the necessity of doing so, away from Edmond? Would she succumb to the new Charlie? Could he love her and satisfy her as Edmond did? Why did you have to come back now, Charlie, and put me through this terrible test?

"If you'll excuse me," she said, interrupting her father who was plying Charlie with questions, "I have to go to the ladies' room for a moment."

The men rose, and Margot heaved a sigh of relief when she realized that Cynthia was not planning to accompany her. She hurried from the restaurant and found a call-box at the front of the hotel. Her luck held again: Edmond was in his office.

"Edmond, darling. Listen carefully. Charlie's back. He surprised us all by turning up unannounced this morning. I'm calling from the Dorchester where we're lunching with Father and his parents. Obviously we can't meet tonight, but I absolutely have to see you tomorrow. I'll insist that I have to go as usual to the Washington Club, and I'll call you from there . . . No, darling, there's no time to talk about it now. I have to get back to the table . . . I'll cross that bridge when I come to it. Just trust me . . . I promise I'll call tomorrow morning. He's going to be debriefed by military intelligence or something and it may last all day. Try to keep your plans flexible. We may have to meet at very short notice . . . Yes, I love you too. Must run now. *Au revoir, chéri.*"

How typical of Edmond, she thought, as she made her way back to the restaurant. His first concern was whether she was going to make love to Charlie that night. She hadn't yet had time to think much about that as an immediate prospect. When she had first heard from Drake and Mouret that he was on his way home, she had pondered the matter and reached only a tentative conclusion. Edmond was hoping that she would decide to deny Charlie his conjugal rights, and she knew full well why; it would precipitate the crisis which he believed must lead to her eventual abandonment of Charlie. But Margot had not then felt ready to be rushed, and she felt no readier now. Charlie would sleep with her and make love to her, and she would just have to find out how well she could take it. The prospect of having two lovers had not struck her as being all that bizarre. In any case, what alternative did she have? She knew she could not abandon Edmond, and she knew she could not be so heartless as to deny her returning husband any opportunity to re-establish his relationship with her. But now, as the hour of the first test drew near, she was feeling nervous and uncomfortable.

When she arrived back at the table, she found the rest of the party ready to leave.

"Can you take the afternoon off from your work?" asked Charlie.

"Of course; I'll call them right away and explain what's happened."

"Good. Then we can go for a walk through the park and pick up a suitcase of clothes from my parents' house and have tea there. And there's some shopping I have to do."

That suited Margot. She wanted to be as busy as possible so that she would have no time to think about the approaching night.

"You can come and see where I work, too, if we have time; it's only just round the corner from home."

They dined and danced that evening at Ciro's, and then went on to the Four Hundred. At dinner she had happily responded to his request that she tell him everything that had happened to her, and talked incessantly. She hardly touched her food, but she drank rather more than she usually did, and by the time they reached the night-club, she was in a very mellow mood. A surprised and delighted Mr Rossi greeted them at the door.

"This deserves a hero's welcome, Mr Garland!" he gushed, and hurried them to a banquette table, giving orders to a waiter for champagne on the house to be brought to them immediately.

"And please tell the band to play 'Just the Way You Look Tonight'," said Margot, squeezing Charlie's hand.

On the opening bars of Charlie's favourite song they moved to the dance floor. Another couple immediately recognized Charlie, and there were congratulations and embraces.

"Seems I'm married to a real, live hero," said Margot pressing her cheek against his. "I wonder whether I can handle that."

Charlie laughed. "Nothing to it, darling. Just keep the adoring females away from me! But seriously, you're just as much a heroine in my eyes. You've been just as battle-scarred as me, and you've survived it all with tremendous courage. I'm dreadfully proud of you."

Margot couldn't think of a reply, so she said nothing. They danced on in silence for a while and then returned to the table. She lit a cigarette as Charlie refilled her champagne glass.

"So, you're really in a hurry to rejoin your battalion?"

"I am. As an ex-POW, I could, I am told, get quite a cushy job in the War Office or something like that, which wouldn't involve me in combat again unless there was an invasion. But I know I'd be bored, and I want to get back into active service with my friends, what's left of them."

"A real glutton for punishment, my Charlie."

"Do you think I'd be being unfair to you? After all, it would mean being away on training most of the time with the prospect of being in on the eventual invasion of Europe if things keep on as they seem to be now."

"No. Not unfair. You're a soldier and you have to do whatever you have to do. I've waited for you once, and I'll wait again, I guess."

Charlie looked at her with a pained expression.

"We really shouldn't be talking about such possibilities on our first night together. I'm sorry."

"No, we shouldn't," agreed Margot. She drank deeply from her champagne glass. I think I want to get really tipsy, she said to herself. "Do you think Rossi grades you high enough as a hero to offer us a second bottle when we've drained this one?"

"Worth a try," said Charlie with a smile. He put a

hand on her knee. "Am I going to have to carry you home?"

"And up the stairs."

An hour and a lot of champagne later, Margot sat on the edge of the bed, giggling. Charlie had just finished undressing her and now stood naked over her.

"What was it like not to have a woman for over two years," she asked, taking his swollen penis hesitantly in her hand.

"Indescribable."

"You must have masturbated a lot." Her words were slurred, and she tried to focus a little better to correct the impression that she was seeing two penises. "Well, did you?" She tugged savagely at him.

"Wasn't much else to do," he said with a nervous laugh. "Come on, angel, onto the bed. You're tired," he continued, lifting her by her arms. Margot turned, sank face downwards onto the bed, then slowly rolled over and held her arms out to him.

"Come and enjoy your first fuck of freedom!"

"The first for both of us since March the twenty-sixth, nineteen-forty."

"Christ! You even remember the date."

She spread her legs and he pushed deep inside her.

"I'm not hurting, am I?"

"Course not, silly!"

Within seconds she felt his climax approaching, and then the warm juices flooded her.

"I'm sorry, darling," he said breathlessly. "I just couldn't contain myself."

"Not to worry."

The room was spinning, and she felt the nausea surging up in her. She pushed Charlie off her and rushed through the bedroom door onto the landing and lurched into the bathroom. She was just in time.

When she got back to the bedroom she found him sitting up in bed, the covers up to his waist, smoking a cigarette.

"Too much champagne and excitement," he said as she climbed in beside him.

284

"Probably."

He put a hand on her breast and gently massaged a nipple. After a moment, she brushed it away.

"We'd better sleep. I have somehow to get to work tomorrow."

Charlie stubbed out the cigarette and switched off the bedside light. Then he leaned over and kissed her on the cheek.

"I'm afraid that wasn't really very great for either of us."

"It doesn't matter, Charlie. It doesn't matter at all."

She turned over and was soon asleep.

Margot managed to steal an hour with Edmond at the end of the following afternoon while Charlie was being debriefed by MI9 on prisoner-of-war conditions in general and his own successful escape attempt in particular.

"So, you think he might be posted away from London?" asked Edmond with unconcealed expectation in his voice.

"He wants to rejoin his old battalion. It's in Scotland at the moment. Jamie's no longer with it, of course, but there are still quite a lot of his friends from 1940 there."

"But wouldn't that mean your going to Scotland too?"

"No. We discussed that at breakfast this morning. I told him that I felt I should be in London to carry on my work and keep an eye on Father. Father, needless to say, didn't agree, but Charlie seemed understanding and said it wouldn't be fun for wives up there anyway. He'd come down some weekends, and I'd go up there to meet him from time to time.

Edmond looked relieved.

"That makes me feel much better," he said. "And please forgive me for saying so, but it doesn't sound as though you and Charlie are desperate for each other's company."

"You're seeing the situation only from your point of view. There must be thousands of wives separated from their soldier husbands in this country, so Charlie sees nothing unusual in that. And then you have to remember

285

he doesn't feel that our marriage is in any way threatened."

They were sitting over a cup of tea at the Piccadilly Hotel, an establishment which Margot felt reasonably sure was rarely, if ever, frequented by people she knew.

"Does that make you feel uncomfortable?"

"At times it makes me feel worse than that, Edmond. It makes me feel positively cheap. So you're going to have to be very patient and understanding with me. I need you, but at the same time I won't have Charlie deeply hurt after all he's been through. He doesn't deserve that. So, for the time being I'm resigned to leading a double life, and you're going to have to get used to that and not get fits of jealousy."

Edmond smiled wryly. "I'll do my best, but it's a lot to ask of a hot-blooded Frenchman."

"It's a hell of a lot harder for me, my love. I simply wasn't cut out for a life of deception, but I've been driven into it."

They had been talking for nearly an hour. Having kept secret from him her meeting with Drake and Mouret, she had resisted the temptation to remind Edmond that he had adamantly insisted that Mouret would have nothing to tell her about Charlie, and she maintained the fiction that his escape and return had taken her as much as anyone by complete surprise. As she had been expecting, Edmond had wanted to know if they had made love that night, and she had told him that they had both been very tired and had had quite a lot to drink and, as a result, had really not done very much. And then she had added that she preferred Edmond to respect her sensibilities by not asking her that sort of question again. He had looked pained and puzzled, so she had reinforced the point by saying that interrogations of that sort would undermine their relationship, and that he would have to learn to trust her judgement on how to handle Charlie.

Margot looked at her watch. "I must go. He'll be home by six and Beaverbrook has invited us, my parents-in-law and Father to dinner tonight. A sort of celebration of Charlie's return."

"Mixing with those sorts of people is very important to you, isn't it, Margot?"

There was more than a hint of bitterness in his tone.

"And to you, Edmond, remember? As long as I have the chance to meet them, I should do so. It's silly to be jealous of that; anyway, you see a lot of interesting people yourself. De Gaulle is not exactly a nobody."

"I know, but it ties you to the Garlands."

"Now, Edmond, who was it who was so insistent that I spread the Gaullist gospel amongst my father-in-law's friends? Don't start getting petty and ungrateful just because Charlie's back."

She picked up her purse, adjusted the silk scarf around her neck, and indicated to Edmond that he help her put on her overcoat.

"My male pride should be offended, *chérie*," he said as he held the coat open for her, "but with you it is always impossible. I am helpless in your hands."

"Nonsense, my love. You're just learning the practical way of handling someone else's wife who insists on the kid glove treatment."

"I'm not sure I understand, but it doesn't matter." He picked up his own overcoat and kepi. "All I want to know right now is when we are going to make love again."

"Shhh!" Margot looked nervously around her. "You'd better start giving me lunch at your flat." She whispered into his ear. "Something simple that can be eaten in bed."

"Now that's more like my Margot," he said as he led her by the arm to the lobby.

23

Maurice Drake watched the cock pheasant haul itself noisily into the air from the dense cover of the brambles. He punched the handle of his ash walking stick into his shoulder, picked up the arc of flight of the climbing bird, gently swung the stick until its tip overtook his quarry's head, and then squeezed on an imaginary trigger. The cock flew on, but in the mind's eye of the would-be hunter, it turned two untidy cartwheels before plummeting sixty feet to the brush and brambles below.

"Damnit, Hugh, I think I miss my regular shooting more than anything else in this wretched war. I'd sell my sainted mother for an assured supply of cartridges."

"Me too. A day's rough shooting when you know you can only pull the trigger a couple of dozen times simply isn't worth the frustration. I prefer to go out and blow 'em all in one good five-minute drive."

Sir Hugh Gaffney, Cabinet Officer adviser to the Prime Minister, waved towards the thickly-wooded far slope of the narrow valley that cut through the centre of his Gloucestershire estate.

"Take Duke's Wood there, for example. Absolutely teeming with pheasant. It's a bloody shame!" He paused to rekindle his pipe, then gestured towards the grey Cotswold-stone manor house that stood at the end of the valley. "We'd better be getting back. Being late for tea ranks second only to treason in Mary's book of capital crimes."

The two men quickened their pace along the narrow path through the underbrush.

"You know, Maurice, what you've been telling me about the BCRA's absolutely lawless behaviour bears out what we've just got from Special Branch in their report to Number Ten. The PM is hopping mad, and now more than ever convinced that he's backed the wrong horse in de Gaulle."

"Then he should expose him and his thug associates for the fascists they are and wash his hands of them."

Drake slashed viciously at a hawthorn bush with his stick.

Gaffney smiled. "I can see how much you'd love to administer a royal thrashing to 'le grand Charles'. Wouldn't we all! But seriously, you know my views, and while I'd be the last to condone the Gestapo-like methods of some of Passy's people in intimidating their rivals, I do see a double risk in the Prime Minister publicizing this and all the other grievances against de Gaulle, even in a closed session of the House. First, the Opposition and even a lot of members of his own party are going to say 'We told you so,' and ask why he goes on backing this anti-British, anti-American megalomaniac. Winston will hate that, and he's simply not politically secure enough to take a major humiliation. Secondly, an attack on de Gaulle may have a result opposite to the one desired: it might actually consolidate support for him in France, particularly if FDR gets into the act. You know how vitriolic *he* is on the subject."

"Damnit, Hugh, these are risks that have to be taken! The man's a bloody menace, and we've no right to be concentrating our aid and comfort on him at the expense of other potential leaders of France."

"But I'm afraid we'll have to go on doing so for now. It's too late to change horses, unless, of course, he forces our hand by doing something even farther beyond the pale than he's ventured so far."

"You can't get much further than he's been, Hugh. But who am I to argue with a Downing Street insider?"

"Someone well qualified to do so, old chap. But it's too nice an afternoon to be worrying our heads further about that now." He paused to tap the ash out of his pipe on the heel of one highly polished brown boot. "Tell me how the salmon have been running in that dream of a Scottish stream of yours."

"Ah, now, there's something to take one's mind off the troublemakers of this world!" said Drake happily, and he raised his walking stick, imagining the supple strength of his favourite salmon rod. The two friends strode on in the gradually failing light toward their tea and scones, chatting contentedly.

Less than twenty-four hours later, Maurice Drake, shaking with anger, stared at the copy of the police report which his assistant had just laid on his desk. One sentence in particular incensed him: "Although no eye witnesses have as yet come forward, the preliminary examination strongly suggests that the deceased had been struck by a vehicle driving in the fog, and that the driver had failed to stop and/or report the accident."

"Accident, my foot!" bellowed Drake, banging a clenched fist on the desk top. "It's those bastards in Carlton Gardens!" He fumbled in his pockets for his pack of Players, found it empty and swore.

"I have Woodbines, sir," said his assistant.

"Keep them, Hawkins; I'm not that desperate. Just get me Sir Hugh Gaffney on the line."

"Yes, sir. May I say how sorry I am about Mr Mouret. A patriot even if he was a communist."

"The two are by no means mutually exclusive, man. Particularly in a war like this."

If the report of Mouret's death brought Maurice Drake to the boil, it sent an icy cold shiver down Margot's spine. She folded the newspaper and placed it back on the table in the reading room of the Washington Club. She felt a sudden need for fresh air and went downstairs, through the lobby, and out onto Curzon Street. It was a cold and cloudy afternoon, and she leaned against the sandbagged portico and tried to chase some horrifying thoughts from her mind. She kept recalling Edmond's angry pledge that evening at the Albert Hall that the Gaullists would not tolerate anyone standing in the way of their march towards the liberation of France. Had Mouret, the communist, stood in their way? As she pondered this frightening possibility, she heard her name being called in the lobby. She quickly went back inside and walked over to the reception desk.

"A call from Scotland for you, Margot."

"Scotland?"

"That's right. You feeling OK, honey? You look as pale as a ghost."

"I'm fine," said Margot, flustered.

Who do I know in Scotland? she asked herself. Plenty of people. Charlie's old battalion, for example. Maybe they were trying to get hold of him through her.

"Did they say who it was, Shirley?"

The switchboard operator leaned out of her cramped little cabin.

"Nope, dear. A man on a pay-phone."

Margot hurried to the booth at the other side of the foyer and lifted the receiver.

"Margot Garland speaking."

"It'd better be after all the time I've been hanging on this line."

"*Larry!*"

"None other, sis. Just flown in. I'm at Prestwick. We landed a couple of hours ago. We'll be down in England in forty-eight hours."

"I can't believe it, darling! It's the most wonderful news imaginable. Have you talked to Father?"

"Just a moment ago. He sounded great."

"You're going to be in London for a while, I hope."

"Three days leave there next week. Once we've parked our B-17s. How's my brother-in-law?"

"Terrific; he'll be thrilled to hear he's going to meet you at last. So come quickly."

"Will do. I've got to go now. There's a line outside this booth. I'll call you all again when we get south."

"We'll have a monster celebration. Take care. Happy landings!"

They rang off, and Margot, beaming broadly, strode back to the reception desk.

"Would you believe that, Candy," she said excitedly to the tall redheaded receptionist. "My brother's just arrived from the States. A new bomber group for the Eighth. Isn't that great?"

"Sure is, honey. And lucky guy to have his big sister over here to keep him out of trouble." She handed a key to an Air Force top sergeant. "Looks like you're getting reinforcements, Perry."

The sergeant turned to Margot. From his watery eyes she could tell that he had been drinking.

"We sure need 'em, ma'am. They took half of our best to North Africa, and when the weather improves, what's left of us here will get kicked into the air every goddammed day."

"Well, help is on the way," said Margot cheerfully.

"Yeah. Tell your brother 'welcome' from me. And tell him by the time he gets his first mission there'll be more Kraut fighter squadrons waiting for him up there than there are whores on Piccadilly on a Saturday night."

"OK, Perry, take it easy now." Candy wagged a finger at him. "Go get yourself a hot meal and a good rest."

The sergeant turned away. Candy leaned over the reception desk and whispered.

"He lost his buddy on a raid last week. I knew him. Nice boy from Tulsa. One day they're here, the next they're gone. Just like that." She snapped her fingers.

The sergeant, lingering a few feet away, examining the contents of his wallet, rounded on her.

"Listen, lady, he wasn't gone just like that." He snapped his fingers in imitation. "Pete sat for half an hour trying to hold his insides in with his hands, and when he couldn't hold them any more they ran all over the floor of the goddammed turret, and he didn't die until he'd seen more of himself on the deck than there was left inside him." He turned and walked away unsteadily to the staircase.

"Don't take it to heart, honey," said Candy soothingly to Margot who was standing there with a stricken look on her face.

"I won't," she said firmly, and strode off towards her office. But suddenly the joy of knowing that Larry had arrived was tempered with apprehension. A typical wartime day, she thought. Something always turns up to spoil the good moments. Such as they are.

24

Margot had gone round to Bolton Place for a drink after work on 23rd December. She had brought her Christmas gift to Edmond, a cashmere sweater, and had received from him a leather-bound volume of Baudelaire's poetry. They had made love rather hastily, wished each other a happy Christmas, and then she had hurried back to Hill Street, where Charlie was waiting to take her out to dinner. The following afternoon they would be taking the train to Hampshire, together with Harland, to spend Christmas and New Year with Charlie's parents at Bowes Court.

On her way to Hill Street from Edmond's apartment, she had told herself that Edmond had to take a back seat in her mind during the holidays. Charlie had spent the last two Christmases in a prisoner-of-war camp, and he deserved, and she owed him, a good one this time. There would be plenty of opportunities to see Edmond when she returned to London in the early New Year. Charlie had just learned, to his delight, that after a period of training as a tank troop commander, he would be posted to the Grenadiers' Second Battalion which now formed part of the new Guards Armoured Division in southern England. The Battalion was based in Wiltshire not far to the west of Bowes Court, and while Margot would continue to don her blue-grey American Red Cross uniform and report daily to the Washington Club, Charlie would be able to join her in the country for most weekends, at either Bowes Court or Verbena Cottage. Edmond had expressed his distaste for her weekday lover, weekend husband arrangement, but Margot reckoned that it would suit her requirements admirably.

She was busy packing on Christmas Eve morning when Edmond made one of his purposely rare telephone calls to her at Hill Street. She was relieved that both Charlie and her father were out of the house when the call came through.

"Margot, I have to see you immediately. It's a matter of great urgency and I can't tell you over the phone."

"But Edmond, we're leaving in a couple of hours!" protested Margot.

"You can't leave until I've seen you again. And you must come now. I'm going to walk down Park Lane to the Dorchester. We'll meet at the entrance and then take a walk in the park. I have to talk to you. If you can leave now you'll be there in ten minutes."

"Can't you tell me over the telephone, *chéri*? I'm awfully pressed for time, and much as I'd love to see you today –"

"No. You have to come. It's imperative."

Margot sighed. "All right. I'll come. I just hope, though, that it's not going to be bad news to spoil my Christmas."

"I'm leaving Duke Street now. Please hurry." He rang off.

A quarter of an hour later, they were walking briskly into Hyde Park with no particular destination in mind. It was a cold morning, and they walked with their heads bowed against a light but chill westerly wind.

"Couldn't we have stayed in the hotel?" asked Margot.

"We couldn't have been properly alone there."

"Well, we're alone now, so tell me what this is all about before I catch pneumonia."

"Very well. I've been posted to Algiers."

Margot stopped dead in her tracks.

"My God! When?"

"I leave two days after Christmas."

"*What*? They give you three days' notice?"

"That's all. They called me this morning."

Margot bit on her lip as Edmond put an arm around her.

"Let's keep walking," he said, "or we'll freeze."

"But why, darling? Why, why, *why*?"

"It's a very important job. I knew a week ago that they were looking for someone from London to do it, but I never guessed they'd pick me." He glanced at Margot and saw the tears welling up in her eyes. "Don't be sad," he said. "I couldn't have stayed in London for ever. Sooner or later every one of us Fighting French will be off to North Africa or taking part in an invasion of mainland Europe. It's just come a little early for me. Naturally I'm distressed by that because of you."

"You sure as hell don't sound it, if I may say so," said Margot, choking back a sob. "Maybe you volunteered for the posting!"

"That's not fair, Margot. Of course I didn't."

"Well, you seem to be as pleased as Punch that they picked you. What are they doing? Making you a Marshal of France and putting you in Giraud's place?"

Edmond sighed. "You're not helping by being sarcastic," he said, unlinking his arm from hers.

"Well at least have the courtesy to tell me what this magnificent new job is all about."

"I will, although some things I have to say won't be too pleasing to you." His tone was icy now. "As I've already told you, you Americans and the British have assailed the honour of France by installing Admiral Darlan as High Commissioner of French Africa. How could they possibly take a former head of the Vichy government, and now Pétain's commander-in-chief of all Vichy forces, and put him in charge just because he says he now thinks the Allies are going to win the war and he wants to be on the winning side? It's an absolute disgrace. That naïve amateur, Eisenhower, is responsible for this. He should be shot!"

"So you're off to Algiers to shoot him, Edmond, is that it?"

"Don't be silly. But don't be surprised if that traitor Darlan gets what he deserves. If he thinks he and Giraud are going to lead the liberation of France and then set themselves up in power, he's in for a big disappointment."

"So you're off to assassinate Darlan?"

"I only wish I was!"

"That's what frightens me; I really think you do wish that."

Edmond smiled. "Well, you can relax. Political assassination is not one of my duties."

"It's somebody's duty among your stop-at-nothing Gaullists. Just look at poor Mouret's so-called 'accident'."

"Not 'so-called'!" snapped Edmond. "I've already told you that, so stop making these silly accusations."

Margot paused and began kicking impatiently at some twigs lying in her path.

"Well, what am I supposed to believe? A man you detest gets killed, and three days later a leading figure in the BCRA gets posted out of the country in a tearing hurry. Are you telling me there's no connection?"

"For God's sake, Margot, are you mad? Are you accusing me of Mouret's death? Do you think that's why I'm leaving for Algiers?"

He had seized her by the shoulders, and his face was white with anger.

"Well, you haven't told me why you're leaving."

"Look, Margot, if anyone had wanted to get rid of Mouret, they wouldn't be so stupid as to do it here under the eyes of our host government. They'd do it in France where there are political scores being settled every day. That's the first point. The second is that I have been entrusted with a very important military assignment in Algiers, confirmed by General de Gaulle himself, which has nothing at all to do with the BCRA. I will be one of the senior military representatives of the National Committee of France Combattante, and my specific duty will be to free from the ranks of General Giraud's armies all those who wish to serve under our Cross of Lorraine. De Gaulle will shortly start work in earnest to bring all French forces, wherever they are in the free world, under his command. That's the only way we can liberate France. I have been commissioned to go and help prepare the way for this in North Africa. And I am promoted to major immediately."

Now Margot felt both relieved and impressed. With a contrite look on her face, she kissed him on the cheek.

"I'm sorry, Edmond. I've been saying some silly things.

It's just that the news of your going so soon is a terrible shock. I'm happy for you; it's obviously a very important job. But you can guess how I'm feeling right now."

"It's hard for both of us, *chérie*. Don't think that I'm not feeling quite desperate at the thought of going so far away from you."

"If you're leaving just after Christmas, we won't see each other again will we?"

"Not unless you can come back here before I go on the twenty-seventh."

"No, I can't do that."

"Because of Charlie?" She nodded and bit on her lip. He looked at his watch.

"We'd better walk back to Park Lane. I have a meeting with Passy in twenty minutes."

As they retraced their footsteps across the park, Edmond explained to her the situation in North Africa as the Gaullists saw it. But Margot was scarcely listening. She was trying to picture life without her lover, and what she conjured up in her mind was far from comforting. Charlie was going to have to fill an aching void without even knowing it, and she was not at all convinced that he could. It wasn't just a lover she was now losing; she was losing another important dimension to her life, her involvement in Edmond's cause. That involvement had been so exclusively tied to his presence and his guidance that, without him there, it would quickly wither. Things just weren't going to be at all the same, and she wished she'd had time to prepare herself for the closing of the chapter.

She interrupted Edmond's continuing diatribe against Darlan and Giraud.

"I do wish you'd told me it could happen as suddenly as this."

"Maybe this is the best way, Margot. Just keep saying to yourself that we're going to see each other as soon as the war is over. Maybe even before; I might find myself back in London at some stage."

"No, you'll go straight from North Africa to France, to fight. That's what you're really longing for, isn't it?"

"That's on the cards, of course," he said solemnly. "But we will see each other after the war."

"Oh sure! If you survive. If I survive. If you come to London. If I go to France. With that number of ifs, forget it!"

"It's a matter of will, not of chance."

"Bullshit! Neither of us can will the Germans not to fill you with bullets or blow me to bits like they did Katie. Anyway, that's not the point. I need you now, not after the war. What happens after this wretched war is much too far ahead for me to think about."

They had reached Park Lane.

"Walk with me just as far as Marble Arch?"

"No, Edmond darling. I must say goodbye to you here."

The tears were welling up again as she let him take her in his arms. They kissed. It was a long slow kiss, and she pressed her lips so hard against his as she tried to control her quivering that it hurt. Then she suddenly drew back, stroked his cheek once, and said simply: "I'm going now, *chéri*. God be with you."

She turned and walked quickly away towards Hyde Park Corner. Edmond stood for a moment, a look of disbelief and defeat on his pale face. Then he shrugged his shoulders and set off in the opposite direction, shoulders hunched against the cold wind.

Margot was barely five minutes' walk from home, but she doubted that her weeping would stop and her tears dry in that time, and having no wish to confront in that inexplicable condition Charlie or her father, either or both of whom could be home by now, she decided to spend a few more minutes in the park, trying to regain control of herself. She passed an anti-aircraft gun emplacement, where two khaki-uniformed ATS girls, leaning against the sandbagging, mugs of tea in their hands, stared at her curiously. Lone women crying in public was not an unusual sign in wartime London, but the beautiful honey-blonde girl in the bottle-green overcoat and black beret must have stirred something in them.

"Like a cup of tea, luv?" one of them called out.

Margot halted and looked over to the emplacement.

"Might cheer you up," the girl added.

"I think it might," said Margot, trying a smile through her tears. "Thank you."

"Not exactly regulations, mind you," said the second girl, pouring tea into a tin mug from a large thermos. "But Dotty and me get bored and like a little company from time to time when the sergeant's not here. Besides, a pretty lady crying on Christmas Eve's just not right, is it?"

"You're very kind," said Margot, taking the tea.

"Husband or boyfriend away?" asked Dotty. "Always feels worse at Christmas time, don't it?"

"No, as a matter of fact he just got back. Escaped from a POW camp in Germany."

"He did? Blimey! Good on him! He must be quite a bloke."

"He is. I'm very proud of him."

"You sound American," said the tea-pourer.

"I am. But my husband's English."

"Wise girl!" said Dotty, putting her mug down on a sandbag to pull the collar of her heavy khaki greatcoat higher about her ears. "They make the best. My George is with Monty in Libya, shoving it to old Rommel. Lovely lad, George. If anything happens to him, I'll marry his younger brother." She giggled. "Stick with good stock once you've found it, I say."

"You look as though you might be a film star," said the other. "From Hollywood or somewhere."

Margot laughed. "Heavens no! But thank you for the compliment. I just work for the American Red Cross."

"London's crawling with your boys, isn't it?" said Dotty. "My sister Eileen's been out with a couple. Very generous, they are, so she says. But with all due respect and that, give me an Englishman every time." She lifted her mug. "Cheers, luv. Good to see the smile back on your face."

Margot finished her tea, thanked them profusely, and set off.

"Take care of that man of yours!" called the tea-pourer after her retreating figure. "I bet he's a smasher!"

Margot hurried to the park exit and across Park Lane into Mayfair. She was feeling a little better, and ready to face Charlie and her father.

When they arrived at Bowes Court that evening, Sir

Walter greeted them with an item of news just culled from the BBC's six o'clock bulletin.

"Admiral Darlan's been assassinated in Algiers. Shot dead by a young Frenchman outside his office this morning."

Margot shivered. At least that young Frenchman wasn't Edmond. She almost blurted out that he had predicted just such an eventuality, but took the wiser course and confined herself to the comment that Darlan probably had what was coming to him.

Throughout their ten days at Bowes Court, Charlie was as lovingly attentive as she had ever known him, and if he was puzzled by her sometimes distracted air and the often wistful look on her face, he said nothing about it, and Margot was content to let him think, if indeed he was so thinking, that she was gloomy at the prospect of their imminent separation when he left to join his battalion. She had made up her mind that she was not going to let Edmond's precipitate departure get the better of her. She would in time grow accustomed to the realization that he had gone forever out of her lfe, and she wanted that time to pass quickly. She felt the pain and trembled before the aching void in her life that he had left, but as the days passed the pain began to subside, and her instant conviction, that cold morning in Hyde Park, that the void would never be filled, seemed less and less tenable. She was still thinking of Edmond when she made love with Charlie, but Charlie's love-making was strong and passionate enough to afford her physical satisfaction, and for that she was grateful to her husband, and showed it.

One nagging regret preyed on her mind uncomfortably often. She had barely said goodbye to Edmond. She had cut the parting cruelly short. Would he understand that she hated lingering partings? Or was he even now thinking bitterly that she hadn't really cared that he was going? That possibility worried her, and she hoped he would write so that she would have an address to which to write him in return, explaining why she had so quickly torn herself away.

25

After several months of absence, the Luftwaffe returned to London on 18th January 1943. It was a sneak raid by six bombers flying in low beneath the radar. Forty children standing in line for lunch at a school in south London were killed when the planes released their deadly cargo. Margot read about it the next morning as she sat in the gloomy waiting room of her physician, Dr Worsley. The agony-stricken face of the bereaved mothers of Lewisham stared accusingly at her from the front page of a newspaper. Distressed, she turned the newspaper over and covered it with a magazine. Twenty minutes later, Dr Worsley, whose hanging judge appearance and manner never failed to intimidate her, solemnly confirmed that she was once more pregnant. Margot thanked him politely.

"Don't thank me, Mrs Garland," he said humourlessly. "I will refer you to my colleague, Sir Horace Pines. You'll need a good gynaecologist to monitor the progress of the pregnancy. Just keep away from air-raid shelter steps." He allowed himself a split-second smile as he rose."And late nights on the town."

Margot left on foot for Curzon Street. The news had not surprised her, but she was nonetheless delighted, and above all happy for Charlie. She wished only that she could, at that moment, drive the image of the weeping mothers of Lewisham from her mind. The Lord was giving to her even as He was taking away from them, and she felt a twinge of guilt at her happiness.

Reaching Bond Street, she spotted the majestic figure of the Dowager Marchioness of Edmonton, swathed in mink, tapping impatiently on the kerb with a walking stick while a red traffic light impeded her stately progress.

Margot caught up with her and greeted her.

"Good morning, my dear," responded the Marchioness, waving her stick at the traffic light. "One spends half one's life these days waiting for inanimate objects to cooperate. The Minister of Agriculture for example. Nothing seems to prevent you from looking quite ravishing, my dear," she went on, casting a pitying eye on Margot's heavy mesh stockings and the beige utility coat she wore over her American Red Cross uniform. "With this wretched clothes rationing, I can hardly distinguish some of my friends from their servants."

"I've just been told I'm going to have a baby."

"How very nice. You must get Charlie to put him down for Eton at once. If it turns out to be a gel, you simply take his name off the list. Hector Broadstairs has booked two places; he's convinced Polly's going to have twins. If Polly's anything like her mother, she'll be lucky to produce even a replica of herself, let alone twin boys. We are now vouchsafed a split second to cross. Come along!"

Brandishing her stick at the halted traffic, Lady Edmonton stepped down from the kerb and tottered across the street.

"I hope the stick doesn't mean you broke something or sprained an ankle," said Margot as they reached the west side of Bond Street.

"No, my dear. My doctor says I have a touch of mild arthritis, by which he really means I'm coming apart at the seams, like one of Mr Attlee's suits. Doctors never tell one the whole truth. They'd take to Cabinet office like ducks to water. I'm going into this bookshop here. We have Italian prisioners of war working on our farms. My estate manager need an Italian dictionary, and the only one we have at Edmonton is fifteenth-century Sienese. Worth a fortune and weighs a ton, but doesn't include the spare parts of the tractor." She paused at the entrance. "Give your Charlie my love. We had a letter from Jamie. He's with the 201st Guards Brigade now, so I suppose he's on the road to Tripoli with Monty. He's been writing rather regularly to the eldest Muirkirk gel.

Naturally he's picked the wrong one; only the youngest doesn't look like the Duke dressed up as a woman. Run along now, and keep that baby warm. And get him down for Eton."

She turned and disappeared into the bookshop, leaving Margot giggling helplessly on the pavement.

Ten minutes later she was in her office at the Washington Club. She knew there was no point in trying to reach Charlie to give him the good news; he was on manoeuvres on Salisbury Plain and had promised to call her that evening. Lois Dell at the embassy told her that her father was in a meeting, so in the meanwhile she decided to try her luck at tracking down Larry at his airbase. Her luck was in, and he whooped with joy when she told him of her condition, and promised to come and see her in London just as soon as he could.

Moments later, her father called her back. He too was thrilled by her news, and urged her to write immediately to her grandparents. Then she heard the tone of his voice change, and in an almost apologetic manner he told her that he had that morning found on his arrival at the embassy notification from the State Department that he was assigned to a post in Washington. He would be reporting there in three weeks' time. First Edmond and now Father, thought Margot miserably, and she told him in a quavering voice how desperately she would miss him.

"Don't get too distressed, sweetheart," he told her. "You've got Charlie and his parents here. And you've got Larry for a while. You'll be well taken care of. Want to have lunch with me? How about Claridge's to celebrate your news and drown our sorrows over mine?"

By mid-afternoon, Margot's spirits had risen somewhat. Over lunch, two important decisions had been taken. The Hill Street house would necessarily be passing to her father's successor, but Margot would keep Verbena Cottage and he would be happy to pay the rent. In the meantime, he had called Sir Walter to tell him of his impending return to the United States, and the latter had immediately offered a choice. If Margot wanted to continue her American Red Cross work for the time being,

303

and therefore needed a *pied-à-terre* in town, she could either be a welcome guest at the Garlands' house, or, if she preferred more privacy, he would be happy to help Charlie pay the rent on a small London flat.

When Charlie called that evening and received the glad tidings that he was once again a father-to-be, Margot relayed his father's offer but added before letting him react that, generous as was the proposal that she join the family at Great College Street, she would really rather have a flat. That suited him too, Charlie assured her, and promised to talk to his parents about it immediately.

It took some arranging, but finally a date was set when both Charlie and Larry could take a brief leave at the same time and join Margot in London to give a farewell party for Harland at Hill Street. A simple buffet supper, largely made possible by Larry's bartering skills on and off the airbase, brought together some twenty guests bent on giving the diplomat a joyful and affectionate send-off.

It was a bitter-sweet occasion for Margot and her father, and as they danced after dinner to the phonograph, she wept softly on his shoulder when the strains of Noël Coward's "I'll See You Again" tugged at her heartstrings.

"I'm being selfish, Father. Forgive me. Mother's going to be over the moon to have you back, but I can be forgiven for wishing that you could have stayed to see the baby born."

Harland cupped his daughter's face in his hands and planted a kiss on her forehead.

"We'll be together again before too long, darling. We're going to win this war, and when we have, we're going to have one helluva Moore-Garland reunion."

"I love you," she said, brushing a tear from her cheek. "Now you'd better go and dance with Marion. She's your date tonight, remember? And since the party's in your honour, Larry and I will look the other way if you want to flirt."

He glanced around. "Looks like Larry's doing the flirting for me. He's welcome to her. I'm not exactly in the mood to be eaten alive, and I'm not sure I've forgiven you for asking her here. When this delightful dance with you is over, I'm sneaking upstairs to my study to enjoy a quiet brandy with Walter. Off limits to women, especially Lady Shears!"

"Chicken, Father!" The dance ended, and Margot went in search of Charlie.

Marion Shears, widow of a Royal Navy Rear Admiral killed in an aircrash, had already decided early in the evening that the handsome young flyer in the USAAF lieutenant's uniform was just what she needed to take her mind off ambulance driving and a lingering migraine headache. She had liked Larry's father the moment she had met him at an embassy dinner party a year ago, but she soon discovered that he became stiff and withdrawn if one began to flirt with him. She enjoyed flirting with handsome men. At forty she felt herself to be at the peak of her desirability, and that it should not be wasted. She was enjoying wartime London too much to want a second marriage, which could likely lead to a second widowhood, and the variety that was spicing her life was not something she would readily exchange for constancy at this stage. The thought of this brave young American boy flying dangerous bombing missions over occupied Europe seemed to be setting other parts of her anatomy as well as her heart aflutter, and she was wondering how direct she must be before he grasped what she wanted of him. As they danced, she looked quizzically into his pale brown eyes.

"I have the uncomfortable feeling you don't like my hair-style, Larry. You keep looking at it."

Her jet-black hair was drawn back and rolled into a chignon at the nape of the neck.

"Oh no, I think it's very nice."

"I can let it down if you prefer," she persisted. "There's a mirror in the hall. Come with me." She led a mildly protesting Larry from the room. "Letting my hair down at a party is a sort of reminder to myself that I've probably had enough to drink."

She giggled as she unpinned the chignon before the mirror and let the sleek locks fall to her shoulders.

"You're not going back to the airbase tonight, are you?" She took a comb from her handbag.

"Tomorrow. I'm due back at midday."

"When you next come up, you should let me know in advance. If Margot doesn't have room in her flat, you can always use my guest room."

"That's very kind of you."

She finished combing her hair and turned to him.

"No, not kind. Devious."

She winked at him, then replaced the comb in her handbag and smoothed the tangerine satin dress over her slim hips.

"I'm staying here tonight," said Larry, hoping to convey in the tone of his voice an appropriate degree of disappointment.

"Of course, dear. But there's always a next time, isn't there?" She patted his cheek.

"Are you seducing my twin brother, Marion?"

Margot appeared in the hall.

"You know I can't resist divine young men in uniform, darling. Count yourself lucky I didn't try to steal that gorgeous Frenchman of yours. I went weak at the knees every time I saw you two together."

Margot froze.

"Oh dear! I said something naughty, didn't I?"

Margot leaned against the wall and sighed.

"You did indeed."

"I think you'd better fill Larry in, then, my pet. No secrets between twins, and no recriminations, I hope, either. Meanwhile big-mouth Marion will go and do penance by dancing with that Grenadier major with halitosis."

Larry looked alarmed.

"What on earth was all that about, sis?"

"I'll tell you, but not here and now," she said, looking very unhappy.

"You had an *affair*?"

"I don't want to talk about it now, Larry. Someone could hear. It was all over long ago. I'll tell you tomorrow, I promise. Let's just thank our lucky stars Charlie didn't hear. Damn Marion!"

Larry took her by the arm. "Let's go and dance."

For the remainder of the evening Margot had difficulty

in getting Marion's *faux pas* out of her mind, and Marion shook her head apologetically in her direction when their eyes next met across the room. When finally the last of the guests were leaving and Marion was putting on her fur coat, Margot managed to draw her aside.

"Don't look so miserable, Marion. It just slipped out. I'll square Larry on it."

"Well, I *do* feel miserable, sweetie. It was unforgivably tactless of me. I'll try to make it up to you by taking you to lunch at The Causerie tomorrow if you're free and still want to see me."

Margot smiled and kissed her on the cheek.

"I'd love that!"

When only the family were left, Charlie and his father-in-law retired to the study for a last nightcap and a chat while Larry insisted on joining his sister and Mrs Watts in clearing the debris of the evening's revels.

"You can tell me now," said Larry, when Mrs Watts went downstairs to the kitchen. So while they gathered up glasses and emptied ashtrays into the fireplace, Margot told her brother, glancing every now and then at the door to make sure no one else was coming in.

"I had a bit of a fling with a young Free French officer who left at Christmas for Algiers. Nothing very serious. He was one of the ones who was at the Café de Paris. He was Katie's friend at that time. I mentioned him to you in at least one of my letters. That's all, Larry. Can you help me put these records away?"

"How could you *do* that, with Charlie in Germany?"

"For Christ's sakes keep your voice down," hissed Margot. "And don't give me any lecture in morals!"

"Did you sleep with him?"

"What if I did?"

"Well, did you? I'm asking."

"Don't ask. Just draw your own conclusions. It's all water under the bridge now, and I really don't want or have to talk any more about it. *Please* help me put these records back!"

Larry walked over to her and put his hands on her shoulders.

"Listen, sis. Don't think me holier-than-thou, but just let me – "

"Then don't act holier-than-thou. These things happen in wartime. I've been in this war over three years, Larry. You've only just joined it. You'll find out for yourself in time that the old rules just don't apply. Charlie didn't get hurt, and I didn't get hurt by what happened. So it's really as if nothing happened, see? And that's the way I intend to leave it. And I suggest you do too. Now go up and join Charlie and Father. I can manage what's left here, and I'd rather do it alone with Mrs Watts."

Larry stared silently at her for a moment, a deep frown creasing his brow.

"You've certainly changed, Margot."

"It's called 'taking control of your life'. You don't wait for everybody else to tell you what to do with it."

She picked up a tray of dirty glasses and walked from the room, heading for the kitchen.

Larry shrugged his shoulders and started sorting out the pile of records.

26

The mid-March afternoon light was beginning to fade as Larry set off across the airfield to the hard-stand where his B-17F Flying Fortress was parked. As he approached the olive-drab bomber, he saw a ground crewman perched on the nose, busy with a cleaning mop. He ducked his head to pass under the port wing and emerge between the propeller blades of the powerful Wright Cyclone radial engines.

"She looks fit to go to a Saturday night dance, Corporal."

"You bet, sir, but the nose insignia could use some touching up. I'll get the paint tomorrow."

Larry scanned the artwork on the port side of the nose. "Nashville Nancy", the swim-suited, dark-haired beauty had lost a small but noticeable part of the underside of one of her prodigiously generous breasts, where a fragment of enemy flak must have struck her

"First time I noticed it. We certainly can't have our Nancy calling on the continent with half a tit missing."

"It will be my pleasure to get my hands on it, sir, as soon as I get the paint."

Larry passed under the plexiglass nose-cone of the bomber and looked up at the two .50 calibre guns recently installed to improve the plane's head-on defence. The B-17 was now truly a "battleship of the air", and Larry had, from his very first bombing mission, decided that if he was going to be scared, he'd rather be scared in a B-17 than in anything else.

He called goodnight to the corporal still busy with his mop and headed back across the cold, breezy airfield to his quarters. As he neared the long, squat Nissen hut, a golden cocker spaniel, the pet of one of his comrades, bounded skittishly across his path, ears flapping. His thoughts turned to Margot. She had offered to buy him a dog as a "welcome to England" gift to keep him company, but he had declined. Right now he didn't want the worry of caring for one. He pushed through the swing doors of the hut and went straight to the room he shared with his command pilot, Jimmy Buckley, the tall Tennesseean, at twenty-three years old the "father" of the crew and captain of *Nashville Nancy*. The room was empty and he flopped on the bed.

He was still finding it hard to believe what Margot had told him the night before in London. How could she let a sleazy Frenchman ball the hell out of her while her own man was locked up in Germany! He simply couldn't grasp how his carefully reared twin could behave so callously. God forbid the rest of the family should ever find out! He loved her with a fierce brotherly love, and while her confession had in no way diminished that love, it had filled him with depression.

As if he were not already depressed. Gloom seemed to have seized all of the aircrews in his wing. Everyone was in a hurry to complete his twenty-five missions and go home, but the appalling weather allowed little prospect of early completion. In all November, Eighth Bomber Command had been able to fly only eight missions; in December only four. Larry had counted himself lucky to have been able to fly even six missions in the short time he had been in England. Morale was further weakened by the chronic shortage of replacement parts for damaged aircraft, new aircraft for those destroyed, and new crew members for those lost. By the time Larry's group had been ready for their first mission in late December, rumours already abounded that the British Prime Minister, alarmed at the mounting losses of equipment and men in the American daylight bombing raids, was putting pressure on the American President to order a halt to them and switch the Eighth Air Force to supporting the RAF's night-time raids.

For Larry and his fellow flyers, the frustration continued unabated. Missions announced and then cancelled because of fog were becoming almost routine. Last week they had been taxiing to take-off when they were called back. All that steeling of the nerves for nothing!

That evening they got the word. It came as usual during supper, as Larry sat in the mess hall with the other officers of his Group, dining off American meatloaf and potatoes. As always, the accompanying Brussels sprouts sat untouched in their dishes along the tables. A few evenings ago, Jimmy Buckley had warned his other crews:

"Some Air Force health adviser has been telling everyone that too starchy food can generate enough gas in your intestines to make you writhe with pain at high altitudes. So cut out the sprouts, he says. Eat spinach instead."

"They sure haven't got the message here yet," his neighbour had complained. "The food these cooks serve could generate enough gas to get a B-17 home with all its engines out."

"Good idea, Harry. If we ever lose them all, we'll stick you in the tail and have you fart us back to base. Pass Harry the sprouts, fellas!"

The public address system crackled and the assembled company fell instantly silent. Larry laid down his knife and fork as a flat mid-western voice launched into a warning order for a mission the following morning. All eyes were turned to the loudspeaker attached to the wall over the entrance as the crew selection came over the wires.

"The whole of our squadron," said Buckley when the order was completed. "How honoured we are!"

"They just think we're getting fat and lazy," said Larry, turning to the table behind him. "Rusty!" he called. "Want to bet my cigarette ration it's the Wilhelmshaven sub pens again?"

A slight, redheaded lieutenant raised a hand to signal acceptance of the wager.

"Sure! You're always wrong. I dreamed last night we were going to Antwerp. A quickie."

"When did you ever have a dream of yours come true, Rusty?" someone called out. "Even a wet one."

Buckley stood up. "Come on, Larry. Let's hit the sack."

"I've got a call to make first. I'll be over in a while."

311

He made his way to a call-box off the officers' lounge and asked the operator for a London number. He was quickly put through.

"Marion, it's Larry. I wanted to tell you how great it was to meet you last night."

"How very nice of you to call. I'm awfully happy I met you, and even happier that you kept my name and number."

"I'm off on a little trip tomorrow. When I next get to London, can I see you?"

"Delighted. But you'd better give me warning. And my offer of a bed remains. I also have friends only two miles from where you are. I think I told you that. I'll invite myself there tomorrow if you're going to be back and can come over and join me."

"Tomorrow?"

"Why not? Do we have to wait until you're free to come to London before we see each other again?"

"I guess not. Give me a number to call there on my return, then."

She gave it to him. "Good luck, Larry. Hope to see you tomorrow."

"God willing."

Sergeant di Martino knocked on the door promptly at five a.m.

"Good morning, gentlemen. Breakfast at five-thirty; briefing at six-thirty; take-off at seven-thirty."

"No fog, Sergeant?" Larry turned over drowsily.

"Sorry to disappoint you, sir. None. Clear as an Arizona sky."

"Then mission number seven, here we come!" Jimmy Buckley sprang out of bed. "Come on, Larry. Our Nancy's hot for some action."

It was still dark when they left the mess-hall after the customary pre-mission breakfast of bacon and eggs. The wind was chill, and Larry pulled his fleece-lined leather flying jacket closer around his shoulders as they set off for the briefing hut. Soon some two hundred men had settled down on the rows of folding chairs facing the dais on which the briefing officer had just appeared. The shuffling of feet and chair legs ceased as the chatting died away. The briefing officer looked intently into the sea of expectant faces. As usual, he was savouring the moment. He half turned toward the huge display map of Western Europe covering the end wall behind him, and raised a long wooden pointer.

"Gentlemen, your undivided attention please!" He tapped the man sharply with the pointer. "The target is Hamburg."

There were excited murmurs from the assembled crews. Larry looked at Jimmy.

"Now that's more like it," he said.

The briefing officer paused to let the noise die down, then he raised his pointer again.

"You're going to have a go at the port installations there."

"Shipping! I was half right," muttered Larry. He leaned across Buckley and tapped Rusty Rabinowicz on the knee. "I'll be a gentleman about it, Rusty. You win."

Nashville Nancy's bombardier grinned back. For someone who smoked fifty cigarettes a day, not going to Wilhelmshaven was a relief. But going back to bomb the hell out of the country that had raped the land of his father and forefathers gave satisfaction beyond words.

"Wolves climbing up to us at eight o'clock! Eight of them!"

The excited voice of Technical Sergeant Rich Losey in *Nashville Nancy*'s cramped ball-turret came singing through the intercom.

"Don't those idiot Red Barons know I've got a heavy date with a titled lady tonight? No honour among aristocrats any more."

"Cut it out, Larry." Jimmy Buckley's voice was firm but calm. "We're coming in to the bombing run. You ready, Rusty?"

"Ready."

Rusty Rabinowicz crouched lower over his Norden bomb-sight in the nose and said his usual short prayer for a steady run and a clear sighting of the target. For the next two and a half minutes, Buckley would have to fly straight and level, at twenty-two thousand feet, so that his bombardier could do what they had come to do. The flak was beginning to burst around them, rocking the plane violently, but no evasion was possible; he had to keep straight and level, a sitting target for the flak gunners below and the Focke-Wulfs closing in on him on his port side. To make matters worse, *Nashville Nancy* was flying in the "Tail-end-Charlie" position, the rear-most left-hand ship in the formation. As such, Buckley and his crew had the dubious honour of being the last to bomb and the least likely to escape damage or destruction.

Buckley clutched grimly onto the controls, battling to keep the Fortress steady as the shock waves of the bursting flak proved too strong for the autopilot.

"Keep her steady, Jimmy," muttered Rabinowicz down below as the ship rocked repeatedly. There they were! The Hamburg docks, vessels lining every pier, dotted with the puffs of exploding bombs, slipped under the crosswires of the Norden sight. He pressed the release. Six bombs fell away from *Nancy*'s belly. He pressed again. The second rack jumped open to release another six, and as it did so, the plane bucked viciously.

"Bombs away!" he shouted, and glancing up glimpsed an FW-190 passing ahead of them on the starboard side. Cannon shells were now crashing against the fuselage. Up above, Buckley responded to the bombardier's call by pulling the yoke over savagely and stomping on the rudder.

"Right, we're getting the hell out of here!" he called to his crew.

Lieutenant Harvey Moss, the navigator, broke in on the intercom, his voice barely audible above the cannon-fire.

"They've got McGee!"

No one had heard any cry of pain from the tail-gunner. He must have died instantly, thought Larry, who was now watching in grim amazement as FW after FW tore past, above, below, and on either side. How the hell are we still flying? he asked himself. He glanced over his shoulder in time to see a stream of cannon shells ripping an orange path across the starboard wing and tearing into

314

the number four engine which now began to jump frantically as if trying to free itself from the wing. Larry cut off the power and feathered the prop.

"Oh boy! We really got that one!"

The exultant shout of Sergeant Stan Ballard, the port waist-gunner, drew Buckley's attention to an FW banking away from them with sheets of flame enveloping the cockpit. It rolled over once before exploding in a ball of fire.

"Shi-i-i-t!"

The oath was barely distinguishable as coming from Losey in the ball-turret.

"I've been goddammed hit in – "

There was a gurgle as the sentence died.

Buckley pulled *Nancy* into a steep bank just as a flak shell burst immediately under her belly, neatly detaching the bloody and pink foam-spattered ball-turret, together with the remains of Losey, and leaving a gaping hole in the belly through which a minus forty-two degree gale now tore into the interior of the ship. As Buckley, with Larry's help, fought to straighten her out again, a Focke-Wulf appeared ahead of them at ten o'clock. Larry turned to his pilot to make sure he'd seen it, and saw the young Tennesseean's head explode in an eruption of blood, brain-tissue and skull splinters. Almost simultaneously, a flak burst rocked the Fortress, almost standing her on her wing again. Cursing, Larry managed to straighten her out, then looked across to his pilot again. The nausea welled up in him, and in a strangled voice he called out to his navigator behind him.

"Harvey, if you're all right, help me with Jimmy."

Lieutenant Moss was picking himself up off the floor.

"I'm OK, Larry." He peered forward into the front of the cockpit. "Oh Jesus!"

He saw Buckley slumped forward over his controls. Between his blood-splattered shoulders was an oozing mess shaped like a half-inflated football where his head had been. His hands still clasped the control yoke.

"Help me get him out," said Larry, snapping off his own seatbelt and shoulder harness.

"You stay put and fly this goddammed plane!"

Moss set about freeing Buckley from his seat and then pulled him by the arms onto the floor and dragged him down into the rear of his own small compartment. Larry heaved himself across into the command pilot's vacant seat, hurriedly wiped the controls clean with a gloved hand, and belted himself in. He could see practically nothing out of his side window; it was too badly shattered. He might just as well have kept his own seat.

"Six 109s coming up at five o'clock!" Coleman in the waist was bellowing into the intercom.

"And bogies at three o'clock high!" Now it was Shockley in the top turret. Suddenly the intercom was a babble of voices.

"OK! OK! I can't hear myself think!" Larry shouted. "Let's keep it orderly. You're using up oxygen. And watch the ammunition; these buggers are going to be with us a long way yet."

They seemed to be flying clear of the flak defences now, but the fighter menace was intensifying. Larry could see the yellow-nosed Messerschmitts sweeping down towards the low squadron. In a moment he heard Shockley's gun above him hammering away at them. The Fortress ahead and above suddenly swung out of the ragged formation, and Larry watched in awe as the port wing slowly began to fold downward. The mortally wounded plane slipped out of sight below and behind them.

"That was Jackie Woodward," said Larry softly, the image of Jackie's cocker spaniel floating in his mind's eye. Just hope he gets out in time, he thought. His concern was wrested back to his own ship as he saw once again the orange trail of cannon fire coursing diagonally across the outer section of the starboard wing and felt the shells ripping into the fuselage. No damage to the starboard engine, as far as he could see. Thanks for small mercies. He concentrated again on his dipping and weaving, struggling to make *Nancy* as difficult a target as he could for the ubiquitous fighters.

"Tail section's hit! Chunk out of the horizontal stabilizer!"

It was Shockley again, swivelling in his top turret.

"Christ! How much more can we take?"

Larry looked desperately at the Fortress ahead and to starboard. It appeared undamaged. He would have to hang on to her. Maybe her gunners could help keep the fighters off the now badly crippled *Nancy*.

"MEs again at one o'clock!"

This time it was Cohn, the radioman, gripping his heavy machine-gun behind the bomb bays, peering aft out of his turret. The plane shuddered as the two top turret guns and port waist-gun opened up in unison on the newest wave of attackers. Larry put *Nancy* into her awkward dance routine again, doubting that in her battered state she could handle the steps without disintegrating.

"Coleman's hit bad!" It was Ballard's high-pitched voice from the waist. "Can someone help? Someone bring morphine. I gotta keep at the bastards!"

Cohn ducked out of his turret and slid his way along the shellcase-strewn floor to see what he could do for the stricken waist-gunner.

Larry watched helplessly as the number two engine shot flames, feathered, and quickly died. He made a rapid mental assessment. Two engines out; damaged horizontal stabilizer; gaping hole in the belly; pilot, tail-gunner, ball-turret gunner dead; waist-gunner hit. On the credit side, for the moment at least, control cables, hydraulics, brakes, wings, vertical stabilizer all more or less intact. Intent on completing his checklist and pondering on the chances of making it back to the British coast, he did not at first notice that the firing had stopped. Nor had he noticed that they were now flying over water. As if aware of this, the navigator brought him up to date.

"We passed over the East Frisians two minutes ago." He read out the exact position. "The bogies have left us by the looks of it."

"Don't be too sure, fellas. Keep your eyes skinned."

But the gods were with them. The fighters had turned back. Now Larry had to get his limping *Nancy* home. He could see two Fortresses well ahead of him, and another half a mile to his port at the same altitude.

"How's Coleman?"

"I'm afraid he's going, sir." Cohn's voice was choking. "His chest is a terrible mess. I can't stop the bleeding, and he's unconscious."

Larry winced. The nineteen-year-old from Muscatine, Iowa, was awaiting news of the birth of his second child, due that week. He'd been as happy as a clam at the prospect; his first had died at three days old.

"Can someone block the ball-turret gap? You'll all freeze to death back there."

"We've got the nose floorboard from behind you on it, held down with ammo boxes."

"Smart boys!"

By the time they crossed the English coast, just south of Lowestoft, Coleman was dead. Larry shared his navigator's view that it would be possible, but not highly probable, that they would make it across Norfolk, West Suffolk and Cambridgeshire to their Bedfordshire base. As they passed just south of the spired city of Cambridge, fire broke out in the dead number two engine and began spreading rapidly, but he had insufficient altitude to order his surviving crew to bale out. He'd just have to keep going. They were, by Moss's reckoning, less than three minutes from the base. They were now skimming over flat fields and rain-soaked villages, and the flames were licking at the fuselage. The comforting sound of landing instructions from the control tower crackled into Larry's headset. He gave final instructions to his crew and wished them luck.

"Get the hell out of her as soon as I manage to pull her up. OK, now, brace yourselves, fellas."

With tyres screaming, they hit the tarmac. The surviving crew were already crouched around the main exit door, and they had dragged the three remaining bodies of their dead comrades to the exit with them. They could tell from the violent vibrations that the tail wheel was gone. To Larry's wild relief, *Nancy* was responding well to his braking, and within moments he had pulled her up. The black, acrid smoke that was now enveloping the cockpit made vision difficult. He snapped off the power of the two functioning engines and began to struggle out of his harness.

318

"Can I help?" shouted Rabinowicz behind him.

"Get the hell out of here, Rusty! She's going up in a second!"

Larry released himself and plunged back down the fuselage. He dropped through the main exit and saw his crew dragging their companions' corpses clear of the plane. Larry managed to get about fifty yards from *Nashville Nancy* before she blew up.

Later that night, Larry slept like a child in Marion's arms. It seemed terrible to her that after the experience which he had just been through he would be expected to be back in the air over Germany almost immediately. But, as he had tearfully told her, clutching his whisky glass in one hand, and stroking her naked thigh with the other, he still had eighteen missions to fly.

27

The summer of 1943 was a somewhat lonely season for
Margot. The Guards Armoured Division had moved from
nearby Salisbury Plain to Norfolk in April, and thence to
Yorkshire in June, taking Charlie still farther away. Now
more than six months pregnant, she had given up her
Red Cross work and was spending more and more time
at Verbena Cottage, looked after by the faithful Mrs
Watts. Charlie came south on leave from time to time,
either joining her at the cottage or meeting her in London
where they would stay at the small Belgravia flat which
was now their London *pied-à-terre*. She occasionally
stayed there alone during twenty-four-hour visits to the
capital for a check-up with her gynaecologist, or when
her brother was in town. And the inseparable Larry and
Marion came twice that summer to spend weekends with
her in the country. She had an open invitation to stay at
Bowes Court, but she confined her visits there to the
weekends when she and Charlie could go together,
which was rare. In July, her old friend Kick Kennedy
returned to England, ostensibly to work for the American
Red Cross in much the same job that she herself had
held, but the true purpose of her return was to be
reunited with Billy Hartington. Margot saw her no more
than a couple of times; the friendship of four years ago
had faded, and the hectic social life of Kick and her circle
was something which Margot, in her condition, felt no
great urge to pursue.

She had long given up her expectation that Edmond
would keep in touch with her by letter, and it therefore
came as some considerable surprise to her when, on the

last day of June, she heard from him for the first time. The letter was postmarked Algiers, and had taken nearly a month to reach her at Verbena Cottage. She heaved a sigh of relief that its arrival had not coincided with one of Charlie's infrequent visits to their country retreat.

My dearest Margot,

I have been meaning to write to you for so long now, and feel very guilty that I have not done so. Something was holding me back, but now I cannot restrain myself longer from letting you know what I am doing and what I am thinking.

An important chapter of my life ended when I came here, a chapter dominated by your presence in my life. It was a wonderful chapter, and I will recall it always with the warmest of feelings.

As I am sure you know, the French National Committee of Liberation has been in existence here in Algiers just five weeks, with Generals de Gaulle and Giraud as co-Presidents. This power-sharing is only a temporary arrangement. De Gaulle will assume supreme authority very soon.

I am to be attached to the Liberation Committee's Military Committee. You know how anxious I have always been to return to France to help the Resistance, but since this is now not to happen, I am at least grateful to be working close to de Gaulle at the seat of authority while we wait for the great day when we can set foot on France's soil again, as a liberating army.

My father and mother, God be thanked, are surviving the occupation with dignity and in reasonable spirits and health. But my dear friend, Weissberg, whom I often told you about, was deported to Germany in March and has not been heard of since. I fear the worst for that noble man. Equally distressing, our *maître de chai*, Grenier, was shot by the Germans for killing a German soldier in the village after an argument. His son, Luc, has fled from Lachaise, and the rumour is that he has gone underground with the *maquis* and will avenge his father's death tenfold.

Enough of this sad news. I wish you, dear Margot,

every happiness. When the war is won, I would count it a great honour if you and your husband would be my guests at Lachaise-Laurent. Our so abruptly ended relationship can be revived as a warm friendship, can it not? It would be a pity if we were to disappear for all time from each other's lives.

I hope that your parents are well, and that Charlie will come through the rest of the war unharmed. In the meantime, I send you my warmest greetings, praying for your health and happiness.

Most affectionately,
Edmond

The letter gave Margot a double sense of relief; relief that, like herself, Edmond looked back with no regrets on their affair, and relief that he was safe and sound. Nonetheless, she felt that he might have expressed himself in slightly warmer tones -- unless, of course, he was now involved with someone else in Algiers. The more she considered that possibility, the more plausible it appeared. It would be unlike Edmond not to be having an affair with someone.

She wrote by return.

Dearest Edmond,

Thank you for writing such a very nice letter. At long last! I had been wondering all these months how you were and whether you were still in Algiers. But maybe you were right not to write. Once you were gone, I needed to concentrate on establishing a *modus vivendi* with Charlie, and your "something" that was holding you back was probably your very fine instincts telling you to give me a chance to do just that. Consciously or subconsciously, you did the right thing, and deep down I'm grateful. At the same time I *was* getting quite impatient to hear your news! So your letter came as a very pleasant surprise.

Your work sounds really interesting, and I'm sure de Gaulle must be glad to have you on his Military Committee.

The big news on my side is that I am expecting a

baby. You can imagine how very thrilled we are, and I count myself very lucky to be a wartime military wife with a husband actually home to see his child born. The other news is that Father is now back in Washington. He left in early February, and I miss him terribly. My brother is still here though. I ran into the dreaded Drake one day on the street. He smiled and raised his bowler, and I smiled sweetly back and kept on walking!

What a lovely idea that Charlie and I should come and visit you in Bordeaux after this wretched war. Yes, why shouldn't we all be good friends? I'm so happy you think that way. Maybe one day you'll be a famous general or even President of France, and we'll be thrilled to say we know you. I especially!

Maybe you can write again some time. Judging by your letter, there doesn't seem to be much censorship your end. So you can give me all the news. But do me one favour, Edmond. Please address any letter you write to me care of The Washington ARC Club, Curzon Street, London W1. I get a little fan mail there from guys who used to use the club and are now back in the States or gone elsewhere (don't be jealous!) and the girls keep it for me to pick up when I'm in town.

I really am pleased you finally wrote. Take care of yourself.

> *Je t'embrasse,*
> Margot

Larry completed his twenty-fifth mission in late July and prepared to fly home. It was a bitter-sweet moment for Margot as she rejoiced that he had survived his tour while facing the stark reality of their impending separation, probably for the duration of the war.

On a perfect summer day in the last week of July, he came, accompanied by Marion, to say goodbye to her at the cottage. Margot awaited their arrival stretched out on a *chaise longue* in the garden, reading the morning papers. The soft breeze leaning against the spread pages of the paper rustled the leaves in the ring of elms round the garden's curved perimeter. The beauty of the day and her surroundings were beginning to soothe her troubled spirit. She had slept little that night. The baby had been kicking heartily, and the knowledge that in less than thirty-six hours' time she would be saying goodbye to her twin, maybe for ever, had stirred up her emotions too much to let her sleep until just before dawn. It was after eleven when Mrs Watts had finally woken her with a breakfast tray. By midday, radiant and refreshed, she was in the garden, basking in the sunshine, and feeling her spirits rising.

The news in the papers was helping the process. MUSSOLINI RESIGNS! IL DUCE OUT! trumpeted the headlines. The King had taken command of the Armies, and Marshal Badoglio had taken up the reins of government. Margot's thoughts turned immediately to Jamie with Montgomery's army fighting its way through Sicily. Maybe the Italians would make peace and there would be only Germans to fight when the Allies reached the Italian mainland. Maybe Jamie was going to survive the war after all; for so long now she had been more or less resigned to the idea that this lovable, funny man was just too good to live through it all.

She heard the village taxi turn into the driveway, and she eased herself up in stages from her prone position on the *chaise longue* to her sandalled feet, the effort leaving her a little breathless. She then walked round the side of the cottage to greet her brother and Marion at the front door.

"You're looking like a million," said Larry, embracing her.

"And weighing it, darling!" she said. She stood back from him, then reached to tap the ribbon of the Distinguished Flying Cross on the breast of his tunic. "I still can't believe my little Larry's a genuine war hero."

"No little Larry he, sweetie!" said Marion, planting a kiss on Margot's cheek. "I've got these terrible bags under my eyes this morning to prove it."

Larry blushed. "I've brought goodies," he said, lifting a bulging canvas bag. "Prepare for an evening of Rabelaisian indulgence!"

They ate a light lunch around a table set up in the shade of the elms, and the merry chatter and laughter

324

pushed the remaining vestiges of the gloom that had tormented Margot during the night into a far corner of her mind.

"Did I hear you mention that Walter had given you some cigars for Charlie?" asked Larry at the end of the meal.

"You did, and I'm sure Charlie would be delighted if you smoked one of them. The box is on my desk in the sitting room."

When he returned a moment later with a cigar, Margot was puzzled by the strained look that had suddenly replaced her brother's cheerful mien. He sat down without a word, pierced the end of the cigar with the point of a fruit knife, and struck a match.

"I trust you take an after-lunch siesta, Margot," said Marion. "I intend to anyway."

Margot didn't answer. She had suddenly realized what must have upset Larry. How could she be so damned careless! Edmond's letter. Folded in its envelope, but lying on her desk with all the identifying information clearly visible. She had taken it out of a desk drawer the previous evening, intending to find a safer place for it in case Charlie visited the cottage while she was in the nursing home giving birth to their baby. Well, at least it wasn't a *pile* of letters and Larry would certainly have not had time to read it, even if he'd had the gall to want to pry into her personal correspondence. Nonetheless, if he was going to be pompous about it, it would spoil the happy atmosphere, and she once again cursed her carelessness.

"Marion asked you a question," said Larry, puffing on his cigar.

"I'm sorry. Yes, of course, I always lie down for a bit after lunch. You two feel free to do whatever you like. Let's just help Mrs Watts by bringing the dishes in."

As they cleared the table, Margot struggled with the decision whether or not to remove the offending letter from her desk top. If she left it there, Larry would be tempted to read it while she was upstairs on her bed. It was a pretty innocent letter, but Larry wouldn't see it that way. And if she removed it now, Larry would notice and

325

assume that its contents were compromising enough to necessitate her hiding it from him.

He pre-empted her.

"I see you heard from your French friend," he said quietly when Marion had set off across the lawn with a pile of plates.

"Yes, he wrote a kind letter inviting Charlie and me to visit his vineyard in Bordeaux when the war is over."

"Jesus, what a nerve!"

Margot felt her temper rising, but determined to restrain herself.

"I didn't take it too seriously. Who knows if any of us is going to be around when this war is over? But there was no harm at all in his writing. I've already told you that there is nothing between us any more."

"Thank God for that. And just make sure, sis, that he doesn't try to insinuate himself into your life again."

"Don't try to teach me how to manage my life, Larry," she hissed. "You may be my twin, but you're sure as hell not the guardian of my soul."

"I never said I was. But I am entitled to express an opinion on what is, after all, a family matter."

"It's not a family matter; it's strictly my business, and you're making a mountain out of a molehill. So please, no more talk of the matter, Larry. I insist."

Marion reappeared, and put an arm around him.

"Are you going to come up and join me after you've finished your cigar?"

"No, I think I'm going to go for a walk down to the village."

"Pity!" said Marion, grinning.

"I'm going up for a rest," said Margot, gathering up the last of the glasses. "See you all a little later."

On her way upstairs, she went into the sitting room and slipped the letter into a pocket in her linen skirt.

That evening they sat down to a dinner of rare excellence for those wartime days, thanks to Larry's foraging skills. They washed down the baked Virginia ham and canned sweet potatoes with two distinguished bottles of claret which Margot forebore to reveal had once lain in the cellars under de Gaulle's office at Carlton Gardens. Larry suspected that their source might have been the Free French, but he preferred to keep his thoughts to himself and he certainly wasn't going to let his suspicions mar his enjoyment of such superb wine. At least he could see for himself that the name of the vineyard's proprietor, inscribed on the label, was not Lemonnier.

Before leaving for London the next morning, Larry, carrying flowers freshly cut from the garden, walked with his sister across the adjacent field to the little church, where they knelt for a few moments in the churchyard by Katie's grave.

"Goodbye again, darling Katie," mumbled Larry as he fought back the tears.

They walked back, arm in arm.

"Promise me you won't worry yourself crazy about me?" Margot said. "You're a wonderful brother, but you mustn't try to take all the burdens on your shoulders. Everything's going to come right in the end. I just know it."

"Twins do worry about each other a lot. You know that. And I'll sure as hell be worrying about you and for you when Charlie has to go again. And that can't be too far off now. But at least you'll have the baby to keep you occupied."

She squeezed his arm and smiled.

"And out of mischief. Isn't that what you wanted to say, you old preacher!"

Larry smiled too. "No more Lemonniers?"

"No more Lemonniers, Larry."

Minutes later they were bidding each other an emotional farewell in the little hallway by the front door while Marion waited discreetly by the taxi. When they emerged, Margot was brushing away tears.

"Marion's going to keep a good eye on you, sweetheart, aren't you, Marion?" said Larry soothingly.

"You can count on me a hundred per cent, darling."

"Take care of yourself," said Margot, still clinging to her brother.

"Of course! Hell, I'm just about out of this war now. It's Charlie we all need to think about."

He gave her a final peck on the cheek and got into the taxi while Marion kissed her and promised to call her in the coming week. Margot waved goodbye as the taxi drew away. Then she went into the kitchen.

"There, there, dear!" said Mrs Watts, putting an arm around her when she saw that she was still weeping.

"I got so used to Larry being here in England," Margot said miserably.

"Well he's out of danger now, isn't he, dear? Think how happy Mr and Mrs Moore are going to be to have him back."

"Yes, Wattie, you're right. I really mustn't be so selfish."

She looked down at her belly and flattened her palms against it, a smile spreading over her tear-stained face.

"Boy, how he can kick. Like a mule!"

One afternoon, just three weeks later, she felt the labour pains start. She had already moved to the Garlands' house in Westminster a few days previously, so her mother-in-law was on hand to accompany her in a taxi to the nursing home in Portland Place where the baby would be delivered. Later that night she gave birth to a daughter whom Sir Horace Pines told her was splendidly formed and in excellent health. The next morning, after a sleepless night sitting up on a train from York, an ecstatic Charlie arrived at her bedside and gazed in bleary-eyed wonderment at his daughter and her mother.

"I've always loved the name Julia," said Margot drowsily.

"Then Julia she shall be," said Charlie.

28

Julia was nearly ten months old when her father returned to war. Since the beginning of May, the Guards Armoured Division, of which Charlie's Grenadier tank battalion was a unit, had been on the south coast of England preparing to play their part in what would be the greatest over-water assault in history, the invasion of Nazi-held France. If Charlie and his fellow Grenadiers felt frustrated at not knowing when the invasion would be launched, Margot had even greater reason to feel frustrated: she didn't even know where Charlie was stationed. So total was the pre-invasion security blackout that wives could not be told by their husbands from where they were arriving on their weekend leave, and each weekend, when Charlie appeared at Verbena Cottage, she would complain of the absurdity of the situation.

"It's a lot of military bullshit, Charlie. Wherever it is you are, the civilians there know all about you, so why can't your wife? And what am I supposed to do if some-thing were to happen to me and Julia?"

It was now the first weekend in June, and Charlie was growing impatient at her constant pressure on him to reveal his weekday whereabouts.

"It's bad enough for me to have to keep the secret," he replied irritably as he shrugged off his service dress tunic and sank wearily into a deck chair in the garden. "There's absolutely no point in burdening you with it as well. And I've also told you, God knows how many times, that if you needed me in an emergency, you have the number of the Regimental Orderly Room in London, and they would immediately alert me. So, please, no more nagging about this. It's not going to go on for much longer; the invasion can only be a matter of days away now, I promise."

Margot handed him a glass of beer and sat down on the grass opposite him, spreading the full skirt of her floral print dress around her.

"You make it sound as though I'm in a hurry to see you off to face the bullets again. That's not fair."

"Of course not, silly! I'm the one who's in a hurry; we all are. We want to get on with it, get it over and get back to our families."

For five weeks, the Armoured Division had been hard at work bringing itself up to battle readiness. Every vehicle, whether on tracks or wheels, had had to be waterproofed for the amphibious landing, and a hundred and one other preparatory tasks performed. The work was now done, and they were ready to go. Some day soon, when the meteorologists could advise the Commander-in-Chief, General Dwight D. Eisenhower, that he had the weather he wanted, the great armada would set sail across the Channel. Until then, the suspense had to be cheerfully endured.

At the end of each weekend, Charlie and Margot went through the increasingly self-conscious ritual of final farewells, knowing that when the Guards were given the order to move, there would certainly be no time for face-to-face goodbyes. And each weekend when Charlie turned up one more time from his secret location, Margot determined to do all she could to give him twenty-four hours of peace and relaxation, but somehow the tension always built up, and she found herself snapping irritably at him. She would then seek to make amends in bed, but she knew she was only making selfish use of his body while it was still there, and the more he told her how much he loved her, and how much he was going to miss her, the guiltier she felt. She could never confess it to him, but she was as impatient for the launching of the invasion as he appeared to be. Of course she was going to worry about him, but since there was now no question of him not fighting, and since that was what he had sought anyway, the sooner he got on with it, the less frustration she would feel. She knew she could now handle having a husband at war; she'd been through it all before. She wouldn't be suffering the way poor Kick would be suffering. It was less than a month ago that she had become the Marchioness of Hartington in a registry office ceremony, to the dismay and discomfort of most of her family, and Billy's Coldstream Guards battalion was similarly poised for the cross-Channel assault. Margot felt deeply for Kick, while facing her own impending separation with equanimity. She had become a fatalist. A lot of brave young men were going to die. Maybe Charlie would be one of them. There was nothing she could do about that except pray that he wouldn't be, and that wasn't necessarily going to help. On the other hand he might survive the war, which surely wasn't going to last much longer anyway, and once again return a hero. Whatever was in store for Charlie, she was impatient to see the war over and done with. She had had as much experience of it as she wanted, and it was now simply a bore. So let Charlie and Billy and Larry and Jamie and Edmond and the millions of their Allied comrades-in-arms hurry up and finish this damn thing off. The romantic view of herself as the brave young bride wondering whether tomorrow would bring tears and widowhood was now four years old and fading. She was already looking ahead to the postwar chapter of her life, and the present inability to know whether she would be entering it with or without a husband was beginning to irritate her. So get on with it, Charlie! And come home covered in glory. Then maybe we'll be able to make something of you!

"How about some Virginia ham for lunch?"

Charlie opened one eye and squinted in the bright sun. "We have some?"

"The last of Larry's cans. If I keep on saving it for the next weekend, you're not likely ever to get to eat it. I'll go and put some potatoes on." She nodded towards the pram standing in the shadow of the box hedge. "If Julia wakes up, take her out and let her romp a bit on the lawn."

When the taxi arrived early on Sunday morning to take Charlie to Windsor station, they kissed each other goodbye, uttering the now ritual words of parting.

"I'm counting on you for next weekend."

"Don't, darling. It could be any day now."

"That's what you always say."

"Take care of yourselves, and keep in touch with my parents."

"And you take care of yourself," she said, opening the taxi door. She grinned. "And stay away from all those Brighton belles!"

Charlie looked thunderstruck. Glancing nervously at the taxi driver, he pushed the car door closed again.

"How in hell did you find out?"

"Because of this."

She fished in the pocket of her skirt and extracted a small rectangle of green paper. He recognized it as the stub of a ticket to a performance of *French Without Tears* at a Brighton theatre.

"Carelessly dumped in an ashtray in the bedroom. So much for your super security!"

"Well, at least you didn't find a pair," Charlie said. "Now you know how well I'm behaving."

"Just keep it up."

They gave each other a parting hug and a kiss, and then he was gone.

The following morning, the village postman handed her a letter with all too familiar handwriting on the envelope. It was from Edmond, and her heart missed a beat when she saw that it was post-marked London. What on earth was he doing there? She had last heard from him in late April: a brief letter from Morocco telling her that he had sought and received permission to join General Leclerc's Second Armoured Division there. She had kept putting off replying and had by now reckoned that it was too late anyway. She knew enough to know that armies did not stand still for long, and he could be anywhere by now. Well, now she knew. He was in London. She tore open the letter, and noted that there was no return address.

My dear Margot,

I hesitated to let you know that I have been back in England for a couple of weeks already because I felt that you and your husband would scarcely welcome my intrusion at this very tense moment. My Division is now somewhere in England (which security forbids me to name) and I will thus be permitted at last to do what was denied me when France was overrun: to go to battle against the Germans on my own native soil, in a tank, as befits a cavalry officer. I am very happy about this.

If, by any chance, you wanted to contact me, you could leave a message with Olwen Vaughan who, as you probably remember, runs my old haunt, Le Petit Club de France in St James's Place. If I don't hear from you, I want you to know that I shall be thinking of you, and praying that we may all get together when this is over. Give little Julia a kiss from me, and be assured that I wish for the safety and well-being of all three of you.

With much affection,
Edmond.

Dear, sweet Edmond, she thought. Such a gentleman. It would be so nice to see him again. Just for lunch and a chat. No harm could possibly come of that, and she wouldn't really be breaking the promise she made to Larry; there was little likelihood of the affair being rekindled. Edmond was presumably in England to join in the invasion, and would soon be gone.

But plans of a visit to London were shelved the next morning. A few minutes after eight o'clock Mrs Watts burst into her bedroom.

"The invasion's started!" she said breathlessly. "It's on the radio. I do hope Mr Charlie is all right."

Margot got hurriedly out of bed and went straight to Julia's room. Her fair-haired, smiling daughter was standing in her cot, gripping the wooden safety rail with pink, pudgy hands. Margot lifted her into her arms and kissed her.

"Your daddy's gone to war," she said. "But he'll be back."

In the event, more than three weeks were to pass before the Guards Armoured Division left England's shores. In the waiting period, all ranks were confined to the Divisional area. Charlie called her several times a week, and on 13th June, the day the first of Hitler's new weapon, the V-1 "Flying Bomb", fell on the southern outskirts of London, Charlie made her promise to stay out of the city. In the meantime, she had called Le Petit Club de France and spoken with Olwen Vaughan. Edmond had not been into the club in more than ten days, and might already have gone to France. Nevertheless, she would, she promised Margot, ask him to call her at the cottage if he came by.

For Julia's sake, she felt compelled to obey Charlie's instruction that she stay away from the city and the Flying Bombs. Had she been on her own she would not have hesitated to move to the Chesham Street flat. The prospect of lengthy isolation at Verbena Cottage depressed her, but not enough to tempt her into accepting her solicitous parents-in-law's suggestion that she move to Bowes Court for the duration. So she put a good face on it, and settled down to await the end, if there was to be one, of the V-1 reign of terror, and for news that Charlie was finally on the move. For that she waited until 2nd July, when she read in the morning papers that the Guards Armoured Division had landed in Normandy. She heaved a sigh of relief that the waiting was over. The curtain had gone up on the final act of Charlie's wartime drama, and through the columns of the newspapers that landed on her front doorstep, she would follow, as best she could, its gradual denouement.

As the Allied campaign in Normandy progressed from the initial assault to the securing of the bridgehead, and finally to the spectacular and bloody breakout, Margot scoured the papers daily for indications that Charlie was in action. The first mention came just three weeks after the news that he had arrived in Normandy. On 22nd July she read that the Guards Armoured Division had been involved in the breakout south of Caen and had suffered losses. She now steeled herself for the arrival of a War Office telegram, but instead, a week later, a cheerful letter arrived from him, full of optimism and humour. It seemed that Charlie was enjoying the fighting.

The following day, to her astonishment and chagrin,

she read that the French General Leclerc's Second Armoured Division had only that day set sail for France. So Edmond had been in England all along! She thought of calling Olwen Vaughan to find out if he'd been into the club and received the message to call her. Then she thought better of it. Even if, like Charlie, he'd been barred from leave from D-Day onwards, he would certainly have called the club to see if there was any message from her. Thus she could only conclude that he had decided against getting in touch with her. So to hell with him!

Mid-August found her, with shaking hand, penning a letter of condolence to Kick. Joe Jr was dead, and the newspapers were full of the courageous exploit that he had failed to survive. He had received his Navy pilot's wings in 1942, and in September of the following year had arrived back in England with the first US squadron to be attached to the RAF's Coastal Command. Through that winter, he flew round-the-clock anti-submarine patrols over the Channel and the Bay of Biscay. By D-Day he had completed his tour of duty and was due to return to the United States. Instead he volunteered for a new assignment, and after some initial disappointments was eventually sent to a top-secret training unit to prepare for a special mission. Code-named "Aphrodite", the mission was a campaign to knock out the V-1 launching sites on the northern coast of France with the Allies' own hastily devised version of a flying bomb: planes crammed with TNT which would be flown part of the way to the targets by pilots, and then, after the pilots had parachuted out for pick-up in the Channel, would be guided on automatic pilot by accompanying planes onto the target. The Army Air Force mounted the first six missions, but none of the "bombs" reached their targets. It was now the Navy's turn to try. Joe Jr flew on the first Navy mission. Over the east coast of England, the massive load of TNT prematurely exploded, blowing the plane, its pilot and co-pilot to smithereens.

Margot's letter missed Kick. On learning of her brother's death, she had immediately hitched a ride on a military transport plane to Boston, to be with her family at this time of grief.

The relative calm with which Margot had been following events across the Channel was broken by Joe's death. She questioned why that should be so, but was forced to admit to herself that it had happened. She trembled now as she picked up the papers each morning, and the crunch of bicycle tyres on the gravel driveway sent her racing to the windows to satisfy herself that it was not a postman delivering a small yellow envelope with a telegram inside.

Summer slid into autumn, and by the first day of September the Grenadiers were on the west bank of the Somme, heading towards Arras and the Belgian frontier. Charlie was now beginning to recognize the countryside from that earlier campaign, and as they crossed into Belgium, not ten miles from Lille, his thoughts turned wistfully to those boisterous evenings spent with Jamie at l'Huîtrière, and those almost carefree months of watching and waiting for the real war to begin. The late afternoon of 3rd September found Charlie waving from the turret of his Sherman tank to the ecstatic crowds gathered outside the Bourse in the centre of Brussels as the long column of his Fifth Armoured Brigade snaked through the city, assembling eventually before the Château Royal, where the Queen Mother of the Belgians was waiting to thank the British liberators of her long and cruelly occupied capital. The following day, after a night of revelry, the Guards were on the move again to liberate Louvain on their march to the Dutch border.

Each day, Margot studied the battle-line maps printed in the papers, and a couple of evenings a week her father-in-law called her to comment on the progress and give her any further information he had culled on events in Charlie's sector. On a grey morning in the third week of September, Margot came downstairs to find Mrs Watts shaking her head sadly over the paper awaiting her on the kitchen table.

"Bad news, Wattie?" she asked anxiously

"That poor girl! First her brother, now her husband."

Margot seized the paper. "Oh, Jesus!"

Billy Hartington was dead, felled by a sniper's bullet in Belgium.

For the first time she felt the conviction that Charlie was not to be spared either. But the days passed and no telegram came, and at the end of September, following the great battle for the Nijmegen bridges across the Waal River, a letter from Charlie reached her. Apart from a sad paragraph about Billy, the letter was written in his usual exuberant style. There was a PS scrawled minutely in the margin which she had difficulty in deciphering: "Stuck my neck out by chance in the right place at the right moment and have been put up for an MC. Will be more careful next time!"

A Military Cross! Margot felt a thrill of pride. Dear, fearless Charlie. Maybe he was indestructible after all. After winning that medal he'd better be.

When General von Rundstedt's massive counter-offensive in the Ardennes caught the Allied armies by surprise, the Grenadiers were resting in a small Dutch mining town between the Meuse River and the German border, after strenuous weeks in the front line. Four days later, as the gravity of the situation mounted, the two Grenadier battalions moved under cover of darkness and in bitter cold back into Belgium. Charlie's battalion spent an anxious Christmas not far from Louvain, listening for the unmistakable rumble of the giant Panther and Tiger panzers; but they never came. The Americans, who had withstood the brunt of von Rundstedt's attack, gradually began to regain the lost ground. The enveloping fog, which had prevented the Allied air forces from breaking the German advance, lifted. Besieged Bastogne was relieved, and General Patton's tanks sliced through the enemy bulge. The last initiative the Germans were to take on the western front was over.

As Charlie spent a cold and anxious Christmas in Belgium, Margot finally succumbed to the entreaties of her parents-in-law that she not attempt to see the winter through in the seclusion of either Verbena Cottage or the London flat. The winter was unbearably cold, and, to make matters worse, coal and electricity were in desperately short supply. Try as she might, she could keep neither the cottage nor the flat warm, and with the forecast of worse cold to come, she capitulated. Her temporary loss of independence seemed now not too exorbitant a price to pay for the comparative warmth and comfort of Bowes Court, where logs from the well-forested estate kept the fireplaces ablaze.

In the third week of January, without warning, but to the great delight of all at Bowes Court, Charlie appeared home on ten days' leave. His excitement at rediscovering his wife and daughter touched Margot deeply, and on their first night together, in the flickering light of a fire dying slowly in the bedroom fireplace, they made love happily and well.

In the days that followed, however, she noticed a disturbing change in him. The initial euphoria which had marked the reunion with his family had quickly given way to a mood of noticeable depression. The exuberance that had shone through his letters from the front was gone, and Margot began to wonder whether it ever had been truly there; maybe he had been wanting them to think that he was in good spirits when in fact he was not. He now spoke only reluctantly, and usually only in the presence of his father, about the fighting he had seen, and he dismissed the circumstances that had led to the sewing of the ribbon of the Military Cross to the breast of his tunic as "something I wouldn't want to live through again or even talk about." He was similarly tight-lipped when his father asked him about casualties among his brother officers. "More than enough" was his only response. They noticed that he was drinking heavily compared to what had been his customary level of alcoholic intake. After the first night, he would fall into sleep, breathing heavily, as soon as his head touched the pillow. On the third morning, Margot gently and smilingly chided him for his nocturnal neglect of her.

"I'm sorry," he said simply. And that was all. She decided to press the matter no further for the time being.

When Sir Walter asked his son whether he had given any more thought to returning to stock-broking after the war, he appeared irritated and said that all that could wait. His only postwar plan was to get out of uniform as soon as they would let him.

"You mustn't be too worried about him, my dear," Sir Walter told Margot one afternoon when they were alone. "We saw a lot of that sort of depression during the Great War, and after it. They snap out of it in time. You just have to be patient and give lots of love and affection. He's clearly very much in love with you, and proud as a peacock about his daughter, but he can't show it very much at the moment. The fighting, to which he's got to return, is just too much on his mind."

"And the drinking?"

"He'll get over that too. It's a release from his tensions. When the fighting's over, so will the drinking be."

Margot was not so sure, but she told Sir Walter that she shared his optimism. Later that afternoon, having persuaded Charlie to relinquish for a while the warm comfort of an armchair before the fire in the library and to take a brisk walk with her through the park, she asked him why he had not so far expressed any wish to spend a day and a night in London.

"What for?"

"Well, I thought you might like to see if some of our friends were there. We could go to a show and dine somewhere nice. Maybe dance at the Four Hundred."

"No. I really don't feel like seeing anyone. London and our friends can wait until all this is over. I just want the peace and quiet of home for these few days."

"Of course. You must spend these few days just as you want to, darling."

They arrived at the edge of the solid-frozen lake which stretched along the northern perimeter of the Bowes Court estate. Half a dozen geese stood motionless on the ice.

"It's a wonder they can survive this cold," said Margot.

"*This* cold? Christ, you don't know what cold is! You should be where I've been these last weeks."

"I know it must have been absolutely awful, Charlie," said Margot soothingly.

"What would *you* know about it?" he snapped.

Margot looked him squarely in the face.

"Charles Garland, snap out of it! Your frightful mood is making it very difficult for all of us to enjoy you these days. What the hell's the matter with you? We're trying to make your well-earned leave a joyful, relaxing and comfortable break for you from this bloody war, and you make us feel about as wanted as lepers. Where did the spirit of those first few hours after your arrival disappear to?"

Charlie poked nervously with his walking stick at the rock-hard ground.

"I'm sorry," he said. "I can't expect you to understand that one can't just stop fighting one day and play the dutiful and loving son and husband the next."

"Some people can, I'm sure."

"Well I can't," he shouted.

"But you *did*! On your first night back – or have you forgotten?"

"Is that all you wanted me back for? A good poke? I'd have thought there was plenty of that available in London for you while I'm away getting shot at."

"Charlie, stop it!" She tugged angrily at the sleeve of his heavy British Warm overcoat, but he pulled away.

"Why can't you all leave me alone?" Jabbing the point of his stick at the ground, he set off with long strides down the path along the lake's edge. "I'll be home late," he shouted over his shoulder.

"Where are you going? It's cold. Let's go home!"

"I'm going to the village – alone!"

"To get drunk, I suppose," she yelled, cupping her hands around her mouth. Charlie marched on. "Damn you, Charlie!" She turned and headed across the broad cattle meadow back towards the house

"He wanted to get something from the village store, but he insisted I come home because of the cold," explained Margot lamely as she joined the elder Garlands.

"More likely gone for a drink at the local," said Lady Garland with a sniff.

"Oh, I don't know, my dear," said her husband, but his look betrayed that he did.

During Charlie's last three days of leave, the relationship between himself and Margot reversed. He made an effort to be affable, even loving, but she no longer felt in the mood to respond in like fashion. She was furious with herself for having gone to the bother of defending him in front of his parents when they knew perfectly well what he was up to, especially after he had been so rude to her. She behaved politely but coolly towards him, and was relieved when her period arrived and gave her an excuse for not making love. Then, on the eve of his departure, as they changed for dinner, his short-lived affability gave way again to his earlier bitter mood.

"I've tried to make it up to you," he said suddenly, his lips trembling, "but you've behaved like a first-class American bitch!"

"What did you expect, Charlie?"

"An effort."

"It took you seven days to make one when up till then no one had said a single unkind word to you. So don't give me that."

She walked into the bathroom and locked the door behind her.

Over the candle-lit dinner table, goaded by a reproach from Lady Garland for her seeming unwillingness to converse with Charlie, Margot felt a sudden urge to indulge in a little reckless taunting of the Garland family.

"I read today in *The Times* that the French succeeded against huge odds in holding Strasburg. Leclerc's division did it. That's the one Edmond Lemonnier is serving with."

"Is he?" said Sir Walter, rising to the bait. "How do you know?"

"He wrote to me when he got to London with the division. They'd been training in North Africa."

"That's the fellow who was with you at the Café de Paris, isn't it?" said Charlie, sounding anything but interested.

"You have a good memory."

"The French have been mostly a bloody nuisance since the invasion. All they're interested in is in retrieving their tarnished reputation. Eisenhower didn't even want Strasburg held: de Gaulle countermanded the American order, the arrogant so-and-so."

"With your Churchill's blessing, Charlie."

"Since when?"

"Read the papers, for God's sakes."

"I didn't know you were such a supporter of de Gaulle," shot back Charlie in a voice loaded with sarcasm. "Forgive me if I offended your sensibilities."

"All right, that's more than enough, both of you," Sir Walter intervened. "I won't have our last dinner together turned into a family squabble."

An uneasy truce was maintained through the rest of the evening. Charlie and his father lingered alone for a good hour over their port while Margot and her mother-in-law sat in the library, Margot flipping over the pages of already read magazines while Lady Garland peered and picked at her needlepoint.

"It's not easy for him, Margot. You must be understanding."

"It's not easy for me either, Cynthia," said Margot calmly.

"All will come right when he gets home for good, I'm sure of that. It's just this awful war; it plays havoc with people's relationships."

"Yes, it does. And I just hope you're right about what will happen when he returns."

They relapsed into a silence that lasted a long while before Lady Garland began a lengthy monologue on how Julia should be dressed and what she should be fed in order to stave off the rigours of the winter. Margot listened in silence, nodding occasionally, unwilling to provoke another family confrontation that evening.

When the two men finally joined the ladies, Charlie quickly excused himself, pleading the need for as long a night's sleep as possible before his wearying trek back to the front started the next morning. Margot rose to accompany him, but Sir Walter waved her back into her chair.

"Stay for a moment, my dear."

Margot looked at Charlie and shrugged her shoulders as he kissed his mother goodnight and left.

Sir Walter helped himself to a whisky and soda off a tray and went to take up his favourite position standing in front of the fireplace. He took a mouthful of the drink, rolled it around his palate, swallowed it, stared at the ceiling for a good ten seconds and then looked Margot in the eye.

"You mentioned Lemonnier tonight, my dear. You didn't see him, did you, when he came to London?"

"No, I didn't. Why?" Margot tried to conceal her irritation.

"I think it's only fair to tell you now that your father and I had a very frank talk about you and this fellow some two years ago. I confess I was concerned about reports that you had been seen together fairly frequently while Charlie was a POW. I expect your father spoke to you about it."

"He never mentioned that he'd discussed it with you, but he and I agreed that Edmond was entitled to our friendship by virtue of his having been Katie's friend and having been with us when she died. That was all."

Sir Walter imbibed again and took another look at some ceiling mouldings much in need of a plasterer's attention.

"Yes. Well, I just didn't want Charlie hurt then, or now. So you'll understand my raising the matter in the light of your remarks at dinner."

All through this exchange, Cynthia Garland had remained silently bent over her *petit point*. Now she spoke up.

"I'm sure Margot would never do anything like that to hurt Charlie."

"Like what?" asked Margot.

"Well, you wouldn't be tempted, is what I mean."

"Everyone's tempted, Cynthia dear, sometime or other," put in Sir Walter. "The point is whether you have the character and the will to resist it."

"Quite so," said Cynthia. "And, of course, Margot does."

"Good!" said Margot, rising rapidly to her feet. "I'm glad that's settled. And now, if you'll excuse me, I think I'll join my husband."

She kissed them both goodnight and went upstairs. But she didn't join her husband. The bed was empty, and so was the bathroom. She left the room again and tiptoed across the corridor to a door under which a light was showing.

"Charlie?" she whispered loudly through it.

"Hope you don't mind. I'm sleeping here," he said from the other side. "See you in the morning."

"That's a bit silly, but have it your own way."

The next morning, he appeared at her bedside, already dressed in his uniform, looking fresh and with a smile on his face. He bent to kiss her on the cheek.

"Sorry, old girl, about last night. I wasn't potted or anything. I just felt a terrible urge to sleep long and deep, and at the moment I find I can't do that unless I'm by myself."

Margot propped herself up on the pillows and shivered at the icy temperature in the room.

"No offence taken, Charlie. But you'd better not use that as an excuse when you come back from the war if you want this marriage to stay intact."

Charlie looked shocked.

"No, I mean it, Charlie. When we have a spat, that's one thing. But I won't have you sleeping somewhere else on the thin excuse that you sleep better that way. I just don't go for sexless marriages."

He made a face at her and left the room. An hour later, after Lady Garland had bade her son a tearful farewell, Sir Walter and Margot accompanied him to the local railway station.

"Take good care of yourself, my boy," said the father, fighting back a tear. "No more heroics; you've got your decoration. Just come back safely." He patted his son on the cheek, shook hands with him and turned away, leaving Charlie and Margot together for the final moments before the train pulled out.

She kissed him on both cheeks, and then lightly on the lips.

"You'd better get in, or you'll miss it."

Charlie got in and pulled the window down. Then he reached down and took her hand and squeezed it.

"Things'll be all right when I get back," he said, blinking. "I need you and Julia."

She smiled. "And this first-class American bitch needs you too."

"I do hope so. God bless!"

A whistle blew, there was a slamming of doors and the train jerked into motion.

"Come back safely, Charlie darling!"

"Will do. I promise."

Margot walked quickly alongside the moving train.

"Do you love me, really?" she shouted above the mounting noise.

"Of course. And you?"

"I love you!"

She could keep up with the train no longer, so she halted, waved once, then turned and retraced her steps to where Sir Walter was waiting. He took her arm.

"He'll come back all right," she said confidently.

Two days after Charlie's departure, a letter arrived for Margot from her father in Washington, and the main item of news in it instantly filled her with anxiety. Larry had returned to combat. She had known for some time that he had converted to the B-29 Superfortress as a command pilot with a captain's three bars on his shoulder, but she had resolutely banished to the back of her mind the assumption that he was being prepared for a second tour of combat duty. Her father's letter came to her as a bitter blow.

For the usual security reasons Larry was unable to tell you himself about this before he left, so I said I would write you immediately. He left last week with the 313th Bombardment Wing for the Marianas. Which of the islands he didn't say. Guam, Saipan, Tinian? Anyway, the chain lies in the Central Pacific (you can find it on the map) and we threw the Japs off them last summer. We've already been hitting Japan from there, so we can assume Larry's gone along to continue the good work and speed the end of the war. I know you'll worry a lot about him being back in combat, but just remember that he's one helluva good flyer and the B-29 is a great machine. I know it must be really tough to have both a husband and a brother in combat, and we're praying for them and for you every day. So try to keep your spirits up. Things are going well for us, and everyone here is confident both wars will be over well before this new year is out. And we'll have some heroes in the family to celebrate, including you, my brave daughter. The waiting wives are every bit as much to be honoured.

Margot was moved but not much comforted by her father's words. It wasn't fair that having barely survived the European war, Larry was now to give the Japs a chance to get him.

Charlie returned to the Dutch-German border where the Grenadiers were lined up with the massed forces of the 21st Army Group, awaiting the signal which would launch them across the great Rhine River and into the heartland of the crumbling Reich. The moment arrived on 30th March, in the early morning of which Charlie's battalion of tanks rumbled across the bridge at Rees. Throughout the month of April they fought their way through the disintegrating but still lethal remnants of the once mighty German army, pushing northwards towards the city of Bremen. On 8th May, arriving in the small Lower Saxony village of Mulsum, some forty miles west of Hamburg, they heard the official announcement of the end of the war in Europe.

That night, Charlie penned his first letter to Margot in a month. It was brief, and, as usual, told little of the fighting he had been through. He ended it thus:

I have come almost to fear moments of great happiness such as this, since there always seems to be some sad price to pay for them somewhere down the line. But maybe this time there really is only happiness to look forward to. Now that this nightmare is over, I can't believe that life with you and our little Julia need be anything but blissfully happy. I certainly promise to try to make it so.

All my love,
Charlie.

Margot was back at Verbena Cottage to enjoy the summer months there when his letter arrived, forwarded from Bowes Court.

Come back soon and show me, Charlie, she said to herself.

29

Margot's hopes that Charlie would be on his way home as soon as the echoes of the last shots fired in the European war had died away were quickly dashed. The armies which had defeated Germany were now called upon to occupy it, and Charlie and his troops soon found themselves relieved of their tanks and placed in charge of a triangle of villages populated by sullen, disarmed Wehrmacht, bewildered foreign forced labourers and resentful local inhabitants.

"I'm not much good at being a sort of pseudo-burgomaster," wrote Charlie to his wife at the end of June, "so I'm damned relieved we'll be leaving here any day now, according to the rumours. But where to I haven't the foggiest, and I doubt our commander has either. But we all know *one* place we're not headed for: home."

The move, when it came, was to the vicinity of Cologne, where the Guards, once again an infantry division, took up what was to be their final occupation area. Demobilization was, however, still far from imminent, and when Margot heard to that effect from Charlie, she decided that the moment had come to make her first postwar visit to the United States. She was impatient to see her family again and to introduce Julia to them. She also felt an urge to exchange for a while the depressing austerity of England for the comparative luxuries and welcome pampering she could expect in her mother country.

She was spending a long weekend with her parents-in-law at Bowes Court when she took the decision. Sir

Walter Garland was in the closing stages of an electoral campaign to retain his East Hampshire parliamentary seat for the Tories. The Prime Minister had called a general election for 6th July, the final results of which would not be announced until nineteen days later when the votes of the servicemen overseas had been received and counted. Sir Walter had so far betrayed no outward sign of doubt about the outcome. Nonetheless, the ritual of a vigorous campaign had to be observed, and that sunny Saturday afternoon found Margot and Lady Garland perched on kitchen chairs atop a flat-bed truck in the local town's market square, from which vantage point Garland was extolling the endless virtues of the Conservative Party and its heroic titan of a leader, and warning of the inexcusable folly of entrusting the conduct of Britain and her Empire's postwar affairs to the likes of Mr Clement Attlee and his socialists. From their demeanour, Margot judged that the hundred or so townspeople gathered below her were almost all supporters of the patrician, grey-flannel-suited orator sporting the outsize royal blue party rosette. The ten-minute speech, to which they listened in respectful silence punctuated by an occasional "Hear! Hear!", was delivered in a resonant baritone which, though mellower than that of his son, nonetheless brought images of Charlie flooding into Margot's mind. As Sir Walter warmed to his theme, she began to see Charlie standing there in his father's place. Yes, Charlie could do it, she thought excitedly. He'd make a wonderful politician. Young and handsome, with that same splendid voice, with his political connections and his impressive war record, surely he would rise quickly through the Tory ranks. Another Anthony Eden. A future prime minister, perhaps. And she would help him. An intelligent, attractive American wife was no handicap to an English politician, as Jenny Jerome had amply proved to Randolph Churchill, and Margot knew that she herself had the potential to play the role of the socially and politically influential wife.

"Attlee was a loyal and hard-working deputy prime minister of our wartime coalition government."

Sir Walter took a deep breath, chest puffed out,

savouring his own generosity of spirit towards the leader of the opposition.

"I am never one to deny credit where credit is due."

He slapped one clenched fist into the palm of the other hand and stared fiercely at his audience as though daring them to doubt the strict accuracy of that claim. The faithful stared back in sheepish acquiescence. Sir Walter enjoyed dealing with unfriendly interrupters and felt mildly irritated at their conspicuous absence from his meeting. No stomach for the fight this time, he thought to himself as he launched into a derisive excoriation of the leadership qualities, or lack thereof, of the man to whom he had just awarded due credit.

Margot held her appropriately admiring gaze on her father-in-law, but her thoughts were still of Charlie. To date she had given no great consideration to the question of what her husband might do once the war was over. On his last leave back from the front, he had bluntly refused to discuss the question until he was home and demobilized. She very well recalled an occasion on which Sir Walter had, in Margot's presence, urged his son to consider the possibility of a political career, an urging that Charlie had politely but firmly resisted by contending that one politician in the family was enough. Margot had given the matter little thought at the time, but now she found herself wondering whether Charlie still held to that view, and if so, how she might set about weaning him from it.

Applause and scattered cheers greeted the close of Sir Walter's speech, and Margot jumped to her feet to join in. Flushed from his oratorical effort and from the heat of the sun, the Member of Parliament beamed happily at his supporters and raised his hand in a Churchillian V-for-Victory sign. Then, indicating that he had something more to say, he signalled for an end to the applause, turned to beckon Margot to his side, and put an arm around her shoulders when she blushingly joined him.

"Before I move on, I'd like you to meet a beautiful young American lady whom my wife and I are proud to have as our daughter-in-law, the wife of our son Charlie, and the mother of our little granddaughter. This is Margot. She spent the whole of the war here, blitz and all, when she could have gone back to the comparative safety of the United States. Instead she felt it her patriotic and wifely duty to stick it out here in her husband's country while he was away fighting and a prisoner of war. Her father was a distinguished diplomat here during the worst of the war and, tragic to relate, Margot's younger sister died in the blitz. But our Margot was undeterred and went to work with the American Red Cross in London. We also had the privilege of meeting her twin brother, Larry, when he came to England to fly a Flying Fortress bomber of the US Eighth Air Force against the Germans. Not content with that, he's now in the Pacific bombing the Japs to their knees."

Margot felt her eyes moistening and a lump swelling in her throat. Sir Walter squeezed her shoulder and went on.

"We owe the Americans an incalculable debt, my friends. They helped us beat Hitler, and they have borne the brunt of the war in the Pacific where we shall soon have the Japs decisively beaten. I suggest we give Margot a rousing cheer so that she can tell her people back home just how much we appreciate what they have done and are still doing to restore peace to this world."

Sir Walter bent towards her and kissed her on the cheek as loud clapping broke out followed by three cheers and some appreciative whistles. A woman's voice shouted "God bless America!" and Margot buried her face in her father-in-law's shoulder for a moment before facing the crowd and repeating "Thank you!" in a strangled voice as she waved acknowledgement.

A man near the front cupped his hands and shouted: "Makes a nice change from your GIs pinching all our girls!"

There was loud laughter in which Margot joined. As it died down, a strong male voice from the back of the crowd cut sharply into the subsiding noise.

"Would the candidate tell us what the Tories are going to do for us working-class people coming home from the war? Are you just going to say 'thanks' and put us on the dole while your type goes on living comfortably?"

Sir Walter withdrew his arm from around Margot's shoulder, and taking the cue, she retreated to her chair. The politician smiled benignly; so the opposition was here after all!

"I'm sorry, young man, that you didn't get here early enough to hear my remarks on that subject, but the hour is never too late to educate the opposition."

His remark was interrupted by the clock on the roof of the town hall behind him striking four, and a ripple of laughter greeted the timeliness of its interruption. Sir Walter paused for the completion of the four strokes, then his face turned solemn.

"We're not going to make the same mistakes the Liberals made after the Great War. You can be sure of that. There'll be jobs and homes for all our gallant servicemen this time. The architect of our military victory will be no less the architect of our peacetime prosperity; prosperity for all with a will to work for it! And if you believe a Labour government can produce prosperity for all of you, I would urge you to recall the chaos in which Mr Ramsay MacDonald left this country's economy at the end of the first – and, I promise you, the last – Labour administration. Trust us! Trust Churchill! We'll give you the opportunity to stand on your own feet!"

There was more applause from the crowd, and a party official stepped forward to whisper into Sir Walter's ear that it was time to move on to his next campaign stop. At that moment a white van bedecked with posters announcing SQUADRON LEADER BILL PERRY YOUR LABOUR CANDIDATE, turned into the marketplace and pulled up outside the town's only hotel. Sir Walter spotted it and grinned broadly.

"Is the young man who asked the question still here?" he boomed. "If so, I suggest he asks the Labour candidate what his party promises the ex-servicemen. He'll promise you the earth because he knows there'll be no Labour government to deliver it! Run over and catch him before he takes off again!"

He chuckled and turned to his wife and Margot.

"Well, my dears, I suggest you two go off home to tea. I'm going to knock on doors for an hour or so in Leefield ward."

"Don't be late for dinner, Walter," said Lady Garland, pecking him on the cheek.

Garland turned to Margot. "Did I do all right?"

"Splendidly! And thanks for the very moving tribute."

"Richly deserved, my dear. Richly deserved."

The two women were helped down off the truck by Sir Walter's supporters. As they walked towards the black Humber parked a few yards away, Margot spotted the young man who had asked the question.

"Oh God!" she said out loud.

She had been able to see only his head and shoulders in the crowd. She saw now that he had crutches tucked under his arms, and an empty trouser leg was folded up and pinned to the waistband of his rumpled grey flannels. She shuddered at the recollection of Sir Walter's jibe that the man "run over and catch" the Labour candidate. She pointed him out to Lady Garland.

"I'd like to go and have a word with him," she said.

"Heavens no, Margot!" said Lady Garland, opening the car door on the driver's side. "There's nothing you can do about an embittered ex-serviceman who's going to vote Labour anyway."

Margot stared at her for a moment, a puzzled and hurt look on her face. There were times when she really disliked her.

At dinner that evening, Sir Walter's mood had lost its earlier ebullience. His afternoon of campaigning had left him with a growing feeling that all was not as well as he had been expecting. He was an experienced and shrewd campaigner who knew his constituency like he knew his own house and acreage. He had already fought three elections there, and each time his confident prediction of the margin of his victory had proved uncannily accurate. But for some days he had been sensing an unfamiliar current runing through the constituency, and he was now more or less convinced that he had identified its nature. Many of his constituents seemed to be suffering from a form of political schizophrenia. They were manifestly grateful to Churchill for leading them out of the long, dark night of war. Every honour that might be heaped upon him they deemed fully deserved. But now there was a different battle to be fought, a battle to change the face of Britain. Emerging from the nightmare of war, the people appeared determined not to go back to what they recalled as the "bad old days" of the '30s. This was the beginning of a new and different era, and it required, they seemed to be thinking, a new and different leadership. The Tory leader had done his job, God bless him. Now it was time to see what the working people's party could do to build a new Britain.

"You're being unduly alarmist," said his wife firmly after Sir Walter had expounded his theory. "British standards of decency and fair play have surely not sunk to the level where even the working class would turn out the man who had saved the country."

Sir Walter contemplated the familiar but always risible juxtaposition of a geometrically shaped slice of spam on his family-crested Crown Derby dinner ware. Then he looked across to his daughter-in-law.

"What do you think, Margot, my dear?"

"I'm not sure, but I do remember Charlie in one of his recent letters saying that the soldiers were sometimes asking whether they had been through all this just to go back to the life they had been leading before. He said he thought the returning servicemen would probably hold the key to what happens in British politics from now on."

"He wrote much the same to us," said Lady Garland, "but Charlie's no expert in political matters."

"I think he'd make a wonderful politician," ventured Margot.

"Yes, he'd probably take to it like a duck to water," said Sir Walter, "and you'd be a great help to him."

Margot beamed.

"Don't you put any such ideas into his head," said Lady Garland sternly. "He'll have a wife and daughter to support when he's out of uniform, and his first priority will be to earn a living. There will be precious little we can do to help you both financially when he gets back, so he'd better put politics out of his mind and get down to work."

"All right, all right, my dear. Don't get worked up about it!" Sir Walter winked impishly at Margot. "I'll find him something in the City again, then later on we can talk about him taking on my seat when I'm too old to stagger into the Members' Bar."

"That'll be the day," said his wife, reaching for a silver hand-bell to ring for the dessert.

"Cold rice pudding with figs," she announced.

Sir Walter groaned. "Such are the fruits of victory!" he said, rising from his chair and heading for the sideboard on which rested a decanter of his favourite port.

Margot went to bed early and lay awake for a long time, thinking about Charlie and politics. The more she thought of him as a Member of Parliament, the more the idea excited her. Why should he have to wait until his father stepped down? The sooner he was elected, the sooner he would rise, and she knew of no bar to a father and son serving at the same time. The question was: could he, and would he, do it?

Margot had always accepted Charlie as a man of modest intellect and not very broad interests. But within the framework of those limitations he was bright and articulate, and from her observation of the many Members of Parliament that she had met, she could conclude with quiet confidence that Charlie need in no way feel outclassed. On the contrary, his good looks, his good speaking voice, his military record, his father's reputation, and his wife, were all assets which, once parliamentary experience had been added, should separate him from the pack and set him on the path to power. So all Charlie needed to get started was a summoning of his own willpower, and a helping hand from family and friends. She would have to see that both of these requirements were met.

First, however, he would have to be convinced to take *her* advice, which was to plunge into politics without delay, rather than his parents', which was to wait. In that matter, she knew that she had a difficult task on her hands. She was fully aware that, fond as he was of his father, Charlie was also much in awe of him and sometimes greatly intimidated by him, and she was far from sure that in an open contest for the mind of her husband she would be able to break his father's hold over him. His parents' argument, however, was that Charlie could not afford the time to follow a political career while pursuing a profession in the City which would furnish him with the income needed to support a family. The obstacle blocking the road to Westminster seemed to be a financial one and by removing it herself, surely she, rather than Charlie's parents, would win his allegiance.

An idea now germinated in her mind. The modest annual allowance which she received from her father derived from a block of family investments designated by him as her inheritance on his death and amounting currently to about $70,000. If she could somehow persuade her father to advance her part, if not all, of that inheritance, Charlie could concentrate on climbing the political ladder while she financed their living costs. The idea excited her greatly, and her last thought before finally letting sleep overtake her was that she should plan an early visit to her parents in Washington.

The next morning she awoke with a mixed feeling of elation and puzzlement. She had awoken from a dream in which she had been lying naked beside the swimming pool at Adamswood. She was on her back, staring up at the sky, legs slightly spread, and the palm of a hand was pressed down hard between them with two fingers moving slowly in and out of her vagina. Every now and then her view of the sky was blocked by a face. The eyes were dark and deep-set, and a lock of unruly black hair fell over the forehead. It was a sad face, and she knew where she had seen it before: it was the face of the young man on crutches with whom she had wanted to speak at the political meeting yesterday. The mouth moved as in speech, but no words were audible. She wanted to touch the face, but her hands seemed to be weighted down so that she could not raise them to it. She felt her climax fast approaching, but then the vision and the sensation had ended abruptly, like a movie screen going white when the reel breaks, as she woke up. She lay still, savouring the moment, then turned to look at her bed-side clock. It was not yet seven, and she decided to try and sleep for another hour or so. She mourned the fact that there was no re-entering the dream. Why could dreams not be like books, to be put down and picked up again at will? She closed her eyes and was soon asleep again.

"If you want breakfast, Margot, you'd better come down quickly before it gets cleared away!"

Lady Garland's voice, accompanied by the swish of curtains being pulled vigorously back, brought Margot back to consciousness with a jolt. She blinked as the daylight poured into the room, and sat up.

"Cynthia, good morning. Is it late?"

Lady Garland pointed at the clock. "After nine-thirty," she said in a tone laden with reproach.

"I've decided to go to the States to see my family. I think I'll go as soon as I can, and I'll take Julia with me. Don't you think that's a good idea?"

Cynthia Garland was standing over the chintz-frilled dresser, sizing up her daughter-in-law's assembly of cosmetics.

"I'm sure they're all impatient to see you both, but don't you think it would be nicer to wait until Charlie is home so that you can all go together?"

The choice of the word "nicer" immediately irritated Margot; it implied unfairness, even disloyalty, in wanting to go without him.

"It may be months before he gets out of the army; I really don't want to wait that long. Besides, we can go together later."

"If you can afford it, I suppose you can." She retreated to the door and said over her shoulder as she went out: "Walter and I will be leaving for church at a quarter past ten. I imagine you'll want to join us, and I can lend you a simple hat if you haven't brought one."

Margot got out of bed clenching her fists and trying to recall the time of the mid-afternoon train back to London.

She wasn't feeling much in the mood for church, particularly not for the vicar of St Etheldreda's in Bowes Green, whose high-pitched, grating voice set her teeth on edge, and whose organist wife transformed the lovely old hymn tunes into a cacophony of wheezing dissonances. But she might try and use the hour in church to compose in her mind a carefully worded letter to Charlie.

In the bathroom, she stared at herself in the mirror. A one-legged stranger masturbating her by the Adamswood swimming pool . . . Christ, Charlie! You'd better get back here soon!

Following an exchange of cables with her parents, who told her that she and Julia would be joyously welcomed whenever they could manage to get over, Margot immediately turned her full attention to travel arrangements. To her intense frustration, she soon found that passage by sea was no less difficult to obtain than passage by air. She began the weary round of the shipping offices, standing in line with impatient GI brides still stranded in Britain and wondering whether they would ever be reunited with their husbands who had already been sent home and demobilized. After two weeks of fruitless search, she was tired and angry enough to give up the whole project, when Julia's godfather at the American Embassy, Alton Shuttleworth, pulled his rank and a few strings and came up with a single cabin on the *Queen Mary* which an army general's wife had unexpectedly relinquished.

And so, with fifteen thousand returning American servicemen and a small group of GI brides, Margot and Julia assembled on the dock at Southampton. A morose and chastened Sir Walter, accompanied by his no less morose wife, were on hand to see them off. Two weeks earlier, Sir Walter had scraped back into Parliament with the smallest margin of victory over his opponent that he had recorded in his long political career. Nationwide, Mr Attlee and his Labour Party had won a landslide victory over Mr Churchill's Tories, and the only shred of comfort that Sir Walter could derive from the debacle, apart from the salvation of his own seat, was the knowledge that his political perspicacity had not been found wanting. He had sensed the change of mood in the country when many of his colleagues, not to mention his own wife, had remained disbelieving of it to the end.

"Tell your fellow Americans not to worry," admonished Sir Walter with a strained smile as he embraced his daughter-in-law. "Attlee's lease on Downing Street is going to be one of the shortest in the annals of British politics, I assure you."

Lady Garland was holding Julia in her arms.

"You do promise to send us pictures of her birthday party, don't you? And you're going to write to Charlie as soon as you get to Washington."

"Of course," said Margot, taking Julia from Lady Garland. She had no wish to prolong the farewells. "I think I should be getting aboard now."

"I just don't know how the boat can hold so many people," said Lady Garland surveying with a disapproving look the mass of waving, cheering troops jammed against the teak deck railings of the huge liner. "I'm afraid it's going to be awfully uncomfortable for you."

"Oh, no. We'll be fine," said Margot, leaning forward to kiss her mother-in-law on the cheek. She then bent to retrieve her vanity case.

"You will take care of our little granddaughter, won't you, dear?"

"I certainly will," said Margot, straightening up and forcing one more smile. "Thanks so much for coming to see us off."

"*Bon voyage*, my dears!" Sir Walter blew a kiss as Margot joined the line of GI brides and assorted families at the foot of the gangway.

Summer storms made the first three days of the crossing even less comfortable than expected for the majority of the *Queen Mary*'s bloated complement of passengers. Margot and Julia, however, were more fortunate and thoroughly enjoyed life on board. Dividing their time between the comparatively comfortable stateroom and the not too congested forward deck area reserved for serving women of officer rank and the wives of officers, they whiled away the hours in relative contentment. For the two main meals served each day, they sat at a table with a group of senior army nurses who made a fuss of Julia and whose company Margot greatly enjoyed.

Less than a hundred miles to the south of the *Queen Mary*, steaming on a nearly parallel course, the heavy cruiser USS *Augusta* was making full speed for Norfolk, Virginia, bearing the President of the United States home from the "Three Power" meeting in Potsdam with Marshal Stalin and the old and new Prime Ministers of Britain, Churchill and Attlee. On board the great grey ship, a concert had just been concluded. The Navy-uniformed bandmaster executed a smart about-face, tucked his conductor's baton under his left arm, and saluted his commander-in-chief. President Truman and his party, seated in the front row of an assembly of the ship's crew gathered on deck, applauded vigorously as they rose to their feet.

"Thank you very much," said the President, raising his voice to compete with the applause and the sundry sounds of a big ship under way at full speed. "That was a fine concert!" He turned to his Secretary of State. "Jimmy, let's get right into that chow line. I'm hungry."

Today, four days out from England, they were scheduled to lunch with the enlisted men in their mess. The President had requested such a lunch during the outward voyage to Potsdam and had thoroughly enjoyed the easy informality of the occasion. The former US Senator from Missouri, transplanted after only eighty-two days as Vice President to the awesome and lonely responsibility of the Presidency of the greatest power on earth, had no intention of losing the common touch.

Secretary Byrnes adjusted his Irish tweed cap and fell in step behind his President as the party made its way down to the mess hall. After standing in line with trays to collect their lunch, the President and his Secretary of State were escorted to separate tables where they were joined by groups of enlisted men. Harry Truman smiled at his young table companions as they sat down together.

"All right, tell me where you're from. Any Missourians?"

It was a minute or two before midday when Captain Frank Graham, the President's Map Room watch officer, entered the mess, looked around for the President, and hurried over to his table. Silently he handed over a message which the President read immediately. It was from the Navy Department, and it was brief. The bomb had been dropped; the target had been Hiroshima; the results were "clear-cut successful in all respects."

The President's face lit up.

"This is the greatest thing in history!" he said, pushing back his chair. "Where's Byrnes?" Looking around, he spotted the Secretary's table and made his way quickly to it. He handed Byrnes the message. "What do you think of that, Jimmy?"

Curious eyes from all around the mess hall were now trained on the two men who stood in animated conversation. Moments later Captain Graham was back with a second message, this time from Secretary of War Stimson. Excitedly the President read it aloud to Byrnes.

"Big bomb dropped on Hiroshima 5th August at 7:15 p.m. Washington time. First reports indicate complete success which was even more conspicuous than earlier test."

Byrnes offered his congratulations again, and the President looked jubilant.

"Jimmy, it's time for us to get home. But right now, I think we should tell these fellows here what's happened."

Conversation in the mess hall had already dropped to a low murmur, and the President had no difficulty in commanding attention. His brief announcement that a powerful new bomb with an explosive force twenty thousand times greater than a ton of TNT had been dropped on Japan brought cheering and applause.

"Come on, Jimmy, let's go tell the officers in the wardroom."

They hurried off, the Secretary wondering why the President had made no reference to the fact that it was an "atomic" bomb.

"Stimson should by now have put out my prepared statement on this," said Truman as they reached the wardroom. "We'll be getting the news bulletins from Washington any time now." The officers, who were lunching, sprang to their feet as the President made his unexpected entrance. "Gentlemen, please stay seated." He grinned broadly at them.

"I've got some news for you."

The news reached the *Queen Mary* by radio that same day and produced a wave of rejoicing among the vast complement of passengers. Margot and the nurses heard it at dinner, and they toasted what they assumed must be the imminent end to the war with Japan.

Midway through the seventh morning of the voyage, Margot, with Julia clutched in her arms, joined the passengers crowding onto the deck as the liner slipped through the Narrows into Upper New York Bay and the mouth of the Hudson River, heading for her berth among the busy piers of Manhattan's West Side waterfront. As the blue-green colossus of the Statue of Liberty loomed on the port bow, the troops massed on the decks offered a noisy ovation to this most eagerly reached milestone on their long journey home from the war. Small craft, one with what appeared to be an all-female brass band aboard giving "One Meat Ball" everything they'd got bobbed alongside, and ships already docked in the harbour blew their sirens in a cacophony of welcome. Margot felt a lump in her throat.

"This is America, my darling," she said, pressing her cheek against Julia's.

"America!" echoed Julia, pulling her head back to look into her mother's eyes and frowning when she saw tears.

"Come on, angel, let's get below and get ready. We don't want to keep Grandmother waiting long for her first sight of you."

Another two hours were to pass before Margot, preceded by a baggage porter with a laden cart, and with Julia trotting wide-eyed beside her, pink teddy bear clutched to her chest, emerged from the Customs shed into the reception area. The cavernous structure already reverberated with the happy cries of recognition as the emotional rituals of reunion were enacted. It took several minutes for her to find her mother in the crowd, and then they were hugging and crying in each other's arms.

"And this is Julia, then!" said Elinor, disengaging herself from her daughter's embrace. "She's beautiful, Margot, and so like you!" She bent down to give the little girl a kiss.

"And this is Pinky," said Julia, holding the bear aloft.

"Well, welcome to New York, Pinky!" Elinor turned again to Margot. "Your father's going to be wild about her. It'll be a real tonic for him, poor darling."

Margot looked alarmed. "Is there something wrong with him, Mother?"

"Not really, dear. Come on, let's go. We're staying the night with my mother, and she's aching to see you both."

On the cab ride across town to the East Side, where Elinor's mother lived overlooking the East River, Margot scarcely looked at the city she had not seen in nearly seven years. She was too busy asking her mother questions, while Julia sat quietly on her knee doing the looking for her.

"Is there something wrong with Father?" she asked again.

"He's horribly overworked, suffering from the particularly hot and humid summer we're having down in Washington, and on top of that he's limping on a stick. Neuritis of the long thigh nerve. It hurts him like hell, poor darling. They really ought to let him take his vacation now before it gets worse, but the European Division just won't let him go. He's a slave to it. But at least they're letting him come up for a long weekend to Adamswood on Friday, so he'll be there for the party."

"Poor Father. That's awful. What's the party?"

"Your doting grandparents are laying out the red carpet for you and Julia. They're planning a party like nothing they've had since Austin's seventieth."

"So when do we go to Adamswood?"

"Tomorrow. There's absolutely no point in your going to that Turkish bath of a capital until you're a bit acclimatized. We'll go down and join your father a little later."

"And what news of Larry?"

Elinor held up crossed fingers. "Still in one piece as far as we know. And still on Tinian we assume. You heard news of our dropping this atom thing on Japan?"

Margot nodded. "The whole ship went wild. Hasn't it stopped the fighting yet?"

"Seems not. But your father's up in arms about the bomb. Says we seem hell bent on destroying Japanese civilization for all time when they're just about to surrender anyway. The dear old softie. He won't calm down until he knows that Larry isn't going to be made to drop one of them as well. Tinian's where it came from, apparently."

"Well, they're bound to surrender soon, then Larry should be home quite quickly. What's he going to do then when he's out? Has he said anything to you?"

"He's not coming out, he says."

"You're kidding!"

"No I'm not. He's decided to make a career of it. Your father says there's no point trying to dissuade him."

"You just wait till I talk to him! I'm not going to see him come through this war just to have him risk his neck in peacetime. He must be crazy!"

Elinor shrugged her shoulders. "Give it a try, honey. Maybe he'll listen more to his twin than he seems to want to listen to his parents. I hate to see him stay in."

"I can tell you, my Charlie just can't wait to get out of uniform."

"And what's *he* planning to do?"

"Follow in his father's footsteps, and further, I hope."

"Politics? Can he earn a living at that?"

"We'll find a way."

"He's awfully young to be starting. What does his father say?"

"He thinks he'd be a great politician. But he'll need persuading that Charlie ought to start right away."

"He'd do better to get a job and earn some money first. He's got family responsibilities now."

Margot decided to change the subject. The last thing she wanted was to get her mother steamed up about Charlie's future before she herself had had a chance to talk to her father.

"Nothing's settled, of course. He may decide to do something completely different. Tell me how the grandparents are at Adamswood."

They chatted on until the cab eventually swung off First Avenue and deposited them outside Number One, Beekman Place.

"Mother's going to go crazy when she sees this little darling," said Elinor, grinning at Julia while she took money from her purse to pay the cab. "And she's *so* good! She doesn't seem at all rattled by all this travel and arriving in a strange land."

"Typical blasé English," said Margot, and they both laughed.

"We dropped another of those bombs on Japan," said the elevator operator importantly as they stepped inside his car. "Just got it on the radio."

"Your poor father," said Elinor, throwing Margot a pained look. "He's going to be apoplectic."

30

"Just mouthwatering!" gasped Margot when she returned to Beekman Place early the next afternoon after a morning's shopping on Fifth Avenue. "Looking at the store windows, you'd never think there were shortages. I could have spent a fortune right there in Bonwit Teller." She unburdened herself of a load of packages. "And Saks! I'd forgotten what it was like to see so much that one wanted."

"So what did you get?" asked Elinor, eyeing the boxes and shopping bags.

"Stockings, shoes, lingerie, cosmetics – and my 'Welcome Home' gift to myself, a divine white jersey evening gown from Bonwit. Classical Greek line, off one shoulder. I expect all the men at the party next week to go weak at the knees when they see me in it."

"I'll have to make sure your grandfather's sitting down when you put in your appearance. Now go sit with Grandma Edith. She's been pestering me all morning to make sure you tell her all about Kick Kennedy and that poor boy before we leave for the train."

They stepped off the train at Poughkeepsie in the early evening to be met by both Austin and Alice Moore with a joyous, tearful welcome. For Margot this was the *real* homecoming. She adored her paternal grandparents, and Adamswood was the only true home she knew in her peripatetic life as a diplomat's daughter. Nothing, she was happy to note, seemed to have changed much in her seven-year absence. Her grandfather, just turned seventy-five, was still the erect, lean, silver-haired gentleman with the handsome, bronzed face, whom she had last seen an easily recognizable figure among the waving crowds on Pier Forty-Three, when the *Athenia* had sailed for Europe in the winter of 1938. Maybe he had lost a little weight, but that was all. Time had been equally gracious to her grandmother, she noted. Alice Moore remained the strikingly regal figure that had always inspired a measure of awe as well as love in her. She was still blessed with the barely wrinkled, enviable skin of a woman a quarter-century younger – they said Margot had inherited her grandmother's skin – and the trim, firm figure of a woman not given to the sedentary life. And as Margot had always remembered, not a wisp of her meticulously swept-up and comb-secured hair was out of place. It was a little greyer perhaps, but that only added to her distinction.

"Things haven't changed too much," said Austin, echoing her thoughts as he escorted her by the arm out to the station forecourt. "You see?" He smiled as he nodded toward the well-polished navy blue 1936 Nash sedan parked at the kerb. "But we've hardly used her. The three-gallon-a-week ration doesn't get us far."

"But you still have her," said Margot delightedly. "That's what counts." The sight of the car brought a flood of memories of herself, Larry and Katie being met by Paul, the chauffeur, at the beginning of the Christmas holidays – always, until 1939, spent at Adamswood, whether the family was resident in Washington or on diplomatic post abroad.

"I do wish Larry was here," she said wistfully as she helped Julia up into the back seat.

"Don't we all!" said Alice. "He'll be heartbroken to miss you. But war is war; what's left of it."

In fact, there was to be very little left of it. On the following Tuesday evening, relaxed and tanned after three days of sunning by the pool, swimming and sleeping late, Margot tucked Julia into her cot, kissed her goodnight, and went downstairs to mix herself a cocktail. The grandfather clock at the foot of the staircase was striking seven as she made her way to the drinks cabinet in a little room off the dining room. Then, armed with a pink gin on ice, she crossed the octagonal hall and walked down the corridor to the library. Her grandfather was sitting in an armchair, and from the radio on a table by him came a vaguely familiar male voice. Austin got up as she entered, put a finger to his lips, and then walked over and silently kissed her on the cheek.

"It's the President," he then said softly. "It's all over. Hirohito's finally accepted the terms."

Within minutes, Harland was on the line from Washington, and Margot cried a little as they talked. She felt the tears coming on again when her grandfather, suppressing his dislike of any religious ritual conducted outside the walls of a church, offered a prayer as they sat down to dinner, giving thanks to the Almighty for having spared Larry, and recalling with love precious Katie's too short but happy life. Then they joyously toasted the peace in champagne – a magnum of the 1933 Krug which had been set aside for this day – and drank the health of the President, "this plucky little man who's filling FDR's shoes a lot less inadequately than I thought he would," as Austin Moore hailed him.

Then Elinor, looking across at Margot, spoke up.

"Have we not forgotten Charlie?"

"How thoughtless of me, dear," said Austin, raising his glass again. "How could I have done such a thing? To our dear Charlie! Brave soldier, loving husband and father. Safe and sound, thank God. Just bring the boy over here, Margot. I have no intention of departing this life without getting to know the man who has made my angel so happy."

Margot smiled, and brushed a tear from her cheek. This was all getting a bit to much for her, and she sighed with relief when the artichoke hearts were served and the toasts suspended.

The next two days were taken up with preparations for the dinner and dancing planned for the Friday night. The end of the war in the Pacific had added new cause for celebration, but Austin insisted that the honour being paid to his granddaughter, which was the purpose of the occasion, be in no way diluted. This was to be, above all, her night. Coming in from the pool one midday, she surprised her grandfather finishing what she assumed must be a long-distance call, judging by the loudness of his voice.

"We'll keep it as a complete surprise, I promise you," was all she heard him say before he rang off.

"What surprise?" she asked.

Her grandfather smiled sheepishly. "Some special entertainment I'm organizing for Friday. So don't be inquisitive."

On Friday morning her father arrived from Washington, intensifying the euphoric state in which Margot now felt herself floating as in a dream. At first she winced to see him limping on a stick, but his immense happiness at being reunited with her and seeing his granddaughter Julia for the first time was so infectious that she soon came to terms with his condition. She would need to choose carefully the moment when she would broach the subject of her plans for Charlie and the financial implications. Although she would have plenty of opportunity when she later joined him in Washington, she felt that the relaxed and convivial atmosphere at Adamswood might induce in her father a more generous and understanding response. She thus decided to prepare herself for a presentation of her case on the Saturday or Sunday.

At her grandmother's insistence, Margot stayed out of the way during the final hours of preparation for the party. Her father was resting that afternoon, so she lay by the pool for a while, swam a dozen lengths, then went in to collect Julia to take her for a walk around the garden. The little girl toddled along beside her as they followed the path down to and around the Dolphin Garden, then through The Wilderness. In nine days, Julia would be two years old. It seemed almost incredible to Margot that the time could have passed so quickly. Poor Charlie! His acquaintance with his daughter had been confirmed to a dozen or so weekends before he went to Normandy, and the ten-day leave spent in a state of deep depression at Bowes Court that last winter. She had seen him little more than that herself. And now, separated from him by an ocean and in the surroundings of her earlier life upon which no imprint of Charlie lay, she felt him to be more remote from her than ever before. Now that he had survived the war, she knew exactly what she wanted from him. She wanted him to cooperate in her master plan to make Mr and Mrs Charles Garland the most important young political couple in Britain. But first he had to be brought back into the centre of her life where she could work her will upon him. She remembered the days in her teens when she would be brought near to tears of frustration in the long field beyond The Wilderness, trying to lure her maddeningly uncooperative pony, Jester, into the halter for saddling. Maybe she was going to face the same frustration with Charlie. His last furlough had shown her that the war had changed him, notwithstanding the deceptively light-hearted letters he habitually wrote. He had changed from the exuberant, uncomplicated young extrovert into an introspective and complex person whose thoughts and actions she could no longer predict nor always understand. She was impatient now to find out just who the new Charlie was, because she had an instinctive feeling that he was emerging from the war a tougher, more self-confident man – even if it proved to be at the expense of some of his boyish charm. That was all right with her. It was his new strength more than his old charm that she would need to harness for the political journey ahead. But could she persuade him to see himself as a young man who could, if he tried, carve a great future for himself at Westminster? That was the challenge that lay ahead of her in London, once the army gave him his freedom. And she was in a hurry to meet it.

Julia fell, grazed her knee and started to cry. Margot cleaned the knee, soothed the tears, and took her by the hand as they emerged from The Wilderness and started across the tract of rough grass toward the carriage drive. Halfway up the drive on their way to the house, she heard a car change gears as it came up the gentle rise behind them. She pulled Julia over onto the grass verge and turned to look. It was the Millbrook taxi. Someone coming to help with the preparations for the party, she guessed, and started to walk on. She was watching over

Julia when it passed them, so she didn't see if it was anybody she knew inside. But presumably it was, because it slowed to a halt a few yards ahead of them. A rear door opened, but nobody got out. Was somebody offering them a ride the last two hundred yards to the house? She took Julia's hand again and walked up to the waiting vehicle. Suddenly a figure leaped out onto the verge, making her jump with fright.

"*Larry!*"

"Reporting in person, ma'am!" He grinned broadly as he saluted.

"I can't *believe* it!"

She plunged forward, dropping Julia's hand, and threw herself into his arms.

"Oh, darling, what a wonderful, wonderful surprise!"

"It was meant to be more of a surprise than this. Grandpa and I decided I'd secrete myself in the house and surprise you in style just before dinner. But who cares? And this must be my fabulous first niece!"

Julia was standing sucking on a forefinger, studying the man in the light fawn uniform and forage cap with an arm around her mother.

"Come and give Uncle Larry a kiss, darling."

Shyly she stepped forward, and Larry squatted down to hold her and kiss her on the cheek.

"She's your spittin' image, sis. Gorgeous!"

"Two in nine days' time. Isn't it crazy that she wasn't yet born when we last saw each other?"

"Barely believable." He stood up, lifting an unresisting Julia into his arms. "Come on. Let's ride up to the house."

Margot snuggled up to him on the back seat.

"It's just the happiest thing ever that you managed to get here. I think I'm going to cry!" Instead she giggled as the tears filled her eyes.

"How are the parents?"

"Mother's fine, but worrying herself silly over Father who's overworked, limping on a stick with his sciatica, and angry as hell about the atom bombs."

"I feared he might be."

"I hope you didn't drop one of them."

Larry laughed. "No such honour, sis. That was the work of the 509th, our neighbours on Tinian."

"Well, thank God for that."

"And my fine English brother-in-law?"

"Sweating it out near Cologne, and dying to get home. I want to talk to you about him. I have a proposal to put to Father about Charlie's and my future, and now that you're miraculously here, I can try it out on you first."

"Not trouble, I hope," he said, frowning.

"Heavens no! Just the opposite. How much leave have you got?"

"Two weeks."

"*Magnifique!*"

Larry patted her on the knee. "So we're still speaking French, eh?"

"Oh, come off it," she said, smiling. "None of that, now!"

"I've never seen you look more beautiful, sweetheart!" said Austin as his granddaughter joined the family in the library for a glass of champagne before the guests began to arrive.

Margot pirouetted in the centre of the room.

"You like my first new dress purchase in New York?"

"Not just the dress," said Larry. "The whole effect. The Aphrodite of Adamswood!"

In keeping with the classical Grecian design of the white gown, she had pulled her hair back, and pinned it so that it fell on the bare shoulder in a single lock into which she had intertwined a string of small blooms cut from white tulle.

"A knockout," agreed her father. "You'll have Congressman Halder grovelling at your feet."

"Oh God! Is *he* coming?"

"Yes, Larry, he is," said Alice, and she wagged an admonitory finger at him. "No repeat of your performance on your grandfather's seventieth, please."

"No need, Grandma. I was proven right." He grinned. "I'll settle for an abject apology."

Some forty guests sat down to a candle-lit dinner in the panelled dining room. Grandfather Austin surveyed the scene happily and turned to Margot, his guest of honour, seated on his right.

"If I'd known the Pacific war was going to be over tonight and that they were going to scrap gasoline rationing the same day, I'd have asked friends from further afield. We could have fed and wined a hundred. Everything you're eating tonight, except this fish pâté, is from the estate and from my cellars, including the pheasant."

"You and Grandma have worked a miracle. And to cap it all, Larry's here."

"Looking well, isn't he? That flying seems to suit him."

"But don't you think he should come out as soon as he can?"

"No, I gather he wants to stay put, and if that's what he wants, who am I to dissuade him? He's a good flyer and he may go far."

"But he still has his senior year to do at Yale. Surely he's not going to pass up a degree when he's three-quarters of the way there. Can't you persuade him to come out and do his final year? He could then re-enlist if he really felt he had to."

"Why don't you try to persuade him? He listens to you with more respect than to anyone else in the family."

"Nonsense, Grandpa. He hangs on your every word. But I'll give it a try."

"Don't be hard on him if he won't do it. He's got a good life in the Air Force, and it's going to be tough on the outside, particularly for people seeking jobs. Peace is going to slam the brakes on this booming wartime economy. The defence industry has given millions good jobs, and wages they never dreamed of. That's all going to wind down just when the boys start pouring back from the war, looking for work. All in all, Larry would do well to stay put for a while. But I can't help agreeing with you that it would be nice if he could take a year out of uniform to finish up at Yale."

"I'll work on him, Grandpa."

"And your own Charlie? What's he going to do?"

"The House of Commons, we hope. Like his father. He'd be brilliant at it, and Britain needs a new generation of politicians now the war's over."

"Good for him! But that takes private means. Does he have an income?"

"He'll get by."

"Being a parliamentarian in England is no bar to holding down a part-time job, as far as I recall."

"True, Grandpa. But if he's going to get to the top quickly, he really needs to devote all his time to it."

Austin smiled. "Who's in the real hurry – Charlie or you?"

"I guess we both are."

"Remember those couplets of Hilaire Belloc?

Towards the age of twenty-six,
They shoved him into politics.

We had intended you to be
The next Prime Minister but three . . .

Margot, dear one, don't be in too much of a hurry. Don't push him into something he may not be ready for. You're both so young, you've got all the time in the world. Enjoy life for a bit; let him make some good money; bring up a nice family. Politics can come a little later."

Margot sipped at her wine. Strike one: Grandpa's against it. Well, it's Father who'll really count in this.

"He can't afford to wait, Grandpa. The Attlee Government isn't going to last long. There'll be another election, and he absolutely mustn't miss that if he's going to get a head start."

Austin chuckled. "I think it's you who really wants that seat in Westminster. I think I've got a budding Nancy Astor for a granddaughter."

"No, no, not me! I don't think the British are quite ready yet to elect a twenty-four-year-old blonde, and another American to boot!"

"Well, I'd vote for you if I could." It was her dinner

partner on her right, Jack Micklem, scion of an old Millbrook family, one-time escort of Margot before she left for Europe and now married to Louise Bayles, the judge's daughter. As a gunnery officer aboard the carrier USS *Yorktown*, he had lost an arm at the Battle of the Coral Sea.

Margot turned to him. "Well, thanks for the compliment, Jack."

"Instead I find myself voting for whichever brave Democrat soul cares to take a mauling from the dreadful Halder over there."

He nodded toward the neighbouring table at which the Congressman sat in a place of honour on Alice Moore's right. Margot could see that he was talking animatedly across the table to the former Elaine Burchett, now the wife of the local veterinarian, Bill Porteous.

"I just don't know why he and my grandparents are such good friends," whispered Margot into her neighbour's ear. "They've never voted for him, so they say, although I rather suspect my grandmother really does although she swears she's a loyal Democrat. Why don't *you* run against him, Jack? You've got a good local name and a fine war record to help you."

"I don't like the idea of attracting sympathy votes for this," he said quietly, tugging at the empty sleeve of his tuxedo. "And that's all it would really be. I haven't any political skills to offer."

"That's defeatist, Jack. I bet you could make it."

"Just not interested. Why not try Larry?"

"Larry, the dear fool, wants to go on risking his neck as a military pilot, unless I can change his mind."

"He's probably right. The vets are going to get shafted as usual. It always happens after a war."

"You have no faith in Truman?"

"I have no faith in any politicians, I'm sorry to say. At least not the present generation of them."

"Then why not be one of the next and get things changed? That's what my husband's going to do when he gets home."

"I wish him luck. But with you as his wife, how can he fail?" He smiled at her. "Can you imagine Louise out on the stump with me? That voice of hers would drive them all away."

Margot was shocked. "That's not at all a nice thing to say about your wife! Really, Jack!"

He smiled and shrugged his shoulders.

"With you, dear Margot, one can't help making dangerous comparisons."

"I'm not sure what you mean."

"Be an angel and cut this pheasant for me, will you? I'm afraid I left half my table manners in the Pacific."

As the dessert was consumed, Austin Moore rose to welcome his guests, and in a short and moving speech, told the assembled company that although one of his three grandchildren had tragically not survived the war, he felt humbled and overwhelmingly grateful to his Maker that Margot and Larry had come through the ordeal.

"Tonight," he said, "it is the privilege of an old man to celebrate youth. I asked you here tonight to honour Margot, not knowing that the Pacific war would already be over; not knowing that Larry would make it here tonight all the way from the Marianas. I am triply and undeservedly blessed.

"My beloved Alice and I, and Harland and Elinor, and Margot too, are enormously proud of young Larry. He did his duty as an American, fighting for the freedom we cherish. He flew courageously in two theatres of war, and bears on his chest the proud emblems of that courage. And he intends to go on serving his country in the armed forces." There was loud applause. Margot clapped her palms together once and held them fast. "So tonight I ask you first to raise your glasses to my grandson, the future first five-star general in the annals of my family!"

The company rose and toasted Larry, who sat biting his lip, eyes glinting, watching over the top of the tall candles the strangely far-away look on the face of his mother across the table.

Austin continued when they had resumed their seats, looking down at her as he began to speak.

"My lovely granddaughter, Margot, faced the horrors of war with no less courage. As you well know, she gave her heart and hand to a fine young Englishman at the outbreak of the European war. When Britain stood alone against the dictators, it was young men like Charlie Garland who marched off to show the world that Britons do not tolerate for long the kinds of injustice and cruelty being meted out by vile men such as Hitler and his gang. He paid a fearful price, spending two and a half years a prisoner of the Nazis until he made as bold and breathtaking an escape from his captors as anyone has ever achieved. And although, as I understand, he could have opted then for a home posting for the rest of the war, he chose to return to fight when the Allies invaded the mainland of Europe last summer. And he won a Military Cross in action. Like his brother-in-law, Larry, he risked all for his country, and emerged a hero."

Margot felt her grandfather's hand rest lightly on her bare shoulder. She was staring fixedly into the candle flame so as not to let her tear-filled eyes meet anyone else's.

"I only wish young Charlie was with us here tonight. But Charlie's heroine, and our heroine, is. Margot fought her war too. A young bride of only three weeks, she saw her husband off to the war, bore bravely the news of his wounding and capture and lived stoically through his incarceration. She suffered in a particularly cruel way the agony of her sister Katie's end, and she lost an unborn child in a senseless accident. But our Margot has an indomitable spirit. She was not going to let any of that beat her down. She went out and put on an American Red Cross uniform, and worked long hours helping bring a little bit of America to our boys over there. The reuniting with Charlie after his escape led happily to the birth of Alice's and my first great-grandchild, little Julia, sleeping peacefully, we hope, upstairs at this moment. A beautiful child. A child born amid the turmoil of war who will grow up to honour brave and wonderful parents."

He looked down and squeezed Margot's shoulder when he saw the tears coursing down her cheeks.

"Though Margot now shares her life with the British, she remains, in my eyes, the symbol of all that is best in America's young people. We are more proud of her than we can say. We wish her and Charlie, and a growing family, a great and joy-filled future. We raise our glasses to you, darling!"

There was a scraping of chairs. Margot clutched at the hand on her shoulder, and stared mistily up at her grandfather. She heard her name called in a chorus of voices, and smiled through her tears.

"Grandpa, you've destroyed me. I can't possibly get up to reply. Please don't insist!"

"Not if you don't want to, sweetheart."

He sat down, and almost at once, at a further table, Larry stood up.

"Knowing my sister as I do," he began, "she'll be too overcome to get to her feet, and I am almost as well. But I just want to thank Grandpa for all the kind words, and that's on behalf of both of us. And thanks for the wonderful party, Grandma and Grandpa. I guess this will go down in the history of Adamswood as one of the happiest events to have taken place here in all its history. How about drinking the health of my grandparents, and couple it with a toast to Margot's and my own beloved father and mother. They're true heroes in our eyes too."

"Good for you, Larry," said Margot, rising to her feet with her fellow diners. She kissed her grandfather on the cheek and raised her glass to both grandparents and parents.

Jack Micklem took her arm as she was about to resume her seat, and when she turned to him, he kissed her lightly on the lips.

"Lucky Charlie Garland," he said. "And now would you care to wager that Congressman Halder will *not* be moved to say a few words?"

"No bet, Jack. He's calling for silence already."

"Dear friends!" The familiar, fruity voice of the Congressman brought quiet to the company again. "This is not the occasion for a speech from a politician."

"Right!"

Margot winced and then joined in the scattered laughter at Larry's intervention.

"Always nice to hear Democrats agreeing with me!" said Halder. "If very rare." There was more laughter. "I just think that this evening would not be complete, given the happy events of the last few days, if we were not to lay aside our partisan differences and raise our glasses to the President of our country."

There was a loud burst of applause and cheering. Halder raised his hand for more silence.

"I don't recall ever proposing a toast to a Democrat in the White House before," he went on, chuckling. "But if for no other reason, I'll propose this one to Harry Truman, because he had the wisdom to drop those two bombs on Japan and end the war. If I'd known those things existed – and by God, I'm glad they do, and that only we have them! – I would have doubted he had it in him to use them. Well, I was wrong. He had it in him, and I want to drink to that. So won't you join me?"

The guests rose once more to their feet.

"To the President of the United States!"

"The President!"

Margot craned her neck to catch her father's expression. It was pained.

The dancing in the octagonal hall began straight after dinner, and Margot danced in turn with her grandfather, with Larry, and then with her father.

"I saw your face, Father, when Halder gave that little performance."

"I hope my disgust didn't show too obviously." He smiled. "Just as well I have difficulty in springing to my feet these days."

"You really feel strongly about it, don't you?"

"I'm afraid I do, honey. You know what they're reporting? We killed over fifty thousand people with that first bomb. Laid waste an entire city. Presumably the second took an equally ghastly toll on Nagasaki. That's too horrible a weapon for anyone to use, even when you have right on your side in a war. And we didn't have to use it. We did it just to impress Stalin, and scare him a little. I can't accept that."

"Did you talk yet to Larry about it?"

"Briefly. He doesn't agree with me. I didn't expect him to."

"Well don't let it get to you too much, Father. Don't

ruin your health worrying about it all the time. What are they saying about it at State?"

"If anyone feels the way I do, they're not saying."

"They're probably wise. You should do the same."

"Well, let's not spoil your evening talking about my hang-ups."

The five-piece band broke into "Sentimental Journey", and Margot planted a kiss on her father's cheek.

"Come and sit with me tomorrow morning in the Dolphin Garden for a daughter-father talk?" she asked.

"Sure, sweetheart. Anything troubling you?"

"Nope. Just want to tell you what Charlie and I are planning for when he gets home."

"More babies, I trust!"

At the end of the set, Margot and her father went in search of champagne and were joined by Jack Micklem.

"May I have the next dance, Margot?"

"Delighted. Just let me have a couple of sips of this first."

Margot looked around and saw Louise Micklem eyeing her balefully from across the room while listening to the veterinarian who was, Margot had been told, well-known for describing in sickening detail to anyone within earshot the ailments of his local patients. Poor, dull Louise with the squeaky-hinge voice. How on earth had she ensnared the so very attractive Jack of the dark, Mediterranean looks and the Gregory Peck voice? Maybe there were hidden traits behind the pedestrian exterior. Maybe she was a wildcat in bed, or a gourmet cook with talents no man could resist. Or maybe she was suffocatingly rich, or about to be, and no one outside the family knew it.

Jack took her glass from her. "Come on, Margot. Time to dance."

They walked along the corridor to the octagon.

"There's something to be said for being a one-armed man," he said as he led her onto the dance floor. "When you dance, you get both of the girl's arms around you!"

Margot laughed. "What a subtle invitation."

She put both hands on his shoulders.

"I'm going to be in New York next week," he said casually. "Will you be?"

"No. I'm not planning to be. I want to stay up here."

"That's a pity."

"Why?"

"I'd like to take you to lunch. Or maybe dinner."

She'd almost forgotten how fast a worker he was, and now she remembered that he'd proposed a visit to his married brother's empty house in Syracuse on their second date, when she was seventeen. She'd refused and he had rarely bothered with her after that, which had upset her only briefly because she had taken up shortly afterwards with Louis, the Congressman's son, from Iowa. Poor Louis, who suffered through the tail end of her first French phase.

"Nice of you to suggest it, Jack. But I won't be there."

"You must be going there sometime on your visit."

"Briefly on my way through to Washington to join Father, and when I sail for home. I'll be staying with my grandmother."

"Can you let me know when?"

"Jack. You're propositioning me, and I don't really think you ought to be."

He smiled. "A little lunch can't do any harm."

"A lot could be read into it by some people if they heard about it, or saw us."

"No one would. We'd be discreet."

Margot was beginning to feel tempted. He was damned attractive, but she didn't trust herself with him. One thing might lead to another. Best put all thoughts of getting laid out of her mind for the moment, and stop dancing with this impossible tempter. He was dancing far too close for comfort from the waist down. She could feel everything, and it was sending the sort of signals flashing through her body which she really couldn't cope with just now.

"Jack, I promised Archie Burge a dance before eleven. He has to leave then to drive to New York."

"Then he's probably already gone."

"But I have to go and look."

"If you insist." They danced to the edge of the floor. "Will you leave a message for me at the Racquet Club if you do have time in New York?"

"I'll see. But please don't count on it. A message, that is. Thanks for the dance, Jack."

He bowed. "My pleasure."

He turned and walked away.

Margot found, to her distress, that Archie Burge was very much there. She'd made no arrangement to dance with the corpulent, heavily sweating manager of the Adamswood estate, but now she felt compelled to; she didn't want to offend Jack unnecessarily.

It was while she was dancing an awkward foxtrot with Burge that the drama unfolded in the library.

"I've just been telling Larry here, Harland, that I'm sorry he wasn't with the Combat Group that dropped our atomic bombs. Now *that* would have been something to be proud of and tell the children!"

Larry looked appalled and hardly dared glance at his father.

"Well, I have to tell you, Congressman, that as his father, I'm mighty glad he doesn't have such an experience to live with for the rest of his life."

He leaned heavily on his stick and glared at Halder.

"They were only following orders, those crews, Father," said Larry a little desperately.

"I know that. It wasn't their fault. It was their bad luck."

"So you don't approve of the way we finished off the Japs?" Halder put his cigar stub back in his mouth and rolled it around in one corner.

"I'm delighted the war's over. But it was going to be over in a matter of weeks anyway."

"At the cost of how many more of our boys' lives, Moore? Maybe including your own Larry's."

"Who knows? But not at the cost of maybe a hundred thousand civilian Japanese lives just to impress the Russians."

"I guess the rights and wrongs of this will be debated until kingdom come," said Larry, attempting a cooling off of rising tempers, if not a reconciliation of views.

"I don't see any wrongs in it, young man," said Halder. "The Japs, all of them, got what was coming to them. And I'm as glad as hell it was us who dished it out to them. But your father's a diplomat, and a good one by all accounts, so I guess he has to think ahead to the time when we'll all need to be pally again with the Nips. I just hope I'm not around to see that."

"I carry no torch for the Japanese warlords, sir, I assure you," said Harland. "I hope they get strung up. But I'm mighty sorry we found it necessary to show the world that we had developed and were prepared to use a weapon of such obscene destructiveness. It will put nasty ideas into other people's heads, and before long, dangerous men will be dangling these over innocent nations and making their blackmailers' demands."

"Then we'd better make damned sure no one else finds out how we make them, eh, Harland?" Halder was all smiles again.

"I'll drink to that, Congressman," responded Harland, attempting a weak smile.

"Of course you will!" He turned to Larry. "Find your father and me a bottle, Captain, if you'd be so kind."

Larry went off to the bar and passed his grandmother on the way.

"No political arguments in there, I hope," she said nodding at the library entrance.

"Nothing serious, Grandma. Just a little skirmish between Father and Halder. But they're all friends now."

"Your father this time! What's wrong with you Moore men?"

She walked on, shaking her elegant head.

Larry relieved a waiter of a full bottle of champagne and hurried back to the library where he filled his father's and the Congressman's glasses, then his own, and retreated. He wanted a dance with his old flame, Elaine. He found her in the conservatory, sharing a wrought-iron love-seat with a local farmer whose name Larry could never remember.

"You promised me a dance, pet," said Elaine, immediately standing up. "Will you forgive me, Tom?"

She didn't wait for a reply from the farmer, but took Larry's arm and hustled him out of the conservatory.

"Thank God you rescued me," she panted. "You haven't talked to me all evening. That sort of neglect on your part only arouses suspicion in the convoluted mind

383

of my Bill. So you'd better come and flirt with me on the dance floor to reassure the poor thing."

Larry laughed. "I'm the one who needs reassuring. I have the strong suspicion I'm going to be raped!"

"You would be, pet, if I didn't know all about your archaic views on sex with married women. You've really got to cure yourself of this."

They walked onto the dance floor and Larry smiled as he felt her amazing breasts come pressing against him. Unusual for a party, their flesh was not visible. They were encased in a tight-fitting powder blue blouse that covered her to her neck. But the shape was unmistakable, and he could almost remember the precise pattern of the blue veins that criss-crossed the area surrounding the large, pale brown nipples.

"Feeling at home, lover?" she asked, smiling as she pulled her shoulders back and pressed in even closer.

Larry looked around nervously but saw the veterinarian nowhere in sight.

"Very much," he said.

"You get my meaning, of course." She moistened her upper lip slowly with her tongue.

"How could I miss it?"

She kissed him on the cheek. "I'm awfully glad you didn't get yourself killed, Larry. It leaves us the chance to have some fun again sometime. Once you've got these stupid ideas out of your head."

"Don't count on my ever doing so."

Elaine laughed. "That's bad news for Bill. I may have to divorce him."

Margot had the last dance, just before one o'clock, with her grandfather.

"It's been one of the happiest evenings of my life," she said. "How can I ever thank you and Grandma enough?"

"Well, we wanted you to have a homecoming fit for a queen, and everyone here tonight agrees that you truly are a queen. That's thanks enough for me. Only the presence of Charlie himself could have made it a still more wonderful occasion for us."

"Grandpa, do you really think Charlie's too young to go into politics?"

"I'm scarcely in a position to judge. But I think you ought to let *him* think this through and listen to his father as well." He smiled. "I know you, sweetheart. You're burning with ambition for him. That's good. But don't cloud his judgement with too much persuasion. Let him work it out."

The music ended, and the remaining dancers applauded. Margot accompanied her grandfather to the entrance hall to join in bidding the parting guests goodnight.

"Feeling tired?" asked Larry, when at last everyone had gone.

"No, wide awake," said Margot. "And you?"

"Awake enough to enjoy a twinly chat with you over a nightcap, when the others have gone to bed. I'm curious to know what this proposal is you're putting to Father about Charlie."

Ten minutes later they were settled into armchairs in the library, Larry with a Scotch, and Margot with a glass of milk.

Margot began by extolling Charlie's potential as a politician: his family background; the political connections, many of which she had herself cultivated during the war; his good war record; his fine looks and impressive speaking voice; and herself as a hard-working consort.

"He's very bright, too!" she added. "I just know he could race ahead of his contemporaries if he made an early start."

"OK, I'm convinced, sis. He's got the potential. So what does he do next?"

"Persuade his father to help him find a constituency, i.e. district, to run in, and then get down to work."

"And supposing Sir Walter agrees and finds him a district, who finances him?"

"It doesn't cost a candidate one red cent to run for Parliament."

"That I know. But who pays the rent and the food bills if he gets elected?"

"He could earn a bit on the side, and I might go to

385

work myself, though I haven't given it much thought yet."

"Doesn't sound too secure to me if you've got a family to support. Would the Garlands help?"

"I don't know."

"And what about while he's looking for a constituency? I don't imagine one's going to fall into his lap the day he comes home. I assume he'll take a job."

"It's possible. Just for a while until he needs to spend all his time on politics."

"So what's this proposal to Father, as if I couldn't guess?"

He smiled and poured himself another Scotch from the decanter at his side.

"I'm going to ask him to advance my inheritance. I'll sell the stocks and use the proceeds to cushion Charlie and myself while he's in the initial stages of his career."

"That's crazy! You'd sell off your capital inheritance to pay the bills while Charlie tries his luck at a seat in Parliament? Whose idea is this? Charlie's?"

"He knows nothing about it. It's purely mine."

"It won't fly, sis. Father will never agree. You know his views on the work ethic. He'll expect Charlie to go to work like any other veteran returning from the war, if there's a job for him. And don't tell me a virtually unpaid job in Parliament is all Charlie is qualified for."

"I'm disappointed in you, Larry. You don't seem to be able to grasp what's at stake. There'll be a whole new generation of postwar politicians jockeying for power. We've *got* to enable Charlie to get out in front! He'll want peace of mind knowing that he's on an adequate financial base. So I want you to back me with Father. Tomorrow."

"First you tell Father what you've told me. Put your case just the way you have now. If Father then cares to seek my opinion, I'll say I think Charlie would make one helluva good politician and that we ought to help in any suitable way that we can. But I'm not going to go ahead of you and start urging him to sell off your inheritance."

Margot stared into her empty milk glass.

"Best you can do for me?"

"Best I can do."

Margot shrugged her shoulders.

"OK. It's better than no support at all."

"Just don't be too upset when he says no."

"Oh, I will be, but it won't be the end of the world. Somehow I'll find the means to bring all this about. I promise you that."

"Good for you, sis. You'll probably make it to 10 Downing Street, and I hope by then you'll have forgiven me enough to invite me to stay. By the way, how's Marion?"

"Not yet forgiven you for having written not a word to her in more than three months. She assumes you're balling the nurses or the WAACs or whatever females you've got down on Tinian. Do you have a girl?"

"A nurse, actually."

"And an older woman, no doubt. That's what you like. What is she? The Head Matron?"

"Don't be bitchy. She's twenty-three, has Betty Grable legs and a cute turned-up nose."

"And good in the sack, I trust."

"I don't know. I've only known her three weeks. Tinian isn't raunchy London."

Margot blushed and then laughed.

"Come on, handsome. Get yourself to bed. You must be exhausted after the flight from the coast."

They walked arm in arm up the stairs.

"It's so good to be home with you, sis," he said, and kissed her on the cheek.

"I'm happy too. Now go and dream all about your sexy little nurse."

Margot slept well that night, and dreamed about Jack Micklem.

"No honey, I can't go along with that, and nor would your grandfather. You might need that money badly one day for something vital to you and your family's welfare. Supposing, God forbid, something happened to Charlie."

Margot kept her gaze fixed on the jet of water issuing from the mouth of the bronze dolphin atop the Florentine

387

fountain. Here we go again! she thought miserably. I'm batting zero and might as well pack up and go home.

Her father, seated on the bench beside her, put out a hand and patted hers.

"Try to understand, honey. I'm delighted Charlie wants to follow in his father's footsteps, but I just can't have you mortgaging your future security to accelerate his political career. He's an intelligent fellow and should be able to work and provide adequately for his wife and daughter. And my guess is that in Britain's changed political atmosphere, he's going to need to prove that he can do that to win the voters' confidence anyway. If you need some money to help you settle into a new apartment, I'm sure I can help. But I'm not going to sell your inheritance and have you living off capital – and I can't believe that Walter would want Charlie doing that either."

"OK, Father. Just forget I brought it up. We'll manage."

She had become weary of her own efforts to have the family see things her way. She'd tried and failed, and that was that. Charlie must go back to the City and take his chance with all the other political aspirants. They'd live in a small apartment, and she'd go out to work if they could afford to keep Mrs Watts. Mrs Charles Garland would have to wait to take her place among the star political hostesses in the capital. And God knows how long it would take to get Charlie into the Cabinet.

"Oh, I never doubted you'd manage, you two. You've already proved you're capable of that. And I'll help where I can. You can count on that."

Margot looked at her watch. "A soothing drink before lunch?"

"Why not? It may help me sleep on the train this afternoon."

She reported back to Larry, and was grateful to him for avoiding any "I told you so" comments. That afternoon they saw their father off on the train, agreeing that the two of them would travel down to Washington together the following weekend to join him there for three days while their mother stayed on at Adamswood with Julia.

388

When they got back to the house from the rail station, Elinor handed her daughter a cable. She tore it open anxiously.

"Well, would you believe it! Charlie's being sent home for demobilization!"

"When?" asked Larry and Elinor in unison.

"September second. Early release for ex-POWs."

"My God, you'd better be getting home," said Larry.

"But the visit to Father! Won't he be terribly hurt? And I haven't properly said goodbye to him."

"He'll understand," said Elinor. "And he'll probably manage to get to New York to see you off on the boat. If we can get you onto one, that is. I don't want you flying with Julia, even in summer."

Thus Margot's first postwar visit to the United States was cut short. As it was, she and Julia arrived back in England only two days before Charlie. The earliest eastbound crossing that they could make was on the *Queen Mary*, going back to England to pick up another vast complement of returning servicemen and GI brides. So Julia had her second birthday in mid-Atlantic.

Her parents-in-law, she quickly discovered, had not been letting the grass grow under their feet while she had been away.

"We've found a suitable place for you and Charlie in Cadogan Square," announced Sir Walter when she went to dine with them on her first day back. "You'll need a proper London place now because my cousin's coming back from Canada and naturally wants Verbena Cottage."

That news upset her; she'd grown very fond of the place and had half been hoping that the owner would have decided to settle permanently in Vancouver.

"It's a very nice third-floor flat with plenty of natural light and minimum redecorating needed. Three bedrooms, two baths, a drawing room and a dining room, and the kitchen is adequately equipped."

Something to start with, I suppose, thought Margot.

"I've bought a long lease on it," continued Sir Walter, "and Charlie can pay me a small rent to start with, maybe rising as he earns more. I've found him a place in a very reputable stockbroking firm in the City, better than the one he was briefly in before the outbreak. They do well there, and the senior partner is an old friend of mine. The pay won't be much, but if you're careful you'll manage quite well on it. The harder he works, the more he'll earn, so we must keep his nose to the grindstone. It won't be all that easy for him at first, adjusting to civilian life, but hundreds of thousands of others are going to go through the same, so there's no reason why he shouldn't settle down pretty quickly."

Margot nodded agreement though she was over-whelmed by the evidence that, from now on, she was going to have to struggle to maintain some independence from her well-meaning but over-solicitious in-laws.

"Do you think you'll really need to keep Mrs Watts on full time, dear?" asked Cynthia. "With you at home, you might be able to have her come in just a couple of hours or so each day to let you get out for the shopping."

And so it went on. It seemed they had left no detail unattended. Arrangements had been made to dispose of the Chesham Street flat. Spare furniture from Bowes Court would furnish – "a little sparsely maybe" – the Cadogan Square apartment. Lady Garland had bought second-hand curtains and carpeting at an auction. A nice young family three doors down ("he had a good war with the Life Guards until he was wounded in Normandy") had two children near Julia's age who would be suitable for her to play with and, in time, take lessons with.

Margot listened and said nothing beyond an occasional "that sounds fine; thank you." And some of it was fine, too, provided that one was accepting, lock, stock and barrel, the elder Garlands' concept of what hers and Charlie's life was going to be. From what she had heard so far, however, their concept and hers were far, far apart. But this, she felt, was not the moment to say so. She was very tired; she needed time to think; and she wanted to talk to Marion. By ten o'clock she had bade her parents-in-law goodnight and gone back to Chesham Street.

*

"Play along with them for the time being," advised Marion Shears, as they lunched together the next day at a Knightsbridge restaurant. "It'll give you a base to build on, and in the meantime I'll get hold of Felix Beale. He's about the best fashion photographer around, and if he doesn't jump at the idea of you doing photo modelling I'll eat my hat. He's bound to have admired you already in the social press."

"Charlie once told me that he abhorred the idea of a working wife, in peacetime at least. He may refuse to let me do it."

"Darling, on what he's likely to be earning, he'll be only too delighted to have the extra income coming into the family coffers. All you have to do is show him that what you have to pay Mrs Watts to look after Julia and the flat while you're working is less than what you are bringing in. Even Charlie's limited mathematical capability ought to be able to grasp that it means some extra money in the bank. Just don't let him spend it on drink, which I gather from your description of his last leave has become one of his little weaknesses. There's no point your slaving away to finance the political launching of an alcoholic nonstarter."

"That was wartime; it'll be different now. My main worry is that he'll let his parents conduct our lives. I couldn't take that."

"You've already made up your mind what you want Charlie to be, and when, but you won't get him there without the backing and consent of old Sir Walter. He's a powerful man who can open a lot of doors for you both. Before you decide to go it alone, weigh that up carefully in the balance."

Which is what Margot did over the next two days as she waited for her husband to come back from Germany. Since her return to London, she had become increasingly aware that she had walked into a situation which she could not easily or quickly refashion to her own design. Charlie had written thanking his father for finding him the job with the stock-brokers, and as she pondered this premature capitulation to his father's will, she realized how naïve she had been, at the comfortable distance of

391

the United States, to assume that their future together was something that the two of them would decide when he eventually came home. In the face of so many *faits accomplis*, the grand strategy would have to be revised. But one element of the strategy she was not going to change: whatever Charlie might earn, she wanted her own, independently earned income. So it was up to this Mr Felix Beale. Unfortunately Marion reported that the photographer was in New York for the next three weeks. Margot groaned; she had wanted to present Charlie and his parents with her own *fait accompli*. Instead, she went to work with her mother-in-law to put the Cadogan Square apartment into shape before Charlie marched through the door.

31

Within a week of setting foot in England, Charlie was out of uniform. And within two weeks, at his father's insistence, he was already at work at the stock-broking firm of Segal and Swinbank. Margot, determined that this new stage in their life together should start off on the right foot, welcomed him home with an outpouring of affection to which Charlie responded warmly. He seemed delighted to be home, thrilled to see his wife and daughter, impressed by the Cadogan Square apartment, and eager to get to work. Margot rejoiced, and kept her fingers crossed. But the honeymoon was not to last. Within ten days, his mood had changed. He became depressed and irritable.

"I'm going to hate the job," he retorted with sudden and unexpected passion one evening when Margot had happened to refer to it.

"But I thought you were delighted with the prospect," said a puzzled Margot. "Is there something else you've decided you want to do more? It's not too late to change, surely."

"No. And for God's sake don't start this politics nonsense again. If you wanted to be a politician's wife so much, why didn't you marry one?"

"Charlie, that's unfair! I told you I wasn't trying to force you to do something against your will; I only told you that I thought you'd make a very good politician and that I'd be your most ardent supporter if you ever decided to do it."

"Well, if I ever do decide to do it, which is unlikely, it certainly won't be as long as my father is still alive. So that's that!"

"Why do you say you're going to hate the job before you've even started it?"

"Because I just know that I will, and don't ask me what I'd rather do instead, because I haven't a clue."

Margot shrugged her shoulders.

"Then I guess, to start with at least, you'll just have to do something you don't like."

That night, for the first time since his return, he left her untouched in bed. Not that their love-making had been particularly exhilarating for her on previous nights. She felt she had been making all the effort as he lay back, silently awaiting the moment when her ministrations aroused him just enough to make intercourse possible, and then, in a matter of seconds, he had climaxed, pulled away from her and rolled over with his back to her, mumbling "goodnight". Frustrated by his selfishness, she would set about bringing on her own climax, and if the movement and the moaning kept him awake, he neither remarked on it nor remonstrated. On this particular night, as they undressed, she had gently asked him if he was losing interest in her body. He had reacted petulantly, asking her in turn whether she any longer got any pleasure from feeling him inside her. She had assured him that she did, but as soon as they were between the covers, he turned away from her and went to sleep.

Then the drinking started, or rather it got worse. She had said nothing about it during his first days back home, although it worried her that he was drinking gin heavily at midday and Scotch after Scotch in the evening. It had seemed to have little adverse effect on him for a few days, but gradually his ability to handle the quantities he was consuming seemed to desert him. She took him home, very much the worse for wear, from dinner parties on two consecutive nights and sought to reason with him the following morning, but he dismissed her concern as unwarranted. Margot urged herself not to worry unduly: Charlie was going through a difficult adjustment period, and would doubtless shape up once he started working.

To a certain extent, her forecast was to prove correct. Charlie seemed to pull himself together as he faced the challenge of his first postwar job. He seemed to be getting his drinking more under control – at least the heavy bouts were no longer an inevitable feature of every evening – and the depression of the past weeks seemed to be subsiding. Margot heaved a sigh of relief and speculated hopefully on the possibility that the worst was now over, and that he was on the road to complete adjustment.

Charlie had been at work about a month when Marion finally succeeded in bringing Margot together with the peripatetic Felix Beale. Over cocktails at the Hyde Park Hotel, she told her photographer friend that Margot was considering a career as a fashion photography model and would be grateful for his advice as to how she might go about it.

"It's very simple, Marion, my dear," he said, his eyes remaining fixed on Margot. "You let me take some photographs of her and, unless my professional eye deceives me, we shall discover that we have a marvellously photogenic young lady on our hands. Then we shall go about teaching her the elements of good modelling, find her a reliable agent, and launch her on a world hungry for beautiful new faces."

Margot blushed and demurely dropped her gaze to her lap. The man sounded a bit too gushing, and he made it all sound too simple, she thought. But he had a great name in the business, and Marion was not the sort of person to expose her to some casting-couch charlatan.

"I'd very much like to try it," she said hesitantly, "if you don't think I'll be wasting your time."

"Good gracious, no! It will be my pleasure. Why don't you come tomorrow afternoon at three to my studio? Bring Marion along if you like."

And so it was arranged. Expecting to feel nervous and self-conscious when she faced Beale's camera in his Bond Street studio, she was surprised to find how relaxed and in control of herself she was as the session started. It was an unexpectedly brief one. He took no more than half a dozen pictures of her, in two of which she wore a black felt mandarin hat.

"Is that all?" asked Marion when he dimmed the lights.

"More than enough to tell me that we have a winner, and enough, I hope, to convince Margot of the same.

We'll look at them tomorrow, and then we can start making plans."

"I know you don't believe it yet, darling," said Marion as they left the studio, "but you're on your way."

"Margot, what on earth is all this about? You know we can't afford to eat in places like The Caprice."

"Just be there, darling. There's something to celebrate and it won't cost you a penny."

"Well, what is it we're going to celebrate?"

"You'll find out when you get there. Twelve forty-five. Don't be late."

"It'll have to be a quick lunch. If I'm late back this afternoon, my life won't be worth living."

"Just be there, darling. Bye-bye."

Charlie replaced the receiver, shrugged his shoulders, and rummaged about on his cluttered desk for his cigarette case. Locating it under four days' worth of unread copies of the *Financial Times* he lit a Craven A and stared out of the grimy window of his office at the bleak buildings across the street. His vantage point was the third floor of an ugly Victorian building at the north end of Old Broad Street where the thoroughfare's continuation northwards was barred by the even uglier, soot-coated monstrosity which was Liverpool Street Station. The stock-broking firm of Segal and Swinbank had occupied the third floor premises since the firm's establishment in 1884, and as far as Charlie could judge the premises had remained untouched and unmodernized save for the introduction of telephones and the conversion of the gas lighting system to electricity. His office was sparsely furnished. On a threadbare and stained beige cord carpet stood his desk, which was in fact a table with one drawer in it. He sat behind it on an armless imitation Chippendale dining chair facing a small bricked-up fireplace in the far wall. Balanced on the mantelpiece, and for some reason never hung, was a back-framed, fading colour print of the Royal Review in Hatfield Park, dedicated to the Most Noble the Marquis of Salisbury and dated 13th June 1800. On the extensively cracked cream wall behind him was a similarly framed black-and-white print, dated 1907, depicting the

396

Governor's Summer Residence, Slema, Malta. A single-bulb light beneath a fly-specked shade hung from the ceiling above the desk. A wooden coat and hat stand stood to one side of the door, and an ancient wooden filing cabinet with three drawers stood on the other side. A disintegrating wicker waste-paper basket completed the furnishings.

The grime on the single window could not conceal the fact that it was a gloriously sunny day outside, but for Charlie it had been anything but glorious on the inside. He had arrived nearly an hour late that morning, nursing a hangover acquired during a bachelor evening on the town with a group of recently demobilized former brother officers. He had then been called in for a "friendly chat" with the senior partner of the firm whose arm had been twisted by Sir Walter Garland just hard enough to secure a job for the latter's son. In the course of the chat, Charlie had been invited to share the senior partner's disappointment that the apprentice stock-brocker seemed to be overlooking the fact that he was there not just to learn the business, but also to bring some in.

"There are good commissions to be earned, Charlie," Mr Hamish Stokes-Taylor had said, directing a rather feeble current of breath at a pile of cigar ash on his blotter, thus distributing it more evenly and less obviously across the leather top of his desk. "You just have to make up your mind to pull your finger out."

"I am trying, sir."

"After all, you know a lot of laddies from good families now back from the war. It shouldn't be so difficult for you to persuade them to dip into their sporrans to purchase a few stocks."

Charlie knew them all right. He'd been amongst the "laddies" himself only the night before, dipping into their sporrans to invest not in blocks of Highland Industrial Holdings Preferred Stock, but in the lowest-priced champagne available at The Purple Parakeet, the return on which investment amounted to a licence to take certain on-the-spot liberties with the establishment's friendly hostesses. The notion that he should have been urging his comrades to conserve their funds for less immediately pleasurable investments struck Charlie as absurd.

"Don't let me and your father down, Charlie," had been Stokes-Taylor's parting, and warning shot.

Margot's summons to lunch was at least an indication that his somewhat disorderly return home at two-thirty that morning had been forgiven, as presumably had also been his rather harsh words to her at breakfast when she had told him that she was seriously thinking of finding a job for herself. He had objected strenuously to any such idea. His earnings at Segal and Swinbank were not exactly princely, to put it mildly, but on them and his army pension they seemed to be managing so far. Furthermore, he'd only been in the job six weeks, so how could she tell already that they needed another income earner in the family? A working wife was wholly alien to his idea of marriage among people of their standing. It might have been acceptable as patriotism in the war, but this was peacetime and Margot's place was in the home. And there the conversation had ended.

Charlie picked his bowler and furled umbrella from the stand and hurried down into the street at twelve-fifteen sharp. A good West End lunch would restore his spirits after that not so friendly chat with Stokes-Taylor. The work bored him most of the time, and his superiors irritated him all of the time, but it was a living. Maybe he'd find something better after a while.

At the bottom of Broad Street he took the Underground from the Bank to Holborn, then changed trains for Green Park. As he eventually emerged into the daylight opposite the Ritz, it began to dawn on him that Margot's mysterious invitation to lunch might just have something to do with what she had said over breakfast about getting a job. The thought annoyed him. If she was going to try to soften him up over an expensive meal, he was going to resist. And if she had had the temerity, knowing his feelings on the subject, to bring along some prospective employer, he'd get bloody short shrift! As he crossed Piccadilly, he squared his shoulders and picked up a proper Guardsman's pace, the tip of his umbrella stabbing the ground at the regulation four-pace intervals.

An ex-Grenadier officer's lady did *not* go out to work!

The Caprice was crowded and it took Charlie a moment or two to spot Margot seated at a corner table, her face half hidden under one of her favourite black straw cartwheel hats. Next to her sat a middle-aged man with slicked-down, rather sparse brown hair, and a baby-pink complexion. He appeared expensively dressed, and Charlie's first impression of him was far from favourable.

"I'm sorry I'm late," he said, forcing a smile as he reached them.

The man stood up and held out a hand.

"I'm Felix Beale. I'm so glad you could come."

Charlie detected a central European accent. Obviously the man's real name was not Beale, he concluded. He shook Beale's hand then bent to kiss his wife on the cheek.

"Sit down, darling," she said smiling. "Felix is a fashion photographer. A very famous one, in fact. I'm sure you've heard of him and seen lots of his marvellous work without knowing it was his."

"It's possible," said Charlie.

"Please have a cocktail, Captain Garland."

"Yes, a pink gin, please."

"And how are things in the City today?"

"Muddling along, thank you. And the fashion world?"

"Unpredictable. Like almost everything else after a long war."

"Were you in the war, Mr Beale?" asked Charlie, injecting just enough incredulity into the tone of his voice to render the question mildly offensive.

"Oh yes. Well, in a manner of speaking. Aerial photo interpretation for the Air Ministry. Nothing like as exciting as your war, of course."

"But very important work, I'm sure," said Margot who was now glaring at her husband.

A waiter took Charlie's drink order.

"Maybe we should order food right away," said Beale. "I understand you do not have too much time, Captain Garland."

"No, I don't, but I don't want to deprive you two of a

leisurely lunch. I shall probably excuse myself before you're finished, if you don't mind."

Margot reached with a foot under the table and dug the point of her shoe hard into Charlie's calf. There was no reaction from him. They ordered their food, then Margot turned to Charlie.

"Since you seem to be in such a hurry, darling, you'll probably want to know right away why we are here."

"Yes, I would." He turned to Beale. "Although I think I can guess what it's all about. Are you going to photograph my wife?"

"I already have. She is a great beauty." He patted Margot's hand. "She is also exceptionally photogenic, and she wears pretty clothes like a dream."

"I know," said Charlie, irritated at the imputation that he might have failed to notice such admirable qualities in his own wife.

"Coming from a real expert," said Margot blushing, "it *is* rather flattering."

"I'm obviously not an expert," said Charlie with a sour smile. "Otherwise you'd be flattered when *I* told you the same thing."

"Oh, come on, darling!" Margot laughed nervously and fiddled with the stem of her wine glass.

"Maybe I should tell you right away what all this is about," said Beale affably. "I think you're going to like what you hear."

As they ate their lunch, Felix Beale set the stage for what Charlie was sure was going to be a proposal to have Margot go to work for him. Here they were, he said, more than six months after the end of the war, suffering in some respects from worse deprivations than during the hostilities. Clothes rationing had actually tightened since the war's end, and English women were right to resent the fact that Britain's most beautiful clothes were being made for export only, while austerity versions of the same collections were all that were available at home.

"It cannot last!" said the photographer confidently. "Denying beautiful clothes to our womenfolk is one of the prices the socialist government insists we pay until

Britain's trade deficit is wiped out. But it's unnatural, and it cannot last much longer; mark my words!"

Charlie eyed his host's immaculate blue pin-striped suit, pale blue silk shirt and pearl grey tie transfixed by a pearl-headed tie-pin, and pondered for a moment on the general economic implications of the government's seeming inability to deny beautiful clothes to Mr Felix Beale.

Beale plunged on with his indictment.

"The Paris fashion houses are under no such restrictions, and yet France was an occupied country! They design what they like with whatever materials they can lay their hands on for whomever will buy. Total freedom, in other words. But we mustn't lose heart over on this side of the Channel. We shall soon be doing the same. And this brings me to the point of our little lunch today." He paused to sip from a glass of claret.

Charlie looked questioningly at Margot, who smiled back sweetly.

"There will, sooner rather than later," continued Beale, "be an explosion of activity in the fashion world here, despite the efforts of Sir Stafford Cripps and the Board of Trade to keep it down. Beautiful women will once again be seen in London flaunting the wonderful creations of Stiebel, Hartnell, Amies, Molyneux and the rest of our geniuses who now can only create their best for export. And with these new fashions must come new faces and figures to show them off to a hungry public."

He paused for dramatic effect, then leaned across the table towards Charlie.

"Your Margot, this epitome of fresh, aristocratic beauty from across the Atlantic, will be one of those new faces, and one of the most admired and successful; I'll make sure of that!"

Beale sank back into his chair, somewhat exhausted by his own rhetoric. "That is, if you will give me your permission, Charlie, if I may so address you."

He pulled a thin gold cigarette case from an inside pocket and offered its contents to his two guests.

Charlie drew a cigarette from the case and lit it. He then looked across at Margot, expecting to confront a heart-melting, appealing look. Instead, to his irritation, he saw her studying her face in the mirror of her powder compact, as nonchalantly as if his accord were already a foregone conclusion.

"Mr Beale, I – "

"Felix. Please call me Felix."

"I assume that what you're telling me is that you want Margot to become a fashion photographer's model."

"I am indeed. She's born to it."

"Mr Beale, I will be frank with you. My wife knows that I am one hundred per cent against her going out to work. There is no need for her to do so, and we have a daughter at home to be looked after. You may think I'm old-fashioned, but I think a wife's place is in the home."

"That's not an old-fashioned notion really, and it has its merits in many circumstances. But the postwar era is bringing many changes to our way of life, wouldn't you agree? I'm not suggesting that Margot work simply to make money, but rather to do something which I know she will do superbly and from which she will therefore derive immense satisfaction and fulfilment, not to mention the pleasure she will give to the fashion world."

"Thank you, Felix." Margot snapped shut her powder compact. "But you should also explain to Charlie that I'm not embarking on a nine-to-five, five-day-a-week job. Bookings will come slowly to start with, as you told me. I'll be at home a lot, even though Mrs Watts will have to look after Julia when I'm working."

"Well, you both talk as if the decision is already made, and that I am here simply to give it my blessing," said Charlie. "Isn't that it, Mr Beale?"

"No, that's not it," replied Beale patiently. "I think you should both talk this over during the next few days and come to a joint decision. But I would urge you, Charlie, to think most carefully before denying to your wife the opportunity to do something really fulfilling. I think you would be very proud of what I know she is capable of doing."

Charlie sat silently, staring at his now empty plate. Margot put a hand on his and squeezed.

"Please, darling. Felix is right. It won't disrupt our home life and it will give me a great deal of pleasure. Mrs

Watts is dying to come to us; she so adores Julia. And the extra money, although it won't be much, *will* come in useful."

"I still don't like the idea as a matter of principle." He drained his wine glass, and then looked from Margot to Beale and back again. "It seems I'm outnumbered two to one. I'll probably live to regret having given in so easily and so quickly, but right now it seems I cannot stand in your way. But I want you to understand one thing, Margot: if it turns out that our private life becomes a mess because of this, I'll insist you stop it. On those strict terms I'm prepared to let you have a go at it."

"That's the spirit, darling. I knew you'd agree."

"Well that's more than I did," said Charlie without smiling. "And now I think I'd better be getting back to the City."

"Won't you stay for one more drink? A brandy maybe? After all, we've got something to celebrate." Beale looked at his watch. "It's not yet two, you know."

"No thank you. I really must go. But thank you for the lunch." Charlie rose and shook Beale's hand.

"I'll take good care of her, Charlie."

Charlie ignored the assurance and bent to kiss his wife.

"Charlie, you're a darling. Remember we're dining at Chips Channon's tonight, so don't be late home."

"I won't."

He straightened up and set off through the tables to the exit.

"Did you really know he was going to agree?" asked Beale as they watched Charlie disappear through the exit.

"No, I certainly didn't. Quite the opposite, in fact. He surprised me. And now, Felix, if you'd care to offer *me* a liqueur, I'll surprise you by accepting."

Beale beamed. "That's my girl!"

I must be out of my bloody mind!

For the umpteenth time since lunch, Charlie silently mouthed the words that seemed best to explain how he had come to capitulate to his wife on a matter of such high principle, and without putting up any sort of a fight. He had spent a miserable afternoon in his office sorting listlessly through a growing mountain of paperwork on his primitive desk, and snapping at both the pool secretary who came to verify, somewhat incredulously, that he still had nothing that needed typing, and at the lady with the tea trolley when she pointed out that he'd used up his sugar ration for the week.

Angry and depressed, he had broken his journey home with a stop at a pub in Sloane Square, and after a couple of pink gins and some soothing words from Hattie, the barmaid, who was used to Charlie's hang-dog look when he'd had a bad day in the City, he had begun to perk up.

"What I like about you, Charlie," said Hattie, pushing a truant hairpin back into her luxuriant mane of peroxided hair, "is that you're the sort to bounce back after a couple of drinks instead of wallowing deeper in your problems."

"Thanks, Hattie, and if that's an invitation to another, I'm in the market."

"No you aren't, Captain. You told me you've got a posh dinner tonight, so you'd better get back to the wife."

"And behave myself."

"You took the words out of me mouth, luv. Now run along."

"You're worse than my mother."

By the time he got home, he had a bare fifteen minutes to change before they would have to leave for dinner. Mrs Watts, who came to baby-sit, greeted him at the door, grinning broadly.

"Captain Garland, you've no idea how happy I am to be moving in with you. It'll be just like old times, won't it, sir?"

"Delighted, Mrs Watts." He hurried past her and went to find Margot in the bedroom. "My God, you don't let the grass grow under your feet!"

"You mean Mrs Watts? Considering she's agreed to make her home here in what amounts to little more than a closet with a skylight, I'd say we were damn lucky to have her. Now do hurry and change, darling. The Duchess of Kent and Cecil Beaton will be at the dinner tonight, so I particularly don't want us arriving rudely late."

"I'd rather we didn't arrive at all," said Charlie glumly

as he pulled a dark blue suit off a hanger. "Fish and chips and a cinema would be much better."

"We should be flattered that we're asked."

"And he should be suitably flattered that we've accepted. He likes pretty women at his table, and a stunner like you, who's an American like he once was, must be irresistible."

He wandered off into the bathroom.

"Don't be cynical about Chips!" Margot called after him. "He's one of your father's closest colleagues in the House, and he can help you a lot when you eventually go into politics."

"It's Segal and sodding Swinbank for me for the rest of my days. I'm leaving you to be the star in the family, remember?"

He shut the bathroom door noisily.

Margot shrugged her shoulders. She knew perfectly well why Charlie was in a sulking mood, and she knew that she would have to lift him out of it before he had second thoughts about letting her work with Felix Beale. She went to her closet and selected a New York acquisition, a ballet-length orchid pink taffeta dress, which Charlie had particularly admired when he first saw it. Tonight she would have to make a good job of humouring her husband.

It was well after midnight when they returned from the dinner party, and Charlie was somewhat the worse for wear. He sat down on the end of the bed and watched as Margot began to undress.

"Don't tell me if I misbehaved, because I don't want to know."

"You didn't, not really. You charmed the knickers off that voracious lady from Fort Worth. She kept telling me 'what a fahn yung hersband' I had. The way she was looking at you, I thought she was going to ask my permission to borrow you for the night. And Chips said you were very funny during the port and cigar session."

"You both flatter me."

"How about getting undressed and making passionate love to your raunchy wife?"

Charlie contemplated her long, naked legs.

"I'll get used to it, I suppose," he said.

"Get used to what?"

"Your being sort of public property. Posing on the cover of magazines and that sort of thing."

Margot slipped her panties off, reached for a pink silk wrap draped over a chair, and put it on.

"My darling, silly Charlie. I'm nobody's property except yours, and never will be." She walked over to the bed and sat down beside him. "You're going to be proud of me, not ashamed of me. I'm not going to do cheesecake, for heaven's sakes!" She laughed. "Although I think I'd be damn good at it."

She parted the silk wrap to expose her thighs and struck a provocative pose.

"Don't you think so? But just for you. I'm your private and personal naughty pin-up." She pulled one side of the wrap away from her chest and cupped a hand under one bosom. "All yours, my handsome, and aching to be enjoyed."

Charlie contemplated her exposed nipple for a brief moment, then got unsteadily to his feet and started to undress.

"I like watching my man strip," said Margot. "You have very good legs, Charlie."

"They're scarred."

"Only one thigh, and I find it sexy. It reminds me that you were a bold warrior."

In a moment Charlie was naked, and he sat on the bed again.

"I know you want to make love," he said, almost in a whisper, "but it's just bloody pointless; you know what I'm like after boozing."

"You're hard work, Charles Garland!" Margot laughed. "But I get you there in the end."

Charlie got up again. "Well, tonight I don't even want you to try."

"As you wish. But how about cutting down the drinking maybe a couple of days a week so that I can have some fun?"

"That's crude!"

Margot felt her temper rising.

"Or is all the drinking a deliberate way of finding an excuse not to make love to me? In the five years of our marriage have I become that unattractive to you?"

"Don't be stupid."

Margot went into the bathroom and shut the door with a bang.

"You'd better stop taking me so much for granted!" she shouted back through the closed door.

There was no reply

Over tea at Marion's house the next day, Margot poured out her frustrations to her friend.

"It just isn't working, and I'm sick as hell about it because I really am very fond of Charlie. I'm doing my best, but he's not responding. It's not just the sex; he doesn't seem to be interested in *anything* – his job, politics, our social life. He adores Julia of course, but he doesn't spend that much time with her. And in his own curious way he adores me too, but he doesn't seem to want to show it."

"It's not difficult, darling, to see what's gone wrong," said Marion, slowly stirring her tea. "You fell in love with this desperately handsome young man who was going off to die for his country. And when he was gone, you fell in love with another desperately handsome young man who was going off to die for *his* country. You're prone to falling in love with your own romantic image of a person, not the real person himself. And when they come home and take their beautiful uniforms off and bare themselves as ordinary, weak, flawed mortals, the dream dies. Charlie had his moments during the war, but now you've discovered that he's basically a weak, rather uninteresting young man who isn't going to fulfil the too high hopes you had of him. You are almost certainly going to be a very successful model: Felix assures me of that. So you have a choice. You can say bye-bye Charlie and decide to make it on your own or with someone else, or you can accept that Charlie is never going to be any of the things you wanted him to be, but you stay married to him because he's socially acceptable, because you're quite fond of him, because he's the father of your daughter, and because, with your own career taking off, it's not vitally important to you whether he makes a success of his or not. What I'm saying, Margot, is that the time has come for you to be ambitious for yourself, not Charlie. And if you plan to keep him, I suggest you find yourself a discreet lover to keep you from going absolutely dotty."

"That I may well have to do in the end."

"Pity Edmond isn't here."

"I don't even know whether he's alive or dead. I've heard nothing from him since the end of the war."

"There are plenty of other fish in the sea."

"Marion, I'm going to have to give Charlie a little while longer to shape up. The drinking may be a passing phase, and perhaps he will find a more interesting job."

"There you go again, sweetie. Think of yourself, not him. Give him six months at the most. And in the meantime, get cracking on your modelling. Heavens, you don't need the Garlands any more to have all London at your feet! You're going to do that yourself."

32

Guided by Felix Beale, Margot signed up with a reputable model agency which quickly found her work, much of it with Beale himself as the photographer. Whether modelling high fashion or casual wear, hats or cosmetics, she displayed before Beale's camera a cool, aristocratic beauty softened by an irrepressible and impish sense of humour – a combination which he translated into such arresting images that designers and other photographers were soon beating a path to her agency's door, and the editors at *Vogue* were congratulating themselves on presenting to the world this engaging new beauty. Surprised and delighted as she was with her sudden success, Margot nonetheless insisted that her duties as a wife and mother not be unreasonably encroached upon. This conscientious approach did not commend itself entirely to her agency, but Beale, who understood her feelings, supported her in her determination not to allow her burgeoning career to overwhelm her family life.

Through that first postwar winter, Margot saw emerging a pattern of existence with Charlie which, if far short of wedded bliss, was at least tolerable under the circumstances. The pleasure she felt at her own social and professional success largely compensated for her disappointment in Charlie as a husband and lover. She sensed that Charlie was aware that he was on probation, and she appreciated the fact that, in escorting her in public, he made every effort to play the part of the elegant and well-behaved husband. As a result, their popularity blossomed, and this in turn diminished the severity of the price she felt she was paying in coping with his occasional drinking bouts at home and the infrequency of his attention to her sexual needs. She thought a lot about taking a lover, and there were candidates aplenty, but in the end she always shied away from such a step, not out of any moral reservations, but because she could not believe that the experience would live up to her experiences with Edmond, and that settling for less could bring her no great joy or satisfaction.

Then, in the early spring of 1946, something happened which threatened to precipitate the decisive crisis in her marriage to Charlie. They had gone to a movie and dined in a Soho restaurant with Jamie, still a Grenadier, just posted back to Regimental Headquarters in London, and a handful of other friends. Charlie chose not to behave that evening. He drank copiously, insulted everyone, including Margot, then announced his intention of going home alone to drink in peace in his own drawing room.

"Let him go," said Margot, when Jamie offered to accompany him to Cadogan Square. "There's nothing anyone can do when he's in that condition."

"Is he often like that these days?" asked Jamie anxiously when he later escorted Margot home in a cab from the restaurant.

Margot nodded.

"Then we've got to straighten him out. I'm damned if I'll stand by and watch him wreck your marriage."

"If he just knew what he really wanted to do with his life, this wouldn't be happening. But he's just drifting. He doesn't give a damn for his job, and I don't entirely blame him for that, but either he doesn't know, or won't say, what he'd rather do instead."

"Well, I have a few other demobbed friends in the same position, but they don't go round getting paralytically drunk and insulting their wives and friends in public. Would you mind if I had a serious talk with him?"

"Of course not, Jamie. It might do some good. He's always looked up to you."

Jamie stared out of the cab window.

"I just can't let him treat you like this, Margot." He took her hand in his, and held it tight for a few moments. He pursed his lips, then took a deep breath. "The reason

I won't tolerate Charlie treating you like this is because I love you very much myself. It sounds so unutterably trite. Trite enough to be comical. But I wanted you to know."

"I don't think that's comical, Jamie. I'm very moved and very flattered."

Jamie smiled. "Aren't you meant to say something like: 'No, Jamie, for God's sake, you mustn't. It's all wrong!' or words to that effect?"

She laughed. "Now that *would* be trite and comical. Real Grade B movie stuff. No, what I would say in this situation to you is: how wonderful it feels to be loved by someone whom one really cares for, and someone one knows isn't going to jump off Tower Bridge just because I still love my husband."

"Couldn't have put it better myself! I really do love you, but I respect the fact that you love Charlie, with all his problems, and I'd hate myself if I ever said or did something to upset you. I just hope my confession of love doesn't fall into that category."

"It doesn't. But dear, dear Jamie, you really don't have to lean over backwards trying not to hurt or upset me. You're never going to upset me by saying that you love me. The only way you'll upset me is by telling me that you find it agonizing to be in this position."

"So far it's not. But it will be, of course, if Charlie goes on treating you badly, because then I'd have no more reason to go on respecting the fact that he's your husband. That's when it would get agonizingly frustrating, so we really do have to get Charlie to pull himself together."

"You're such a love, Jamie, but you know, you really are a bit too good for your own good! Come over here and give me a nice kiss."

Jamie did as he was bidden, and Margot let it go on until he finally wanted to draw away.

"I liked that," said Margot.

"Me too!" Jamie laughed a little nervously.

"It was naughty, fun, and perfectly harmless," she said. "And perfect timing," she added as the cab came to a halt outside her Cadogan Square address.

"Do you want me to come up and see if he's all right?"
Jamie asked as he handed her out of the cab.

"No, I can manage."

"Good for you." He smiled happily. "Sleep well."
Then he turned and jumped back into the cab, and was
gone. She watched the cab disappear round the corner
into Pont Street before going in. Upstairs she found
Charlie snoring in bed. There was a scrawled note on her
pillow.

PLEASE FORGIVE MY GROSS BEHAVIOUR TONIGHT. I DRANK
TOO MUCH BECAUSE I HADN'T GOT THE COURAGE TO TELL
YOU THAT I GOT THE SACK FROM FUCKING S & S THIS
AFTERNOON. I'LL TELL YOU ALL IN THE MORNING. C.

Margot sat down on the bed and put her head in her
hands. What is everybody trying to do to me? she
whispered angrily to herself.

Lying in bed, she didn't know on which of the two
latest predicaments to train her confused thoughts.
Charlie was going to be in terrible trouble with his father;
that was clear enough. As for Jamie, she pondered briefly
on the thought that, under other circumstances, she
might have become the Marchioness of Edmonton instead of plain Mrs Charles Garland. Then sleep overtook
her.

Charlie's explanation, as he sat swathed in a bathrobe
at the dining room table, cradling a cup of tea in quivering hands, was succinct and unapologetic.

"I had a bit to drink at lunch, and when Hamish called
me in to tell me that I'd forgotten to do something that
morning which he thought important, but which really
wasn't, I more or less told him to get stuffed. He took not
too kindly to that, and the next thing I knew I was being
handed a month's salary by some gnome in the administration office and being told to clear out my desk by five
sharp."

Margot sighed and shook her head.

"You're really self-destructive, aren't you, Charlie?
Can't you understand what all this drinking is doing to
you?"

He reached towards the toast rack and then changed his mind.

"I hated Segal and Swinbank anyway. I'm free now to find something more congenial."

"Being fired from a job for drunkenness is not the best recommendation for picking up another," said Margot impatiently. "Does your father know yet?"

"I checked with Mrs Watts. He didn't call while we were out last night, so presumably he hasn't yet been informed by his spies at S and S."

"Then I suggest you bite on the bullet and call him before they tell him."

While Margot dressed for a morning's work with Felix Beale and Hardy Amies, Charlie called his father and not unexpectedly received, as he put it, "the worst bawling out since Major Ritchie and Auntie Jean took exception to my ambulance ride." He was ordered to report to the Carlton Club for lunch the following Monday, by which time he should be ready to inform his father what steps he had taken towards finding new and gainful employment.

"And how are you going to go about that?"

"Well, for starters I think I'll toddle along to the Guards Club for lunch and chat to a few people there."

"Remember that you just picked up your last pay-check," said Margot sourly.

"Earned with blood, sweat and tears, my girl. Don't you worry; I'll find something. We won't starve."

"No. But if you'd had your way and kept me from working, we probably would."

As Margot made her way to the West End, she decided to put Charlie's problem out of her mind. There was nothing that she could do about it, so it was best left to him and his father to sort out. She was angry enough at this latest manifestation of Charlie's casual lies and irresponsible attitude to life, and Marion would no doubt tell her that this should be regarded as the final straw and that he should be told that the marriage was over. For the moment, however, she simply didn't want to bother with it. Charlie was fast becoming an irrelevance, and she had no intention of allowing his problems to slow the momentum of her own professional and social progress. For the time being she would ignore him, and if he came to his senses, got a job, and showed a little responsibility, he might once again become relevant to her scheme of things. If he didn't, the marriage could properly be declared dead.

Charlie duly kept the lunch appointment with his father the following week. It was a somewhat sombre meal to which they sat down at the Carlton; and Charlie felt that the club servants were eyeing him with disdain, as if they had read the look of displeasure on his father's face and were loyally associating themselves with it. He had all too little to report: a contact in Armstrong Siddeley's fighting vehicle division; a possible lead through an Eton friend to the paper manufacturing business; an opening with a wine merchant, albeit one where he had an outstanding bill too large to settle at the moment; an offer of an interview for a junior post in the management of Bertram Mills' Circus. At the mention of this last prospect, Sir Walter had laid down his knife and fork and asked his son whether he was joking.

"I have to look at every possibility," replied Charlie defensively.

Sir Walter shrugged his shoulders.

"It looks like your old father is going to have to come riding to the rescue again."

"I'm sure you can safely leave it to me."

"I'm far from sure. Good jobs aren't easy to come by with the country in the parlous state Labour has dragged it into."

To Charlie's relief, his father's mention of the Labour Government led the Member of Parliament off on a detailed cataloguing of the miscreant Attlee's latest errors, and no further mention was made of Charlie's own misdemeanours until they were taking leave of each other on the steps of the club.

"You know," said Sir Walter, dusting a trace of cigar ash from the lapel of his black jacket, "a father has to worry about his son. It's human nature. You had a good war and I don't like to see you go adrift in peacetime like so many young officers did after the Great War. You'll get your second chance all right, although after your ill-mannered performance in the City you'll probably have to steer clear of there for a while. And when you've got that second chance, for God's sake make the best of it. One day you'll want to follow me into politics, so keep your nose clean in the meantime. All right, old boy?"

Charlie had been listening to the paternal homily with head bowed respectfully and with a properly mournful look on his face. Now he looked up and smiled at his father.

"I won't let you down, I promise."

"Don't let yourself down. Now run along and go to it. I'll tell your mother to stop worrying so much, and you give Margot my love. Quite a celebrity now, isn't she, what?"

"So it seems."

Sir Walter gave his son an encouraging pat on the back and turned his attention to hailing a cab on St James's Street. Charlie thanked his father for the lunch and crossed the street, heading northwards towards his tailor to cash a small cheque.

Once back in the Palace of Westminster, Sir Walter went straight to a telephone and called his daughter-in-law.

"Margot, my dear. I've just come from giving Charlie lunch, and I think we've cleared the air a bit, but I want your help."

"Of course. You know I'd do anything to – "

"Quite so, quite so, my dear," cut in Sir Walter who had no wish to yield the floor at this juncture. "Now, he told me about one or two of the ideas he has but they seemed pretty vague and some of them just stupid. So, what I want you to do, my dear, is help me convince him that he's got to find something to do now that will restore his good standing after he's made such an ass of himself in the Stock Exchange. None of this circus nonsense, or sitting in a St James's wine merchant's swilling sherry all day. He has to do something that will be a stepping stone, not a barrier, to politics one day. You see what I mean? You must stop him from wasting his time pursuing unsuitable jobs, and for heaven's sake keep him away from the whisky bottle.''

"I'll do my best, Walter, but it isn't going to be easy. It's hard enough to control his drinking at home, and there's nothing I can do about it out of the house.''

"I understand, my dear. Now I forgot to tell Charlie over lunch that Winston and Clemmie are coming to dinner on the fourteenth, and you two are invited. I know they'll be delighted to see you again.''

"Thank you very much. We'd be delighted too.''

"Good. Cynthia said she saw some very nice pictures of you in a magazine at her hairdresser yesterday. Jolly proud of you, we are.''

"Well they're keeping me busy, which is good. Especially with Charlie out of work.''

"Don't let him use that as an excuse to drag his feet. I've got to run now. Meeting of the '1922 Committee'. Give my granddaughter a kiss from me. Goodbye, my dear.''

They rang off, and Margot went to prepare Julia for a walk in Hyde Park. Winston and Clemmie! My God, Charlie, if you get potted and shame us all at this one, I'll never, ever, forgive you! You've already killed any chance you ever had to make it in politics, however much blind faith your father may have in you still, but I'm damned if I'm going to let you undermine my name and place by association with your recklessness.

As it turned out, Charlie was on his better behaviour the night the Churchills came to dine with their friends, the Garlands. The sole embarrassing moment came when Mr Churchill asked him at the dinner table what he was doing to earn a living, and Charlie replied that he had that very afternoon accepted a job offer from an estate agency in Brompton Road, helping to write prospectuses on London properties. This information he had, for some reason, seen fit to withhold from both Margot and his parents, and while Margot, for form's sake, pretended that she had already learned of this from him and was generally approving, Sir Walter could not conceal a disappointment bordering on anger. When she asked

Charlie later why he had said nothing of the job until it was drawn from him by the Leader of His Majesty's Loyal Opposition, he told her that he thought it would be amusing to break the news that way. Margot had shaken her head in amazement.

For her part, she enormously enjoyed the occasion. The former Prime Minister had plenty to say about the Council of Foreign Ministers of the Big Four Powers that was taking place at that time in Paris. Thence the conversation turned to de Gaulle who had dramatically resigned the Presidency of France just four months earlier.

"A miscalculation of historic magnitude," declared Churchill with an impish smile. "He believed his services to be so invaluable to the French people that they would immediately clamour for his re-enthronement on any terms he cared to exact. How little he knew his own people!"

"And you think he will never return now?" asked Margot.

Another impish smile.

"It is not unknown for a people to change its mind about a leader it has ungratefully and injudiciously removed from office." There was approving laughter around the table. "But it is rare to accord that second chance to one who has petulantly removed himself."

Poor Edmond, she thought. The end of his hero.

In the early days of July, Harland Moore brought Elinor to Europe. They stayed in London for ten days, just round the corner from their daughter and son-in-law, at the Cadogan Hotel, and were much fêted by both generations of Garlands. These were Margot's happiest days in a long while, and the joy of seeing her parents again, of finding her father seemingly restored to full health and vigour, and the relief that Charlie was still in his job by the time they arrived and behaved discreetly while they were there, all combined to strengthen in her the hope that her marriage would be saved. She had confided in neither her parents nor Larry the troubles she had been through with Charlie since he came home, and in the light of the greatly improved atmosphere prevailing at the time of her parents' visit, she felt that her decision had been fully vindicated.

After their London stay, the Moores were due to spend a week in Paris. Margot would dearly have liked to accompany them there, but she had rented a cottage on the Sussex coast for a couple of weeks to ensure some sea air for Julia before the close of summer. It was while she was down at the cottage that she received a brief letter from her father, from Paris, with an enclosure. The enclosure was a page clipped from a magazine article about the owners of some of Bordeaux's better-known vineyards, and one of the photographs accompanying the text was of Edmond, standing among the vines, with Château Lachaise-Laurent in the background. Her French was rusty, but with the aid of a pocket dictionary found on one of the cottage's bookshelves, she translated the relevant section of the article. Her heart began to beat faster as the story emerged:

Since his father's death in November 1945, the young Colonel Lemonnier has been the proprietor of the well-known St Julien vineyard of Lachaise-Laurent, the widow of the late Georges Lemonnier, former Deputy and Mayor of Bordeaux, having invited her son to assume full ownership.

Edmond Lemonnier was one of the earliest to rally to General de Gaulle in London in 1940, and served with the "Fighting France" headquarters there until joining General Leclerc's famed Second Armoured Division in Morocco, with which formation he then went on to participate in the liberation of France. He was awarded the Croix de Guerre for gallantry at the recapture of Strasbourg, and at war's end was one of the youngest full colonels in the French Army. He is also decorated with the Order of the Liberation. Colonel Lemonnier resigned with honour from the Army on the death of his father in order to take over his responsibilities as *propriétaire* of the Third Growth vineyard. A loyal supporter of former President de Gaulle, the thirty-year-old colonel spoke widely in the region at the time of the national referendum on the draft Constitution, urging, as did his distinguished mentor, its rejection. Politics runs in a Lemonnier blood. Will he, the third generation of this family to own the vineyard, emulate his father and combine wine-making with statesmanship?

Well, good for you, Edmond, thought Margot. You survived. So why didn't you tell me? She looked again at the photograph. He didn't appear to have changed much. Maybe his hairline had receded a little, and he looked a bit thinner in the face. A colonel? And all those decorations? You did well, Edmond. No mention of a wife in the article. But you seem to have forgotten all about me, and that should be remedied. That same day, therefore, she sat down and wrote him a letter.

My dear Edmond.

My parents were briefly in Paris and they sent me the *Paris Match* article about you. I suppose it's one way of finding out whether you ever survived the war, although a letter from you would have pleased me even more!

Anyway, congratulations! You seem to have emerged quite a hero (which doesn't surprise me) but I do have a bone to pick with you. You never got in touch with me after I had left that message for you here in London before you went off to win all those medals. Why? I was hurt.

I was sorry to note in the article that your father had died. But I am sure you are running the family vineyard with great success. I'd love to come and see it one day.

Charlie works in a real estate office, and I have taken up fashion photo modelling, and am enjoying it very much. It's possible you've seen me gracing the pages of English *Vogue*, but then what would you be doing looking at English *Vogue*?! I do both *haute couture* and cosmetics, not that there's a great deal of either in supply here yet. People say they live worse here now than during the war. So much for socialist government.

I'm sorry that General de Gaulle has wound up his political career. Or has he? Winston Churchill thinks he

419

has; I had it from the horse's mouth! Churchill, of course, has not. If you find time to write, tell me what you think.

I'm keeping my fingers crossed that my work will bring me to Paris before too long. I will not fail to look you up, but maybe you'd better write in the meantime and confirm that no mention of a wife in the article means you indeed don't have one! Not that that would inhibit me from calling you, but I would be more comfortable knowing.

I have no idea what your Paris address is, or even if you have one there, so my wine merchant kindly gave me the address of Lachaise-Laurent. I hope it's where you can be reached. And you must not fail to let me know if you are planning a visit to London.

A bientôt, j'espère!
Margot

She went out and posted the letter without delay, just in case she had second thoughts later about re-establishing contact with her wartime lover.

33

One morning in mid-September, Margot awoke to hear Charlie telling someone over the telephone that he was sick and would not be coming in to work that day. She got out of bed, went to the drawing room, and was surprised to find him fully dressed.

"What's all this about your being sick?"

"I'm not. It's just that I have something I need to do today, and the only way I can get the day off is to say that I'm ill."

He fiddled nervously with his tie and stared at his well-polished shoes.

"Well, out with it; what is it that's so important that you have to play hookey from your office?"

"I'm afraid I can't say now, but I'll certainly tell you later."

"Charlie, if you're about to do something that's going to end in you losing your job, you'd do better to stay right here, sick or not."

Charlie put his hands on her shoulders and kissed her on the cheek.

"Just trust me. I'm not getting into any trouble, I promise."

"Well, if it's not trouble, why in hell can't you tell me?"

"I'll tell you soon. Just don't ask me now."

"Will you be back for dinner?"

"Of course. I must run now."

Slowly shaking her head, Margot watched him leave the apartment. Then, remembering that she was being picked up by Felix at nine to be taken to Hampton Court for a layout of winter coats and hats, she hurried to her room to get ready for the day. Whatever Charlie was up to, be it on his own head. She had work to do.

Margot's career had got off to a rapid start. Given her special relationship with Beale, and the fact that he worked principally for *Vogue*, she had fast become a favourite of that journal's editors. Meanwhile she was rising fast up the list of models on her agency's books most in demand for both advertising work and fashion editorial.

For this, she knew how much she owed to Felix. He had taught her much, flattered her often, given her self-confidence, and sought no price from her other than her commitment to do her work well. As he had explained to her at the outset, he never saw a model as a mere display device, and no model worth her salt saw herself as such. He saw her as an individual, living personality whose relationship to the clothes she wore and the surroundings in which she showed them was always believable, however striking the image. As Margot had quickly discovered, the purpose of his endless chatter as he worked with her, interspersing his instructions with comments on what he knew of her life, her likes and dislikes, was to prevent her from forgetting for a single moment while she faced the camera that she was a real person, not a clothes-horse.

The results, they were both happy to admit, were stunning, and fully justified Beale's initial confidence that she had the potential to become a star model. She had been approaching her twenty-fifth birthday when they met, an age considered by the profession to be unusually advanced at which to be starting a career. But, as Beale was quickly able to show, her cool, aristocratic beauty was enriched by such a variety of expressive, photogenic moods that he was capable of presenting any image of her ranging from a casual, wide-eyed innocent just turned nineteen to a worldly sophisticate, wholly aware of her elegance and beauty.

On her way out to Hampton Court that morning with Felix, she enquired casually what the chances were of her ever getting work in Paris. The day before she had received an answer to her letter to Edmond. He had apologized for not repsonding earlier – he had been on a visit to Algeria – and had renewed his wartime invitation to bring Charlie and Julia on a visit to the château. He had then added that he had no present plans to visit London, but hoped very much that her work would soon bring her to Paris. Although mildly irritated that her initiative had not sparked a rather warmer, more urgent reaction from him, and that while she had said that *she* wanted to visit the vineyard, he had included Charlie in the renewed invitation, she was nonetheless pleased that he had finally written. It was now all the more urgent that Felix use his contacts and ingenuity to ensure that a visit to Paris on assignment was no further delayed. She was more than ever curious to see what effect the old Edmond magic, in its new clothing, might have on her.

"Be patient, my child," said Felix. "We will work over there before long, I am sure." He paused and pulled a white silk handkerchief from the pocket of his tweed jacket. "Your impatience wouldn't by any chance be connected with a certain young wartime acquaintance?" he asked as he dabbed genteelly at his nostrils.

Margot looked at him curiously. "How might you know about such a person, Felix?"

"Marion," he replied, returning the silk square to the interior of his left pocket.

Margot laughed nervously. "I might have known! It's not the first time she's let that particular cat out of the bag. Thank heavens you're the soul of discretion. You are, aren't you?"

"Discretion itself, my dear."

"Then I might as well tell you the whole story."

She finished just as they arrived at the gates of the palace.

"Almost worthy of a novel," said Felix, chuckling. "I like the Drake character; might have come straight out of John Buchan."

As they drove into the immaculately kept royal palace grounds, she confessed to herself that her impromptu revelation to Felix of the details of her affair had been her little revenge on Charlie for being secretive about what he was up to that day.

To her surprise, Charlie came clean on his return that evening.

"I've spent the day at a film studio."

"What on earth for?"

"I was invited to watch a film being made."

"How very nice. I suppose it never occurred to you to invite me along, and why all the secrecy if that's all you were up to?"

"A few days ago, I ran into a fellow who was in my POW camp. We met in a pub – "

"Naturally!"

"Do you want to hear, or don't you?"

"Go on."

"He's called David Hughes-Webb, and he's an Assistant Director at Concord Pictures, one of J. Arthur Rank's acquisitions. They use the Rank Studios at Denham, and he asked me if I'd like to go down and see a film being made. He said the best day would be today, so I went."

"And?"

"They were shooting interiors for a film called *Devil's Dawn* or something like that. Not very exciting, actually, because the stars weren't involved in that particular scene, but quite interesting to see how they did it."

"I didn't know that you were interested enough in watching movies being shot to risk losing your job."

"Well, to tell you the truth, David had hinted when we talked in the pub that there was someone he wanted me to meet at the studio."

"Oh, so we're going into the movies now, are we? Or was he lining up a nice little starlet for you to play with?"

"Damnit, Margot, I'm not going to tell you what's been happening if you're going to be so bitchy!"

"Well, why can't you come out with it straight, then, Charlie. You didn't go down there to watch a bunch of bit players stumbling around the lot; you went because your friend wanted you to meet someone. So don't beat about the bush. Who is this someone and why did he want you to meet him?"

"I'm flattered by your interest. I thought that since I told you I didn't want to be the youngest prime minister since Pitt, you never gave a damn about my career!"

"All right, I'm sorry, Charlie. I had a tiring day and my nerves are a bit on edge. Be an angel and refresh my Scotch while you keep talking."

She handed him her glass.

"Well, David gave me lunch in the studio restaurant, and we were joined by a man called Vernon Shonfield who's Concord's casting director. At first we talked about the war because he'd been a signals officer at Alex's headquarters in France in 1940, and so we'd sort of covered the same ground. He stayed with Alex throughout the war and met Jamie in North Africa. Then we talked about making films, and he suddenly asked me if I'd ever thought of being an actor. I thought he was joking, and told him that apart from a walk-on part in *Julius Caesar* at Eton and some knock-about stuff at Christmas in the camp, I'd never set foot before an audience. Anyway he said that the film industry was looking for new faces, and one or two had been found amongst people of my background coming out of the services. He even mentioned an ex-Grenadier, but I don't remember the name and I didn't know him. He'd never acted in his life before either."

He handed Margot her drink.

"And he thought you might be one of the new faces?"

"David said he thought I had the looks and seemed in good physical shape – "

"He obviously hasn't seen your liver!"

" – and I have a good speaking voice. They also thought my war record, such as it was, could help."

"I thought acting ability had at least something to do with it as well."

"That one can learn. Anyway, the upshot was that Shonfield said he could probably get me a screen test if I was sufficiently interested. No commitments, of course, but he thought it would be interesting to find out how I

425

came across. He told me to think about it and call him back this week. That's all."

"So what are you going to do?"

"I'd like to do it. What do you think?"

Margot got up from the sofa and walked over to the windows to draw the curtains.

"Well, what do you think?" repeated Charlie.

"Listen, Charlie," said Margot. "I gave your father an undertaking that I would do all I could to help you get and stay in a job which could eventually be a stepping stone not an obstacle to politics, and – "

"Oh fuck politics! Why is it always politics? I don't give a damn about them!"

"I know that, Charlie. And although I used to think you'd make a very good politician, I've long since changed my mind. You're weak, unreliable, and a chronic drinker."

Charlie laughed bitterly. "Sounds like good material for Parliament to me."

"I've given up all ambition I had for you in that direction," she said, returning to the sofa. "On the other hand, if they think you might make it in movies, I'll back your decision to give it a try. But you've got to promise me two things. First, you can't do a screen test if you're sauced, so you lay off the booze. Second, you don't breathe a word of this to your parents unless and until you've taken and passed the screen test. There's absolutely no point in making your father apoplectic now if it's not going to come to anything anyway. You can give him the bad news if you're accepted by Concord – and believe you me, it will be very bad news to him."

"Both promises will be kept, old girl."

"Then come and seal them with a kiss." He bent over her and kissed her lightly on the lips. "Christ, Charlie, you'd better do better than that on screen if you're going to be in the money."

The next morning, before leaving for his office, Charlie called Vernon Shonfield and told him that he'd like to do a screen test, if one could be arranged. When he had left, Margot called Jamie at the Grenadiers' Headquarters and asked him if he remembered meeting a Vernon Shonfield when he was at Alexander's headquarters in North Africa.

"Yes, I remember him. One of the signals fellows. An ex-actor. He got sent elsewhere when a rich Egyptian tried to shoot his balls off for rogering his actress wife in a Shepheard's Hotel in Cairo. Rather a splendid chap."

"Well, he's now a casting director in the movies here, at Concord Pictures, and – "

"Don't tell me you're going to be a film star! How absolutely super! You'd be marvellous, old girl!"

"Not me, Jamie. Charlie."

"*Charlie?* You're joking."

"I'm not. He's met your lusty friend, and they've arranged a screen test. Nothing may come of it, of course, but they're giving it a try. I was calling you to find out if you thought Shonfield was a serious type who wouldn't lead Charlie up the garden path. From what you've told me, he sounds anything but serious, but I guess there's no harm in Charlie having a go."

"Of course not. But, Charlie! I'd just never have thought of him as an actor. Knowing Walter's likely reaction, I really think you should go and do a little advocacy on Charlie's part. Walter listens to you, and I'm sure it would help."

Margot devoted the remainder of the morning and the afternoon writing letters to her parents and Larry. She felt it was premature to mention Charlie's involvement with the film studio, and she was far from sure that her parents, if not Larry, would take any more kindly to the idea of her husband becoming an actor than the Garlands would. She paused in mid-letter to ponder on how she might follow Jamie's urging and intercede with Charlie's parents if he was indeed to enter the acting profession. She relished not one bit the prospect of alienating her father-in-law, as she was bound to do in backing Charlie. The elder Garlands were important to her. The political circle into which Sir Walter had so enthusiastically invited her never failed to fascinate her, whatever Charlie's jaundiced view of politics might be, and the thought that she might find herself henceforth excluded by an angry father-in-law who felt he had been betrayed alarmed her. On the other hand, if she sided with Sir Walter, Charlie would go ahead anyway, if only out of pique, and all she would have succeeded in doing would be to worsen the atmosphere at home and maybe precipitate the end of her association with the Garlands altogether. It was obvious that she would have to play her cards very, very carefully indeed.

To Charlie, Cole Mallinson looked more like a rumpled professor than a film producer, and the tortoise-shell frame of his spectacles was held together with elasto-plast.

"Let's take a look at you," he said, switching roles from professor to physician as he came round from behind his desk. Charlie wondered if he would be asked to step behind a screen and strip. On second thoughts, it was an adjutant's inspection, so he drew himself up to attention and stared rigidly ahead.

"I can see you were a Guardsman, Mr Garland." Charlie smiled gratefully. "Relax old chap. Loosen up a bit. You're too tense."

Mallinson perched himself on the front of his desk.

"A touch of young Redgrave, don't you think, Vernon?"

"Yes, I think you're right there."

"Would you take your jacket and tie off, Mr Garland?"

"Yes, of course."

Charlie took off the jacket of his grey flannel suit and and went to work on the knot of his tie which, for some inexplicable reason, he had knotted tighter than a parcel string that morning. After a brief struggle, which set him perspiring, he prised it loose, and stood clutching jacket and tie in one hand while he delved for a handkerchief to mop his brow. Shonfield stepped over.

"I'll hold them for you. Just unbutton a couple of shirt buttons."

Charlie wondered whether Michael Redgrave could possibly have gone through this humiliation.

"Good! Good!" said Mallinson, giving Charlie no hint whether he was expressing pleasure at what he saw or merely applauding Charlie's ability to undress to order. A silence which seemed like an eternity ensued, and then Mallinson slid down from his perch.

"Sit down and tell me all about yourself."

He led Charlie over to a sitting area in one corner of the office and motioned him to an armchair. For the next twenty minutes Charlie talked about himself, prompted with questions and comments from his two interlocutors, at the end of which the producer asked him why he wanted to be an actor.

"Because I think I'd enjoy it."

"And what makes you think you can be one?"

"I don't know that I can be. I'm hoping you can help me find out."

"Well, for a start, we'll go and see what you look like on camera, young man. We're borrowing a corner of the *Devil's Dawn* set which I understand you visited last week. You'll be doing a short scene with a pretty young lady called April Astor whom we recently put under contract. It won't take long."

They escorted him from the building and, one on either side of him, marched him briskly towards Studio C. Charlie felt like a condemned man on his last walk. His knees began to weaken and he tried desperately to formulate in his mind a few simple words that would express his overwhelming desire to go no further with this wholly mistaken venture.

"Do you read Sax Rohmer?" asked Mallinson.

"I don't believe I ever have."

"Really? I thought everyone your age had. Inventor of Dr Fu Manchu, the greatest literary creation of the genre ever. Rohmer's not his real name, it's Ward. Birmingham Irish. You should read him, Mr Garland. One day he'll part with the film rights. That's the day I'm waiting for. Every English male lead under thirty-five will be on his knees begging to get the Nayland Smith role. That's the Doctor's nemesis, you know."

Charlie threw a puzzled sideways look at Shonfield who grinned and winked back.

"I've certainly heard of Dr Fu Manchu," said Charlie as he followed his two escorts into the studio.

"I'm glad to know that," said Mallinson, looking pleased. For a moment Charlie speculated grimly on what might have been in store for him if he'd said he'd never heard of the oriental villain.

The set was lit and a camera crew stood ready.

"Morning, Archie," said Mallinson to a thin man with a shock of red hair. "Meet Charles Garland." Charlie was beckoned forward. "This is Archie Buck who'll direct this little test. Got the script Archie?"

A single typewritten sheet was handed to Charlie.

"April will be here in a moment," said the director, who spoke with a heavy Scottish accent. "You're a young man of upper-class background who's met this girl on the train that takes you both to work in London each morning. She's a hairdresser, and she's agreed to meet you for a pub lunch. You've just finished your lunch, and you're now trying to persuade her to stay up in town that evening and go to a cinema with you, but she's putting up resistance. All right? When she gets here you can read it through together a few times before we shoot the scene. Then I think Mr Mallinson wants us to do some short takes of just you alone."

"I see," said Charlie, barely audibly.

A pretty blonde girl in beige slacks and a green shirt hurried across the studio floor towards them.

"Sorry to be late," she said breathlessly. "I broke a strap on my bra. Do I look uneven, love?"

"Not that it tells," said Archie with a grin.

"Hello! You must be Charles Garland."

Charlie shook the extended hand, painfully aware that his palm was sweaty with panic.

"Nice to meet you," he stammered.

"All right April," said Mallinson, stepping forward. "Let's not waste more time. "Take him off in the corner and read it through."

Charlie and April walked a few yards away to a couple of chairs and sat down.

"Nice name, Charles Garland. Don't let them change it," said the girl with a friendly smile.

"So's yours. Might you by any chance be related to Mary Astor, the actress, or any of the other Astors?"

April Astor laughed. "Heavens, no! My real name's Mavis Batty. Come on, let's give this masterpiece a quick read through."

Forty harrowing minutes later, Charlie was shaking hands with Cole Mallinson outside the studio.

"Thank you very much, Mr Garland. Thank you very much. It wasn't such an awful ordeal, was it, now?"

"I'm afraid I've been wasting your time, Mr Mallinson," said Charlie, "but I really appreciate your having given me the opportunity to try."

"No waste of time at all. I have to hurry to my lunch. Vernon here will see you safely off. Read lots of Rohmer, Mr Garland. *Fu Manchu's Bride*, which he wrote in '33, is the best in my opinion. We'll be in touch, I hope." He walked briskly away.

Vernon Shonfield took Charlie by the arm.

"I'll buy you lunch. Come on."

"Oh, you really don't have to. I can go to a local pub on my way back to the bus."

"Nonsense. It'll be my pleasure, and you probably need a drink straight away."

As they set off toward the main building, Charlie opened his mouth to ask the question to which he already knew the depressing and humiliating answer, but Shonfield spoke first.

"Dear Cole's a bit of a bore with his Fu Manchu. I should have warned you. He's written treatises on him; it's an obsession. He's read every word Sax Rohmer's written God knows how many times, and he'll never rest until he can get to make films of his stories."

Charlie laughed nervously. "Thank heavens I at least knew who Fu Manchu was even though I've never read any of those books. I'd hate to have failed that test as well."

"You didn't fail either test, Charlie."

Charlie stopped in his tracks.

"You're joking! I made an utter balls-up back there in the studio. It was the most embarrassing hour I've ever spent."

"Cole disagrees. So does Archie Buck, and so do I.

You're totally untrained, and that shows, but it's all there to be mined."

"But Mallinson didn't say a single word afterwards to make me think that I'd been anything but a failure."

"Precisely. But he didn't say you'd been one either. He did, however, tell *me* that you were worth taking a gamble on and that he's going to take up the question of putting you under contract. The final decision will be South Street's – that's headquarters in London – but his recommendations are rarely turned down. So relax."

"Heavens! I'd never have believed it."

"He and I will be looking at the print of that test tomorrow morning, but I'm damn sure his mind's already made up."

"And you agree with him?"

"Yes, I do."

They reached the restaurant and ordered drinks first at the bar. Shonfield raised his gin and tonic.

"Here's to you, Charlie. Let's hope you get a contract soon. In the meantime, you'd better get yourself an agent. That's another thing we can talk about over lunch."

Charlie lifted his glass.

"Thanks very much. Just keep your fingers crossed that my father doesn't murder me before I get to sign on."

Vernon Shonfield had correctly read the producer's mind, and a week later he was able to telephone Charlie to inform him that the powers-that-be at South Street were accepting Mallinson's recommendation – subject to an interview at headquarters which would be more or less a formality – that he be put under contract to Concord. The pay was likely to be in the region of twenty pounds a week.

"More ammunition for your father," said Margot gloomily. "That's a fiver less than you're getting in your present job."

But in fact she was very pleased for Charlie. For the first time since taking off his uniform, he had picked up a challenge and come out on top. Maybe at last he had found his feet.

Charlie's parents, predictably, did not see it that way at all. At Margot's urging, Charlie went round to his parents' house alone to break the news and to tell them that he had his wife's full support. She herself would telephone them when he returned.

"*If* I return," said Charlie unhappily. "I wish to God you'd come with me to hold my hand."

"No. You've absolutely got to show them that you're your own man with your own mind, and that it's made up."

So Charlie braced himself for the onslaught and set off for Westminster.

He returned an hour later looking pale and very unhappy, and poured himself a large Scotch before vouchsafing a single word on what had happened. Slumped in a chair, and after two long draws at the soothing liquor, he finally spoke.

"They were perfectly bloody about it. My father said he would absolutely not permit me to sign any contract. He raged on about my throwing away a respectable job just to fulfil some schoolboy fantasy. I reminded him that one of Winston's daughters was an actress and was even married to an Austrian comedian, but he just told me not to be impertinent."

Margot started to laugh.

"It's no laughing matter. When I told him you were supporting me, he wouldn't believe it. Said I was lying. You should have been there, you see."

"Don't worry. I'll set them straight on that. They can't stop you signing the contract, and they know that, so the sooner you do it, the sooner they'll come to accept that their son has a right to organize his own life. Christ, Charlie, you're a grown man who's been through one helluva war!"

"It isn't as simple as that."

"Why not?"

"They had me against the wall," he said miserably. "I agreed to wait and think it over some more."

"You did *what*?" Margot got to her feet and came to stand over him. She sighed deeply before speaking.

"Charlie, Charlie. You let yourself down again, didn't

you? Not to mention letting me down as well. For once in your civilian life you've done something you can be really proud of, and you're now hell-bent on throwing it all away because your parents tell you to. You're going to sign that contract if it's the last thing you ever do, and immediately it's ready – or you and I are through. I mean that, Charlie."

Charlie signed the contract three days later. In the intervening period, his father had made one more determined effort to convince his son that acting was best left to the likes of Ralph Richardson and Laurence Olivier who knew what they were doing, and that a young man who could wear both the Old Etonian and Brigade of Guards ties was a fool not to exploit such credentials in areas of activity where they were considered second to none as guarantees of preferment. But Charlie believed Margot when she posed her ultimatum, and had no wish to be abandoned by his wife at this somewhat precarious juncture of his life. So this time he bit a little harder on the bullet and told his father that he was going ahead, promising him at the same time that he would work hard to make both his wife and parents, and eventually his daughter, proud of him. Sir Walter bestowed what he intended to be the lowest grade of blessing that could be bestowed by a father on an errant son, and stalked off in a dark mood to the House of Commons to commune with a more rational type of human being than his offspring.

Margot heaved a sigh of relief and wrote her parents-in-law a note thanking them for their "generosity of spirit" in the matter, a gesture which did not come too easily to her, but which seemed to have some tactical merit. And then she wrote to her parents to inform them that her one-time soldier then stock-broker then estate agent husband was now a movie actor.

With Vernon Shonfield's help, Charlie acquired an agent, a taciturn ex-vaudeville producer named Greville Viner, who proceeded to disabuse his client of any high-flown notions he might have of playing Margaret Lockwood's lover for starters. With luck Concord might throw him a small part within the next two or three months, or he might be lent out to some other studio for a specific role, but neither eventuality was to be counted on. In the meantime, he would be enrolled in a small film acting class run from a shabby terraced house in Hammersmith by a German director who had left Berlin in 1925 with Ernst Lubitsch but, because of a romantic attachment, had chosen London instead of Hollywood and had found obscurity instead of fame. Emil Neumann had, nonetheless, built himself a reputation of a sort in the growing British film industry as a good teacher of technique before the camera, and the three mornings a week which Charlie was to spend at his class would, it was hoped by the studio, prove to be time and money well spent. Charlie, with nothing else to do, was happy to give the time. He was less happy to find half the cost of the classes deducted from his unprincely wage packet of twenty pounds a week.

At the end of six weeks of arduous training at the hands of the demanding Neumann, Charlie, though buoyed by his teacher's far from discouraging assessment of his progress, began to fret over the absence of any sign or mention of a film role. His friends' enquiries about when he would be going before the cameras were beginning to embarrass and annoy him, and the inevitable "I told you so" attitude of his father riled him horribly. Margot urged him to accept that these were early days in an embryonic career, and should be endured with patience and determination. But, as the days passed, she could see that Charlie was slipping into a depression, and after three months, as 1947 approached, it was clear that he was drinking as much as the residue of his pay packet and the hospitality of his friends would allow. Once again the writing was on the wall, and she wondered whether she had not, after all, made a ghastly mistake in siding with Charlie rather than his father.

34

"Stanley, come and meet another of our young actors who's just come under contract." Tommy Hull, head of press relations at Concord Pictures, beckoned the correspondent of a national tabloid. "Stanley, I'd like you to meet Charles Garland."

"Pleased to meet you, Mr Garland. What'll be your first picture?"

"I don't know yet."

"We're working on that," interjected Hull.

"I see from the handout that you're the son of the MP Sir Walter Garland. Been any other actors in your family?"

"Not that I know of."

"And your wife is Margot Moore, the model."

"Correct."

"She here?"

"No, I'm afraid not."

"What sort of roles are you hoping to get?"

"At the moment, anything."

"Nice to meet you, Mr Garland."

"My pleasure."

Charlie forced a smile and moved away into the crowd.

"Talkative bloke, isn't he?" observed the journalist.

"Strong, silent type, old boy. The women will just love him."

Looking around him, Charlie could spot no more than three or four familiar faces. Cole Mallinson, his spectacles still unrepaired, hovered over a short, effeminate-looking young man, no doubt testing him on his knowledge of Fu Manchu. The redheaded director who had handled the screen test was there, but to Charlie's disappointment there was no sign of the delectable Mavis Batty, alias April Astor. Maybe she would be along later. The private room at the Dorchester in which Concord was throwing a party for the press to introduce those newly under contract was filling up rapidly, and Charlie was afraid that he might miss in the crush the two people he really wanted to see – his agent, Greville Viner, and Shonfield, the casting director. Not that he had anything particular to say to them himself: what he really hoped to see was the two of them getting down to business over a drink on what to do about one Charles Garland who was getting pretty sick of telling film and gossip columnists that he hadn't a clue what Concord intended doing with him.

He drained his Scotch and soda and craned his neck to identify the most direct route to the bar.

"Come and meet the *Daily Mail*, Charlie."

It was Tommy Hull's assistant, a young man fighting a losing battle to grow a moustache, whose name persistently escaped Charlie.

"A refill first," said Charlie firmly.

"OK. We'll wait for you over under that chandelier."

Charlie set off towards the bar, only to find his way blocked.

"Which one are you?" asked the obstacle, a stout lady peering through thick spectacles at her publicity handout while keeping a firm grip on Charlie's sleeve.

"Charles Garland."

"Ah, yes, I have you now." She transferred her myopic stare from the sheet to the living object of her curiosity. "But you *couldn't* be any relation to Judy Garland," she said with the accusing tone of a prosecuting counsel.

"Nobody's claiming that I am, madam," said Charlie easing carefully past her. He found his way blocked again, this time by a giggling brunette with an impressive cleavage.

"I'm Gloria Horn. I've just been signed up by Concord."

"Good for you, Gloria."

"And you're Charles Garland, the one they all say looks like Michael Redgrave. Do you see the likeness?"

Charlie felt his gall rising.

"Frankly, I think I look like Charles Garland."

The girl started giggling again, and Charlie squeezed past her bouncing bosom, ready now to trample underfoot anyone who barred his way to the bar. With a sigh of relief he reached it and replenished his glass. He turned to survey the scene and cursed as he saw Shonfield slipping out of the door. Of Viner there was still no sign. He decided to forget the instruction to join the *Daily Mail* under the chandelier and to hover instead by the bar. Noticing his Brigade of Guards tie, the waiter smiled at him.

"Scots Guards myself, sir. Mess corporal at Chelsea Barracks until a couple of months ago when I got out."

"A good deal more civilized than this circus. I was a Grenadier, and I'm beginning to wonder what the hell I ever did leaving."

"In the films now, sir?"

"That's the general idea, but at this rate they'll be on their fifth remake of *Beau Geste* by the time I get anything to do."

"Can't be that bad a life, sir. Lot of nice crumpet around, by the look of it."

"If you like full bosoms and empty heads." He drained his glass and handed it to the waiter for a refill. "That's about all you'll find here."

"Not quite, I hope."

Charlie turned to see to whom the female voice belonged and found himself facing a blonde with a deep suntan.

"Clearly not," said Charlie, grinning sheepishly.

It was an attractive rather than a lovely face, meticulously made up, especially around the large brown eyes. Soft blonde hair fell not quite to the shoulders, and was held at the left temple by a diamanté clip. She wore a full-skirted ruby-red faille dress with a lace embroidered bodice which looked to Charlie to be extremely expensive.

"Paris?" suggested Charlie, looking approvingly at it.

"Balenciaga. Are you a fashion expert, by chance?"

"My wife's a model. One gets to recognize them."

438

"Would madam like a drink?" asked the waiter.

"Madam would. A Scotch on the rocks with a little water please."

"My wife's an American, too."

"And who is this American model's English husband?"

Charlie grinned and snapped to attention.

"Charles Garland. Not yet working film actor, by kind permission, or oversight, of Concord Pictures."

She held out a sun-tanned hand.

"Melissa Hooper. Hollywood screenwriter. Working, I'm happy to say."

"How nice to meet you. Are you working for us?"

"No. I'm working from Hollywood researching a script for MGM. Terry Loudon, the head of your script department, is an old friend. He asked me along here tonight."

"First Hollywood type I've ever met."

"Don't be over-impressed; I'm a very small cog in the machine."

"But a working cog, nonetheless."

"Don't despair. You wouldn't be here tonight being thrown to the Fleet Street wolves if they didn't plan to use you."

"I hope you're right. What are you working on, if that's not a secret?"

"No real secret. I'm working on a script about an American airman who escapes from an Italian prisoner-of-war camp and ends up a deserter in Switzerland after falling for a mountain guide's daughter. It's not really as awful as it sounds."

"I'm sure not. I escaped through Switzerland myself."

"No kidding! From Italy?"

"Germany, actually."

"Well, you and I must do some talking while I'm here in London. You can give me some authentic background before I head for Switzerland. Can I persuade you to lunch with me tomorrow, for example?"

"I'd be delighted. May I – "

"You're definitely my guest. Don't worry. I'll make you sing for your supper all right. I'm staying at Claridge's. I suggest we meet at The Causerie there at one. In case of emergency you can leave a message for me. Melissa Hooper. Room 202."

"I really look forward to it."

"So do I, Charles."

"Charlie, actually."

"Charlie." She glanced at his full glass of Scotch. "I'll be expecting total recall at lunch tomorrow, so no hangover please." She flashed him a dazzling smile and walked away.

"Actors 'ave all the luck, don't they, sir?" The waiter grinned at Charlie. "Nice bit, that one. Hollywood an' all."

"I'm inclined to agree. And on that happy note, I think I'll make good my escape. Thanks for your excellent service; they must miss you at Chelsea."

Out of the corner of his eye Charlie saw Tommy Hull heading in his direction.

"Hell! I'll never get out of this place," he muttered.

"Ah, Charlie! There you are. I have a whole bevy of people who want to meet you. Bring your drink, old boy."

Charlie sighed, then, fixing a dutiful smile on his face, fell in behind the head of press relations.

Fortified by a couple of pink gins at the Guards Club *en route* to Claridge's, Charlie presented himself punctually at The Causerie and found Melissa Hooper waiting for him at the table, reading a magazine. Dressed in bottle-green silk with pearls, she once again radiated the sensual elegance that Charlie had found so immediately seductive the evening before. She wasted no time over small talk. Over cocktails Charlie was requested to give a brief account of his life, both in and out of war, and then, over chicken crêpes and wine, she interrogated him in detail on his escape from Germany, jotting down an occasional note on a pad by her plate.

Charlie was impressed. Obviously there was a very sharp mind behind the chic exterior. He put her age at somewhere between thirty-five and forty, and money and self confidence, he concluded, had furnished her with the wherewithal to transform what he imagined might have once been a rather plump, not very striking-looking girl into the exceedingly attractive woman.

As they drank coffee, Melissa talked about herself. She had been born and raised in San Diego, the daughter of a prominent local attorney, had majored in English at a small private college in Southern California, and had then gone to work for a local newspaper. At twenty-six she had married a screenwriter three days after their first meeting, and had joined him in Santa Monica. Impressed by her writing ability he had taken her on as his full-time collaborator, but the childless marriage had ended after four years, in 1940, when he blew his brains out on hearing that he had incurable leukaemia. The trauma had driven her to alcohol and near-suicide herself, but by the time the Japanese had blasted Pearl Harbor, she had pulled herself together and gone to work in Navy public relations, writing recruiting movies for the WAVES. In 1944 she had been hired by Paramount's script department but had left a year later when her father died leaving her, an only child, with sufficient money to set herself up as an independent scriptwriter. It was, she said, the best decision she had ever made, and the rewards had so far proved handsome.

Charlie was disarmed by the candour with which she recounted her life story, and found himself encouraged to fill in some of the gaps he had left in his own account, especially the agonies of self-doubt that afflicted him at this time as he waited and waited for his own big decision to bear some justifying fruit. Disappointing and offending his parents had been a painful price to pay, and had it not been for Margot's support, he could never have taken the step.

"My sister American must be one helluva woman," said Melissa. And then, to Charlie's mild discomfort, she added: "but she shouldn't let you drink so much."

She signed for the lunch while Charlie stared into the bottom of his coffee cup.

"I'd like to help you, Charlie, if I can. I'll talk to a few of my friends in the movie business over here. If your Mr Neumann has taught you anything at all about acting, you ought to be getting good parts soon. You fit nicely into today's popular image of the solid, handsome good-guy Englishman."

"You think so?" Charlie began to perk up.

"Just don't try to be the swashbuckling type like Stewart Granger. Speaking of whom, would you care to escort me to his new movie this afternoon?"

"Well, yes, of course, I'd be delighted."

Charlie silently thanked his lucky stars that he had just enough money left to pay for two good seats and one taxi fare.

"The afternoon's on me as well, Charlie. Don't look so worried!"

She smiled sweetly at him, and he felt himself blushing puce as they left the restaurant.

When Charlie got home that evening, Mrs Watts informed him that his wife would be working late and would not be home for dinner.

"There's a nice macaroni and cheese if you'd like it."

"No thanks, Wattie. I think I'll go out."

Since the fair Melissa Hooper had spared him the expenditure of his last thirty shillings, he saw no reason why some should not be devoted to sausage rolls and drinks and a friendly chat with Hattie the barmaid.

"Could you read Julia a story before going?"

"Of course."

Charlie went to his daughter's room. The little girl was sitting up in bed, and the sight of her startled him.

"Wattie!" he shouted. The housekeeper appeared in the doorway. "Why the hell has her hair been cut so short? It's dreadful! She looks like a boy!"

"Mrs Garland thought she'd try a new style. Julia likes it, don't you darling?"

Julia nodded assent a little uncertainly.

"Well, I think it's awful. In future I wish to be consulted before anything as drastic as that is done to my daughter."

Mrs Watts shrugged her shoulders and beat a retreat, while Charlie sat himself on the edge of the bed and sighed.

"Come on, let's read a story, little one. Which one do you want?"

"*The Tale of Peter Rabbit.*"

"Excellent choice."

He reached up to a bookshelf above the bed and pulled the Beatrix Potter volume from the row of books.

When Charlie returned home shortly after closing time, he found Margot writing letters at her desk in the drawing room.

"Where the hell were you?" he asked.

"Working," she said without looking up. "By the sound of it I don't need to ask where the hell were *you*. How much money into Hattie's till this time?"

"How I spend my money is my business. On the other hand, what you do to my daugher's hair is definitely *not* exclusively yours. You've ruined it!"

"It is not ruined. We were going to cut it this next summer anyway. I'd told you that already."

"Well bloody well ask me next time."

Margot spoke again with sweet reasonableness.

"I suggest you go to bed, Charlie. You've obviously had a tiring day and evening."

He hovered over her as she sat at the desk.

"Love letters? No, of course, I forgot. You only like those pansy photographers and dress designers. Do they wear their own dresses at home?"

Margot put down her pen, and still without looking up spoke slowly through clenched teeth.

"Charlie, I don't want a row with you when you're drunk. If you wish to insult me, wait until morning. I shall also have something to say to you then."

He turned and walked towards the drinks tray.

"No, Charlie!" she said firmly. "You are *not* having another drink."

Charlie paid no attention and picked up a whisky glass. Margot sprang to her feet and dashed across the room.

"Put that glass down!" she shouted, tears now welling in her eyes.

Charlie picked up the whisky bottle with his free hand, and as Margot made a lunge for it, he swung it behind his back and put up his left hand, with the empty glass in it, to ward off her attack. The glass caught her on the right cheekbone, splintered, and she felt a stab of pain as the broken edge tore her cheek. She staggered back pressing the palm of her hand to the wound as blood began to run down to her jaw. Charlie stood frozen to the spot.

"You shouldn't have done that, Margot," he stammered.

Margot, panting with the effort to regain control over herself, fixed him with a contemptuous glare.

"You seem to forget, you miserable, drunken bastard, that my face is just about our only livelihood at this moment. Or maybe that doesn't bother you."

She turned and walked hurriedly from the room. Locking herself in the bathroom, she began to administer first aid to the cut on her cheek. Mercifully it appeared to be not too deep despite the difficulty she was having in stopping the bleeding. She would have to go to her doctor first thing in the morning, and for the time being an adhesive bandage would have to suffice. She dabbed cold water on the wound until the bleeding slowed, and applied a strip of bandage. She then went into the bedroom and undressed. Charlie had not joined her by the time, with eyes still wet from silent weeping, she fell into a troubled sleep.

Margot returned from a visit to her doctor the next morning much comforted by his assurance that the injury would leave only a barely perceptible hair-line scar, if any at all. Fortunately it was close to the weekend, which meant she would have to cancel one booking before she was able to remove the bandage and camouflage the healing wound with carefully applied cosmetics.

Charlie, who had spent an uncomfortable night on the drawing room sofa, was up and dressed by the time she returned. He came to meet her in the hall as she entered.

"Darling, let's sit and talk for a moment," he said. "Please!"

"Fine. I want to talk to you too," she responded coldly.

He followed her into the drawing room and shut the door.

"I want to say how sorry I am about what happened last night. I really am desperately sorry, and it won't happen again, I promise."

"You're dead right, Charlie. It won't happen again because the marriage is over. I've had enough; more than enough."

Charlie gaped at her.

"Over? I don't understand."

"Yes, over or is that word not in the actor's vocabulary these days?"

"But I was just about to give you a piece of good news."

"Oh, I thought you already had: that you weren't going to slash me up with a broken glass any more when you get drunk."

"No, listen! Everything's going to be all right. Viner just called. I'm being tested for a good film role the day after tomorrow. It's a Concord picture, a comedy about soldiers returning from the war. If I get the part, which he says is practically certain, we start rehearsals in a week and location shooting a couple of weeks later. The long wait is over!"

"I'm happy for you, Charlie, but it doesn't alter my decision. My mind is made up. I'll talk to a lawyer and find out how best it can be handled, but I want a divorce, and that's final."

Charlie sank into an armchair, white as a sheet.

"You can't do that, Margot," he said faintly.

"Oh yes I can."

"You've got no proper grounds."

"I'll find some. Maybe your blonde girlfriend can help."

Charlie looked up. "What blonde girlfriend, for Christ's sake?"

"Don't take me for a fool, Charlie. You obviously never learned to keep extra-marital activities out of the public eye. It saves an awful lot of trouble."

"Just what the hell are you getting at?"

"What I'm getting at is that it's damned silly to walk around the West End arm in arm with a blonde who isn't your wife and with a silly smirk on your face! You're not the Invisible Man, you know." She strode to the door. "I hope you two enjoyed the movie," she added. "But it wasn't very smart of you to pick a theatre just two doors down from my agency. Now I'm taking Julia to the dentist."

Charlie followed her quickly to the door.

"Do you really mean to tell me that you want a divorce because I took a Hollywood screenwriter to a see a film after she'd very kindly given me lunch to talk about my future?"

"That's not the reason I want a divorce, and you know it. It's not your stupidity, it's your drinking. I just can't go on living with a violent drunk, and I'm not having Julia living under the same roof with one either."

"All right, Margot! Have it your own way," he said. "I will leave today."

"Don't play the martyr; I'm not throwing you out on the spot. I'm simply giving you notice that I want this marriage ended. If it can be done amiably, so much the better, and you can go on living here until you've made other arrangements."

"And what if I don't agree to give you a divorce?"

"Then we'll just have to live apart while remaining married, which isn't a very tidy arrangement."

"Damn you, Margot! Do you realize what you're doing?"

"I do indeed, Charlie. I've stood by you as long as I can. Your performance last night was the last straw; that's all."

Charlie pushed his way roughly past her, dashed across the hall and left the apartment, slamming the front door hard behind him.

As on other occasions when she felt in need of moral support, Margot turned to Marion and Felix, who immediately agreed to meet her for lunch at the Berkeley.

"Say no more," said Marion, when she saw the strip of sticking plaster on Margot's cheek. "If that's what it's come to, you have no alternative but to ring down the curtain on the marriage."

Felix was somewhat more cautious.

"You're absolutely sure that you don't love him enough any more to see whether the shock of realizing what he's done to you may pull him together?"

"I can't help being fond of him, and I'm also very sorry for him, but I just cannot go on in this marriage."

"But now that he's finally got his first film part," persisted Felix, "don't you think that might change him for the better? Forgive me, darling, but you've got to be absolutely sure."

Margot looked from one to the other and spoke the words slowly.

"I am absolutely sure."

"Then it's settled," said Marion, patting Margot on the hand. "The question now is: what grounds? Cruelty? Adultery?"

"I don't want to talk about that just yet," said Margot wearily. "The basic decision has been taken; let's rest on that for the time being, and maybe you could order me another drink."

When Margot reached home late in the afternoon, Mrs Watts informed her that Charlie had arrived back at midday, had packed a suitcase, and left again.

Margot sighed.

"Come into the drawing room for a moment, Wattie dear," she said. "I have to explain to you what's going on."

"You were lucky to find me home, Charlie," said David Hughes-Webb, taking his suitcase from him at the door of his Earl's Court flat. "I had a wisdom tooth out yesterday and didn't feel like working today. Come on in and make yourself at home. I imagine you want a whopper of a drink."

"You're a real Good Samaritan, David," said Charlie sinking down onto the sofa.

"You can sleep on that for a few nights until you find something better. I'd say stay as long as you like, but it would rather cramp my style with April."

"April? April Batty Astor?"

"None other, old boy. The sweetest fuck I've known. Whisky and soda?"

447

"Yes thanks."

"So the dazzling Margot Moore gave you the old heave-ho! You must have been a terribly bad boy. Were you caught in flagrante what-not?"

"No. She just decided she'd had enough of the marriage. Typical bloody American. They don't think they've made it in society until they've been in and out of two or three marriages."

"Well, I won't probe, old boy, but if there's some gorgeous girl in your life, don't be shy about introducing her to the Good Samaritan."

Charlie grinned. "That reminds me. May I use your telephone?"

"Help yourself."

Charlie called Claridge's and left a message for Melissa Hooper to call him at the Hughes-Webb number when she returned in the afternoon.

"I met this Hollywood screenwriter at the press party the day before yesterday. Melissa Hooper. Do you know her? A friend of Terry Loudon."

Hughes-Webb shook his head. "But if she's a friend of Terry's, she probably rogers like a rattlesnake. That's his condition of friendship. What's she like?"

"Very good-looking, elegant and probably ten years older than me. She bought me lunch at Claridge's yesterday to pick my brains about POW camps and escaping. She's working on a script for MGM."

"You lucky sod. Did you do any brain-picking in her room?"

"No. We went to the cinema. That's all."

"What a waste. Are you going to see her again?"

"I hope so. I just left a message for her."

"I'll be back at Denham tomorrow. If you want to bring her here during the day, you're welcome. Just don't block up the loo with used freddies."

"Christ, David! Is there ever anything else on that brain of yours?"

"You forget, old boy, that I did the full five-year stretch at Oflag XIV C. I've got a lot of catching up to do. Finish your drink and we'll go down and have a bite and a pint at my local, and you can tell me all about the par you're supposed to be getting. The story sounds positively juvenile."

Charlie was staring at the floor, a look of boyish bewilderment on his face.

"Let me have another Scotch first, will you?" he said, still not looking up. "I think it's just hitting me what the hell's happened this morning."

And then he dissolved into tears.

Hughes-Webb answered the telephone in the early evening when Melissa Hooper called back.

"He's sleeping at the moment; he got monumentally drunk this afernoon, I'm afraid."

He then went on to explain why, and Melissa, after expressing her concern asked him not to disturb Charlie, but to have him call her anytime at Claridge's that evening. If Charlie felt up to dining with her at the hotel, he was more than welcome.

"If he does join you, please don't keep him up too late," urged Hughes-Webb. "He's reading for his first part tomorrow morning."

Charlie eventually awoke, feeling like death, towards nine o'clock that evening. After drowning a cup of strong tea, he called Melissa and told her that he would have loved to dine with her but that right now he felt in no shape to stir from his friend's apartment.

"I really am dreadfully sorry to hear what has happened," she said.

"Bit of a bloody mess, I must say."

"Is this a temporary break, do you think?"

"It doesn't sound like it. She seems to have made up her mind that it's all over."

"Are you very unhappy about it, Charlie?"

"I don't know yet; it's only just hit me. What I feel now is anger. I feel like an unwanted toy thrown away by a capricious child."

"I'm leaving tomorrow night on the boat-train for Paris and will be going on to Geneva forty-eight hours later to do some local research on the script. Would you like to come with me?"

There was a long pause, then eventually he spoke.

"I wish I could but if I get the part tomorrow, I'll have to hang around here for rehearsals to start."

"Then why not just accompany me to Paris and return here when I go to Geneva? Don't worry about the cost; I'll cover that. It'll do you good to get away from London for a couple of days."

"It'll rather set the seal on my situation, won't it?" said Charlie uncertainly.

"I gathered from what you just told me that it was already set. But if you'd be nervous about it – "

"No, no. I'll come."

"Well then, get a good rest tonight. No more hitting the bottle. Good luck with the reading tomorrow morning, and come and pick me up at Claridge's at six. I'll have your ticket. Have you got a passport?"

"Yes."

"All right then, Charlie dear. I'm thrilled you're coming. We'll make it a fun-filled two days."

When she rang off, Charlie filled in the details of the conversation for David.

"You lucky bugger, Charlie! Not only will you get to dip your wick into the good lady, but in Paris to boot, and all for free. Some bastards have all the luck. Now don't tell me you're not enjoying the single life, old boy. And this is only Day One!"

As Charlie lay pondering on what he had let himself in for, Margot was telling a stunned Sir Walter, who had called to speak to his son, that the marriage was finally on the rocks and that Charlie had disappeared into thin air. The conversation was brief, and Sir Walter's tone far from sympathetic.

"He'll be back," he said firmly, after recovering his composure, "and mind you let him into the flat. You've both obviously behaved in a very silly and headstrong fashion, and the sooner you come to your senses and make up, the better. There's absolutely no question of a divorce."

"I'm afraid there is," said Margot frostily, "but I can see that this is not the moment to discuss it. I will let you know if and when I hear from Charlie."

And with that, she rang off.

The following morning, Margot received a handwritten note from Charlie, slipped under the door. In it he announced that he was leaving for the continent that evening for a stay of forty-eight hours in connection with his film role. On his return to London, he would be staying with friends and would get in touch with her to arrange a discussion of their immediate future.

Margot shrugged her shoulders and went off to work. There was nothing she could do about the situation, even if she had felt inclined to do something. The ball was now squarely in Charlie's court, and she would wait to see what he did with it.

What he eventually did with it came as a shock even to her. For five days she heard nothing from him; then, on the sixth day he called and told her in a quaking voice that he had come to a milestone decision: Melissa Hooper had invited him to accompany her to Hollywood to try his luck in movies there.

"I thought you were supposed to be going into the movies over here," said Margot, trying to conceal her astonishment.

"I didn't get the part after all."

"But I thought it was a certainty! Don't tell me you drank yourself out of it." There was a silence. "All right Charlie. It's your life. Just remember you have a daughter, and I think it would be nice if you came and said goodbye to her before you run off with your girlfriend. That's all I have to say."

She put the receiver down, and then called his parents. It was his mother who answered, and Margot told her simply that their son was going to Hollywood with a girlfriend and would probably not be coming back. There was now no way in which the marriage could be saved and a divorce avoided. She then politely rang off, leaving Lady Garland fighting to find words adequate to the awful moment. Her next call was to Felix Beale.

"Felix, dear. I need a stiff drink and a good lunch, and above all, your soothing company. The Ritz at one?"

"To hell with Charlie Garland!" said Felix Beale. "You're well rid of him, my angel, if you'll permit me to say so, and this lunch is not going to be a maudlin affair, raking over the ashes of a dead marriage. I've got something much more important to talk about."

A waiter brought Margot a whisky-sour.

"Good. Distraction is just what I need."

Beale pulled some newspaper and magazine clippings from an envelope and handed them to Margot.

"Christian Dior," he said, savouring each syllable. "The man's an absolute bloody genius! Look what he's done! Turned the fashion industry on its head and proclaimed the supremacy of Paris."

The clippings which Margot now pored over were reports, with artists' sketches and a few photographs, of the collection unveiled just three days ago in Paris by a young French designer of whom few people, if anybody, outside the Paris fashion world had ever heard until now.

"Isn't it too exciting for words!" gushed Felix. "He's kicked out the window that awful square, spare masculine wartime cut and given us instead this glorious feminine shape."

Margot looked at the illustrations and saw immediately why Felix was so excited: natural shoulders, full bust, wasp waist and long, full skirts with hems only about a foot from the floor. After so many years of austere self-denial, this was truly a feast of luscious feminity that Dior was offering.

"It's stunning, Felix," she said. "They're going to love it over here."

"Of course they will." He took a sip from his pink gin and beamed again. "Of course, we can count on this idiotic government to condemn the use of so much material during this interminable and quite unnecessary shortage, but if the 'New Look' is sufficiently publicized over here, the manufacturers and designers are simply not going to be stopped. If the French who were under occupation all through the war can do it, so can we!"

"I certainly hope so."

"Margot, sweetheart, you're going to look just divine in Dior's clothes. We have got to rush you over there and do a splendid layout for *Vogue*. I'm going to call them

452

today and tell them that they absolutely must have you to do it."

"Now, that's what I've been waiting to hear!" said Margot happily.

"And you can see your Edmond whatever-his-name-is."

Margot wagged a finger at him. "Now, now, Felix, don't rush me, you wicked old thing!"

Beale raised his hands in surrender.

"Forgive me, sweet child. Business before pleasure, I agree."

"Of course, I'm not ruling out combining the two," she said, modestly lowering her eyes and restraining her smile.

With Europe gripped in the cruellest winter since 1848, so the experts assured everyone, Margot was not overjoyed at the prospects of a Channel crossing, but the opportunity to do the Dior layout to which *Vogue* instantly agreed, was one surely not to be missed. It would be professionally helpful to her, would take her mind off the upheaval in her domestic life, and would, last but not least, provide her with the chance to find out whether Edmond still felt anything for her. And vice versa.

35

In the lobby of the Hôtel Meurice, Margot sat flipping through the pages of a fashion magazine, trying to compose herself as the moment when Edmond would appear drew nearer. She had slept late that morning, exhausted by two hectic days of work on the Dior collection. Felix Beale, as was his wont, had insisted on exterior locations for his photographs, and she had been rushed by taxi from one place to another, each time in a different costume, until *Vogue*'s and Beale's requirements had been met. She had, however, been handsomely rewarded. Monsieur Dior himself, confessing to being totally enchanted by *"la ravissante américaine"*, had pressed upon her, at a fraction of his quoted price, a day suit and a short taffeta evening dress, with the urgent request that she be seen wearing them as often as she dared. Beale had moaned at the prospect of paying a king's ransom in customs' duty at Dover, but Margot was savouring the delight too much to be concerned about that. She agreed with the couturier that his "New Look" might have been made especially for her, and as she now sat waiting for Edmond, wearing the grey wasp-waisted suit with its full, pleated skirt, she felt confident that he would find her appearance stunning.

She had called his Paris apartment number on her first evening in the city, and had been disappointed to learn from the housekeeper that *"monsieur le colonel"* was in Bordeaux for the remainder of the week. She left her name and hotel address, asking that he be given them in the event that he should call the apartment.

Within twenty minutes he had called back.

"What a splendid surprise, Margot! I forbid you to leave Paris until I get there. I will leave on the train tomorrow night and we will have lunch the following day."

"I'd love that, Edmond, but are you sure you can get away from Bordeaux as soon as that? In any case, I was supposed to be leaving for London tomorrow night."

"No, I beg you to stay. I have to be here for an important political meeting tomorrow afternoon, but I will definitely be in Paris Thursday morning. If you will permit me, you will be my guest at your hotel for as long as you can stay."

"No really, Edmond, you don't have to do that."

"But I insist. I will call you on Thursday morning as soon as I arrive. Now you must excuse me; I have to rush to an appointment in Bordeaux. *A très bientôt, ma belle!*"

She had had no alternative but to accept, although she realized when she rang off that she would be missing a theatre party with Marion on Thursday evening. Well, Marion would understand, and at least she would not be absent from any photo bookings.

"I'm very glad to hear it, dear one," Felix had said when she told him of her change of plans and the reason for it. "It or rather he, should do you a world of good."

"I wish you'd stay long enough to meet him, Felix."

"I wish I could, but I have masses of work at home. Besides," he'd added, grinning broadly, "I'm sure you're going to give me plenty more chances to do so."

"*Bonjour*, Margot."

"Edmond!"

She jumped to her feet, and he bent to kiss her hand just as she leaned forward expecting a cheek to cheek embrace, so that her chin scraped his brow. They both laughed self-consciously as he straightened up to kiss her on both cheeks, and then he stepped back to feast his eyes on her.

"*Ravissante comme toujours!*"

"And you are as handsome as ever, Edmond. You've put on a little weight, and it suits you."

She noticed the poppy-red thread of the Légion d'Honneur on the edge of his left lapel. His thick, dark hair had, as she recalled from the photograph in the magazine, receded a little, and there was a thin purple scar, about three inches long, curving like an inverted eyebrow beneath his right eye.

He looked at his watch.

"I have a table at Pré Catalan, in the Bois de Boulogne. Shall we go?"

"It sounds wonderful, and I'm hungry."

"So, you are a famous mannequin now," he said as they settled into the back seat of a taxi. "I see you are wearing Dior. It becomes you."

"Thank you."

"He came at the right moment upon the scene to cheer us all up. Paris is a rather gloomy place these days. But while you are here, we will make it sparkle! Tonight I will take you to hear a marvellous new singer called Yves Montand. He's a protégé of Edith Piaf, and he sings at Les Ambassadeurs. You'll like him. Then tomorrow evening, if you can stay – "

"Edmond, I really do have to get back tomorrow. I have booked a sleeper on the evening boat-train."

"Well, that still gives us the day. There is a ceremony at the British Embassy in the afternoon where the Ambassador will be decorating a number of our wartime *résistants* for helping the British, and my man from Lachaise, Luc Grenier, is among them. You should come with me. Before that we will have a little lunch at my apartment – Josette is a resourceful cook in these days of continued rationing and happily my household is never short of wine! – and you may want to do some shopping in the morning."

"Edmond, you are overwhelming me with your hospitality. You really didn't have to go to so much trouble."

He smiled at her. "After four years of not seeing you, you begrudge me forty-eight hours?"

"Of course not."

As the cab sped up the Champs-Elysées, Margot fell silent for a while, staring out the window. Her thoughts were leaping too far ahead for comfort. Supposing she was married to the man sitting next to her, and this city was her city? What would she really be feeling now? They'd probably be on their way to lunch with some important political figure, in their own chauffeur-driven car, and they'd be discussing little Pierre-André's end-of-term report, or how boring the Marquis de So-and-So's dinner had been.

"Edmond, it really is good to see you again, and I'm longing for you to tell me over lunch just what you're doing now."

"And you have to tell me too. I should be polite and ask you first how your husband and little daughter are."

Margot had no wish to drop the bombshell in the back of the cab. That could wait until they were both mellowed a little by a glass or two of wine.

"They're fine," she said. "Julia's the light of my life."

Through the first part of their lunch, and as the comforting red wine began to relax her, Margot encouraged Edmond to do the talking, and when he had finished recounting his war experiences after leaving England, she congratulated him on his fine record and on having emerged unscathed.

"Except for this." He tapped the scar on his cheek.

"Yes, that. What was it?"

He grinned. "A flying champagne glass in a Strasburg hotel."

Margot laughed with him.

"I left the army," he went on, "and returned to Bordeaux to find my father dying of cancer, a secret he'd kept from me. I promised him I would take care of my mother and the vineyard, but that I also intended entering politics. I argued that France needed the firm, strong leadership which de Gaulle could give but he'd never changed his mind about him and was shocked that I wanted to work for him. But then, on the morning that he died, he gave me his blessing and told me to do what I believed was right. He smiled through his pain and said that he always thought our name looked better on a bottle of fine wine than on a ballot paper. Dear Papa! Then he just closed his eyes and died. I miss him terribly.

He was a wonderful father, and I'm so sorry you never met him."

"Believe me, so am I," she said softly.

Edmond reached across the table and placed a hand on top of hers for a brief moment.

"I'm sure of one thing; he would have loved you."

Margot stared down at her plate.

"Do go on, Edmond."

"Well, after we buried Father, I went up to Bayeux to hear the General's great speech on the need for a strong new constitution. The one he outlined was far better than the one we eventually got. I immediately started working for the nomination as a Union Gaullist candidate for a seat in the new National Assembly. I got the nomination in a consituency in the Gironde, near home. The party did badly in the November elections, and of course I was not elected. But de Gaulle was not about to give up. I came to Paris to talk to some of his aides, and they told me that the General was certain that America would never use the atom bomb against the Russians and that the Russians would therefore surely overrun Europe, just as Hitler did."

"Just look what they've done to Poland, and what they have tried to do in Persia. De Gaulle is not alone among the Western statesmen who sense the danger, but he's certainly the only leader in France who's ready to sound the alarm good and loud. He's not spoken in public since November, but now he's planning a huge personal campaign. He'll lash out at the French Communist Party and remind his audiences that the Red Army is only three hundred miles away from our borders. He says we must lay aside our differences with America, and accept her military protection as well as her economic aid, and if de Gaulle's prepared to say *that* about America, you can be sure he feels we're near to war."

Margot studied Edmond's face with a mixture of fascination and alarm. Edmond the Gaullist in civilian life seemed just as much a fanatic, if not more so, than Edmond the Gaullist in uniform.

"You really believe he'll return to power?"

"Of course! You just watch the municipal elections later

this year. That will be the first step when we gain control of the cities and the towns. Next will be the National Assembly and the reins of power."

Margot smiled. "I find your political passion as awesome as ever."

"You don't have to be afraid; at bottom all makers of good wine are peaceful, convivial types. But I've been talking too much. Now I want to hear all about you."

Margot took a deep breath.

"Well, Edmond, you might as well get the big news right away." She swallowed a little wine and watched his expression which registered no change whatsoever. "My marriage is over. Charlie has run off to Hollywood with a woman screenwriter, and God knows if he'll ever come back. He'd got himself put under contract to a British studio as an actor, but he drank himself out of his first role. That was his trouble: drink, leading to violence. I couldn't take it any more."

Edmond had kept his eyes fixed on his empty plate all the while that she spoke, an embarrassed look on his face.

"I am very, very sorry, Margot," he said almost inaudibly without looking up.

"I am too, Edmond. I put a lot of effort into trying to help him make something of his life after he came out of the army, but he let himself down all the way along the line. I wanted him to go into politics, but he was changed when he came home from the war. I had thought that a handsome young man of his background, with a Military Cross and a distinguished politician for a father, would be just what the Conservative Party needed, but I had not realized how much the war had changed him. His father got him a job in a stock-broking business, but he got fired from that for drinking. Then he went into real estate, and then a wartime friend got him a screen test. I supported him to the hilt when his parents objected violently to his going into movies because I thought that here at last was something that he really wanted to do and could do well. But the months of waiting for his first screen part were too much for him, and he went to pieces again. I felt sorry for him in a way, but I couldn't go on living with him. He'd shattered too many of my dreams."

"When did this happen?"

Margot looked at him and bit on her lip.

"Not quite three weeks ago."

"*Mon Dieu!* As recently as that! My poor Margot, you must still be suffering the shock."

"No, not really. I'm sad that my Julia has been deprived of her father, but I'm otherwise rather glad he's gone to Hollywood. It should convince his parents that the marriage really is at an end and that I'm entitled to a divorce. At the moment they're kidding themselves that he'll come back and apologize and we'll start over. But as far as I'm concerrned, that's just not on the cards. I will, however, wait a few months until it's crystal clear to everyone that he's not coming back. Then no one can accuse me of rushing him to the divorce court before he's had time to repent and come home."

"You think he will marry this lady?"

"Probably. I don't see him surviving there alone."

"And you will go on living in London?"

"Oh, I think so. That's where I'm now well established in the modelling business and where I have my friends. I thought briefly about going back to New York, but the idea doesn't attract me enough to go through the upheaval, at least at present."

"Well, I think you should consider coming here. This is where the most exciting things are happening in the fashion world."

Margot laughed. "I'm sure I'll be working over here from time to time on the collections, but I don't think I'd survive living here. You know how inadequate my French is."

"You would learn quickly enough."

"I suppose so, but – "

"Think about it, at least."

Margot smiled and reached in her purse for her cigarette case.

"When will you come and visit me at Lachaise-Laurent? Can you come this time?"

"No, I told you I have to get back to Julia and my work.

But I would love to come sometime, on a future working trip."

Edmond struck a match to light her cigarette.

"Tell me, Edmond," she said, after the first puff, "why did you never respond to that message I left for you at the French Club in London before you left for Normandy?"

"I never got the message."

"You called that lady who ran it?"

"I may have done, but I can't remember. I know I never went to the club again. We had no more leave after D-Day, so I couldn't have seen you anyway."

He could have at least called me, thought Margot, but decided it was pointless to question him any further. It no longer mattered that her ego had been pricked at the time.

"How about coffee and a cognac?" he asked. "They're still stingy with the coffee, as in all restaurants, but the taste here is about the best in Paris. Afterwards I will deliver you by cab to wherever you wish to begin your afternoon. A gallery, maybe? With this wretched newspaper strike, you just have to look at the billboards on the streets to know what there is to see."

"I'll go to the Louvre, I think. There's so much there that I want to see. Then I can walk back to the hotel and rest up a bit before our evening together."

"Excellent. I will fetch you at half-past seven. We will have a glass of champagne at my apartment before we go to dine and hear Montand."

He summoned a waiter and ordered coffee and cognac.

"Tell me, Margot, do you have other friends here in Paris?"

"Apart from acquaintances in the fashion business, the only people I know here are the British Ambassador, Duff Cooper and Lady Diana. But they are really friends of my parents-in-law. Connie de Creçy went to live in Nice when Henri died in 1941, and then got out before the Germans occupied the rest of France and has lived in Palm Beach ever since. You remember I told you during the war that I had been born in their apartment on the avenue Hoche."

"Well, since you know the ambassador, why don't you accompany me tomorrow?"

Margot laughed a little nervously.

"I don't think that would be very wise. My appearance with you would almost certainly become known to the Garlands back in London, and that I do *not* want to have happen."

"Am I that notorious?" he said, smiling.

"Let's just say that until the divorce is through, I must be seen to be behaving impeccably. Walter and Cynthia would *not* regard my turning up at the embassy on your arm as impeccable behaviour, I'm afraid."

"Then I must bow to your proper sense of caution, my dear. And you are certain that Charlie will not come back and that there will be a divorce?"

"I know my Charlie. He might regret what he's done, but he wouldn't be able to bring himself to face the music back in London. His father would murder him. Besides, I think he knows I'd never take him back even if he did return."

The coffee and cognac arrived.

"Let's not talk any more about Charlie," she said. "Tell me more about your political plans."

Edmond sniffed at his cognac and took a sip before replying.

"You know me, Margot. One defeat at the polls has only whetted my appetite. I'll get to the National Assembly one day, and I'm not one of those people who enters politics with no ambition to get to the top."

"Good for you, Edmond! That's what I tried to get Charlie to see, but he didn't want to take the first step."

"You've always wanted to be in the thick of politics, haven't you?"

"Yes, I confess I like being where the power is." She smiled. "But I'm a hard-working fashion model now. I just don't know how I can be involved in British politics. I still have my friends among the politicians, but my ambitions for Charlie were what was really driving me. Once I knew he had no interest, I just became a spectator."

"There's always France," said Edmond, staring into his cognac.

"And you, you mean? It's a little early to be talking like that, I think."

"But the idea is not without its attractions."

"I really hadn't given it any thought."

Edmond raised an eyebrow and smiled, confirming her fear that she had sounded totally unconvincing.

Later that afternoon as she wandered through the galleries of the Louvre trying to concentrate on the masterpieces she loved so much and hadn't seen since a vacation visit to Paris in 1935, her thoughts kept darting away to Edmond. In the Galérie Medicis, amongst the Flemish and Dutch works, she thought seriously of staying on in Paris for a few more days, and to hell with her work in London that week! She wanted to speed up the process of getting to know the new Edmond. But later, standing in wonder before Giotto's St Francis of Assïsi in the Grande Galerie, her homage to the Italian master was interrupted by a signal suddenly flashing in her mind: get back to London! Give yourself time to think away from the man!

When she got back to her hotel room, undressed and lay down on the bed, she found that her mind had not changed. She must stick to her plan and go home the next day. And if Edmond suggested, which she was certain he would, that they renew their physical relationship before she left, she was simply going to say no. Once that started, she would probably never get out of Paris. Moreover, the layout she was booked to do for Victor Stiebel the day after tomorrow was just too important to miss, and her reputation for reliability too valuable to damage. Tonight, you've got to try to stand firm, she told herself. Just because he's your former lover, you don't have to drop your panties for him on the first date in four years. Show him he's got to earn his way back into them. After all, who was it who took the initiative in making contact again after the war? He'd made no attempt to trace me, so why should I hand myself to him on a plate now? Next time, maybe. No, next time, certainly, provided he keeps in touch with me in the meantime.

At seven-thirty promptly, Edmond collected her from the hotel and drove her in a cab to the rue de la Faisanderie on the edge of the Bois de Boulogne. The size and elegance of the Lemonnier family apartment on the second floor of a fine nineteenth-century building almost took her breath away.

"I adore tapestries," she said dreamily, as, champagne glass in hand, she accompanied her host on a tour of the spacious residence.

"This one here was woven in Brussels. It's late fifteenth-century," he said, pausing in front of an imposing depiction of a sylvan hunting scene covering one entire wall of the room. "But wait until you see the tapestries at Lachaise. They are even better." They passed on through the apartment until they reached his bedroom. "Heavens, Edmond, what a bed!"

"Well, as you've noted already, my father was an enthusiastic collector of nineteenth-century Empire furniture. Most of it used to be in the apartment in Bordeaux, but I sold the place and moved the contents here."

Margot stared with an amused smile at the massive sample of Napoleonic craftsmanship, a vast double bed with elaborate gilded mouldings and decorative pilasters which looked to her more like a stately horse-drawn sleigh from one of the tsars' winter palaces.

"It was made for one of Napoleon's marshals. I was born in it," he added importantly, leaving Margot with the impression that it had thus acquired a sanctity which overrode any considerations of mere comfort. He looked at his watch.

"We should be going," he said.

"Not until you've given me one more glass of champagne. I'm enjoying myself for the first time in weeks – no, months."

He took her by the arm. "That makes me very happy, then."

They returned to the salon and Margot took a second, more leisurely tour of the big room, gazing in awe at the gilt-framed paintings.

"I'm surprised Goering didn't make off with them during the Occupation."

"They weren't here. We hid them in cellars in Bordeaux well before Paris fell."

"It must be wonderful to live amongst such beauty. My grandfather has some nice English watercolours at Adamswood but nothing, of course, to touch this."

Edmond put a hand on her shoulder.

"Someone as beautiful as you should always live amongst beautiful things."

"It would be nice," she said, staring at a Sisley snow scene. "Shouldn't we be going to dinner?" she added, draining her glass.

They dined well in an unpretentious but rewarding restaurant on the Left Bank, on the edge of the Champ de Mars, where Edmond was clearly a favoured customer, after which they repaired to the Ambassadeurs to drink more champagne and listen to Paris's latest nightclub hit, the Italian-born ex-factory hand, Yves Montand, singing his passionate working-men's songs with a lean and hungry look and much use of his expressive hands.

"I think he's wonderful," whispered Margot snuggling close to Edmond.

"He's very political, if you can understand the words," said Edmond. "The clientele here cannot much like what he is singing about; they just like his music and his voice."

Margot stifled a laugh. "You're so serious, Edmond. I always liked your voice better than your politics!"

He squeezed her hand. "Then you don't understand my politics, *ma belle américaine!*"

"Then teach me," she whispered in his ear.

The song ended, applause broke out, and the singer took a break. Margot was beginning to feel the succession of champagne on wine going to her head, but she made no protests when Edmond reached for the bottle in the cooler beside him and refilled her glass.

"You have to give me the chance to teach you. You seemed to learn rather fast in London."

"Oh, I'm pretty bright when it comes to understanding politics." She was aware that she was slurring her words somewhat, so she concentrated hard on what she wanted to say next. "Tell me one thing Edmond. One thing I've always wanted to know. Did you become my lover in

London because you really had a passion for me? Or was it just because you thought I would be useful to your Free French cause?"

"*Mon Dieu*, what a question! You certainly helped us by singing the praises of de Gaulle amongst your political and diplomatic friends. But I wanted you for yourself, *chérie*. Above all for yourself. I thought you never doubted that."

Margot swallowed some more champagne.

"Well, maybe at the time I didn't. But sometimes since then I have asked myself that question."

Edmond was staring straight ahead with an impassive expression on his face.

Oh, damn! thought Margot. I've offended him now. Why didn't I keep my silly mouth zipped? She fumbled under the tablecloth and put a hand on his knee.

"Forgive me if I asked a stupid question. It's only the champagne talking."

He turned to her and smiled.

"I'm not hurt. It's just that you never asked that question when we were together in London, so I was a bit taken aback when you asked it now. That's all."

She took another sip of champagne.

"I think I'm getting us into deep water. Can we dance before I've had too much to drink to be able to stand?"

They made their way to the dance floor, but after few moments Margot began to feel dizzy.

"Edmond, I think you'd better take me home. I don't want to disgrace you here."

"You've had a tiring three days," he said gallantly. "Would you prefer to sleep at my apartment? Josette can go over to the hotel tomorrow early and pack your things."

"Thank you, Edmond, but no."

She saw the big sleigh bed in her mind's eye. I'd never be forgiven if I was as sick as a dog in that heirloom, she thought. Next time.

"But are you sure you'll be all right alone in the hotel?"

"In my condition I'd really rather be alone," she said, taking his arm as they left the crowded dance floor, "I'm very sorry. I was enjoying myself so much, I didn't notice how much I was drinking. You should have stopped me, you wicked man."

They collected their coats, and the doorman found them a cab. She sat slumped with her head on his chest, saying nothing all the way back to the Hôtel Meurice, and praying that the rising nausea could be contained until she was in the privacy of her bathroom.

He saw her into the lobby, where she kissed him on the lips and thanked him profusely for a lovely evening.

"You're sure I can't persuade you to accompany me to the embassy tomorrow?"

"Absolutely not, *chéri*. For one thing I doubt that I'd be in any shape to go anywhere respectable tomorrow, except straight back to London. You'll see me off?"

"Of course. I'll be here at five-thirty. Will you be all right the rest of the day?"

"I'll sleep all morning, I hope. Then I'll amuse myself in the afternoon. Don't worry about me. Now I'd better hurry upstairs. See you tomorrow!"

She hurried into the elevator and sighed with relief when the operator pulled the doors closed. She made it to her room and bathroom just in time.

Downstairs, Edmond went to a telephone booth, looked up a number, made a quick call, then hurried to a waiting cab. He gave an address on the rue des Acacias, and the ancient Citroën rattled off northwards towards the Arc de Triomphe. He had only himself to blame for the fact that he was not now on his way to his own apartment with Margot. He should have skipped the nightclub and taken her straight home after dinner. Well, never mind. He'd made good progress, he reckoned. She had obviously been suitably impressed with *le Colonel* in his natural habitat, and would be eager to visit him soon at Lachaise-Laurent. That would be the next stage in his campaign to secure this treasure for himself. Thank you, Charlie, thank you, for setting her free . . . and thank you, Miss Hollywood, whoever you are, for taking him so many thousands of miles away. What a day of good news this had been! Thank God also for *Paris Match*. But for that article, they might never have come together again. True, he had often thought of trying to get in touch

with her, but the feeling that too much time had passed
and that his original invitation to her and Charlie to come
to Lachaise was really pretty silly in hindsight, had
always stayed his hand. And then she had come and
fallen into his lap! Pity about the champagne; he'd far
rather be making love to her now than paying a call on
the absurd Henriette. But at least he wouldn't be scolded
for failing to visit her on her birthday, as he had promised
before he knew that Margot was in town. And since he
felt in the mood for some more champagne, what better
plan than to go and open the magnum he had sent to
Henriette as her birthday gift?

Five minutes later he was climbing the stairs of the old
building which housed Henriette and her two Persian
cats, having ascertained to his chagrin that the rickety old
elevator was once more out of commission. He knocked
on the door of her third-floor apartment and waited.

"*Un instant, cheri!*" came a shrill voice from within. A
few moments later the door opened a crack and a face in
stage make-up peered round it.

"At last," said Henriette, pulling the door open while
concealing herself behind it. Once Edmond was in, she
pushed it shut with a flourish and struck a theatrical
pose.

"You like it?"

Edmond surveyed the ensemble which at first sight
struck him as minimal Moulin Rouge. Black silk stockings
encased her not very slim legs and were held up by a
frilly black garter belt and bodice combined, from out of
the top of which spilled her impressive milk-white
breasts. A single orange-dyed feather sprang from her
piled-up henna-darkened hair. Tottering on six-inch
heeled patent leather black shoes, she led the way into
the living room as Edmond complimented her on the
trouble she had taken to appear festive, and eyed
morosely the quivering globes of her generous *derriére*.

"I'm sorry to be so late," said Edmond as he shed his
overcoat and dropped it onto a velvet upholstered prayer
stool just inside the living room door.

Henriette stepped forward to plant a chaste kiss on his
lips.

"Powder on your collar, *mon petit Colonel*. I think you are the biggest cheat in all France, but how can I resist you – or rather how can I resist *this*?" Scarlet-tipped fingers clutched at his groin for a moment, then she drew away. "Thank you for sending round the champagne and the flowers, *chéri*. Are they my only gifts?"

Edmond felt in an inside pocket of his jacket and pulled out an envelope.

"Happy birthday," he intoned as he handed it to her.

She tore it open and extracted a thin wedge of newly printed notes. Between thumb and forefinger she counted them with the dexterity of a bank-teller.

"Not bad at all, *mon chou*. You made a real effort, and I appreciate it. More than makes up for what I could have earned instead of waiting for you."

"By about ten times," said Edmond, trying not to sound too irritated.

Henriette went to a desk in front of a draped window and secreted the bank notes in a drawer.

"Open the champagne, *mon petit*! What are we waiting for?"

She tottered towards him, surveying her bouncing breasts as she came. Edmond busied himself with the bottle.

"I have a special birthday game for us tonight," she said in a conspiratorial whisper as she joined him in the alcove and pressed her whole body against his. "It is the most exciting way to taste champagne."

"Oh, really?"

Edmond strained to remove the resisting cork.

"Only with you would I do this, *mon chou*."

The cork popped.

"Liar!"

"It's true!"

"I hope it doesn't spoil the champagne. This is good vintage Veuve Clicquot."

"Well, I'm not going to use the whole bottle," she giggled.

"All the same, I'll drink mine from a glass."

"Stupid spoilsport!" she shouted angrily.

"Calm down, Henriette. I was only pulling your leg. I'm sure it will be sensational."

He handed her a glass of champagne, and the somewhat mollified Henriette smiled.

"I'm glad to hear that. For a moment I thought you were going to tell me that my little game was going to offend your patrician Bordeaux senses, because if you had, I would have reminded you that you, *mon amour*, have precious few senses capable of being offended. That's why you come to me."

Edmond laughed.

"You said it; I didn't!"

Margot was awoken, as she had feared, by a splitting headache. She took a couple of aspirin and lay back on the pillows with a towel soaked in cold water pressed to her forehead. She couldn't remember when she'd last let herself get into such a state and shuddered at the recollection of some of the things she'd said to him. She lifted the telephone and ordered coffee to be sent up at ten o'clock, in an hour's time. Then she closed her eyes again in the hopes that sleep might once more overtake her.

By midday, after a soothing hot tub and a visit to a coiffeur on the Faubourg St Honoré, she felt sufficiently restored to do some window-shopping, eat a *croque monsieur* in a brasserie, politely fend off two elegant male predators who tried their luck with her, one after the other, while she ate, and spent the early afternoon back at the Louvre, picking up from where she left off the previous afternoon. Then she went back to the hotel to pack and be ready for Edmond.

At five o'clock he called her to confirm that he'd be with her in half an hour. He sounded cheerful and enquired solicitously about her health.

"I paid my debt this morning," she said. "I hope you're no longer angry with me for my miserable performance last night."

"Do I sound angry? You were a delight."

"But I think I said a lot of ridiculous and maybe even offensive things."

"You didn't, so don't worry. I'll see you shortly, I have some amusing news for you."

"Tell me now!"

"Patience *chérie*, I'll tell you at five-thirty."

Margot hurried to finish her packing. Usually a neat packer, she found herself this time throwing her clothes in carelessly. Even the Dior evening dress was accorded less respect than she would normally grant her more workaday apparel. Her irritability seemed to be mounting by the minute. Edmond was playing games with her, and she didn't appreciate it one bit. His sweet reasonableness annoyed her. She hadn't at all been a "delight" the previous evening; she had been an ugly inebriated bore, so why didn't he say so? Why did he, her former lover, have to be so goddammed polite, as if they'd never met before? Why hadn't he come round to the hotel this morning, blasted her for behaving like the proverbial martini-swilling American divorcée, and then made it up to her by balling the living daylights out of her? Instead he was coming round to sit her down in the lobby and tell her some "amusing news" before putting her on the train, like giving a goddammed kid a candy to keep her happy on the way back to school! Well, she had only herself to blame, she finally admitted, as she jammed the lid down on her over-stuffed suitcase and fought to close the latches. She had played hard to get, by stifling her emotions and then by getting sauced to ensure she didn't get screwed. Still, having come all the way from Bordeaux to see her, he might have made the effort to spend more time with her. Then things might have worked out differently. Next time – and by God there was going to be a next time! – she'd make damn sure she didn't scare him off as she'd obviously done this time. It had been downright silly of her to believe that she could only take the measure of her feelings for the rediscovered Edmond by running away to think about him. She needed to be with him to decide whether or not they had a future together. She should at least have stayed in that gorgeous apartment with him, even if only for a paltry twenty-four hours.

Still smarting with self-reproach, she called the

concierge to have her suitcase taken down, then left the
room.

Edmond arrived promptly at the appointed hour. He
kissed her lightly on the lips, told her she looked divine,
and ordered *thé au citron* to be brought to them at a table
in a quiet corner of the lobby.

"You've no idea what happened at the embassy,"
he said, grinning broadly. "The ceremony was a short
affair, and afterwards I handed my man, Luc Grenier,
over to his *compagnons de la Résistance* and told him to be
back at Lachaise drunk or sober by Monday night. I
talked briefly to the Ambassador and Lady Diana Cooper,
and then an Englishman approaches me and introduces
himself. And who would it be but our old nemesis
Maurice Drake!"

"You're kidding!"

"Honestly! He was very amiable; he never referred
once to my having been in London during the war, but
simply asked me whether I thought the General would be
launching a new Gaulist party and what role I might be
playing in it. I was a bit cautious, but I told him about the
two meetings at the end of this month and the beginning
of April, and that seemed to satisfy him."

"Well, thank God I didn't accompany you there. I
assume he didn't mention me."

"No, not at all. But I'm puzzled that he recognized me
so easily; he never once met me in London."

"Oh, come on, Edmond! You're underestimating
British Intelligence. They probably know about the mole
on the inside of your left thigh."

She blushed at her own remark, and Edmond laughed.

"Only if you told them, *chérie*."

"I resisted the temptation. But what a coincidence . . .
or was it? That man sends a shiver up my spine."

"Well, let's not worry about Monsieur Drake now. He's
not a very agreeable subject for our last conversation
before you disappear out of my life again."

"I won't disappear unless you want me to. Or unless
there's someone else in your life you haven't told me
about."

"There's no one else, I can assure you. And I most certainly don't want you out of my life. Quite the contrary."

"Then you absolutely must keep in touch. I know you're terribly busy with your political activities and the vineyard, but if you want to build on this renewed relationship, you've got to work at it. No out of sight, out of mind nonsense."

Edmond smiled. "And that goes for you too?"

She nodded. "Of course!"

"Margot, haven't you asked yourself the question: how does one renew a relationship with someone living on the other side of the Channel?"

"We have to find out how much we need each other and for what purpose. We must write a lot, telling each other what we think we mean to each other, and what we expect of each other. Maybe it simply won't add up to enough. We'll just have to see."

"That's a sensible view to take. And if you want to know, *chérie*," he added, putting a hand on her knee, "I'm an incurable optimist."

"I'm very glad you are."

He looked at his watch. "I'd better get you to the Gare du Nord."

"How was your morning?" she asked brightly as the cab drew away down the rue de Rivoli.

"Very constructive. I met some Gaullist colleagues, including my fellow Bordelais, Chaban-Delmas. He made a great name for himself in the Resistance, you know. Anyway the General is going to make a major speech at Brunéval on the thirtieth, his first since last November. It will be a huge rally of former Resistance workers and Free French, and it'll mark his return to the political arena. Chaban and I will be mobilizing supporters from our region to come to the rally. Then there'll be another one the following week in Strasburg. That one's a ceremony to honour the American soldiers who died in Alsace. Pity you can't be there."

"I wish I could."

She couldn't help being swept up in his burning enthusiasm.

"So we're really on our way. It's all very exciting, as you can see."

Margot tucked an arm through his.

"My gorgeous fanatic! How about you and me running France after de Gaulle's had his second round?" She giggled and kissed him on the cheek.

"Did you think I had any other plans? Have you been labouring under the delusion, *chère madame*, that only your body is of use and interest to me? Shame on you!"

She put her lips to his ear. "On the contrary, shame on *you*. You put it to no use at all these past two days!"

Edmond laughed nervously. "I didn't want to appear the impatient lecher on our first reunion."

She tapped him on the cheek with the palm of her gloved hand.

"Don't let it happen again. Whatever you think I may be thinking."

They arrived at the Gare du Nord with little time to spare and after locating her sleeping compartment and leaving her luggage in it, the two of them stood together on the platform, waiting for the last call to board the boat-train.

"I've loved every minute of it, Edmond, really. And you were so generous to pick up the tab at the hotel."

"It was my pleasure. I just wish we could have more time together. You will have to plan quickly for a visit to Lachaise."

"I'll do my best. But it has to be combined with work in Paris. That's the only way I can do it with these damned currency restrictions."

"But you won't have to spend anything while you're here. Just count on me."

"You're a darling."

He put a hand on her shoulder and pulled her close. There were shouts of *en voiture*! As he kissed her she put an arm round his neck and let her cheek rest against his for a few moments. Then she drew back, blinking as she felt moistness in her eyes.

"*A bientôt, chéri*," she said, and turned to hurry up the steps into the train.

"*Au revoir!*" he called after her.

474

A Wagon Lit attendant pulled the door shut behind her, and through its window she blew Edmond a kiss before retreating into the corridor and secluding herself in her compartment.

Edmond turned to walk back down the platform, unaware of the pair of eyes that briefly followed him through the corridor window of the next coach to slide past him as the train moved slowly out. Even if he had been aware, there would have been nothing he could do at that juncture to rectify the error he had made in putting Margot on the same London-bound train as Maurice Drake, and in treating him to a ringside seat at their tender farewell.

Maurice Drake was nothing if not the soul of tact. When the dining-car attendant appeared in the doorway of his compartment to enquire whether monsieur wished a table for dinner at the first or second sitting, he told him he preferred to have a light meal brought to him in his compartment, if that was not too much trouble. He did not wish to risk embarrassing Margot by revealing his presence on the train.

36

Sir Walter Garland rose from his seat at the meeting in Westminster Central Hall the moment Sir Stafford Cripps, the morose and ascetic president of the Board of Trade, had concluded his speech to the assembled businessmen and union leaders. The cabinet minister's appeal for a massive export drive had sounded hollow and hopeless in the wake of the chilling review he had just offered of the worsening economic crisis. Garland had no wish to hear the rest of the speeches: if there was anything he needed no more of that week, it was bad news. Once outside, he walked the few yards to Victoria Street and stood at the kerb opposite the Great West Door of Westminster Abbey, tapping irritably on the pavement with the tip of his folded umbrella as cab after cab swept by with their flags down.

"Hello, Walter. Shall we share one if by happy chance we ever get one?"

Garland recognized the voice and turned to greet his fellow Tory MP, Reggie Kempton.

"Morning Reggie. What fit of masochism drew you to that little gathering, assuming that's where you were?"

"Good excuse to get out of the house, old boy. Thursdays are Hilda's canasta mornings; like a bloody hen-house. Even Stafford Cripps is preferable to that. Where are you off to?"

"Carlton. Care to join me for lunch?"

"Bless you, but I have a lunch at White's. Here's a cab; I'll drop you off."

Once inside the cab, heading for St James's Street,

Kempton offered his commiserations over the publicity in the social columns devoted to Charlie's defection.

"You'd have thought the Beaver, being a close friend of yours and all that, might have called his hounds to heel by now."

"Can't blame him really, Reggie. Charlie and Margot aren't exactly the King and Wallis Simpson. They're fair game for his mud-stirrers, I'm afraid."

"Had she already asked for a divorce before he pushed off with his Hollywood moll?"

Garland winced. "Yes, she had. Apparently his drinking had got out of hand. I just can't think what's got into the boy; he never settled down when he got back from the war. I did all I could, but he seemed bent on self-destruction. Dreadfully sad; awful waste."

"Maybe Margot should have stuck it out with him."

"Maybe, but I can't really blame her seeing how he's behaved since. I was so damned angry with the boy for going into this film nonsense that I rather took it out on her for not stopping him. But she probably couldn't have. Now I feel I really wasn't fair to her; she's a good girl. All of us are very fond of her and she's made a great hit with a lot of people like Winston and Clemmie. And she's a good mother to that precious little Julia."

The taxi drew up outside the Carlton and Sir Walter got out.

"See you soon, Reggie, and thanks for the lift."

"Spirits up, old boy!"

The taxi drew away, and Garland climbed the steps to the club. Within a few minutes he was ensconced in an armchair, whisky and soda to hand, and a copy of the *Illustrated London News* held high in front of his face as a warning to other members that he had no great wish to be disturbed. He was not, after all, in the most sociable of moods, but it had been the prospect of staying at home listening to his wife's increasingly hysterical commentaries on their son's behaviour that had driven him to risk the embarrassed and embarrassing expressions of sympathy of his club friends on the misfortune that had been visited upon him.

If there was one thing which Sir Walter could not tolerate, it was having the honourable name of Garland dragged in the mire and held up to public ridicule. The Garlands had remained free of even the slightest taint of scandal since the early 1860s when his great uncle Jasper had wrongly accused a Scottish duke of cheating at cards, and had languished for the next decade in a ship-broker's office in Bombay. Now his own son's name was being bandied about in the popular press and in the drawing rooms of London and country houses, not to mention in his own clubs and the Commons, as a first-class bounder who hopped it to Hollywood with a blonde nearly old enough to be his mother, leaving a much admired and beautiful wife and three-year-old daughter behind him. No wonder the gutter press were having a field day! To be thankful for small mercies, or in this case large miracles, there had as yet been no mention in the public prints that he had sunk his chances of a first film role in a sea of Scotch, but that, no doubt, would be vouchsafed to the drooling public at any moment, just to complete the humiliation. Distasteful as the thought of his son being a film actor had been to him, it was bearable in comparison to the labels now being affixed by all and sundry.

Sir Walter slapped the magazine shut, drained his glass, hauled himself out of the chair, and stumped off, head lowered, towards the dining room. His chances of remaining unmolested by sympathizers were about nil, he reckoned, but a man had to eat somewhere.

A few minutes after Sir Walter had left the club, Sir Hugh Gaffney emerged with his lunch guest on the front steps. With identically timed movements, worthy of a couple of well-rehearsed hoofers, they popped their bowlers onto their heads and hooked their umbrellas over their left forearms as they sauntered in step down to the pavement.

"It was awfully good to see you again, Maurice, and I'll certainly take you up on that fishing invitation," said Gaffney as they prepared to move off in different directions. "And thanks for your confiding in me over poor old Walter's family problem."

Maurice Drake unhooked the umbrella from his arm.

"Well, you know Garland well enough to know what, if anything, to say to him about it. And thanks for the lunch."

They nodded to each other and went their separate ways.

For the rest of the day, Sir Hugh Gaffney wrestled with the decision whether or not to pass on to his old friend, Walter, the disturbing information just imparted to him by Maurice Drake. He had no liking for meddling in other families' affairs. On the other hand, he was very fond of the Garlands, and it distressed him to think that, in their ignorance of all the facts, they were forced to conclude that their son bore the exclusive blame for the scandalous situation that had arisen in his marriage, and that their daugher-in-law's behaviour had been above reproach. Gaffney knew how fond Walter and Cynthia were of their American daughter-in-law, and the news could therefore come as a bitter shock to them. But he would be failing in his duty as a true friend if he did not alleviate them of the burden of thinking that it had been their son's fault alone.

By the morrow, Gaffney's careful reasoning had joined his instinct in tipping the balance decisively in favour of informing his friend that his daugher-in-law had been seen in Paris in the company of none other than former BCRA officer, Edmond Lemonnier, and that the manner of their parting, as observed by Drake, had suggested a continuing relationship quite incompatible with the position of a woman claiming to be the innocent party in a marital dispute.

He therefore called Sir Walter and, intimating that he would be within the precincts of the Palace of Westminster that afternoon, got himself invited to tea in the House of Commons.

Margot's face was ashen as she started to read the letter from her father-in-law, but by the time she had finished it, it was flushed with anger.

Dear Margot,

By what means I came into possession of this information I have no intention of revealing. Suffice it to say that it comes from an impeccable source, and I have judged its worth accordingly.

There can be no doubt that you have either revived, or never abandoned, a wholly improper relationship with the Frenchman Lemonnier. How otherwise could you account for the displays of affection last week in Paris, only days after Charlie had left you and we had, in good faith, recognized you as the wronged person in this unhappy affair?

I had my doubts during the war, while Charlie was languishing in his POW camp, but your respected father, no doubt deliberately misled by you, assured me that there were no grounds for suspecting that you were carrying on an affair with the man. I might add that your choice of person with whom to conduct an adulterous relationship (can you deny that it was one?) astonishes me. My source of information, who seems to know all about Lemonnier and his and your "friendship", has a very low opinion of him indeed, and who am I to question that?

These revelations would have been distressing enough under any circumstances, but the mounting evidence that you concealed your own unacceptable behaviour while allowing my son to assume all the blame for a broken marriage has cut me to the quick. I would have thought so much better of you. If you can satisfactorily prove to me that these accusations are wholly unfounded, I shall be more than abject in my apologies and more than generous in making restitution. But I am more or less certain that you are in no position to do that, and under the circumstances it seems only fair to Charlie that he be put in possession of these unsavoury new facts, so that he can have them taken properly into account when the divorce proceedings are begun.

I am sure that you will understand that our

relationship can never be the same again after this. My wife and I feel horribly betrayed, as no doubt will Charlie. But you remain the mother of our granddaughter, and as such it is necessary that, with Charlie abroad, we remain in contact with you. For our part, we will seek to keep such contact as devoid of acrimony as possible, for Julia's sake and as befits people of a certain upbringing, and we trust that you will reciprocate.

If you have appointed a solicitor to handle your legal affairs here, I suggest that he not delay in consulting mine, Mr Gerald Fortland of Lowsley, Fortland & Fitch, who will be representing my son's interests in what I now regard as a highly desirable move to end this marriage as quickly as possible.

Yours sincerely,
Walter Garland.

"That bastard Drake!" shouted Margot out loud. "Bloody little creeping spy!"

She threw the three pages of handwritten letter onto a table and went to the kitchen to make herself a soothing cup of coffee. How dare Walter Garland wrap himself and Charlie in a cloak of self-righteousness like that! All right, her father-in-law had put two and two together and come up with what happened to be the right number. She wasn't going to waste time trying to deny it. But he didn't have to be so bloody sanctimonious about it when his own drunken son had run off without so much as a goodbye with some easy lay from sleazy Los Angeles! God, those Garlands have a nerve! Well, she'd show them; she'd damn well marry Edmond if he wanted her. That would give them something to talk about!

She burned her finger lighting the gas stove and started to cry. She stuck the finger into a pat of butter and felt the pain ease. The telephone rang and she was comforted to hear Felix Beale's voice on the line.

"Welcome back, beautiful. The Dior pictures are an utter dream, and *Vogue* are over the moon about them. They'll have pride of place in the up-coming issue. How was the rest of your stay?"

"Very pleasant, Felix. It was marvellous seeing

Edmond again, and we got on very well. It was just like old times."

"Sounds promising. We'd better get lots more work in Paris, and we probably will."

"The sooner the better."

"The papers here don't seem to be letting up on you and Charlie. They've interviewed him in New York on his way to the West Coast. He says he hasn't touched a drop since boarding the boat at Liverpool, and he's serious about making movies in Hollywood. Meanwhile the blonde beams happily at him. It's in yesterday's *Graphic* if you can stomach reading it."

"I doubt if I can. I just want to do lots of work, Felix, to take my mind off the whole miserable affair. I'm going round to talk to Stella at the agency now."

"Then come on to the studio afterwards and we'll crack a bottle to celebrate your stunning enhancement of friend Dior's little masterpieces and my magical capturing of it for posterity.

"Bless you, sweetheart, I'll be there."

37

The November skies over south-western France were grey, but there was no rain, and as the Paris to Bordeaux express cut through the perimeter of the suburbs of Poitiers and entered the calm, rural landscape of the Vienne, Margot awoke from a brief after-lunch nap, and contentedly watched the fields and villages slip past her. In a couple of hours she would be in Bordeaux. She was, at the moment, feeling anything but nervous at the prospect of her reunion with Edmond, but she wondered, nonetheless, whether this equanimity would survive the final stages of the journey.

Following their Paris reunion little time had passed before they were exchanging letters. Margot had made haste to write to him in the wake of Sir Walter's outburst, and had informed him, with many apologies, that thanks to the dreaded Maurice Drake, their wartime relationship and recent meeting in Paris had now become an open issue in the marital collapse, and there was a possibility of his name being dragged into the court case if Sir Walter got his way. Edmond had responded promptly. He was sorry to hear of these new problems, and assured Margot that he himself was not embarrassed by the linking of their names; indeed, he had never for a moment believed it could be avoided in the event of a divorce. He was only sorry for the anguish which she must be experiencing, and he promised to do whatever she asked of him to ease her way through the divorce proceedings. In the meantime he was deeply involved in the municipal elections campaign in his area, and he would be in touch with her again as soon as the October vote had taken place.

Margot's relief at Edmond's very understanding reaction was matched by her relief on reading a letter from Charlie which arrived a few days later. In it he assured Margot that he had no intention of fanning the flames by taking advantage of his father's distressing revelations. The fact remained that it was he who had provoked the crisis which ended in the break-up, and he had no desire to visit more problems upon his estranged wife and daughter by reversing his original decision to play the guilty party in the case. While he was saddened to learn of her wartime affair, he felt that Julia stood to suffer the most eventually if it became public knowledge, and that, at all costs, they must try to spare her until she was old enough to understand and accept it. In the meantime, life with Melissa in Hollywood was bringing him much happiness and a sense of fulfilment. There was an excellent chance that he would shortly be signed by MGM, and once he was earning again he would be in a position to send a modest amount monthly to help pay Julia's expenses. He wished Margot every happiness and prayed, for Julia's sake, that they could, despite everything, treat each other as friends.

Margot had cried a little over that letter. It was the old Charlie; tender, concerned and responsible. This Melissa must be having a good effect on him, and for that she was happy. The divorce case now went ahead as Charlie had agreed and over the strenuous objections of his father as to the choice of guilty party. Margot's solicitor informed her that the provisional decree could be expected to be handed down at a court hearing in the first quarter of 1948, with the decree absolute, making her a free woman, following six months later. In the meantime, through the spring, summer and early fall of 1947, she worked as hard as her agency and her schedule could allow her. Resigned to the fact that she would not see Paris again until the autumn collections were presented by the fashion houses there, she continued to hope that Edmond might be able to visit her in London, but his preoccupation with the forthcoming municipal elections prevented him from doing so. They exchanged a number of letters recounting their respective activities, but neither seemed ready to commit to paper such feelings as they felt for each other. It was as if there was an unspoken agreement to avoid discussing the future of their relationship until the divorce was granted.

One morning in October, Margot read in her newspaper of the Gaullist triumphs in France's municipal elections, and a week later she received a letter from Edmond. In it he recounted the stunning successes of his hero's newly formed political movement, the Rassemblement du Peuple Française, or RPF. Nearly forty per cent of the votes cast had been garnered by the RPF and the scattering of groups fighting under the Gaullist flag. Gaullist mayors took over the town halls of half of France's principal cities and towns, including Paris. As Edmond exulted: "We have conquered the cities; now we shall conquer the whole country!" And then he added: "My happiness can now only be multiplied by the joy of welcoming you as my guest at Lachaise-Laurent as soon as possible."

Margot hastily acknowledged his letter, congratulating him on the success of the RPF, and telling him that she would be in Paris in the second week of November to do a layout of Pierre Balmain's latest collection, after which she would be delighted to come to Lachaise for a few days.

Thus did she find herself, that overcast afternoon, bound for Bordeaux, wondering at her own calmness as she approached what she now felt must be a major milestone in her life. Her visit to Lachaise-Laurent would be, she was sure, decisive in the matter of her relationship to Edmond, and the more she thought about it, the more confident she became that she could overcome the last remaining doubts she had that marriage to her was what Edmond both wanted and needed. Of her own wants and needs in the matter, she no longer had the slightest doubts. The prospect that marriage to Edmond offered of a comfortable life without financial worry, of recognition and excitement on the climb to political power, and of a highly satisfactory sexual relationship, was far too attractive to abandon. Besides, she really felt that she was once again in love with the man, as she had been during the war. There was only one matter, therefore, to be settled, and it was the crucial one: did Edmond want and need her enough to enter into this partnership with all seriousness? She had no intention of letting him "give it a try" just to please her. He had to want it as much – no, more – than she did if it was going to work. And he had to convince her that was so. If she took this step in the face of what she was certain would be vigorous parental and brotherly opposition, she wanted to eliminate the risk of being told later that she had been played for a fool by a callous adventurer.

As the train rattled through the outskirts of the great port city, and the conductor popped his head into the compartment to announce arrival in Bordeaux in three minutes, Margot felt the nervous thrill of an athlete impatient for the crack of the starting-pistol. She had a bare five days in which to work her will.

"Welcome to Bordeaux!" said Edmond, rushing forward to greet her as he spotted her descending to the platform. He hugged her to him and kissed her on both cheeks. "You must be tired although you don't look it; you look as fresh and beautiful as ever."

Margot beamed. "I'm feeling fine; it was a restful journey, and I'm all the better for seeing you."

Preceded by a baggage porter, they walked arm in arm out to the station forecourt where Edmond indicated a large maroon convertible with a white canvas top.

"What a perfectly gorgeous car!"

"It's a Renault Minerva Grand Sport. Very rare these days. It spent the war hidden away from the Germans in small pieces. We had the devil's own time putting it together again."

Darkness was falling as they drove out of the city and headed northwards towards the Médoc country.

"How did your modelling work go in Paris?"

"Very well, I think. Balmain's created some really fabulous clothes. I wish I was a rich woman; I'd spend an absolute fortune on *haute couture*."

"At least you'd do honour to the clothes. It's the clothes which normally do honour to the rich Parisians who buy them. What you need, Margot, is a rich husband worthy of you, but you must be very selective."

"Oh, I shall be! Don't you worry about that." Margot laughed nervously. "And your politics?"

"Very exciting. If those municipal elections had been an election for the National Assembly, we'd be running the country by now. The people obviously want de Gaulle back, and somehow or other we have to put him back, no matter what that wretched Assembly says."

"Heavens, Edmond! It sounds like you're plotting a coup."

"Nothing so dramatic or immediate, I'm afraid," he said. "Let's just say that one day it might became necessary to bypass this ridiculous constitution in order to give the General the reins of power before the country collapses into the hands of the communists. You must have been reading about the plague of strikes that they've inflicted on this country, and the chaos they're creating to please their Kremlin masters."

"Yes, I have. It sounds pretty bad."

"Well, all that's going to have to stop." He banged his fist down on the horn as the car swept by two elderly bicyclists whose reproachful faces Margot fleetingly caught in the failing light. "Do you realize that this is the first time I've ever driven you?" he said, grinning at her.

"Except in Kay's pony cart, which you drove as though you were Ben Hur in the Colosseum. And since you like to drive this particular vehicle as though you were John Cobb, maybe you'd get your eyes back on the road."

As they continued northwards, Edmond recited the names of the vineyards whose entrances were visible in the car's headlamps, and before long they were turning left off the main road in the village of St Julien and running westwards down a narrow road through the vines towards the outer reaches of the commune. Moments later they passed through a large stone gateway and Margot gasped as the headlamps illuminated the façade of the château.

"Edmond, it's beautiful!"

"I knew you would like it."

They swept round a circular driveway and pulled up before tall oak doors at the head of a flight of stone steps.

Edmond tapped on the horn before switching off the engine.

"Wait a moment, Edmond. Before we go in, I wanted to ask you something. What have you told your mother about us?"

"That you're an old friend from London, the one whose sister was killed in the Café de Paris; that you are divorcing your English husband who's gone off to Hollywood; and that I am very fond of you."

"That we were once lovers?"

Edmond put a hand on her sleeve.

"I think she figured that out for herself. Anyway, she's impatient to meet you, and I think you're going to get on very well. Her English is almost non-existent, so try out your French on her. It'll be good for you."

A porch light went on and a servant with gold epaulettes on his white jacket came through the door and down the stone steps. Edmond opened the car door on his side.

"Come on, my beauty. Nothing to be afraid of!"

Margot smiled as the door on her side was opened. "This is Etienne, Margot."

"*Bonsoir*, Etienne."

"*Bonsoir*, Madame Garland."

The frail, still beautiful, Giselle Lemonnier welcomed Margot with open arms. In her halting English she told her how beautiful she was, how much she was grateful to the Americans for their help in winning the war, and how happy she was that her beloved son had such a wonderful relationship with his friend from wartime London. Margot thanked her profusely in French and told her what a privilege it was to be a visitor to the lovely château, and finally to meet its charming mistress.

"Edmond will show you everything tomorrow, my dear. I am sure you are tired after your journey, so we shall dine early and send you upstairs for a long night's sleep."

They ate an excellent *coq au vin* accompanied by a

magnum of Lachaise-Laurent 1933, at the end of which Margot felt her eyelids becoming heavy, and she was glad to be encouraged to retire.

"My mother likes to read a little in front of the fire before going to bed," said Edmond, taking her by the arm, "so I will accompany you to your room to see that Chantal has provided you with all you need."

In the ornately furnished bedroom with its broad, canopied bed, everything was found in order.

"Tomorrow I will run you off your feet showing you everything inside and outside, so you must sleep well," he said, placing his hands on her shoulders. Then he drew her to him and their lips met in a long and searching kiss.

"Now that's more like it," said Margot softly as the kiss ended. "And better late than never."

Edmond smiled shyly. "Lachaise is the perfect place to begin again."

"So begin. Or maybe I'd better wait until tomorrow to see 'the impatient lecher' at work!"

Edmond looked puzzled and then laughed.

"You remember that."

"How could I forget?"

He kissed her lightly on the lips and turned to go.

"Pull the bell rope by the bed when you wake up, and Chantal will come to hear whether you want breakfast in bed or downstairs. Now sleep well, *chérie*."

"You too."

"You've no idea how happy it makes me to have you finally under my roof," he said as he closed the door.

The next morning, while Madame Lemonnier nursed a migraine attack behind the closed shutters of her bedroom, Edmond gave Margot a tour of the château, detailing the history of the fine eighteenth-century mansion and its impressive display of antique furnishings and exquisite pictures. Next, he led her through the vineyard, carefully explaining the layout of the growing areas with their rows of vines, the annual cycle of grape-growing, the properties of the soil that ensured the Médoc's fame as one of the world's greatest sources of noble wines; and then in the vineyard's building and cellars he taught her about the making of the wine and introduced her to the delights of comparing the recent vintages in the barrel and the more mature wines already bottled. In the *chai* where the newest vintage was housed in long rows of polished oak barrels, he showed her a plaque on the wall commemorating Aristide Grenier, *maître de chai*, shot by the Nazis in 1943, and then, with Aristide's son, Luc, resistance hero decorated by both the French and British governments, now successor to his father as *maître de chai*, they tasted the new wine and agreed that both old Grenier and Edmond's father, Georges, would have been proud of it.

That afternoon, Margot was given a tour of the great neighbouring châteaux, tasting the wines at Château Lafite and a half-dozen other notable vineyards in the area, and ending the tour at Château Margaux where, amid the Empire splendour of his home, the courtly proprietor smilingly urged Margot to consider changing the spelling of her name "so that your incomparable beauty and my incomparable wine may be forever linked." Margot thanked him for his exquisite compliment and basked in the look of consummate pride on Edmond's face.

"What an enchanting gentleman!" she said as they drove away. "I could have hugged him."

"You should have done. We old wine-growing families are rather special people, although I say it myself. We try to be as noble and worthy of esteem as our finest vintages. Like the vintages, we sometimes fall short of our highest expectations. And as with the wines, it's not always our fault."

That same evening, Edmond gave a dinner in Margot's honour at the château. Madame Lemonnier apologized in advance for the fact that food rationing and shortages would prevent her cook from presenting a meal of the standard of cuisine for which Lachaise-Laurent had been justly noted in pre-war days. To Margot, however, the dinner to which twelve sat down in the candle-lit Louis XV dining room was a feast of rare excellence, and she was touched that Edmond had produced for the occasion some of the very greatest bottles from his father's cellar.

For the first time during her visit, she felt that her nerves were not altogether subdued. She knew that she was going to be carefully scrutinized by the guests, and she was anxious to give a good account of herself and be a credit to her host. Dressing for dinner, she had begun to panic at the thought that Giselle Lemonnier might find the plunging neckline of her midnight blue velvet gown too lacking in modesty, and she had refused to go downstairs until Edmond had come to her room to pass judgement on it.

"You are a vision of loveliness," he declared. "All the men will be at your feet tonight."

"And the women at my throat?"

He smiled. "I, at least, will feel flattered. Come down soon. Our guests will be arriving."

After a glass of champagne and a fulsome compliment from Giselle on her appearance, Margot's nerves settled down, and by the time that the last of the guests had arrived, she was in good spirits. Edmond had thoughtfully selected guests who could communicate at least tolerably well in English, and had included, as a compliment to Margot, the American consul in Bordeaux. Seated at table between the consul and the curator of Bordeaux's Museum of Fine Arts, she plied her neighbours with questions about life in the region and talked vivaciously of her work as a fashion model and of her family back in America.

"I have to congratulate you, Edmond," she overheard one of the male guests say as they left the dining room. "She is exquisite and charming."

She watched Edmond blush with pleasure.

"Would you give me the pleasure of sitting with me for a while, madame?" said a female voice at her shoulder as they crossed the hall. "We had no opportunity to talk at dinner."

Margot turned and saw that the request came from a strikingly handsome woman with whom she had exchanged only a few words of greeting before the dinner.

"I'd be delighted."

"You've met rather a lot of strangers in these past days, so I won't at all hold it against you if you've already forgotten that my name is Diane de Villambeau."

She smiled pleasantly at Margot, who confessed that the name had indeed escaped her. In the salon they selected a Louis XVI sofa beneath a vast tapestry depicting the crowning of Charlemagne and sat down.

"You speak excellent English," said Margot.

"My first husband was an English banker with a passion for climbing in the French Alps. He was killed there, unfortunately, back in 1934."

"I'm so sorry. I believe you've known Edmond for some time."

"I was born in Bordeaux, and I returned here after my first husband's death, and saw quite a lot of Edmond in the years just before the war. I married again just after the war started. He was a doctor and we moved to Paris because he was determined to stay close to his aged parents during the Occupation. Henri was a wonderful but headstrong man. He got himself killed during the liberation of Paris, trying to drag a wounded *résistant* out of the path of a German tank."

"You have had a tragic life, it seems."

"In some ways." She pushed a lock of rich copper hair behind one ear before flipping open a gold case and offering Margot a cigarette. Margot thanked her and took a cigarette, which Diane lit with a gold lighter before lighting one for herself at the end of a long black and gold holder.

"Edmond has talked often about you, Margot, and he has certainly not exaggerated in his description of your beauty."

"That's very sweet of you both," said Margot. "I can certainly return the compliment."

"And he's very much in love with you."

Margot exhaled smoke slowly, giving herself time to think how to respond calmly.

"You obviously know all about our meeting during the war, and what we meant to each other then."

"Oh, yes; I know all about it. He told me everything and I was delighted. But your use of the past tense when speaking of what you meant to each other was not intended to tell me that it is all over?"

"Well, to tell you the truth, Edmond is being very coy on the subject. He is being terribly kind to me and making me feel wonderfully at home and relaxed, but he has said little about where he sees us going from here on. So I just have to wait and see."

"And do you love him? Forgive me for being so direct." She laughed. "That's me, I'm afraid!"

Margot smiled. "Oh, yes, I love him. But I'm not sure that I understand him right now."

"I think he's a little afraid of scaring you away with a marriage proposal before you're divorced. He thinks you might think it not proper."

"After all that we've already been through together! He really shouldn't be so timid. He's certainly not timid in his politics."

"You're right. In that, he's a headstrong fanatic."

"Are you a Gaullist?"

She was anxious to get off the subject of Edmond, having revealed more than she had intended.

"No. I think de Gaulle's a very dangerous man. He's hinting at revolution because he's too impatient to seek power through the ballot box. But he'll fail. The people will prefer a bad republic to a good tyranny any day."

"So, Edmond's backing the wrong horse?"

"I happen to think so. But he seems to be getting an awful lot of fun and satisfaction out of it, so who are we to stop him?" She laughed. "As long as he doesn't end up in front of a firing squad!"

Margot looked unhappy. "Is de Gaulle really talking about revolution?"

"Read his speeches of the last few weeks, my dear. At least, read between the lines. What he's saying is that if the National Assembly won't do what he wants it to do, the RPF will somehow destroy it. So now everyone else is rallying to the defence of the Assembly. He's gone too far and he'll pay for it."

"Oh dear. Edmond was painting such a rosy picture of the RPF's future."

493

"Well, fanatics never like to admit to making mistakes, do they?"

Out of the corner of her eye, Margot saw Edmond approaching.

"I think I should break up this cosy tête-à-tête," he said, taking her by the hand and lifting her to her feet. "Diane, you must excuse us. I have to share her with my envious gentlemen guests."

As the guests were departing a little after midnight, Diane took Margot aside and urged her to come and see her in Paris the next time she was there.

"And good luck with Edmond," she whispered into her ear. "I think you're going to have to take the initiative!"

"I'll certainly think about it," she said.

"That is, if you really want him."

Margot smiled and shook Diane's proffered hand. "Thanks so much for your friendly advice. I certainly hope we meet again soon."

"Then come back to Paris soon. You're welcome to stay at my apartment, whether I'm there or not."

"That's very kind, Diane. I may well take you up on that."

After everyone had gone, Edmond escorted his weary mother to her room, asking Margot to wait in his downstairs study where he would join her for a nightcap and a chat about how the evening had turned out.

The study was a comfortable, book-filled room upon which Edmond had clearly set his mark. There was a large silver-framed, unsigned portrait photograph of General de Gaulle on the *directoire* desk, dominating smaller photographs of his mother and late father. On a table in front of the velvet-draped windows stood a scale model of a Sherman tank bearing the insignia of General Leclerc's Second Armoured Division and the name "Lachaise-Laurent" painted on its side. Beside it, arrayed in a small glass showcase, were his decorations for gallantry and his campaign medals.

Margot settled into a comfortable armchair near the cavernous fireplace in which the embers of a log fire still glowed. She was impatient to find out more from

Edmond about his friend Diane de Villambeau. She had taken an immediate liking to the chic and pretty widow whom she judged to be somewhere in her late thirties. It occurred to her that if she was eventually going to find herself living in France as Edmond's wife, Diane could well fill the role of confidante which Marion Shears now filled in London.

"You enjoyed yourself?" asked Edmond, striding into the room bearing a bottle of champagne in a cooler.

"Loved it; your guests were charming, especially Diane."

"I'd better be honest with you," he said, reaching for two champagne glasses in a cabinet. "I had my first serious affair with Diane, although she was older then me. It was before her second marriage. Are you embarrassed to hear that?"

"Heavens! Why should I be?"

"Of course, why should you? It ended eight years ago."

Margot stared into the embers of the fire.

"She said a funny thing. She said that she could see just by looking at you that you are very much in love with me. What do you suppose she sees that I don't see?"

"*Ma chère*, you mustn't take Diane too seriously. She likes to play games with people."

"Are you playing a game with me, Edmond?"

"How do you mean?"

Margot glanced up and saw the look of surprise on his face as he handed her a glass of champagne.

"Have I done something to offend you, Margot? If I have, I – "

"No, no. I didn't mean to imply that. You've been a perfectly charming, wonderful host. But you're holding back on something, Edmond, and since I'm leaving here the day after tomorrow, I want all the cards out on the table before I go."

Edmond pursed his lips and stared at the floor. Then he said:

"You're absolutely right. All cards on the table."

"Fine. I'll show mine first. I'm in love with you,

Edmond. Very much so. For the second time in my life. I want to know whether you're in love with me."

He looked into his champagne glass as he answered.

"Of course I'm in love with you, *chérie*. I've never really stopped being in love with you. But I've been afraid, ever since you told me about Charlie, that you might reject me if I asked you too soon to marry me when your divorce comes through."

"But you could still have told me you loved me," she protested. "You behaved as though you did, when we were in Paris, but you never said as much."

"Well, I've said it now. I just didn't want to shake the bottle and ruin it."

Margot got up and walked over to him.

"Then why don't you uncork it and enjoy it?"

She giggled as she put her arms around his neck and then pressed her mouth hard against his in a hungry kiss.

"When I've finished this glass of champagne," she said breathlessly a moment later, "will you take me upstairs and make up for all that lost time?"

"With the utmost pleasure."

She sipped at her champagne, her eyes twinkling at him over the rim of the glass.

"I hope champagne is good for my health," she said. "It's all I ever seem to drink these days."

A single bedside light burned. Margot stood in the middle of the bedroom, head thrown back, eyes closed, as Edmond undressed her. She stepped out of the long velvet gown as she felt it slip to her ankles. Eyes still closed, she smiled as his fingertips traced the swelling of her breasts over the top of her brassiere and then, as his lips pressed against her throat, she felt the fingers move around and down, over her garter belt to the silk-enclosed cheeks of her backside, and she became aware of the stiffness of his penis, still confined in his clothes, pressing urgently against her. His hands moved up again to unhook the brassiere, and she held her arms forwards to let him pull it away.

"Kiss them! Kiss them!"

She moaned as his lips closed over one already erect

nipple. She reached for the collar of his jacket and pushed it back over his shoulders. He drew back from her breast and pulled his jacket off. She reached for his bow tie and tugged impatiently at it.

"Let me do it; it'll be quicker," he said.

Margot stepped back and watched, her hands kneading her breasts, her tongue massaging her upper lip, as Edmond rapidly removed his clothes.

"You have a beautiful body," she said breathlessly. "That little bit of extra weight has made it perfect – No! Let me!" She darted forward as she saw Edmond slip his fingers into the waist of his shorts. She sank to her knees and eased the shorts over his hips, letting them drop to the carpet. She took his erect penis on one hand, closed her mouth over it and sucked hungrily on it until he urged her to pause. She got to her feet and let him slip her panties off her.

"I'm ravenous for you. You can see that, can't you darling?" she panted, running her hands through his hair as he bent to unhook her stocking tops from the garter belt. In a moment she stood naked, and he led her to the bed and was quickly astride her. She moaned and rocked her head back from side to side as he entered her, and their first orgasms were fast in arriving.

For nearly two hours the cycle of love-making and resting in each other's arms repeated itself until, over Margot's drowsy protests, he slipped out of the bed.

"Don't tell me you're weakening already!" she muttered, and giggled into the pillow.

He turned and slapped her playfully on the behind.

"I have a very early meeting with Luc in the morning. If you're good and sleep now, I'll bring you breakfast after my meeting."

"And some more of him?"

She grasped his penis and leaned over to kiss the tip of it. He pulled gently away and slipped his pants and shirt on. Then, having gathered up the rest of his clothes from the carpet, he bent over and kissed her lightly.

"Sleep well, for what's left of the night."

He turned and walked to the door.

"Edmond darling," she whispered, "thank you for

making me feel what it's like to be a real woman again. I feel I'm floating in space."

"Well, when you come down to earth eventually, please make sure you land on the spot where I am, and stay there. For ever."

Margot sat up.

"Don't tell me I finally heard a proposal!"

Edmond hesitated, then he came back to the bedside.

"Yes, I suppose it is." He laughed. "I could have put it better, though."

"It sounded fine to me. You really want to marry me once I'm divorced? Will your mother approve? I mean, I'm not French and I'm not even a Catholic."

"You're going to marry me, not my mother, and she's already told me she'd approve anyway."

Margot clutched at his arm.

"And you promise you're really, really in love with me?"

"Yes. Now go to sleep before I change my mind."

"Well, at least you can seal it with a kiss!"

He bent and kissed her on the lips.

"Do you have to sleep in another room, then?" she asked a little breathlessly.

"Good Catholics don't sleep with their fiancées."

Margot swung playfully at him with a clenched fist.

"Then get out of here, you pathetic puritan, and don't you dare forget when you wake me tomorrow that as of now we're engaged to be married."

"I'm sure you'll remind me, *chérie!*"

He was laughing softly as he left the room.

Margot cried tears of happiness in the dark until she fell asleep.

She passed the rest of her short stay at the château as if in a dream. Giselle Lemonnier hugged and kissed her when Edmond told her that Margot would one day soon be her daughter-in-law.

"But it has to be kept a strict secret, *Maman*," admonished her son. "Otherwise it could cause difficulties for Margot back in England."

On her last evening there, Edmond took her to the

ballet in Bordeaux, after which they ate as good a meal as the city had to offer at Le Chapon Fin. Then they hurried home to make love.

The next morning, he drove her to Bordeaux to catch the *rapide* to Paris.

"Are we really going to be able to stand the waiting, darling?" she asked him as he raced the Minerva through the villages of the Médoc. "After all, I don't see my divorce coming through for at least six or even eight months."

"We'll manage. I'll try to get to London to see you, but we'll have to be discreet. And I imagine you'll be coming to Paris on assignments between now and then."

"I'll try to swing it," she said. "But, God! That's going to be a long, long eight months!"

38

"If you're both really sure you're in love with each other, you should certainly go ahead and get married as soon as you're free to do so," said Marion Shears, when Margot called her on her return to London. "I assume," she added, "the prospect of living in France holds no fears for you."

"None that I can think of. The language will be a problem for a while, but I'll start French lessons right away here in London; I already speak a little."

"Well, it's all terribly exciting, darling. I can see you already as France's first ever American First Lady! I'll insist on an early invitation to the Elysée Palace."

"Don't be surprised if you get one. You've no idea how determined Edmond is, and how well they think of him already in Gaullist circles. God, how I love a man who's going places, especially in politics!"

"It takes more than political victories to make a good political marriage, my sweet. What was it like to be back in bed with him?"

Margot smiled. "He's lost none of his old touch, I can assure you. I just can't get enough of him!"

"Then the marriage bids fair to be a whopping success."

"So you don't think I'm crazy?"

"Not I, darling, but your parents surely will. In fact I assume they'll be what you Americans call 'mad as hell', won't they?"

"I rather fear so, but I'm not going to tell them until the divorce is through."

"Good girl! In fact, you'd best not tell anyone. British divorce court judges are like bloodhounds when it comes to sniffing out that sort of thing. If you're sueing Charlie for divorce on the grounds of his adultery, you must absolutely not let the judge think you couldn't care less what Charlie was up to as long as you were freed to marry your own lover. You have to appear to be furious and deeply hurt. It's all a game, really, but it's one you can lose and wind up without a divorce if you play your cards carelessly."

"I have to tell dear Felix; not that he wouldn't worm it out of me anyway in the end. But no one else. God help me if it gets to Walter's ears."

"Keep your fingers crossed, darling."

Which was what Margot did for the next two months as she waited for the case to come to court. In the meantime, she met her solicitor to discuss the awkward matter of the "Discretionary Statement". As Rowland Barnard gently explained to her, British matrimonial law required the "innocent party" in a divorce case to furnish the presiding judge with a written confession of any adultery committed in the course of the marriage from which that party now sought release.

"It's a simple statement handed to him in court in a sealed envelope. Only he and we will ever know what's in it. But he will decide, on reading it, whether you deserve the divorce."

Margot went white. God Almighty! Marion never told me about *that*!

Barnard shifted uncomfortably in his chair.

"Were there – " he paused to pull a handkerchief from his pocket, dab genteelly at his nostrils, and replace it – "Were there such indiscretions, Mrs Garland?"

Margot shrugged her shoulders in resignation.

"If you've got to know, you've got to know, I guess. There was something during the war, and – "

"If you'd prefer to write it down and let me have it at your convenience – "

"No, no. I might as well tell you now. I *did* commit adultery with someone."

"These things happen in wartime, Mrs Garland. Judges are understanding of a little lapse."

The handkerchief came out again.

"Or was there," he enquired as it was returned to the pocket of his black jacket, "was there a, shall we say, a pattern of indiscretion?"

"Oh, no. Just one person."

"But on more than one occasion."

"Yes. Does that matter?"

"Less than having more than one lover, Mrs Garland. Nonetheless, I venture to hope that we can advise the judge that your liaison with the gentleman was of a spasmodic rather than habitual nature."

Margot smiled nervously.

"How many times is spasmodic, Mr Barnard?"

The solicitor moistened his upper lip with tip of his tongue as he carefully lifted a piece of fluff from the lapel of his jacket.

"I am sure your indiscretions can be counted on no more than the fingers of one hand."

If you count the same fingers several times over, thought Margot to herself.

"I am sure they can be, Mr Barnard."

"Shall we say three?" He pushed a piece of paper across the table to her, and pulled a fountain pen from an inside pocket. "Name and approximate dates will suffice."

"Real name?"

Barnard nodded silently as Margot took the pen. Then he turned in his chair to gaze discreetly at the rain-spattered windowpanes, as Margot penned the details of her adultery. What on earth could a judge deduce of her character from such a bare-bones record of her affair with Edmond? Precious little, she hoped.

As Christmas drew near, Margot began to fret about where she and Julia should spend the holiday. She dreaded being alone in the Cadogan Square flat. Sharing it with Edmond was out of the question, and Marion would be in Scotland with her ageing mother. She thought briefly of appealing to her parents for travel funds to join them at Adamswood, but then dismissed the idea. She had modelling bookings right up to the week before Christmas, and the divorce was now set for hearing on 23rd January. Two midwinter transatlantic voyages for so short a stay held little appeal.

Jamie Edmonton came to the rescue, and wrote:

> You absolutely must come to Edmonton with Julia. Mother will be delighted. You'll have to put up with hordes of my relatives, from senile aunts to puking infants, but tribal Christmasses at the hall are really rather fun. And don't worry. Uncle Walter and Aunt Cynthia *won't* be there. They are always at Bowes Court for Christmas, as you know. My family all love Charlie, but they know how rottenly he's treated you and feel great sympathy and affection for you and Julia. So you *must* come! Pack warm clothes. The only time you'll get within ten feet of a fireplace is when the men are out slaughtering pheasants. And watch out for my uncle Tommy. He has ten pairs of hands, none of which he keeps to himself when there are pretty girls about.

Margot was delighted. She and Charlie had spent many enjoyable weekends at Edmonton Hall. He had always seemed to behave much better at Edmonton than at Bowes Court, drinking less and being kinder to her. She put it down to Jamie's good influence. Jamie had always treated him as an extra younger brother rather than a cousin, and Charlie, though he would never admit it, clearly held his cousin in deep affection and respect. Margot suspected that Charlie had been more distraught by the knowledge that he had shocked and disappointed Jamie by his "disappearing act" – as it was referred to in the family – than by the reactions of his own wife and parents. She knew that Jamie had written him a scalding letter which must have cut him to the quick. But since the "disappearance" Margot had never heard Jamie refer to his cousin in any terms other than those of sorrow.

"Mother is up to her matchmaking again," Jamie added in his letter. "She invited a girl called Charlotte Winter, who is a lady-in-waiting to Princess Elizabeth. Her father's governor of one of our East African colonies, and he and his wife are her old friends. They consider me suitable altar fodder for the girl, and Mother very much likes the idea of a daughter-in-law whose parents are usually no less than three thousand miles away."

It was Christmas Eve, and the assembled company, the gentlemen in black ties, the ladies in long gowns, were taking before-dinner cocktails around the huge fireplace in the Red Drawing Room. Margot recalled how, on her first visit to Edmonton, the Dowager Countess had briefed her on every one of the impressive number of family portraits adorning the silk-hung walls of the several reception rooms. Politicians, soldiers, diplomats and bishops, and the occasional wife, immortalized by the brushwork of the likes of Kneller, Romney, Reynolds and Gainsborough; the lives and times of each forebear were explained to her in pithy oral sketches every bit as revealing as the protraits themselves. And as Margot now sipped at her pink gin, she recalled with amusement the Dowager Countess's terse comment on the eighth earl, whose portrait by John Singer Sargent hung over the fireplace. "That arrogant lady-killer," she had announced, waving towards the elegant figure posed in silk hat and hunting attire, "that was Jamie's grandfather. He'd have been in Lord Salisbury's cabinet in '95 if he hadn't been caught rutting with his doctor's wife in a second-class railway carriage. It was the class of carriage which was inexplicable."

"What do you think of her, Margot?" enquired Jamie, nodding towards the pretty, raven-haired girl, engaged, a few feet away, in conversation with the wide-eyed Uncle Tommy.

"Charlotte? I've hardly spoken to her yet, but she seems very nice. And she's certainly something to look at."

"I suppose she is."

"Any romance?"

"Romance?" Jamie grinned and put an arm round her shoulder. "Don't you know I only go for divorced American models?"

"Steady Romeo. I'm not divorced yet!"

"Just as well with me around. Come on, let's rescue her from Uncle Tommy before she gets pinch marks on that alabaster skin of hers."

The following morning, walking back from Christmas services at the family church across the park, Jamie detached himself from Charlotte and drew Margot away from his mother.

"You really do like her? Charlotte, I mean."

"Yes, Jamie. I really do."

"Everyone around here seems to know what's best for me. It's a little irritating, frankly."

"You sound as though you're being put under pressure. What's the hurry?"

"Mother has a maddening habit of getting her way on family matters in the end. She told me last night that as far as my continuing bachelor status was concerned, her patience was exhausted. She sounded like Hitler talking about Czechoslovakia!"

"Well, don't be pushed into anything you don't want."

"Don't worry, love. I'll never let that happen."

"What does she feel about you?"

"Heaven knows. She just smiles sweetly at me and tells me how much I make her laugh."

"How about asking her if she feels anything?"

"Not much point in that. No, what we've got to do is see if she's jealous of *you*. I'm going to flirt outrageously with you for the rest of your stay."

Margot felt herself blushing.

"You haven't stopped since I got here. But you're *not* going to use me as your instrument to torture her with."

"Come on! Be a sport, old girl. It's the only way to find out. Not that I really care."

He took her arm and kissed her lightly on the cheek.

"God, your cheeks are cold."

"It's a freezing day, or hadn't you noticed?"

"Not until I kissed you."

Margot shook her head.

"You English! You're all totally crazy!"

Margot returned to London with Julia, refreshed and in high spirits. Her warm reception by Jamie, his mother, and the rest of the family had delighted her. She had found Jamie's light-hearted flirting amusing, particularly since it didn't seem to be upsetting Charlotte. And that didn't seem to upset Jamie.

"Plenty more where she came from, old girl," he had said with a grin after the lady-in-waiting had taken her leave to return to her royal duties.

The distractions of Christmas at Edmonton Hall had kept her mind off the court case, but a letter from her solicitor awaiting her on her return brought it back. In it he informed her that he had thought it wise to retain a barrister, Mr Lewis Crocker, KC, to appear for her. The case was to be heard by Mr Justice Barstow, a judge with a reputation for terrier-like persistence in his pursuit of the truth. Counsel of less exalted standing were liable to be intimidated. Lewis Crocker, KC, so Rowland Barnard insisted, was not.

For the first time, Margot now began to feel nervous about her court appearance, and by the appointed day, despite daily encouragement from Marion and Felix, and loving letters of support from Edmond, she was contemplating her imminent appointment with Mr Justice Barstow with all the terror that might afflict an accused with a water-tight murder case brought against her.

Over a hasty lunch in the Strand, close by the law courts, Crocker, assisted by Barnard, rehearsed her in the testimony which the barrister would elicit from her before the judge. Pushing her food around her plate, and taking barely a mouthful, she listened carefully to Crocker's line of questioning and the gist of the answers he expected her to give.

"You must be prepared, dear lady, for His Honour to put one or two questions to you directly," said Crocker in a tone of voice and with a look which suggested that to be spared such an eventuality was something for which they should devoutly beseech the Almighty.

"Look him squarely in the face," he went on, "keep your voice up, and be brief and strictly to the point in your replies. If you run into heavy seas, I will risk bringing down his lordship's wrath on my head by sailing to your rescue."

He smiled thinly before raising a last mouthful of baked apple and custard to his lips.

"I think I'd like a brandy," croaked Margot in a strangled voice.

From the public gallery, populated mainly by inveterate divorce case spectators of the ageing female variety, Felix Beale and Marion Shears smiled encouragingly at Margot as she entered between her counsel, now wigged and gowned, and her solicitor. Advised by Barnard to dress with sobriety, she had chosen her flared navy-blue overcoat with a modest black fur trim at the collar, and a black velvet beret spiked with a pearl hat-pin. Single-pearl earrings were the only other visible pieces of jewellery.

"Perfect understated elegance," purred Beale approvingly.

"Heart-melting!" added Marion.

"Usual widow's weeds," muttered a journalist in the press box. "They'll do anything to look innocent and put-upon."

The court usher brought all present to their feet as the tall, stooped figure of Mr Justice Barstow entered and took his seat. The case of Garland versus Garland was solemnly announced to him.

When the moment eventually came for Margot to enter the witness box, the judge belied his reputation by smiling benignly at her. This wholly unpredicted gesture caught her off guard and after gaping at him for a moment in wonderment she found herself stammering as she took the oath. Then, from the well of the court, came the measured voice of Mr Crocker, leading her gently through the examination.

When did she notice that her husband was drinking heavily? What were her feelings about his apparently growing reluctance to engage in sexual intercourse with her? Would she describe the circumstances in which her cheek became cut? Had she been supportive of his decision to become an actor even though his parents expressed their displeasure? Was the lady in whose company she saw her husband leaving the cinema the same lady whose picture appeared in an article in the New York

Herald Tribune reporting on their arrival in New York on 28th March 1947?

The questions continued, without interruption from the judge, and Margot deduced from the nod which Crocker gave her at the end of each answer that she was giving satisfaction. It was when she was confirming that her husband had admitted to her over the telephone that he had committed adultery with Mrs Hooper for the first time in a Paris hotel that the judge intervened.

"Mrs Garland, had you ever raised the subject of divorce with your husband *before* he began his association with the lady with whom he now lives?"

Margot glanced anxiously at her counsel. His impassive look affored her no guidance. She looked back at the judge.

"Over his drinking, for example," he added.

"No, your honour. I believed his drinking problem could end and our marriage continue happily once he had settled into a career that he really enjoyed and did well in."

"And did you believe that an end to his drinking might mark the restoration of normal sexual relations between the two of you?"

"Yes."

"In the meantime you would accept, albeit reluctantly, this absence of all sexual activity?"

Margot hesitated, her eyes riveted on the judge's.

"Yes, I suppose I – "

"If your honour pleases – "

It was Crocker's voice she heard.

"I have not finished!" snapped the judge.

Margot felt her palms growing clammier as she gripped the front of the witness box.

"Mrs Garland, I imagine you were subjected, like many, to long periods of sexual abstinence during the war. Was that a burden which you found difficult to bear?"

"Yes, it was very difficult, your honour."

Her voice was barely audible.

"I don't think the court clearly hears you, Mrs Garland. You must speak up."

"I said that it had been very difficult, sir," repeated Margot, raising her voice.

"Thank you. Now what is it, Mr Crocker?"

"I just wanted to remind your honour that there is a Discretionary Statement for your perusal."

"Later, later! Proceed with the examination."

"I believe no further examination of the petitioner by me is required."

"I agree. Mrs Garland, you may step down."

"Thank you, sir."

Not daring to glance up at the gallery, Margot returned to her seat next to her solicitor who gripped her hand reassuringly.

"You did well," he said simply.

There followed submission of eye-witness testimony of a Cunard steward to the effect that the respondent had shared a first-class cabin on the *Queen Mary* on an east-west crossing of the Atlantic with the lady in whose name, Melissa Hooper, the cabin had been booked, and that the two had been served breakfast in bed on each day of the voyage. And on that the petitioner's case was rested. A clerk now handed the judge the envelope containing Margot's Discretionary Statement of adultery. Before opening it, he polished his glasses with a small square of chamois leather. After what seemed to Margot to be an eternity, he replaced them, opened the envelope, and seemed barely to glance at its contents before placing it to one side, and looking across the court towards her.

"One does *not*," he began sternly, "dissolve marriages lightly here, although I am aware that in some countries divorces are wont to be granted on what I would characterize as woefully inadequate grounds."

Margot played nervously with her pair of black suede gloves.

"The petitioner has chosen to petition for divorce on the grounds of her husband's adultery, and on the evidence presented I am satisfied that the adultery, as described, did take place and was not condoned by the petitioner. I would add, however, that I find the desertion of a young wife and child by the father under the circumstances described even more abhorrent than the adulterous act."

Margot suddenly felt a pang of sorrow for Charlie; he had been willing to assume the role of sole guilty party, for which she was very grateful, and now he was being rewarded with a tongue-lashing *in absentia* of which she really deserved to bear a share.

"Mr Crocker, I note here that the respondent is currently providing the equivalent of only six pounds a week to support the abandoned family."

"It is our understanding that the respondent's financial situation is at present precarious, your honour."

"A film star in Hollywood?" asked the judge incredulously.

Crocker smiled. "With respect, your honour, he is not yet a star, by any means. In the meantime we have the assurance of those representing him that his support of the family will be augmented as and when his circumstances permit. For the time being, my client, who has her own career, has been generous enough to accept the current sum as adequate."

"I see. Then I will grant a decree nisi. The costs are awarded against the respondent."

At that the judge rose, bringing the court to its feet, and without more ado withdrew.

"So that's that," said Marion to Felix. "Only one nasty moment."

"She charmed the old boy out of his knickers!" grinned Beale. "Come on, let's collect the dear girl and try to save her from the jackals of the popular press."

The newspapers had their day. The following morning, only *The Times* and the *Financial Times* of the myriad journals appearing daily on London's streets bore no photograph of an unsmiling Margot, on the arm of her solicitor, and with Felix and Marion visible over each shoulder, leaving the law courts. "TOP MODEL WINS DECREE"; "MP'S ACTOR SON BEHAVED 'ABHORRENTLY' SAYS JUDGE"; "GRENADIER HERO LEFT ONE AMERICAN BEAUTY FOR ANOTHER"; "COSY CABIN ON THE 'MARY' ENDS MODEL'S MARRIAGE"; DRINK AND HOLLYWOOD BLONDE TOO MUCH FOR MARGOT".

"It can't do your career any harm, dear," said Felix

510

soothingly over lunch on the day the papers were giving Margot top billing.

"I dare say," she said, "but I really feel I want to get out of London for a while. Maybe I'll go to Washington, if I can afford it."

"Out of the frying pan into the fire, if you ask me."

"Well, I daren't go to Paris. Barnard says I've got to remain on my very best behaviour until the decree absolute comes through at the end of July, and I wouldn't trust myself in Paris."

"Nor would I trust you, dear one," said Felix with a broad grin. "So I suggest you stay here under mine and Marion's watchful eye, and do lots of work. Don't forget you've got that Ponds Cold Cream contract coming up, and Stiebel's collection. There's plenty to keep you busy over here for the next two months, and after that the dust will have settled."

So Margot stayed in London and went back to work. She wrote a long letter to Edmond telling him how much she loved him and that they both had to be patient until she was truly a free woman. She wrote also to Charlie to say she was sorry that the news coverage of the divorce had been so obviously hurtful for him to read, and wishing him much success and happiness in Hollywood. To her parents she wrote a letter describing the divorce hearing and assuring them that, with that ordeal over, she was very much at peace with herself and working hard again. Of her plans for the future, she said nothing.

The six months would pass very quickly, wrote Edmond in his prompt reply, especially since both were so busy, she with her modelling and he with his politics. In the meantime, he would like to know if an early August wedding followed by a honeymoon in Italy would suit her. Her parents, acknowledging her letter with some relief, urged her to come to visit as soon as possible. From Charlie, she heard nothing.

Despite Edmond's prediction, the six months of waiting for the final decree did not pass nearly quickly enough for Margot. As the weeks dragged by, her desire to be with Edmond turned from longing to frenzy, and although she busied herself with as full a schedule of photographic assignments as her agency could book for her, she found herself on numerous occasions on the verge of throwing caution to the winds and booking a seat to Paris. Then caution would prevail, and with a sigh she would tick another day off the calendar.

In mid-May, Kick Kennedy died in a private plane crash in the south of France, and Margot pondered on the unhappy fate of a young American girl who had married a European against her family's wishes. She decided the time had come to compose a letter to her parents, for mailing after the divorce. She had drafted it several times by the time she was satisfied with it, and each succeeding draft she made shorter than its predecessor. The more she thought about it, the less she felt a need to justify her decision at any length. It should be enough for her parents to be assured that she and Edmond loved each other very much, that she was not at all intimidated by the prospect of living in France, that her financial situation would be entirely secure, and that Julia would be lovingly cared for. What more was there to say?

On the due date, her solicitor called her to inform her that the Registry of the High Court of Justice was now ready to issue the certificate making the decree nisi absolute. She was free. She placed a call to Edmond and was frustrated to learn from his housekeeper, Josette, that *"le colonel"* was on a political mission to Clermont-Ferrand for forty-eight hours and had left no telephone number. It upset Margot to think that he could have forgotten how important a day this was. She was due at eleven that morning to model a Rahvis evening gown in the unusual setting of a bombed-out mansion in Grosvenor Square, following which Felix had promised her what he called an "Independence Day" celebration lunch at Prunier's, her favourite restaurant. In a somewhat sulky mood, she prepared herself for the photo assignment, and was at the front door, ready to leave, when the telephone rang. To her relief and joy it was Edmond. Barely audible over a humming and crackling line, she heard him congratulate her, pledge his undying love for her, and propose 12th August as their wedding day. Tears of happiness rolled down her cheeks as she shouted her assurance that she

512

heard what he was saying and that it made her the happiest woman in the world. The call over, she hurried to the bedroom to repair the damage wrought to her make-up by her crying before speeding in a taxi to Grosvenor Square, stopping on the way to post the letter to her parents.

For the rest of the day, she was in the highest of spirits, and even the eerie coincidence of Maurice Drake's presence at a nearby table at Prunier's did not spoil her enjoyment of her first day as a divorced woman free to marry the man she loved.

"And how are your dear parents?" enquired Drake as he stopped at her table to greet her on his way out.

"They're fine, thank you. Just fine."

"Or, at least they are for the moment," she said to Felix with a wry smile after Drake had left. "They haven't got my letter yet!"

39

Elinor Moore cried when she read her daughter's letter, and only when she had pulled herself together and drunk a cup of strong coffee did she telephone the State Department to inform her husband, in a still unsteady voice, of its alarming contents.

Harland Moore sighed deeply before putting his immediate thoughts into words.

"Well, well, well! I can't say I'm wholly surprised any more than I can say that I'm wholly delighted. But she's a grown woman who presumably knows what she's doing. I guess we just have to be philosophical about it, dearest."

"Well, I think you should talk her out of it. I've nothing in particular against the young man, from what I remember of him, but I'm *sure* she doesn't know what she's getting into, going to live in France and marrying a Frenchman."

"From what you just read to me, it sounds as though she has no qualms about that, and I think that if we were to try to stop her, we would only reinforce her determination to marry him and risk losing her affection and trust. No, Elinor, we just have to grin and bear it. What choice do we have? She's a twenty-seven-year-old divorced mother of one. She's no longer a baby."

Moore could hear his wife sobbing quietly.

"Come on, angel. Don't upset yourself so much. He'll probably turn out to be a good husband to her. She's a sensible girl and I don't believe she'd rush headlong into a second marriage without having thought it out very carefully."

"You should make her think longer about it. She's being impetuous."

"She's known him for at least seven years, my dear."

"They first met seven years ago, and have hardly met each other since. No, Harland; I don't think she really knows what she's doing. I'm very upset."

Harland sighed. "Listen, sweetheart, we'll talk about it again this evening. I have to go now. Just keep calm. I'm sure it's all going to work out for the best."

"Come back early then."

The conversation ended, and Harland put the receiver down.

My Margot's Edmond! he thought. I might have known it! No point in trying to stop her; she's too strong-willed. Elinor knows that as well as I do, but she'll never admit it. Well, the sonofabitch had better make a damned good husband, or I'll personally come and fling him off the top of the Eiffel Tower!

Harland now wondered if Margot had written to her brother. He decided to call Larry and find out. He knew that the news would be particularly unwelcome to him, and he wanted to persuade his son not to fire off an angry letter, which he would doubtless have in mind to do.

In the fall of 1946, to the delight of the whole family, Larry had availed himself to the GI Bill and returned to Yale to complete his unfinished junior and his senior years. After a difficult period of adjusting to the life of a college undergraduate after the more than three years of combat flying, he had settled down, enjoyed himself, worked hard, and graduated *cum laude*. That had delighted the family too, especially his grandfather Austin. But on the subject of what he would do on graduation, Larry had kept his counsel. Margot was not the only family member fearful that this silence meant that he intended to re-enlist in what, since July 1947, was now the United States Air Force, a separate arm of the nation's defences. His mother badgered him with queries as to his intentions, but the reply was always the same: "I haven't decided what I want to do, and won't until I'm out of school." His father accepted that.

Just four days before Margot's bombshell had fallen

515

through the mailbox of the Moore's P Street residence in Washington's Georgetown, Larry, just a month out of college, had dropped his own bombshell. Returning from a weekend of sailing on Chesapeake Bay, he told his parents that he was declining their graduation gift of a trip to Europe. He was re-enlisting.

"Is this just an emotional reaction to what's going on in Berlin?" asked his mother bitterly. The Soviet blockade of Berlin had begun four weeks earlier, and the airlift of food, coal and other vital supplies was already under way.

"No, Mother, that's not fair. And I certainly don't expect to be flying on the airlift. I'm not checked out on the C-47. I'm going back because I would never have left if there hadn't been an opportunity to finish up at Yale. I want an Air Force career, that's all. Flying is my life."

"You can't argue with that, Elinor," said Harland. "Larry's got a good future in the service."

"I thought the Air Force had been reduced to practically nothing," she persisted. "What sort of future is there in that?"

"Well, I can't expect you to have studied the report of the President's Air Policy Commission, Mother," said Larry with more than a hint of sarcasm. "It calls for a seventy-group air force, fully equipped and ready by New Year's Day, 1950. I intend to be in on that."

Harland reached his son at Adamswood, which he had more or less made his home during his final years at Yale. No, he had not heard from Margot, and the news of her which his father now reported left him stunned and then enraged.

"Easy on her, son," Harland had urged, sensing his intention to vent his wrath on his sister. But Larry was in no mood to be easy on her. A vigorous two-hour horseback ride along the valley cooled him off for a while, but by nightfall his rage had returned. Over dinner with his grandparents, he railed against his twin sister's choice of second husband, referring to him as an "unprincipled wife-stealer", and later, out of his grandmother's earshot, as "that fornicating Frog". Austin and Alice Moore, taken aback though they were by their granddaughter's news, counselled restraint. Margot was a sensible woman; she wouldn't marry a complete bounder, so this fellow had probably emerged from the war a better person than Larry depicted him. But Larry was not impressed by such speculation, and when his grandparents had retired to bed, he settled down in the library and wrote to his errant twin.

Dearest Sis,

This has to be the most difficult letter I ever wrote, but somehow it has to get written. Father called me today and passed on to me the news you wrote about your marriage plans.

You know that your happiness and well-being have always been of supreme importance to me. I think that's natural with twins, and I certainly know and appreciate how much you have always cared about my own. Life has played you some pretty crazy tricks over the last seven or eight years, and you came through them all with spirit unbowed and your head firmly screwed in place. And that has made all of us proud of you.

In the matter of what you do with your life, you may think I ought, even as your twin brother, to mind my own business a bit more. Maybe it's partly because Uncle Sam has been taking good care of me for so long now, whether in the military or college, that I have too much inclination to worry about you who are more vulnerable. Be that as it may, the worry is motivated only by love, and by a deep desire to see you happy.

Preface over: now straight to the point. Why, oh why are you marrying Edmond? Are you really so in love with him that you cannot live without him? I thought you'd gotten over him long ago. And does he feel the same way about you? Convince me of that, and despite the fact that I have no time for the fellow, I will never question your decision again. I may question your judgement, but I'll accept and make the best of what you will have done.

I suppose a decorated young colonel from a good

French family might on the face of it seem to be not at all a bad catch. But we know, don't we, that that's not all Edmond is! For one thing, he's a political fanatic with a pretty murky record back in London according to Father, and Father's no slouch when it comes to research into that sort of thing. No doubt he'd claim he was only doing his patriotic duty. Well, shameful things done in the good name of patriotism can fill a hundred history volumes.

But what really worried me about your marrying him is this. During the war, when he was in London, he had not the slightest hesitation in starting an affair with somebody else's wife, while that somebody happened to be a prisoner of war. And why was Charlie a prisoner? Because he'd been fighting to keep the Germans out of Edmond's own Goddammed country! Now what sort of man is that? I tell you, he's not a man, he's a creep! He was *using* you in London because of your position and because there was sexual gratification to be had at the same time. Now he's about to do it again, and that you're aiding and abetting this makes me sick to my stomach. And since he's already shown us what he thinks of the sanctity of marriage, what guarantee have you that he won't be treating his own marriage with the same disregard for honesty and faithfulness?

For heaven's sakes, sis, darling, screw that beautiful head of yours back on straight and take a hard look at where you're headed. You *must* be able to see that this smarmy Svengali is not for you. He's a lethal threat to your future happiness however irresistible he may appear to you at the moment. He's jumped on you while your resolve has not yet recovered from the blow of Charlie's unhappy behaviour. So push the man off. Don't throw yourself away like this!

Enough said. And forgive the harshness of the tone; it's the only way I can express myself on this matter.

My own news is that I'm back in uniform as of the end of the week after next. Back to B-29s for the time being, with Andersen Field on Guam (20th Air Force) my almost certain destination, unless they find out over the next few weeks that I've forgotten everything about flying!

Give Julia a hug from me. I'm thinking about you all the time and praying you'll see the light.

Love and kisses,
Larry.

When Margot received the letter, she burst into tears. How could her darling brother be so cruel, so lacking in understanding, and unsupportive! She called Marion and went round to see her.

"Don't upset yourself, darling," her friend insisted. "Treat Larry as though he'd never written the letter. Write him a blissfully happy letter on your honeymoon, showing him that way how wrong he is."

Margot took her advice, and left the following week for Paris, and marriage to Edmond.

40

"La Pergola"
Porto d'Ischia
Napoli
20th August 1948

Dearest Larry,

Well, I won my bet with Edmond! I just knew you
would go back into the Air Force. I've always had my
worries about you spending your life thousands of feet
up in the skies, especially at times when nasty people
are trying to knock you out of them. But I realize now
that you can't hold a good flyer down on the ground
for long. You obviously have a great career ahead of
you, so what else can I do but wish you good luck,
darling boy, and happy landings!

I learned from Father that you'd graduated *cum laude*,
a detail you forgot to mention when you wrote. Like
Father, I think that's pretty good considering the three-
year break, so congratulations. I imagine it can help
you in the Air Force.

All this has no doubt kept you very preoccupied, so
Julia and I forgive you for having missed her fifth
birthday last week, just the day after our wedding. I
insisted on bringing her here with us, and Edmond
doesn't mind – he adores her – and there's a treasure of
a housekeeper to help take care of her.

The wedding went very well, not least because it
was a perfectly beautiful day. First there was a civil
ceremony in the morning at the Paris *Mairie*. Short
and to the point. I wore a mushroom-pink satin dress

520

(fashionable long hem) and a matching velvet side-beret. There were just eleven of us: the happy couple; Edmond's mother; his sister and brother-in-law from Nice; Julia, of course, looking divine in pink with a white straw boater; darling old Felix, rather tearful, and Marion, escorted by a lovely old sugar-daddy called Henry Avingham. Absolutely, she tells me! He made it in South Africa and has just returned to live in England after thirty years. He picked her up at a party three weeks ago and hasn't left her side since. Last but not least, my new French girlfriend, Diane de Villambeau (you'd drool over her, knowing your taste for older women) who's an old pre-war flame of Edmond's. And Edmond's attorney, a rather sinister little man with a colossal nose, called Maître something-or-other who – surprise! surprise! – was with the Free French in London. Diane gave a champagne reception at her apartment afterwards to which another dozen of Edmond's friends, mostly Gaullist politicians, came. Jacques Chaban-Delmas, the mayor of Bordeaux and a leading Gaullist, couldn't make it, but he sent magnificent flowers.

My French is improving, but I'm not really going to enjoy politics properly until I've got much better. Edmond's very patient and helpful, and we talk French together a great deal now.

I had rather too much champagne at Diane's and cried a lot when Felix proposed a tear-jerker of a toast. He gave me a lovely crayon portrait done by an artist friend of his from a photo of me. And Marion, the darling, gave me a magnificent pair of pearl earrings.

In the evening, Marion's generous Henry took us, Felix and Diane to dinner at Grand Vefour. Sumptuous it was, but food prices in Paris are insane, and it must have set the old boy back about 3,000 francs a head, according to Edmond. Edward G. Robinson was at the next table and drank to our health when he overheard we were newly-weds. He comes to Paris to buy paintings.

The journey down here was very tiring, particularly the bit between Rome and Naples. The villa is perched high up on the winding coast road above the port. It's cool, comfortable and full of flowers. Marta, the cook-housekeeper, cooks like a dream. Each morning, around eleven, we drive in a battered old jeep (relic of our conquering heroes of four years ago) to a stretch of rocky private beach owned by the landlord of this villa, and we have a picnic lunch there followed by a long siesta back home. The weather so far has been perfect except for one day, and we're off tomorrow to explore Capri.

When I get back to Paris, I'm going to talk to the *Vogue* people, at Felix's and my agent's insistence. But I'm not going to be rushed into a decision about going to work.

Well, I'd better stop. We're off to dine in a little trattoria in the port this evening as it's Marta's day off.

I want you to know, Larry dearest, that I am blissfully happy. Edmond is the sweetest, most caring husband imaginable, and wonderfully stimulating company. I love his intelligence and his drive, and I just know he's going places in politics. It's going to be fantastically exciting being there with him.

Take care of yourself; you're very precious to me. If you speak to the parents around the time you receive this letter, do please tell them I'm writing to them next. Probably tomorrow. We return to Paris on Thursday of next week.

Hope it's not too unbearably hot in the Texas sunshine.

Love and kisses,
Margot

PS Does it really have to be so far away as Guam? What a pity you couldn't have gotten yourself a posting in Europe. France is crawling with our boys in blue, a lot of them around Bordeaux. Maybe next time?

41

Returning from a week's stay at Lachaise-Laurent, Margot found a cable from her father announcing his imminent arrival in Paris. A letter from him reaching her a few days later explained that he would be briefly joining the State Department's advance team which had already arrived in the French capital to prepare for the meeting of the Four Powers' Council of Ministers, due to open at the Palais Rose on 23rd May 1949. He would be staying at the George V, and expected to be in the city about a week before returning to Washington shortly after the arrival of Secretary of State Acheson.

Margot was elated. In addition to the pleasure of seeing her father, she was relieved that he would finally have an opportunity to get to know Edmond as a son-in-law. He had always written encouragingly to her about the marriage, expressing his delight at her happiness, but she suspected that this was more his paternal generosity than a conviction that she had done the right thing. Now he would see and learn for himself that her choice had been fully vindicated and that her happiness was assured.

Moore arrived on the fourteenth, and after a day conferring with his leader, Ambassador at Large Jessup, and State Department Counsellor Bohlen, he repaired for dinner to Edmond and Margot's apartment on the rue de la Faisanderie.

It was a joyful reunion. Margot hugged her father tearfully; Julia jumped up and down with delight, and Moore smiled bravely as his son-in-law embraced him on both cheeks with Gallic fervour.

"I've never seen you looking lovelier, my darling

daughter," said Moore admiringly. "Marriage and Paris seem to suit you."

"I'm thriving on it. I've never been happier in my life!"

Over a candle-lit dinner, the three exchanged news from both sides of the Atlantic as Edmond proudly presented a succession of Lachaise-Laurent's finest vintages in honour of his father-in-law. Over dessert and Château d'Yquem, the conversation turned to politics and Margot listened with quiet pride to her husband's softly spoken articulation of the Gaullist position on subjects ranging from the Atlantic Pact to the price of gasoline. Moore gently led him on from issue to issue, saying little himself, but acknowledging gracefully Edmond's expressions of gratitude for the vital supplies of food and fuels that had been arriving from the United States for France under the European Recovery Programme. Only when the conversation turned to the future of Germany did Moore take issue with his son-in-law and question vigorously General de Gaulle's assertion that the Germans had probably learned little from what they had been through, and that the Allies' determination to establish a strong central German government in Bonn would lead to the emergence of a Fourth, and potentially dangerous, Reich.

"No heated arguments on our first night together!" said Margot firmly, rising to her feet. "Father was up all last night on a plane, and I'm sending him back to his hotel right now."

"Of course. Forgive me," said Edmond, and left to find a cab.

"He's a fine young man, your Edmond," said Moore on hearing the front door close.

"But?"

"No 'buts' really. I can see that you're happy, and that's what counts in my book."

"But you don't like his politics, do you?"

There was no rancour in her voice.

"Well, the adminstration back home doesn't have much time for de Gaulle. We all reckon he's had his days of glory. A few people out on the far right in Congress carry a torch for him, Taft, Halder, that sort of people. They like his strident brand of anti-communism."

"And you, Father?"

"I just don't think he's very relevant any more. He benefits from a big protest vote, but the things he says he wants to do with the constitution frighten people enough not to want to give him all that power he seeks."

Margot smiled. "I'll remind you of that little lecture, Father, when he's back in the Elysée, and when Edmond's one of his ministers!"

"Oh, Edmond may well go far; he's very bright and very ambitious. So are a lot of Gaullists. But I think they'll find themselves another leader and a more reasonable policy to follow."

"That's all right with me; I married Edmond, not de Gaulle. It's where *he* gets to that counts."

Moore drained his cognac glass.

"I like your loyalty and enthusiasm, sweetheart, but a word of advice from your old father. Don't let your very natural ambition for his political success take over as the alpha and omega of your relationship. There's much more to a good marriage than that."

"You're talking like dear old Marion. Don't worry. I love him; he loves me and Julia. His political prospects are the icing on the cake." She giggled. "It had just better not melt, that's all!"

Moore sighed and then smiled.

"Why do I bother? My advice was superfluous in London; it probably is again here."

Margot got up and crossed to where her father was sitting.

"I'll *always* listen to you, you darling old wise man," she said, bending to kiss him on the cheek. "But I can't promise to do what you advise. That goes for Edmond, too."

"Poor Edmond!"

"What does he think of me now?" Edmond asked as they undressed for bed.

"He likes you very much, *chéri*. Really he does. He just thinks you're backing the wrong leader, but that you Gaullists will find a new one anyway in the course of time."

"That's pretty naïve."

"Edmond! You don't talk of my father like that!"

He dropped his shirt on the bed and walked over to where she sat at a mirrored dresser, naked but for garter belt and stockings, removing her make-up. He bent over and cupped her breasts in his hands.

"He probably said the same about me."

"No he didn't. He was very complimentary." She made a face at him in the mirror. "Hands off, lover. I can't get this make-up off while you're doing that to me."

"Then don't take it off."

He took her under the arms and lifted her roughly to her feet so that she toppled backwards over the stool into his embrace.

"Edmond! Stop this King Kong stuff!"

But he had lifted her into her arms, and he now carried her, protesting weakly, to the bed, and dropped her onto it.

"You love it, don't you?" he said, sliding his underpants off.

"Can't get enough of it."

She stretched her arms up to receive him.

During the rest of Moore's brief stay in Paris, he managed to see his family no more than three times. The pressure of work in preparing for the deliberations of the four foreign ministers had become intense. Margot nonetheless put what little time she had with her father to good account. In particular, she took advantage of his invitation to Ambassador and Mrs Bruce's reception for the Secretary of State to make herself known to the senior embassy officers and their wives, and to members of the American community in Paris whom she had so far had no occasion to meet.

"How delightful to discover you, Margot," said the exquisitely elegant ambassadress, admiring in turn her beautiful compatriot. "We had no idea that Mr Moore had a daughter married here in Paris. We must make up for lost time, and you must let us get to know your husband."

Margot blushed happily and wished that Edmond had been able to be there with her. The Gaullists were holding their national council of the RPF out in the suburb of Vincennes. Late in the afternoon he had called to say that the proceedings were running behind schedule and the General would be delivering his closing address late. Regrettably he would not, therefore, be able to join her and her father at the embassy reception. In fact, it would be better not to count on him for dinner either.

Margot had therefore decided that she and her father would dine alone that evening. It was his last night in Paris. With the four foreign ministers – Acheson, Bevin, Schuman and Vishinsky – launched on their difficult discussions on the future of Germany, Moore's modest role in the preparations was at an end, and he would be leaving the next morning for Washington.

"It seems you were something of a hit there," said Moore approvingly, as they eventually took their leave and emerged onto the avenue d'Iéna. "Both Murphy and Bohlen complimented me on having such a strikingly beautiful daughter, and the enchanting Mrs Patten decided you were the secret weapon that would bring the Gaullists back to power!"

"How nice of them. Edmond has always insisted that the American diplomatic community here treats all Gaullists like lepers. I'll be happy to report to him that that's not one hundred per cent true."

"Do you think he ever intended coming tonight?"

"Oh, no. He really did have to stay to hear the General. I know he would have come with us otherwise. He wouldn't miss a chance like that to do some propaganda for the RPF in such exalted American company."

"All right if we dine at the George V? I feel a little too weary to go out on the town."

"Fine with me, Father. We can walk there."

The subject of Larry came up in the early stages of their dinner.

"Are you two on writing terms again?" queried Harland.

"Certainly! He's written three of four times since he got to Guam. They're never long letters because, as he says, there's really very little to report. I guess his letters to you are much the same. Did he tell you about

527

his latest nurse? First it was older women, now it's always nurses."

"You think he's accepted Edmond?"

"He'll never accept Edmond, Father, but since the letter I wrote to him on our honeymoon, he's never said another unkind thing about him to me. His only references to him are 'I hope you are both well' and that sort of thing."

"He'll come round eventually, I'm sure."

"I hope you're right, but I doubt it."

"Did he tell you about his letter to Halder?"

"No. What was that?"

"Halder put out a pretty silly statement a couple of months back saying that the Berlin Airlift was simply saving the Russians from the trouble and embarrassment of dealing with a starving and rebellious city. He said we should have shot our way through the blockade on the first day, regardless of the possibility of it leading to war. I sent the text of the statement to Larry, and he wrote a stinging rebuttal to the congressman. He saw it as a slur on the Air Force among other things, and his dander was really up. It was a good letter; Halder sent me a copy with a snidely worded covering note telling me that my son's manners hadn't improved with the experience of war. Can you beat that? Of course, he didn't himself have the good manners to reply directly to Larry, at least not as far as I know."

"Typical Halder! The man's a real pain in the ass."

"And a strong supporter of de Gaulle," added Harland with a grin.

"With friends like that, the General's in trouble. Isn't he also a member of that dreadful House Un-American Activities Committee?"

"Very much a leading light on it. He sees Communists under every bed in the country, not excluding Harry Truman's. And he regards my boss, Dean Acheson, as Karl Marx reincarnated."

"You know what we ought to be doing, Father: we should be persuading Larry to quit the Air Force to make a run for Halder's House seat. He'd make a damned good congressman, I promise you. Besides, I'd rather enjoy having a brother on his way to the White House while Edmond's on his way to the Elysée!"

Moore laughed. "My sweet Margot, I've thought that if the good Lord were ever looking for someone to be a power behind His throne, you'd be the first in with a job application!"

"Naturally! But seriously, Father, don't you think he'd make a good politician?"

"He might, but I doubt we'll ever find out. He wants those Air Force general's stars more than anything else. Besides, he'd be a bit young for Congress."

"Nonsense, Father; he'd be thirty by the time of the 1950 congressional races, and Jack Kennedy was only twenty-nine when he won his seat in '46."

"Jack had the Kennedy name and the Kennedy money. It takes that for a young man to unseat a long-time incumbent like Halder."

"Well I'm going to write to Larry about it anyway."

"Certainly no harm in doing that, honey. But I doubt you'll persuade him any more then you were able to persuade Charlie. You've got Edmond in politics; why not settle for that?"

Margot smiled. "Not enough, Father. Not enough."

Harland shook his head in amusement. "To change subjects, what news of Charlie?"

"He seems fine. He wrote about a month ago and sent some clothes for Julia. Did you catch his movie? The war movie, *Four Days to Rome*?" Moore nodded. "He wasn't bad, was he? But I hated the way they'd bleached his hair."

"Do you think he'll make it as an actor?"

"Why not? He tells me he's getting work quite regularly now. And the best news is that he's coming to shoot a movie here in Paris in the fall. It'll be his first big chance as a second lead. He's thrilled about it. And it'll be wonderful for Julia to have him around for a while. They were finally married, you know – in January. He seems very happy with his plump little Santa Monica matron."

"Typical ex-wife's comment!" said Moore. "I wanted to ask also after Edmond's mother. How is she these days?"

"In pretty poor health, the darling. I'd like to get down

to Bordeaux more often to see her, but it's not easy. She's been so kind and welcoming to me; I adore her. Maybe when you are next over you can come down to Lachaise to see her."

"And how is the vineyard?"

"Doing well, despite some problems with the new manager. He and Edmond have rather fallen out, I think. But he doesn't talk to me much about the business side. I do love it down there; it's so peaceful, and the château is a dream. Julia loves it too."

"So all in all, I can report home that our Margot is as happy as a clam."

"You can indeed."

He fiddled with his coffee cup.

"I think I should come now to the question that your mother told me to ask on pain of awful retribution if I forgot or chickened out."

"Which is?"

"What about children? Anything planned? You never mention the subject in your letters, and I know your mother's getting a little concerned."

"I should have told you about it. We've decided to wait a bit. Or rather Edmond has."

"Wait? Why?"

Margot shrugged her shoulders.

"He just feels he'd rather wait until he's won his seat in the Assembly. He says he's not sure he can cope with being a father of a newborn while he's concentrating on getting that seat."

"But the elections are two years away, sweetie! What do *you* feel about this?"

"Disappointed, I have to admit. But as it's what he wants, I'm going along with it."

"You'll be in your thirties."

"I really don't worry about that. My gynaecologist says I'm in excellent shape and could produce without difficulty for some years to come."

Harland sighed. "Your mother's going to be very unhappy about this. Would it do any good if I talked to Edmond?"

"No, Father. Don't do that. He's a very proud husband

530

and head of the family. He might take it badly, and I don't want it to become a bone of contention. Everything else is really so wonderful between us."

"Well, I guess that's important. I'll square your mother, but don't blame me if I can't stop her writing you a not very happy letter about it."

Margot smiled. "I know how to cope with not very happy letters from the family!"

Three days later, after her father had left for Washington, Margot brought up the subject of children again with Edmond, and reported that her parents were unhappy about the delay in starting a family.

"I'm sorry, *chérie*, but I'm not changing my mind," he told her. "There's plenty of time, and in the meantime, if you wanted to, you could always pick up your modelling again."

"You wouldn't mind?"

"Mind? Heavens no! It could help me a lot to have you on magazine covers and that sort of thing."

"Well, I'll think about it, then."

She did, and the idea began to appeal to her the more she thought about it. Is this what Larry would call "being used" by Edmond? So what? She'd get a lot of fun out of it, a lot of publicity, and, of course, a nice supplement to her spending money. She wondered now why on earth she'd been hesitating.

42

The audience at the Folies-Bergère gasped in wonder and then burst into applause as phosphorescent stained-glass windows suddenly appeared on three sides of the theatre, enclosing them in a veritable Gothic cathedral. The stage began to fill with figures luminously costumed in Elizabethan attire, gathering at the foot of a great staircase, at the head of which the heavily veiled figure of Josephine Baker, reincarnating the just-beheaded Mary Queen of Scots, launched, insouciant of the anachronism, into Schubert's "Ave Maria".

"Only Paris could think up something so exquisitely tasteless," whispered the American diplomat seated on Margot's left.

Margot forced a smile. She had been looking forward so much to this evening. Josephine Baker's triumphant return as leading lady at the Folies had been keeping the theatre packed for weeks, and Margot had finally managed to secure six tickets and organize a party to see the show and dine afterwards in Montmartre.

But now Edmond had wrecked their evening. He had not come home by the time their four guests had arrived at the rue de la Faisanderie. He was still unaccountably absent when the time had come to leave for the theatre. And there had been not a word of explanation by telephone as to what was delaying him and whether he intended joining them at all that evening. Embarrassed and apologetic, she had insisted to her guests that some important political business had overtaken him, and that they should proceed to the theatre without him. She left his ticket at the box-office, just in case, but now the performance was close to the final curtain, and the seat on her right was still empty. Mortified and worried to death, but trying to conceal at least the latter emotion, she took her guests off to dinner.

From the restaurant she called Josette at the apartment; there was still no sign of, or word from the Colonel. She barely touched her food, and her guests, sensing that she was anxious and impatient to get home, hurried through their dinner. By midnight she was home.

Helping herself to a stiff Scotch, she decided that the time had come to inform the police that her husband was missing. She went to Edmond's study to find the number of the Commissariat de Police of the Seizième Arrondissement but, on the point of dialling, her courage failed her. There had to be some simple explanation, and the most likely one was that he was closeted in some highly important political conclave and unable to send word out to her. If he had been taken ill or injured in the street, the identification he always carried would have ensured a speedy telephone call to his home. He was always a very moderate drinker, so the probability of him incapacitating himself in some city bar struck her as being very remote indeed, and the equal improbability of him spending the evening with another woman was reinforced by her certainty that, in such an event, a man of Edmond's experience would have the wit to try to cover his tracks by calling her to reassure her that he was engaged in some entirely innocent but nonetheless aggravating activity. It *had* to be some political business, but it worried her all the same that he should not have made a superhuman effort to get in touch with her at some stage in the evening.

She returned to the salon, put her feet up on a sofa, and began to thumb listlessly through a pile of mostly read magazines. The ormolu clock on the mantelpiece showed ten minutes to one when she decided she was too tired to wait up any longer. She again briefly considered calling the police, and once again rejected the move as premature; they were not likely, she reckoned, to mount a manhunt at this hour of the night. Clinging to the hope that he *was* about some vital political business, while at the same time growing more and more apprehensive as to what might be involved, she retired to bed.

She slept fitfully, waking from time to time to reach across the bed in the hope of feeling his body next to hers, and then lying awake worrying when she realized he was not there, until sleep briefly overtook her again. When the light of another sunny day made it impossible for her to sleep any more, she got up and dressed, and then called the police. Less than an hour later, a young plain-clothes detective and an elderly uniformed officer were at the apartment door. Seated with them in the drawing room she patiently answered their questions touching on his work habits, his health, his friends, his political affiliations, his relations with herself, particularly during the last twenty-four hours, and finally his propensity to pursue, if indeed she had knowledge that he did, such pleasures as drink and/or other women.

"In other words, madame," observed the detective as he slapped shut his notebook at the end of the questioning, "your husband is a gentleman whom one would not normally expect to disappear mysteriously."

Margot sighed. "That, monsieur, is precisely why I have summoned you."

Speaking slowly to make sure that she understood, he assured Margot that should any information as to her husband's whereabouts, whether in happy or unhappy circumstances, reach the ears of the police, they would be most diligent in informing her right away. In the meantime, she would do well to remain at home so as to be in a position to invite the police to close the file the moment he walked in through the door, which, the detective concluded with an indulgent smile, was what usually happened, sooner rather than later, in these unfortunate little cases.

"So you're not going to look for him; is that what you're telling me?"

"We shall be making appropriate enquiries, I assure you, madame."

Feeling not at all comforted, Margot bade them good-day and settled down to pass a nerve-racking morning. She wondered if she should call one or more of the few political colleagues of her husband whom she had actually met, but decided not to. The chances were that they were involved in whatever Edmond was up to, if indeed he was on political business, and would therefore be either unavailable or unwilling to talk. If there was no word from him by evening, she would certainly have to start calling his political friends. In the meantime she would give him a few more hours' grace, provided her nerves could stand it.

Morning turned to afternoon, and then, at five o'clock, she turned on the radio to listen to the news bulletin. The leading news item confirmed her fears: sixteen RPF members had been arrested on suspicion of plotting a coup d'état. The names of those detained would be released later. For the time being there was no futher details or information to announce.

"I knew it! I knew it!" she cried as she rushed to the telephone to call Diane. The maid informed her that Madame de Villambeau was away until the following morning. Margot asked where she could be reached since this was an emergency, but was told that she had left no number. She began to panic.

"His lawyer! His lawyer! Why didn't I think of him earlier?" she muttered as she rushed to Edmond's study to look up the number. She called the *cabinet* of Maître Savournet, praying he was still there. He wasn't; he was at his nephew's wedding in Rouen. Could a colleague help? Breathlessly Margot explained that her husband had been missing from home and that she had now heard about the arrest of the sixteen as yet unnamed RPF members. Maybe he was among them. Someone must find out immediately. Please!"

A voice at the other end of the telephone sought to calm her. One of Maître Savournet's colleagues would call the Ministry of the Interior right away, and the Maître would be alerted in Rouen if the name Lemonnier was on the list. Madame would be kept informed, and in the meantime she should talk to no one about it.

"Thank you, thank you very much," she said. "And please act quickly. I'm desperate."

"About what, *chérie*?"

She swung round, receiver in hand.

"Edmond! Where the goddammed hell have you been?"

She threw the receiver back onto the telephone and jumped up, glaring at him and clenching her fists.

"Calm, Margot! Calm!"

He walked towards her, and she noticed that he had recently cut himself shaving.

"Calm? How the hell can I be calm? You disappear without a trace. You stand me and our friends up all evening without so much as a call to say what's happening! You stay out all night God knows where, and all today without a word to me, and here I am listening to radio reports that they're arresting RPF people in some coup d'état plot. And you ask me to be *calm*!"

She was shouting now, and the tears were welling up in her eyes.

The telephone started to ring, and Edmond stepped past her to the desk and picked it up.

"Yes, I am here," he said. "No, there is no problem. I trust you have not disturbed Maître Savournet. Thank you."

He replaced the receiver and turned to Margot who was standing, shaking, in the middle of the room.

"Sit down, darling, and let me explain."

"By God, you'd better," she said, mopping at her eyes. She slumped into a chair.

Edmond struck a nonchalant, confident pose, hands thrust into the pockets of his business suit jacket.

"I owe you a big apology, Margot, but what I am about to say is strictly between you and me, and when I have said it, you will understand what happened and why, and we need neither let it upset us further nor refer to it again."

Margot frowned. "Then it *was* to do with the coup attempt."

"There's been no coup attempt. But there might have been, and I spent most of the last thirty-six hours travelling to and from a distant part of France to talk to a man who might have become directly involved in something stupid like that, and I talked him out of it."

"De Gaulle?" asked Margot, her voice trembling. "You went to talk *him* out of a coup? *You?*"

Edmond laughed nervously. "Of course not. He was in no way involved. I'm afraid I cannot betray a trust by telling you who."

"Well, if there was no plot, why have all these people been arrested?"

"There had been some careless and foolish talk, but it adds up to nothing, and they will certainly be set free."

Margot's lips started to shiver again, and she fought back new tears.

"Edmond. You have *got* to tell me. Why are you involved in all this? How do you know so much about it? I tell you, you're frightening me to death with all your inside knowledge about plots and arrests, and your secret missions to God knows where. I want to know."

"I am involved only because I believe in the mission of de Gaulle and his movement, and I'm not going to see it wrecked by a lot of reckless hotheads. I am a person of no importance in the hierarchy of the movement, as yet, but I have certain responsibilities in addition to preparing myself for the National Elections in 1951. That is all, and I beg of you not to concern yourself."

He sank into a chair opposite her. Margot could see that he was exhausted and she could feel sympathy welling up inside her. But there were still some matters to be straightened out in her mind.

"Why did you not call me from wherever it was you went? You must have known I was going out of my mind with worry. And what precisely are these 'certain responsibilities'?"

Edmond pursed his lips, then smiled wearily.

"The reason I could not telephone you was because I did not want there to be any possibility of my whereabouts being traced or known about later."

"That, Edmond, is exactly what I don't like about your 'certain responsibilities'. It's all cloak and dagger stuff for the movement – like what you were doing in London, isn't it? Well, I want you to know that I married a man who, I thought, was a peaceful vineyard proprietor who happened also to be an admirer of de Gaulle and wanted to serve in the National Assembly under his flag. I didn't know, and you didn't tell me, that you were still engaged in the shady side of politics."

"You're jumping to ridiculous conclusions."

"Am I? Secret journeys to warn mystery figures against joining in plots? Plots of which you have prior knowledge? Don't take me for an idiot, Edmond."

"You're making far too much of it, *chérie*. Now calm down." He slapped the arms of his chair and stood up. "You must trust me, that's all." He bent over her and kissed her on the cheek. "Now I have something really important to tell you," he said with a grin.

"What?" She sounded less than interested.

"No more politics for ten weeks. I want time alone with my little family, so this is what we're going to do. We're going to spend two quiet weeks at Lachaise. It will be a rest for all of us and my mother will be so happy to have you and Julia around. Then we will go to the beach. There is a comfortable little house close to Arcachon, right on the shore, which my parents have rented before. We can have it for all July and August. You'll love it. How does that sound?"

"If it's for two months, I certainly hope it's a nice place. I don't want Julia and myself stuck alone in some crumbling old beach cottage for weeks on end. You know you can't stay away from politics that long!"

Edmond looked hurt.

"Margot, *chérie*, what on earth's the matter with you? I tell you, it's a charming house in a beautiful spot. Josette will come with us, so you will be comfortable. And I mean it when I say that I am going to be on vacation. Right through August. *Mon Dieu!* I thought you'd be delighted!"

"I'm sorry, Edmond. I *am* delighted if you really mean what you say. I'm snapping at you because I've been angry and frightened since last evening, and I haven't got over it yet."

She reached up from her chair to take his hand and squeeze it.

"But you do want to go to the beach?"

"Of course, *chéri*. And Julia will love it."

It took Margot most of the time they were at Lachaise-Laurent fully to recover her spirits. Edmond's disappearance without trace, albeit brief, and his subsequent explanation, had unnerved and then depressed her. The restoration of her tranquillity was delayed when, the day after their arrival at Lachaise-Laurent, Edmond confessed that he would, after all, have to spend much of the two weeks on political business in the region. To add to her depression, the summer skies remained obstinately overcast and the rain fell every day through the first week. Each morning she lingered late in bed, listlessly reading well-thumbed Erle Stanley Gardner paperbacks shipped over by her mother, and resisting Julia's pleas that she get up and dress and keep her company downstairs. In the afternoon, during a break in the showers, she would take her daughter by the hand and stroll silently down the narrow road bordering the vineyard to the village of Lachaise, where the little girl would charm old Madame Moutier at the village shop into giving her candy and letting her play with two dusty kittens in the back room.

"Is something wrong *ma chère*?" Giselle asked shortly after Margot's arrival at the château.

"Not really, Giselle. Maybe I'm just a bit tired. I'll be fine when we get to the shore, provided the weather clears up."

"Is everything all right between you and my son?"

"Oh, certainly! But he had promised to leave his political work alone these two weeks, and I suppose I'm a bit angry that he hasn't."

"You must be patient with him, my dear." She smiled and took Margot's arm as they walked to the dining room for lunch. "It's not easy being married to a politician. Particularly someone as infatuated with his leader as Edmond is with that crazy General de Gaulle. My Georges always said that one day Edmond would see the light and recognize that de Gaulle was a man for the war but not for the peace."

Margot kept her counsel; she had no more desire to

argue with her mother-in-law than she had to be disloyal to her husband. Nonetheless, she felt that her confidence in Edmond's political judgement could do with a little bolstering. Outside the circle of Edmond's political cronies, she met with disconcerting rarity these days anyone who had a good word to say for either the General's current behaviour or his chances of making a political comeback.

Towards the end of their time at the château, the sunny weather returned, and with it Margot's good humour. Coming into breakfast one morning after an early tour of the vineyard with Luc Grenier, Edmond was relieved to hear the welcome sound of Margot's pealing laughter upstairs, and a moment later, Julia, giggling frenziedly, came rushing down, pursued by her mother.

"The little witch has been at my make-up while I was in the bath," said Margot breathlessly, and collapsed into Edmond's arms. "What a gorgeous morning it is, *chéri!*" She planted a kiss on his lips. "Will you drive us into Bordeaux? I want to buy a new floppy straw hat and a sexy pair of shorts."

Edmond beamed. "First you have breakfast with Maman. Then I'll drive you to Bordeaux."

"*À vos ordres, mon Colonel!*" she said solemnly, and executed a smart salute.

"Well, we are in good spirits today, aren't we?"

"You bet we are! Come on Julia; come and join me and Grandmère at the table."

"By the way," she said later as they climbed into the Minerva and started off for Bordeaux, "I've made up my mind. I'm definitely going to go back to work as a model."

"You are?" said Edmond, throwing her a quick glance as he steered the big convertible through the gateway. "Then I applaud your decision. If that's what you want to do, I'm delighted."

"Well, I see no reason why an American can't become Paris's best known photographic model, do you?"

Edmond smiled, and patted her knee.

"None at all, *chérie*. None at all."

He turned onto the road in the direction of St Julien and pushed down on the accelerator.

"You just wait and see, Colonel Lemonnier!" she shouted, coiling a bare arm round his shoulders as the car rapidly and noisily accelerated. "You're going to have the most desired and photographed wife in all France!"

From the last week of July to the first week of September, they summered happily on the Atlantic shore. The modest two-storey white stucco house stood on the edge of a small village, a hundred yards from the sandy shore and a ten-minute drive from the outskirts of the port of Arcachon. Josette was brought from Paris to cook and keep house, and Giselle Lemonnier, whose chronic headaches were aggravated by over-exposure to sea air, was driven over from Lachaise-Laurent each Sunday by Luc Grenier to spend the day with her young family.

Fanned by the Atlantic breezes, Margot, Edmond and Julia spent long days lazing on the beach and venturing, when the sun was at its apex, into the bracingly cold water. Some evenings, Edmond and Margot would dine in Arcachon at a favourite restaurant near the port, then stroll arm in arm along the Boulevard de la Plage for a nightcap at the Casino. Near the end of August, they made the two-hour drive to Biarritz, where they stayed for three days at the Miramar, and where Edmond, to Margot's amusement, was compelled to enlist the cooperation of the management in keeping a love-lorn Italian duke from dogging their footsteps from morning to midnight.

Back at the cottage at Arcachon, Margot's best loved time of the day was the early evening when she and Edmond would sit at a table on the stone-flagged terrace overlooking the shore, sipping glasses of the local dry white Graves, and talking about the future. As the days passed, Margot found her doubts about Edmond's politics slipping away as he gently but persuasively talked of the condition of France and of its people; of the threats from within and without; of the yearning of ordinary people for strong, stable government, and of the genius of Charles de Gaulle, the only man capable of matching the demands of the times. Yes, she believed once more in Edmond as fervently as she had believed before. He was destined for the pinnacles of power; of that she was now more certain than ever.

As they talked, she would ponder on how immensely gratifying it was going to be to have a famous husband. But how much more gratifying to match his fame with fame of her own! Most women with celebrated husbands were content to bask in the reflected glory. She knew she was not such a woman. Certainly she wanted glory for Edmond, just as she wanted glory for Larry. But she wanted them to owe it, at least in part, to her. That, above all, would give her satisfaction.

Such thoughts prompted her to delay no longer in setting in motion her return to the world of fashion photography, and in mid-August she wrote to Felix Beale.

Can you be an angel and write to Irina Malinovska saying I badly want her as my agent? She's by far the best but, as you know, you don't just walk in on her. She's *very* choosy. I know you can swing it as an old friend of hers. Anyway, I should be considered quite a catch, shouldn't I?

On that, Felix Beale heartily agreed.

How could Irina be anything but thrilled to handle you, dear one? I shall write to her immediately. She spends her Augusts on the Costa del Sol as guest of a rather disagreeable, elderly Spanish general. They sit under a huge parasol sipping Valdepeñas and plotting the restoration of their respective royal houses. She refuses to receive him in Paris because she says he insults all her friends. I will give her your Arcachon address in case, as I suspect, she feels like contacting you without delay. She can be a little intimidating on the surface, but underneath it she has all the sweet sentimentality of old Russia. You will come to love her as I know she will quickly come to treasure you.

Felix was as good as his word. Two weeks later, as Margot and Edmond were packing up for the return to Lachaise-Laurent, a letter arrived with a Malaga postmark. Madame Malinovska would be delighted to have Madame Lemonnier come by the agency for a discussion on her return to Paris.

At the end of the first week of September Margot took Julia back to Paris, leaving Edmond to attend to vineyard and political matters in Bordeaux. She would return to him at the château in the last days of the month, in time to be at his side when General de Gaulle visited the city.

In the third week of September, Charlie arrived in Paris to shoot scenes for his new picture. Melissa, he explained, was too busy meeting a script deadline to accompany him. Margot was relieved that Edmond had tactfully found the pressure of work enough to keep him in Bordeaux until the General's arrival. With neither Melissa nor Edmond around, the reunion would be rid of much of the strain that she had otherwise anticipated.

It took place at the Berkeley Hotel, where Charlie was staying, late in the afternoon of his arrival, and Margot felt the emotion of the occasion more strongly than she had expected. Pretty little Julia, in yellow organdie and white ribbons, brought tears to her mother's eyes as she leaped into her father's arms. My God! Hollywood's brought out the best in him, thought Margot as she stepped forward to kiss Charlie on the cheek. The California sun had lightened his hair, and on his sun-tanned face there was no hint of the puffiness that she remembered from his drinking days. The cut of his navy blue blazer with gleaming brass Grenadier buttons showed how trim his figure was, and the cream silk shirt and brand new suede shoes spoke of an expensive shopping spree in London *en route* to Paris. Margot caught a glimpse of the three of them in a mirror in the lobby and thought what an incredibly handsome trio they made. Obeying a sudden superstition, she had chosen an outfit which Edmond had yet to see her wear: a pencil-slim wool dress, and a check jacket with a Peter Pan collar. A black velvet beret tipped over her forehead, and black patent leather boots completed the ensemble.

"You're looking *sensationnelle!*" said Charlie, as he took her by the arm and led them both to a small lounge where he ordered a bottle of champagne and some ice cream. They chatted easily about the picture he was making while they watched Julia unwrap a box of gifts, and Margot began to feel more relaxed. The talk turned to life in Hollywood and life in Paris, and an hour sped past.

"I must take Julia home," said Margot eventually, glancing at her watch.

"Will you come back later and dine with me?"

Margot looked surprised.

"Aren't you tied up with your movie people?"

"I told them I had family business. We'll make it an early dinner because I have to start at six tomorrow."

"OK. Why not?"

"And then we can discuss when and where I can see more of Julia while I'm here."

"Of course."

Margot had decided before coming that she would accept an invitation to a discreet lunch alone with him during his stay, but that she would rather not dine with him. She was anxious that none of Edmond's or her friends spot her out in the evening with a handsome young man, even though she could truthfully say that she was discussing with her ex-husband their daughter's welfare. Now she gently reprimanded herself for this lapse in self-discipline, and, feeling absolved, began to look forward to the evening.

At her suggestion they dined at a small restaurant near the Parc de Monceau where she had been once or twice with Diane de Villambeau and never seen anyone she knew. Diane, she was certain, was in Bordeaux.

Over oysters and *coq au vin* they exchanged more news of their lives, with no reference to the days of their life together until Charlie mentioned his visit to his parents in England on his way to Paris.

"My father's retiring from the House," he said. "He won't contest the seat at next year's election. He hasn't been too well, and Winston's promised him a peerage."

"Well, good for him." Margot smiled and ran a fore-finger round the rim of her wine glass. "So I'm dining with the future Lord Garland."

Charlie looked embarrassed.

"I'm afraid so. Not that I'll use the title in Hollywood."

"Come on! Don't deprive Melissa of the pleasure of being called Lady Garland."

"Father's far from dead yet," said Charlie, a trace of irritation in his voice.

"Did your parents ask about me?"

"Certainly."

"And?"

"Father said he doesn't think you're making enough effort to let them see Julia."

"That's damned unfair! They had her for a whole week when I went over for Marion's wedding, and I just haven't been able to get over there since. Why don't they come and see her here? I can't haul her over there every school holiday just to suit them."

"Don't get upset; I defended you. Anyway, when Father's out of Parliament they'll have more time to travel, and I'm sure they'll come here."

Margot drank some more wine and let her irritation subside.

"How's Jamie?" she asked.

"In great form, and he sent his love. He came very close to getting engaged to Charlotte Winter, then backed away at the last moment. Apparently she was very upset and rushed off to her parents in East Africa. I think he should have married her, but he swears that she has absolutely not a brain in her head."

"I didn't think that would bother him."

"He's become rather a serious type. Lord Salisbury's taken him under his wing in the House of Lords and is making him speak on foreign affairs. He seems to be enjoying it. I think he was getting bored running Edmonton for his mother."

"Well, good for Jamie. I was wondering whether he'd ever get off that elegant butt of his and use his talents."

"He seems very fond of you."

"And I of him. I won't ever forget that he was the one

member of the family who went on treating me affectionately after we split. And his mother, I suppose, as well."
She stretched a hand across the table and touched one of Charlie's. "Don't let's talk about the past, Charlie. It's all worked out wonderfully well for both of us in the end. I'm blissfully happy, and it sounds as though you are too. We're both leading exciting lives and going places, I hope. And Julia's happy, although I wish she could see more of you. When she's a little older, she can come and visit you and Melissa in Hollywood."

"That would be splendid," said Charlie softly. "I'm so glad you see things this way. No regrets. No recriminations."

Margot smiled. "Oh, I don't know. I think I'm rather annoyed that I'm not going to be Lady Garland one day!"

"Incurable snob! How about a nightcap at L'Éléphant Blanc?"

"How do you know about that place?"

Charlie grinned. "Melissa ruled it strictly off limits! She says the world's most beautiful women are to be seen there."

"You don't have to go anywhere else for one of those. You've got one right here."

"Touché! Are you flirting with your ex-husband by any chance?"

"A little. I don't often get taken out to dinner by a handsome Hollywood star."

"Correction: a not-so-handsome, bottom-of-the-rung, take-anything novice."

"You always sell yourself short. That's why you need strong women in your life."

"And one at a time's enough, sweetheart. Now, how about that nightcap?"

"No. Anyway, don't you have an assignation with that sexy little French actress you're playing opposite?"

"Heavens no! She's a spoiled, bad-tempered little brat, and she hates the English. Besides, she's got a Corsican boyfriend. They're lethal."

"Well, I'm not going to L'Éléphant Blanc. But you can take me to your hotel, if you like. For a cognac."

"Is that wise?"

"Don't look so worried, darling. I'm not propositioning you. It's just that I'm enjoying your company and don't want it to end so early, but I'd rather not be seen around in public nightspots with you. Your hotel room's not peopled with gossiping busybodies."

"We could go to the Latin Quarter."

"Your hotel or nothing."

Charlie sighed "This could lead to trouble."

"For old times' sake? I don't think so. Pay the check and let's go."

"You're sure?"

"Do you have a room or a suite?"

"A small suite."

"Then there's no problem."

Charlie shook his head in puzzlement, and summoned a waiter.

Fifteen minutes later they sat facing each other in Louis XV chairs across a coffee table, sipping cognac from balloon glasses. Charlie was questioning Margot about Edmond's political career, and she was aware that her answers were becoming progressively perfunctory. She leaned forward to put her glass down on the low table, and sensed he was staring at the cleavage she was revealing. She straightened up and flicked a stray lock of hair back from her temple.

"Charlie, would you be very shocked if I told you that I would like you to make love to me?"

She examined the scarlet lacquer on the nails of her left hand.

"Not shocked," he responded quietly. "But I'd rather like to know why. It doesn't seem very consistent with what you were telling me at dinner."

"No?" She examined the nails on the other hand. "To tell you the truth, I'm just curious to find out what the new Charlie is like – the new, successful Charlie. It's just curiosity, that's all. Sort of unfinished business. Is that very wicked?"

Charlie shook his head and lit a cigarette.

"Not really, I suppose. But not terribly flattering to me, either."

"Oh, I didn't mean – "

"You don't have to explain yourself. I just don't think it's a very good idea."

Margot got to her feet. "You're probably right. Forget I even said it."

As she looked around for her handbag, Charlie rose and came to her. He put his hands on her shoulders and pulled her close.

"No hard feelings?"

Margot said nothing, but curled her arms around his waist and rested her head on his shoulder. They stood there silently for a moment, and then she looked up into his face.

"That was dumb of me," she said. "It was the drink and the fact that I find you so goddammed handsome now. Not that you weren't before, but now you're really irresistible. Christ! I'm sounding like a lovesick bobbysoxer!"

She laughed.

"You're giving me a swollen head," he said.

"I wish it was a swollen something else!"

She found herself pressing her pelvis against his groin.

"No hard feelings Charlie!" she giggled. "How very unflattering of you!" She pulled away from him. "Call me in the morning about Julia," she said, walking towards the door. "You must see more of her."

Charlie followed her, picking her coat off a chair and putting it round her shoulders.

"I can see myself out." She turned and kissed him on one cheek. "Thanks for a lovely dinner," she said gaily. "I really did enjoy our talk."

"So did I," said Charlie, looking mystified.

"Good luck with the shooting tomorrow."

She opened the door and left without looking back.

"Goodnight!" Charlie called out to the retreating figure.

Margot walked past the elevator and hurried down the staircase.

"Idiot Margot!" she repeated to herself in a mutter as she descended. "A real *idiot!*"

Leaving Julia in Josette's care, Margot hurried back to Edmond at Lachaise-Laurent on the eve of General de

Gaulle's visit. She told Edmond that Charlie's visit had gone smoothly, that Julia had been thrilled to see him, and that she herself had had a pleasant lunch with her ex-husband to discuss Julia's upbringing and relevant financial matters.

The self-recrimination over the incident with Charlie had not lasted long. She had seen him a half-dozen more times during his stay, but only briefly, and always with Julia. There was no reference to her behaviour that night, and no embarrassment. She had written the whole episode off as a simple and probably common enough case of a woman wanting, on the spur of the moment, to make love with a man she had frequently made love with in the not so distant past. That they were divorced and remarried had no real relevance in the particular circumstances. No harm had been done. She had simply had a bit to drink and had felt like finding out what it was like to get laid by the new Charlie. And he had said "no". End of story.

The night of her return to Bordeaux, she and Edmond dined alone at the château, although there was an invitation to a large dinner at Château Margaux. Margot pleaded tiredness after the train journey and a desire not to have to share her husband with anyone on her first evening back with him. Edmond felt flattered, and was only too happy to present abject apologies to their would-be host at Margaux. When dinner was over, they called briefly on Giselle, who was confined to her south-wing apartment with a bad cold, to bid her goodnight. Then they had repaired to Edmond's study for a nightcap.

"Lock the door, *chéri*," said Margot as they entered the book-lined room.

"What on earth for?"

"Just lock it."

Edmond shrugged his shoulders and complied. Margot turned round the wing chair at his desk and sat down.

"Why didn't you come to make love to me when I went upstairs to change for dinner?"

"Because you said the train journey had exhausted you." Edmond came and stood over her.

"That's not much of an excuse. I want to make love right now, Edmond."

"Fine. Let's go upstairs."

"No; here."

"*Here?*"

"Right here."

"But it's not comfortable, *chérie*."

"Don't be so goddammed unromantic! It doesn't have to be."

She started to unbutton the front of her grey silk blouse.

Edmond laughed nervously. "What's this little game all about?"

Margot stood up and unbuckled a thin diamenté belt around her waist.

"It's about a man doing what a woman asks him to do."

"In that case," said Edmond, executing a courtly bow, "madame's wish is my command."

"Good," said Margot, letting her long black taffeta skirt fall to her ankles. "Hurry up and get your clothes off."

As Edmond began to undress, she pulled the chair away from in front of the desk, pushed some papers on the desk top aside, removed her bra and panties, then lifted herself agilely into a sitting position on a large leather-framed ink blotter.

Edmond shook his head in disbelief, but Margot smiled and swung her stockinged legs provocatively at him.

"Why not?" she asked, with a grin, then turned to pick up the framed photograph of General de Gaulle which adorned the desk. The General, in uniform, sat at another desk, forearms resting on another blotter. His long delicate fingers cradled a fountain pen poised above a document. The hooded eyes stared impassively into Cecil Beaton's camera, and the legend at the foot of the portrait read "Londres, 1940". Margot stared back into the humourless face, then wagged a finger at it.

"This is not for your eyes, *mon Général*!" she said, giggling, and replaced the portrait, face downward, on the desk. "And now, to it, lover!" she sang out, dropping lightly from her perch, then pirouetting to present Edmond with an inviting rear view. "Right here, over the desk," she said. "And fuck you, Charlie!" she added under her breath.

The following morning, in Bordeaux's Esplanade des Quinconces, before the monument of the Girondins, Margot and Edmond sat on the platform amongst the local RPF notables, awaiting the arrival of the General escorted by Mayor Jacques Chaban-Delmas. Margot, in high spirits, was enjoying being peered at shamelessly by so many curious people, and was excited to see with what deference her husband was being greeted by party officials and other Gaullist supporters.

"I never realized what a big fish *mon Colonel* really was," she said, clutching his hand.

"That's because you only think of me in sexual terms," he whispered, grinning.

"Oh, shut up!"

A moment later they were on their feet applauding the arrival of the General and the Mayor. The preliminaries over, the General rose to speak.

"It's a hard century we live in," he began. "In ten long years I have never said to the French: 'Good people, sleep in peace.'"

A fit of giggling seized Margot, and she had to pull a handkerchief from her handbag and press it to her mouth. Looking mortified, Edmond squeezed her hand hard. In a while it subsided, and she sat listening intently, increasingly mesmerized by the hypnotic eloquence of her husband's hero. At one point she winced and frowned when the General charged that America could not be counted on to send her armies ever again to the rescue of Europe. But by the time his closing "*Vive la République! Vive la France!*" rang out, she was won back, and she joined ecstatically in the clapping and cheering which now filled the square with thunderous noise.

"You *will* be like that one day, won't you darling?" she shouted above the din to Edmond.

Edmond grinned at her and took her by the hand.

"Come on! We've got to get through this mob to the General. Chaban's expecting us to greet him."

It took them time to force their way to the cordoned-off area where the General was receiving the congratulations of the notables. An RPF aide recognized Edmond pushing his way forward with Margot, and brutally cleared a path for them to the General.

"You know Colonel Lemonnier, *mon Général*," said the Mayor.

"Indeed I know the Colonel," said de Gaulle, holding out his hand. "We are grateful for your efforts in this region. I hope you will shortly be serving in the National Assembly."

"I fully intend to, *mon Général*," said Edmond beaming. "May I present Madame Lemonnier. She is the daughter of a distinguished American Foreign Service Officer."

Margot stepped forward, and the General took her proffered hand and inclined his head towards it, straightening up again some six inches short of the target.

"That, Madame, is an Atlantic Pact in which one might have some confidence," he said. There was a fleeting hint of a smile, then he turned to greet another couple.

"Congratulations, *chérie*," said Edmond, as they moved away through the crowd. "Not many people have induced de Gaulle to crack a joke."

"I thought it rather banal, actually," said Margot. "But I forgive him. He's so damned impressive."

"That's why he'll lead France again."

"But you'll do it even better one day, darling, and you'll crack better jokes."

"Monsieur Lemonnier!"

A young man, panting, caught up with them. Edmond recognized him as one of the staffers from the Mayor's office.

"I have been trying to reach you with a message," he stuttered. He looked agitated and unhappy.

"Well, what message?"

"Monsieur Grenier has been calling from your home. I have the unhappiness to report that he has very bad news for you concerning your mother."

"My mother?"

The young man pursed his lips tight as if trying to prevent the escape of words that he knew must be uttered, and which were now on the tip of Edmond's tongue.

"She's dead, then," said Edmond with certainty, and crossed himself. Then he turned away.

43

January 1950 found Margot in a flurry of activity in Paris. Christmas and New Year at Lachaise-Laurent had been celebrated with some restraint in the aftermath of Giselle Lemonnier's death, and the return to Paris in early January had been something of a welcome relief for Margot. While she had presented herself at Irina Malinovska's agency for a talk with the proprietor in early October, and had been enthusiastically signed up on the spot, she had bowed to Edmond's request that, in recognition of the period of mourning for his mother, she should refrain from appearing before the cameras until the New Year.

She worked very hard during January, and soon she was gracing the cover of French *Vogue*. Margot Moore, the star model, was back on top again.

Felix Beale wrote her a congratulatory letter.

Back to where you belong, darling one, looking more ethereally beautiful than ever. Dear friend Dior must be speechless with pride at the way you show off that really rather unbecoming "envol" line. But you, of course, transform it into something it doesn't deserve to be.

I'm insanely jealous of those Parisian photographers, and must hurry out to Paris and bend these ageing knees before the goddess who got away from me. All I beg of you is not to join that monstrous regiment of women who feel they will be condemned to oblivion if they do not adopt the darling Zizi Jeanmaire's "gamine" haircut. It's all right for her. But a classical aristocrat like you should eschew such frivolities.

Margot was delighted with her swiftly regained recognition, and she threw herself into her work with unbridled enthusiasm and energy. At the same time she was anxious not to deny time for her burgeoning social life. More and more of "*le tout Paris*" wanted to meet and get to know the exquisite American and the handsome, politically ambitious young war hero and vineyard-owner at her side. Invitations to luncheons, dinners, receptions, balls, first nights and *vernissages* poured in in bewildering numbers. As the year progressed, Margot's visits to Lachaise-Laurent became fewer and of shorter duration, and even then she would be impatient to return to Paris. Edmond began to complain that her demands for his presence in Paris to participate in the hectic social life was causing him to cut back inadvisedly on his political activities in the region that was expected to send him to the National Assembly in a year's time.

"You worry too much, *chéri*," was Margot's invariable response. "How can they possibly not elect you? You're known as one of de Gaulle's up-and-coming young men, and they know that you need time in the capital which is where everything's happening. Besides, I can't possibly go to Charlie de Bestagui's fabulous party next week without you, and we're lunching with the Bruces out at their Versailles house this weekend. And don't forget we paid a king's ransom for those tickets to hear Flagstad in *Götterdämmerung* on Tuesday. So just stop worrying, darling. I need you here."

The gossip columnists and photographers needed them in Paris too. The envelopes bearing Margot's letters to her parents in Washington were stuffed with clippings from the papers and glossy magazines. Entreaties from the recipients that she and Julia, and Edmond, if his political and business commitments would permit, pay a visit to the United States during the summer were gently rebuffed:

You know how much we'd love to , but we're both just too horribly busy. You may have read that the fashion business is in the doldrums at present because of the very high price of fabrics, all brought on by excessive union wage demands. But all it really has resulted in is shorter skirts (which Edmond certainly appreciates!), and I'm as busy as ever. Not to mention the cosmetics business which gives me plenty of work too.

I suppose my letters and clippings *have* given the impression that we do nothing but go to parties, but of course that's not really true. Caring for Julia and Edmond, and doing my work conscientiously, are really my top priorities. What time is left over for Paris society is not all that much. I suppose it just seems that way because we get mentioned and photographed almost every time we set foot in a gathering. But don't worry: we're not trying to outdo the Windsors! Edmond's *very* serious about his political work and about keeping up Lachaise-Laurent's superb reputation as a vineyard. And I'm very serious about being a first-class wife and mother, and staying at the top of my profession for as long as age will permit.

Harland Moore's reaction was to suggest to Elinor that they pay a visit to their daughter and her family sometime in July, a suggestion which Elinor greeted with enthusiasm. Margot was delighted when she received news of this, and immediately began making plans for her parents' entertainment in both Paris and Bordeaux. They would want to be in the capital for the *Grand Nuit de Paris* with its spectacular fireworks display, and she, anyway, had to be there then for the French collections. They could go to Bordeaux later in the month, and that would allow time to have the principal guest suite at the château entirely redecorated.

The parental visit, however, never materialized. Three days before the Moores were due to board the *Queen Mary* for the eastward crossing, the North Koreans invaded South Korea, and the State Department cancelled Harland Moore's leave. Five days later, the first American combat troops were ordered to the war zone.

"Damn! *Damn!*" exploded Margot when she received her father's apologetic cable. She had been looking forward to her parents' visit, and had programmed it with infinite care. Now, in addition to the disappointment, she began to fear for Larry. She had no need to resort to her atlas to know that the Twentieth Air Force, based on Okinawa and Guam, must inevitably be involved, and that meant that Larry's Nineteenth Bombardment Group of B-29s would, sooner or later, be carrying her brother back into combat. She tried to comfort herself with the thought that it would almost certainly be a short war. The North Koreans would surely be forced to the negotiating table by an outraged United Nations, whatever the Russians might say. And if Larry had survived against both Germans and Japanese, would he not survive this time too?

Over the next weeks, it seemed to Margot that every Frenchman, and not a few French women, were anxious to advise any American they encountered on how to handle the situation in Korea. It irritated her, as did the French newspapers' recurring complaint that the American intervention in Korea risked precipitating a Russian invasion of western Europe. Edmond was little comfort; he agreed with the newspapers. And, as the news worsened in the fall, she began to fear he was right.

Margot pulled the turned-up collar of her coat closer around her as she realized that winter had finally arrived in Paris. It was a grey, cold October day at the close of an unusually long and mild autumn, and she had noticed that morning from her bedroom window the season's first hoar-frost whitening the rectangle of lawn in the interior courtyard of their building.

They were walking the short distance to the avenue Foch where they would be the guests at lunch of one of Edmond's Gaullist colleagues, a young textile magnate of considerable wealth. Margot had met him twice before, and had found his extreme political opinions almost as disagreeable as his barely veiled intimations that he would like to have an affair with her. She would gladly have passed up the invitation to lunch but, after a mild protest to Edmond, she had submitted with a pout to the call of duty.

She had been somewhat comforted for the moment by a long letter from her father, received that morning, telling her that growing fears in Europe of an imminent world war were unwarranted. MacArthur's brilliantly conceived and executed landing of US Marines to the enemy's rear at Inchon had, he wrote, turned the tide in the Allies' favour, and unless the Chinese decided to rush immediately to the help of their communist comrades in Korea, the war there would be over in a matter of weeks. Bitter pill though it would be for the Russians, they remained, for all their rhetoric, profoundly reluctant to risk a world war for the sake of reversing a defeat for communism in south-east Asia. And so, wrote Harland Moore to his daugher, she should tell her European friends not to write the world off just yet.

Margot hoped desperately that her father was right. Edmond was certain that he was wrong, taking his cue from de Gaulle who was busy telling his fellow Frenchmen that the Korean War, far from being almost won, was the prelude to Armageddon.

They arrived at their destination, and Margot paused before the tall wrought-iron gate which gave onto a small formal garden, on the other side of which rose an imposing mid-nineteenth-century apartment house.

"Edmond, before we go in, I want to warn you that if our host, Hervé, insists on pushing his usual anti-American line, there'll be fireworks from me because I'm in no mood to hear that sort of thing. And that goes for anyone else there. And I don't care how important they are."

Edmond took her by the arm and led her through the gate.

"I hope that won't happen. A man as rich as Hervé is very valuable to our movement. He needs to be humoured."

"So do I, by God!"

Hervé Mayence was a short, slightly built Alsatian in his early forties. He spoke in a high-pitched voice while a cigarette dangled, in the manner of his hero, from the corner of his mouth. His wife, Janine, was a diminutive, dark-haired girl who, as Margot recollected, rarely spoke in her husband's presence, preferring to listen wide-eyed to whatever he had to say, which, on any subject susceptible to political comment or analysis, was a great deal.

As the party went into the dining room for lunch, Margot decided that she would seek to deflect from herself all political conversation. Even armed with her father's reassuring news from Washington, she felt in no mood to get into a wrangle over the war. Thus, when Hervé Mayence, on whose right she was placed, enquired about the state of the RPF in Bordeaux, she adroitly swung the conversation round to what she knew was a topic second only to politics in proximity to his heart: Alsatian cuisine.

Flushed with the success of her preemptive tactics, Margot struck again when the moment arrived for her attention to be sought by her neighbour on her right.

"How dangerous are the communists in America, madame?" he enquired.

"As dangerous as anywhere else, I'd suppose. But tell me, Monsieur Josselin, how your daughter enjoys playing Shakespeare in French? I hear she is having a great success in the new production of *Le Conte d'Hiver* at the Comédie Française."

Monsieur Josselin's face lit up.

"How kind of you to remark on it! Our little Stephanie's role is not one of the most important, you understand, but she certainly makes the most of it. It is the second act that gives her the opportunity to show her histrionic talents."

"You must remind me of it. It's too long since I last read the play."

So far, so good. But she knew her luck could not last. When Monsieur Josselin paused in his exposition of the second act to ingest another mouthful of *turbot braisé au Riesling*, Margot cocked an ear towards the conversation in progress across the table. As she suspected, they were talking of war, and she suddenly found herself drawn into the conversation by Mayence.

"I think you would be interested to hear what Tarpeau has to say about Korea since I understand that your brother is a bomber pilot with the American Air Force there. Tarpeau is something of an expert in world affairs."

Margot looked across the table at a balding man in thick, rimless spectacles who sported a Hitlerian moustache and a badly tied navy blue bow-tie. He put down his knife and fork and dabbed at his mouth with a napkin before speaking.

"I'm sure Madame Lemonnier is aware of the very desperate situation of the United Nations' forces, which are of course principally American, in that unhappy campaign. Any day now, the Chinese Red Army and Air Force will strike, and MacArthur has neither the men nor the material to withstand them."

So far he had addressed his remarks to his host, as though it would not be wholly proper to address remarks about anything so masculine as war directly to a lady. But now he turned to her.

"Either you will have to use the atomic bomb on them, madame, or you will be driven from Korea. In the first case you will almost certainly start a third world war; in the second you will, of course, lose all the military and political prestige accumulated since 1941."

With a little sniff, he reached for his wine glass.

"Well, how fascinating!" said Margot, complementing the note of heavy sarcasm in her voice with an exaggerated grin.

"It most certainly is," chimed in Mayence. "It's such a pity to see such a great nation as the United States risking utter humiliation when it is only trying to do something honourable like saving South Korea from the communist North."

Margot leaned sideways to allow a maid to remove her plate, then, as she straightened up, she spoke.

"Why, may I ask, are you so sure that we risk humiliation?"

It was Tarpeau who responded.

"Because you have made a grave military mistake. You have gone to fight a war too ill-equipped and too undermanned to cope with a Chinese intervention."

"Thank you for your advice," said Margot, feeling the blush of anger spreading over her face. "I must accept that you are, of course, experts in these matters. How many years is it now that an ill-equipped and undermanned French army has been bogged down in Indochina? Three? Four? I suppose you hope that we might learn from your errors."

She noticed that she now had the entire company as her audience, and that Edmond, looking anguished, was giving her agitated little signals to stop.

Tarpeau removed his spectacles and wiped them with a handkerchief before returning to the attack.

"Your demonstrated weakness in Korea, madame, could prove fatal for Europe. You have picked up a burden you cannot bear, and you risk dropping it on our heads."

"Would you not agree, Margot?"

It was Mayence, and feeling his hand patting her well above the knee, under the tablecloth, she brushed it off.

"Thank you, Hervé, but I have nothing to add except that I find America being lectured by France on how to win a war in south-east Asia, or anywhere else for that matter, a little hard to take. Even over a delicious lunch like this."

She inclined her head towards Janine Mayence at the other end of the table, causing her to blush and stare rigidly and mutely at her plate.

A short, embarrassed laugh from Edmond broke the silence.

"I'm sure you will all excuse my wife for any unintended insult to her adopted country."

"*Insult?*" Margot was now seething. "If any country has been insulted it's America!"

"That's enough, Margot."

"Indeed it is, Edmond."

Margot pushed her chair back and rose quickly to her feet. She held out her hand to her host.

"Thank you for the lunch, Hervé. I'm sure you can all continue your discussion better without me."

Mayence rose too, holding her hand.

"But you must not leave us. We mean no disrespect to your country, my dear."

Margot pulled her hand gently away.

"I'm sorry, but I think I must go."

She walked quickly down the dining room towards the double doors, where Edmond cut her off.

"Sit down immediately," he hissed through clenched teeth. "You are making a fool of yourself."

Margot didn't answer, but pushed her way past him and let herself out of the room. Edmond followed her.

"Margot, you are gravely insulting our hosts and embarrassing all the guests, not to mention me."

She found her coat on a rack by the front entrance.

"Don't say I didn't warn you, Edmond," she said, and swept out of the front door, closing it rapidly behind her.

Back on the avenue Foch, Margot set off at a brisk pace towards the Arc de Triomphe, and by the time she had reached the Place de l'Étoile she had recovered her composure and was beginning to savour the high satisfaction she felt at her performance. Her father and Larry would have been proud of her. So, for that matter, would the American ambassador, although he might not consider her departure in the middle of lunch to have been particularly diplomatic. But what do you do when people treat Uncle Sam like a global village idiot? She realized she would be facing a furious Edmond on her eventual return to rue de la Faisanderie, and they were dining that night with the Baron and Baronne de Cabrol. Such an evening was definitely not to be spoiled by petty family feuding.

She bought a newspaper at a kiosk and scanned the movie theatres. A new picture by René Clair, *La Beauté du Diable*, was showing, so she hailed a cab and spent the next two hours forgetting what troubles lay ahead at home.

She arrived back at the apartment just before six o'clock, having passed by the Malinovska agency on the avenue Montaigne to discuss bookings. The usual flattering number of requests for her had been reviewed, and she had picked and chosen with care, relying, as always, on Irina Malinovska's unfailingly sensible advice. She had left the agency in high spirits; the money would be substantial in the coming months, and both *Vogue* and *Elle* had her booked for covers in December.

Her spirits sank, however, when she walked into the salon at rue de la Faisanderie and saw the look of thunder on Edmond's face.

"Sit down Margot," he said coldly.

For almost the first time in her memory, she felt afraid of him. Trying to maintain a nonchalant, even impertinent air, she flopped down into a chair and kicked her high heels off.

"I'm exhausted! I've walked kilometres!"

Edmond ignored her remark.

"I am sure you will understand," he said, returning from closing the large double doors, "that such inexcusable conduct cannot go unpunished. I owe it to my friends and colleagues, whom you have so gravely insulted, to take measures which will ensure that there can be no repetition of such gross behaviour."

Margot began to feel very uncomfortable, incapable of deciding whether to show fiery defiance or abject contrition. She stared at her stockinged feet and wondered what punishment he had in mind. A beating? Being kept in on the night of Marie-Laure de Noailles' next costume party?

She looked up and was astonished to see Edmond with his back turned toward her and his shoulders heaving. Was the man crying? For God's sakes, he was laughing!

She leaped up and pulled him around.

"You bastard, Edmond! You actually got me scared!"

"I'm sorry, *chérie*," he said, still shaking with laughter. "The temptation was too great." He pulled a handkerchief from his breast pocket and dabbed at his eyes. Then he put an arm round her waist and led her to a couch.

"You really were very naughty," he said, pulling her down beside him, "but after a while I began to see the funny side of it. Tarpeau's face was something to be seen, and he never uttered another word until he left. And Mayence really can be a pompous little man. On reflection, it really was quite a performance."

Margot pulled her legs up onto the couch and lay her head back in Edmond's lap.

"You haven't told me the one thing I want to hear from you," she said stroking his cheek.

"What's that?"

"That you'd have done the same thing if you'd been in my country and they'd talked about France like that."

Edmond nodded. "I probably would have done."

"Good. You're a human being after all. Now, since we have a couple of hours before we have to be at the Cabrols', less the time I need to say goodnight to Julia and dress for the party. I suggest that you think of a nice way to make up for the fright you gave me."

"Champagne?"

"In bed."

"You're decadent, Madame Lemonnier."

"And I intend to remain so. All the way to the Elysée."

"Thank God Yvonne de Gaulle doesn't know all about you. I'd be drummed out of the RPF."

As the year drew to a close, Margot was ready to count her blessings. She was as happy as ever in her marriage; she was riding high in the fashion world as one of Europe's best known and admired photographic models; their social life was glittering; and, thank God, Larry – many times in combat that year – was still alive and unharmed. Yet the full enjoyment of these blessings seemed permanently threatened. Talk of a third world war had grown all year and showed no signs of abating. The Kremlin's patience, people insisted, must surely be close to exhaustion. And then what? Margot agonized over a long letter from her mother pleading with her to send Julia to America until the threat had passed. In the end she wrote back saying that the general consensus among knowledgeable Americans in Paris was that, if the worst happened, New York and Washington were likely to be as vulnerable as any European capital. She was not sure she believed that, but she wanted to try to justify in her mother's eyes, if not in her own, her determination to keep her only child with her. She had written earlier to Charlie on the same subject, and he had endorsed her feeling that Julia's place was with her mother. Her decision confirmed, she turned her thoughts to the year 1951: the year that, God willing, would see her Edmond enter the National Assembly and his leader, maybe, return to power. But, greatest of joys, 1951 should also see the end of Edmond's self-imposed ban on the fathering of the child she so longed for. It promised to be a landmark year for the Lemonniers.

44

It was Larry's lucky Christmas. In the third week of December, his B-29 was badly damaged by a Chinese MiG-15 while bombing the bridges on the Yalu River over which men and material were pouring from Manchuria to supply the Chinese Red Army pushing southward through Korea. Larry was unhurt, but while his Superfortress was under repair he seized the opportunity to apply for leave long overdue to him, and managed to get ten days. Allowing three and a half days to get to the East Coast of the United States and the same back to Andersen Field on Guam, he could spend three days at Adamswood where his parents would be joining his grandparents for the holidays. On his third try, he squeezed aboard a C-124 transport headed for Tokyo, and his luck held. After ten hours on Japanese soil he was airborne again, courtesy of the Army, on his way to San Francisco through Hawaii. On the evening of 23rd December he was in New York, where he stayed overnight with his grandmother Edith. The next morning his elated father drove down from Millbrook to pick him up.

"Let's get the combat debriefing done before we're amongst the womenfolk," said Harland with a grin as they sped northwards out of New York City. "You know how easily upset they are."

So Larry brought his father up to date on his part in the air war over Korea.

"That's certainly no picnic you're on, my boy," said Hartland after Larry had described the desperate efforts to knock out the bridges over the Yalu River.

"It's as frustrating as all hell. As fast as we knock

them out, Chinese engineers throw up pontoon bridges alongside them, and the little yellow bastards and their equipment just keep streaming over. And in places where it's frozen over thick, they just drive across. But the real frustration is Truman and the Joint Chiefs' stupid order that we're not allowed to attack targets on the Manchurian side of the river. Can you imagine what it's like to watch those damn Chinese and North Korean MiGs coming up at you from their bases on the other bank which we're not allowed to attack? Even with our Sabre and Thunderjet escorts we're going to be sitting ducks once those pilots learn to shoot straight. We could get them on the ground if Washington would only let us. Boy! How I'd love to get the Joint Chiefs, even old Harry himself, up over the Yalu."

"I can understand your frustrations, Larry. I really can. But the Soviet border's just too damn close. We cannot risk triggering off something there. It could lead to the sort of trouble that no one can control."

"Well, it doesn't make sense to me to have to fight with one hand tied behind your back. No wonder MacArthur's chewing the rug."

Harland smiled. "If MacArthur had his way, son, you'd be bombing Peking. And then what price the survival of this planet?"

For the rest of the way to Millbrook, they talked about the war. Larry thought his father sounded generally disillusioned, and more than once his comments suggested that he might be tired of his government work.

"Do I get the feeling that you've had enough of Washington and State?" Larry eventually asked as they turned in through the Adamswood lodge gates off the old Dutchess Turnpike.

Harland hesitated for a moment.

"Maybe. We can talk about that later."

The three generations of the Moore family celebrated Christmas in the traditional Adamswood style, attending midnight mass at the parish church, and exchanging gifts before their Christmas lunch the following day. A call booked to Lachaise-Laurent came through as the goose was being served, and the family broke from the table to wish Margot, her husband and Julia a happy Christmas and New Year.

Later that afternoon, Harland suggested to his son that they take a walk through the woods. As they proceeded past the stable-block to take the path across the grazing meadow on the edge of the woods, Harland, limping less these days as Larry was happy to notice, cleared his throat and adjusted the brim of his brown homburg.

"I have some news to break to you, old fellow," he said. "You may not think it very good news."

Larry looked startled. "What is it, Father?"

"I'm resigning from State."

"You are? Well, is that necessarily bad news?"

"It is in a way, because under other circumstances I would not have decided to go."

"What other circumstances? What's going on?"

Larry opened the gate into the meadow and they walked through.

"I'm quitting, Larry, because I want to avoid putting the family through a lot of unpleasantness which I see coming down the pike. Some silly accusations were made against me in the department some time ago. Someone told the FBI that I was disloyal. So the – "

"*Disloyal!* You disloyal! What sort of an idiotic joke is that?"

"Hear me out, Larry. Then tell me what you think. Anyway, the department's Loyalty and Security Board took up the case, investigated it, and cleared me. That was four months ago, and since the Board's decision had gone the way I knew it must, I didn't see any point in bothering you or anyone else in the family about it. But someone somewhere didn't appreciate my being cleared, and the case ended up being reviewed by the President's Loyalty Review Board."

"That kangaroo court!" Larry exclaimed. "Nothing but a goddammed McCarthyite star chamber."

"I share your view, and predictably they overturned State's findings and declared by a vote of three to two that I had indeed failed the loyalty test."

His voice was full of bitterness now.

567

"And what, for Christ's sakes, do they say you're being disloyal about?" Larry shook his head. "This is all absolutely unbelievable!"

Harland stopped and leaned on his stick. "They say," he said, staring off into the woods ahead of them, "that there was reasonable doubt about my loyalty. And 'reasonable doubt' in their terms means suspension from duty. So I'm suspended from duty until the Secretary is back in town to decide my fate. Knowing Acheson, he'll certainly refuse to fire me. He has as much contempt for that Board as you and I have, and McCarthy's vicious and senseless attacks on him and the Department have roused him to the point where he'll fight back like a tiger on a case like this."

"So where's the need to resign, Father?"

"He knows I'm not disloyal, but by jumping to my defence he'll attract a whole lot of publicity to the case. I can't face that, and don't intend to let the family face it either. Given the present mood in the country, those ready to believe every damned lie of McCarthy's and his gutter cronies about communists in government out- number saner Americans by about ten to one. We'd go through hell, Larry. So I'm quitting. And that's that."

"But you can't give up like that, Father. That's playing into their filthy hands!" Harland shrugged his shoulders and resumed walking. "And you haven't yet told me why they're saying there's reasonable doubt about your loyalty. And who in hell's accusing you?"

"The FBI and the Board aren't required to tell you who's informing. My attorney, Phil Haskell, tried to get it out of them, but they clammed up."

"That's outrageous. They're behaving like goddammed Nazis."

"The charge was that because I'd been known to be against the dropping of the atomic bombs on Japan, and because they also knew that I favoured the Soviet Union being eligible for Marshall Aid if they wanted it, I must be a disloyal American and a communist sympathizer."

"But Marshall himself was in favour of them getting a share; they know that! It's sheer Alice in Wonderland."

"And look what names Senators McCarthy and Jenner

are calling *him* these days over the Korean war. Traitor, liar, murderer . . . should I expect any better from them?"

"But why did they wait all this time to accuse you?"

"Well, you know as well as I do how fast the hysteria's growing. McCarthy has a lot of support out in the country. Hell! Even Bob Taft's waving him on in his communist-under-the-bed witchhunts. They're greedy for some more victims and someone turned up my file and thought I'd be a convenient one. State's one of their top targets."

"But you haven't done one single disloyal thing, Father! I've told you, by quitting, you're handing McCarthy and his mob an easy and totally undeserved victory."

"Well, first of all, the Loyalty Boards aren't just looking for disloyal acts. They're looking for disloyal thoughts that could sometime in the future lead the person with those thoughts to act disloyally."

"My God!" said Larry. "What's disloyal about an honest difference of opinion on policy? What's America come to?"

"A good question, son."

They had reached the far side of the meadow, and as they passed through the gate and started up the woodland trail, Larry took his father's arm.

"You don't have to sacrifice yourself for the family, Father. And I mean that. We can take whatever comes, but you have got to fight. You owe it to all the decent people in government to fight. Can't you see that?"

"Larry, I appreciate the brave words. But I've talked to your mother about it, just three days ago when the news came through about the Review Board's decision. She wants me to quit. She's worried my health won't take it, and Dr Macready down in Washington would probably agree with her. I didn't have too cheerful a report from him last time."

Larry fell silent for a while.

"Well," he eventually said with a sigh, "your health is, of course, a prime consideration."

"It isn't for me, but I have to think of Elinor."

"Otherwise you'd have fought?"

"I think so."

"That's what I wanted to hear, Father." He squeezed his arm. "But tell me, who do you think was your accuser?"

"I can't, of course, be certain, but I've got a pretty good idea who it might have been. Our friend on the Un-American Activities Committee."

"Halder! My God, I bet you're right. Just the sort of thing the swine would do, no matter that it's a member of a family which welcomes him to their home. Have you told Grandpa about all of this?"

"Not yet. I didn't want to spoil his Christmas. I didn't want to spoil yours either, but you're leaving tomorrow."

"Halder – of course it's him! He stored up in that diseased mind of his the argument you two had at the party when Margot was over at the end of the war. And then he waited until the witch-hunting hysteria was at its height to use it and gain some kudos amongst his nasty little accomplices on the Hill. Jesus! I wish I had time to track the bastard down and confront him with this. If he confessed, I think I'd kill him!"

"Steady, son. Let's not rush to judgement. That's their evil little game. It could have been someone else."

"I'm damned sure it wasn't. Underneath that veneer of friendliness, he's always disliked us, just like he hates all FDR New Dealers. He loves being invited to Adamswood so that he can have the double pleasure of wining and dining well and sneering behind our backs."

"Colleagues in the department knew of my views on the bomb and on Marshall Aid. I could have been denounced by one of them."

"Don't be naïve, Father. They are your friends, and just as threatened as you are by the McCarthyites."

"I wish I could be so sure." He looked at his watch. "Up to the stone bridge, Larry, then we'd better turn for home. I mustn't be selfish and keep you away from your mother when you're here for such a short time."

As his father had reported, Elinor was adamant about the resignation when Larry discussed it with her that evening before dinner.

"It's sad, but it's necessary," she said simply. "He's really not fit enough to carry on with that overload of work at State in any case. If he'd been rather less devoted and indispensable to his department, they'd probably have sent us off to a comfortable ambassadorship somewhere. Such are the fruits of dedication and hard work," she concluded bitterly.

Larry wanted to discuss the matter with his grandfather, particularly the suspicion that rested on his local Congressman, Halder. But Harland insisted that he didn't want his parents troubled with this just yet. It was therefore in a certain mood of frustration that Larry took leave of his mother and grandparents the next morning to drive with his father to the airport. As he expected, his mother shed tears, and he sought to comfort her.

"I promise I'll be back to see you all again before too long. And they won't keep me there for ever anyway."

"You've done more than your fair share already," said his grandmother.

Austin embraced him. "Darned proud of you, Larry," he said in a quavering voice. "Give 'em hell and come back safe and sound." Then he winked. "Don't worry about the womenfolk back here. Your father and I will take care of them."

Larry had stayed awake late the previous night, his head too full of thoughts about his father's predicament to let him sleep. And an idea, at first seeming outrageous, had begun forming in his mind in the early hours of the morning. By the time he had fallen asleep, at well after two o'clock, the idea was no longer seeming so wild.

"Halder's bound to seek re-election in '52 isn't he, Father?" said Larry as they drove towards Long Island and Idlewild Airport.

"I would imagine so."

"What would you say to the idea of my quitting the Air Force to run against him?"

Harland shot a quick look at his son, "You're serious?"

"Dead serious. I'd have to work hard for the Democratic nomination, of course, but I think you mentioned last night that his opponent in this last race wasn't up to much."

571

"They rarely are. Everyone around here reckons he's got a lock on the seat, so it's hard to find a willing candidate who's any good – or a good candidate who's willing. But I thought you had general's stars in your life plan. Since when have you been thinking about politics? Not, I trust, only since our chat yesterday. I've never thought revenge a very good platform for anyone to run on. For heaven's sake don't give up a good flying career just to have a go at Halder on *my* behalf. You've got to have a better reason than that. You've got to want to serve the people, not just your family."

"I'd be serving the people simply by removing Halder from Congress. What better reason for running can you find than that?"

"And the Air Force?"

"I've had a good run, Father. Three theatres of war in eight years, and I guess I'll have my major's oak leaves up by spring. I can come out in the fall feeling pretty good about myself. And I think I do want to come out. It's not just Halder and you. I'm finally getting a little tired of living in Quonset huts, eating military food and competing for whichever of the WAACs and nurses are known to be ready and willing."

Harland smiled. "You have a point there. But what about the flying?"

"I'd miss it, of course. But I might get work with an aircraft manufacturer which would keep me flying. If I didn't get to Washington, of course."

"It's a big decision to take, Larry, and only you can take it. If you're that keen to make it into the House, I sure as hell wish it wasn't Halder you were going to try and unseat. For all sorts of reasons, subjective and objective."

"But if I decide I want to, will you and Grandpa scout out the local party scene for me?"

"You bet! I'll have time on my hands very soon. It'll give me something to do."

"You really are going through with this resignation?"

"As of this moment, yes. Acheson's a helluva persuasive man – well, he's a lawyer, isn't he? – but I think I've got the strength to defend my decision. Yes, I'll quit."

"Then, I'll run."

Harland looked at him.

"Then we'd better make damn sure you win." He grinned. "Can you imagine what that sonofabitch would be like if he defeated you?"

"My son-in-law, Edmond, probably wouldn't agree with you," said Harland Moore, smiling at his lunch companion across the table at Washington's Metropolitan club. "From what I understand from Margot, he's rather in favour of Joe McCarthy's strategy, even if he allows that the tactics have unfairly ensnared his father-in-law."

"Harland, I raise my glass to you. I've never known a man with so little rancour in his heart in the face of so great an injustice."

Philip Haskell raised his glass of wine and looked his client deeply in the eye as he sipped from it.

"A noted attorney such as you, Phil, should be irritated beyond words by my unwillingness to fight, and I really appreciate the spirit in which you have accepted my surrender. But I have to tell you that nothing in my foreign service career has given me more satisfaction than my Secretary's efforts to persuade me this morning. He was ready to fight all the way, as I told you. But he agreed with me that McCarthy would simply have the charges renewed. He even offered to have a blue ribbon panel review the conflicting findings of the two Boards. But I said no. I didn't want to go through any more of this nonsense, nor did I want his, Adrian Fisher's and the department's time taken up with my case. My resignation on grounds of ill health can be backed up by my physician. I'm going because I want to go, and Acheson now understands that. I feel I've let him down by not fighting, but he's too big and admirable a man to rub it in. As far as I'm concerned, Phil, Dean Acheson is the greatest American gentleman of our time."

Phil Haskell felt a lump in his throat as Moore finished, and he sought to drown it with another mouthful of wine.

Harland Moore smiled at him. "Sorry, Phil. Unlike me to get emotional like that. Let's drink to my boy, Larry.

He hasn't yet convinced me that he's serious about leaving the Air Force and going for the nomination. And if he does, I'll always worry that he gave up a great career just to avenge my misfortune. But at the same time, I'll be as proud as hell if he manages to unseat that neanderthal Halder. By God, Phil, I'll be as proud as a peacock!"

On Guam, Larry waited until he received the expected letter from his father. Then he sat down and wrote to Margot. Her reply amused and pleased him vastly.

This is the best news ever! Of course I was appalled when I got Father's letter about his resigning and the reasons for it, and my heart bled for the darling. But why in hell didn't he tell me you'd discussed the possibility of a run against Halder in '52? *I* discussed your doing exactly that when he came to Paris for that Minister's meeting! You remember? I wrote you about it. He never mentioned that to you? Sometimes I just don't understand Father. Anyway, it is now your *duty* to run. Halder must be annihilated for good and for all. You'll be a great Congressman, I just know it, and I'll be on top of the world with a husband in the French Assembly and a brother in the US House of Representatives. What more could I ask for? Lots, on reflection – but all in good time. Get the family raising money quickly. It'll take time; we're not the Kennedys, after all! But I'm sure Grandpa knows some people to tap. Last but not least, you've *got* to find a suitable wife, so the sooner you come home the better. A sexy little Florence Nightingale from the base hospital just won't do. Since you should be aiming for the White House eventually, you don't want to make the wrong choice now. Promise you won't pick anyone until I've had a chance to look her over!

"What's your real amibition in life, Grace?"

Larry rolled over off his back and propped himself up on one elbow. He flicked some sand from his fingers before reaching out to stroke the firm, bronzed tummy of the girl stretched out on the beach towel beside him.

"To lie on a beach like this for the rest of my days. With you, or better still someone like you in all respects except for this absurd mania for flying four-engined coffins to places where you're not welcome."

"Thank you, Lieutenant Fullbright, for your frankness."

"You're welcome, lover boy. When this tour's over, you'll find me back in Malibu Beach where I belong, and the only thing I intend to nurse from then on is the occasional pleasurably earned hangover."

"What sort of girl do you imagine wants to be married to a politician?"

"An escapee from a mental institution. Why? Don't tell me you've decided that running for President is more laughs a minute than being shot at by MiGs!"

"I'm thinking about it."

"You must be getting too much sun. I'd better get you back to that so-called hotel and turn your thoughts to something healthier. Besides, I'm feeling horny again."

"When do you ever not?"

"I guess I'd make a good Washington wife. Isn't that all they ever do?" She sat up, drew her knees up under her chin, and stared at Larry through the blue lenses of her sun-glasses. "But you wouldn't get me to Washington, not in a thousand years. Southern California's my territory, and I ain't going any place else but there."

"I'm relieved to hear that, sweetheart."

She reached over and slapped him on the thigh.

"Don't get smart with me, lover! Come on, now. I have to be back on the base in two hours."

"Two hours! So what's the hurry?"

"Oh, Jesus, Larry! Why don't you date that red-head, Wilma or whatever her name is? She's one of the ones who doesn't *like* getting into the sack with anyone. Remember? Just wants to be fed and watered."

"A nice, normal girl."

"Glad *you* think it's normal. Come on, move it, Major."

"There's something so divinely romantic about you, Grace," he said, climbing slowly to his feet.

45

There was little cloud in the April sky as the formation of
B-29s of the 19th, 98th and 307th Bomber Groups roared
towards the familiar target on the Yalu River, the seemingly indestructible bridge at Sinuiju. Larry had lost
count of the number of times he had paid it his personal
attention in recent months, but it stubbornly declined to
disappear into the murky waters. He could think of no
good reason why it should be any different today, so
what the hell were they all doing up there at eighteen
thousand feet, heading toward a nasty little reception
committee of General Liu Ya-Lou's MiG-15s?

In the aircraft commander's seat, Larry glanced up
through the overhead port at the Sabres of the Fourth
Wing flying top cover. The longer this war went on, the
more experienced and dangerous these Chinese MiG
pilots were becoming – as both bombers and fighter
escorts were learning to their discomfort. On his last raid
on the bridges two weeks ago, Larry had watched with
amazement as a squadron of the swept-wing fighters
flashed with ease through the 19th Group's escorting
screen of F-80s and badly damaged the B-29 just behind
him.

They were now seven minutes away from the target.
If the pattern of previous engagements held, the MiGs
would come at them from across the river as the leaders
in the formation flew in over the target.

But today it was different. The voice crackled into his
earphones.

"About four-squadron strength, coming up dead
ahead."

"Damn rude of them to come up this early without warning."

Christ! he thought. That makes about fifty of the sonsabitches. This is going to be some party . . .

A two-week nationwide transportation strike had killed Margot's plans for herself and Julia to join Edmond in Bordeaux for the Easter holidays. Instead, Edmond had willingly made the long drive to Paris to join them there for a brief respite from his campaigning. The national elections were then some ten weeks away, and from now on Margot would be spending as much time with him in Bordeaux, once the strike was over, as she felt she could. She was torn between her desire to be seen at her husband's side as he criss-crossed his Gironde district, and her reluctance to leave Julia alone in Paris – albeit in the reliable care of Josette – during the school term, and had finally decided to spend the working days of every other week with Edmond, and weekends in Paris with Julia.

Paris, usually bustling with foreign and provincial tourists over the Easter weekend, had been strangely empty and quiet. Owners of cars were able to move around the city with ease. Many other citizens had reverted to the habits and equipment of the Occupation and had hauled rusting bicycles out of cellars and garages.

"All grist to our Gaullist mill," Edmond had declared with satisfaction on arrival at rue de la Faisanderie. "Another nail in the coffin of this pathetic government!"

He had been in high good humour throughout his five-day stay in the capital over Easter. Soundings in his electoral district were suggesting a growing RPF allegiance among the voters, and while reluctant to sound over-confident, he had begun to speak of his election, at least within the family, as more likely than not. When he had set off in the Minerva, three days after Easter, on the return drive to Lachaise-Laurent, Margot had promised to join him there as soon as the strike was over for a week of campaigning.

She had been able to keep her promise in the first week of April, and had had her first real taste of campaigning, finding it thoroughly enjoyable. Edmond's charisma as a platform speaker thrilled her, and his easy manner with the people he spoke to in the village streets and on the farms and vineyards convinced her that he was a natural politician. She prayed that Larry would prove the same. In the meantime she was aware that she was herself something of an attraction at Edmond's side, and the well-rehearsed, if brief, appeals for support for her husband, delivered in her increasingly fluent French, brought lively applause and cheers. It was therefore with some reluctance that she took a break from the campaign after a week on the hustings to return to spend ten days with Julia in Paris.

She arrived to find Paris agog with the news, which had broken that day, that President Truman had fired General MacArthur for insubordination. Without exception, the Paris newspapers reported the event with comments highly approving of the American President's action. The General's manifest desire to widen the war with China had been scaring the French for months, convincing them that it could only lead to a third world war. Therefore, while not omitting to praise his past glories, they heaved a collective sigh of relief at his departure.

Margot would have given anything to know what Larry was thinking at this time. Ever since his combat duty in the Japanese war theatre, he had spoken with reverence of MacArthur, but his admiration for Truman was also unstinted except, as he wrote in his letters, in the matter of the President's prohibition on raids on the enemy's airfields on the Manchurian side of the Yalu River. With her twin brother's fortunes constantly on her mind, Margot could not but share his reservations.

She found herself explaining this to her two dinner partners the following evening. As was so often the case these days, the talk had turned to the debate raging in France between the "neutralists" whose voice was the newspaper *Le Monde*, and the "anti-neutralists" championed by the rival daily, *Le Figaro*. The war of words over whether France should declare its neutrality before the United States triggered a real war with Russia, leaving Western Europe a radioactive pile of rubble, or whether the Atlantic Pact should be vigorously supported, had been waged since the turn of the year. The anti-Americanism of the "neutralists" cut Margot to the quick. On the other hand, Truman's conduct of the war in Korea didn't seem to be improving Larry's chances of surviving until the day he could return to run for Congress. Meanwhile Edmond, loyal to de Gaulle's view of the matter, insisted that America was putting French civilization at risk, whether or not Larry and his comrades were allowed to bomb China. In a quandary, Margot had decided simply to stay out of the debate wherever and whenever it surfaced.

Tonight, however, the editor of *Le Figaro* was seated on her right at dinner, and the warmth of his feelings expressed toward America and its President had emboldened her to break her rule.

"I try to be loyal to my husband's position as an RPF candidate, Monsieur Brisson," she said with an engaging smile, "but as an American I cannot help agreeing with you that France would be making a terrible mistake if she tried to go it alone outside the Atlantic Pact."

"Well said, madame. But do not worry: the 'neutralists' are not going to prevail. And, with due deference to your husband, de Gaulle is not about to come back into power."

Margot quickly changed the subject and talked of her brother's experiences in the Korean war and his plans to run for Congress. The gentleman on her left, who looked to her to be much too young to be, as her hostess had informed her, an appeals judge, quickly revealed himself to be an ardent admirer of Senator McCarthy.

"Maybe you do not fully appreciate what he and his like are up to," commented Margot coldly.

"Then tell me, madame, please," he urged, gazing intently at the décolletage of her olive-green Dior gown.

So Margot told him what the witch-hunters had done to her father, and the telling was spirited enough to induce the judge to revise somewhat the extent of his admiration for the senator, and to offer his sympathies to the daughter of the senator's and the congressman's victim.

The judge had just made his handsome amends when

a white-gloved waiter leaned over her shoulder to inform her quietly that there was an urgent telephone call from her husband to be taken. Excusing herself to her two neighbours, she followed him to a telephone in a room near the dining room.

"I'm sorry to have to bring you from the table, *chérie*," she heard Edmond say. "Your father just called me here at Lachaise hoping to reach you. He has something urgent he wants to talk to you about tonight and suggests that you call him as soon as you yourself get home this evening."

"Heavens! If it's that urgent, didn't he tell you what it was all about?"

There was a pause.

"He just wants you to call."

"Edmond, darling, I'm frightened. It could be bad news about the grandparents, or Larry, or Mother."

"Don't jump to conclusions, *chérie*. Call him as soon as you get home, and then call me. Promise?"

"Promise."

"Then go back and enjoy the rest of your dinner party."

Margot returned to the table, trying to convince herself that it could be something to do with Larry's political plans. But she was beginning to feel queasy, and by the time they rose from the table, at which she had barely spoken since returning, she was convinced that it had to be very bad news.

"I'm afraid my daughter is not at all well," she explained to her hostess when she enquired if something was amiss. "Would you be very understanding and excuse me if I hurry home right away?"

"Of course, my dear. It was gracious of you to remain with us to the end of the meal."

She booked the call immediately on arrival at the apartment, then sat nursing a Scotch and water in the salon and distractedly turning the pages of a magazine.

It took forty minutes to make the connection, and then she heard her father's voice.

"I thought it better, sweetheart, that I rather than Edmond give you the news which I gave him a little earlier. By now he will be on his way to you from Bordeaux." She could sense the strain in her father's voice, despite the distance, and she had already started to weep when he said next: "I'm afraid our darling Larry is gone. He died when his plane was damaged in a raid yesterday."

"Oh no, Father! Please no!"

"I'm so sorry, honey," said the choking voice over the wires. "You've got to be brave about it."

The tears were streaming down her cheeks, and she was shaking so much she could hardly keep the receiver to her ear.

"They're flying him home tomorrow, so we'll be able to put him to rest at Adamswood. That's a comfort to us all."

"Father, I can't talk. I'm sorry," she stammered, then the weeping convulsed her.

"Don't try to, darling. Let me just tell you this: Mother's bearing up wonderfully, so don't worry about us. Edmond is getting an air ticket for you first thing tomorrow, so that you can come over the next day. We'll have the burial the day after you arrive. Can you hear me all right?"

"Yes, Father," she managed.

"Well I won't talk more now, honey. I'll call again within the next forty-eight hours. Before you leave anyway. Take a sedative and sleep. Is Josette there?"

"Yes, Father." She struggled to say goodbye, but couldn't. So she put the receiver back, and collapsed face down on the sofa, sobbing uncontrollably.

46

Margot was in an exhausted and emotional state when her father met her off the plane from Paris on the eve of Larry's funeral. Edmond had excused himself from making the trip with her, pleading the pressures of the campaign schedule, but she knew that the real reason was his rarely referred to awareness of what his late brother-in-law thought of him. Margot didn't mind; this would be essentially a Moore gathering.

Her father's comforting presence by her side and his gentle words of encouragement on the long drive to Adamswood helped to calm her down, and by the time they arrived, she was composed enough to greet her mother and grandparents without losing her self-control. After a fortifying drink, and before retiring to her room to rest before dinner, she asked her father to accompany her to the little parish church to which Larry's flag-draped casket had been brought that afternoon from New York by Air Force personnel. For a while she knelt with her father in a pew, urgently asking God to take away the anger she felt at Him for not sparing her brother in the end. And what had the Moore family done to deserve to lose both Katie and Larry? And why had *she* been spared? She got up and went to stand by the casket, resting a hand on the Stars and Stripes. She tried to imagine him inside. Her father had told her that he had not been badly maimed. A shell fragment had pierced his left temple, killing him instantly. The co-pilot had completed the bombing run before turning the damaged but still air worthy plane for home.

"Didn't they send his medals back with him?" she

whispered to her father. "They should be on the casket here."

Harland put an arm round his daughter's shoulder.

"His personal effects have not yet reached us."

She turned and laid her head against his chest.

"Father, what would he want us to do now?"

Harland frowned.

She was crying softly, so he left her puzzling question unanswered.

The morning was sunny and warm when they laid him to rest in the family plot. Following the church service, they slowly followed the casket to the grave dug on the sloping north side of the churchyard, next to the small horizontal stone marking the last resting place of Harland's younger brother Eliot, dead of scarlet fever at the age of six. The family ranged themselves on one side of the open grave, friends and neighbours on the other. Elinor had requested no mourning clothes, a request which all save the former Elaine Burchett had elected to honour. Margot herself wore a pale grey two-piece suit over a pale blue silk blouse; on her head was a black straw cartwheel hat. She stared with bemusement at Elaine on the other side of the grave, in a clinging black sheath dress, sheer black stockings and a black turban. Did she think she was giving poor Larry a last thrill? Even her veterinarian husband looked ready to disown her.

The final prayers over, the casket was lowered, and Margot, fighting back her tears, sought to comfort her distraught mother. A uniformed Air Force top sergeant from the local recruiting office folded the flag and presented it with a salute to Harland. Then, after the assembly had filed past the grave to pay their last respects, the cars were started up for the short journey back to Adamswood.

At the house a buffet lunch was served, and when the last of the guests were gone, Margot retired to her room to close her eyes for a while. As the first numbing shock of Larry's death had begun to ease, the troubled thoughts pouring in on her mind had included the angry realization that Congressman Halder was going to get

583

away with it now. Her father's calvary would go un-avenged – and there was nothing she could do about it.

On Sunday, 17th June 1951, eleven years to the day after Marshal Pétain had capitulated to the invading Nazis, Edmond Lemonnier was elected to the National Assembly. And Margot let out a whoop of delight.

De Gaulle's RPF had done a lot better than even the optimistic Edmond had expected, emerging as the largest single party in the Assembly with 118 of the 627 seats. The new deputy from the Gironde celebrated with his wife, friends and supporters at a champagne supper at the château two days after the election. Telegrams of congratulation arrived from Washington and Adamswood, from London, and even from Hollywood. But the celebration of Edmond's personal victory, which had been impressive, was tempered by the realization that the Gaullists were not about to take power. The parties of the old coalition Government still had a clear majority over the RPF and the Communist Party combined, and none of the coalition parties felt like breaking away to help the General form a government.

"So it's business as usual, I'm afraid," Edmond reflected bitterly after the first euphoric flushes of victory.

"It's a scandal!" said Margot. "Four million people voted for de Gaulle!"

They were lying in each other's arms, naked. It was a hot night, and they had thrown the bed covers back.

"Never mind, *chéri*. The important think is that you are now in the Assembly. Your time will come."

She laid her head on his chest and let her hand wander down over his flat stomach.

"We *have* to have a new constitution. France cannot continue this way. We *have* to do something!"

"Now remember, no undercover plots and dark conspiracies. You promised."

Edmond laughed. "You forget; I'm now a respectabl deputy."

"I doubt that would stop you. But I can and I will."

"How?"

"Like the Sabine women." Her fingers closed aroun

584

his stiffening member. "First sign of skullduggery, Mr Deputy, and I withdraw my favours."

"Oh God! How cruel a woman!" moaned Edmond in mock despair.

"Just try it and see what happens."

She eased herself down the bed, her tongue tracing a moist trail over his abdomen.

"Except, of course, that I want that baby now."

"Patience. You'll have it soon."

In the two months following Larry's death, Margot had welcomed the distraction of the political campaign. But now that it was over, and despite Edmond's victory, she began to feel her spirits sinking again. By the end of June she was in a deep depression. The void left by her brother's death seemed progressively less supportable; her yearning for a child seemed destined to remain unrequited for the time being by Edmond's procrastinating; her energy and enthusiasm for life were at a distressingly low ebb.

A letter full of her problems to Marion Avingham brought an immediate response. Margot must travel at once to London where her friends would see to it that her spirit was quickly restored. Edmond readily agreed that a few days in London might do her much good and she packed a couple of suitcases and took the Golden Arrow to London, promising to be back within ten days.

Henry and Marion Avingham received her at their elegant Wilton Crescent home with an outpouring of affection and fulsome hospitality. At the dinner party they gave for her on her first night in town, Margot gasped with excitement as the guests – whose identity had been kept as a surprise – arrived at the house to honour her. Whatever Walter Garland may have had to say to his political colleagues about his erstwhile daughter-in-law, her popularity with the parliamentary establishment seemed undiminished. Friends she had shared with Dick Kennedy during the war greeted her joyfully, as did her friends from *Vogue* and the fashion industry.

"You see?" said Felix Beale hugging her, "London will always be at your feet!"

"And so will I," said Randolph Churchill. "We must steal you back from the French."

Barbara Goalen, *Vogue*'s favourite model, kissed her on the cheek. "Your Balenciaga is stunning," she said, taking in the extravagantly flared lines of her black satin taffeta gown.

Margot beamed happily at everyone around her. Dear Chips Channon, the handsome Ormsby-Gores, Willie Douglas-Home, several Astors, and, hovering attentively by her, beloved Jamie Edmonton.

"I'm in seventh heaven!" she told Henry Avingham as he escorted her in to the dinner set at six candle-lit tables decorated with pyramids of cut flowers. "I do wish Edmond was here to see this."

"You've no idea what fun all this is for us, my dear. We're going to have a splendid ten days with you here. I feel twenty years younger at the prospect of it!"

For Margot, they were indeed ten days of unending entertainment: theatre parties, racing at Goodwood, a glittering evening at the Festival of Britain's South Bank exhibition; a convivial lunch at the House of Lords with Jamie, including a peek into the Commons and a sighting of Sir Walter in the Chamber. She drew upon reserves of energy she had forgotten she had, and when the day on which she had promised to return to Edmond and Julia arrived, she realized how totally restored she felt.

"Marion, darling, you did it!" she exulted as she said goodbye to her friend. "I'm feeling terrific, and I can't wait to get back to Edmond now and get on with my life."

To Margot's surprise, Edmond was not at the Gare du Nord to meet her on her return. Feeling a little hurt, she took a taxi to the apartment where Josette informed her that the Colonel was down at the National Assembly on urgent business, and Julia was at a school friend's birthday party.

"Quite a welcome home," she said sourly, picking up a pile of mail and taking it to the bedroom. She stretched out on the bed and began to open the envelopes. They were mostly invitations, and not many of them looked particularly interesting. She set aside two for acceptance in early September: a weekend invitation from the formidable American-born Princess Chachavadze – or

586

always accepted her invitations – and a much coveted invitation to Charlie de Bestegui's costume ball in Venice.

The bedroom door burst open and Edmond hurried to her.

"*Chérie*, I'm mortified I couldn't get to the station to meet you! How are you? Was it marvellous?"

Margot flung her arms up to embrace him.

"Oh, angel, am I glad to see you! Yes, it was really a fabulous visit. And how have you been? Is everything all right? I've been missing you terribly!"

Edmond stopped the flow of words with a long kiss on the lips.

"I've been fine," he eventually said, sinking down onto the bed beside her. "I'm sorry I couldn't meet you, but it was a big day in the Assembly. Would you believe that we finally have a government? Since a couple of hours."

"About time too! Who got the nod?"

"That colourless relic, René Pleven. He put together an old-hat coalition of the centre-right which made the right noises on the school reform issue. We're not part of it, of course, but then – "

Margot put a hand over his mouth.

"Politics later, *chéri*. First, you close the door, then you take your clothes off, and then – guess what?"

Edmond grinned. "I can't imagine."

Margot pushed the open mail onto the floor and sprang agilely to her feet.

"God, if you knew how much I've been wanting this!" she said as she unzipped her dress.

They dined later that evening because Margot kept Julia up way past her bedtime, delighting in hearing every detail of her life since their last parting. And then, since it was a balmy evening, she had insisted on a walk to the edge of the Bois, and an apéritif in a sidewalk café on the rue de Longchamp. Over a Pernod, she told him all about her stay with the Avinghams, and of all the old friends whom she had seen.

"Now don't be jealous, darling," she said, patting his hand when she saw the slight look of irritation on his face as she recited the names.

Over dinner they had an argument. Edmond had no wish to go to Venice in the first week of September for Charlie de Bestegui's costume ball.

"Quite apart from the fact that I want to be down at the vineyard at that time because the Assembly won't be sitting, I find the whole idea of this ball very vulgar."

"Nonsense, Edmond! Everyone says that it's going to be the greatest party in Europe since the war."

"Precisely! There are millions of very poor people in Italy, and such a conspicuously lavish display plays right into the hands of the communists."

"But, darling, the money Charlie spends will be going into the pockets of the Venetians! And so many of our friends will be going; the de Cabrols, the Pol Rogers, the von Hoffmannsthals, Cecil Beaton, Dior – "

"I know, I know. But that doesn't make it any more acceptable to me. The world's on the brink of war, and all Paris society can think about is which Paris hairdresser will make it to Venice to look after them, and how much Barbara Hutton's costume is going to cost."

"You're just a spoilsport, Edmond. You really are." Margot sat pouting. "I'm going to go, anyway," she said. "People will expect me to be there, and I'm damned if I'm going to disappoint them."

"*Mon Dieu!* What arrogance, my pet!"

"Oh, forget it for now. I don't want us quarrelling on my first night back."

"And your last but one night before going away again," said Edmond bitterly.

"Business is business, darling. Chanel pays big bucks for my face and figure. And it's only for a few days. Why not come too? You like Antibes."

"And politics is politics."

Margot shrugged her shoulders.

"Then we'd better make the best use of our time together here."

She winked at him and stuck a finger, childlike, in he mouth.

"Sex maniac!" he said, pouring himself another glass o Yquem.

47

Marianne Tricot caught the nine o'clock ferry from the Pointe de Sablanceaux at the tip of the Ile de Ré, and twenty minutes later she walked ashore at La Pallice, and took the bus for the five kilometre ride into the Atlantic port of La Rochelle.

Madame Tricot always enjoyed her monthy trips to La Rochelle to see her widowed sister, Jeanne. But this was not one of her regular visits, and she would not have time to enjoy a leisurely lunch of Jeanne's mouthwatering *mouclade au pineau*, washed down with a bottle of Muscadet. Today she was planning to spend no more time in the town than she was required to get to Dr Sinard's office on the rue Gambetta, pick up the drugs, and head back to La Pallice to catch the next ferry returning to the island.

When she had propped her husband, Marcel, up on the pillows that morning to feed him his bread soaked in milky coffee, he had complained of worsening pains. He looked worse too, she decided. They both knew that the pervasive cancer had all but completed its fatal work, and the only thing that mattered now was to keep the dying fisherman's last days and hours as free of pain and suffering as was medically possible. After eating her own breakfast, Marianne discovered to her chagrin that the packet she thought contained a replenishment of the supply of the pain-killing drug prescribed by Dr Sinard was, instead, a packet of laxative pills. Hence her hurried journey across the water to La Rochelle.

Meanwhile, in the white-washed fisherman's cottage close to the small boat-lined quay in the village of

Ars-en-Ré, Marcel Tricot lay staring through the open window at the sun-drenched white walls of the cottages across the narrow street. Most of them had their green shutters closed to keep the rooms cool, but Marcel was determined to keep looking out onto the world outside as long as light and life permitted. Today, he was convinced, was his last day on earth. He sensed that his body was finally giving up the unequal struggle, and everything was quietly and inexorably closing down. It was like his fishing boat when he cut the engine and let it slip silently into its berth. No noise, no vibrations, no churning water at the stern. Just a peaceful, unaided, slowing down until it came to rest.

He no longer had any regrets. He had at first been shocked and angry to find out that he would be dead of cancer at the age of fifty-one, but he had outlived both his younger brothers: one dead on the beach at Dunkirk, the other shot against a wall on orders from the Gestapo chief in Nantes. Now there was only one matter left to be dealt with if he was to leave this world with no unwanted baggage, and that required a short talk with Père Rémy, the village priest, who had promised to look in later in the morning.

With weakened fingers he lifted a small leather satchel from a chair by the bed and pulled an envelope from it. He checked the contents: a quarto-size folded sheet of paper, handwritten on both sides, and ten one-thousand franc notes. He replaced the contents, tucked in the flap of the envelope, which bore the priest's name, and propped it on the bedside table between the lamp and his glass of water. He felt tired by the effort and let his head sink back on the pillows. He closed his eyes.

Père Rémy cursed his ill luck. Why today, of all days, did his fellow priest in La Flotte have to succumb to food poisoning and call on him to take the marriage service that afternoon? Given the impossiblity of cutting the wedding feast afterwards without causing the gravest of offence, he did not see himself getting back to Ars-en-Ré much before five, which meant he would miss the visit of the organ repairer. And then hadn't he promised t look in on poor Marcel Tricot? Well, he'd make a point of going tomorrow morning after first mass.

Marianne Tricot missed the bus to La Pallice and resigned herself to taking the midday ferry instead. With time to kill, she went to the café opposite the bus stop and ordered a cup of strong coffee. She was happy to get off her feet.

Unlike his mother, Bertrand Tricot had arrived by car at La Pallice in time to catch the eleven o'clock ferry. He was running well ahead of time. He and his girlfriend had had a blazing early morning row, and he had left her apartment on the outskirts of Poitiers, a ninety-minute drive from La Rochelle, without staying for breakfast. The clock on the black and white spired tower of the church in Ars-en-Ré showed twenty minutes to midday when he turned down a side street running off the market square and drew up before his parents' cottage.

The front door was, as always, unlocked, and he went in, calling his mother as he entered. No one answered. He climbed the narrow staircase to the upper floor. He might as well not put off the less than agreeable moment when he would have to sit at his father's bedside and make polite conversation to the dying man, and try to pretend, for form's sake, that he was distressed at his father's worsening condition.

Bertrand Tricot and his father cordially disliked one another. The young man had come back from the Indo-China war convinced that the French had no right to try to dictate the future of the country and its indigenous peoples. He also came back with a healthy admiration for Ho Chi Minh, and within weeks of his return and demobilization he had joined the French Communist Party and gone to work for a communist journal of opinion in Paris. This was more than a disappointment to his father: it was, in Marcel's view, an unacceptable insult. It had always been understood that the boy would join his father on the fishing boat on his return from Indo-China. It had also been understood that he shared his father's loyalty and devotion to the person and cause of Charles de Gaulle. The son's apostasy and the father's reaction to it had embittered relations to the point where even when

591

Bertrand eventually got a job with the Poitiers newspaper, he paid no visits to his parents just 130 kilometres away. The newspaper had fired him that summer in embarrassment over his increasingly extreme communist views, and his girlfriend, the daughter of a well-to-do but left-leaning local businessman, had been supporting him while he eked out less than a living as a freelance journalist.

A call from his mother confirming that his father was close to death finally persuaded him to make the journey to the Ile de Ré, if only for his mother's sake. Now he would make an effort to be polite and unargumentative in his dying father's presence.

"*Bonjour, Papa!*" he said brightly as he pushed open the door of his father's room. Marcel was staring out of the window and made no move to recognize the arrival of his son. Bertrand approached the bed.

"I said '*bonjour*'. Are you going to be civil and respond, or am I wasting my time coming to see you?"

It was then that he saw his father's eyes.

"*Merde!*" he exclaimed. "All this way, and he's as dead as a doornail!"

He walked round the bed to take a closer look at his late father.

"Poor bastard," he said, surrendering for a moment to sentiments of filial sympathy. "It can't be nice to die alone in the daytime."

He gently closed the lids of his father's eyes, thinking bitterly of how the last time he had done that to a dead person, it had been his closest friend in that criminally useless war.

Then his glance was caught by the envelope by the bed. He picked it up, and could see at once that it contained money. What the hell was he giving that amount of money to the priest for, he wondered, as he counted the bills. Then he turned his attention to the handwritten page of cheap writing paper.

Father [it read],

I write this in case I die before being able to tell you face to face what is on my mind as I prepare to meet my Maker. I shall be sorry if that has to happen, but at least I shall die knowing that you will take this letter seriously.

I have a confession to make, and since writing tires me so, I will keep it brief.

In the winter of 1943, in London, when I was with General de Gaulle's France Combattante, I was an accomplice in the murder of a French *résistant*. He was a communist, we were told, and a mortal threat to de Gaulle's efforts to build up the secret army in occupied France. The man, Pierre Mouret (whose name must be familiar to you because he became something of a posthumous hero) was run down in the fog after being lured by us into a trap. I was not in on the planning of this – I only obeyed orders – but I drove the car to the rendezvous and drove it back after the killing. For reasons I needn't explain, I was not at the wheel when Mouret was deliberately run down. A man called Captain Lemonnier did the driving and there was a third man with us, but I don't remember his name.

If I die before you give me extreme unction and absolution, and whatever else you do, will you promise to say a special mass for me, asking the good God to forgive me for that mortal sin? I am not a bad man, Father, but sometimes in war you get told to do things which you know are wrong but which you have to do. I heard afterwards that Lemonnier decided on the killing without higher authority knowing. They all went on thinking it was an accident in the fog. Anyway I kept my mouth shut these years because I was scared. But maybe I should have confessed to the church before now.

I enclose ten thousand francs for the mass and for whatever other good works it might help pay for.

Lord, forgive me!
Father, pray for me!
Marcel Tricot

Bertrand Tricot took a deep breath when he'd finished reading his father's confession, then let out a sharp whistle. Captain Lemonnier! Gaullist Deputy! It *had* to be him!

He folded the letter, put it back in the envelope, and stuffed the envelope into his pocket. Some editor would pay a fortune for that letter, he thought happily. But that was not how he was going to play it.

48

Edmond remained adamant on the subject of de Bestegui's
Venice ball. The Médoc vintage was likely to begin any
time after 13th September, and since the selection of
the date to start picking the grapes was the most momen-
tous decision a vineyard proprietor made all year, there
was no question of him not being at Lachaise-Laurent
when the day of decision might be only a week away.
His vineyard and cellar workers would be returning
from their pre-vintage holidays that week, and his *maître
de chai*, Luc Grenier, was already back, poring over
weather reports from the Bordeaux meteorological office,
checking the maturity of the grapes, and preparing for
the arrival of the teams of Spanish pickers who had to be
accommodated and fed during the two to three weeks
of the harvest. Accordingly, Edmond left Paris for
Bordeaux on 6th September, bidding Margot a rather
tepid farewell.

Margot had remained adamant too, and had proceeded
with her plans to attend the ball in the company of
friends. There was no shortage of single males anxious to
escort her once it became known that Edmond would not
be in attendance. But Margot refused to be hurried into
a decision, and her caution was rewarded when she
received a letter from Felix Beale in London saying that
he would be at the ball, and enquiring whether she and
Edmond, who must surely have been invited, would be
there as well. Delighted, Margot wasted no time in calling
Felix and asking him to be her escort, a proposition to
which he responded with great enthusiasm. Her choice
of a gentle middle-aged homosexual friend of the family

to be her escort did little to mollify Edmond, who continued to insist that the risk of being cuckolded in the city of canals weighed far less heavily on his mind than the certainty that the well-publicized association of the name Lemonnier with what he saw as an ostentatious display of misused wealth would be noted with surprise, if not displeasure, in inner Gaullist circles.

"Don't be pompous, Edmond," said Margot, summarily dismissing his objections. "It doesn't suit you."

She now turned her mind to the question of what costume she would wear to the ball. Felix Beale would be dressed as a mid-eighteenth-century bewigged gentleman based on the self-portrait by Maurice-Quentin de Latour. Diana Cooper, the famed beauty who was the wife of the British ambassador to France, was going, Margot had heard, as the Cleopatra portrayed in the magnificent Tiepolo fresco at de Bestegui's Palazzo Labia. And some other notables of Paris society were having period costumes specially designed for the occasion by leading Paris couturiers. Margot decided therefore to consult Christian Dior on the matter.

"My dear, with your classical beauty, you must not overdress," the designer told her. "Some of the ladies are going to look like extravagant wedding cakes, but that is not for you."

He showed her a book on French eighteenth-century paintings.

"This is how you should go," he said with a flourish of the hand as he found among the pages Fragonard's Young Woman Reading a Book. "She is ravishing in her simplicity and the yellow dress is a dream. No comical wigs or distracting accessories. Just natural. I will find you a pretty little book with the pages hollowed out which you can carry and use as a bag. Go and talk to Antonio, or whoever does your hair, and show him a copy of the painting; he will easily give you this swept-up style. Come to me for a fitting of the dress in ten days. My dear, you are going to be too hauntingly beautiful for words, and Felix will be the envy of all!"

Margot left the avenue Montaigne establishment in high spirits. She would be leaving in the afternoon for

596

Antibes to do the Chanel advertisement. That, happily, would pay for the Fragonard dress that Dior would now make for her. She could hardly have asked it as a gift from the disapproving Edmond.

Crossing the avenue George V, she smiled pleasantly at the driver of a car waiting at the traffic signal when he blew her a kiss. How lovely it was to be beautiful and noticed on a perfect early September day in her favourite city! All she needed now was for Edmond to stop sulking about her trip to Venice. She'd call him in Bordeaux as soon as she reached Antibes, and tell him how much she loved him and missed him. Dear, wonderful Edmond!

49

At about the time that Margot's flight was landing at Nice Airport, Bertrand Tricot swung his battered Citroën onto Route National 10, on the outskirts of Poitiers and sped past the sign announcing that Bordeaux was now 218 kilometers to the south. He would, he reckoned, be in the port city within three hours at the most, and at Lemonnier's vineyard some thirty minutes later. He had some time, then, to refine his plan of action.

Basically it was very simple. He had had no difficulty in establishing that the Deputy was indeed at Lachaise-Laurent. Where else would a vineyard proprietor be than amongst his ripened grapes at this moment of the year? He had also ascertained without difficulty – a call to the apartment on rue de la Faisanderie and its cooperative housekeeper – that Madame Lemonnier, the American model, was on the Riveria on a professional assignment lasting at least three days. This, then, was an ideal time to visit the killer of Pierre Mouret. He had briefly toyed with the idea of calling him for an innocent-sounding appointment to discuss Gaullist ambitions in the south-west, but had rejected it. An unheralded visit would likely throw his quarry off guard and create the best condition for an "on the record" confession by the distinguished murderer. That was what, and that was all, Tricot sought. To what use he would then put this confession was still only generally outlined in his mind. It was going to make headlines somewhere, and those headlines were going to mean two things to Bertrand Tricot: sweet revenge for the murder of one of his heroes, and a handsome sum of money in the bank.

He reached the northern outskirts of Bordeaux on schedule, then headed north towards the Médoc vineyards. Clouds had gathered, and the first drops of rain began to spot his windshield as he entered the village of Margaux. About ten kilometres to go now, and the adrenalin was running. He pulled up outside the Étoile, the village's restaurant on the main street, and went in to use the telephone. He dialled the number of the Lemonnier château.

He was in luck.

"Monsieur Lemonnier?"

"Yes?"

"I have an urgent letter for you from the Conseil Inter-professionel du Vin. I wanted to be sure you were there before coming over to deliver it by hand."

"I see. You'd better come over then. Are you calling from Bordeaux?"

"Margaux."

"Then I'll expect you shortly."

Tricot hurried out to the Citroën and set off northwards again through the vineyards. In St Julien he found the turning to the left that would take him the last two kilometres to his destination. The big moment of his life was upon him.

At Lachaise-Laurent, Edmond replaced the telephone receiver, frowned, scratched his head, and then walked briskly from his study and climbed the staircase to the first floor. He was wondering what it was that the CIVB wanted to communicate so urgently that they would send a man out from Bordeaux. Something to do with pricing, he supposed, but the urgency puzzled him. The Bordeaux wine trade wasn't known for frenetic activity of that sort.

He pushed open the door of a guest bedroom.

"You have a choice," he said, addressing a figure curled up under a sheet on the bed. "If you can be up and dressed in five minutes, you can come downstairs. If not, you must stay in here until I say you can come down."

"Why?"

Diane de Villambeau rolled over and sat up, letting the sheet fall away from her naked breasts.

"There's a man coming from Bordeaux to see me. I don't want you wandering round the house half naked while he's here."

"What time is it?"

"Nearly eleven."

"Good God! Were we up that late last night?"

"Until three."

"I have a hangover," she said, rubbing her forehead. "Be a darling and get me something for it. And while you're downstairs, you'd better look in the study for my panties." She giggled. "I seem to remember having rolled them up in a ball and thrown them on top of bookcase. Don't ask me why."

"You were potted."

Edmond came over to the bed and bent down to kiss a large brown nipple. Diane's arm went round his neck and she tried to pull him down.

"No, you wicked woman! Not now. I've got to get downstairs to fetch your aspirin."

"And panties."

"And panties."

"Come back soon."

"But not to stay. I'll call you when the man's gone."

"Are your servants here?"

"I'm not that reckless. I sent them off early to Bordeaux to shop. They'll be out all day. You can stay for a cold lunch, if you want, but then you go."

"Yes please, lover boy. Any chance of having it in bed?" she smiled coyly.

"If you're a good girl."

Five minutes later, Edmond heard the crunch of wheels on the gravel in the courtyard. He went straight to the front door and outside onto the stone steps. A youngish man in an ill-fitting grey suit was emerging from a Citroën which had seen far better days. Edmond went down the steps to meet him.

"You are the gentleman from the CIVB, with the letter?"

The man held out his hand. "Good morning, Colonel. My name's Bertrand."

Edmond shook his hand, mildly irritated that a mere letter-deliverer felt it necessary to be so formal.

"You have the letter?"

"I do, but it will require a moment or two of explanation. Might I come in?"

Edmond shrugged his shoulders. "Please follow me, monsieur."

He led him into the house and straight to his study. On the way he remembered that he had not taken the aspirin up to Diane. She would have to wait a few minutes.

"Please take a seat," he said, waving his visitor to a chair as he settled behind his desk. "May I see the letter, please?"

Tricot put a hand into an inside pocket and withdrew two sheets of waxy-looking paper. He coughed, and stared out of the window as he spoke.

"Colonel, I am not from the CIVB. I am a journalist who has come into possession of some important information which needs corroboration. I believe you can help me, so I'd like – "

"I must ask you to leave instantly, monsieur," cut in Edmond sharply, rising from his chair. "I have no time to give to someone who enters my house under false pretences." He started to walk towards the door.

Tricot made no move.

"I said I wish you to leave!"

"Colonel, did you deliberately run down and kill Pierre Mouret one foggy night in London in 1943?"

"Certainly not!"

Edmond stood sentinel-like at the open door, his face betraying no emotion. Tricot got up and walked towards him.

"Read this."

He handed him the two sheets of paper.

"What is it?"

"The confession of Marcel Tricot that he was an accomplice, albeit an unwilling one, in the murder of Mouret. He names you as the murderer."

Edmond scanned the first page, frowning.

"It is obviously a worthless piece of paper. A forgery. Who sold it to you?"

"No one. I am Tricot's son. He died ten days ago, and I came into possession of the confession which he had addressed to his priest. My father was your driver that night, as you can read."

"I remember a Tricot on our staff," said Edmond, suddenly pale. His hands shook as he turned to the second page. "But I do not remember him being there on that occasion."

Suddenly the awful realization of what he had said struck him, and he felt physically sick.

"On *what* occasion, Lemonnier?" A look of triumph spread over Tricot's face.

At that moment, Diane appeared in the doorway, dressed in a bath towel.

"Ooops! I didn't know anyone was around." She retreated rapidly down the passage, calling over her shoulder: "The aspirin! I'm suffering!"

Edmond ignored her. He was staring at the two sheets of paper.

"It's true, isn't it?" said Tricot. "By the way, when does your wife return?"

"Next week," said Edmond weakly.

"I see. Then, er – " Tricot nodded towards the door held open by Edmond, giving on to the passage down which the betowelled figure had just retreated.

"A house guest." The man's impertinence suddenly pulled Edmond together. He left the doorway and strode purposefully to his desk and sat down.

"I take it, monsieur," he said, opening a drawer and pulling out a cheque-book, "that you have come to negotiate a price for that highly suspect document. I am prepared to consider purchasing it, because its contents, if made public, could be widely misinterpreted. You are obviously hard pressed for money, otherwise you would not be playing this stupid game; so, I am prepared to set a principle aside for a moment, and indulge you. How much?"

Tricot began to laugh.

"What an absurd man you are, *Monsieur le Député*! You really think I came all this way with this confession of my father's just to sell it to you! I came here to have the contents confirmed. You have obliged me, and now I can oblige you by leaving, as requested." He turned and hurried through the door.

Edmond sprang from behind his desk and dashed after him. Tricot was now running for the front door. As Edmond bounded down the steps after him, his quarry was agilely swinging himself in behind the wheel of the Citroën. Edmond seized the door handle on the passenger's side. It was locked. Tricot had started the engine as Edmond jumped round to the front of the car to block its forward movement. Gripping the headlamps, he stared ferociously through the windshield at Tricot.

Tricot smiled for an instant. "You want me to kill you the way you killed Mouret?" he shouted.

Then he threw the gear lever into reverse and jammed his foot down on the accelerator, leaving Edmond sprawled on the gravel. By the time Edmond had staggered to his feet, the Citroën had made the half turn and was disappearing through the arched gateway. His first thought was to run to the garage and give chase in the Minerva; then, to his chagrin, he remembered that Grenier had not yet returned from Pauillac with a new fanbelt to replace the one that had snapped the day before. He swore loudly and, brushing himself off, hurried back into the house.

Back in his study, he closed the door and slumped into an armchair.

"What, in God's name, am I now going to do?" he exclaimed out loud.

He clenched and unclenched his fists as frightening thoughts poured into his mind. He had no idea where to find Tricot again; the man had left him with not the slightest clue as to where he came from. The fact that he came by car could have provided the answer, if only, in his state of excitement, he, Edmond, had not omitted to check the registration plate whose initial digits would have indicated the *département*. The man had got clean away, headed God knows where, in a make of car so common that the local police would laugh at him if he were to try to enlist their help in tracking it down. By now he was well on his way to wherever he was headed, no doubt composing in his mind the sensational piece he would be delivering to his newspaper. "DEPUTY IMPLICATED IN WARTIME MURDER OF RESISTANCE HERO." And that would be that. The stupid public would be more ready to believe the confession of a dying man than the protestations of innocence of a politician.

"Damn! Damn! *Damn!*" he shouted in his frustration and anger, leaping up from the chair and beginning to pace up and down the room. How in God's name was he going to get to this man, Tricot, before he handed in this piece, this death-warrant?

"Grivault!" he exclaimed suddenly, and rushed to his desk to pull open a drawer. The third man in the car . . . he knew Tricot *père* well enough. He must know where he had gone to live after the war. Grivault must be contacted immediately.

The study door opened. "May I come in?"

It was Diane, this time more modestly attired in one of Margot's bathrobes.

"What do you want?" asked Edmond sharply as he continued rummaging through a drawer in the desk.

"Is something the matter? I heard raised voices, and then that car took off like a robbery getaway."

"Nothing's the matter, except that you might have avoided presenting yourself half naked to a man who knows you're not my wife."

Diane giggled. "I'm sorry, *chéri*. I didn't know he'd arrived, honestly. Will he cause a scandal? Does he know Margot?"

"Probably. Now, for heaven's sake get dressed and out of here."

"Already? I'm still waiting for my aspirin, remember?"

She sank into the armchair recently vacated by Edmond, and let the robe fall away from her long, slim legs.

"And we were going to make love again."

"That's out, now," snapped Edmond, then sighed with relief as he identified the piece of paper he had been searching for. "Please go and get dressed and go back to Bordeaux. I'm going to be extremely busy from now on."

"Something is wrong, isn't it? Did that man bring you some bad news?"

"It's really nothing to do with you."

"It is! My lover's in trouble, and I have a right to know what's happening."

"You have no right whatsoever," said Edmond angrily. "And I'm not your lover. You came here last night wanting to get fucked, and you got fucked. That's all!"

"Christ! What's got into you?" She rose from the chair and walked towards the door. "I can see I'm not wanted around here. Well, screw you, Mr Deputy! I hope that man, whoever he was, has a load of fun telling everyone in Bordeaux that the master of Lachaise-Laurent has naked girls running around the château when Madame is away!" She flounced out.

Edmond followed her as far as the door and slammed it shut. Then he hurried back to the desk and picked up the telephone. He dialled the local exchange and asked to be put through to a number in the Finistère region. A female voice came on the line, and he asked to speak to Monsieur Henri Grivault. But Monsieur Grivault was on business in Corsica until the following Tuesday, four days away. No she didn't know how he could be reached there. Did she by any chance know of a Monsieur Tricot? No, she didn't. Was she Henri Grivault's wife or daughter? Neither. She was his niece, and she came over from a neighbouring village every day when her uncle, who lived alone, was away, to feed his dogs. Would she promise to tell her uncle, as soon as he returned, to call Colonel Lemonnier at the following number as a matter of extreme urgency? And if he called her from Corsica in the meantime, would he please get in touch with him immediately from there? She promised to do so.

Edmond wiped beads of perspiration from his brow as he replaced the receiver. He was stymied. All he could do now was wait and pray. If Grivault came through before the story was in print, his career, reputation and marriage might yet be saved. If not, then it was all over for him. He knew his fellow Gaullists too well: there would be no rush to his defence. He would be left to fend for himself against a tide of righteous wrath and recrimination. Nor could he expect Margot's faith in him not to be shattered. Her dreams of seeing him elevated to the pinnacles of political power would be utterly destroyed, and he was only too aware what essential underpinnings to their relationship those dreams were. Tricot, moreover, could be counted on to rub salt into the wounds by titillating the prurient curiosity of his reading public with stories of half naked women running through the corridors of the Deputy's château while the mistress of the house was away. He would be spared nothing. The wreckage would be total. Yet, he had no regrets for what he had done. He was simply shattered by the realization that he had, in the end, not got away with it. Chance had tripped him up, and the humiliation was more than he could bear.

He got up and went to the window to stare out across the rows of grape-laden vines stretching into the distance. The rain had stopped, but dark clouds still hung low and threatening over the vineyard. The vintage would be late, for sure, he thought. Maybe he would not live to see it. Quite likely the year of his death would be recorded in the wine annals as a rotten year for clarets. He smiled grimly at the irony, and then hurried from the house. For the next hour he paced up and down the paths between the vines, desperately trying to convince himself that there was not yet any solid reason for surrendering to despair. He heard Diane's car start up. He was not surprised that she was leaving without saying goodbye, but it added to his sense of abandonment. He decided to go back to the château and see if he could reach Margot by telephone in Antibes. There was nothing he wanted to say to her about Tricot's fateful visit; he just wanted to hear her voice and steal some comfort from her while she was still in ignorance of the tragedy now likely to befall them.

For his part, Bertrand Tricot was in the highest of spirits and hummed loudly if tunelessly as he raced through the northern suburbs of Bordeaux and picked up Route National 10 bound for Angoulême and Poitiers. His fingers were itching to get to his typewriter. In a matter of days his name would be a household word in political journalism, and the Communist Party would hail his sensational revelations as a mortal blow to the would-be dictator, de Gaulle. And his girlfriend back in Poitiers would now treat him with rather more respect than she had been showing of late. By dying, his father had finally done him a signal service. He could at least be grateful to him for that.

50

Felix Beale was already installed at the Hôtel Lotti by the time Margot arrived back in Paris from her Antibes assignment. The message left at the rue de la Faisanderie informing her of this also enquired whether she would care to dine with him that evening. Margot called back and accepted the invitation. She then called Edmond at the château.

"How did it go?" he asked.

"Rather a trial: the photographer was a lecherous little rat. How are the grapes coming along?"

"It's going to be late. The weather's still lousy and the crop's going to be disappointing. Early October is my guess."

"Damn!"

"Why?"

"Because I wanted to be there, of course, darling. I hate to miss the *vendange*, but Irina has early October packed with bookings. Maybe I can get down just for a couple of days on the spur of the moment. Are you going to stay down there from now until it starts?"

"Yes, I have to. You're leaving for Venice tomorrow?"

"No, the next day. But I suppose I won't be seeing you now until I get down to Lachaise. If I get down. That's depressing, *chéri*."

"Your choice. You didn't have to go to that ridiculous party."

"Oh, darling, let's not start that silly argument again. I'll be back in Paris in five days."

"Stay longer, if you feel like it," said Edmond irritably.

"Edmond, *chéri*, you sound in dreadfully low spirits.

What's the matter? You can't have a superb vintage every year. Is that what's worrying you?''

"No. It's probably because I'm missing you."

Margot paused before responding. Then she sighed.

"You're making me feel guilty now, and that'll spoil my visit to Venice. If you're lonely and need cheerful company, why don't you find out if Diane's in Bordeaux? You can take her to the ballet or something. I'm not jealous."

"I may do that."

"Yes, do, darling. I have to run, now. I'm dining with Felix tonight, and I want to take Julia to have her hair cut. And before I forget, we're running low on claret here. Can you ship some more up?"

"Yes."

"Cheer up, *chéri*. I'll be with you again soon."

"Goodbye, then."

"*A bientôt*, darling."

Edmond replaced the receiver and rose from his desk. He had a sinking feeling that that might possibly have been the last time he would ever hear his wife's voice. He felt a great urge to rush to Paris to see her before she left for Venice, but he knew he had to stay at the château waiting for Grivault's call. Only Grivault could save him. He was due back in Concarneau either tonight or tomorrow, according to his niece. Then he would call immediately.

Edmond looked at his watch. Nearly three. He was desperate for something to take his mind off Tricot. Maybe he would call Diane and suggest a rendezvous at her place for an hour or two. He hadn't spoken to her since his abrupt dismissal of her from the château nearly a week ago, but he knew she was still in Bordeaux, and he was quite certain she would welcome a restoration of relations.

He picked up the receiver and asked the operator for the Bordeaux number.

Margot wore one of her Dior favourites that evening, an accordion-pleated white crêpe dress, when they dined expensively at Allard. As she expected, every head turned as she entered on Felix's arm and, as usual, she felt a warm glow of satisfaction. She knew she would never, ever get bored of being admired or become blasé about the looks of longing on men's faces. She enjoyed each time as if it were the first.

"Poor Edmond's feeling lonely, and I'm feeling guilty," confessed Margot at one point during dinner. "But what can I do about it?"

"Nothing, dear one," replied Felix. "Men who marry top career models should know the risks, and they're not dissimilar from those that you take in marrying a politician. So don't feel sorry for him. What do you think of the *canard aux olives*?"

The subject of Edmond's morale was not raised again that evening.

Edmond knew that he was really too drunk to drive himself safely home from Diane's apartment in Bordeaux, but there was no question of him giving in to her entreaties that he stay over until the following morning. Grivault may have called already, and Edmond was anxious to get back to the château before the lateness of the hour compelled him to postpone the return call until the next day. He had meant to leave Diane's apartment at no later than six o'clock, but that hour had found them both locked in each other's arms on her capacious bed, and he had subsequently succumbed to her urging that she be allowed to prepare him a simple chicken and mushroom supper. Throughout the evening, he resisted the growing temptation to tell her of the appalling and probably fatal dilemma which now confronted him. As long as the smallest hope of deliverance from the clutches of Tricot remained, the fewer the people in whom he confided the unhappy facts, the less trouble he would have later when, he prayed, the matter would be disposed of. He told Diane, therefore, that he had been having problems with Margot and with the vineyard, and that while these problems would surely be resolved in the course of time, they had left him depressed and in need of the sort of comfort which she could so expertly provide. Diane had been only too happy to oblige once again, but she had difficulty in understanding why he was so determined to sleep the second half of the night in his own bed.

Twice on his drive through the darkened villages of the Médoc, he nearly fell asleep at the wheel, recovering each time as he felt the big Minerva begin to swerve out of his control. He heaved a sigh of relief as he finally swept through the château's gateway. Too tired even to garage the car, he stumbled up the steps and pushed his way through the oak front doors into the still lighted hall. There was a note from Etienne, the butler, on a silver tray. Grivault had called and could be called back at any hour of the day or night.

Edmond hurried to his study to arouse a sleepy operator at the St Julien telephone exchange. In moments he had Grivault on the line. After apologizing profusely for the lateness of his call, Edmond asked him what he remembered of the Marcel Tricot who had been with them on the night of Mouret's death. Grivault thought for a moment, then spoke hesitantly.

"Well, *mon Colonel* – or do I call you *Monsieur le Député*? I'm unfamiliar with the protocol – I saw him only twice after London; once in Algiers, and once, just three years ago, at a Free French reunion in Nantes."

"Nantes? Why Nantes?"

"General de Gaulle came to speak there. People came from all over the region to hear him. Tricot came up from La Rochelle. From the Ile de Ré to be precise. We talked about that because I have a brother-in-law who's a policeman in La Flotte; that's on the island."

"And Tricot lived there too?"

"Nearby, at Ars-en-Ré. He told me he had his own fishing boat. I suppose he's still there. We said we'd keep in touch, but we haven't."

"He's dead. I learned that from his son, Bertrand. Do you know where his son lives?"

"No. But I understood from the father that they were not on speaking terms. Marcel told me in Nantes, when we went for a drink together after the speech, that his son was a communist journalist, and that he had no time for him."

"He didn't say for what newspaper he wrote?"

"Can't say that I remember him telling me. Are you trying to reach him?"

"Yes, as a matter of fact I am."

"I've got Marcel's address somewhere. His widow must know. But I do remember him telling me that he had no telephone."

"Can you give me the address? Not that they won't know in a small village where his house is."

"I'll have to do some searching. Maybe I'd best call you back in the morning."

"I'll call you. I'm much indebted to you, Grivault. Goodnight."

"Goodnight, *mon Colonel*. A privilege to hear from you after all this time . . . Er, by the way, sir, there's no trouble for us, is there, over that Mouret thing?"

"None at all, Grivault. None at all."

"Good. Then, goodbye, *mon Colonel*."

Henri Grivault replaced the receiver and went into the kitchen to open a bottle of beer. Sitting at the kitchen table, he began to puzzle over the conversation with the Colonel. He had said that he had learned from Tricot's son that the father was dead. But he'd also said that he didn't know where either father or son lived, and somehow that didn't tally. He lit a Caporal and inhaled deeply.

"I smell trouble," he murmured to himself.

He stared as the two German Shepherds, nuzzling together on a rug by the door, sleepy but still watchful.

Tomorrow, when he talked again with the Colonel, he would try to find out a bit more. After all, if someone was on to the Mouret business, and if that someone was by chance a communist journalist, he, Grivault, could be in big trouble too.

"*Merde!*" he swore, then drained his beer, stubbed out the cigarette, and went up to bed.

Edmond slept well that night, and opened his eyes at his usual waking hour of just before seven o'clock. It was another grey day, and he grieved for his vintage. He threw a bathrobe around his shoulders, stepped into bedroom slippers, and went downstairs to instruct

Etienne to have breakfast ready for him in the dining room at a quarter to eight. He then repaired upstairs again to shave and dress. Later, over breakfast, he pored over a map, plotting the quickest route to the Ile de Ré. Then he consulted the *Guide Michelin* for information on the ferry service to the island. Satisfied that he could be in Ars-en-Ré by early afternoon if he left the château at nine, he went to the study to call Grivault again.

The man sounded agitated as he gave Edmond Marcel Tricot's street address, and he interrupted his expression of gratitude for the information with a request for reassurance that the Mouret matter was not about to resurface. Edmond promised him that his enquiries had absolutely nothing to do with the dead resistance leader, and brought the conversation to a close.

By nine o'clock sharp, he was on the road to La Rochelle.

Ten minutes after he had left, the telephone rang in the château, and Etienne hurried to answer it.

No, he told the caller, Colonel Lemonnier had just left for La Rochelle and had given no precise time for his return. No, he did not know where he could be reached in La Rochelle. Would the caller care to leave his name and number? He would not. Etienne shrugged his shoulders and replaced the receiver.

In the editorial offices of *L'Hummanité*, the French Communist Party's national newspaper, a small group of men huddled round a desk, waiting anxiously for the one of their number speaking on the telephone to finish the call.

"That's it!" he said triumphantly, ending the call. "He's gone to La Rochelle. That means the Ile de Ré. He's trying to track you down, Tricot. Somehow he found out where your father lived."

"So where do we go from here?"

"We print the first story in tomorrow's edition. Meanwhile you go with a photographer to the Ile de Ré and find him. Then we have our reaction story. And that should do it. So get going!"

Edmond drove the great maroon convertible off the ferry at the Pointe de Sablanceaux, and twenty minutes later reached the main square in Ars-en-Ré. He pulled up outside the church when he saw a priest chatting with a parishioner at the entrance. He got out of the car and waited until the parishioner took leave of the priest, then he hurried over to catch the cleric as he turned to re-enter the church.

"Excuse me, *mon père*. Might I trouble you for a piece of information?"

The priest adjusted the black biretta on his head.

"Certainly, monsieur. *Bonjour*."

They shook hands, and Edmond asked directions to the street that Grivault had indicated.

"Runs behind the hotel there," said the priest, pointing across the square. "But it's very narrow. I wouldn't try taking that big car into it. Which end do you want to go?"

"The late Marcel Tricot's house."

"The near end, then. A minute's walk. You would be looking for his widow, I presume."

"I am."

"Well, I'm afraid luck has deserted you, monsieur. Madame Tricot left on the bus this morning. She has almost certainly gone to see her sister in La Rochelle, and that means usually that she's not back before eight o'clock in the evening."

"You wouldn't by any chance have her sister's name and address in La Rochelle."

"I'm afraid not."

"Well, thank you very much. Forgive me for disturbing you." He was about to turn away, when a thought halted him. "*Mon père*, you would not, by any chance, have met Marcel Tricot's surviving son?"

"Young Bertrand? Not in a long while. His relations with his family were, alas, not of the best. He was very rarely here. But he did come for the funeral. In fact, it was he who found his father passed on."

"You wouldn't know where he lives, then?"

"In Poitiers, so he told me. He's a journalist there."

Edmond shook his head in anticipation of the answer to the question he now put.

"You wouldn't know his address, or the newspaper."

"No, my son. I can't help you there."

Edmond thanked the priest again, and hurried back to his car, aware that the curious gaze of the priest was following him. He got into the car, and as he switched on the ignition, he wrestled with the choice of two courses of action. Either he could wait for Madame Tricot and get her son's Poitiers address from her, which would mean not reaching Poitiers until late that night or the following morning. Or he could drive straight to Poitiers now and take a chance on finding out Tricot's whereabouts for himself. The former course commended itself as the more prudent, but time was not on his side. He would have to gamble on finding Tricot before the end of the day.

He opened the glove compartment on the dashboard and lifted the route map out from under the heavy service revolver wrapped in a brown silk scarf. He consulted the map for a few moments, then dropped it on the passenger seat, depressed the clutch and eased into bottom gear.

The priest was still watching him as he swung round the square and headed for the road back to the east end of the island.

Three hours later, he parked the car behind a small hotel on the boulevard Grand-Cerf in Poitiers, and went inside to consult the local telephone directory.

He clapped his hands in delight; the gamble had paid off. Tricot, Bertrand lived on the rue Naintré and had a telephone. He called the number and a female voice answered. Edmond's face fell and he suppressed an oath as he heard her tell him that Bertrand was in Paris on business and would be back later the next morning. He had not said where in Paris he would be conducting his business or staying the night. No, he had no office in Poitiers; he worked at home. Monsieur should call the number again around midday.

Edmond thanked her and went into the hotel bar. He needed to think. He ordered a *pastis* and settled down at a corner table. If Tricot was in Paris, that meant only one thing: he was trying to sell his story. But to whom? No responsible newspaper would print it without double-checking with the subject. Not even that communist rag *L'Humanité*.

He got up from the table, asked the barman to keep an eye on his barely touched drink, and went back to the telephone. The operator put him through first to Paris, and Josette answered. Madame Lemonnier had left on schedule at midday. There had been several calls that morning, one of which, taken by Josette, had been from a gentleman asking for the Colonel but declining to give his name.

Edmond called the château, where Etienne had a similar report to make. The man would not identify himself. Yes, thought Edmond, returning to the bar. He'd wager a fortune that some editor was after him. Well, let the bastards wait. The sort of money he was bringing to Tricot in hard cash was more than enough to persuade him to withdraw the story as a cruel hoax perpetrated upon him, the journalist. And if, as seemed most improbable, the money left him unmoved, it was the end of the road for both of them. He would at least allow himself the satisfaction of shooting the bastard. He would have nothing to lose by doing that. Confident, however, now that he had run Tricot to ground, that it would not come to that, he sat back and savoured the *pastis*, and pondered on how he might fill in the time before Tricot's return.

A middle-aged woman with rather fat legs but a pretty face and inviting bosom looked in a friendly way at him as she walked to the bar and bought a packet of Gauloises. Edmond smiled at her as she returned by his table.

"Might I join you for a drink, monsieur?" she asked.

"By all means."

Edmond rose and pulled back a chair for her. They shook hands after both were seated again.

"André Fourcard," said Edmond.

"Nanette."

"It was clever of you to find me," said Tricot affably over the telephone. "Meanwhile, I was looking for you in Paris. So I suggest that you come to my place. I have some more questions I'd like to put to you."

Edmond marvelled at the man's impertinence. He found the small apartment house on the rue Naintré and parked opposite. From under his driver's seat he pulled a leather briefcase and opened it. It had two compartments. One contained three fat envelopes, the other was empty, and into this he now placed the wrapped revolver. Then he rebuckled the straps on the case and got out.

A distressingly thin girl with large, dark eyes opened the door when he rang, and led him wordlessly to a small living room. Tricot sat on a sofa, reading a newspaper.

"Thank you for coming," he said, neither rising nor offering his hand. "Please take a seat."

"I prefer to stand," said Edmond. "I will be very brief. I have not come here to answer questions; I have come to conclude a deal which I think you will not want to pass up."

Tricot sighed and shook his head.

"Listen, Lemonnier, I've already told you – "

"No, you listen to me." Edmond was unbuckling the briefcase as he spoke.

Tricot watched him and put down the newspaper.

"Ten million francs, cash."

"What?"

"Ten million."

Tricot whistled. "I'm impressed," he said.

"So you damn well ought to be. You wouldn't make that in ten years. It's yours in exchange for your father's note of confession, your immediate withdrawal of any article already given to a publisher on any pretext you care to invent, and a written undertaking that you will never seek to publish or otherwise reveal the contents of that confession or your dealings with me. If after taking the money you break any one of these conditions, I can assure you that you will be a dead man within hours of my hearing about it. I am not without the necessary means and friends to have you hunted down and taken care of. I can assure you of that."

Tricot stared at him silently, his face visibly twitching.

"Dix millions, Bertrand," said the girl in a hesitant, husky voice. *"C'est . . . c'est énorme!"*

"Tais-toi!" barked Tricot, not taking his eyes off Edmond.

Edmond stared back. God, make him accept! he prayed. You just can't refuse that much!

"You have the money here?"

Edmond pulled out the three envelopes and tossed one to him. Tricot pulled open the flap and fingered the tightly packed bundles of new notes.

"If you've got all ten million there, you have a deal, Lemonnier."

"Produce your father's confession and you can start counting the money."

Five minutes later, Edmond was back in the car. He sat motionless behind the wheel for a full minute, saying a silent prayer of thanks. Then he switched on the ignition.

"And if you doublecross me, you bastard – "

He left the sentence unfinished as he slipped the car into gear.

André Fourcard bought Nanette a cheap dinner at the hotel and then spent the night at her apartment behind the church of St-Hilaire-le-Grand. She had an interesting wardrobe of provocative clothes, and if she lacked the real expertise of his favourite Paris whore, Henriette, she was nonetheless able to distract him entertainingly enough. After a bottle and a half of local wine had been rapidly consumed, the wretched Tricot was fast receding from his mind.

He left early the next morning. It was a straight 250-kilometre drive due south on a good road to Bordeaux, and he reckoned on making it to Lachaise-Laurent in time for a late lunch. In Angoulême, he stopped at the post office to call Etienne and advise him of the hour of his arrival and order lunch.

"Thank heavens you called, *mon Colonel*! The calls are driving me crazy. Everyone's looking for you, and they say you must go straight to Paris to your attorney's office. Maître Savournet has been calling since nine about every ten minutes. And then the newspapers – "

"Wait! What the hell's going on? What did Savournet say? What newspapers?"

As soon as he asked, he knew the answers, and he suddenly felt physically sick.

"It's very bad, *mon Colonel*. Something about you in *L'Humanité*."

"Etienne," said Edmond weakly. "Go to my study and get the Maître's number."

"He gave it to me. I have it right here – Trocadero 8869."

"I'll call you later, Etienne. Don't tell anyone where I am or where I'm going. I'm going straight to Paris."

He rang off and slumped against the wall of the telephone booth. Tears of anger began to roll down his cheeks. In a quaking voice he asked the operator to get him the Paris number. Savournet was brief and to the point.

"The front page piece is headed: PIERRE MOURET WAS MURDERED BY GAULLIST CLAIMS SON OF EYEWITNESS. The next line: FATHER'S DEATHBED CONFESSION TO BEING ACCOMPLICE NAMES NATIONAL ASSEMBLY DEPUTY LEMONNIER. It's pretty strong stuff, Edmond. And this man Tricot says you personally admitted to him that you were the instigator and at the wheel of the car. If you feel up to driving, get here quickly. If you're too shaken, take the train. I won't go home before you arrive."

"Listen, Maître, I want to tell you – "

"Don't tell me anything now. It can wait. Just get here as fast as you can."

"All right. I'll get going."

Pale and shaking, Edmond left the post office, walked across the street to a café and went in to order a drink and a cup of coffee. Margot would be arriving about this hour in Venice, if the train was on time, he thought. How quickly would she learn of what was happening in Paris? His hands were shaking so much, he spilled coffee on the table-top and cursed. He put the cup down and picked up the cognac, draining half of the measure.

First things first, he told himself. The double-crossing Tricot would certainly have gone into hiding the moment he had left, so there was no point him chasing back to Poitiers. It would take time and organization to flush him out and kill him, despite his earlier boast of seeing him dead within a matter of hours. That had been an idle threat on which he had not seriously expected to have to make good. He had no alternative but to follow Savournet's instructions and return to Paris to face the music. The thought sickened him, and he ordered another cognac.

By the time he was back in the car, he was on the verge of tears again. It would be a long drive from Angoulême to Paris – some 450 kilometres. A long time to be alone with himself and his petrified thoughts. Why was he going to Paris anyway? It was all over for him. Savournet could do nothing for him. His purchase of Marcel's written confession and Bertrand's "silence" was only further proof of his guilt.

Headed northwards once more on Route National 10, he began to sob. He wanted to see Margot one last time, but it had to be now. He couldn't wait. He murmured her name over and over again between sobs, and told her how miserable he was to have brought all this unhappiness on her. The tears were beginning to blind him, and he reached into his pocket for a handkerchief. A stone railway bridge arched over the road ahead, and suddenly he knew that a force stronger than himself had taken control. The force pushed his foot down on the accelerator and then, a second later, it pulled the wheel over to the right.

"*I love you, Margot!*" he shrieked as the big maroon car exploded into the massive stone structure and disintegrated in a burst of orange flame and flying debris.

Crowds were packed along Venice's Grand Canal as the motor launch bore Margot and Felix to the landing steps of the Hotel Europa. Happily, Margot acknowledged waves and an occasional wolf whistle. Then a voice cried "Bestegui" and there was laughter.

"They're waiting for a regatta to begin," explained Felix, "but they seem to know why we're here, and they seem to like it."

Margot laughed. "My silly old Edmond thought they'd be pelting us with rotten vegetables."

Inside the Europa, at the reception desk, Margot was informed that she should telephone a Maître Savournet in Paris without delay.

Margot went pale.

"What is it, dear one? You look as though you'd seen a ghost." Silently she handed Felix the written message. "Oh dear! Is that trouble? Look, let's go to my room right away. They can send your stuff up. I'll put through the call, if you like, and find out what's the matter."

"Yes, please do that for me, Felix. I'm suddenly afraid to do it myself."

She clutched at his arm, her lips quivering, as Felix gave instructions to a bellboy.

Upstairs in his room, he placed the call, while Margot sat, twisting her fingers nervously.

"It has to be something about Edmond. I hope to God he's all right!"

She felt tears beginning to well up in her eyes.

"It'll take about ten minutes to get through, I'm afraid," said Felix replacing the receiver. "I'd better order us a soothing drink. Some champagne?"

Margot nodded, biting on her lip.

Felix called for champagne, then walked to the open windows looking out onto the canal.

"It's so pretty. Come and look."

But Margot had lain down on the bed, and was staring at the ceiling.

"It must be very serious for Savournet to call. And something *has* happened to Edmond, otherwise he'd be calling himself."

Felix sought to reassure her, not to jump to alarming conclusions. But she was not easily comforted.

The telephone rang and Felix leaped to pick it up. He soon had Maître Savournet on the line, and in his halting French explained who he was and that Margot was by his side. Is it bad news? he enquired. Margot watched his face and saw the frown creasing his brow.

"What is it?" she asked urgently.

"You'd better take over, dear one. My French isn't up to this."

He handed her the receiver and sat down beside her on the bed. Margot listened, and as she did so, the tears began to course down her cheeks.

"How despicable of them! You're obviously going to sue." She stretched a hand out and clutched Felix's. "Yes, I'll come right back," she said in a choking voice. "He'll need me. If he contacts you before he reaches me, please tell him I'm on my way."

She started to weep uncontrollably. Felix took the receiver from her and spoke again with the attorney.

621

He repeated his name and the room number and rang off.

"We have to go back, Felix," she said. "At least, I do."

"Tomorrow. And I'm certainly coming with you."

He held her close and let her sob against his shoulder.

There was a knock at the door, and Margot retreated to the bathroom while the waiter uncorked a bottle of champagne. She sat down on the closed toilet lid and put her head in her hands. What had Savournet really meant when he said that the communists "think they've pinned a wartime murder on your husband"? And what did he mean when he said that she'd best come home immediately to "help him through this very painful moment"? The communists always told lies about Gaullist politicians, and no one took it too seriously. But murder? Would they really go as far as to accuse him of murdering Mouret without being quite certain that he had?

"Edmond," she moaned. "Don't tell me you really did kill him!"

She heard Felix call out to her to come and have some champagne and she got up and walked to the hand basin to take stock in the mirror of her ravaged face. She dabbed a little cold water on her eyes and cheeks, dried them, and decided to do no further repair work until she'd had a drink. She returned to the bedroom and took the proffered glass from Felix.

"I just can't think straight for the moment, darling," she said, slipping into an armchair, "so you'll have to do my thinking for me."

"Of course, dear one. Just stay calm, and we'll make the necessary plans. First of all, we're going to withdraw from the de Medicis' dinner. The hotel can get us train reservations, and by the time Edmond is back in Paris and in communication again, and we've had a chance to talk to him, we'll be all ready to leave. So just relax and let Uncle Felix take care of you and everything."

"Darling Felix! What would I have done without you? Damn politics! I was so looking forward to this."

"Well, it will all get quickly cleared up, I'm sure. Maybe Edmond will pronounce it a storm in a teacup and insist that you stay here."

"No, I couldn't do that. If Savournet says I must return, it has to be pretty serious for Edmond."

"Well, I suggest that when we've done justice to this Veuve Clicquot, you go and unpack what you need for this one night, take a rest, and then we'll dine quietly here at the hotel."

"I don't want to see anybody, and the hotel's crawling with people I know who are here for the ball. Can we have dinner sent up?"

Felix smiled. "I'm sure the management will not read anything into such a request that is not there! Now drink up; it will do you good."

They were just finishing dinner in Felix's room when the telephone rang and he answered it. It was the receptionist confirming their train reservations for the following morning. Margot had hoped it would be Edmond, and her hopes were immediately rekindled when the telephone rang again the moment Felix put down the receiver.

"It's Savournet," he told her. "Maybe all is well after all."

"Hello, Maître. Yes, this is he."

Margot watched Felix's face for the tell-tale expression. It was quick in coming. He winced visibly and drummed a clenched fist against the carved bed-head.

"I'm so sorry," he said in a strangled voice. "Yes, we'll be in Paris early the day after tomorrow. Don't worry, I'll handle it. Thank you, Maître. Goodnight."

He put the receiver back.

Margot was standing over him by the bed.

He took both her hands in his and looked up at her, straight in the eye. He could see that she already knew. So he simply nodded.

"I'm afraid so, dear one. He's no more. He crashed his car on the way back to Paris. That's all they could tell us."

"Then it was true what they were saying about him," she said quietly. "Edmond wouldn't have died unless there'd been nothing to live for."

Then she collapsed into Felix's arms.

51

In the opinion of the Angoulême police, Colonel
Lemonnier's car had gone out of control when, at very
high speed, it had hit a patch of oil. The coroner recorded
a verdict of accidental death, having stated that in the
dramatic and tragic circumstances surrounding the
deceased at the time of his death, it was to be expected
that suicide should be initially considered as the cause.
But he was impressed by the expert police evidence, and
wished to give the Colonel the benefit of the doubt. The
Church would therefore welcome his burial in consecrated
ground.

Edmond was duly laid to rest in the little churchyard
abutting the north end of the Lachaise-Laurent vineyard.
The police came in force to keep a battalion of press
photographers and journalists, and a swelling throng of
curious locals, from the churchyard which Margot had
insisted be off limits to them. She had it announced in
advance, through Maître Savournet, that the burial was
to be a strictly private affair. No friends, no flowers.
Above all, no Gaullists; her rage when it was reported
that General de Gaulle could not remember ever having
met the deceased had yet to subside.

And so it was that she stood by the graveside, supported by Felix Beale and the faithful Marion Avingham.
The only other people present were Edmond's sister
and her husband, from Nice, and Maître Savournet from
Paris. Grenier, *maître de chai*, was the sole employee
on the estate invited to pay his last respects. Diane de
Villambeau was the only other person invited, and she
failed to appear.

624

With Edmond laid to rest, Margot, accompanied by Felix and Marion, took the train to Paris. Marion had urged her to come to London, bringing Julia with her, to escape the persistent and nerve-racking attentions of the press. But Margot had made up her mind that she was not going anywhere. For the time being she intended to stay at the rue de la Faisanderie, keep Julia in school, and try to put her life together again. It would not be easy, she confessed, but she had no intention of running away. Her husband had been hounded to his death for a wartime act that only implacable political enemies would dare call murder. She was not now going to give those enemies the satisfaction of seeing her life destroyed as well. Paris was her home now, and in Paris she would stay.

Marion Avingham was not the only person to try and fail to lure Margot away from Paris. Harland Moore, now in premature voluntary retirement, urged her return to the United States, and Charlie wrote saying that it would be better for her and Julia to be almost anywhere else in the world than in France. Friends at the American Embassy counselled at least a temporary change of scenery, and Irina Malinovska offered her the use of her country cottage near Chantilly. But Margot would not be moved.

"I'll be fine," she assured Marion and Felix on the day that they reluctantly relinquished their watching brief over her and returned to London. "I'm going to work this out for myself. Hell, I'm the owner of a fine vineyard, and I have a successful career here which I'm going to resume."

"I admire you, darling," said Marion, embracing her with great emotion. "But just remember that you can always pick up the telephone and say you're coming running if things get too tough."

That evening Jamie Edmonton called from London, inviting her and Julia to come over for Christmas.

"You know how welcome you'd be, and this time we'll keep all the ghastly relatives away as I'm sure you'll want it to be very quiet."

Margot thanked him profusely and said that she would like to make up her mind a little later. She was very much inclined to come, and would let him know her final answer by early November.

She now settled down to put her life in order again. Through the two weeks of her widowhood, *"L'affaire Lemonnier"* had filled the press and airwaves, and the furore showed little sign of abating. Across the political spectrum it seemed generally accepted that Marcel Tricot's confession was no forgery, and that the late deputy had stood accused; but now the principal parties were all dead, and the majority of politicians felt that the affair was best not pursued further. It was hardly a Dreyfus case, and the government of the day was in no way implicated. It involved the Gaullists and the Communist Party, and since the Gaullists were anxious to have the whole wretched story buried and forgotten as soon as possible, it left only the communists to keep the affair before the public eye. And the public seemed to welcome it. As far as they were concerned, the popular press could not print enough about the rising young Gaullist star and his glamorous American wife; about the Colonel's very questionable activities in wartime London; about his dramatic unmasking and his violent and suspicious end; and finally about the beautiful widow whom the photographers caught in their lenses as she came and went to and from her luxury apartment in the Seizième, head held high, but with never so much as a good morning for the quote-hungry reporters who day and night lay in wait for her and dogged her every footstep.

After a week of crying herself to sleep, and of struggling to hold back tears the next morning at the breakfast table with Julia, Margot found herself coming to grips with her loss. She was certain that Edmond had deliberately taken his own life when he realized that the unveiling of the truth about Mouret would be the end of his political career. But she was also haunted by the thought that he might have despaired of her ever forgiving him, and that this may have been a stronger inducement to self-destruction than his political disgrace. That thought she could not bear, for she had often pondered on the possibility that he had been involved in Mouret's supposedly accidental death, and she had long since made up her mind that he love for him would survive any subsequent revelation. But she had never suspected that the revelation would be public. She had simply considered the possibility that he might one day, in confidence, tell her the truth.

When Marion and Felix left, Irina Malinovska, who had been tactfully waiting in the wings, invited Margot to lunch at her apartment and told her the best thing she could do would be to return to work as soon as she felt that respect for a proper mourning period had been observed and that her physical and emotional state permitted it.

"Are you sure you want me back?" asked Margot, much touched by her agent's concern. "Might they not think I'm a bit too controversial now?"

"Of course I want you back! Everyone wants you back! You have been through a great personal tragedy, but you have emerged with courage and grace. We all recognize that. It couldn't have been easy not to run away, but here you are in Paris, taking your daughter to school each day, braving the gauntlet of the press, leading your daily life with great dignity and calm. It's magnificent, my dear!"

So Margot promised her that as soon as she felt ready, she would happily return to work. In the meantime, there were family matters to attend to. She would shortly have to visit Lachaise-Laurent, of which she was now the proprietor, and discuss the future of the château and the vineyard. The accountant in Bordeaux had addressed an agitated letter to her saying that "the usual subventions" were overdue. Having no idea what that meant, she consulted Maître Savournet who told her of the Swiss bank account from which funds were drawn to help meet the costs of running both the château and the vineyard. She asked for details of the account, which Savournet immediately obtained from the bank in Geneva. The balance had been dramatically reduced by a recent withdrawal of the equivalent of ten million French francs.

"The timing of the withdrawal," said Savournet, "suggests that your late husband might have been intending to buy someone off, or had actually bought someone off, in connection with the Mouret revelations. That would most likely have been Tricot."

"And if he has it, can we get it back?"

"I'm afraid not."

"Then Lachaise-Laurent is in trouble."

"Unless the money is in his safe down there."

"Then I'd better go and look."

Margot left for Bordeaux the next day and met the accountant at the château. The safe contained only a few documents related to the estate, a copy of the will that Maître Savournet had read to Margot and her sister-in-law, Solange, and some papers concerning the establishment of the Swiss bank account.

"I fear, Madame," said the accountant mournfully, "that the poor harvest we expect will add to our woes. If the usual subventions are not forthcoming now, you will have to consider borrowing from the Bordeaux banks."

Margot left the accountant poring gloomily over the books and went outside for a stroll among the vines. She found Luc Grenier there and asked him what he really expected from the harvest.

"Not much, madame," he said twisting his weather-worn black beret in his gnarled hands. "This is going to be a very poor year. The weather has been the very devil."

"But next year could be great."

"Certainly." He smiled. "Wine-makers are optimists."

Margot walked on for a while, deep in thought. She loved the château and the vineyard, but Edmond had been so much a part of it that she now harboured serious doubts as to whether she would feel the same about it for much longer. And if she was going to be plagued with financial problems trying to keep it going, she would certainly lose her enthusiasm for the place. With the money Edmond had left her, and her own earnings from modelling – for as long as there were any – she would have no problem in maintaining the Paris apartment and leading a pleasantly comfortable life there. But if the style of her Paris life was going to have to be trimmed to meet the demands of Lachaise-Laurent, she would be most unhappy. On the other hand, she might marry again and if it were to someone of substance, she might regret having given up Lachaise-Laurent prematurely.

She was in a quandary, but escape from it came just three days later, albeit in circumstances that plunged her into a well of despair.

In his will, Edmond had, rather to Margot's surprise, bequeathed to Diane de Villambeau one of the oil paintings in the château of which Margot was inordinately fond. Moreover, it hung in their bedroom. It was a beach scene by Boudin, and was of both sentimental and material value. Margot had decided to enquire of Diane whether she might consider accepting some other painting or paintings in its place, and had invited her to a drink at the rue de la Faisanderie for this purpose.

"No, Margot, I'm sorry. He wanted me to have it, and I cannot go against that."

Diane lit a cigarette as she spoke, and Margot noticed how much her hands were shaking.

"It really is of great sentimental value to me, Diane. It can hardly mean the same to you, with all due respect."

"Well, that's where you're wrong, I'm afraid. Let's not talk about it any more. It's in the will, and I'm sure that in time you'll come to accept that Edmond's wishes really ought to be respected."

Margot felt her gall rising. This long-time friend of hers was treating her in a patronizing manner and talking as though she, rather than Margot, was best placed to interpret Edmond's wishes.

"After all, Margot," she added, "I had known Edmond for a very long time."

This was too much.

"Who in the hell do you think you are, Diane?" she exploded. "You're talking to Edmond's widow remember? I don't give a damn how long you've known him. He may have been my husband for only a few years, but that doesn't give you or anyone else the right to speak for him now that he's dead!"

She was on her feet now, pacing up and down on the Aubusson carpet.

"Don't be childish, Margot. It doesn't suit you."

"Childish! I'm simply telling you that I won't have you

behaving as though you were more important to Edmond than his own wife. You may have had your little fling before the war, and I've never held that against either of you. But that was in the past, and over and – "

"Not so, Margot," broke in Diane quietly.

Margot swung round, eyes blazing.

"What the hell do you mean by that?" she shouted.

"Well, since you're obviously in the mood for a confrontation, I might as well lay my cards on the table. The affair never really ended."

Diane inhaled calmly on her cigarette and then slowly expelled the smoke through her nostrils.

"Say that again," hissed Margot, standing over her, arms akimbo, her whole body quivering with rage.

"We were occasional lovers all the way through your marriage, if you really want to know. We were last together two days before he died. At Lachaise-Laurent."

"You're lying, Diane. Why, God only knows. What do you expect to gain by stupid lies like that?"

"Nothing. It happens to be the truth. Now that he's dead and neither of us can have him, you might just as well know it."

She got to her feet, stubbed out the cigarette in an ashtray, and started to walk towards the door. "I think I'd better be going."

Margot, looking suddenly panic-stricken, stood rooted to the spot.

"No wait, Diane," she said, her voice barely a croak. "We've got to have this out. You mean you remained lovers all that time?"

"Yes." She turned in the doorway. "I'll see myself out. I'm sorry, Margot."

"You filthy whore!" Margot seized a silver ashtray and hurled it in Diane's direction. It clanged against the door frame as Diane retreated to the hall and ran to the front door. "Get out of here!" shrieked Margot after the retreating figure, half choking on her sobs. "Don't ever come near me again! Ever! Ever! Ever!"

The front door slammed as Josette appeared, wiping her hands on a dish-cloth and looking thoroughly alarmed.

"Madame, are you all right?"

She hurried to the sofa in the salon onto which Margot had collapsed face-down, weeping uncontrollably. Josette patted her back.

"Don't distress yourself, madame. Can I help you?"

Margot shook her head, and fought for breath between sobs. At that moment, Julia came running into the room herself in tears.

"What's the matter, Maman?" she cried, her little shoulders heaving as she stood over her prostrate mother.

"The bastard!" moaned Margot. "And with someone he said would be my best friend!"

Josette gently took Julia by the arm and pulled her away.

"Maman wants to be alone for a while, my pet. She'll be all right in a moment. You come with me."

Sighing deeply, the housekeeper led the little girl away to the kitchen.

Irina Malinovska became worried. For three days her calls to Margot had been answered by the housekeeper who told her curtly that Madame Lemonnier was indisposed.

"But you have to tell me what is wrong with her!" insisted Irina.

"She is overtired and has not been feeling too well, madame."

"Has a doctor been to see her?"

"No. She says it's not necessary."

"Well, then, I'm coming round immediately."

Josette started to protest, but Irina had rung off.

"She hasn't said she would see you," said Josette defensively, when she opened the front door to the tall, grey-haired lady.

"She doesn't have to," replied Irina coldly. "I'm here and I'm going to see her." She put gloves and a handbag down on the hall table, and turned again to Josette. "Please show me to her room."

Josette suddenly felt intimidated by the very determined visitor, and meekly led the way. Irina knocked on he door.

"Margot, it's Irina. Can I come in?"

631

She opened the door without waiting for a reply.

"Oh, heavens!" she exclaimed in an exasperated voice as she surveyed the scene.

Margot sat propped up in bed, red eyes staring from darkened hollows, skin mottled and hair tousled. She held a glass of amber liquid in her hand, and the sweet-sour odour of consumed and unconsumed Scotch whisky assailed Irina's nostrils. A tray of untouched breakfast lay on the other half of the big double bed.

Irina walked over to the bed and silently took the glass from Margot. There was no resistance.

"You must be rather shocked to see me in this state," said Margot in a matter-of-fact way. "Well, it happens to the best of us. If you like I'll tell you how that bastard of a late husband of mine made it happen to *me*."

She waved Irina to a small armchair near the bed.

"How long have you been lying there in this condition?" asked Irina sharply as she sat down.

"A few days. A week. Does it matter?"

"Yes, it does. And I want you to start by telling me what's gone wrong, and then we'll discuss how it's going to be put right so we can get you back on your feet, and quickly."

For years, Irina had been confronting the emotional crises of the beautiful women whose modelling careers she managed. Broken hearts, marital breakdowns, professional jealousies, terror of ageing, hypochondria; she knew and had dealt with them all. There was no reason, therefore, for her to doubt that she could wrest Margot from this pitiful crisis into which she had plunged.

Encouraged by her, Margot now unburdened herself in a rambling monologue, full of contempt for Edmond and pity for herself.

"Do you know what I did last night, Irina?" she asked at one point. "I called Edmond's sister and brother-in-law in Nice and told them that I was putting Lachaise-Lauren on the market, and that if they wanted to keep it in the family they'd better come up with a damn good offer right away."

"Was that wise?"

"Wise? What's wise got to do with it? That whore d

Villambeau was laying my husband there – God knows how many times! I'll never set foot inside the place again."

Irina sighed. "Don't do anything in haste which you'll regret later, my dear. You're in no condition to be making big decisions like that."

"Oh, yes I am!" said Margot defensively.

Irina patiently heard her out, and then told her firmly that her career was more important now than ever before. She was the most admired photographic model in France, probably in all Europe, and at the height of her powers. She owed it to herself and her daughter to use her God-given gifts for as long as she could, and to the best advantage.

Margot listened expressionless, staring at the chipped nail varnish on her fingers.

"Thanks for your confidence, Irina," she eventually said. "But something's broken in me; I don't think I'll be good at it or enjoy it any more."

"Nonsense, child," scolded Irina. "I won't listen to such inanities." She got up. "The next time I see you I expect to find you up, dressed, properly made up, and ready to talk about your work."

"I can't promise. I'll see how I feel."

"You can and you will promise." She bent down to kiss her on the cheek. "You stink of Scotch. Go and take a bath, and don't you dare touch another drop of the stuff before I get back! I won't stand for this childish self-destruction."

Margot made an effort the next day. She let Josette accompany Julia to her school, but by ten-thirty she was herself up and dressed. She felt none too well and had refused anything more than a cup of coffee for breakfast, but she found the strength to speak to Maître Savournet over the telephone about her intention to sell the vine- yard and château, and to resist firmly his entreaties that she think again before instructing him to proceed with the sale.

"I have made up my mind, Maître," she said firmly. "I've decided I just don't want the bother of it."

"But you have a perfectly competent manager to do all the work," pleaded Savournet, "and the banks will almost certainly be happy to help you through a difficult period."

"No, Maître. Edmond's sister says she wants the place so if she makes a good offer it's hers. And if she doesn't we'll find another buyer. That's all I have to say on the matter."

By midday, her spirits were flagging again, and she sought to bolster them with a couple of stiff drinks. She refused any lunch and started collecting the framed photographs of Edmond and of Edmond and herself together which were displayed around the apartment, and she threw them into the back of the closet. Then she flopped onto her bed and napped for a while. Her daughter awoke her at five, and the two lay locked in each other's arms for a while. It was a brief moment of unalloyed happiness for Margot. Julia was all that mattered to her now. From now on she'd devote her time and energy to earning the means to give her daughter the best of everything. They would be inseparable, and God help anybody who came between them!

52

The following morning, Margot called Irina, told her she was fine, and promised to come by the agency within the next two days. She was, however, in a mood to leave the confines of the apartment and dine out alone that evening. Since Edmond's death, her friends and acquaintances had respected her wish to be left alone until such time as she indicated that she was ready for a resumption of her social life. But the secluded existence which she had imposed on herself was beginning to pall, and while she did not yet feel ready to face her friends, she did feel an urge to be amongst people again. So, after Julia had had her supper and gone to bed, she put on a simple skirt and blouse, threw a light overcoat around her shoulders, slipped a pair of dark glasses into her bag, behind which to hide in the restaurant, and set off to find out whether being alone in a crowd in the evening was any worse than staying alone at home with her thoughts.

She found a small and not too crowded restaurant near the Porte de la Muette, and ordered a bowl of onion soup and a cheese omelette which she consumed while flicking through the pages of magazines purchased at a nearby kiosk. It came as no surprise to her that they all carried photographs of her, eyes hidden behind dark glasses, escorting a sad-faced Julia to school. Nearly a month after Edmond's death, the Mouret-Lemonnier affair still attracted the attention of the popular press, particularly those sections of the press intent upon keeping Gaullist embarrassment alive. The focus had switched, however, from the affair itself to its innocent and surviving victim, the deputy's widow. There was manifest sympathy for the beautiful young American model and her golden-haired daughter. She had become embroiled in a political scandal of which she could have had no knowledge, and in which she could not possibly have been implicated. As long as this remained the tenor of their comments, and as long as there was no disturbing intrusion into hers and Julia's private lives, Margot felt no cause to feel maltreated by the press. Nonetheless, for the time being she felt more comfortable incognito, and she felt relieved that evening that the disguise offered by her severely swept-back hairstyle, her lack of make-up, and the large dark glasses was effectively sparing her the stares and whispers of the curious.

Her frugal dinner finished, she decided to extend the evening by going down the Champs-Elysées to catch the last showing of Daniel Gelin's new movie, *Edouard et Caroline*. Her head buried in a magazine, she stood nervously in line for a ticket for some fifteen minutes before escaping with relief into the darkness of the theatre, still unrecognized.

It was nearly eleven o'clock when she emerged onto the still crowded sidewalk and started walking from the Étoile, wishing to stretch her legs for a moment before picking up a taxi at the Rond Point. As she walked, she became aware of a young man keeping level with her and casting furtive glances at her. She was used to that when she was looking her normal best, but in this deliberately dressed-down state she had expected to attract n admirers. Paying no attention to him, she quickened he pace slightly. She cursed silently to find, on arrival Rond Point, that there were no taxis waiting on the stand She hesitated for a moment, wondering whether she should try the avenue Montaigne, when a voice behin her said:

"There don't seem to be a vast number of cabs on th streets tonight."

The accent was unmistakably New England.

She turned and saw that it was the young man who h been her unsolicited escort down the Champs Élysées

"Oh, there'll probably be one along soon," she sai refraining from commenting on the fact that he h addressed her in the native tongue. She gave him a fleeting glance, and saw a tall young man, probably in his early twenties, dressed in a brown tweed jacket and grey flannels, with buttoned-down shirt and club tie. Curly dark-brown hair framed a strong-featured face with aquiline nose and large dark eyes.

"Well, you were here first by a neck," he said cheerfully, "so you get the first one."

"Thank you," said Margot, not looking at him.

"How did you like the movie?"

She looked round. "Very amusing."

"My French isn't up to catching all of it, but I enjoyed it a lot all the same. Your French, of course, is very good."

Damn! thought Margot. He's recognized me.

"What makes you say that?"

The young man shrugged his shoulders.

"Since you're Margot Lemonnier, you must speak it fluently."

"Are you a reporter?"

He laughed. "Heavens, no!"

"Then, why are you following me?"

Her tone was curious rather than accusatory.

"I recognized you coming out of the movie. I'm a writer, and – "

"I might have known!"

"No, no, don't get me wrong. I'm not looking for an interview or anything like that. I write fiction, and I happen to be a great admirer of yours."

"I can't say I see the connection."

"It would take a little time to explain."

"Yes, I guess it would."

"You see, I dropped out of Cornell in my junior year to come here to write a novel. I've been here just six months, and it's going pretty well so far, but – "

"Well, here's my cab. I hope I'll read your book one day. What author's name will be on it?"

"Joseph Wiley. That's me. No pseudonym." He stepped forward to open the cab door for her. "Since we both now each other's names now," he said, his hand resting n the door handle, "couldn't we have a drink somewhere?

We could walk over to the Relais Plaza. Maybe you'd like to eat something there?"

"Hardly the sort of place struggling young writers should be frequenting. Anyway, no thank you. I must get home."

"*Alors!*" The driver leaned over to protest through the window at the delay.

"Where are you headed?" asked Wiley, opening the door.

"Rue de la Faisanderie."

"Near avenue Foch? I'm on rue Berlioz, on the other side of the avenue."

"Quite a way on the other side. You'd best take your own cab."

"But why don't I just take this cab on?"

Margot sighed. She looked around and saw that there was no other cab in sight.

"All right. Let's go before we lose this one."

As the cab swung into the Elysées, Margot, somewhat against her better judgement, decided to probe.

"You have an opportunity now to explain how you recognized me and what your following me has to do with your writing."

"Your disguise couldn't fool me. I'd know you anywhere. I must have about a hundred photographs of you at my place, mostly from the fashion magazines."

Oh God! thought Margot. Why did I have to get into a cab with one of those? He seemed harmless enough, and rather charming. But she'd read that people obsessed with particular celebrities could, in extreme cases, be a danger to them. She decided to humour him.

"I'm very flattered. But why?"

"Well, when I started writing this book, I found I needed a sort of model for my heroine. Somebody whose picture I could look at and pretend that it was she. I saw your photograph on a magazine cover, and read inside that you were an American married to a Frenchman. I knew immediately that you were the model for my Thea."

"And is Thea an American married to a Frenchman?"

"Yes, but it's a very different story from yours."

"Lucky Thea!"

"I only took you as the visual model, really. Thea is married to a French scientist who collaborates with the Germans during the war, so she leads a secure life under the Nazis. Then she falls in love with a German army officer who turns out to be a part of the opposition to Hitler, secretly plotting his assassination. The Gestapo come to suspect him, and when they find out about the affair, they try to make her get the names of army plotters from him. But she now sympathizes wholly with the cause, and she turns the tables on them, planting false evidence on her collaborator husband to make it look as though he is really a resistance leader, while at the same time warning her lover of the danger he is in. Word gets around that a resistance leader has been betrayed by his American-born wife, but before they find out that the scientist is, in fact, a collaborator, a group of *résistants* kidnap Thea and plan to execute her. Her German lover tries to track the kidnappers down, and in doing so inadvertently gives himself away to the Gestapo. The *résistants* get proof of Thea's true loyalties when they are about to execute her, and they spirit her through Spain back to the United States. But her lover, Bernd, is hanged."

"On second thoughts, unlucky Thea. She seems to have had an even worse time than me."

The cab was approaching the foot of the avenue Foch.

"There's a very nice little bar near my place," said Wiley. "*Please* let me buy you a nightcap! It's really not that late."

Margot hesitated, looked at her watch, shook her head, then said:

"Oh, what the hell! Just a quick one, then."

The bar was comfortable, dimly lit with pink lights, and womb-like. It reminded her suddenly of the Four Hundred in London, except that there was no dance floor.

"How about some champagne?"

"Heavens! Can you afford it?"

Wiley looked taken aback.

"Sure. I may be a struggling writer, but I'm not destitute."

"No offence meant. By the way, what do I call you? Joseph? Joe?"

"Joe. May I call you Margot?"

"You may. Where do you come from, Joe?"

"Bedford, Mass. My father's an architect, but not a very successful one. At least, he's not well known outside Bedford. My mother's a Capel from Boston."

Margot smiled. "That explains the champagne. Smart father!"

A waiter appeared and champagne was ordered.

"How did they take your dropping out of Cornell? And why did you do such a silly thing?"

Wiley looked hurt.

"It wasn't silly. I was wasting my time there. I've always wanted to be a writer ever since I could read, and I don't need a college degree for that. They were just wasting money on me. They took it very badly, of course. In the end, they agreed to finance me for just one year in Paris. After that I'm on my own. I'll make it."

"You have a publisher for the book?"

"Not yet. I've only written five chapters."

"In six months? You'd better stop collecting pictures of me and get back behind that typewriter!"

"Now that I've met you, I'll be inspired."

The champagne was uncorked and poured.

"Here's to you, Margot. May all the unhappiness in your life be now behind you, and may there be nothing but joy ahead."

Margot felt a lump in her throat.

"Thanks a lot Joe. I wish you the same, and good luck with the book. What's the title going to be?"

"*The Flowers of Treason*."

"To *The Flowers of Treason* then." They raised their glasses and drank. "Forgive me coming back to it, Joe but why so many pictures of me? It sounds like a obsession."

Joe stared into his glass.

"I guess it is a bit of an obsession. You see, to me you' really Thea. I only keep the pictures that don't to

640

obviously root you in a particular moment in time that would not be Thea's time."

"But the fashion photographs root me very definitely in a particular time spot. Wartime fashions were nothing like this."

"Well, I'm not much of a fashion expert, so I overlook that. I guess I mean that I don't keep photographs of you with other people if they remind me of a particular time and place which Thea would not have known. That's all."

"I see."

"Tonight you're the perfect model for Thea. Thea on the run."

"On the run?"

"She was running from her enemies. You're running from your grief."

Margot felt uncomfortable. She took a long draw on her champagne, felt the fizziness invade her nostrils, then swallowed slowly.

"How old are you, Joe?" she eventually said.

"Twenty-two."

"You're very young."

"So?"

"Listen, Joe. Would you resent it very much if I told you that I don't like the idea of being someone else in your mind? I'm Margot Moore. If you're plastering me all over the walls of your apartment, you're plastering Margot Moore, me, on them, not some figment of your imagination. I haven't yet had time to think about whether I mind being all over your place as me. But I know I don't like being there as someone else. Does that make any sense?"

Joe pursed his lips and fiddled wth the stem of his champagne glass.

"I guess it does," he said softly. "You must think me very childish. I'm sorry."

"No, don't be sorry."

She stretched a hand across the table to touch his.

"Believe me, I don't mean to hurt or put you down. I'm very happy for you that you're writing this book, but Thea isn't me, and I'm not Thea. Oh hell, forget it! I'm

641

being too sensitive, and I don't seem to be able to say the right thing to anybody these days. And now I'm lecturing someone I only met less than half an hour ago. I think I'd better just shut up and drink. That's what I seem to be best at these days."

Joe smiled. "You'll find me an enthusiastic accomplice. After all you've been through, you need to let your hair down a little."

"No sooner said than done."

She reached to the nape of her neck and pulled some pins from the tightly coiled chignon of honey-blonde hair. Then she let the hair fall and shook it out.

"Is that better?"

"Stunning. The Margot of my picture collection. Now tell me how you first got into the modelling business."

The bottle of champagne was finished by the time Margot had completed her account of her entry into the world of high fashion photography and her rapid rise to the top. It was the first time in weeks that she had really talked with anyone, and she began to feel a great sense of release. This eager young man, hanging on her every word, was pulling her out of her despondency, just by smiling and listening to her.

"I'm still thirsty. Let's have another bottle," he said.

"You're crazy. I've already had too much."

"Nonsense. The night is young, and I have only a few steps to stagger to my front door."

"Well, what about me?"

"You can stagger with me to the same front door, if you wish. Otherwise I shall have to pour you into a taxi."

Margot wagged a finger at him.

"You're trying to lure me to your bed, Mr Wiley. I hereby promulgate 'Margot's Law'. Having turned thirty, I do not sleep with men under twenty-five."

"Entirely unconstitutional. I shall definitely have to have some more champagne to compensate for this blatant discrimination. *Garçon!*"

Margot laughed. "No wonder you're so behind in your writing. You're probably soused in champagne every night."

"Not every night, but as many as possible. I just like the taste of it."

They had consumed half of the second bottle by the time Margot announced that if he was going to show her his picture collection, he had better do it now before she was no longer able to walk to his apartment.

"An eminently sensible decision," he said, and called for the bill.

Outside Margot shivered in the cold night air.

"I hope it's not far."

"Less than two blocks."

He took her arm and led her off down the rue Pergolèse and onto rue Berlioz. He unlocked the heavy wrought-iron and frosted-glass front door of an imposing apartment house, and took her in an elevator to the third floor.

"We have to walk up the last flight," he said. "I'll lead the way."

At the top of the house was a single apartment, small, low-ceilinged, but comfortably furnished. A large skylight in the living room gave it the air of an artist's studio. Wiley took Margot's overcoat and laid it on a chair.

"Make yourself comfortable," he said, pointing to a deep armchair.

"Do your skills run to making coffee? I really need some."

"No problem. You will have it immediately."

Margot settled into the chair while Wiley went off to the kitchen. She looked around her. There was no sign of any photograph of herself on display. In that case, she surmised, they must be in his bedroom. She looked at her watch. Twenty to two. A decision was called for. If she wasn't going to let him make love to her, she'd better go immediately after restoring herself with a cup of coffee. If she was going to let him, she'd have to stay the night, because once she'd got her clothes off, she knew she wouldn't have the strength to dress again later and go out into the night. She got to her feet again and found her way to the small kitchen in which Joe was heating coffee.

"Can I use your bathroom?"

"Last door on the right on your way back to the living room."

643

"The coffee smells heavenly. Bring it quickly."

She found the bathroom and used the toilet. Washing her hands, she looked disapprovingly at herself in the mirror. She had brought no make-up with her, so there was no way she could do something about her face. She must be a terrible disappointment to this young man who knew her only through the over-glamorized photos in his collection. She left the bathroom and opened the door next to it. When she switched on the light, she caught her breath. The whole of one wall was covered, floor to ceiling, end to end, with pictures of her. Magazine covers, fashion pages, cosmetics advertisements, the only two lingerie layouts she had ever agreed to do, all were there. He must have somehow got hold of back numbers of English *Vogue*, because she recognized many of Felix's pictures from '47 and '48. The decorated wall faced a broad, low divan bed. He must lie there, just staring at that gallery she thought to herself. She marvelled at the way in which he seemed to be controlling his excitement at finally having the genuine article, in flesh and blood, right there in his apartment.

She switched off the light and returned to the living room and the armchair. She closed her eyes, the better to commune with herself about the decision she must immediately make. Common sense called for a rapid return to rue de la Faisanderie. If she failed to appear at breakfast, Josette would panic. On the other hand, the champagne had been doing its work and the prospect of making love again after nearly a month of forced abstinence was becoming more and more appealing by the minute. She was wondering what was taking Joe so long when she began to feel herself sinking into a twilight world of half consciousness. The welcome aroma of freshly made coffee wafting close to her nostrils brought her back, and she heard a cup and saucer being put down on a table next to her. Slowly she opened her eyes.

He was standing over her, legs apart. The bottle-green silk bathrobe was not quite drawn together by the loosely knotted sash at the waist so that she could see his nakedness under the robe. She stared for a moment at what he obviously intended her to see, then looked up into his face.

There was a hint of a smile on it, but she could tell from the quivering corners of his mouth that he was nervous.

"Aren't you taking things a bit too much for granted, Joe?" she asked quietly.

"Well, I thought that – " He paused and closed the robe around him. "I thought that if I made the first move, you might find it easier to make up your mind."

"About what?" She realized that she wanted him, but his presumption irritated her, so she decided to stall a while.

"To stay here with me."

"To sleep with you, Joe?"

He nodded.

"And you think I want to?"

He looked uncomfortable now.

"You came up here, didn't you?"

"For this," she said, reaching for the cup of coffee.

"Then enjoy it and go home!" he snapped.

"You'd better be good, Joe."

He looked puzzled.

"By that I mean *this* had better be good," she said, reaching with her free hand between the folds of his robe.

Joe swallowed hard as he felt her fingers close around him.

645

53

Charlie Garland swung the blue Studebaker onto Santa
Monica Boulevard and headed westwards towards Beverly
Hills, home and Melissa. He could hardly wait to tell her
the good news, and, since they would be going to the
Van Johnsons' party that night, there would be plenty
of people with whom to share it. He had just completed
the fourth year of his seven-year contract with MGM, and
up to now his screen career had consisted of being lent
out by Sam Goldwyn to any other studio that would give
him work. He had worked for Paramount, Universal and
Warner Brothers in roles that never seemed to get any
bigger or better. But the picture he had partly shot in
Paris had apparently caught Goldwyn's eye, and just
when Charlie was becoming resigned to the certainty that
MGM would decide that they'd made a mistake and
finally exercise their periodic option to terminate his contract, the miracle happened. He had been called in to the
studio that morning and told by Goldwyn himself that his
days of wandering from studio to studio were over. He
was to be cast in a major MGM production with two of
his biggest stars. And his contract would be rewritten
accordingly.

By the time he reached the small house in Coldwater
Canyon that had been his and Melissa's home for the past
two years, he had already made a mental shopping list of
long-wanted items for the house and gifts for Melissa and
himself that he could now afford. Whistling happily, he
parked the car under the lean-to carport and hurried into
the kitchen. He found Melissa making lime marmalade in
the kitchen.

He kissed her long and passionately until she broke away to catch her breath.

"Heavens, Charlie! To what do I owe this very welcome outburst of passion?"

"It's finally happened!"

"They fired you?"

"Absolutely not! Your struggling English actor has at last hit the big time."

He opened a closet and pulled out a bottle of Scotch.

"Let's take drinks onto the terrace, and I'll tell you all about it."

"Fine, sweetheart, but I hope I won't be spoiling the fun if I tell you that there has been an urgent call for you from Paris. You're to call the international operator as soon as you get in. Do it now, get it out of the way, then we can relax with your good news. The operator's number is over there on that pad."

"Who was calling me? Margot?"

"I don't think so, although it's her number the call came from. I guess it's urgent because it's the middle of the night over there."

"Oh Jesus! That blessed girl attracts drama like a lightning rod."

He went to the living room and called the international operator. Five minutes later the call was through, and the voice at the other end announced in French that she was Josette, Madame Lemonnier's housekeeper. Charlie urged her to speak slowly so that he could be sure to understand her. Julia, reported Josette, was in a state of great distress because her mother seemed to be spending a lot of her days and most nights away from the apartment. No, she was not down in Bordeaux; she was definitely in Paris. Josette hesitated to say this but Madame had been drinking a lot recently, and her behaviour was greatly upsetting to the little girl. Julia had finally told her mother that she wanted to go and see her father in America because she was so unhappy. There had been a row and a reconciliation, but the child had then woken up in the middle of the night crying inconsolably and calling for her father. Her mother, as usual, was spending the night elsewhere so in desperation she, Josette, had taken it

647

upon herself to call Monsieur Garland, having found his number in Madame's address book.

"You did quite right," said Charlie, rubbing his forehead in consternation. "You have no idea where Madame goes at night?"

"None, monsieur. She says nothing to me when she returns in the morning."

"That's very irresponsible of her. She should at least leave a number where she can be reached in an emergency. Is Julia still awake?"

"*Oui, monsieur.* Do you wish to speak to her?"

"Yes, but before I do, I want to tell you that I will call my cousin in England, and ask him to go to Paris and find out what's going on. I can't, I'm afraid, come myself. But Lord Edmonton will come and sort it out. All right?"

"Thank you, monsieur. Shall I get Julia?"

"Yes, please."

In a moment she was on the line. Her voice breaking with emotion, she pleaded with her father to let her come to him in America.

"You will come very soon, darling," he assured her, brought close to tears himself by her heart-rending plea. "Cousin Jamie will come over from London to see you, and then everything will be fine. Mummy's been through a terrible time and is probably not at all well at the moment. But you mustn't worry, angel. She'll be all right soon. Tell her to call me here, as soon as possible."

When he eventually put the receiver down, he buried his face in his hands and wept tears of frustration, anger and pity for his Julia. What the hell was Margot up to? It was simply not like her. She worshipped the child, and had so far been an impeccable mother. Clearly the strain of the past few weeks had finally overwhelmed her, and she was seeking solace in some man's arms.

He mopped at his eyes when Melissa came in.

"Sorry," he said. "I just got rather upset by what I wa told from Paris."

"Poor darling," said Melissa, sitting by him on th couch and taking his hand. "Do you want to tell m about it?"

648

"Of course."

"Well, you're quite right to send Jamie, darling," she said when he had finished. "Your parents would not have been the best people to involve at this stage."

"There's nothing more I can do about it from here until tomorrow morning. I'll call Jamie then. If he can't go, maybe Ivor can."

"Of course Jamie will go."

"Well, his government whip's job in the Lords ties him down a bit, but I'm sure he'll make the effort."

"So now you can come with me onto the terrace and tell me all the good news about the studio. Then I'll need half an hour to change for the Johnsons'." She got up and pulled him to his feet. "Come on, pet. Sit yourself down out there and I'll refresh your drink."

Charlie watched her retreat towards the kitchen with his glass. What a superb woman! he thought. Christ knows what my life would be like if I was still married to that gorgeous but utterly trouble-prone Margot. I'd probably already be dead of drink!

He went out onto the terrace, counting his blessings, and calling out to Caesar, his white Pyrenean, to come up from the lower garden and show his master some affection.

"I'd absolutely love to see you, Jamie," said Margot, pressing her free hand against her right temple, trying to squash the pain of her excruciating headache. "But there really isn't a crisis. Charlie seems to have got a rather over-dramatic picture of what's going on. He probably didn't understand Josette's French too well."

She shifted the receiver to her other ear and went to work on her left temple, grimacing as she did so.

"Well that's good news, old girl, but I sort of promised Charlie, and I can certainly get away the day after tomorrow for a couple of days. Besides, it's been far too long since I saw you, and I've got to persuade you to come over for Christmas and the New Year."

"OK then. You'll be very welcome. I'll book you into the Alexander, then you'll be walking distance from here."

"I'll be over on Thursday at midday, then. I'll pick you up at one and take you to lunch."

"Who is this marquess fellow? A former lover?"

Joe Wiley lit a cigarette and pulled the sheet up over their two bodies.

"No, stupid. I've already told you. He's my first husband's first cousin. He's a very dear friend."

"Sounds like a bit of a busybody."

"Well he isn't. Charlie panicked when Josette made that idiotic call, and the result is a visit from Jamie. Personally I'm delighted, and if you think you can't do without me for forty-eight hours when you've done without me for twenty-two years, I'm not impressed."

"And can you do without me?"

"I fully expect so."

"Thanks a lot. Maybe it's only the marijuana you'll miss."

"You know damn well I'll miss your love-making. What woman with an ounce of sensitivity wouldn't? But there's a difference between missing something and having to do without it for a while."

"I still say you could easily come here nights after he's gone back to his hotel."

"I'll think about it, but I don't want Julia upset again. And I'm certainly not coming here during the day. Jamie gets my full attention so long as he's here."

"Lucky fucking Jamie!"

"Don't be childish."

"I am a child. Isn't that what you keep telling me? I thought that was part of the attraction. Yesterday afternoon you told me that the very thought of being screwed by someone who was still in nursery school when you had your first period was enough to soak your panties."

Margot blushed at the recollection.

"That was the reefer talking." She looked at her watch. "Do you realize that it's nearly six and you haven't typed a single damn line of the book all day? You promised you would work while I read in bed."

"And you never kept your appointment with that Irin

woman, your agent. Serve you right if she kicks you off her books."

"Well, it can't go on like this." She pushed the sheet back, planted a kiss on his slack penis, and swung her legs off the bed.

"This round-the-clock fucking is going to kill me. Right now I wish you were a truly lousy lover whom I could walk out on with no regrets."

"Well I'm not, and you're not going to walk out on me. I'm enjoying balling America's most famous and beautiful model. It'll look good on my sexual résumé. Besides, you're hooked."

"Not permanently, Joe. You're good therapy for me right now, but I don't have any long-term plans for us."

"Holy shit, Margot! My cock's the only thing that's good enough for you, isn't it?"

"I said it, not you. Actually I find it very charming when you're not being vulgar or getting drunk out of your mind."

"Look who's talking!"

"And you may turn out to be a good novelist, and I like people who make a success of their lives. So it's not just your manly attributes below the belt that appeal to me. It's just that I don't somehow see you being to me what I will probably need and want when I'm back on my feet. And you won't want or need me either. You can't go on screwing older women all your life."

"You certainly have a way of making a person feel great!" he shouted after her as she went into the bathroom and closed the door.

When she emerged, she found him wrapped in the bedsheet, hammering away furiously at the typewriter.

"That's a good boy," she said, bending to kiss the nape of his neck.

"Don't be so fucking patronizing!"

She pulled the sheet from his shoulders and pressed her breasts against his broad back while curling her hands around his abdomen. Joe stopped typing.

"Who was complaining about me not doing any writing today?"

"Freshening up put me in the mood again, lover boy."

"Surprise, surprise!"

"Be an angel and get me another Scotch. Then come back to bed. I'll still get to see Julia before her bedtime if we make it a quick one."

"Women are so goddammed inconsistent," he said, ripping the sheet of paper from the typewriter.

"Oh, Jamie, I'm so sorry to be in this state on your arrival. And we were going to have such a nice lunch together. Why don't you come round at four, when Julia gets back from school? We can spend time with her, and then you can take me out to dinner if you like."

Jamie agreed, and, with a sigh of relief, she sank back on the pillows again.

Well, it hadn't been entirely her own fault, she told herself for the umpteenth time. She had agreed to have a quiet dinner with Irina the evening before, for the purpose of discussing her return to work, a discussion that had been postponed three times already. Irina had expressed such shock at Margot's appearance that she had rushed to look at herself in the nearest mirror.

"I suppose I look a little tired," she said lamely.

"*Tired?* You're a wreck, my child. What on earth have you been up to?"

"Just surviving."

"Well, you can't go back to work in that shape. I'm going to send you out to my Chantilly cottage for a week of complete rest and isolation. My housekeeper will take good care of you."

"That's very kind of you, Irina, but I have Julia's godfather arriving from London tomorrow for two days."

Irina sighed. "Then you'll go as soon as he's gone."

Margot nodded reluctant acquiescence.

"I can see that you've been abusing yourself with alcohol again. It's written all over your face. You really are ou to destroy yourself, aren't you? It's got to stop."

Throughout dinner, Margot listened with growing exasperation to her agent's lecturing. Finally she said:

"Please Irina, don't think I don't truly appreciate all th care and concern you feel for me, but *please*, no mor scolding tonight!"

"As you will, my dear. Now tell me about this god-father of Julia's."

When she finally escaped after dinner, Margot went straight to the rue Berlioz.

"God, how I need a drink! Get me a large one, quickly, darling."

Joe was stretched out on the couch in the living room, and the air was pungent with the aroma of marijuana.

"Want a puff?"

"Not now. Just a drink."

He fetched her a Scotch.

"Margot, I need help?"

"Help? What sort of help?"

"Money."

"I thought you had no problems in that department."

"Well, I do now. I owe a lot, it seems."

"You have expensive habits: champagne and reefers. Have you been borrowing to support them?"

"Yes, I have. My parents' allowance ran out a long time ago."

"Who did you borrow from?"

"The people who supply this." He held up the reefer.

"Oh Christ! I can just imagine what sort of people *they* are."

"I need four hundred thousand francs by tomorrow evening."

"*Four hundred thousand!*"

"You've got to help."

Margot sighed. "On one condition. No more marijuana."

"I thought you liked it."

"I can easily do without it."

"All right. It's a deal. But you'd better bring the money to me tomorrow midday."

"Jamie arrives then."

"Then come early afternoon after you've lunched with him."

"I'll do my best."

She took a mouthful of Scotch and stared at Joe.

"Why does everything always turn sour on me these days?"

That night she got very drunk, and she didn't get

home to rue de la Faisanderie until after Julia had left for school.

With the lunch with Jamie now cancelled, she hauled herself out of bed, showered, dressed, made herself up, and took a taxi to her bank on the avenue Victor Hugo to withdraw four hundred thousand francs.

The manager apologized profusely.

"You recall, madame, that you left instructions for Maître Savournet's fees to be paid direct from the account. That has been done. At present there is just over two hundred thousand in the account."

"Then can I borrow two hundred thousand."

"That can certainly be arranged. It will be in your account by tomorrow afternoon if you care to sign the papers now."

"Can't I have it today?"

The manager pointed to the clock on the wall.

"I fear not, madame. I trust that does not inconvenience you unduly."

Margot pondered for a moment. No, Joe could wait until tomorrow for the balance. She could give him half today. That should keep his creditors at bay for twenty-four hours more.

She was at his apartment by three-fifteen.

"I can't stay. Jamie's coming around at four. Here's two hundred thousand. You get the rest tomorrow."

"Goddammit, I told you I needed it all today!" he exploded.

"Well you can't have it," she shouted back. "I've got to borrow it from my bank and they can't give it to me until tomorrow afternoon. Just be grateful for what I'm doing for you."

She held out the envelope of money. With a swing of his hand, he knocked it from hers to the floor.

"It's useless! It has to be the full amount, you stupid bitch! These people don't fool around."

Margot's anger welled up.

"Pick that up, Joe," she said icily.

"Pick it up yourself," he said, turning away, "and come back with the full amount by six."

Margot bent to pick up the envelope.

654

"You just lost the whole amount, Joe. You can fend for yourself." She turned back towards the front door.

"Goodbye, Joe. I hope they don't beat you up too badly or break too many bones."

He turned and came towards her, wiping his lips with the palm of his hand. Then he hit her across the face with as much force as he could muster. She sank to the floor, and her two hands rose quivering to her mouth as the blood began to drip onto her beige overcoat. She caught a tooth as it slid over her lower lip.

"Stupid bitch," said Joe, and walked into the living room, closing the door behind him.

Margot pulled a silk scarf from her neck and held it to her mouth as she strugged to her feet. Then she left the apartment, went down stairs to the street, and walked unsteadily to the cab stand at the corner of the rue Pergolèse. There were few people on the street, and they watched her progress with curiosity. One man coming out of a building asked her if she was in need of help. Silently she shook her head, but he walked alongside her anyway, and when he realized that she was heading for the cab stand, he raced ahead to make sure that the single cab waiting there was at her disposal. He held the door open for her.

"You are going to a hospital, madame?" he enquired solicitously.

She took her head and pulled the bloodied scarf away from her mouth. The man winced.

"Rue de la Faisanderie," she murmured through swollen lips.

The man passed the instruction on to the driver. In ten minutes she was home.

"No irreparable damage," said the doctor. "I can assure you of that."

He began to pack the paraphernalia of his profession back into the big leather bag.

"Well, that's good to hear," said Jamie cheerfully. He smiled at Margot and bent to take her hand.

"I'll call round tomorrow. You'll probably be feeling up to seeing your dentist the day after," said the doctor as he took one last look at Margot. "They shouldn't build swing doors that can do that sort of damage to a person," he added, shaking his head. "It's scandalous." He saw himself out.

Jamie sat down on the bed.

"Don't try to talk any more, old girl. We'll speak tomorrow when you're less sore. Julia wants to come in to see you now. I'll stay and have supper with her, and then come and say goodnight to you."

"Bless you, Jamie." The tears streamed down her cheeks. "I'm so glad you're here!"

By the time Jamie returned to the apartment the next morning, Margot had made up her mind to tell him everything. She told him about Diane's revelations concerning herself and Edmond; about her resort to the bottle; about her decision to sell Lachaise-Laurent to Edmond's sister as soon as possible. She told him about her chance encounter with the young Cornell drop-out, and their brief and violently ending affair. She spared no detail, no self-recrimination. She wanted it all off her chest: drink, drugs, despair, the lot.

Jamie sat silently by her bed, his expression varying from surprise to horror, from sympathy to sadness.

"My God!" he said, as she concluded the catalogue of her woes. "You poor, poor darling! That's more than any woman should have to go through in an entire lifetime."

They talked on for about an hour, and then Jamie looked at his watch and told her that if he was going to be back in London in time for an important evening sitting in the Lords, he'd have to get going.

"I'm going to call Charlie from London tomorrow," he said. "What would you like me to tell him?"

"Tell him Julia's fine. I had a bad reaction to Edmond's death, but I'm through it now. You don't have to tell him the rest; that's between you and me."

"And you will come to Edmonton for Christmas?"

"Absolutely! It's a promise."

He bent and kissed her on the forehead.

"God bless, old girl. Take care of yourself and my little god-daughter."

"Jamie, darling, I can't tell you how important it's been to me that you came, even if only for a day and a half. You caught me as I was going under for the third time."

"Nonsense! You're one of life's strongest swimmers. Just make sure you're headed for the right shore." He blew her a kiss from the doorway. "See you at Christmas."

It was at that moment that the thought first seriously entered into her mind: Marchioness of Edmonton. Forget it! she told herself. You're just too controversial for that family, however fond Jamie may be of you.

She picked up a magazine, and busied herself reading all about the dinner party the Duff Coopers had just given at Chantilly for Princess Margaret.

"What on earth have I been doing with someone like Joe Wiley?" she said out loud, and suppressed a laugh because she knew it would hurt her very sore mouth.

To her relief, Joe Wiley made no attempt to contact her. Two days before leaving for England, however, she read in a newspaper that he had earlier been arrested and charged with stealing travellers' cheques, and had now been given a six-month suspended sentence and put on a plane back to America. Poor, stupid Joe! she thought. Maybe one day he'd write *The Flowers of Treason* and redeem himself. It was a good story. On the other hand, he may have stolen that too.

54

When Margot set out from Paris with Julia to journey to Edmonton Hall for the Christmas holidays, one question was uppermost in her mind. Would Jamie take the initiative and raise the subject of marriage with her, or would she have to steer him towards it? One way or another she was going to have to find out what her chances were, because the more she thought about it the more convinced she became that marriage to Jamie, at the earliest acceptable moment following a period of decent mourning for the wretched Edmond, would be the perfect next step in her life. A second, related, question of almost equal importance was whether she could count on the support of Jamie's mother, the Dowager Marchioness. Over tea and crumpets before the blazing log fire in the Great Hall on her first afternoon at Edmonton, Margot detected what she thought was a hint of encouragement from her potential mother-in-law, now confined by arthritis to a wheelchair which she propelled about the ancient mansion with all the élan of a getaway driver.

"You've been through a perfectly ghastly time, my dear," she sympathized. "Personally I've always adored the French, but they can be rather troublesome and unpredictable at times. Amy Shropshire married a perfect charmer for her first husband, and they got on like a house on fire until she discovered he was a defrocked priest and still married to a waitress in Le Havre. Marry another Englishman, dear. They're dotty all right, but rarely devious."

Jamie proposed on Christmas Eve.

"I'm deeply flattered," she said with becoming modesty

"but do you really think that someone with my track record is for you?"

"Mother thinks so, and so do I, but I was afraid you might not want another politician in your life."

"But I *adore* politicians, darling! Particularly handsome English ones who are going to the top."

"So you're saying 'yes'?"

"I am."

"Gosh, that's fabulous!" Margot started to laugh. "You English!"

"When shall we announce it?"

"Remember I've been a widow barely three months."

"We can announce it officially – put it in *The Times* and all that – in early March, and marry in early April. How's that?"

"A decent enough interval, I'd say."

"But we'll have to let close family know beforehand."

"Of course." Margot beamed. "I can't wait to see Walter's face when he hears who his favourite nephew's wife is going to be!"

"Then why don't you tell him and Cynthia yourself? You'll be seeing them in a few days' time."

"It will be the sweetest of pleasures."

On the day she and Julia were due to visit her former in-laws, or "the outlaws" as she had dubbed them, Marion Avingham, with whom she and Julia were staying, joined Felix Beale and Margot for a celebration lunch at Claridge's.

"Well, well," said Marion, "as I said to you last night, you certainly don't let the grass grow under your feet, do you?"

"Are you really in love with him?" asked Felix, to whom the news had been broken only as they sat down to lunch.

"Oh, I will be, darling, I just know that he's the sort of person whom one can learn to love very easily. Right now, I'm desperately fond of him. I know he's been in love with me for years, but from my side it's always seemed a sort of brother-sister relationship. Now of course I'm looking at it in an entirely different light. He's been absolutely wonderful to me. In fact, he literally saved my life." She smiled. "I think he deserves me!"

"Saving a life is not normally an unassailable reason for tying a knot, my beauty," said Felix, lifting a pink gin to his lips. "My cook saved my life once when I choked on a chicken bone, but I didn't rush her off to the altar in a fit of exaggerated gratitude."

"Oh, come on, you two! Jamie's a divine man, and if I'm not yet head over heels in love with him, I know it's still going to work beautifully."

"We're playing devil's advocates, darling, that's all," said Marion soothingly. "What about sex?"

"A perfectly normal, healthy young man, I'd say, judging by the way he can hardly take his eyes off my body. Charlie always said he had a one-track mind when they were in the army together and was constantly picking up girls, and, so he always boasted to Charlie, 'doing 'em proud'. So unless he's lost his touch, he should be all right."

"Thank God for that, angel," said Marion. "As the saying goes in London these days, attributable, I may add, to one of your about-to-be sister marchionesses: 'The harder they are, the harder they are to come by!'"

"Enough, you harridans!" said Felix. "You're putting me off my lunch. I want to know if Margot's going to work again over here."

"I may do, darling, if Jamie agrees, and if I do, I'm all yours whenever you want me."

Felix beamed happily.

"Well," said Marion, taking the menu offered by the waiter, "I'm sure it will all work out just marvellously. He's got everything you could possibly want: good looks, pots of lovely money, a title predating the Restoration, several lovely homes, a very bright political future, and no previous marriages. It's a miracle Princess Margaret hasn't snapped him up. She's certainly looked him over."

"Honestly, Marion, you make me sound so grasping!"

"We know you, pet. He's just what you want and need, and we're tickled pink that you've got him."

"Yes, but – "

Margot suddenly looked embarrassed and a little annoyed.

"But nothing, darling," said Marion smiling, and putting a hand on Margot's. "I think you were really born for Jamie. It's a pity you had to go through what you've been through on the way, but that was probably in your stars, too." She took a pair of spectacles from her bag and began studying the menu.

"She's right, you know, Margot," said Felix. "This is definitely the man for you."

"Well, I'm relieved we all agree," said Margot with a wry smile. "I have only one reservation, and that is that as a peer, he can never be Prime Minister. Foreign Secretary, very likely, but not the absolute top." She smiled. "I think I would have adored Number 10!"

Felix threw up his hands in mock despair.

"There you are, you see! The girl's incorrigible. She gets the most eligible marquess in the country, and she's dissatisfied because the price of a coronet is bye-bye to Downing Street. Really, darling, you're impossible!"

Margot was laughing. "Dear, sweet Felix, that was my little joke!"

"But nearer the truth than fiction, darling," said Marion. "You don't fool me for a minute. Now let's eat. I'm starving."

Late in the afternoon, Margot picked Julia up at the Avinghams' house and set off for the Westminster home of her recently ennobled ex-father-in-law, now Lord Shelbroke. It would be hers and Julia's first meeting with Walter and Cynthia in over a year, and it was one to which she was looking foward with the keenest of anticipation.

As the taxi drew up outside the Queen Anne house on Great College Street, she gave Julia last-minute instructions.

"Curtsey to them and kiss them both on the cheek, darling. Don't be shy about talking; your English is perfectly good enough. And don't mention Cousin Jamie and our plans until I do. Promise?"

"I promise, Mummy. Can I ask them if they've heard from Daddy?"

"Of course. Come on, now. Let's go in." She paid the cab, and the butler opened the door as soon as she rang. "Good afternoon, Locke," said Margot cheerfully. "You remember my Julia, don't you?"

"Good afternoon, madam. Yes, indeed I remember the young lady. She's certainly grown. Good afternoon, Miss Julia. May I take your coats? His lordship and her ladyship await you in the drawing room."

"Thank you, Locke. We will make our own way up."

Margot primped her hair in a mirror, checked the ribbon in her daughter's, then, taking her by the hand, led her up the staircase to the drawing room.

"Ah there she is!" said Cynthia, coming forward to greet her granddaughter, and giving Margot, at the same time, only the hint of a glance of recognition.

Margot nudged Julia forward.

"Good afternoon, Margot," said Walter, maintaining his stance in front of the fireplace, in which a log fire burned.

"Hullo, Walter. Nice to see you."

Margot, too, held her ground in the doorway, and watched approvingly as Julia bobbed a curtsey to her grandmother, and stretched up to kiss her on the cheek.

"How pretty you are!" exclaimed Cynthia. "And grown so fast!"

Walter advanced towards his granddaughter who greeted him in like fashion. Then the little girl turned and looked appealingly at her mother.

"May I come in, Cynthia?" said Margot.

Lady Shelbroke glanced towards her.

"Of course. How are you?" There was no warmth in the voice.

"Come and sit down," said Walter.

"If you'd prefer, I can leave you two alone with Julia for a while, and come back and fetch her."

"I've ordered tea, Margot, so I hope you will stay."

The tone suggested to Margot that her possible enjoyment of the tea took second place in Cynthia's order of consideration after the inconvenience of having only three people consume a tea which her staff had gone to the trouble of preparing for four.

"Thank you, then I'll stay."

She walked briskly to a sofa near the fireplace and settled comfortably into it.

"I have a couple of late Christmas presents for Julia, if she'd like to come with me to my room," said Cynthia.

"How very generous of you, Cynthia," gushed Margot. "Darling, go along with Granny and see what she's got for you."

Hand in hand, grandmother and granddaughter left the room. Between Walter and Margot there was a moment of silence, which Margot eventually broke.

"I haven't congratulated you on your peerage, Walter," she said affably.

Standing rigidly, hands clasped behind his back, Walter allowed himself a faint smile.

"Miss the Commons a great deal, of course. But the Lords keeps me quite busy, you know. Committees and that sort of thing."

He unclasped his hands and brought them round to start fiddling with the heavy gold watch-chain which hung across his waistcoat.

"I imagine you run into Jamie quite a lot then."

"Oh, yes. He's one of the whips, you know. Well, he must have told you that while you were staying there for Christmas. He'll probably go far. Winston's got an eye on him, and so has Anthony. And Salisbury thinks a lot of him. All he needs to do now is make a good marriage. Pity he let that Winter girl go; just right for him."

Margot suppressed a smile.

"Listen, Margot, there's something I ought to say to you before Cynthia returns. I owe you an apology. I should have written at the time of your husband's death. Very remiss of me. It must have been quite awful for you."

"No apology needed, Walter. I suspect that Cynthia discouraged you from writing."

Walter looked extremely uncomfortable, and moistened his lips with his tongue.

"I wasn't really expecting a letter," she went on, anxious

663

to add to his discomfort. "After all, he was scarcely a friend of yours."

"No, but – "

"Well, I'm over the horror now, and so is Julia. She's been a great comfort to me, as you can imagine. So has Jamie, and Charlie's letter was very sweet."

Walter began to rock gently up and down on the balls of his feet. She noticed that his lips were quivering in anticipation of some pronouncement that was painfully slow in coming.

"Funny how things sometimes work out, what?" he finally vouchsafed.

Margot frowned. "How do you mean, Walter?"

"Well, you know," he continued uncertainly, "just that unpleasant episodes in one's life have an end just as pleasant ones do."

"By unpleasant episodes, you mean my marriage to Edmond, I imagine."

"Please, don't think me – "

"It's all right, Walter," she cut in. "The marriage itself was a very pleasant episode in my life. I'm just glad that Edmond died before I found out what a real bastard he actually was. A lousy, womanizing cheat!"

Walter looked profoundly shocked, and was stunned into speechlessness.

At that moment the door opened and Julia ran into the room, holding in display across her chest a dark blue velvet party dress with a lace collar.

"Look what Granny gave me, Mummy," she said breathlessly. "Isn't it lovely?"

"It certainly is, darling. I hope you thanked her very nicely."

"I also got some English books."

"Lucky girl. Come and sit down, now."

Margot glanced up at Walter.

"Yes, very lucky," he croaked, still struggling to regain his composure as he saw his wife rejoin them.

"Tea is on its way," she announced, and lowered herself into an armchair. "Julia tells me you have recent news of our Charlie, Margot."

"A letter about three weeks ago. He's loving making

the film for Goldwyn. I think he's really off and running now. And he seems to have a wonderful circle of friends there in the movie colony."

"So he told us when he wrote. I can't quite imagine him hob-nobbing with all those actors and actresses. I suppose he's become rather American," she concluded with a sniff of disapproval.

"Charlie American?" exclaimed Walter. "Absurd idea! He gets parts because he's so English. That's his strength. I always knew he'd do well at that."

Like hell you did! thought Margot.

Locke arrived with the tea tray which he set before Lady Shelbroke, who began dispensing hot buttered scones and cups of China tea.

"Well, when you return to live in America," she said to Margot as she handed her her cup, "Julia will, I hope, get to see lots more of her father. I assume you will not be against that."

"Why on earth should I be against it? On the contrary, the more they see of each other, the happier I shall be. And from what I hear, Melissa will make her very welcome when she goes out to Los Angeles."

"I'm glad to hear that," said Cynthia dryly.

"But, of course, I'm not going back to America to live."

Cynthia looked at her with a puzzled expression.

"Surely, after all you've been through in France," intervened Walter, "you'd be less than happy staying there."

"I've no intention of staying in France. I've sold the vineyard to Edmond's sister, and the Paris apartment goes up for sale as soon as I get back."

"So where are you going? I hope nowhere unsuitable for Julia," said Cynthia, a look of alarm beginning to spread over her face.

Margot paused, savouring the moment to the full.

"Julia and I are coming to live in England. Isn't that nice?"

Walter and Cynthia exchanged glances.

"Well," said Cynthia, groping for words, "I certainly welcome the idea of having Julia so close."

She put down her teacup.

"Where will you live?" asked Walter.

Margot took a buttered scone from a covered silver dish and laid it on the plate balanced on her knee.

"Where will we live?" She raised the scone to her mouth and bit into it. Masticating slowly, she looked from Cynthia to Walter, and then winked at Julia. She swallowed, then tapped at the corners of her mouth with a small napkin.

"At Edmonton."

"At *Edmonton*?" Cynthia looked thunderstruck.

"At Edmonton," repeated Margot.

"Is Dorothy renting you a stable flat, or something?" enquired Walter incredulously.

"Don't be absurd, Walter!" shot back his wife. "She's never done that."

"It's very simple," said Margot, smiling angelically. "Jamie and I are getting married in April."

Cynthia froze, her face turning ashen white, her eyes locked into a squint of total astonishment and panic.

"Well, I'll be damned!" said Walter quietly.

"Aren't you going to congratulate me?" asked Margot, taking a second bite of the scone. She winked again at Julia, who was smiling uncertainly.

"Since when was this decided?" asked Walter, noting that his wife was still incapable of speech.

"He proposed at Christmas. Christmas Eve, actually."

"Who proposed to whom, I'd like to know!" Cynthia had suddenly found her voice, although it was barely recognizable, even to herself, so painfully high-pitched did it sound.

"As I told you," said Margot patiently, "he proposed to me on Christmas Eve, and I accepted joyously. I'm really taken aback that this seems to have hit you as unwelcome news."

"It's a shock, that's all," said Walter.

"How come Dorothy never told us, or Jamie himself?" protested Cynthia.

"They knew I was coming to see you, so they thought it would be nice if I told you myself. Well, maybe it has come as a bit of a surprise, but I want to assure you that it's all going to turn out just beautifully. Jamie and I are over the moon about it, and so is Julia."

"And Dorothy?" snapped Cynthia.

"I was there when Jamie told her. She said, 'Good for you, Jamie! She'll keep you on your toes!' Then she embraced me warmly, told me he was lucky to get me and vice versa, and urged me to stop him putting so much brilliantine on his hair."

Julia giggled, and Cynthia cast her eyes heavenward.

"Well!" said Walter, and took a deep breath. "I suppose that's that, then."

"So smile, Walter!" said Margot gaily. "Let's all be happy about it."

Walter looked appealingly to his wife, and saw to his distress that she was biting on her lips, fighting back incipient tears.

"Does Charlie know about this?" she said in a choking voice.

"I wrote to him yesterday. We both did. I've no reason to believe he'll be anything but overjoyed. After all, how could he not be delighted that Jamie will now be Julia's stepfather?" She looked at her watch. "Come on, Julia darling. We must go. Remember we're going to the pantomime this evening. You can wear the pretty dress Granny just gave you."

Margot put her plate down and got to her feet.

"Thank you for the lovely tea, Cynthia. We'll be here for another couple of days, so maybe Julia can come again, since this has been such a short visit."

Cynthia offered no reply. She got to her feet, bent to kiss Julia on the cheek, and then, with a mumbled "excuse me", she dashed from the room.

Margot shrugged her shoulders and gathered up her bag from the sofa.

"Please forgive Cynthia," said Walter in a despairing voice. "This has been quite a shock for her."

"For you both, judging by the reception my announcement got."

"You must give us time to adjust to the idea."

"Of course. I can see that you need it." She walked with Julia towards the door. "We can see ourselves out, Walter, if we can just get our coats from Locke."

Right on cue, the butler appeared at the foot of the staircase, the coats over his arm.

"Kiss Grandpa goodbye, Julia."

Julia obeyed, then Margot held out her hand to Walter. He took it and shook it, his face a picture of mournful solemnity.

"Don't look so damned tragic, Walter!" She leaned forward and kissed him on the cheek. "I'm going to make your nephew very happy."

She turned and led Julia down the stairs. Just before the front door closed on them, she heard Cynthia's voice calling out to her husband.

"Walter! Call Dorothy this instant!"

"Call her yourself. All I want now is a bloody stiff drink!"

A door slammed somewhere upstairs, and downstairs Locke hurried the two visitors out onto the front step.

"Can I find you a cab, madam?"

"No, Locke, thank you. A little walk will do us no harm. We'll pick one up in Parliament Square."

The front door closed, and Margot began to giggle.

"Come on, my little princess," she said, taking Julia's hand. "Now it's your turn to be entertained."

Margot became the Marchioness of Edmonton on 3rd April, the marriage being solemnized quietly at Caxton Hall Registry Office, after which a luncheon was given by the Avinghams at their Wilton Crescent house. Lord Shelbroke attended the luncheon, drank a lot of champagne, and was utterly charming to his old wartime friends, Harland and Elinor Moore. Lady Shelbroke, meanwhile, had chosen to go into hospital the previous day to have a varicose vein attended to.

The press had a field day.

55

Resplendent in her purple velvet robe, the Imperial Crown on her head, the Sceptre clasped in one hand, the Orb cradled in the palm of the other, Queen Elizabeth II glanced at the serried ranks of her Peers of the Realm, gathered near the throne, as she began the long Recession back through the Abbey of Westminster at the conclusion of her Coronation Service. The choir of four hundred voices, accompanied by organ and orchestra, launched into the National Anthem. And the Right Honourable Lord Shelbroke, damp-eyed with loyal emotion and encouraged by his fellow barons flanking him, who were singing lustily if none too tunefully, added his own reedy voice to the joyous noise.

Heart-warmed and moved as he was to see his Queen well and truly crowned, a measure of his delight was reserved for the thought that, after long hours, he was within minutes of being permitted to remove the suffocatingly heavy ermine-caped, ruby-red velvet robe, and to loosen the silver buckles below the knees of his black Court Dress breeches which were biting into his flesh, despite the assurances of his Savile Row tailor that his lordship might anticipate no such discomfort.

A level below him, to the left of his group of barons, stood the smaller group of marquesses, amongst whom he could easily recognize his nephew, the Marquess of Edmonton, by his height, tempered by the familiar stooping but alert stance which suggested that he was about to take flight.

The splendidly robed peeresses with their glittering tiaras were out of his line of sight. But he could vividly picture his wife, Cynthia, risking a pulled neck muscle as she strained to watch the comportment and reactions of her one-time daughter-in-law, now Marchioness of Edmonton, who, on arrival in the Abbey on the arm of the Marquess, had caused a twitter of excited whispering, not quite all of it benevolent.

Magnificent in her cream-brocaded gown, ermine-trimmed ruby-red robe with eight-foot train, and the Edmonton tiara of diamonds and rubies set forward of the crown of her swept-up coiffure, Margot thrilled to the occasion. Never had she seen such pomp and ceremony, heard such stirring and beautiful music, or felt so transported by the sense of a truly spiritual and uplifting moment in history. Nor even in the headiest moments of her career as a supremely admired model had she ever felt her own beauty and poise being more admired than on this day. And when the Archbishop of Canterbury had placed the St Edward's Crown on the Queen's head, and all the peers and peeresses had put on their coronets, Margot had allowed herself a little *lèse-majesté* in seeing this as her crowning moment too.

When the two-mile long Royal Procession finally set off amid blaring bands and the clatter of horses' hooves on its long route through the rain-sprinkled streets of London jammed with cheering citizenry, Lord and Lady Shelbroke gathered up the hems and trains of their robes, tucked their coronets under their arms, and hurried in as dignified a manner as was possible under the circumstances to their house just round the corner from the Abbey.

They were entertaining to lunch some two dozen family and friends, and at Jamie's insistence had hired a television receiver on which the guests could follow the Royal Progress and the nation's celebrations, while lunching off smoked salmon, cream of chicken, and desserts.

Margot and Jamie arrived, giggling, under a capacious umbrella. The butler relieved them of their ermine robes and coronets, and Margot checked her coiffure and make up in the hall mirror.

"How do I look, darling?"

"Marvellous," said Jamie. "Your rivalry to the Queen's beauty came close to treason."

"And I felt all right on my feet." She patted her stomach. "Not bad for four months pregnant."

She turned to her husband and picked a hair off the gold-threaded collar of his scarlet Grenadier tunic, and straightened the medals on his chest.

"Come on, your lordship, I'm dying for a drink. Let's join them."

Julia came running from the television set as she saw her mother enter the drawing room.

"I saw you! I saw you both!" she said excitedly.

Margot bent to kiss her daughter and straighten the ribbon in her hair before turning to greet the rest of the company.

Cynthia Shelbroke took her in charge and escorted her round the room. She found she knew everyone there, including the two government ministers and their wives.

"And you know Sir Maurice Drake, of course," said Cynthia in a dramatically lowered voice.

"Well hello, Sir Maurice!" said Margot gaily. "What a pleasure to see you."

She held out her hand, which he shook warmly.

"A great pleasure for me too, Margot. I imagine you are well settled back into English life by now."

"Oh, absolutely. And I'm loving it."

"Well, it's good to have you back."

Margot laughed. "Are you sure about that, Sir Maurice?"

She took a glass of champagne from a waiter's tray and sipped from it, watching Drake blush.

"Tell me, Sir Maurice," she said, bending to his ear. "Who have you got watching me these days?"

Drake grinned. "With your beauty, my dear, is anyone not watching you?"

"Well said!" On an impulse, she kissed him on the cheek. "Friends?"

"Friends, of course," he said.

Margot turned and saw her mother-in-law, the Dowager Marchioness, entering the room in her wheelchair after being transported up the stairs by a posse of panting chauffeurs and footmen. She went over to kiss her.

"Did the son and heir kick up during the service?" She tapped Margot's belly. "And he's down for Eton?"

"Don't tempt providence, Dorothy," said Margot, grinning. "It may well be a girl."

"Nonsense, child. Edmonton first-born are never gels. Go and get me a particularly strong whisky and soda."

Across the room, Walter took Maurice Drake aside.

"You know, Maurice, it's all a bit bizarre," he said, nodding in Margot's direction. "Actually, Cynthia has a rather less flattering description of the situation. I fear she'll never come round to it. But to have that amount of both bad luck and good luck, is really pretty rare."

"Exceptional, I'd say."

Walter grinned. "Actually, old boy, I think it's rather fun. Or is that just the champagne talking?"

"I don't think so. After all, I share your view and I haven't yet been offered a glass of champagne!"

"Good heavens! I *am* a bad host." He looked around him for a waiter, and saw none. Then he spotted Margot. "Margot, my dear," he called out, beckoning to her.

She came over to them.

"We've neglected Sir Maurice's needs. Do be an angel and fetch him a glass of champagne."

Drake looked embarrassed.

"No, really, Walter, I can get it for myself."

"But I'd be happy to," said Margot grinning. "Don't look so worried, Sir Maurice! I'm Margot Edmonton, not Lucrezia Borgia!"

She turned and left them.

"That girl!" said Walter, shaking his head. "That girl! I hope Jamie knows what he's doing. My God, Maurice, he'd better!"